The Old Bunch

THE
Old Bunch

Meyer Levin

1937

Rancho Lazarus Publications

ISBN: 978-0692234600

A note about "style":

This text has been transcribed from old print editions. The original presentation has been preserved and all word usage, punctuation, and in-line formatting of the text is as it was in the original publication and reflects the writing style, spelling variants, and editorial preferences of the author, Meyer Levin, and the original publishers.

Much care has been taken in this transcription to ensure that new errors were not added in the process. Other reprints of this work have been found to be full of a distracting number of typos and errors that were not part of the original book. We have endeavored to produce a clean text, free of errors that were not the author's style choices. If you find something in this book that appears to be an error, and is not of the nature of an old spelling variant or stylistic choice, please email us at OldBunch@rancholazarus.com so we can verify if it was a choice of the author that was present in the original printing, or correct it for future printings.

Footnotes have been added in certain places to enhance understanding of the relationship of the story to major historical events. Those footnotes were not part of the original text and are copyrighted by the current publisher.

Thank you and enjoy this wonderful book.

Rancho Lazarus Publications
Payson, Arizona

Cover art adapted by Celia Megdal

Publisher's Note

THIS book speaks for itself, and requires no introduction. These words are for a prospective reader.

Meyer Levin was a Chicago-born Jewish author. His best-known book is "Compulsion", which is a novelization of the notorious Loeb and Leopold murder case of 1924. Levin was in a special position to tell the story, because he was personally acquainted with the perpetrators. Levin is also famous for bringing Anne Frank's diary to light. But "The Old Bunch" may be his greatest work.

"The Old Bunch" was written in the mid-1930's, and it tells the tales of the kids of a Chicago Jewish ghetto coming of age and stepping out into the world. It's presumably something of a fantasy autobiography, echoing Levin's own adventures -- Levin was born in 1905, and the events in this book take place beginning in the year 1921 (when the "bunch" is graduating from school), and running through to 1934.

The book is compelling for its individual stories and for its living window into times past. Because it was written prior to the horrors of WWII, it's a very pure view of the pre-war era. (Anything written later will necessarily be done with hindsight, and will likely de-emphasize "unimportant" details in favor of those that connect to major war events.) But the history is merely a fascinating byproduct of the vivid human stories that fill the pages.

"The Old Bunch" is surprisingly unknown today, which is a shame. This really is one of the great novels, and it belongs up there with Tolstoy and Steinbeck. It conveys the entirety of the era: The people, the culture, the economics, Chicago politics (very dirty!), and global trends (some characters travel to Europe and Palestine). It covers the Roaring Twenties, Prohibition, the Great Depression, and the New Deal. To read the book is to live and breathe in these bygone days.

Most importantly, Meyer Levin depicts events without agenda or judgment. Characters may be Democrats or Republicans or workers or bosses or religious or atheistic or many other things, but all are portrayed with depth, and none are simple heroes or villains or symbols. These are, in the end, tales about the very personal and individual transitions to adulthood, and the elusive quest for wisdom. It is the same challenge that every generation must face.

Enough said. Now start reading and let "The Old Bunch" take you where it will.

TO MY WIFE

Author's Note

It has become customary to introduce realistic novels with the statement that their characters and events are imaginary.

I shall not attempt a discussion of the relations between fiction and reality here, except to point out that the realistic novel by its very nature depends upon the use of human materials, and it follows that those materials must in every case fall within the possibilities of human experience.

Perhaps people who lived in the time and places described will expect to identify themselves with the characters in this story. Such identity is entirely mistaken. Certain human traits, problems, and life patterns are recurrent within the society that I have attempted to depict. The use of this type of material is within the granted province of the novelist.

I can say that to my knowledge no real individual is the counterpart of any character in this novel, with the exception of those who are named by actual name. And even they appear in their legendary rather than in their living aspect. Believing that such figures as Samuel Insull, Big Bill Thompson, and Al Capone have become part of the legend of Chicago, I have taken the liberty frequently used by writers of realistic fiction, and introduced their presence. I think my furthest liberty is to have caused Mr. Insull to appear at a wedding of one of my characters.

It seems hardly necessary to say that there is not the slightest malice intended or implied in this work.

In short, if anyone expects to find out anything about anyone's private life from this book, I can assure him at the outset that he won't.

--M. L.

CONTENTS

The Bunch

THE BOYS:

MORT ABRAMSON. *His parents manufacture millinery.*

SAM EISEN. *His father is a buttonhole maker.*

ALVIN FOX. *His father* SOL (the Old Fox) *manufactures folding chairs.*

JOE FREEDMAN. *His father owns a flophouse on South State Street.*

LOU (Big Ears, Second-the-Motion) GREEN. *His father* MR. GREENSTEIN *is a barber; Lou is the* Shadow *of*

LOU (the Sharpshooter) MARGOLIS. *His father is a pawnbroker.*

BEN (Droopy) *and* SOL (Chesty, Speedy) MEISEL. *Their parents own a tailor shop.*

HARRY (Pearly Gates) PERLIN. *His father is a fur worker; Harry has a brother named* VIC.

DAVE (Runt) PLOTKIN. *His father is a cigar maker.*

RUDY STONE. *His father is a shoemaker.*

MITCH WILNER. *His father is an insurance agent.*

THE GIRLS:

SYLVIA ABRAMSON. *Mort's sister.*

ALINE FREEDMAN. *Joe's sister.*

EV GOLDBERG. *Her parents own the Evelyn Shoppes.*

ESTELLE (Red) GREEN. *Lou's sister.*

ROSE (Skinny) HELLER. *Her father owns a furniture store; she has a sister named* MAE.

LIL KLEIN. *Her father is a real estate operator and money lender.*

CELIA MOSCOWITZ. *Her father* RUBE *is a politician and in the scrap iron business.*

THELMA RYSKIND. *Her parents own a grocery store.*

PLACE: *Chicago, New York, Paris, Palestine, Greece, Poland.*
TIME: *1921 to 1934.*

BOOK ONE

Boys and Girls Together

FLAPPERS AND JELLYBEANS[1]

AFTER graduation, there was no place or no excuse for Harry Perlin to meet anybody, except taking a walk down Twelfth Street—pardon me, Roosevelt Road—on the chance of running into somebody looking over the movie stills in front of the Central Park.

Harry meandered as far as St. Louis Avenue, taking a squint through the drug store window to see if Rudy Stone was behind the counter. Rudy wasn't there. Harry turned on St. Louis, thinking maybe he'd run into Lou Margolis, who lived in one of the newer three-story red brick fronts that were stuck in, breaking the gray rows of identical two-flat houses. Fellows like Lou Margolis had something that always kept a crowd turning around them; in fact they had to make excuses to get away from people.

Kids were playing peg. One of them slammed a peg that hit Harry's ankle. "That's all right," Harry forgave, glad to see the scared look fade off the kid's face. The kid doubled down and began to count the sticks. It had been a good long hit.

These summer days, kids stayed out late, playing. The twenty-first was the longest day of the year. It gave Harry a kick to remember facts like that. Motorists turn on lights at 7:40. Automatically, he looked at his wrist-watch. It had the latest radium-lite numerals.

Now it was getting towards dark; the air was the same dirty gray as the stone building fronts. Suddenly he heard a bunch of kids yell: "Yay!" then realized the street lights had just gone on. He had used to yell Yay himself, and straighten up with wonder every time the lights went on.

Now he turned up Douglas Boulevard. Naturally this was a sweller street; most of the buildings were six flats, six-room apartments, red brick sunparlor fronts. Occasionally there remained a large private residence, built when the Irish ran the neighborhood.

Signs hung in the lighted basement windows of many of the apartment buildings: Spartan A.C., or Bluebirds, or Aces. The Lawndale Sportsmen even had a special blue and white electric-box sign, but they could afford to be fancy, they were in good with Rube Moscowitz, who even gave them baseball uniforms. A bunch of fellows would be hanging around in front of each club, making cracks at girls who paraded in pairs along the street. Just taking a walk. On Friday and Saturday nights a lot of the clubs would have victrolas going, and the girls, having accidentally met the fellows, would stop in for a while; there would be dancing.

---

[1] "Flappers" were the young Western women in the 1920's who wore short skirts, bobbed their hair, listened to jazz, and challenged traditional social mores. A "Jellybean" or "Jelly-Bean" was a slang American term of the 1910's and early 1920's for a young man who dressed stylishly but lacked other merit (similar to the older slang terms, "dandy" and "fop").

It was Harry Perlin's idea not to have a club like those other clubs: most of them existed only for a baseball team or to have some fun with the broads. But Pearly thought if fellows like Lou Margolis and Rudy Stone and maybe Mitch Wilner and Joe Freedman could be drawn into the club, serious-minded fellows, they would have a club of a higher type, and they would keep something alive.

Turning again onto Independence Boulevard was like walking up the last side of a rectangle bounding that world. Almost everybody lived inside that rectangle. Well, Sam Eisen lived down on Troy Street, and the Meisels over on Sixteenth; but the half mile square that he had bounded was somehow warmer, full of life, it was the body containing the guts of the neighborhood though there might be limbs spreading outward.

Across the parkway that ran in the middle of the boulevard, making it such a swell street, Harry could see some of the girls gathered on the stairs of the Moscowitz house. He blushed, even though they were at such a distance.

It was funny how on some streets one side seemed dead, the other alive. Take in business. Rudy Stone had told him that Mrs. Kagen's drug store was a dying proposition because it was on the wrong side of Roosevelt Road. Rents on the other side were twice as high, but worth it. The Central Park was on the busy side.

But further along the boulevard, when he saw Joe Freedman getting into the Buick, he waved and crossed over. They circled around to Garfield Park and back, Harry listening to the motor. The valve tappets were making a racket again. "I'll come over Sunday morning and tighten them up," he offered. He got out and lifted the hood of the engine; he could just make out the valves popping. If there had been a little more daylight left he would have started to work right away. Joe was a lousy driver and was killing the car. Between him and his sister Aline what chance did a car have? But you could hardly blame Aline as girls are always hard on a car.

"She had it out yesterday," Joe complained. "Every time she has it out she comes back with something on the blink."

Aline emerged. She was wearing a bright red little skirt, like all the girls were wearing. It had white buttons. Through her georgette waist he could see the straps of her chemise. "Well, what's the matter now? Hello, Harry," she said, and he could feel her standing near him. He wanted to offer to drive her wherever she was going, but after all it wasn't his car.

She was just going over to Rose Heller's but Aline was so lazy she had to take the car even if it was around the corner to the grocery. She admitted it: "What's the use of walking if you have a car?"

As she clashed gears, the fellows looked at each other, wincing.

The Freedman house had one of those high English basements, ideal for a clubroom. Harry figured he could build a crystal set and have it at the club; everybody would take turns listening on his set.

"Say, nobody uses that basement of yours, do they?"

"No," Joe said. "The old man has some ideas of renting it, but you know how he is, he wouldn't spend the dough to fix it up first."

"It's got a nice entrance all right."

"Yah. My mother has got it in her head that I ought to be a doctor, just so I could have an office there," Joe said sarcastically.

"I'll bet it would make a swell clubroom," Harry said.

Joe cast a glance at the dark windows. "They don't want a club in the building. It's supposed to cheapen the building." He grinned.

"Greetings and salutations. What can I do you for?" Rudy was wiping glasses behind Mrs. Kagen's soda fountain. He came out and sat down with Joe and Lou Margolis, ready for a conference.

The first idea was to limit the club to ten.

"If we have it at all," Joe Freedman said, "it ought to mean something to belong. I mean we want something different. We don't want just another club."

Joe's idea was to have each member represent some different field of interest. For instance, Rudolph, going into medicine, could represent that. And Lou naturally would be the law. Joe, himself, would represent, well, the arts. Everyone would bring something to everyone else.

That was a good idea, Rudy agreed, but wouldn't it cut out too many good fellows? For instance, they would want Mitch Wilner.

"Oh, sure."

"Oh, sure."

But that would make two doctors.

"Well, it wouldn't have to be strictly that way, I mean . . ."

The main idea was fellows that would do something. Fellows that weren't just ordinary.

Each leaned back a little. Now they were looking around themselves, seeing what fellows they would go with, whom they would recognize.

"How about Sam Eisen?" Lou offered. This was strange coming from him as everyone had thought Lou and Sam were on the outs. Something funny had happened between them when Lou, as editor of the *Ogdenite*, refused to support Sam for re-election as school mayor, and put in that *goy* McGowan instead. But that school stuff was all over. Lou, at least, was showing that he harbored no grudges.

"Sam's a fine fellow. He'll get somewhere," Rudolph agreed.

They discussed Mort Abramson.

"All Mort would be in for would be the social end," Joe pointed out.

"Well, I haven't anything against being social," Rudy said, "but—"

"Well, I mean, according to that idea we had—what could Mort contribute? He'll probably end up in his old man's business."

"It might be a good idea to have one business man!" Lou Margolis cracked.

Just then they realized that Dave Plotkin had come into the store.

"What is this, the Black Hand?" Runt said, sitting down with them. Trust him to horn in on anything.

He put in Sol Meisel, because Sol was a star athlete, and had been on the championship basketball team—Dave Plotkin, manager. Then they had to have Ben Meisel, because he was Sol's brother.

That made nearly ten.

Harry Perlin was almost left out, as there was nothing special about him, but his friend Joe Freedman insisted that the club had been Pearly's idea in the first place.

Lou Margolis pulled in his shadow, Big Ears Lou Green, who wasn't much. Big Ears soon had another name. It was Second-the-Motion.

"The Ten Aces," Chesty Meisel offered for a name.

"How about the Ten Spot?" Runt Plotkin said.

"The Decas," was Mitch Wilner's studious idea.

"The Ten Turks," Lou Green suggested, with his eyes hopefully on Lou Margolis.

Lou went his shadow one better and said: "The Ten Terrible Turks." There was laughter, but Second-the-Motion thought it was a good name, seriously.

"The Ten Spot," Runt Plotkin insisted. Once he got something in his head! "I move we put it to a vote!"

"Any second?" Lou Margolis asked.

"Point of order!" cried Droopy Ben Meisel.

"There's a motion on the floor."

"A point of order is always in order," Ben argued, and they argued about that. Finally Lou conceded: "Well, what's your point of order?"

"I forgot," Droopy said, and he didn't hear the last of that all night. Whenever an argument about anything got hot, Lou Margolis would mimic: "I forgot," and that would send the fellows into convulsions.

Other names suggested were the Ten Stars, the Ten-Alls; then somebody said did the name have to have Ten in it, and they thought of the Rainbow, the All-Stars, the Independents, the Kibitzers Klub, the Eagles, the Hawks, the Lions, the Tigers, the Bears, the Black Cats, the Blue Elephants, ha ha ha, now get serious fellows, the Arrows, the Owls, the White Owls, then Harry Perlin said:

"How about the Big Ten?"

"Naw, that's—well, that's conceited."

"No, I mean like the Big Ten colleges." Some of the fellows had never even heard of the Conference; but Harry suggested that each club member could represent one of the schools.

Runt Plotkin said it was no better than the Ten Spot. Sol Meisel, to kid Runt, suggested the Little Ten, and Ben Meisel made a motion, Lou Green seconded the motion, and Big Ten it was, six to four.

"Point of order," Lou Green said, as the vote was counted.

"What's it about?"

"I forgot," Lou burbled, convulsed with his own laughter. But somehow the joke wasn't as funny as when the Sharpshooter did it.

Harry offered to calcimine the place if some of the boys would come over Sunday morning and help him. It was okayed for him to go ahead and buy the stuff and the club would repay him.

He came over and did the job, but there was only one brush so Joe Freedman mostly stood around watching. Runt dropped in just as the job was finished. The calcimine had cost 74 cents and Harry gave the bill to Runt, who had somehow become Secretary-Treasurer. It was never paid. He could take it out of his dues, but that would make him feel a piker.

In the Morning, in the Evening

Lil beaded her lashes. With her round little face stuck almost against the mirror, and her big round eyes, everybody said they were big round eyes, held hard open, she fingered the twitching lid and carefully brushed a drop of the black goo onto the edge of her lashes. My, she had long golden lashes, but what good were they if they didn't show? After the stuff had hardened she moved her eyelid slowly downward in an experimental wink at herself. She turned quick to catch herself unexpectedly. She dropped a quick wink. She ran her palm up her arm to feel the delight of herself. All up and down her arms and along her sides she felt little wiggles and jumps of delight. . . . In the morning, in the evening, ain't we got fun! . . . She had many kinds of lipstick. Her father owned the building on the corner of St. Louis and Roosevelt, in which there was Mrs. Kagen's drug store, and she liked to vamp old Dr. Meyerson who was always hanging around the drug store. Mrs. Kagen had a special little drawer, where she dropped the samples that salesmen left. Lil would go into the store and rubber through the counter; every time a salesman left a new lipstick, trust her to get hold of it. Kissproof! That was the latest. "What do you want with Kissproof?" Dr. Meyerson growled. "Wouldn't you like to know!" and she stuck out her lips at him. It was all for Rudy Stone's benefit, he was afraid of her. He always hid behind the prescription partition. "Look at the little vampire!" Dr. Meyerson would remark, trying to slap her behind as she skirted past him. "Would you believe it, only last year she would come in here to steal all-day suckers, now lipstick! Kissproof! Flappers!" he would philosophize. He was a nice man with a fat bald head and she had him completely vamped. "I'll tell your father!" he would promise, all the while Mrs. Kagen sighed resignedly.

Now Lil had got the Kissproof on her mouth, she put her lips out toward the mirror. "Oh, you beautiful baby," she said. "Oh, you beautiful baby," keeping her mouth out in the shape of a kiss. They said that in swell finishing schools for society girls the girls had to sit for two hours a day saying prunes and prisms so their lips would come out in a bow. Prunes and prisms, oh, baby, her lips were a perfect cupid's bow! It just comes to me natural!

She jumped up, bent over to straighten her stockings.

"Flappers!" her father would say. "Sixteen years old! flappers!" And while he was lecturing her, she would bend down just like this to fix the roll of her stocking because that was what got him mad and yet he couldn't say anything. Stockings had to be pulled up every so often and she liked to do it right in the street. Right when standing talking to Mort Abramson or Lou Margolis she could just bend down and pull up her stockings and they tried to keep on talking making fresh and clever remarks.

Lil set the stocking an inch above her knee, so that almost any movement swishing around would flash the naked flesh above the stocking. It almost scared her sometimes, being so daring. I've got rings on my fingers and bells on my toes. . . . She stared at her face in the mirror lid of her big box purse, licked her lips, worked her beaded lashes carefully up and down. . . . That would be a cute idea, bells on your toes. Little weentsy sleigh bells. Gee, if she only dared start a fad like that! She touched the tip of her finger to her tongue and slicked the golden spit curl that made an S on her forehead. She had practiced and she could make it into an O for Oscar but she didn't know any Oscar. It would be terrible if she fell in love with a T or a W! But S was her natural. Who it stood for was a secret. It might be Sol Meisel. Or maybe Sam Eisen. Boo, wouldn't Sam die if he knew! Serious Sam. Two S's. It was nice when her head went back into the cup of a boy's hand. Sol had great big hands, he was an athlete. Lil shivered and danced with herself, she felt so full of life, and she had a big green-stone ring that she put on her engagement finger to kid the kids, rings on my fingers and bells on my toes, and as she walked out onto Roosevelt Road she felt she could almost hear the little bells of herself ringing all around her as she walked. . . . The rich get richer and the poor get . . . (children!). . . Oh, but honey, ain't we got fun!

Passing Rosen's barber shop, Lil Klein looked inside because at a certain angle you could see your whole figure mirrored, and who should be sitting there but Estelle Green! She was getting a bob! Celia Moscowitz was standing beside her holding her hand and giving directions to Mr. Rosen.

Oh, mygod, Lil thought, if I had beautiful red hair like that I would never have it cut! And why didn't Estelle have her own father bob her hair, he was a barber and they didn't have dollars to throw away. Bet she would catch it when she got home!

Mr. Rosen, finishing, held up a mirror for Estelle to see the back. Estelle's shoulders began to shake; Lil couldn't tell whether she was crying or laughing. Then Estelle jumped out of the chair and ran for the door.

"Kid, I've gone and done it!" Estelle burst out, meeting Lil. She stood trembling as if one word would make her cry.

"It's beautiful!" Lil said. "Honest!"

"Oh! Does it look all right? Honest?" Estelle clutched Lil's arm.

"Honest, kid! Oh, it's awful cute! It makes you look so snappy!"

"Honest?" Estelle said, staring first at Lil and then at Celia. And suddenly she wailed: "Oh, my mother'll kill me!"

"Oh, don't be a gump," Celia said. "You look cute."

"Oh, you don't know my mother." She began to tremble all over. "I can't go home. She'll kill me!"

Lil and Celia had to pull her into a side street, as everybody was stopping to stare at Estelle.

"My mother didn't like it either at first," Celia said, "but now she says she's going to get her own hair bobbed."

"Anyway, what can she do, it's cut," Lil pointed out.

But that only made Estelle wilder. "Oh, you don't know my mother," she wailed. "She said if I ever cut my hair she'd cut my head off, she's got some crazy idea only bad women do it, oh, she just wants to ruin my life, she just wants me to sit in the house and be crazy like her, oh, you don't know what I have to stand for—"

"I know what, kid," Celia said, putting her thick arm around Estelle and leading her like a child; "listen, you come to my house, and we'll have my mother call her up and break it to her."

The Moscowitz house was fancier than any house in the neighborhood. Mrs. Moscowitz was up to date and you would never see a Yiddish newspaper in her hands. She dressed spiffy with wrap-around sport skirts, and even rolled her stockings, just like the girls. The apartment was swell, too, with a full-width sunparlor and French doors. Near the gas log fireplace was a grand piano—not a baby grand. A great red and yellow Spanish shawl was slung over its propped-up top. There were at least a dozen lamps, floor lamps and table lamps, and Celia's mother was always buying marvelous new lamp shades at Field's. Yellow silk shades with domes growing out of domes, and pagoda shapes with gorgeous long bead fringes. There was a big oriental vase that was always full of flowers. The only time Estelle ever had flowers was at graduation, and she supposed she would get some when she got married.

Well, the Moscowitzes could afford it. With his political pull, Rube Moscowitz made plenty of money.

Just to sink into the beautiful overstuffed sofa, made Estelle feel better, safer.

Mrs. Moscowitz looked at her sitting there bawling, and burst out laughing.

"Why, a great big girl like you!" she said.

Then Mrs. Moscowitz marched around her inspecting her bob from all angles. She even stepped up and arranged a lock of hair.

"Why, I think it looks *very* cute," she said. "My, if Celia only had red hair like that!"

"I wish I had hair like that!" Lil agreed, waiting for someone to cry: "What! With your golden locks!"

"I think it brings out the color to cut it," Mrs. Moscowitz said. "Anyway, why have long hair? It's such a bother. Believe me!"

Estelle stopped sniffling. She began thinking of a campaign to make her mother buy a new frontroom set.

"Now, dearie," said Mrs. Moscowitz, "I'll talk to your mother if you want me to, or why don't you just walk in and surprise her? That's what Celia did to me."

"Oh, you don't know my mother!" Estelle began all over again. "She— well, she doesn't understand things the way other people do."

"That's right!" Lil put in. "Didja read in the paper only the other day some Polack caught his daughter with a bob and he broke her nose? Honest! It was in the paper! He was arrested and fined five dollars!"

"They should have broken his nose for him," said Celia.

"Can you beat that!" said Mrs. Moscowitz. "But some people are such ignorants! They just can't understand this is a free country and a girl can bob her hair if she wants to. They're greenhorns[2]." There was a strained moment; Estelle blushed as red as her hair.

When the telephone rang, Mrs. Greenstein was sitting on a kitchen chair, waiting for something terrible to happen. Fear of the strange forces of this outside world had been in her ever since, as a girl, she had left her village in Poland in a horse-drawn cart, to go on trains and in the dark thrumming hold of a terrifying boat, for the new country. It had seemed that the trains must collide, that the boat must sink.

Twenty-two years of this life had passed, and yet it was a strange life to her. First one lit gas jets and then one turned on electric lights, but still the only real life, the only safe life, was under the glow of the oil lamp, those first sixteen years back home.

She sat in her kitchen, just another dumpy West Side mother, in a shapeless housedress. Although she kept her house clean, she let herself go sloppy around the house, tying strips of rags just under her knees to hold up her stockings, no matter how many pairs of garters Estelle bought her. Mrs. Greenstein's mouth was fallen, her eyes always wore an expression of deep inner tragedy.

---

[2] "Greenhorn" was an epithet often applied by Americanized Jews to immigrant Jews that retained the attitudes of the Old World.

"What is so terrible in her life?" Estelle would sometimes burst out. She would think of all the mothers who had had sons killed in the war; they really had something to be tragic about!

Now, waiting for trouble, Mrs. Greenstein sat looking out at the crisscross of gray painted stairways and back porches. A gang of kids were walking a fence; each seemed to be her boy Louie, who was walking on a thread agonizingly stretched from one point to another of her own heart, and would surely fall and break his neck.

When the telephone rang she was startled exactly as if she had seen one of the children fall. The telephone must some day bring her news of a terrible disaster; each time it rang might be that time.

But it might be a boy calling up Estelle for a date. Perhaps she could find out who; from her daughter she never learned anything.

"Hahlo," she said carefully. "Who is this?"

"Hello, mother." With the others listening, Estelle said mother instead of ma.

Mrs. Greenstein said: "Yeh?" and waited.

"I've got a surprise for you," said Estelle, and a nervous giggle came out of her.

"What kind of a surprise?" said Mrs. Greenstein. Then she could bear the strangeness of it no longer, this telephone, what was the girl trying to tell her, what terrible thing—had she run away with a *goy*?

"Where are you?" she cried.

"Oh, I can't tell her!" wailed Estelle, putting her hand over the mouth of the phone. "She'll kill me!"

"Where are you? What is the matter?" cried Mrs. Greenstein.

"Listen, ma, don't get sore—I'll tell you if you won't get sore."

"What has happened!"

"Don't get sore! I had a bob!"

"Hah?" said her mother.

"A bob! I bobbed my hair!" Estelle shrieked, and began to giggle.

"No! I told you not to do it! How many times did I told you not to do it!" Mrs. Greenstein's whole body was trembling. It was just as if her daughter had called her up to say she had done something bad with a man. The wildness of her. She saw the nakedness of her daughter, the young, white, evil flesh, the girl naked with shorn hair under the lustful eyes of men. Her daughter would become a whore in the streets, her daughter with the breasts that she had seen budding, and been ashamed to tell her daughter anything, with the hips that she had felt rounding under her own fingers every time she made her daughter a dress; but how could she talk when even their languages were different, how could she tell a girl such important things when she couldn't think of the English words for them, while in Yiddish you always felt you were talking up, not down to your children? And the girl would laugh at her. The girls knew everything

15

already, with their smart eyes, and their tongues licking their lips. Such young snips, wild, they were wild, something wild in them, like wild animals.

"Well, aren't you going to say something?" Estelle said.

"Where are you?" Mrs. Greenstein sputtered. She wanted to get a stick, a whip in her hands, and hit until red welts were raised. Then she would know! That Esther!

"I'm at Celia's. I—I—" Oh, it would have been better if she had gone straight home.

Now Mrs. Greenstein understood. Now it was all clear. It was the others who were leading her daughter. Mrs. Moscowitz, fancy and stylish, who had a *shikseh* in the house. And her daughter with the great bulging breasts that a girl should be ashamed to show in the street.

"All right! You are by Mrs. Moscowitz! Stay there! Don't come home, do you hear me, you haven't a home any more! I should never live to see you again!"

Estelle began to bawl. "Listen, ma, listen, ma, oh, stop it! stop it!"

"Why, what's the matter, Estelle? Here, let me talk to her." Mrs. Moscowitz took the phone. "I know how you feel, Mrs. Greenstein, but, honest, it isn't so bad. All the girls are doing it and you ought to see, Estelle looks real cute."

"Listen, Mrs. Moscowitz," Estelle's mother shrilled, "you don't have to tell me how to raise my children. Your girl you can raise like you want. But let me tell you there are still some people maybe they are not so swell and stylish but they are still respectable. For your girl she should go around painting her face and staying out all night with the boys, all right! Her family shows her the way! But as long as I am still alive I would not let my girl be such a cheap, fresh, dirty thing! You know what I mean! Whores and pimps—"

Mrs. Moscowitz turned yellow. "After all I have nothing to do with it!" she shrieked. "I was only talking for your own good!"

"You and your girl and all your kind, you are taking good girls and making them—"

"You can't talk to me like that! You can't—"

"All right, you want her, keep her! Maybe you can do business with my girl and your girl too!" Mrs. Greenstein's voice was one long hysterical shriek. "Maybe your husband the politician can collect good money for them! In the flats all over the neighborhood! White slaves, *nafkehs*--"

Mrs. Moscowitz hung up the receiver.

It was a while before Mrs. Greenstein knew that no one was listening. She sat, shuddering, staring at the wall.

Estelle was crying and crying. Celia took her into her bedroom and pulled back the orchid taffeta spread, and Estelle lay on the sheet and sobbed.

For a while Mrs. Moscowitz held off, but then, realizing the poor girl's mother was nothing but a greenhorn, and plain crazy, she came and stroked Estelle's hand. Estelle only cried harder, to think that some mothers could be so understanding.

Lil Klein sat on the edge of the bed, feeling just full of things to tell. She had just started out for a walk, and here she was in on everything!

The phone rang and it was Thelma Ryskind wanting to know if Celia was going to the social at the boys' clubroom. Thelma didn't want to go by herself, but if the rest of the girls were going . . .

Just the thing to make Estelle snap out of it! "Oh, kid, wait till I tell you what happened!" Celia said. "Meetcha here."

For once, Harry Perlin stopped work on time. By five-thirty he was at the rusty sink in the rear of the Albany tire shop, rubbing mechanic's soap into his knuckles, trying to wash out the little black grease lines that stayed there no matter what he did.

> "Sweet personality,
> Full of rascality . . ."

He whistled the tune, and the words kept hopping through his head.

"My, my, my, Pearly must be stepping out tonight. Don't do anything I wouldn't do," the boss kidded him.

At home, without waiting to eat, Harry grabbed his crystal set and stuffed some wire and some tools into his coat pocket. He dashed over to the clubroom.

On an old golden-oak dining table which the Freedmans had contributed to the club, Harry set up the radio.

> In the morning, in the evening,
> Ain't we got fun . . .

At last Harry put the earphones over his head and listened. Nothing. He tried one spot and another. Suddenly he heard a crackling and sputtering. Static. His set was working.

Then Harry realized someone was standing behind him. He blushed before he turned: it might be Aline.

> Ain't got much money,
> Oh, but honey . . .

It was Joe. "Does it work?" Joe said, putting on the other set of earphones. Harry watched his face.

"What's all that noise?" Joe said.

"That's static."

"Sounds like a tin lizzie. Is that all there is to it?"

"Well, you have to wait until something comes on the air," Harry explained. "There ought to be something tonight." He was beginning to feel anxious. Maybe Aline had a date somewhere else tonight. He could pretend he had to go through the house to fix the aerial, and see if she was there.

"Say, can't you get rid of that static?" Joe said, taking off the phones.

Harry fumbled with the contact, trying to find a clearer spot. The main idea was the set worked. Couldn't Joe get the main idea? Everything else could be cleared up, in time.

The two Lous, Lou Margolis and his shadow Lou Green, came in with the Meisels. Lou Green had brought along a portable vic. He set it up and put on "Old Pal, Why Don't You Answer Me?"

Runt Plotkin came in, rubbing his hands energetically in imitation of a Maxwell Street business man. "Well how's about it boys, how's about it?"

"Say, did anyone see my sister?" Lou Green said. "She had her hair cut and, boy, is she going to get it! The old lady is sore as hell."

Runt spotted the radio set. "Say, Harry, can you broadcast from that? How about having a special broadcast for the club?"

"Bring on the broad and I'll do the casting!" Lou Margolis the Sharpshooter cracked.

That was a howl.

They were standing around and it began to look like maybe the girls wouldn't show up after all.

Lou Margolis grabbed the earphone and talked into it as though it were a mouthpiece: "You are now listening to the Big Ten club in a special program. If anybody has seen a redheaded baby who answers to the name of Estelle Green, tell her to go home 'cause her mama's getting mad! All is forgiven. Positively, Mr. Gallagher?"

"Absolutely, Mr. Shean!" Lou Green responded.

Harry Perlin suggested having the business meeting while they were waiting.

"Have we got any business?" Lou Margolis said blandly.

"How about paying some dues? Come on, out with the shekels." Runt Plotkin rubbed his hands.

"Hey, what time did you tell them to come?" Sol said.

"Eight o'clock."

"Yah, Jewish time," snapped the Sharpshooter, and there was a general snicker.

Then a cluster of girls arrived. Four of them: Celia, Thelma Ryskind, Lil Klein, and Estelle Green. They came giggling, sniffing, down the three steps, peeking in as if they had never met any of the fellows before, and then the place was suddenly full of girls. Aline Freedman finally condescended to come down; skinny Rose Heller was with her. The girls were all chirping and jumping about Estelle, examining her bob. It was as if the fellows had nothing to do with the place.

"Oh, you look cute, you look darling!" They all brushed her hair and fluffed her hair.

"I don't dare go home, my mother'll kill me!"

"Oh, she'll be all right when she sees how cute you look. . . ."

Pearly pretended to be absorbed in his radio. Aline was right near him talking to Lou Margolis. "Doesn't Estelle look cute! Do you think I ought to have mine cut?"

"I like yours the way it is," Harry Perlin blurted.

Aline snatched up the headphones. "Earmuffs!" she said. "Does it work?"

He got dizzy from her being so near.

"I don't know if there's anything on the air just now," he managed to say. She had got her hair all tangled under the earphones, and he had to free the locks with his excited fingers.

Now the ripples of girls seemed to spread outward from redhead Estelle, the girls spreading through the room, sniffing and sensing to feel what a boys' place was like. "They ought to have curtains," Sylvia Abramson observed. Aline looked to see if Syl had come with her brother Mort, Syl was such a kid she didn't really go out yet. But Sylvia was with Alvin Fox, the Duke. Mort must be peeved because the boys hadn't asked him to join.

Joe Freedman, being artistic and chairman of the house committee, was called over to discuss curtains. Joe and Sylvia knew each other from school of course, though Syl was still there, in the class of '22. Aline noticed the slightly embarrassed feeling that fell between the two kids; they were looking each other over as if meeting for the first time, and she could practically see them getting a crush. It would be cute if Syl went with Joe; maybe she'd see more of Mort.

"You could make them out of checkered gingham, it's awfully cheap, too," Sylvia suggested.

"Say, that would be just the thing," he said. They decided she'd come over after school some time, for the measurements. A star-struck silence fell. They drifted apart into the crowd, as though not quite sure they were finished talking.

The fellows were herded at the rear end of the room, the girls pretended to be interested in the decorations, nobody quite knew whether they should start dancing, or what. Mitch Wilner saved the situation by putting on some records Thelma had brought over.

"They're classical," she said, handling them as though they were made of platinum. "That's Caruso. That's my favorite record. *Pagliacci.*"

"Did you hear Caruso died[3]?" Alvin the Duke interjected.

---

[3] Enrico Caruso died August 2, 1921 at age 48.

"No!" Thelma gasped.

"Sure, it was in the paper."

"That's right! It's a fact!" Runt Plotkin had seen it too.

"Oh, my God!" Thelma clutched the record.

"Say, I'll bet those records will be worth something now," Runt said. How could he think of such things at such a time!

The whole bunch had gathered around the victrola. "Play it anyway," the Duke suggested.

"Oh, it would be like a ghost!" Lil squeaked.

Harry Perlin wound the victrola. There was a kind of reverent silence. It was as if all of them for the first time together were brought into the presence of death. It made them all feel glowingly united, not just flappers and jellybeans, but a new young generation capable of facing the serious things of life.

When it came to the part where the clown laughed, Thelma stifled a sob.

"She's putting on an act," Estelle whispered, to break her own feeling.

Joe Freedman had moved nearer to Sylvia Abramson; when the record was over they were standing like mates, side by side. Embarrassed, they moved away from one another.

"That man was a great artist," Mitch Wilner stated.

"My God, it gives me the creeps," redhead Estelle cried out. "Put on something snappy."

Harry Perlin put on "My Man," and a few couples began to dance.

Thelma Ryskind took her Caruso record upstairs for safety.

Lil Klein was dancing with Sol Meisel. Gosh, how thrilled she had always been by him, the star athlete. Now he was out of school, would he still be that, a star athlete? She pressed her hand against his back, feeling the muscles. She pressed her forehead against the warm scratchy harbor under his chin. This way, he would breathe the scent of her hair, right under his nose.

While dancing with Lil, Chesty Meisel had his eye on that redhead. Boy, he could certainly fall for Estelle.

He was certainly dumb at conversation, Lil thought, and he was a bum dancer too. You would think being so speedy on the basketball floor he would be light on his feet, but he carried her as if he were carrying a ball and had to stop and look around to see which way the coast was clear. To fill the silence she began singing under her breath:

"Oh, my ma-an,
I love him so,
He'll never know . . .

"How do you like my new spit-curl?" she asked Sol.

He examined it. "Boy, that's hot." But he didn't catch on. "Can't you read?" she said.

"Huh? Oh. Is that supposed to be an S?"

"Guess who it stands for."

Sol grinned. He was waking up. "How about Sol?" he said.

Lil tried toddling a little but he didn't follow.

"Is it Sol?" he said.

"Lots of names begin with S," she said, giving him a long look through slanted lashes. She could make him wake up if she wanted to. "Say, doesn't Sammy Eisen belong to this club?"

"Yah, he's a member."

"Well, I don't see him around."

"Oh," said Sol. He wished the record would end so he could get next to that redhead. But every time it nearly ended Lou Green would put the needle back somewhere in the middle, and har, har.

Lil decided she liked fellows with brains, like Lou Margolis or Sam Eisen. But Lou Margolis was too conceited, and had a terrible Jewish nose. She began to hum again:

"I love him so,
He'll never know . . ."

Sam Eisen wasn't so sure about the club. Rudy Stone, Mitch Wilner, Joe Freedman were all right. What he was leery of was the smart alecks and cake eaters, like Lou Margolis, or Sol Meisel, the flapper's delight.

Oh, no, he wasn't holding any grudge against Lou Margolis. From now on things had to be judged from a grown-up standpoint, and maybe that affair in school had only been kid stuff.

It was funny, though, after the swell way he and Lou had worked together the first half of the year, running the school between them; boy, how they had made those kids do things! Big Bill Thompson had nothing on them! Throw away your hammer and get a horn! Boost Ogden High! Some of the excitement was still in his blood, though of course now he knew it was only kid stuff. Still, the school had never piled up such a record before, it was a kind of winning fever they had shot into the kids, Lou Margolis pounding the idea of win, win, in every issue of the *Ogdenite*, while Sam inflamed the students at mass meetings. After cleaning up the lightweight football championship and the soccer championship the school swept on in a kind of hysteria to cop both basketball shields, to win in debating, swimming, and a dozen minor sports.

But then Lou had got funny, refusing to support Sam for re-election. It was beginning to be said that the Jews were running everything, Lou hinted. That was beginning to make bad feeling. So Lou's school weekly came out for Chuck McGowan for mayor. Sam Eisen was defeated.

All kid stuff. Jealousies. Lou had wanted to be the whole cheese and maybe make fifty bucks on the class pins and senior prom. Sam Eisen put it all out of his mind. But one thing he had learned from that experience. Look how even in that kid stuff at high school the power of the press had been demonstrated! And look at Hearst. They said he was going to run for President.

Now Sam was going into the world, and that school stuff had shown him what he could do. . . . To run people! To feel the power of the crowd surging in himself, to feel that he was making them do big things, good things, that they never could have done scattered. Not exactly politics. Certainly he didn't mean to become a cheap ward politician, a Rube Moscowitz. And even to be a Clarence Darrow wouldn't fulfill his want. But that was more like it.

And he had thought those fellows in the club were the ones that were going to amount to something, to do things! But here the first thing the club did was to run dancing and socials like all the other pastime clubs in the neighborhood. Those dizzy flappers that hung around with lazy Aline Freedman would be there. Lil Klein with her golden curls and baby eyes. He wasn't afraid of girls, but what he hated was this monkeying around. There was no use pretending; he wouldn't be ready for girls for several years.

He would drop in and listen to Rudy Stone's talk, and leave right afterward.

At 8:30, Rudy went into the little closet, hung up his white coat, and washed his hands. As he put on his jacket he checked up on his notes, in the pocket. Two sheets covered with minute but perfect handwriting. He had put in some time preparing his talk for the club, since he believed that any task undertaken, no matter how small its significance, should be accomplished to the best of his ability.

"Well, madam, is everything under control?" he repeated his parting formula to Mrs. Kagen.

"Go on, go on, nobody needs you," the old lady chirped.

"Over the river, Mrs. Kagen," he said. "Don't take any wooden nickels."

Rudolph walked up to Dr. Meyerson's office. He had not wanted to borrow the microscope in advance as there was no sense in taking extra responsibility.

"Greetings and salutations," he said as Dr. Meyerson stuck his head out from the inner office door. The brushy white eyebrows jerked upward. "Ah, Rudy." Dr. Meyerson emerged. "What are you after, huh? I know you did not come for the pleasure of imbibing my wisdom!"

With his sprouting white eyebrows, Dr. Meyerson looked like Theodore Roberts in the movies. A brusqueness of speech, a slight eccentricity of manner, went with the character. It was expected of him. He had come to expect it of himself. The neighborhood doctor. Years and years and all that baloney. The babies that he had pulled out of their mothers' bellies now coming to him with ulcers in their own bellies. For twenty years he had been sending all of his prescriptions to the Kagen drug store. Mr. Kagen, *olav hasholem*, had sent the doc his first patients.

Between Dr. Meyerson and Rudolph there were no ceremonies. That was his first command. "No ceremonies. Don't show me any respect. It makes me feel too old." He approved of Rudolph. At least once a week he announced to Mrs. Kagen, so Rudy could hear: "So he wants to be a doctor? Well when he gets out I will turn over my practice to him. By that time I'll be old enough to retire if I don't go crazy first. Maybe it won't be fancy enough for him. But let me tell you, Mrs. Kagen, plenty of these fancy young squirts just out of the medical schools would be glad to get five bucks for curing Mrs. Schmaltz's bellyache. A doctor is a doctor, that's all, for a bellyache or for cancer. Now they are all specialists. If you have to have your adenoids out, go to Prof. Dr. Applebaum in Philadelphia! If you have ingrowing toe-nails, go to Rochester! I am a specialist in monkey bites! I handle only cases of people who have been bitten by a monkey! . . . Rudolph will be a doctor, and my families will need a doctor, and a case of piles, begging your pardon, is the same on Twelfth Street as in the Drake Hotel!"

Rudolph could say of Dr. Meyerson: "Well, maybe the old guy stopped reading the *Courier* ten years ago, but you have to admit he gets around, he has a lot of patients, he is in the hospitals, he knows what's going on."

They went into the little office with the roll-top desk and the jars of pickled embryos. "Well, here it is, not so up to date and maybe a little dusty." Dr. Meyerson blew imaginary dust from the cover of the microscope. "So you are going to make a bunch of Pasteurs and Kochs out of your pals?" He bent over the scope, squinting ferociously, his eyebrows sticking out like spears. "It's a fine thing, Rudolph. A remarkable invention. I can remember the excitement when people began to do things with the scope." He tapped the tube. "At that time I was not even a medical student yet. When I came to this country I was like your father, a shoemaker. Yah. And a fine one. Well, you know at that time we didn't have to go eight years to school to be a doc, and I didn't learn so much. Never mind. It is better now. Better you should learn in school than on your patients. So Koch came out with his tubercle bacillus. My, was I excited! Pasteur finds the cure for rabies. Oh, what excitement!" Meyerson dropped his knotty fingers over the scope. "You know what it was going to do, this little tube? It was going to make an end to all diseases. Yep, it was going to put us out of business forever. Complete. We smear a little blood on the glass, we find the bacillus—presto! We make a serum. Finish! All that would be left for the docs to do would be maybe to saw off a leg once in a while. So we shot everybody full of serums." He paused, cocked an eye at Rudy. "If a doctor kills somebody, well, we know he would have died anyway. Hah?"

"That's usually the case," Rudy said, uneasy at the old man's intensity.

"Oh, serums are a fine thing. Maybe the greatest thing man has ever produced. They have saved millions of lives. Stopped epidemics. So if we had a little trouble until we learned to use them, and if even now we have a little trouble every once in a while—" He put his hand heavily on Rudy's arm. "I had a little experience myself, once. When I was a young practitioner, and didn't know how to take those things . . ."

In a moment, Rudy thought, he would be told something of the secret, deep truth about being a doctor. But Meyerson ticked his lips, like one who decides he is not yet ready to sum up his life and die.

He coughed, breathed noisily. "So you understand, they haven't found out even the germ for a common cold, yet! All the big heads rushed to the laboratory and they haven't taken their eyes away from the eyepiece for forty years, and what have they got? We can cure diphtheria and we can prevent scarlet fever and I still have to put up little red signs on the door for scarlet fever, like in the Middle Ages, and do you know how many children died from diphtheria last year? Right here in America! And we can see this little louse of a tubercle bacillus, but what can we do about him? We can put the patient in bed. So they can gaze in their eyepieces, and meanwhile old *kakers* like me have to crawl around and give pills to diabetics and a lot of good it does them. . . . Nah. Here is your wonderful machine, Rudolph," he snorted. "If your hoodlums break the lens I will break your neck."

Opening a drawer, with his jerky, emergency-brake abruptness, Dr. Meyerson pulled out some slides. "These are mostly tubercles. Once I was intending to do some work on the subject; among our little *landslait* in the shops there are plenty of specimens. I was going to find out why operators more than bosses get the louse." He looked at a marking. "Ah, Yankel Feinberg. Well, he won't mind if you exhibit his sputum. Papa Feinberg is where he don't have to worry about Meyerson's bills any more. . . . And this little worm is typhus, and this—well maybe you have some nice young girls in your club, huh?" He chuckled, a sound more like a gargle, and put aside the slide marked *Spirochaeta pallida.*

"Thanks very much, doc," Rudy said, taking a last look to make sure everything was in order, before sliding the scope into the box. "Well, over the river."

As he walked down Roosevelt Road, holding the box out stiffly to keep it from bumping his leg, he was listening again to Meyerson's outburst. What got him was the way he knew the old doc really felt. The doc wasn't belittling the wonderful things research had accomplished. It was just a disappointment, a sorrow to him, that the cure-all had not really been discovered. Working in one drug store or another, after school, and full time in summers, Rudy had got to know almost every doctor in the neighborhood, and Doc Meyerson was still, to him, the man that tended the sick. It was a good solid feeling to know that the doc was behind him; he even had a practice waiting for him. Sometimes, putting on his hat, Rudy looked at his face in the mirror; he saw the simple round contour of his cheeks, the few honest pimples that came and went, and whose cause he knew. He got a feeling not so much of self-satisfaction as of trust in himself; all this work that he was doing, day and evening, all this being good, was really the only way; the trust of someone like Doc Meyerson gave him that same clean satisfaction. He hoped some day to find a wife who would have that kind of faith and trust in him.

". . . The whole night through I pray to you . . ."

Rose Heller was a scream! So good-natured, always jolly! She sang in a comical nasal tone, throwing out her long skinny arms:

"My arms embrace an empty space;
Old Pal, why don't you answer me?"

"I'm enswering!" Lou Margolis mimicked. "Vot number do you vant?"

"Wrong number!" Rose came back. Was she a scream!

". . . Sure he'll fight. But who's he gonna fight? There ain't anybody can last two rounds with Dempsey. He'll make hash out of Gibbons!" Sol was arguing with Plotsy.

"It was Fatty Arbuckle in *The Traveling Salesman*. Oh, boy, was he funny!"

"Is he the cat's pajamas! When Fatty started to make love I thought I'd die!"

"He takes the hand-crocheted soup-spoon!"

"Hey, do you know how a fat man does it?" Runt said to Sol.

"Ask Dad, he knows," the Sharpshooter cut in. The fellows sputtered.

"Welcome, stranger," Lil said to Sam Eisen.

"Oh, hello," he said and sort of wandered off.

She had known it! He was afraid of her! Serious Sam! . . . Old Pal, why don't you answer me? . . .

The bunch was collected around the two Lous, who had been prevailed upon to do their Gallagher and Shean imitation. They certainly had it down pat, practicing all the time at the Sharpshooter's house. They made a perfect team. Lou Green was the taller of the two and, with his happy red cheeks, he was such a comical combination for snappy-eyed Lou Margolis.

Lou Margolis was supposed to have made up this verse himself. It was about a girl who

"came home at three a.m.,
and her papa said a-hem,
can you tell me pliz, my Rosie,
vere you been?"

And in falsetto, Lou Green chirped:

"I took a joy-ride on a hack,
And the boys made me walk back."

"Posilutely, Mr. Gallagher?"

"Absotively, Mr. Shean!"

Lou Green always bust out laughing himself on the "absotively."

Rudy Stone appeared in the doorway. "Greetings and salutations," he said.

Now the lecture would begin. Some of the kids had to double up on chairs. "Hey, Red!" Sol called to Estelle. "Plenty of room." He patted his knee.

"Hey, here's a soft seat," Alvin Fox called, and offers arose from every side. Estelle promised to sit on each lap for five minutes, starting with Sol's.

Sam Eisen found himself squeezed onto one chair with Lil. "Pardon me," she said devilishly as she pressed her warm little thigh against him, and he said: "Oh, I can bear it if you can," and looked straight into her eyes. They both had to laugh. He had to put his arm around her to keep her from falling off the chair; she thrust her face up at him, with an outward movement of the cupid's bow lips, and said: "Gee, I bet you're even human."

Suddenly Sam decided he would be like the other fellows and sneaked his fingers against the softness under her unfettered little breast.

"Why, the verra idea!" she lisped, giving him a Lillums hoity-toity stare, while she lifted off his hand like a bug. Then she pulled her skirt down over her knees, and turned her attention forward.

Sam felt sore. She let everybody else. He had watched her dancing. But afterward he worked his hand back there, and she settled into it.

Mitch Wilner seemed to have appointed himself general assistant to Rudolph. They had the cover off the microscope, and were bending their heads together at the eyepiece.

"What kind is it? A Zeiss?" Mitch asked judiciously.

"Spencer," said Rudolph, showing the name-plate.

"Those German ones have marvelous lenses," Mitch said. "The Americans can't touch them."

"I don't know about that," Rudolph said. "He's got a pretty good lens in here."

Lou Margolis called the meeting to order and said: "Any old business, any new business, any old clothes, suits, umbrellas, a motion is now in order to adjourn."

All the members waited for Lou Green to say "Second the motion," and when he did there was a howl. The members tried to explain the joke to the visitors.

Lou Margolis then introduced Rudy as the illustrious Dr. Stone.

"Thank you, professor," Rudy came back. He cleared his throat and said ponderously: "Ahem." There was a laugh. He drew forth his notes and spread them on the table.

"We have here," he said, "an instrument commonly known as a microscope. Now, I think it is safe to say that the study of medicine did not really begin until the invention of the microscope. Before that, if you got sick, the learned doctors held a consultation and decided to bleed the patient. But in 1660 a Dutch lens-grinder by the name of Leeuwenhoek . . ."

"He's cute but too serious," Aline was thinking, looking at Rudy's honest round face, with the pimples. As he talked, a cowlick of hair came down over his forehead, and she wondered how he would act if he were alone with a girl. . . . Lil fastened her round eyes on the speaker. Sam would see that she had some brains, and was so interested she didn't even know his hand was there.

That old Dutchman had never even thought of a removable slide, Rudy said. By the time he died he had six hundred microscopes standing around his shop, with everything from a raindrop to a hair fixed in them.

It was the thought of that little Dutchman making his six hundred microscopes that stopped Harry Perlin. He was sitting near enough to reach and touch the finely adjusted brass knobs. Harry could imagine that Dutchman sitting on a worn stool before his immaculate workbench, his set of tweezers, his clamps, his grinding tools all laid out in precisely their proper places. He must have had a fine shop for himself, everything kept in order. Each time he finished one, he must have experienced a sort of sadness with his pride, and not felt good again until he had started on another microscope, to be better than the last. When each new lens was finished, he rustled around for something different to look at, just as each time you tried out a new hook-up on a radio you wanted to pick up something in the air, to check the way it worked. The kids all laughed, but there was nothing funny about those six hundred microscopes, sitting around the walls of the Dutchman's shop.

Listening, Mitch checked off each thing Rudolph said against what he already knew. Of course Rudy was just giving them the elementary stuff that they had practically all had in high school; but still it gave Mitch a safe feeling to realize that so far he knew everything that Rudy had to say, even with his year of premedic. On the other hand, he wouldn't have minded learning something tonight.

Now Rudy was going to demonstrate the scope. He tipped a drop of oil onto the tubercle slide. Mitch had to know what kind of oil was used.

There was a hush as Rudy bent over, looking into the scope, adjusting the focus. His stubby fingers seemed suddenly delicate, touching the brass screw. It was strange how they sat there fascinated. In high school, any science teacher would have been tickled to show them how a microscope worked. But now, doing it for themselves, they felt as though they were investigating some deep and occult science.

Rudy straightened up, and Mitch bent over the tube. He tried to keep both eyes open, as he had heard that experts didn't have to shut the unused eye. He pressed so close that the eyepiece was against his glasses. Although the scope was already focused, he couldn't help putting his fingers on the small screw, turning it up a little, watching the slide go vague and out of focus, then turning it back until the view was sharp, trying to get it even sharper than Rudy had left it. There. He had done the focusing for himself. Now.

"Do you see the tubercles?" Rudy said. "The little red buggers?"

Mitch saw the field of sputum, grayish-greenish splotches, some scattered dark flecks and bits of streaky crooked lines; this that he was doing was nothing, kid stuff, and yet he felt his heart pumping. He was so excited he couldn't analyze, at first.

"There's a few right near the center of the field," Rudy said. Mitch wished he had found them without Rudy's direction, and felt he would have if Rudy hadn't spoken. He made out three red specks in a clump, like a hen track. To the left there was another group. Suppose he were Koch, looking down for the first time upon the germs that he had isolated! He began to count the germs.

It seemed to him that there was nothing for him to learn about this instrument, but only to remember; it seemed that this had all been a part of him some long time ago.

"I counted fourteen," he said, straightening. "That guy had t.b., all right."

"He must have. He died of it," Rudy said.

Lou Margolis took a squint and cracked: "Hey, are you sure those things are dead?"

There was a big laugh. But Rudy explained seriously that the dye on the slides killed the germs.

"They dye to die!" Lou Margolis cracked, and was that a howl!

Plotsy looked and couldn't make out the red things they were talking about, but finally he let on that he had seen them.

A hair was one of the things they looked at. Aline thought she would have a fit when Rudy solemnly grasped the cowlick that hung so comically over his forehead.

"Oh, lemme do it!" she begged. He stood patiently like a little boy while she singled out a hair and gave it a yank. Rudy was sweet.

He put it on a slide. "This hair is too dark," he said. "All you can see is the segmentation. Is there a blonde in the house?"

"How about a redhead?" Sol cried, and yanked a couple of hairs from Estelle's head. She yipped, and jumped a mile. Sol guffawed.

Mitch contributed a blond hair. Then they examined the three kinds of hair. The blond showed best.

One after another, they uttered cries of astonishment and wisecracks, seeing the hair growing out of itself in segments, seeing something actually inside a hair!

The novelty gone, some drifted away. But there remained a group around the table, Mitch and Rudy, Sylvia Abramson and Joe Freedman and Harry Perlin, with Alvin Fox sardonic on the fringe; and spreading among them was a kind of wonder and excitement.

"Like an insulated wire," Harry Perlin thought. The hair-nerve in the center was the live wire, and then packing all around, and a shell outside. This was where all of man's ideas came from—from nature.

He wanted to communicate his idea to someone, to Aline maybe, but was abashed.

Joe Freedman stared through the eyepiece. The orderliness of the hair-structure, one piece growing out of another, an endlessly repeated design, an endlessly repeated birth. He raised his head and smiled to Sylvia Abramson.

"It makes you feel a human being is so natural, like grass," she said to him.

"Or trees," Joe added. They thrilled.

"Joe is getting a crush on Sylvia," Aline observed to Rose Heller.

Then they decided to look at blood. "Anybody got a pin?" Rudy asked.

Skinny Heller performed some tricks under her dress, and brought forth a tiny safety pin.

"I'm not responsible for the consequences!" Lou Margolis warned Skinny.

Rudy lit a match, sterilized the pin, and pricked his finger.

"Ugh!" Lil cried, hiding her face in Sam Eisen's coat. They all watched the spot of blood well up on Rudy's finger-tip. He smeared it onto a slide.

Aline Freedman studied it first. "My, is Rudy a red-blooded man!" she announced.

"Those are the red corpuscles," Rudy said. "Can you see the white ones?"

Impatiently Mitch Wilner waited for that dumb flapper to get out of the way. He glued his eye to the scope. The yellowish, spotted miasmic field was nothing like the diagrams in physiology books. And it quivered; these were living cells, in their jellying, aqueous motion! He had a shock of affinity, of touching knowledge. He would be a doctor all right; he would know everything about this flecky, crowded fluid. Why, if he could stay right here, and keep his eye fixed until he had analyzed every particle within the clotting greenish threaded mass, every cell, every organism, he would know all of life.

"I think I see the leucocytes," he remarked.

"Are we impressed!" Rose Heller said.

Now Mitch could make out the separation of the red cells. They were forming into clumps, neat as rows of checkers in a box. The precision of it! The mysterious absoluteness, the certainty of their movement! To separate themselves out of the confusing, floating mass, to gather and range themselves in serried ranks! You couldn't actually see them move, yet if you blinked and looked again, you saw that the red clumps had become larger. So that was coagulation.

"You can see the coagulation!" he announced.

"Give someone else a chance," Sylvia pleaded.

For a moment three heads were bent together by the microscope. Alvin Fox noticed the pretty sight: Sylvia's dark sleek hair between blond and brownish thatches of Mitch and Joe. He saw them turn their faces toward each other for an instant, and he saw an intimate smile pass among all three, as though they had mysteriously met inside the secret earth, and shared the knowledge of its wonders.

The look on the girl's face then was so pure, so cool. Ah, that rare thing, Alvin grandiosely reflected: an intelligent female!

He neared the group and struck a cynical attitude.

"A pretty picture," he commented.

But they paid no attention to him, except that Sylvia said: "Do you want to look? It's fascinating."

"No," he drawled. "I'm not interested in delving too deeply. It destroys the beauty of illusion. Just think what a beautiful young maiden would look like under the microscope."

He knew it was a wrong, an asinine tack. They laughed briefly, but were already away from him, among themselves.

One more thing Mitch Wilner had to see: the inmost movement of the particles that he had read about.

"Do you think we can see the Brownian movement in the blood?" he asked Rudy.

"What's Brownian movement?" Sylvia looked first to Mitch, then to Rudy, respectful of their great wisdom.

"It's the movement of the electrons inside the molecule," Rudy explained. "They rush around, just like the planets in space."

Could they see that too, through the microscope? the inmost movement of the universe?

"You can't actually see the electrons in motion," explained Rudy, the all-wise, "but you can see the effects of their motion when they hit a large particle. Just as you can't see the wind but you can see a barn door swing when it is hit by the wind. We don't know what electrons are," he said. "They may be just blind charges of pure energy, shooting around."

"Then what keeps them together?" Rose Heller asked. "How do they keep from shooting out all over the place?"

"It's electricity, that's what they are," Harry Perlin said.

The molecule contained two kinds of forces, positive and negative, Rudy explained. The positive forces stayed put in the nucleus, and the negative forces were the wild, excited electrons that whirled and bounced through the vast open spaces of the molecule.

Male and female, Alvin reflected, the females always trying to keep the males in place, curbed, bound in their orbits.

There were uncontrollable electrons too, negative particles that would not move in orbits, but zigzagged, and sometimes went shooting off outside the boundaries of their own molecule, banging into other molecules.

Alvin exchanged a glance with Joe.

For one small shivery instant the thought of the universe was clear to all of them; molecule and universe, from the largest to the most minute, the pattern was the same. And people, too! Each particle balanced among innumerable other particles, forces canceling each other, forces accidentally accumulating in a sudden direction, but throughout time the steadying, indrawing pull of the positive-charged nucleus.

For one instant, to Alvin, Mitch, Joe, Harry, Rudy, Sylvia, Rose, it seemed clear how you could use these same construction pieces, these molecules, these chaotically assembled balances of positive and negative charges, female and male charges, static and erratic charges, you could put them together to build stone and to build flesh and to build thoughts; the relationship of people was in the same plan.

"Can I see it?" Mitch said.

Rudy the reliable had brought along a little bottle of potassium oxalate, so they could put blood into non-clotting solution. Now he placed a drop of the blood solution on a bit of glass, which he turned over so that the blood-drop hung on the bottom side. There was a special microscope slide containing a penny-size pit. Rudy placed the sliver of glass over this pit, the blood-drop hanging free inside.

"So that's what they call a hanging drop, huh?" Mitch said. He was learning fast.

Then Mitch hunched over the eyepiece. It was motion he had to look for. Some quivering, trembling motion that would be the result of the wild bombardment of electrons. If he could put all his power, all his judgment, into his eye, and see what he needed to see . . . Rudy had seen it. Mitch touched the small screw, so as to focus in a deeper plane in the hanging drop of blood. Motion was everywhere, he stared into the midst of it, and yet he could not see it. The thing to do was to concentrate on one spot, concentrate.

Now he saw. The thing was all in knowing what you were after. There was a fleck, a grayish dot, just below the center of the field. It danced.

Joe looked, but couldn't recognize any movement. Sylvia looked, and saw it. Joe looked again, and saw it.

It was electricity, Harry Perlin thought. At the bottom of everything was electricity.

"Any more questions?" Rudy asked.

"Yes," Lil Klein piped, showing her interest in serious things. "What's more important, a telescope or a microscope?"

"You're cuckoo!" Sol yelled at Lou Green. "I would give six of those sluggers for one pitcher like Alexander. That guy Babe Ruth is just having a lucky streak, that's all."

Runt Plotkin offered to bet a buck Babe Ruth would hit fifty home runs by the end of the season.

"Owo! don't give me charity!" Sol howled.

"I'm no-no-body's ba-a-by!" Estelle sang at Sol.

Plotsy rubbered along the row of books some of the boys had contributed to the club. *The Four Horsemen of the Apocalypse, Judge Priest*. A book by Maxim Gorky. *The Genius* by Dreiser. Deep stuff, all right. He would get a lot out of belonging to a club with serious-minded fellows like Joe and Rudy.

"Coming out Sunday morning?" Sol asked. "We're gonna play some ball. Say, how about organizing a club team, Plotsy?"

Everything in a state of flux, in motion, quivering. This atom to change and change again, but always to remain the same atom; to drift during the years through the anatomy of the city, to lose particles and to draw in particles: but always remaining safe, tight in the center, in the static nucleus, the girls that become women draw husbands to themselves, always the pull and the repel between safety and freedom, always the center, and those in their path-worn orbits, and the erratic bodies going and returning, the giving-off, and the taking-in.

> He isn't good, he isn't true,
> He beats me too, what can I do?
> Oh, my man—

"Oh, I can't stand jazz," Thelma says to Lou Margolis.

And Mrs. Freedman brings down cake. Celia Moscowitz takes only half a piece, she's reducing. Estelle is certainly getting wild, look at the way she's shimmying. Somebody ought to speak to her.

> In the morning,
> In the evening . . .

Somebody is shaking the door-handle.

Not much money,
Oh, but honey,
Ain't we got fun . . .

It is a moment before the kids realize she has burst into the room. Without a hat, her hair flying around her red, excited face. Estelle's mother! Estelle is dancing with Sol, her belly pressed to him, his paw clamped on her back accidentally clutching up her skirt so that every movement shows a flash of her legs.

Oh, but honey . . .

A turn of the dance brings her face to face with her mother. Estelle lets out an involuntary sound, half-scream, half-laugh. "Don't hit me! Don't hit me!"

"So! Here she is!" Mrs. Greenstein cries. "You—you—" She can't find words. All the young faces staring at her drive her wild.

"You—you—you dirty thing!" she yells at her daughter, and goes up and grabs her by the arm.

Poor Estelle! Her mother just doesn't know better than to make a scene like that. Poor Estelle, she'll feel so mortified she'll never be able to look anybody in the eyes again. How silly, to go crazy like that because Estelle had a bob.

Well, poor Mrs. Greenstein. She simply doesn't understand. And you have to see her side too. Estelle is kind of a wild kid.

Oh, don't be silly, Estelle isn't wilder than anybody else. She's just lively that's all.

But we weren't even doing anything, we were just having a lecture.

Go on, kid. Go on home with her, humor her, that's the best thing. We know how it is. We understand.

Lou, do something, pacify your mother. Oh, he's such a lummox.

Thank God they've gone. If it lasted any longer I'd have screamed. Oh, she won't do anything to her, what can she do? Poor Mrs. Greenstein, she acts as if she's still in the old country.

Hot Saturday Night

Mrs. Freedman opened the door. She was one of those large cushiony women whose hands seemed always to be damp from doing something in the kitchen. "Aline is still in bed, the prima donna," she complained. Best of all Aline's friends, Mrs. Freedman liked Rose Heller. This girl had such a clear face. The other girls all looked like they knew too much, their lips were always like still wet from kisses. Maybe it was because Rose was so skinny she looked cleaner. Her cheeks were always bright and dry.

"Hey! What's the idea?" Rose yanked the pillow from under Aline. "It's ten o'clock."

Aline stretched. Her lips peeled slowly away from each other as she yawned. "What's the rush? I believe in taking life easy."

33

"It's terribly hot out," Rose said as Aline was dressing. "I'm not wearing a thing."

"Well, you don't have to." Aline picked up a bandeau. "Oh, the dickens with it," and dropped it.

They began to jabber about Estelle. That crazy mother of hers.

Mrs. Freedman interposed: "She should have asked her ma first. My girl wouldn't do a thing like that."

"Oh, wouldn't I!" Aline said. "I think maybe I'll bob my hair today. It's terribly hot."

Mrs. Freedman's face flamed. "Lena, if you cut your hair, I will—"

"No, ma, I was only kidding, honest . . ."

"Rose, you shouldn't let her! I rely on you—" and on she raved, almost as bad as Mrs. Greenstein.

"She just can't take a joke," Aline apologized to Skinny Heller in the bus. The bus was bumpy and slower than the El, but classier.

"My mother is just the same," Rose said. "They're all alike."

Aline felt a thrill of real friendship. Rose understood, Rose came from the same kind of family.

Mrs. Freedman had given Aline five dollars to get a Ferris waist. "Even if it isn't a regular corset. You got to have something to hold you together."

"I wish I had a figure like yours," Aline declared. "Kid, I'm going on a diet."

They saw an ad in the paper for the cutest knickers, at Field's.

Aline sucked in her lip. Mygod, would she dare!

It wouldn't hurt to look at them. They could go to Field's first, then look in at Mandel's to compare prices.

"That's just what I always do," Rose said.

They were simply steaming under their dresses by the time they got through, just stopping in the Boston Store to make sure they hadn't missed anything. Aline was worried the knickers would get home before she did, and would her mother have a fit!

They went to Rossman's to get some slippers for Rose. They had hardly stepped inside the door when Skinny clutched Aline's arm.

"What's the matter?"

"I forgot Lou works here," Rose whispered.

"Well, what of it? I bet he'll give you a rakeoff."

"Oh, no. Oh, kid—let's go to O'Connor and Goldberg's." Rose was ablaze with blushes.

"Why, kiddo! You've got a crush on him!" Aline accused. A delicious, chummy feeling spread through Aline. Imagine! Rose, with her innocent ways!

She steered Rose right into the store and sat her down. "He'll wait on us," she said, catching Lou's eye on the run.

"Oh, hello, why hello, Skinny!" Lou tossed at them. "Say, wait a minute and I'll take care of you. You'll have me kneeling at your feet," he kidded.

"Now I ask you," Rose blurted. "Is that nice?"

Lou Margolis was the speediest salesman on the floor. And the way that kid could knock out p.m.'s was a riot. The fellows said he would rather sell a p.m. than a straight pair of shoes even if there was no extra commission on the sale, just to show he could put it over.

Some fellows had to remember a line to give their customers . . . now there is a stylish article, ma'am, and yet serviceable. But Lou had a different line for every customer, the words just rolled out of his mouth. He would certainly knock them dead in the courts when he was a lawyer.

When he had debated in high school he could take either side of an argument, like: Resolved, the government should own and operate the railroads; he could make you feel he believed heart and soul in what he was saying, either side.

Why shouldn't he sell p.m.'s? The customer saw what he was getting, didn't he? There was really nothing wrong with those shoes, was there?

"Whatya take, Skinny, a four?" Lou said, looking intently at her foot.

"Three and a half," she chirped.

He pulled off her shoe and looked. "That's right, by God. I didn't realize your feet were so small."

Was she thrilled!

Rose had seen a slipper in the window, with a bow, and she wanted military heels because high heels just made her look taller and skinnier than she was already. But she couldn't tell him.

"I've got just the number for you," Lou said, and darted away.

"Kid, look at those alligator skins, aren't they *cute!*" Aline squealed, but Skinny's mind was filled with something she had read in the Inquiring Reporter. "How many times a day should a husband kiss his wife?" At breakfast, she thought. And when he comes home from the office. Her father never kissed her mother, though, regularly like that. Or at all? She wondered if Aline's father . . . ? Well, their fathers and mothers weren't educated; in real American families the husband kissed the wife every day.

Lou Margolis went right back to the stack of p.m.'s; he stood whistling, bobbing his knees, snapping his fingers, oh, but honey, ain't we got fun, and snaked out the box he wanted. They were high-heeled black pumps, but the flappers all wanted bows this summer. This lot hadn't been selling at all.

Mickey slid over, commenting: "Say, that's some pair of broads you got there. Boy, I'd like to cop a feel off that little one. I hear those Jewish babes are hot."

35

"You said it." Lou pulled a shoe from the box, and went out.

Skinny's heart fell when she saw the slipper; she knew she wouldn't have the nerve to bother Lou to show her something else. Of course there was no shame in anybody's working, and yet she couldn't help feeling funny at the thought of his stooping at other people's feet like a menial. Of course it was just a summer job.

"Kid, didn't you want bows on them? Or tassels?" Aline reminded her.

"Oh, I don't know," Rose said. "Everybody's wearing bows. I think I'll be different."

"What do you want high heels for? Mygod, you're tall enough as it is," Aline whispered.

Rose flushed.

"That's a good buy, Skinny," he said. "It's a special."

"I think they're cute," she murmured, wishing only to get away, oh, she couldn't have him kneeling at her feet. "They fit all right, too."

In a moment Lou had the box at the counter. "Chalk up another p.m.," he said to the cashier, grinning.

On Saturday night if they had no dates none of the kids liked to admit they had nothing special to do; they always waited until the last minute in the hope that something new would happen and make this a real Saturday night.

Joe Freedman's sister Aline was trailing around in her teddies and a half-open dressing gown. First she had paraded around disgustingly in those knickers that looked as though they were pasted to her behind. "All right, all right, I'll take them back Monday!" she replied every time the old lady started to complain. Girls wearing pants! In the street! No! Even that redhead Estelle Greenstein didn't do such things!

"All right! I'll return them!" And then Aline discovered she had lost the check.

Finally Aline took off the knickers and settled down to the slow piecemeal process of fixing herself up for Saturday night, taking a bath, prying at her cuticles, sitting around half naked.

Joe ate some cold *schav* off the edge of the dining room table. Nobody ever bothered to set the table. It was too hot to live.

He went out and drifted down the street.

He drifted into Mrs. Kagen's drug store. "How's your lung and liver?" Rudy greeted. "What can I do you for?"

"Doing anything tonight?" Joe said.

Rudy wasn't sure but what he'd be on until closing.

Joe called up Mort Abramson, thinking his kid sister Sylvia might answer the phone. But Mort answered. Mort thought he might pick up some gash and go to the Entertainers. Joe backed out of the invitation to come along, saying it was too hot. Especially for a nigger joint; it would

36

stink, he added, proud of that touch. Though for once he'd like to call Mort's brag about those wild pickup dates. Anyway it would probably cost a lot of jack. And he wasn't sure he wanted his first experience to be like that. With some picked-up punk.

He didn't ask to talk to Sylvia.

On the corner there was the usual crowd listening to Isaacson, the soapbox atheist. Every Wednesday and Saturday night he held forth. Lots of times he started hot arguments with Jews who still had some religion. Clumsy-tongued men, buttonhole makers, cigar makers, would raise up their voices from the crowd and say: "I don't know, but there is some kind of a God in the world."

Joe spotted Alvin Fox on the outskirts of the crowd. Foxey was all duked up wearing white duck pants and a silk shirt; his curly hair was slick with axle grease, as usual. His eyes X-rayed the summery dress of every girl that hesitated near the crowd.

"What's doing?" they greeted each other.

"They saved the world for democracy," Isaacson sneered, screaming, "and what do they get for it? A kick in the pants! They are standing in the breadlines. . . . God, they say, give us bread! . . ."

A group of girls had just come out of the branch library and were hesitating about coming over. . . . At moments like this, the Duke could hardly keep himself from jumping up there and starting a brilliant speech *à la* Oscar Wilde. But why waste himself on a dumbbell crowd like this? . . . The girls had gone away, a confusion of birdy ankles.

"Aren't you going to wear your new shoes, Rose?" Mrs. Heller asked. "Better put them on, your old shoes are shabby." It sounded as though she had just learned the word shabby.

As Skinny put on the new shoes her mother said: "Why did you get high heels? It only makes you look bigger."

They had gone over that when Skinny brought the shoes home. "Can't I wear high heels if I want to!" she cried, exasperated. "Mygod, you'd think I was the Wrigley Building!"

"Where are you going? Going out?" Mrs. Heller said hopefully.

"Oh, just out with the girls. Over to Aline's."

There were two main reasons why Harry Perlin didn't have the nerve to call up Aline Freedman that Saturday: 1. He had taken her out the Saturday before; maybe she didn't want it to seem that he was her regular Saturday night date. 2. He didn't have a car.

Anyway he had given his mother all of his salary to use in paying the rent; his father's diabetes had the old man flat on his back again.

He sat near the front window reading *Popular Mechanics*. There was a diagram of a hookup for a loudspeaker. He could pick up an old phonograph horn in a junk shop. Might as well look over the radio in the clubroom.

"What do you want to wear a coat for?" his mother asked. "It's hot."

Harry started to take off his jacket, but changed his mind and wore it in case he should meet somebody.

A lot of old people spread out on the front stairs spoiled the looks of a property. Especially on the boulevard it looked cheap, Mrs. Freedman thought. Douglas Boulevard was already cheap because of slovenly gossips spreading themselves in front of the best apartments, and loud fresh boys and girls dancing in the basement clubs. Now Independence Boulevard was the classiest place in the neighborhood and such cheap things shouldn't be allowed on Independence Boulevard.

Yet on a hot night like this what was there to do? She herself went to sit out for a while, careful to put on a fresh dress and a hairnet. It was true that she herself had talked her husband into letting the boys have a club in the basement; but these were the smartest boys in the neighborhood, they would all be lawyers and doctors. Aline was a grown girl, and it was better to have young people coming around her own house than that she should run around God knows where.

There came Harry Perlin. Did he have a date with Aline? "Good evening, Mrs. Freedman," he said. "Well, is it hot enough for you?"

"Oh, it is hot enough for anybody," she said.

He looked toward the basement. "Well, I guess none of the boys are there."

"Joey went out," she said. "I think Aline is in the house."

He flushed.

Aline, still undressed, was collapsed in a chair. She could hear her mother and Pearly Gates talking outside and she felt angry and yet satisfied that Harry had come hanging around. If nothing exciting happened, at least he would be there.

Soon she heard Skinny Heller talking to her mother. Mygod, those old people were spread out in front of the house like a ghetto.

"I heard you bought new shoes, let me see. Oh, they are nice, so nice and plain. But what for did you get such high heels?"

As Rose came up and rang the bell, Aline heard her mother going on to the neighbors: "Such a pretty face, it is a pity she is taller than all the boys."

Mygod, didn't she realize Rose could hear her?

Rose wanted to do something, go for a walk at least. Aline yawned. "That pest Harry is downstairs in the clubroom," she said. "I don't know why he follows me around."

"Oh, come on, don't mope around," Rose said. She wanted to go to the Central Park, she was crazy about Harrison Ford. Celia had seen the show in the afternoon, *Wedding Bells*, and said it was swell.

"I know what, let's make him take us both," Aline said with sudden pep.

"Oh, I'm not going to be a *shlepalong*," Rose cried.

"I'll die if I have to listen to that simp all night! Come on!"

In twos and threes, floating and drifting, gravitating toward Roosevelt Road, past the Central Park to see what's playing. William S. Hart is across the street at the Twentieth Century. Down a few blocks to the Star Theater, but it sweats and stinks and only cheap skates go there. Just walking down Roosevelt Road to see what's doing, to see the dresses and hats. Sylvia Abramson walked along, thinking she would get a jumbo ice cream cone at Tannenbaum's drug store. Who should she run into but Lil Klein and Estelle, Estelle looking as though nothing in the world had happened. And they all stopped at the edge of the crowd where Isaacson the atheist was raving, and who should they meet there but Joe Freedman and Alvin Fox.

"Just listen to that loon!" the Duke sneered. "I could refute every one of his arguments without trying!"

"Well, why don't you go up there and talk?" Estelle said.

"Why should I waste my time talking to these nitwits?"

"Well, I like that!" Lil bridled.

"Aw, you're just backing out!" Estelle kidded him.

"All right, what'll you give me if I do it?"

"Oh—anything I've got," Estelle daringly insinuated.

"Hear that! I got witnesses!" Foxey snapped. Lil doubled over, giggling.

Just then Isaacson, hoarse from an hour of discourse, came down off his step-ladder to pass among the crowd and sell Robert Ingersoll booklets. "You'd throw away a dime for an ice cream sandwich; here, feed your brain for a change."

And Alvin found himself climbing, half pushed, up the ladder. For an instant he felt watery. But he scorned himself for this weakness. He was certainly smarter than anybody in that crowd. By the light cast from the corner store window he could see the form of Estelle's young breasts, the warm nipples pressing moist against her dress. Anything I've got!

Then he heard his own voice, high, almost falsetto in pitch, saying: "I was going to call you all a bunch of damn fools, but I'm just as much of a fool for being up here as you are for listening!" A laugh and a puzzled angry murmur went around. He was a success! He suddenly realized that they would have to stand down there and take what he gave them! He climbed to the very top of the ladder, and steadied his voice, trying to deepen it away from that boyish quaver.

"I am not going to say that I believe in a god, or a supreme being, or whatever you call it. But the gentleman who preceded me claims to be an atheist. I maintain it is just as foolish, just as childish, to believe there is no god as to say there is a god!" Alvin made a piercing commanding glare come out of his eyes. "Let me ask," his voice rolled on, "does the speaker believe in free will? No! He is a disciple of Schopenhauer, and Schopenhauer did not believe in free will! Then how can he be an atheist if he does not believe in free will! He has contradicted himself!" On this glowing word, Alvin's voice reached its peak. In high school debating he could always flabbergast his opponents by accusing them of self-contradiction.

In a sour, angry mood Sam Eisen stood at the border of the crowd. The Duke was up there showing off. Instead of hearing Alvin's words, Sam kept hearing the endless duet between his father and mother. "But I tell you I only make twenty-eight dollars a week. Twenty-eight dollars, not fifty." "But can I help it if the girls need . . . ?" "What do you want me to make, money out of my finger? . . ." "I can't make shoes out of my fingers either. . . ." And so on every day, every week, from childhood. For a moment Sam's eyes focused on Alvin's slick hair, which shone greenish under the street lamp, then on the buttery contours of the Duke's face.

Sam looked around the crowd. These were their true faces, relaxed; no thought of hiding themselves. He got the queer idea of checking on the number of happy faces in the crowd. To his right: an oldish man with a fallen, patient mouth, making him think at once, angrily, of his father. No happiness there. A fat woman, just flesh. Another man with a sneering pimpled face. On and on, one next to the other in the crowd, ugly and tired faces, sarcastic, stupid, tight-mouthed, bleary-eyed, sunken-eyed, dirty-eyed, all ugly, all wearing in the twist of the mouth or the hang of the cheeks the story of some main thing wanted and ungotten; maybe a few of the younger faces showing some eagerness, but even among the younger faces, there under the sharp relief of the street lamp, already the beginnings of the twist, the leer, the shrinking of the flesh that would deepen with every season. To take such people, to blow some life into their faces! . . . Some of the kids in the bunch were standing nearby, but in their faces too he suddenly saw the same traces as in the others. The redhead, with her lips fat at the corners, and Lil, nothing but flesh, sure she was pretty, but nothing but flesh, and that Sylvia Abramson kid, cool and sweet, but already something calculating in the tilt of her head. It was worse than he expected; there was hardly one really happy face. Not a one. And this was Saturday night. What was wrong with them? What the hell was wrong?

He became conscious of a head stuck mockingly beside his head, following his stare.

"My, such deep thoughts," said Lil. "I bet they're worth at least a nickel."

The Duke was down from the platform. "Well, how was I?"

"Gee, you were wonderful! Lemme touch you!" said Estelle, and mockingly put her hand on his chest.

In seemingly playful return, he put his hand on hers, but she pulled back snickering just as he felt the hard point against his palm.

Isaacson shrieked from the ladder: ". . . and my learned young friend should go and read Schopenhauer before he quotes him—"

"Aw, what's the use?" Alvin said. "He contradicts himself all the time. You can't argue with a fanatic."

"Then what did you go up there for?" asked Joe Freedman.

"I just wanted to show myself I had the nerve. It takes something to get up there in front of a lot of people older than you, and make them listen."

"Of course," Sylvia twitted. "People always stop to listen when they hear a baby crying!"

She laughed to Joe. The scent of her came up to him; he could feel her slender breathing, separate and cool, through the steamy sour-fleshed crowd. Perhaps it was really true that there was a destined woman in the world for a man, and that, like an animal, he would know her by her scent; all others would be the same to him, but she would be different.

The bunch were all going to the Central Park.

"Coming along?" Joe asked Sylvia.

"I just came out for some ice cream," she said. "I'll have to call up my mother."

While she was phoning, he got two jumbo ice cream cones; they were beautiful with winding streaks of green, orange, white. He presented her with her cone, bowing mock-gallantly.

His first gift to me, Sylvia thought happily.

Mort Abramson had waited until his kid sister Sylvia was out of the house before beginning the argument about his money.

His father was stretched on the davenport, as usual, chain-smoking. He would lie down right after supper and would hardly move an arm or say a word all evening. He was like a burnt-out log, still giving up a stream of smoke; one good poke and he might dissolve into ashes.

Mrs. Abramson was still bothering around in the kitchen. Mort stationed himself where she too could hear. "Listen, I want to take care of my own money," he announced. "I'm not a kid any more. If I wasn't working for the family, I'd be getting my full pay every week and I want it to be just the same."

That brought his mother out.

His father opened his eyes and looked wearily at Mort. "Isn't ten dollars enough to spend?" he said.

"What's the matter, Mort, got a new girl?" Mrs. Abramson half joked.

Mort said a fellow wanted to be his own boss, that's all. If he was making twenty-five, he wanted to have it.

Mrs. Abramson's eyes lightened. This was really his only reason. She could feel.

"Listen Mort, if you want the money you can have it," she declared. "Only don't make a mistake now. In the business, you always have time to start. But later, you won't be able to start in college."

"I'm not going to the U now, that's settled," Mort said. "Maybe I'll take some evening courses, or go next year. But I'm in the business now and I don't want to be treated like a kid any more. What do you want to do, keep a dime bank for me all my life?"

Suppose he got into a poker game, suppose he wanted to—well, any number of times a fellow wanted twenty-five in his pocket instead of ten. He might use it one week and put it in the bank the next. They knew he wouldn't throw away his money.

"Listen, I understand how you feel," his mother said. "Only you know yourself, if we hold the money the firm can use it, and in a bank it just lies there."

"Well, I can lend it to the firm if I want to, just like anyone else."

"At six percent?" his father sneered, coughing.

"After all, it isn't like you were working outside, you are living at home, too," his mother said.

"Do you want me to pay board?" Mort cried hotly.

Her look shamed him. Somehow against his mother the victory always became hollow. Mort was conscious of his father slowly closing his eyes and turning his head to the back of the davenport, as if the argument was settled.

"I won't turn it in every week," Mort said with a last clutch at freedom. "Whenever I've got a hundred dollars, I'll add it to the loan."

"Any way you want," his mother smiled. "Only, Morty, don't spend all your money on one girl."

The Oakland was hitting on all six. Just past Kedzie, Mort drew up to the curb, to figure out his plans for the evening. Should he get another fellow? The Duke? But he was just a bluff. Joe Freedman? Aw, Joe was getting silly about sis. All the fellows in the bunch made him sick. A bunch of lily-white virgins. Bet they all were virgins. The Big Ten, the Ten Friggers, that's what they were. He wouldn't have joined if they had asked him.

The idling motor seemed to have a warm, panting beat. He shoved her into gear. He didn't want to pick up anything in Douglas Park. Jewish broads wouldn't come across. His shirt was stuck to the back of the seat. It made a sucking noise as it peeled away. His coat lay beside him. He felt to make sure of his wallet. Twelve bucks. Good he hadn't taken more along. This way he couldn't lose much.

Images of women flowed before him. Christ, he was hot for tail tonight. Some of the Polish girls at the factory who spread their knees while they sat working, for coolness, oh, boy, where they wanted the breezes to blow. Maybe dark meat tonight. They were supposed to be swell. The wheels sucked on the tarry pavement, softened by the day's heat. The motor rumbled like a running dog. Nostrils full of the wind of the bitch. Down Twenty-Second Street, maybe pick up a Polish broad.

He coasted along the curb. The trouble was you couldn't see their faces until you were past them, who cares about faces, you can always throw a towel over their faces, through their flimsy waists you saw their breasts riding as they walked. . . . Better stop and get some protection first, you couldn't stop at a drug store after you had picked up the gash. . . . If there was a woman clerk? He pictured the girls in the bunch, skinny slats all trying to get skinnier, they didn't know their main attraction; the only one was Celia Moscowitz, with her big muskmelon bosoms, oh, boy, could you go to sleep there, bet she wouldn't mind either. . . . Suddenly he was trying to picture some fellow, some strange fellow, with his sister Sylvia, but stopped himself.

He was on Cottage Grove, and coasted, coasted through niggertown, but the real opportunity never seemed to come, and before he knew it Mort was up to Sixty-Third, and saw the blaze of the Tivoli lights: Constance Talmadge in *Wedding Bells*. The Tivoli was supposed to make the Central Park look like a nickel show. Those Balaban and Katz boys were certainly going strong. Maybe he could sit down next to some hot South Side broad, an Irish baby, give her the knee during the show, maybe cop a feel, get started.

Anyway it was cool inside; and when he got out it would be just late enough to pick up the real stuff.

Wedding Bells. That ought to have some hot scenes. Connie Talmadge was hot stuff. The cashier wore a georgette waist. He was sizing up her bubs but someone behind pushed him.

"One," Mort said, and the ticket jerked out.

At nine o'clock Mrs. Kagen's married son came around. "Go on, Rudy, go out, have a good time," Mrs. Kagen cried, shooing him out of the store. He called up Joe Freedman but nobody was home, so Rudy dropped into the Central Park. Constance Talmadge in *Wedding Bells*.

Harrison Ford isn't really my type, the Duke was thinking. I'm more like Elliot Dexter. . . . After a while Harry Perlin couldn't control himself and clasped Aline's hand. She let him, but didn't respond at all. The orchestra played the "Poet and Peasant Overture." There was a wisecracker named Jack Rose who crunched up a straw hat after every joke. He had the place in stitches every time he threw in a Yiddish word. Harry Perlin counted eighteen busted hats. Even if he got them wholesale the cost must mount up.

When the show let out, practically everybody was there in the lobby. Aline spotted Rudy Stone, too. Good, now Rose would have someone to take her home. Rose announced she was hungry. "You ought to examine her, Rudy," Aline kidded; "I bet she has a tapeworm."

They had to put two tables together in Kantor's delicatessen. The place was crowded and noisy and jolly, the whole Kantor family was working, all of them fat and juicy ads for their corned beef.

Bernie Kantor finally took their orders. They all wanted corned beef sandwiches and pop, except Pearly, who just wanted pop. He hadn't figured on having to buy three movie tickets.

Boy, those were some sandwiches. Plenty of juicy meat, on that light yellow-crusted rye. Bernie Kantor put on his act, hacking a knife down that yard long loaf as easy as slicing a banana. But, behold, there was a new-fangled slicing machine for the corned beef. Everybody crowded to the counter to see the invention.

The sour tomatoes were hard and just right. And chocolate soda was just the drink to go around a corned beef sandwich.

Lou Margolis and his shadow Lou Green drifted in, with the Meisel twins.

"Hey, Red, how does it feel to sit down?" Sol Meisel yelled at Estelle. Was he dumb! Just when they had finally made Estelle forget all about it.

"I'll show you!" she screeched and jumped up and gave him a kick in the pants. He caught her wrists and squeezed and commanded: "Gonna be a good girl? Huh!" She sputtered, laughing and struggling, and everybody was laughing at Sol and Estelle cutting up. Finally she bit his hand. "Now behave!" she said, and sat down, suddenly sedate. Sol grabbed her sandwich and crammed it down in one bite.

The boys had been downtown and seen George Arliss in *Disraeli*. "He was a big cheese in England," Lou Green explained.

"Wasn't he a Jew?" Sam Eisen asked.

"A Jew could never get to be President of this country," Alvin said.

"Oh, I don't know about that," Rudy Stone put in. "Everybody has a chance."

"Don't you believe that bull," Alvin stated.

"He don't believe anything, he's an atheist!" Lil proclaimed.

"I'm not an atheist, I'm an agnostic," Alvin declared proudly, and that started a big argument. When they asked Lou Margolis what he was he ended the argument by telling a funny story, in a Yiddish accent, about a little old Jew who came up to heaven and was asked, "What are you?" and he said, "I am an atheist." So God whispered to him: "Shh, don't tell anybody. I am an atheist too."

Then in walked Mort Abramson. Where'd he been? "Oh, around," he hinted lasciviously. "Say, anybody seen Celia Moscowitz? I got a ticket."

"What for?"

"What do you suppose?"

For speeding, he let on, though it was for parking in front of a fireplug.

Estelle said she was going to Celia's in the morning, and could leave the ticket for Mr. Moscowitz.

"Oh, would you do that for me?" Mort gave her the eye.

"Why, sweetheart, I'd do anything for you!" she came back.

Rudy Stone took the check for everybody and the fellows squared with him. He insisted on paying for the girls, but let Harry Perlin pay for his own soda. "Boy, that saved my life," Harry Perlin thought.

Just Like a Rainbow

All the kids in the bunch thought of Joe Freedman as the artist because he used to draw such swell covers for the *Ogdenite*, and in the class prophecy by Lou Margolis it was predicted that Joe would paint the portrait of the President; but one thing Joe hated was to be thought of as becoming an artist with a velvet tie living in a garret and all that crap.

He knew his parents talked about him at night. Did he want to be a lawyer or a doctor? An artist? Yah, the boy maybe had talent, but did an artist make a living in America?

Artists had lots of love affairs. When an artist met a woman he would ask her to come to his studio and pose for him, and pretty soon he would get her to pose naked and then, oh, boy!

Once Mort Abramson brought something to show Joe. "This is artistic, you ought to appreciate this!" he said juicily. He pulled out one of those thumb-it movie booklets. It was of Harold Teen and Lillums. Harold was an artist and Lillums was the model. As Mort buzzed the pages through his fingers, Joe could feel the blush spreading over his face like oil spreading over water. This was the idea her brother had about artists.

Sylvia brought over the curtains she had made. "I made them simple without any ruffles or anything," she said, "seeing as how it's for a boys' place."

She was so appealing sitting there with the open package, waiting for his approval. "Just stay like that, I want to draw your picture," Joe said.

Now he would coolly analyze her features, showing himself that her nose was too prominent and her chin too small. But that only gave her face such an eager, pointed look.

"Do you think I ought to bob my hair?" she asked.

Joe studied her seriously. "Let me see you with your hair down."

"My, we're getting romantic," said Sylvia. She let her hair down. It flowed around her shoulders, dark-radiant under the unshaded bulb.

"How old are you?" Joe said.

"Sixteen."

"Sweet sixteen and never been kissed," they both remarked at once. They held out their little fingers, crooked, to make a wish.

I wish, I wish, she thought, and the totality of her wish surprised her, warmed her like a rush of blushes all through her body. Oh, it was so soon to wish something like that. And they were so young! "I wish nothing happens unless it is the real thing."

Joey had put down the pad and was approaching, diffusing like a close-up on a screen. Her heart was on a point like when you are in an automobile and it skids and before you know it you have skidded and you are still pushing down with your toes as if to gain control and it's over.

It had been a quick childish kiss.

He had not said: "I love you."

Joe walked abruptly back to his chair and took up his pad. He glared at her, to see her only as something to draw. He could tell the whole youngness of her form, the adolescence of her breasts, the tender narrowness of her shoulders.

He threw down his pencil.

"I can't draw," he said. "I'm no artist."

"Oh, I'm sure you can," she said, womanly and encouraging. "I'm sure you can do anything you want."

"Oh, I don't know. I don't think I'll go to the Institute."

He wished he could explain to her, to Sylvia. Like, the other night, sitting around with the fellows, he had noticed a face shaped in the cigarette smoke. Like a jackass he had called attention to it, and Mitch had said, admiringly: "It takes an artist to notice things like that." That was what people would think of him, an artist, a dreamer seeing things in smoke. He would lead a chained and tortured life, like Dreiser's *The Genius*, and being an artist he wouldn't be able to be faithful to any woman.

Jews were always wanting their children to be artistic. Yet if he went to be a real artist he knew he would be driven nuts by their anxiety for him. And what of Sylvia? They were just kids, sure, and he would leave her.

If you studied law or medicine or became a C.P.A., no matter if you were the best or the worst, you were something. In art, you either had it, or didn't have it.

For a vacation job, Joe was working at Donnelley's where hundreds of young fellows sat at tables alphabetically sorting telephone directory slips. And among them were several driveling old men, whose fingers constantly trembled. Fifteen bucks a week. Would he end up like them, if he tried to be an artist?

"Don't do that," he said as he saw Sylvia putting up her hair. Yet he fixed this pose in his mind: her arms upcurved to her head, her expression preoccupied, in this timeless pattern of womankind. Like a little wife in the morning in the bedroom, with her hairpins so intimately held in her mouth.

"Someone might come in," she said, calmly taking the last pin. "Anyway you're not going to draw."

Mammy Song

In the mornings, Mrs. Freedman took a look in the clubroom. What did boys know about taking care of a place! Besides, it was as though by touching their victrola records, wiping their books, she could feel what they were doing and thinking. What did children tell their parents nowadays? . . .

New curtains. Hemmed by hand. A neat girl's stitching, too.

From the floor, Mrs. Freedman picked up the piece of paper on which Joe had begun to draw a picture.

There were only a few marks, lines as undefined and soft as fallen hairs. And yet Mrs. Freedman knew. This was that nice little girl, Sylvia, daughter of the Abramsons who had a ladies' hat factory. Mrs. Freedman could feel in her own thick fingers the excitement behind her son's random pencil strokes. She sank down on a chair and tears came into her eyes, as though she were weeping at a nice Jewish wedding.

Look how you could recognize the girl's face! Her boy was a genius.

But why had he thrown away the picture?

She took it upstairs and put it in the second drawer of the bureau, down under everything.

It was a busy hour in Kovarsky's butcher shop. Mrs. Plotkin hung back and waited. She only wanted chuck meat. Let him take care of the others first.

To the little old woman with the *shaitel*—the orthodox wives' wig of the old country—Mr. Kovarsky sang out: "Good you came, Mrs. Wilner. I have saved a spring chicken for you"—he smacked his lips—"sweet as butter."

They all knew Mrs. Wilner. In the butcher shop she would always say: "The best. For me, nothing but the best. So it costs a penny more. We are a small family, I have only one son and he is not a big eater, so let it be the best." Their son Mitchell had come to them late, after two other children had died.

Mrs. Wilner inspected the little fowl carefully, looking for flecks on the skin, prodding the meat with her thin, stiffening fingers.

"Where will you find such a beautiful fat young spring chicken?" Mr. Kovarsky cried, in his lip-smacking Yiddish. "Only you yourself surpass her!" he flattered heartily, while with his eyes he told a luscious young housewife the remark was really for her. "As soon as I saw it I said this is for Mrs. Wilner. I put it away."

Mrs. Freedman approached and pressed her fingers to the breast of the chicken. "It is really a fine chicken," she judged. "I would buy it myself."

The telephone rang.

The woman listened to Mr. Kovarsky take an order. It was a good order, steak, and a five-pounder, from Mrs. Abramson.

"Tell me," Mrs. Freedman said, smiling, "that is the Abramson that has a little hat factory downtown?"

"That's the one. They live on Avers Avenue in their own building."

"A six-flat," Mrs. Klein detailed, rolling her head in her chins.

"She is up to date, she telephones in her order," observed Mrs. Freedman.

"A busy woman. She goes down to the factory every day. She wears the pants," Mr. Kovarsky said. "You know them?"

"My children know their children," said Mrs. Freedman, wanting to tell more, but holding herself in.

Kovarsky chopped zestfully through a set of ribs. "Who's next? You?" he called, confronting Mrs. Plotkin.

She shrank back, withdrawing before all these women with their orders for the fattest, the best, the top cuts.

"Wait on her, wait on her." She indicated Mrs. Freedman. "I only want a few pounds' chuck meat."

His face lighted up. "Mrs. Freedman, I know just what you want. For you I have a whole bull!"

The housewives' laughter rang through the shop and the butcher cleared his great red arms, and rang his knife against steel. That Kovarsky!

"Better you should cut out your own tongue, that's a slice I could relish!" Mrs. Freedman retorted good-naturedly. "Well, Kovarsky, come on, with your sweet words you don't fool me, I want to see a good piece of breast."

"Breast! the wives should ask me to show them breast!" the ribald butcher shouted, howling with merriment at his own jest. He threw a slab onto the counter. "Here! This will make bones in your children, and maybe it will make a few children too!"

Mrs. Plotkin's wide, reddened nostrils trembled as though she were actually sniffing the fine cuts of meat on the counters, on the sawing block, the fat chickens that hung from the hooks. As always, Kovarsky's butcher shop thrummed with the high ringing hum of gossip. Here the good mother tongue was spoken, here they were free of the superior, American watchfulness of their children. And here the truth about everybody was known. What goes into their bodies, what goes into their flesh, first cut, second cut, or chuck meat and scraps? Oh, the fine ones were building their children out of the best, out of fat, fat chickens and geese; here you were known for what you were: Mrs. Klein buys veal today; Mrs. Becker takes a cut that has been lying around here for a week, it is already black with rot, but he gave it to her a dime cheaper; Mrs. Levinson, the stingy, buys two pounds of ribroast for a family with five people, as if they can't afford to eat!

And Mrs. Plotkin was thinking, maybe this time instead of chuck meat she could buy roundsteak. With six children and a husband who didn't give out mortgages you couldn't always buy the best. It would come to maybe a quarter more.

She eyed the fine, pink-blooming slab that Kovarsky had cut for Mrs. Freedman, firm, tender, unblemished flesh.

That was meat!

BEGINNINGS OF WISDOM[1]

RUNT PLOTKIN, chewing on a fat cigar, strolled into Mrs. Kagen's drug store. So casually, Rudy could tell he was after something.

"How's business, Rudy?" he asked.

"Exqualafadocious," Rudy replied.

"Say, that's a way to use up empty bottles," Runt said, referring to the Arbuckle case. "Is that straight, could a thing like that kill her?"

"Better be careful," Rudy admonished, cocking his head professionally.

Runt lipped his cigar. "Legally, I don't see how they can prove anything on him." Then he mimicked, " 'Roscoe hurt me!' " and broke into a farty laugh.

He leaned over the cigar counter. "Say, where do you get these ropes?" he said, and pulled a cigar out of his vest pocket. "Have a good cigar," he offered.

Rudy sniffed it, lifted his brows appreciably, and put it in the pocket of his white coat.

Runt's proposition was to supply Rudy with refills for the cigar boxes, at less than wholesale price. Rudy could get a cut on them, and the store could make something too.

"We got a lot of old customers, doctors," Rudy said. "They know their brands."

"Listen, I can duplicate any brand," Plotkin declared. "I can get the bands, too."

"You can't duplicate brands, Plotsy," Rudy said in a friendly way. "You'll get yourself in a jam."

Runt put up his chin, with a wise expression. Where he got the stuff was nobody's business.

What was the sense in his old man slaving in some lousy cigar maker's shop on Division Street, out of work half the time with strikes and unions? For a long time Runt had been trying to jack up the old man's nerve, make him go out on his own, get a table in a store window, sell direct to the customer. But the old man was a *dreck*. He would sooner get two dollars a day from some lousy Mr. Schmelofsky than make five bucks a day on his own.

Now Runt's idea was to get a few outlets, a couple of drug stores, and Jake's poolroom, then the old man could make the stuff at home without paying for licenses and union graft. He could undercut everybody and still make dough.

---

[1] Proverbs 9:10 "The fear of the Lord is the beginning of wisdom: and the knowledge of the holy is understanding."

"I couldn't do anything on my own responsibility," Rudy passed the buck. "I'd have to ask the old lady. You know how she is. But maybe I could pick up some orders for you straight. Just loose cigars. You don't need any brands. Some of these doctors know a good cigar."

That idea didn't appeal to Runt so much. Chickenfeed. But Mitch Wilner came in, and Runt dropped the subject. Anyway he saw Rudy wasn't taking to the idea.

Mitch looked worried. His forehead bulged from long concentration. "Say, Rudy, I want to ask your advice," he said.

Runt hung around, listening.

Mitch was worried about which university to go to. He had practically decided on the University of Chicago for his premedic but now he was full of doubt again. It seemed to him to be a decision that would shape his whole life. He couldn't sleep, worrying about it. He weighed Carlson of the U. of C. against Arey of Northwestern, Ranson of Northwestern against Wells of Chicago. The U. of C. was the place for big names, specialists, but then they said Northwestern gave a fellow more practical training. . . . The problem was driving him crazy. For Rudy, it was different. He was scrambling through, working his way. But if a fellow had his choice, he had to be sure to pick the absolute best, the top in every field!

"What you want is Johns Hopkins, Columbia, and the U. of C. rolled into one," Rudy kidded.

It was a joke, but something quivered inside of Mitch. Johns Hopkins; why should he be content with anything less?

"Say, how about the City Medical College?" Plotkin put in helpfully. "I know a guy going there. Harry Marcus."

Mitch groaned, and Rudy said with mock seriousness: "Well, Plotsy, I've heard tell as there are better schools, but none quicker, by golly!"

Plotkin looked from one to the other. He felt queer, kind of stepped on. Aw, the boys didn't mean anything; he was just dumb.

Mitch said he was going to take a little vacation before the big plunge; his folks had a cottage at Benton Harbor, and it would be vacant after Labor Day. Joe Freedman was coming along, and maybe Rudy wanted to join them?

Rudy figured he could use a vacation but it was a difference of fifty bucks in pay and he would need the dough in school.

"We'd certainly be glad to have another guy. There's plenty of room," Mitch said.

"Say, I might take you up on that," Runt Plotkin put in.

Mitch was a little surprised but after all he had nothing against Plotsy.

"Sure," he said. "Come on out."

Runt said okay he would, in a couple of days. He had some business to take care of.

As they went out of the store, Runt pulled a handful of nickel Blue Books out of his pocket. "Say, Mitch, ever read any of these? This Nietzsche is pretty deep stuff. I got a whole flock of these, I'll bring them along out to Benton Harbor, huh?"

That Blue Book guy made something of an idea, Runt Plotkin reflected. He, too, had to find something. Hitch onto something. There was plenty of dough floating around even if times were supposed to be tight. Schmutz Schmaltz, who hung around Jake's place, made over a buck a dozen on fishskins. But he wasn't going to peddle rubbers, and anyway he couldn't horn in on Schmutz's trade. And these damn kids in the bunch didn't even know what rubbers were for. He had to get something. Every time he walked into the house, he felt like walking right out and not coming back till he had a flock of dough. He was the oldest, damn it. He was no slob with love for his brothers and sisters and the old man and the old lady but the whole layout disgusted him and he wanted to throw some kale in there and set it right. Once he got hold of a good thing he would work night and day, develop an organization. Runt could see himself sticking a perfecto in his mouth, walking out of his office through a room full of blonde stenos with their legs crossed, they'd uncross them for him! Their heads would all turn following him as he marched out, taking the afternoon off at his box seat at Cubs' Park, or at his golf club.

The big little guy, they would call him. Eventually he would be bigger than all those smart guys, Lou Margolis and Sam Eisen, the coming lawyers. He would be a lawyer too. Going to law school nights, studying nights. As he strode along, his fingers spread strong like to hunk onto a pile of dough.

The big Moscowitz girl and Skinny Heller were walking toward him. He waited for them to recognize him. That juicy *zaftig* Celia Moscowitz. He would have more pull than her old man, Rube Moscowitz!

The girls passed without noticing him.

So he was just a runt, too small to see, huh?

Celia and Rose were so absorbed, whispering about the Arbuckle case[2], they didn't even see him pass. Rose was so disturbed by the front page stories in the papers, by the hints of what had been done, that she nearly felt sick when talking about it, yet couldn't stop, wanting to know exactly what was it they had done? Exactly.

Celia pretended to know all about it. Just how it was done. Within herself, she was scared. There were certain things she did herself, when feelings overcame her. . . . She would stop it from now on.

---

[2] Movie star comedian Fatty Arbuckle became the center of a national scandal in September of 1921 when a woman was injured at Arbuckle's party and subsequently died, apparently as a result of sexual excesses and possible assault. Arbuckle was tried for manslaughter but not convicted.

"It was a real wild party," Celia said to Rose. "I heard my father talking about it. His pals knew all about it. You know, they get the inside stuff. Well, you know, that kind of a girl, they'll do *anything*. . . ."

A bottle! Rose tried not to picture it. Suddenly it was as if the thing had been done to her own body. She felt she was going to be sick right there on the street. She clawed Celia's arm.

"Kid! What's the matter?" Celia tried to take Rose into the drug store. Rose wouldn't go. Leaning against a store window, she got control of herself.

Oh, but always all her life she would feel the horror, the revulsion of this moment . . . oh, if any man ever came near her she would think of that, the wild bestial drunkenness, the bottle, oh, how could she ever love, it would always make her sick!

Joe and Sylvia could have laughed at themselves because they were in puppy love. They went walking in Garfield Park, and she brought along her kodak.

Joe took funny poses, like Napoleon, like a senator, twirling a mustache. They laughed and laughed. But suddenly their kidding mood vanished. "Now be serious," she said, "I want this one, I want you to look like you." Joe stood looking straight at her, now this was himself, standing in the park with his shirt open at the throat, feeling young and fine and looking at the girl he loved. And she saw him with his long bony wrists, his humorous bony nose, and his eyes, warm like Dick Barthelmess. . . .

It was like a ceremony; they exchanged places, she handing him the kodak as they passed. "Did you turn the film?"

She looked so—so—standing there—an overpowering feeling came into his hands, to crush, and at the same time to hold delicately, carefully, perfectly the bloom of her face, the cool of her lips.

He went up to her and kissed her but she pulled away, still laughing girlishly, my, in the broad daylight, anyone might see, some of the bunch might be in the park.

They stood apart for that instant, flushed, looking directly into each other's face, with complete openness and recognition. . . . It was like that time in the basement when she had put up her hair. . . . Joe felt a kind of premonitory fear, that his life was going off all wrong, on the wrong track. She was really different, a different person than he was seeing, in the glow of love. Why, it was silly, they were just kids, and this could not be final. Yet he felt a chill fear, for in the life of every artist there was always a fatal love.

"You're too civilized," Joe said, hardly knowing how the words had come to his lips, or what they meant.

Then they were both frightened. They waited, listening, as though the echo and meaning of the words would come to them from the future.

"Talk to me, Joe," she said.

Joe couldn't think of a word to say.

Perhaps this was the feeling that was called Weltschmerz . . . what was life anyway? As Ben Hecht said in *Erik Dorn*, man was but a scrap of paper blowing in the wind.

Momentarily, Joe envisioned his old man's flophouse on South State Street. The sour, soaked smell, the alky-sodden face of Mike the helper, the bums sitting in their own spit. That was the end of life. Ben Hecht saw that too. Life was an obscene gargoyle.

These were the feelings he needed to talk out of himself, lying there on the grass in the open sunshine, with Sylvia looking seriously and tenderly into his face. But he couldn't think of anything to say.

She began to talk about his vacation; he and Mitch should get along well together. All at once Joe envied Mitch.

There was a fellow who knew exactly what he wanted, and went straight for it. At the same time Joe felt somewhat scornful.

"What does a fellow like that get out of life?" he said, waiting almost jealously for Sylvia's answer.

She agreed with him. "Mitch is too studious. He ought to be more human. But of all the kids in the bunch, he is really the best," she said, feeling grown in judgment, and settled in a sweetheart, with whom she shared a friend.

But Joe grew even more gloomy. "What are you thinking of? Oh, why are you so despondent, Joe?" She stroked his hand. Perhaps it was because he was an artist, and felt life more deeply than ordinary people. "Oh, sometimes I'm so afraid for you."

In the mornings, Mitch and Joe walked along the boards over the sand, walked past closed hot dog stands and hibernating souvenir shops, up into town to ask for mail. Right after Labor Day, Benton Harbor was deserted; they had the beach practically to themselves.

Joe's letters came from Sylvia every day. At first they were the formal notes of a girl, tenderly shy, as if she stood bashfully beside him. On the second day she added: "Oh, I miss you so much. All the chatter chatter chatter in the parlor, and I miss you."

Joe wrote about the beach and the lake and the stars, and drew scratchy idiotic pictures of himself all covered with lumps like hills, from mosquito bites.

The swell thing to Joe was how Mitch did not kid him about Sylvia's letters. The long hours when they lay with their elbows in the sand, or at dusk when they walked along the country road, and discussed things, books like this *Growth of the Soil* Joe was reading, a book that made you feel you wanted to be bound into the earth like a tree: those hours the boys felt like brothers.

Joe was still worrying about what to do with himself. Maybe go to law school with all those other fellows, become something quickly, a lawyer in a couple of years, get at grips with life.

"You don't want to be a lawyer," Mitch said. "Why should you waste your talent? Why don't you do what you want to do!"

"I don't know," Joe said, envious of the certainty, the directness, of his friend. Why, becoming a doctor would take ages, eight, ten years, a fellow would be twenty-six or seven by the time he could start to earn a living. To have to be supported all that time by his parents. Suppose he wanted to get married, or something?

It was woman that he wanted. The desire bothered him, never let him alone for a moment. How did a fellow like Mitch stay so cool? Even here, lying with his elbows on the beach, reading, Joe could not help being bothered by the thought of a couple of girls who had appeared among the season's stragglers. They would come out of the water chasing each other, shrieking laughter. They would come just near enough so the boys could tell they were young. And their figures in the wet bathing suits.

"I guess they don't want us to notice them," Joe said ironically.

"They are about as coy as a couple of elephants," Mitch said. "But they can't help it. The female of the species is burdened with the instinct of race preservation."

"They might be good-looking, at that," Joe said. He tried to keep on reading.

On the fourth day, Runt Plotkin showed up. Mitch had forgotten about asking him. But of course it was okay. "Swell you could make it," he said.

After supper Mitch was on the porch reading the *Outline of History* by H. G. Wells. Boy, that was some book! He had read a hundred pages and man hadn't yet appeared on the scene. Plotsy came onto the porch and sat on the cot. He lighted a cigar and began to smoke. The acrid smoke bothered Mitch; he went out and stood in front of the cottage, breathing clean air again.

Plotkin came out and stood beside him, looking across the beach at the water. The sky was coming dark, with a beautiful afterglow. Runt stood with the cigar in his mouth, pointed at the water. "Certainly beautiful, isn't it?" he said.

Mitch felt somehow annoyed. "Guess I'll take a walk," he said.

"Mind if I come along?" said Runt.

"Hell, no," Mitch said, and called to Joe. It was their evening walk. Runt walked along with them, smoking his big cigar.

In the evening, Joe and Mitch played chess. Runt watched, trying to catch onto the rules. What he'd like right now would be a game of pinochle. He listened to insects bouncing against the screen. Outside, the crickets were chirping loud as a tin can factory, the sons of guns. He went outside and stood still with himself, puffing another cigar, letting the smoke up into the night. The stars were great. This was the way to get out, sometimes, made you feel clean right into your guts.

He was wrong to think the boys were trying to high-hat him. They were just guys like himself. What the hell, Joe Freedman's old man ran a flophouse. He was a couple of years older than the boys and that made a difference. Besides, Joe was a kind of genius, and Mitch was a smart guy, and they weren't as simple to get along with as other guys. But he'd get along okay.

When he had copped some dough for himself he would have a country place on a lake like this, come out by himself sometimes, just to sit and take in the stars.

Runt Plotkin felt a great friendliness rising out of himself and having nowhere to go. He felt as if at this moment he could talk to someone heart to heart. The feverish suspicion, the fear all the time that people, the world, life, would put something over on him if he wasn't on his guard, left.

The girls were on the beach again. "Hah! what do I see!" cried Plotsy, shading his eyes like a mariner.

"You can see plenty!" Joe said, with an air of experience.

"Hot mama! That broad in the red suit is pretty *zaftig*," Runt said.

Mitch went in for a swim. Joe monkeyed with the firm wet sand, modeling a female shape.

"What you need is a model," Plotsy said, smirking.

"Yeah? They ain't hard to get," Joe knowingly observed.

In a couple of minutes Runt was back with the two broads, giggling and chattering.

"Oh, my, ain't he some artist!" the one in the red bathing suit exclaimed in a high-pitched noisy voice. She had a Yiddish accent. Her toes were ugly, bumpy and spread, Joe noticed right away. Close up, neither of the girls was attractive. They had bad teeth, their skin was coarse with a yellowish ghetto tinge, they were older than the boys, and they talked like cheap Maxwell Street broads.

"Meet Maymie and Esther," Plotsy said.

"What is this supposed to be? A horse?" Maymie said to Joe, putting her unlovely foot on the shape he was molding. She laughed, screaming at her own joke.

"No, a cow!" Runt bantered.

Runt started a sand throwing game with the girls, and soon he was rolling over with Esther, wrestling.

When the fellows got back to the cottage they talked knowingly of the girls.

Runt hadn't been quite sure what line to take, but the boys certainly talked as if they knew what it was all about. Hell, it was a perfect setup, Dave thought, a house to themselves! It was a shame to waste it!

"I bet they could put on some party," he remarked.

"Well, the house is yours," Mitch said.

It was no surprise to meet the girls strolling along the road at sundown. Plotsy said they ought to see the cottage. They consulted together for a moment, laughing screechily, then came along.

They put a record on the victrola:

"I'm the sheik of Araby,
Your love belongs to me. . . ."

Maymie strayed into the kitchen. "Yoo hoo," she called, and Runt grabbed the chance. He winked at the fellows as he went. Their bedroom was right off the kitchen.

It didn't take him long. "Say, what kind of a girl do you think I am!" she protested. But his arms were tight as steel cables. She heaved and wrenched against them, but never raised her voice, never screamed, keeping up the argument with him in a compressed undertone. So he knew she would give in.

"Aw come on, aw be good to me, aw say I'm nuts about you honey! Come on you know what you came here for, what did you come here for if you don't come across, aw come on honey I'm dying for it honest I'm nuts about you . . ." The words tumbled out of him harsh and whining, crazy, pressing her back and down all the time, till at last she let him.

"Don't think I'm that kind of a girl," she kept repeating all the time. "Wait. Be careful. Be careful."

That was all right, too. He made it a principle never to get a girl into trouble. They let you have it, and that was the least you could do for them in return. It was only white. He was a white guy.

On the porch, Esther put one record after another on the portable victrola. She snapped her fingers, her hips writhing. "I'm no bodiis beeeehbi," she intoned with the wheezing record.

The two boys didn't know what to do. It was hard to think of anything to say to her. They pretended not to notice the scuffling and murmuring from the back room.

Finally Plotsy emerged with Maymie. She was fixing her hair. Plotsy figured maybe one of the boys had already torn off a piece. Now the other could take his pick. But the minute he saw the boys he sensed that in some strange way he had behaved wrong.

Everybody stood around strainedly.

"All by myself in the morning,
All by myself in the night. . . ."

When the record was finished, the girls said they had to go. Plotsy offered to walk them back.

"Well, I guess Runt had a hot time," Joe observed.
"Yah, he can have them," Mitch said.

"I don't see any point to it," Joe said. "For me, there has to be something more with a girl."

"A rag, a bone, and a hank o' hair," said Mitch.

Joe said: "Their skin was coarse. And those yellow teeth! That would spoil it for me."

"Well, you know some guys will take anything." Mitch's voice was flat, touched with disgust.

The next morning, Runt came right out with it.

"Say, listen, if I'm spoiling your vacation I'll leave. I didn't come down here to spoil your vacation."

"Oh, no," Mitch said hastily. "What's the idea, Plotsy?"

"I just had a feeling that we're not getting along, that's all. You fellows and I—well, that's all."

Mitch said: "Hell, Dave, the only thing gets on my nerves is those damn cigars you smoke all the time."

"Well, that's too bad about that," said Runt. "You shoulda told me. I don't believe in spoiling other people's pleasures."

Even under their assurances was the feeling of difference that he had sensed as soon as he got off the boat. All the years they had known each other in the city was one thing. But coming out here was like carrying a couple of bolts of cloth into the sunlight, and finding that the colors that seemed the same in the murky shop are entirely different outdoors. Their folks owned real estate, did business, had dough. Everything was going to be sweet and fine for them. He had already knocked around a bit in the world. They were swell and pure and they couldn't sully themselves with a couple of broads like Maymie and Esther, though they could talk plenty dirty and must of had wet dreams about the girls. He didn't get onto that kind of behavior.

"I think if we want to go on being friends I ought to pull out," he said. "No hard feelings at all."

Well, if he insisted, nobody was going to stop him, Mitch said, though he certainly was welcome to stay.

"Well, the girls are going home anyway," Runt said, passing it off with a laugh.

The fellows took him down to the boat and they parted shaking hands and wondering just what they had got into an argument about.

Mitch and Joe, turning away from the pier, felt as though an embarrassing situation had ended. It had been like sitting at table with some guy who eats with a knife.

Now they were together again.

The next morning Mitch and Joe were on the beach early.

Joe lay against the clean sand, letting a web of laziness come over his body and over his mind, trying to stop feeling guilty about Runt.

Mitch was plowing steadily through the *Outline of History*. Four hundred pages already. There was a fellow that never wasted time. No fuzzy futzing around.

"I'm going in," Mitch said, rising. "I'm going to swim out to the pier today. I want a workout."

Joe pulled himself erect, shook sand from his hair. The pier looked very far away, across the inlet. "Say, that's at least a mile," he said.

"Just about," Mitch affirmed.

"Ever swim it before?"

"I used to do a mile easy in the Institute tank."

"Yah, but that was in a tank."

"Well, here's your chance to be a life saver," Mitch kidded, and ran into the lake.

"Wadya think I am, a boy scout?" Joe called after him.

Suppose Mitch got a cramp. There wasn't even a boat around. Joe walked along the sand, keeping opposite the swimmer. Turn them over and dump out the water. Pull their arms up and down. Of course nothing could happen. A mile was no trick, and if Mitch said he could do it he would do it.

After each froglike thrust of the legs, Mitch let his body float full distance under water. He swam with a full, regular breast-stroke, unhurried, feeling himself from the first moment of launching into the water drawing steadily nearer to his objective. The water had a sweet taste when he let it flow through his mouth.

When he got out he would run all the way back to the cottage. That would be a good workout. His mind would be clear as his mouth felt now, clean, and like his body without an excess ounce of fatty waste. There was waste everywhere. For instance everybody ate too much. The idea was to create enough energy for use, and use it. Sure, he too was bothered a little by girls but if he couldn't have them the way he wanted them he would use up his energy, keep himself cool, until he could have them the way he wanted them. Joe was an intelligent guy but even Joe let himself slop around. Steadily under and up over the water. Mitch opened his eyes under water and saw the clean blue water and felt the water wash clean against his eyeballs. If he wished he could turn over on his back and float awhile, to rest, but he had estimated his energies correctly and this even stroke, without rest, would carry him exactly to the end of the pier, would leave him empty. It was like draining a vessel, clean.

He could feel the muscles of his arms, the tendons down into his fingers, all being worked, all being used. He looked to see the end of the pier, had expected to see it closer. But he did not quicken his stroke. He would get there, in due time.

As Joe walked along the shore, sometimes losing sight of Mitch, watching anxiously for that sun-sleek head to bob up again, he reasoned with himself that this was nothing uncommon, just a swim; and yet some obscure premonition seemed to throw a meaning far forward into his own life, their lives. He too could certainly swim a mile if he set himself to do it; practice up a few days, and then launch himself for the pier. What had got into him lately that he kept measuring himself against Mitch? What was so perfect about Mitch? He was as bright as Mitch Wilner any day. He could be a doctor if he chose.

The small lapping waves rode over the sleek head endlessly. What if he should get a cramp? Suddenly Joe felt angry. Mitch had no right to throw this responsibility on him. Joe ran out onto the pier; if anything happened he could try from there. He ran up and down along the pier, in bare feet, waiting.

When Mitch got there Joe leaned down to pull him out of the water, but Mitch scrambled up onto the pier by himself. He was puffing. The two boys laughed, and avoided each other's eyes, except for a glance. Mitch's teeth began to chatter. He started to trot down the pier, and onto the sand, running at an even pace through the soft sand where the going was heavy. Joe ran along for a while and then gave it up and walked. Mitch was just a demon for punishment. When they got back to the starting place Joe looked across the water to the pier again; it didn't seem so terribly far.

Life Is Just a Race

"Aha, he is going already. Where are you going, mister?"

Sol Meisel didn't even look back to answer his mother. The same words came every Sunday morning, the minute he stirred out of the house. He unchained his bike.

"Instead of running around all over the streets with his bike, we got suits to deliver. No, for that he hasn't time!" he heard her complain to the world.

"Ben can deliver them for a change," Sol called back. "What does he do all the time?"

Every day, even Sunday, the same hollering and arguing around the house. His old lady never got tired. Since he was a kid he remembered. First they lived in the back of the store on Twelfth Street and Laflin, now they lived in back of the store on Sixteenth and Millard. His mother always ready to rush out the minute she heard a *yachneh* arguing with the old man about a dress that was spoiled by the cleaner, and she would sue.

Sol liked to ride way out on Ogden Avenue to where there were no streets or houses yet, only sticks with street-names. He could ride a bike faster than any kid he knew. Or, pumping hard, he would catch up with a truck and hold on, getting a free ride, getting still further out, way out far from everything.

He liked speed. He had swell wind.

On Sunday morning there were always a bunch of guys hanging around Jorgenson's bike shop. Sometimes they went for a grind together. Frank Swiadow was there.

"Hi, Swede," Sol said. The joke about Swede was he was really a Polack.

"Hi, Solly," the fellows called.

Pop was in the workshop back of the store. He had a racing bike taken apart to the bare bones; he was truing up the triangular framework.

"Hey, Solly, how would you like to trade in that delivery wagon of yours?" Pop said.

"Yah. Fat chance," said Sol. They were always kidding him because of that big basket on his bike.

"You know who rode this baby?" Pop tapped the framework.

"No, go on, tell me," Sol said. He had heard it a hundred times. Pisano, the Wop Whizz.

Sol picked up a wheel, spun it. A couple of boys came in and started talking about Alderman Monahan's bike races in Humboldt Park. "Hey, Solly, why don't you go in?"

The riders had to represent sport clubs. Well, he had played baseball a lot with the Aces. Suddenly he had a nutty idea. He would say he was riding for the Big Ten! Pop had a blank, so he put that down.

The park drive was lined with cars. Every rider seemed to have a whole family out to watch him. There were five or six guys he knew in the lineup; still, Sol felt kind of strange. He was no grandstand player; still, he felt all alone.

He hung around near Swede, who was also riding. "See that kid in the green jersey?" Swede said. There were four guys in green jerseys, from the Shamrocks. The little kid with the laughing face was Charley Witczik, who had won the race last year.

Some politician made a speech with a lot of baloney about fair play in sport and fair play in politics. There were some cute-looking babes. Sol guessed that was what was going to ruin him, girls. He saw Pop Jorgenson squeezing his way through the line of officials. He would have asked redhead Estelle to come only what if he didn't win. The guy with Pop was Pisano, the Wop Whizz! The last couple of years the Whizz had been laid up with a leg that went out of joint every time he got out of the hospital.

Pop came alongside. "That's your old bike," Pop said. Pisano put his hand on the bar for a minute as if he could recognize the feel of it. "Don't be afraid to turn on the steam," he said to Sol.

The gun sounded, and Sol raised out of his seat, digging in the pumping strokes for his start. But he didn't kill himself. Some of those guys were the flashy kind, he saw right away, standing up to gallop on their pedals, their bikes wobbling with the strain of forced speed. The green-shirted kid Witczik was one of the kind that leaned low, doubling over his handlebars like a jockey on a horse. Sol slipped into a spot toward the forward end of the string, riding a wheel behind Swede; on his left was a kid in a Spartan A.C. jersey. Sol automatically carried along in the race, while his eyes shuffled over the riders. Witczik had already stuck his nose out in front and evidently intended to stay there till the finish. That was the only way some guys could ride: with a bee on their tail. Other guys had to have something in front of them, to catch. The speed hitched up a notch, and Sol's legs went along with the increased tempo. He felt fine. The air was cool, washing past his face. There was a sucking whir of wheels. The wind began to break up his hair. He felt all full of power, using up nothing, being carried along.

Off a bike, he was always wanting something, noticing something wrong, worrying or being sore. When he got on a bike, especially in a race, everything seemed taken care of by his eyes and his legs; the old lady didn't bother him, or the redhead, or the girl across the alley, he could sometimes see her shadow when she was undressing, or what would he be when his brother Ben was a university graduate.

The race was breaking up now with Witczik and three other riders drawing away from the rest. The dividing line was just in front of Sol. He fastened his eyes on the green jersey back, knowing his legs would respond and shoot him straight along the line of his sight as though it were a charged wire. But as he tried to break away from the gang another rider in a green jersey swerved toward him. So they would try to pocket him! Shamrocks! This is a free country dammit and if a guy can ride let him ride! Sol hoisted himself up off his seat and laid forward with stabbing downstrokes of his legs. His head swung from side to side like a wind-banged door. He shot daringly between the two riders and skewed left, cutting in on that man. There was one instant flash of danger, that moment so fast it cannot be distinguished from the preceding and following moments, when he was off balance and felt he might spill. Then he was straight again. He had torn himself loose from the gang. He pumped savagely, his head still knocking from side to side. He could feel the strength of his legs pulling on his guts. That was the way to ride.

Witczik darted a look backward and saw him. That was enough. The green jersey jackknifed even lower upon his bike. He didn't seem to use his legs, but to be shooting head first through the air.

Some girls were screaming.

Sol knew he could win. This was the best part: being a little behind and knowing he would pull up and win. There was no meaning to anything but win. There was no second place, only win. He could feel his legs now pulling on his heart. It was nearly time. He didn't want to get up there too fast. He didn't want to be chased. His eyes had to have something to catch, not to look back on.

Now his eyes fastened on the finish line; his gaze was a steel cable along which he spun, to the line. All of him was in the race. The cords in his neck were tight; muscles in his skull, pulling on his ears, were tight. He drew alongside the leader. That kid could ride. That Witczik scooted like a low-slung roadster.

For a moment they battled side by side, their legs matching stroke for stroke. Sol caught a last sideways flash of the kid's face. The same face with the frozen laugh. But it was sore.

In a last wild attempt the green jersey swerved toward him, to prevent his passing. That was enough. The rage went up in Sol; he could feel it pressing against the roof of his head. By the time he could see through his anger, he was ahead of the other guy and over the finish line. Nobody was going to block him.

For a moment he felt alone because Ben wasn't there. You'd think at least somebody'd be around to see him win. Another guy he thought of was Runt Plotkin who used to run onto the floor with the gun at the end of the basketball games, and slap the boys on their sweating backs.

He should have brought the redhead, oh, boy, if she had seen him pass that Witczik bastard.

He had come to a stop straddled over his bike, resting without dismounting. Swede pulled up alongside and said: "Nice going, Solly."

Sol began to grin foolishly; he never knew how to answer praise. More people were around him now and there was a hubbub because nobody knew who he was. He began hearing his name repeated: "Meisel, Sol Meisel." And a girl's voice piped out of the crowd: "I guess he's Jewish. That's a Jewish name, Sol."

He liked the slow manly walk back to the shed, wheeling his bike with his hand on the warm saddle, and on the other side of the bike walked Pop Jorgenson and the Wop Whizz, Pisano. Pisano limped, gabbing: "Well, you feel pretty good, huh, kid? You did pretty good. Say, maybe we can make a rider out of this kid, hey, Pop? You got out all right, but watch it you don't let them box you in like that again." The Wop continued with his twist of a smile, so you couldn't tell if he was kidding or what: "You don't want to be a rider, look what you get. You break every bone in your body and you break your head too. Look at me, hey, Pop? There ain't a nickel in it. Don't let 'em kid you."

When he got home Sol announced it to the house: "Well, I won. I won the race."

"Huh? What did you win? A medal?" His mother's voice held, way back somewhere, a right to be angry in spite of good news.

"A cup," he said. "A silver cup."

"Well, where is it? Let's see?"

He didn't have it yet. They had to engrave his name, and his club's name, and have a presentation. He was practically the champion bike rider of Chicago, but it would be hard to explain that to her.

Sol went to the drug store to call Estelle.

"Come on over and tell me about it," she said.

That was the only thing, to win.

Within the Law

In the hallway, Lou Margolis met Melvin Coyne, who lived on the top floor. Coyne had studied law but never practiced, seeing he could make more money in business. His frame was cushiony; his red cheeks were always bunched up in a wise little sneer.

Pulling one of the books from under Lou's arm, Coyne looked at it sardonically. "Yah, yah, the same old crap. Say, is that crook Donohue still handing out the bull?"

"Sure. I've got him," said Lou.

Coyne emitted a soft laugh. "Did he tell you the one about the *ganef* and the Catholic priest?"

"Hmh?"

"I thought he told that one every term. It's a smart one," Coyne promised. The story was about a thief who saw in the paper that a certain priest had a certain golden goblet at his house. "So this Greek figures he can get a price for it from some pawnshop fence on North Clark." Lou caught the crack about his father's business. "Oh, yeah?" He didn't let himself be kidded. Coyne resumed: "This Greek was a professional. He'd been jugged in eighteen states. So he gets inside the priest's house—"

"Unlawful entry," Lou glibly spotted the crime.

"Wait a minute. This *ganef* hears someone coming, so he dodges behind a door. Two big fat priests are walking down the hallway. One of them sees the *ganef* through the door crack. Boom, the priest lays himself against the door, nearly squeezing the life out of the poor *ganef*. The other priest calls the cops."

Lou snorted appreciatively.

"You ought to hear Leaky Donohue tell this. He defended this crook. You know what the defense was? He asks the *ganef*: 'Are you a Catholic?' Sure! the *ganef* is a good Catholic—"

"I got it. Any Catholic got a right in the priest's house!"

"Wait!" Coyne said. "The joker is, you know they got regular Catholics, and Greek Catholics, and a Greek Catholic to a Roman Catholic is worse than a *goy* to a rabbi! But in court Donohue kept his mouth shut, and the dumb S.A. never asked this *ganef* what kind of Catholic he was. So Leaky got away with it!"

64

Lou blinked his eyes, appreciatively.

Coyne handed back the book. "Say, what do you want to be a lawyer for anyway? You're a smart kid. Go into business."

"Well, I don't know," said Lou. "Law is a business too."

"One thing, a law training is never wasted. You can always go straight afterwards!" was Coyne's parting shot.

Lou Margolis had a way of slumping back in his chair, with a sharp attentive look on his face, as if he were cleverly considering the instructor's every remark.

"Bear in mind, gentlemen"—Donohue's large fleshy mouth gave him the appearance of always smacking his lips over some choice idea—"that in cases of unlawful entry it is absolutely up to the state to prove felonious intent. For instance, in my practice some years ago—" and Lou heard him recounting the tale of the Greek. The class roared at the picture of the fat priest squeezing the life out of the poor prowler. "For once, he was glad when the police arrived."

Then Leaky described how he had handled the defense. "It was my contention, before the court, that since my client was a Catholic he had a right of entry into the priest's house . . . and as they could not prove felonious intent, the judge was obliged to acquit."

Donohue surveyed the faces of his students, with a knowing, withholding leer.

Lou said: "Excuse me, sir, did you say your client was a Greek?"

"Yes." Leaky Donohue leaned forward.

"Then wasn't he a Greek Catholic? And the priest a Roman Catholic?"

"You've got it!" Leaky grinned.

All the heads in the room squirmed toward Lou Margolis. Nothing ever got past that guy!

Up to that moment Sam Eisen had been listening carelessly. But now he came suddenly to attention, not quite sure he had understood what was said. He questioned the instructor, "Point of ethics." Had he known his client was a Greek, not a Roman Catholic?

"It was certainly not my part to bring this out," said Donohue. "The State's Attorney should have disclosed that fact. As he failed—"

The fellows were staring at Sam as if he belonged in kindergarten.

"Oh, I see," he said hastily. He didn't want them to think he was so dumb as to miss the cleverness of the trick. But in this case the lawyer knew that his client was guilty. Sam came out with the whole thing. "But suppose an attorney has evidence proving his own client is guilty. Is he then under obligation—I mean, can he withhold that evidence? And defend his client?" He ended lamely. He perfectly well knew the answer to this question.

Donohue drew back the corners of his mouth. "I am glad you asked that, Eisen," he said. "It usually pops up about this time. Mr. Eisen"—he sucked a tooth—"you are really asking this question of yourself, not of me. You ask yourself whether, in all conscience, you could defend a client you knew to be guilty. Well, you know that a lawyer is ethically bound to provide the best defense at his command for his client." He arose from his chair, and his voice now began to flow in the rolling periods characteristic of his courtroom speeches; before he was finished with his speech, he was striding back and forth, flinging his arms.

"The whole trend and evolution of the law, gentlemen, has been for the protection of the innocent man who might be unjustly convicted of wrong. It is an accepted principle of American justice, gentlemen, that it is far better to allow ninety-nine criminals to go free rather than convict a single innocent man out of that hundred! Every accused man is entitled to a full and competent defense. I can't impress too strongly upon you this fact. Why, the very constitution of our law provides that if there is so much as a choice of conclusion, between guilt and innocence, the judge or jury must find a defendant innocent. Now"—he leaned on the side of the desk, as one getting down to cases—"up to the moment when the jury goes into the juryroom, the accused, to you and to everyone else, must be treated and thought of as an innocent man! That's the law! And you must apply the very letter of the law. For instance"—his voice dropped to the conversational level, his knowing, smacking lips hung loose again—"take so simple a matter as venue. I had a case once of a—burglary let us say, on Clark Street. In examination, the prosecution failed to specify what Clark Street. It might have been in Evanston, for all the charge said. I let that omission go into the record and was able to secure an appeal on the ground that the prosecution had not proved venue!"

Runt Plotkin noted that down. He could see himself pulling a smart technicality like that in some important case in the future.

Sam smiled inwardly. Donohue had never really answered his question. That had been clever.

It was raining. They made a dash for it. Runt got his pants splashed by a Checker. "Sue him!" The Sharpshooter laughed as they piled into Raklios's, shaking the rain off their hats and faces.

"Ham sandwich," Lou Margolis decided.

"Make it two," said Lou Green.

"Two on," the counterman chanted.

Lou Green was still trying to figure out that trick about change of venue.

"But what's the use of it?" he persisted. Mygod, what a dope! "Suppose you get a new trial. They'll just go over the same stuff, and convict the guy again, won't they?"

"But that's the whole idea of law!" Lou Margolis snapped. He put his sandwich saucer over the mug to keep the coffee from spilling in transit. "Why, before the new trial some of the witnesses might die or go away or you might get new evidence or anything might happen. Why, you could stall it a year or two. And all the time your fees pile up. That's the whole idea."

The Shadow's face brightened. This time he got it.

Plotkin sat himself next to Lou Margolis. "Say, Lou, you sure caught him on those Catholics. Where do you get to know so much about Catholics?"

"Oh, well." Lou let a smart look come into his eyes. "I thought there was a catch to it somewhere."

All of a sudden they were arguing again about defending a client you know is guilty. Plotsy brought it up. Lippy Davis said, what the hell, if a guy had such a conscience he could pass up the case.

"Oh, no!" Lou Margolis twinkled. "Why, it's your duty to provide the client with the best possible defense, isn't it? And you believe your own defense is better than anyone else's, don't you? So . . ."

The fellows laughed.

They filed out of Raklios's, Old Ganzy, the cashier, murmuring: "Well, looks like you young men are going to get wet," and taking their dimes and quarters. Sam Eisen, with one of his flashes of sentiment, took a look at the old man's cheeks, and as he passed out into the rain he had one of his youthful spasms of feeling the sick unsafety of this fourflusher's world.

The guys were still arguing. Sam heard Runt remark: "I don't give a shit how guilty the guy is, it ain't his fault. Either he's broke or can't get a job or something, that's what makes a criminal. I figure I'm always justified in defending a criminal!"

"Hear, hear!" the fellows kidded Runt. "Clarence Darrow the second!"

When Sam got off the street car, the rain had abated to a drizzle. He had three blocks to walk. He pulled off his hat, so as to let the rain wet his forehead.

He was still bothered by that idea, defending people you were certain were guilty. This was ridiculous, he knew, because mygod half of law practice must be like that. He was no damn fool idealist, he told himself. This, tonight, was just one of those surprise encounters, part of learning. After all, it was all right. Yes, he could see it now and it was really all right, it was necessary. He could feel a vast experience behind the procedure. He could feel it going back, evolving out of the earliest laws, all through common law, up to now, this sense of giving a man the utmost chance, the utmost play for freedom. There were guys who went to Harvard Law School or even the U. of C. and got a lot of other stuff besides what he was going to get. Of course most of it was theory, impractical. He wouldn't need it. Still, he felt a need of something, more knowledge, a deeper basis for his thoughts, so that when he came up against a problem of this kind he would have the real stuff and could cope with it; maybe he didn't even belong in law, a fourflusher's game. If he wanted to be clever like Lou Margolis he could do that too. But maybe he ought to get something else, some real university stuff, besides this surface stuff of law. For the first time

Sam felt there was more to this and to everything about civilization, America for instance, than you got on the surface, than you got just grabbing hold.

You could defend anybody, Plotsy said, because a criminal wasn't really to blame for what he did. Sam smiled wryly. Good old Plotsy. Sometimes in his simple way he clamped onto the truth, but was it really so simple?

On another night, Plotsy, with his nose in a book, rode past his street and only realized it when he felt the lights of the Central Park through the street car window. It was just as well. Sadie would be sitting in the front room and his mother would be gabbing in the kitchen and Hymie would already be asleep in the bed they shared so he couldn't put on the light to read, there was no damn place in that house for a fellow to study. He got off the car and went into Jake's place and got himself some coffee. He sat down and spread open his case-book.

The noise in a place like this didn't bother him as much as the noise of one voice at home. A shadow fell over the pages and a heavy hand landed fraternally on his back. It was Maxie Novak, a lawyer himself, who did a lot of business with boys that came into Jake's place. Maxie flicked Runt's volume, laughing. "Say, what the hell good is that crap going to do you?" He was in a fine, generous mood, and hunched down next to Runt. "Lemme give you a steer, kid. It ain't the number of books you read. It's the people you know. That's what you got to know in the law business, people. Say, all the law that's in the books don't talk as much as a good box of cigars. That stuff ain't going to get you any customers." He slammed the book shut for Dave.

By this time, Runt could be sure of a personal nod from Jake himself when he came into the place, he could roll the dice for his check, and he could wander back there and watch the poker game. But now he was with Maxie Novak! A couple of Checker drivers, Davy Long the Battling Hebe, Schmutz Schmaltz, were in the game. There was about five bucks in the pot. Maxie Novak pulled up a chair and got in, grunting: "Say, I hear you had a little argument with a Yellow," to one of the Checkers.

"Aw, it was nothing. I only sliced off his front wheels," the Checker modestly admitted.

Runt pulled up a chair for himself. Now he was in.

He didn't do so bad. Came out a buck ahead, after a couple of hours.

He Worked His Way through College

Harry Perlin had taken the bell off his alarm clock and fixed it so the clappers hit a little piece of lead, just loud enough to wake him, as the rest of the people in the house didn't have to get up at five o'clock.

The first month he had used to shake himself out of sleep and feel good, feel a song coming on his lips. There had been the thought, "Working my way through school," always as a refrain to whatever he was doing. But now the truth was he felt run down and tired as hell. Some guys seemed to be able to tend furnaces and sling hash and still be full of pep, ready for jobs, friends, studies, and even school activities; maybe he was not the stuff such heroes were made of. Crouching, he shook the clinkers out, his head averted so as not to get ashes in his eyes and nostrils.

Another thing wrong was that he was outside the real life of the university. Oh, the guys in raccoons and girls in raccoons cavorting in a topless flivver—Family Entrance, Open All Year Round, Girls Wanted, If Nature Won't, Lizzie Will! There was a carefree *goyishness* about such kids. . . . No, Harry corrected the thought, for there were plenty of Jewish boys sporting around in crushed hats and raccoons. Then he told himself they were the guys with dough; but no, there were even fellows who were working their way through, who managed to get that carefree collegiate effect. You couldn't say money was the only thing.

He didn't want to be a male flapper, no, but there was just something about that kind of collegiate life that he longed for, a feeling that he was young and getting a kick out of things too.

Why couldn't there be a mechanical stoker? he thought as he dug the shovel under the coalpile. The iron scraping on the floor was a noise tearing him out of his uncompleted sleep.

His mind began to fumble with ideas of gravity feed, maybe some heat-sensitive trigger that would automatically open the coal chute. . . . If he had time, and a little workshop. . . .

Yes, he would say, swiveling in his chair and looking across the desk at the interviewer—invention is born of necessity. My idea came to me in the basement of a rooming house, where I was shoveling coal, working my way through the university.

Joe stopped into the lab for Mitch. Mitch was staying overtime finishing up some kind of experiment on a frog, because his partner was such a dope. They had the back of the frog's head cut away, and as Mitch delicately approached a salt-tipped probe, the cream-faced boob said: "Come on, don't be stingy, let's use a little salt. It dun't cost you nutting," he mimed, sticking his fat finger into the salt and into the frog.

Mitch flamed, but said nothing. He put down his probe and left with Joe. After this he would watch what he got for a partner. "And that thinks it's going to be a doctor!" he groaned. "*Goyishe kopp!*"

Mitch had an invitation to a smoker; Joe was included.

"You don't want to join a frat, do you?" Joe was horrified.

"Why not? This is one of the best Jewish frats on the campus. They made first place in scholarship the last three years."

A Jewish frat?

Mitch had to laugh when Joe declared that if he ever did consider joining a frat, it would certainly not be one that practiced racial segregation! Mitch explained the situation to him.

At that, Joe was dumfounded. He hadn't even known Jews were excluded from other fraternities. He fumed. He raged. Now he knew he had always been right about fraternity snobs.

How could any decent person join, under such conditions? "Mitch, you aren't going to join, are you?"

"They haven't asked me yet," Mitch replied. Sometimes Joe got on his nerves. What was wrong with a little fraternal fellowship? The Jewish frats hadn't started the racial issue, had they? Joe had to make an idealistic problem out of everything. People weren't supposed to be angels. Why not see things as they were?

Mitch Wilner took it all in good spirit. "Here! Service!" a brother bellowed. Mitch received the scalding soup plate from Esmeralda, who mercifully tipped him off with a grimace. The moment he got to the impatient brother, someone on the other side of the table yelled: "Hey! Where you going with that? It's mine!" So, impelled by the flick of a paddle, Mitch started around the table. But when he got to that side, a brother at the end of the table yelled: "Hey, stupid! Come here with that soup!" Encouraged by a few more paddle-whacks, Mitch made the end of the table.

"Hey, you flat-footed, elephant-toed, worm-brained louse with the face of a red-assed baboon! Can't you follow simple instructions? Bring me that soup!" howled Marcus Proskauer from the head of the table. Whack! whack! on his journey, but Mitch could hardly keep from laughing at Marcus's string of epithets. Finally he landed the soup in front of Marcus, who stuck his fist in it and howled: "This soup is cold! You blundering, stuttering, club-footed, hare-lipped, lop-eared . . . Lithuanian!" Whack! Whack! Whack!

Mitch Wilner took it all in good spirit and the brothers were therefore fairly easy on him. Besides, this was not the Z.B.T. and they were just a bunch of good fellows, no snobs. All of a sudden the pledge-ragging atmosphere would vanish and a quiet, friendly fellowship, like the quiet that falls between fits of hysterical laughter, would descend upon the house. Mitch would sprawl in the parlor, a couple of fellows would be smoking, and Proskauer would be talking to him as if there had never been such a thing as the soup-scene at the table. Just gab about courses and this and that. "I see Peterson is giving Chem 12 in the spring quarter. Better wait and take it then. He's good." Tips like that. The feeling of being steered right.

This was a Friday, and one of those cold bright afternoons when the whole lab seemed spotlight clear. Mitch was nearly through with his set of nitrogen-oxide experiments. The gas was bubbling peacefully into the last bottle.

Mitch took the bottle of nitric acid, intending to pour a few drops into his flask.

"Just look at him," observed Weintraub, the class kibitzer. "What control! What precision! I'll bet that's how his mother fed him his milk. An inherited characteristic, eh, doctor? Aw, come on, Mitch, loosen up. Give it another drop!" Laughingly, he jarred Mitch's elbow. Some acid splashed onto Mitch's wrist.

"What the hell, guy! Can it. I'm trying to run a reaction here." He washed the acid from his wrist and went on working. In a few moments, his wrist began to itch. Then he noticed that the spot of skin had turned yellow. "Say, look at that," he said.

"Yah. It always does that. Even the fumes can do it to you," Weintraub observed.

"I know that, chump," Mitch said. "But why does it do it?"

"Because nitric acid turns skin yellow," Weintraub elucidated. "It's a stain."

Mitch looked carefully at the yellow spot. The itching had stopped, but the thing continued to puzzle him. Finally he went up to the assistant.

"I was just wondering about this," he said, showing the stain. "Is there any explanation for it?"

"Well, yes," the assistant said. "It's a reaction with the protein in the skin. It's called the xantho-proteate test. Nitric acid is a good test for protein. It always turns the protein yellow."

"Oh," Mitch said. "I see."

He went back to his nitration. But every few minutes he raised his wrist and looked at the yellow spot. Nitric acid. Protein. Yellow. Absolutely. Deep, almost too far within himself to reach and examine, was a feeling of safety. A different sort of safe feeling from the one he had when sitting with the fellows in the house, feeling safe in their fellowship. This was deeper, greater. This was a reassurance that there was an absolute truth, and that absolute truth was science. Sometimes the truth was simple to find, sometimes the truth might be confusing on the surface, but once you traced it down, it would always be the same. It wouldn't turn on you. It was absolute.

Standing there watching the gas bubbling up through the water into the bottle he felt glad, very glad. The brightness and coldness of the day was like a spotlight on this first discovery of certainty. He was on the right track.

Joe had a theme assignment: "Describe your favorite building on the campus," and he stalked the grounds in twilight, seeing the gray Gothic masses as towers of the soul. He would write not of one building, but of the whole Gothic symphony, with its themes of arches, gables, spires, its fluting variations, its grace notes of gargoyles. He was a spirit walking alone, absorbing all this greatly into himself, the miauling campus kids could not see as keenly as he saw, with the understanding eyes of an artist. Gothic was purity.

The smart alecks could be modernistic and jeer about those medieval towers, built to house modern knowledge in Chicago! They could repeat the joke about the janitors having been ordered to leave the tower windows unwashed, so that Harper Hall might acquire an air of antiquity. They were young jackasses, hooting at tradition just to be different. But he was mature.

The purity of this unified and stylized beauty filled him with an elated sense of power. He too could do things like this: carve enduring stone, in a timeless, Gothic mood, free of all passing turmoil! Only the pure endured. This entire university was a quadrangle of sculptured stone, beauty, and learning together in classic peace; these forms would live forever, when the silly stunts of modernism, the twistings of the Szukalskis and the tricks of the futurists were forgotten jokes.

The studio of the celebrated sculptor, George Norcross, was across the Midway. Sections of molds, chunks of castings, lay about the yard. The building had a vaguely institutional appearance; troops of schoolteachers were frequently seen visiting the place. Once Joe followed such a group into the studio.

The doors were a reproduction of the gates of Ghiberti. Around the walls stood plaster casts of the great cathedral sculptures: Reims and Florence. Joe told himself this was like coming home.

In the huge central shop was a scaffolding around a wooden rough of a monument. A couple of young fellows were whacking on clay, while the goateed sculptor modeled the actual surface. He climbed down to greet the visitors: a gentle, small man wearing an immaculate light blue smock. He had a civic air.

The helpers, too, clambered down. The shorter one was of an Indian cast of features. Joe approached him. "Smoke?"

The fellow made an involuntary motion to light up, checked himself, and grinned. "We better go out. The old man doesn't like to have the atmosphere polluted."

Joe shared the humoring grin. "Say," he said, "how does a guy get hooked up here?"

Slowly curling smoke, the fellow eyed Joe shrewdly. "What kind of stuff do you do?"

"Oh, heads and stuff," Joe responded.

The Indian shrugged, accepting Joe as of his own world. "You know the old man, he is still a Florentine master with disciples and apprentices crawling around his feet. Bring around a piece to show him and shoot him a line of bull. He'll let you work for him for nothing. But at least you'll have a shop to use, and clay." He flicked away the cigarette, and returned to the studio.

The instant they got inside the doors of the Coliseum and heard the rubbery buzz of the bikes, the Wop Whizz came to life. He talked a blue streak, as if Sol knew all the guys he was talking about. He had a pair of ringside passes, but he practically jumped over the barrier. "I'm a son of a sea cook, there's that lousy Dutchman, Voss. Holy Jesus, that bastard has spilled more guys!" He yelled and waved, and the rider, spotting him, waved back.

In a minute a whole bunch of trainers and bike boys and a couple of riders were around the Wop, shaking his hand, thumping his back.

"Hey, where's your crutches?" Voss tossed as he rode by.

"Take off that wooden leg!" Pisano retorted.

Pisano took Sol around, having him meet lots of riders, trainers, big shots, champions. Guys whose names were uttered with respect in Pop Jorgenson's bike shop. And at each stand, the shop talk, the kidding, say what happened to Gus Dietrick, he broke a hip in Berlin, too bad that guy rode a pretty race in Milan, say is that blonde still trailing Happy Hooligan, you mean tailing, say I hear Voss is holding out for three hundred smackers a day for the Garden . . .

This was the place he belonged. This made sense to him. A guy in a bunk having his legs massaged. A rider gulping coffee and tossing the can off the track. And he met Carl Stockholm. The big Chicago rider squeezed his hand and said it was nice going the way he had copped the Humboldt Park Derby. Sol flushed and said: "Aw, it was just kids."

Then the Wop saw some pudgy, hurrying guy on the track.

"Hullo, Pisano!"

"Hullo, you Abe Kabibble!" They pounded each other laughing. It was Abe Cooperstein, the manager of the race. "Here, you schmaltz herring, here is one of your own Abies for your stable," the Wop said, pushing up Sol. "Say, this boy could beat your fuckn Voss riding a pushcart!"

Pudgy Cooperstein chuckled, and gripped Sol's hand.

"You ought to have a Hebe," the Wop said. "That's one thing you ain't got in your menagerie."

"Well, bring him up. Come up and talk to me," the promoter said. He pulled out a wad of passes and handed a couple to Pisano, a couple to Sol. "Well, come in and see me, I'll be here all week, come around."

Driving home, the Wop talked all the time. "Take it from me, Solly, it ain't such a bad graft. Why, the last night the fuckn preems are a hunerd, two three hunerd bucks, and that starts to be dough, huh? It's the same like anything else, you gotta be good, but if you're good, there's dough in it. Only one thing. You gotta watch out for the girls. That's the one thing that's finish for a bike rider. Girls. Say, what do you think finished me? Say, I could get over this fuckn leg. But I'm all shot to hell. You got to watch out for the girls. That's my advice to you."

Sol nodded sagely. About girls, did Pisano mean like some fellows let on, if you had nothing to do with women the strength of the stuff went right back into your blood, and you were stronger? Or maybe Pisano just meant about a dose you caught from girls. Or maybe only what the basketball coach had meant, running around, getting soft?

"Sure," Sol said. "I know. I never have much to do with them."

"That's the idea. Say, lemme tell you a rider can get plenty of stuff. Say, the letters they send you. Say, I could tell you one time I was riding in Paris. Oh, boy. But you don't want to do that. You want to watch out. It pays in the end."

Sol saw a flash of himself in blue and white jersey sprinting ahead of the field to whiz by the flag, copping one sprint after another, saw a flash of himself driving a speedy yellow Marmon roadster, saw a flash of himself in foreign cities, Berlin, Paris, London, Rome, sending checks home to his brother Ben, to send him through college.

Let those smart guys in the bunch study law and be doctors and all the rest of that crap, a good athlete was just as important.

The Wop offered to train him and maybe get him into the next Chicago grind. "I ain't saying you're going to cop off the big dough but there is always a chance and we want to have this straight so we won't get in any scraps with each other. We want to have an understanding."

There was a pause. The Wop paid attention to his driving.

"Well, how about fifty fifty?" Sol offered.

Pisano looked at him and laughed. "See, kid, that's what I mean, you don't know the ropes at all. For a kike you sure are generous with the kale. Some guy that wanted to take you could just take you up on that and hold you to it. That's too much to give away. You're doing the riding, see? I ain't a regular manager, but I'm gonna steer you just because I like the way you handle a wheel. I'd like to see you get in the game. I'll make it a fourth, twenty-five percent, how is that?"

Sol said: "Sure, anything you say is okay with me," feeling almost dizzy the way things were going. Pisano sure was a square guy; he was lucky.

Just because a girl was beautiful, did that prove she had to be dumb?

Sol was a cute fellow, but sometimes Estelle wondered why the more brilliant fellows in the bunch didn't think she was worth talking to.

And among the girls too it seemed taken for granted that she was just a Dumb Dora. Sometimes she almost thought it was spite, because they were afraid she was too much competition.

Like that time Aline and Rudy Stone were discussing that new book, *If Winter Comes,* and she asked if she could borrow it. "Well, if you want to," Aline said, "but I don't think you'll be interested, it's kind of deep."

Of course Celia Moscowitz could have gone to the swellest U, with her father's money, but instead she was going to the Downtown Business

College with Estelle, learning stenography and typing, just for something to do.

They rode downtown on the El together, every day.

"Gosh, if I were you I'd certainly go to college, it makes a difference the kind of people you associate with later on in life," Estelle insisted.

Celia was reading Harold Teen. "I'm sick of school," she said. "I know enough to get what I want out of life. Look, aren't these cute?" Lillums was wearing fur bootees. Galoshes were passé. "Let's see if the stores have any like them, we can go to Field's during lunch. I'm dieting anyway."

The girls were over at Aline's.

Aline said she was sick of being a home girl, sitting around all day, and so she was going to start in at the U next semester. Northwestern, so she would have to live away from home; and there was real campus life at Northwestern.

She could just see herself a real campus co-ed in jersey things and a pleated sport skirt. The best Jewish sororities had chapters at Northwestern. And anyway she felt in need of meeting a whole new set of fellows. It happened even to the most popular girls—times when suddenly after being rushed with a choice of several dates for almost every night, there was a period of no calls. Most girls never let on, pretended to be busy, but it happened to them all. And nobody knew just why. And suddenly the thing would pass and a girl would be popular again. Anyway it wouldn't hurt to meet a whole new set.

"My folks want me to go to normal, like Rose," she said, "but what's the use of slaving for two years to be a teacher, and then just when you get started teaching, you go and get married, and it's all wasted. I'd rather just go to the U, and take it easy."

"I think every modern woman should be able to do something, to have some interest in life, even after you get married," said Thelma, who was studying at the conservatory, and never let you forget it. But with her hard luck with boys, she ought to have something to fall back on. No matter how much the girls coached her, she never knew how to keep fellows interested.

Sylvia Abramson said any girl that expected to marry a college man ought to go to college too, or the marriage would never be successful.

"Then I guess Estelle must be gunning for a college man," Celia laughed. "All she talked about is going to the U."

Estelle, coming in just then, heard Lil's haw haw.

"Why, she can't go!" Lil's voice was strident, indignant. "Estelle has to get a job. Her folks can't send her to college, why they need the money she could bring in as it is!"

How It Is between Brothers and Sisters

The subject came up between a bunch of the girls: what were their brothers like to them?

Thelma Ryskind had two younger brothers. "They can be real sweet sometimes and I can make Jerry do anything I want but Nate is just a fiend. A kid brother is just a nuisance," she said. "Anyway, when you get to be our age, a fellow and a girl haven't got very much in common."

"You mean a brother and a sister," Estelle meaningfully cracked, and the girls screeched, Skinny Heller's horsy snicker audible above the others. Quieting, she said she had always thought a brother would be kind of chummy.

"Joe is a good kid but we aren't so chummy," said Aline Freedman. In her heart she had often wished she had a sister instead of a brother; a sister you could have intimate talks with, lying awake in bed. What was the use of having a brilliant brother, when he thought you were too dumb to talk to? "But you know how Joe is, he never talks much," Aline excused their lack of chumminess.

"Oh, Joey talks a lot," Sylvia said innocently.

Hoots greeted this.

"I suppose he's just like a brother to you!" Aline remarked in a tone between catty and kidding.

"My brother talks to me," Sylvia said. "He likes to come into my room. Sometimes he sits on the bed just before I'm going to sleep, and we talk."

"Mort!" the girls shrieked. That was a good one on Mort, the slick lady-killer! Telling bedtime stories to his kid sister!

But she felt she couldn't really explain to them the brotherliness of Mort, and how nice it was to have him treat her like a kid sister all the time. Sometimes they both came in late from dates; and he would look into her room. "Where have you been, did you have a good time?" The other night he had asked her: "Say, Syl, are you in love with Joe?" and her eyes had brimmed, looking into her brother's. It touched her inexplicably to have Mort sitting on the edge of her single bed, and everything in the room, she suddenly realized, was girlish, and pure, to Mort it was his sister's room, white and maidenly. The pink-shaded lamp warmed her face, and he looked earnestly at her. He wanted to know everything about her and Joe, what they did together, and she wanted to be able to tell her brother, but when it came to talking of her feeling for Joe they would joke away from the subject, and Mort would get up and go to his own room.

"Well, I think brothers and sisters should try to be friends," Estelle Green contributed. The truth was she and Lou were like people who work for years in the same office but are shy of getting acquainted. Their strangeness had a peculiar abashed quality that was due to the fact that each secretly remembered how as children they had slept together in one bed. But when Estelle had that row about bobbing her hair, Lou had stood up for her, yelling and outyelling his hysterical mother, yelling that it was all right, everybody was doing it, even yelling in a hard impersonal way that for his part she looked better with her hair bobbed. "Fellows like to act as if they didn't have any feelings," Estelle said, "but a girl can tell. Lots of times I think brothers and sisters could be more friendly."

"Well, of course I'm friends with my brother," Aline said. "Only I mean, you know, there are certain things and it's different. It's different than you thought it would be. I mean I could always rely on Joe as a brother. But there are certain things a girl doesn't even want her brother . . ."

Rose Heller wondered if things like seeing each other was what Aline meant. Sometimes when she came into the Freedman flat Aline would be calmly walking around in her stepins, with the door of her room open, and Joe in the house. Didn't brothers and sisters think of each other in that way? Rose flushed, guilty with her thoughts. She was glad she had no brother. It would scare her. Though sometimes she wished she had a little brother, just a kid, like Thelma's kid brother, the rascal, kids were so cute.

It felt so intimate to be talking like this. This was the thing about getting together with the girls, sometimes it was just shrieks and cries about new dresses and dates and spilling a little dirt, and sometimes as they talked they got a warm, real henlike feeling, nestling down into this female intimacy. Testing it bit by bit, like testing the warmth of bathing water, and then sinking into the steamy enveloping bath.

In each of them was the feeling that maybe here, maybe now, would come some understanding of what was missing at home, where parents and brothers and sisters seemed so unlike what you read about in the stories in the *Saturday Evening Post* where parents were chums with their sons and daughters. They felt this warmth of settling into each other, discovering that other girls' feelings were like their own.

A brother could help a girl a lot, telling her what fellows liked in girls, so she would know how to act. Do fellows tell on girls? Syl, does Mort tell you about the girls he goes out with? Aline, does Joe tell you about Sylvia, or ask you how he should act with her? To get inside those mysteries that fellows have, of what they really think of you.

And now in their talk they almost let out the inner fear, the inner panic; you could tell each girl was reaching and feeling in the dark, fearfully exploring the treacherous, mysterious realm of being a girl. You couldn't ask too much or you would give away your secrets, in your asking. And the whole world was secret, fellows and girls were secret, even in this lush intimacy, in this rare good feeling of a bunch of girls talking like naked to each other, each felt that the final true secret of how to behave, how to catch and keep a fine man, was held from her by her sisters.

How far should a girl let a fellow go? Doesn't Mort come back and tell you all about the girls that let him do it to them? Do they really let him? Oh, those *shiksehs* Mort Abramson goes out with.

77

"It doesn't make any difference if they are *shiksehs*," is Sylvia's opinion. "They can be nice girls too. Of course there are some girls in any race . . ." she implied with disdain and horror.

But no, not Jewish girls. Jewish girls never let fellows.

"Fellows like a girl that lets them play around," Estelle said, "but they don't respect a girl that lets them go all the way."

Did that knowledge come from her brother Lou? You could bet Estelle was talking from experience. Lord knows what she had let Sol Meisel do. But no, she couldn't have let him go all the way. If she had done it, you could tell. There would just be something about her, that you could tell.

The girls looked, each to her best chum, and around at all the others. They felt themselves still all together, all still pure. Jewish girls didn't let fellows do it to them. But how far could you go without doing it? That was what their glances, their eyes on each other, sought to ferret out. Mouths on mouths, and tongues, and letting hands explore under your dress, and a hand, even lips on your bared breast, but even that wasn't doing it; writhing close in the back of a car, with only a film of cloth between; but even that wasn't doing it, you were still pure, still a virgin. You could let them do anything except—you know—and you saved that for your husband.

"My brother got married last year," Lil Klein said, "and since then he's a total stranger."

Daughter and Mother

Estelle looked down upon the creased flesh of her mother's neck, the scraggly hair, the squat back bulging the yellow print housedress. She had to repress an impulse to wrench herself away from the feel of her mother's thick hands upon her, pinning, smoothing the folds of the new dress.

She was ashamed of it, but her mother made her sick. She stood there enduring the touch of those hands, the dumpy woman crawling around her, shaping the new taffeta.

—Holy cats, she doesn't have to be like that she doesn't have to scrub the floors like a Polish washerwoman we have enough so she could pay a couple of dollars for someone to do the heavy work, she doesn't have to have her stockings falling! And if she washed her hair and dieted a little, if she only tried to take care of herself . . .

—Well, I certainly am a hell of a one! Here she has given her whole life slaving away for us kids and I . . .

—Who asked her to?

—Well, she does it anyway. Here she is on her knees fixing a new dress for me to go out in. She never goes out herself.

—Who tells her not to? Mygod I wish she would go out and have a good time once in a while! Believe me I'm never going to let myself get like that! What for? For who?

—For the kids. For us.

—Thanks, keep the change. Why doesn't she have a life of her own? It's always where am I going, and who am I going with, and what will I wear, why doesn't she worry about her own clothes a little!

Her mother clambered to her feet to get a piece of trimming.

—Ugh look the sloppy way her petticoat hangs, how can she be like that! We're grown up. She can spend some time on herself!

As her mother's back was turned, Estelle studied the woman. Her shape was all gone. The flesh was not fat with eating, but a kind of sickly puffy flesh of dull self-neglect. . . . If she should become like this! People said that in their faces a resemblance could be seen between mother and daughter. Shuddering, she worried: how did a person get this way?

Estelle remembered when they were kids, her mother had not been like this, and the house had seemed homier, visitors used to come and drink tea and gab in the kitchen, and there was always Yiddish laughter about *landslait* in the old country. When had it changed? Since they had gone to school and started talking English in the house and grown up? Her father wasn't so bad. He took an interest in life. At the table he and Lou were always discussing the fight news and baseball news, the old man was even better up on the stuff than Lou, being a barber. Naturally he talked in English but the old lady still jabbered in Yiddish. When the old man and Lou exchanged opinions about the Dempsey fight, over the table, she padded back to the stove, fussing with the pots; it was all a dead world to her. She understood the English words, yes, but she seemed to shut herself to all their talk, hostile.

Again her mother stooped to hem the dress; the fight would come now about the length.

"That's too long," Estelle wailed.

"What do you want, to go around with your *pupik* showing?" her mother barked.

"They're wearing them even shorter. Mygod!"

"Maybe so you can ride on the boys' bicycles, you *nafkeh*!" her mother snapped venomously.

"Oh, for cry sake!" It had just been a joke—the other day in front of Rose Heller's house, when a lot of the kids were hanging around, Sol had dared her to ride his bike. Of course when she straddled it a lot showed, and Mrs. Heller had to see her.

"I know, I know everything!" her mother cried, nevertheless angrily pinning the hem up another inch. "You think you are so smart you don't have to tell your mother anything. Go on, go on, do like you want. I will not be able to look in the faces of the neighbors, in my old age. Nothing I am supposed to know. Who you go out with, it's none of my business. Come home when it is light already! What do they do, all night long, such fine children, the girls in their naked dresses and the boys with their automobiles."

"Oh, mygod, she's starting again," Estelle wailed as if to an audience.

"I have to slave day and night, silk dresses to make her. . . ." She began to splutter her words, half in Yiddish, half in English, and suddenly to cough. It was a queer, mouthy cough, as if she were trying to clean her mouth of the foulness of her life, of her daughter, of the pollution of strange America.

Estelle went and got her a glass of water. Pity for her mother came up within her anger; oh, the whole thing was such a mess. Why did her mother make such an unhappiness of all their lives, when they might just as well be happy?

Occasionally when the girls came to the house and they had a gathering, her mother would fix cakes and coffee and would serve everybody and would stand around, lingering in the back of the hall or in the kitchen, listening to their young voices, coming in every once in a while to admire their dresses, and then her mother seemed quite happy. She would even fix herself up, comb her hair, and look neat and decent. But being alone in the house with her drove Estelle crazy.

She was always trying to get inside of Estelle's life instead of having a life of her own.

The phone rang; Estelle ran to be the one to answer. It was Sol, about tonight.

Sure enough, she had hardly got back when her mother had to know: "Who was it?"

"A fellow."

"Are you going out tonight?"

"Yes."

"Well, who are you going out with?"

"Sol," Estelle surrendered.

That started it again. . . . Boys like Mort Abramson, they called her up too, why couldn't she encourage them, plenty of fine smart boys she knew but she had to pick the one that was no good, a bicycle rider! A bicycle rider!

Estelle listened without comment; if you talked back it would last forever.

Next time she wouldn't even tell her mother who had called.

Sol might be dumb but, oh my gosh.

Flaming Youth

Sam knew that the bunch already took it for granted he was going steady with Lil Klein. All a fellow had to do was to walk a girl home once and he was ticketed. That first night after the movie, he was silent and grumpy. He had felt sore at the cuteness of Lil, the bangs golden shiny, the saucy eyes, and the penciled eyebrows, just another flapper trying to look like Bebe Daniels in *The Speed Girl*. And himself another sucker in the trap of sex. Except, he had a feeling Lil could be different. She could be a real person, she even had some brains. Why did she have to be a dumb flapper like Aline and the rest of that crowd? Why couldn't she be herself?

"What's the matter, Mr. Philosopher?" Lil teased.

"Nothing."

At the door, turning for good-night, she had said in her soft little-girl voice: "You don't like me, Sam, do you?"

"Maybe I would if you washed your face!" he burst out.

"Thanks for the advice, Mr. Eisen," she flared. "There are plenty of people that like it the way it is."

"You ought to be spanked!"

"Oh, yeah? I'd like to see you try!"

And before he knew it he had seized her and turned her down on his knees. He sat on the stairs, and started to spank her. She wriggled madly. "You! You! I'll scream!"

Embarrassed, dizzied by the liquid pressure of her body on his thighs, he hesitated. Lil squirmed around and slapped his face. She was still sitting on his knee. Real life had come into her eyes, the vapid affected gaze was gone. They stared at each other. Her cupid's bow mouth was parted. "Oh, did I hurt you?" she said. Her head was cupped in his hand, and she bent backward till he thought she must break, while they kissed.

They had dates every Wednesday and Saturday night. But every time Sam left her, walking home, he was disgusted with the way they had behaved, the gluey kisses, the squirming on the couch and worrying her folks would come in, worst of all the having to hold himself in all the time.

Jumping up if they heard her folks moving around, and putting on a record.

"She's got hot lips . . ."

Everything went but the real thing. Lil let him play with her breasts, while she lay back with a strange hypnotized stare. And they would have those long wet tongue-kisses. For hours they would go on like that, teasing themselves. And he would go home disgusted.

Walking home late, walking hard to get the devil out of himself, Sam would figure it that all this crap about flappers and flaming youth was a lot of hooey. Either he and Lil would have the real thing or cut off.

In the dark stretches between lamp posts he would see a couple squirming in a parked car, or against a wall, and then he would get a sudden clear feeling of knowing in advance what sort of people would come out of this. They would get used to half-ass acceptance, squirming their way through life, never quite getting what they wanted, never letting go in a full natural way. Whetting their appetites and letting the steak be taken away from under their noses.

So he skipped a Wednesday, and when he phoned the following Saturday Lil told him she had a date, who with? oh, someone. Late that night he couldn't stop himself from walking casually up St. Louis Avenue.

There she was parked in front of the house in Mort Abramson's car, both of them crunched into a corner of the seat, their faces glued. One glimpse made Sam sick. He walked away.... They were all kids, loose undeveloped kids, like some kind of spawning matter floating in warm water.

When Sam stopped seeing her, Lil had an orgy of petting, with all kinds of fellows. She got a kick out of driving fellows crazy. She was a real wild modern girl.

Lil was a hot kid, and Mort decided to take her out on a wild date, and see how far she would go. He took her to Colosimo's. She was impressed all right. Watching that red-hot floor show, they got dancing awfully hot; and yet there was something warily withheld about her always.

When they parked on the darkened street he began the usual game. She made no effort to stop him, letting him put his hands under her stepins, but it was strange, this time there was something strange emanating from her different than he had ever known in other girls: it was associated with the femaleness of her, and vaguely with disease—as if there were something wrong with her. There was an uneasiness in Mort, a feeling of contact with some unhealthy female plasma that he had never known before. He could not think of it in the same mind with the airy sweetness of his sister, or with the meatiness of whores he had laid; he thought maybe she was falling off the roof, maybe that had something to do with it.

No nice girl had ever completely given in to him. Jewish girls never let you. What would he do if she let him go all the way? Had Sam Eisen been having it?

"Do you want to come up?" she said a bit hoarsely; and he kissed her in the hallway, feeling a sucking, female quality in her mouth.

Lil was scared and yet couldn't stop herself, acting like in a trance. An overpowering curiosity possessed her, she had to know how bad she was, she had to go to the very edge and look over. Mort, the experienced man! She felt her flesh melting, in burning panic—a wild modern girl! No, she must be true to her future husband. . . . And even if it should be Mort, he would never marry a girl who had let him do it. They stopped to kiss again. With his lower lip thrust forward, glistening moist, and his dark eyes passionately intense under his dark olive face, he was like Rudy Valentino. Suddenly she went heavy on his arms.

She had fainted.

Mort was scared stiff. The weight of her was heavy on his arms; he let her down slowly, his muscles trembling, till she rested on the stairs. Should he ring the bell? Yet, with his fear, was his pride of prowess: Kiss them and they pass out! Maybe she was really sick, falling off the roof, a girl shouldn't go out in that condition. Or maybe she was pregnant, maybe Sam had knocked her up and now he would get the blame. A globule of sweat broke in his armpit and rolled down his side.

"Lil! Lil!" he called huskily, afraid to wake someone. He shook her, and her head lolled crazily from side to side. Should he slap her face? Then he thought of his flask. Not really much of a drinker, he was always forgetting he carried a flask. He dribbled some gin across her lips. She came to.

"Whuh?" she said. "What happened?" She started to get up.

"Here, are you all right? Is anything the matter?"

"It's all right," she said. She was safe. It hadn't happened. Something had saved her. Now she was sure it was Sam she loved.

Mort got her up the stairs half-lugging her, and was he glad when she was finally inside that door!

The experience opened vast dark tunnels into which Mort dared not look. Things about girls. For the first time Mort felt there was something about all women, a kind of organic female imperfection, that a man simply couldn't understand. At moments like that, some spark went out of them and they turned back to clay.

After that Mort always waited for Syl to come in from her dates with Joe. When she was out late, Mort would sit in the frontroom, till he saw the lights of Joe's car. Then he could tell how long Syl and Joe stood in the hallway.

Build Chicago!

The Chicago Theater was the triumph, the central diamond in the lavaliere that Balaban and Katz had strung around the city! And they had started right on Roosevelt Road with the Central Park; then the Riviera, the Tivoli, and now the Chicago Theater!

The entire Moscowitz family were guests of the management on the opening night! It was just a palace, Celia reported. Oh, she couldn't find words for it. There was a special eight-page section in the paper, but even that didn't give you an idea of the splendor!

And a new Norma Talmadge picture!

Mort knew all the places to park. He turned into the alley between Wabash and Michigan, and slipped the Oakland neatly into a space hardly a foot longer than the car itself.

"How's that?" he asked, squirming around for applause from the back seat.

"Oh, you're wonderful," Sylvia conceded.

"You just have to know how," Mort said.

As they flocked down Randolph Street, Thelma Ryskind— Mort was giving her a break—had to stop and look at fur coats in Field's window. "Squirrel is the only thing I would have!" she said to Syl who was wearing her new raccoon. "Anything else looks cheap beside it!" Yah, let her old man buy her squirrel coats out of his two-by-four grocery.

As they turned into State Street, the Chicago sign blazed at them. Boy, was that a sign! It made daylight of the whole block. Eight stories high. Three thousand bulbs spelled CHICAGO!

"It's beautiful," Thelma said. "You know what it reminds me of? Beethoven's *Moonlight Sonata!*"

They had come early so as not to have to wait, but there was a line of people four abreast curving way around Lake Street.

A crummy old building occupied the actual corner.

"Just goes to show, you can't be too smart," Mort said. "Those guys with the corner lot heard B and K were going to build, and held out for half a million. So B and K just built the theater around them. Now they are stuck with the lot!"

After a wait of forty-five minutes they got inside the lobby. Everything white and gold and mirrored!

Up on the promenade was a grand piano, all in white!

"Daddy, buy me one of those!" sang Thelma Ryskind.

A man in a tux sat down at the piano and began to play "Hortense."

"It's sacrilege!" Thelma said. "To play anything but classical music on a beautiful piano like that!"

And overhead, a magnificent chandelier! The largest in the world! Six tons!

Joe, however, was critical. "Chandeliers are relics of the days when they had to use candles to light up a place," he argued. "It's so heavy it's unsafe and it's a bad lighting fixture...." Then he became sarcastic about the gilded ornamentation and the jelly-roll pillars. "They don't belong in buildings made of structural steel," he proclaimed.

Sylvia was overwhelmed. "Gee, I bet you would make a wonderful architect," she said.

Why hadn't he thought of that himself? Architecture was the thing! A real profession, better than medicine or law; and he could make big money too, instead of being a starving bohemian like the boys at the studio. Even this big, glittering new Chicago, for all its vulgarity, was exciting, vastly proportioned! The hell with that old fossil Norcross and his medieval stones. He could sculpture with skyscrapers! It took Sylvia to discover him to himself!

"No waiting for balcony seats. This way for balcony seats, please."

They herded between red plush ropes.

Inside, they were just in time to see the marvel of the entire symphony orchestra sinking mechanically into the pit.

Chicago, noisily white and glittering! The Wrigley Building, bursting the Loop! A new city of skyscrapers would rise around the river-bend! He would be one of those who would fling them into the air!

Oh, beautiful Norma Talmadge!

They sat in the back of the car, not cuddled close, because Mort could see them in the rear-view mirror. There was something about tonight. All of herself was poised like a song in her throat. The signs on stores and the headlights of oncoming cars fluttered across her eyes. Why, old-fashioned girls in times of romance fainted of love (what Mort had told her of Lil's fainting but that was ugly not like this, this was love this tender wild lovesickness that trembled in her tonight). It thrilled her so, because she could influence him, show him his way. She felt a real woman now.

In the house they hardly spoke but sat kissing those long white kisses. At the end of a kiss she sat up. Listen. Wait.

Sylvia went into her own bedroom. From a little jewel box in the top drawer of the dresser, without turning on the light, seeing through a luminosity that seemed to come right out of her heart, she took a small, plain gold ring.

In the frontroom, Joe had hardly moved. She sat herself by him again. The ring was in her closed hand. "I've got something for you," she said.

"What is it?"

She opened her hand. She tried to keep her voice from quivering. "My mother gave me this. It's something her mother gave her. She said I should save it until I knew the man I loved, and give it to him."

She held it out. She was so sweet. So sweet and a girl. How did she know? How was she sure?

"It doesn't mean anything," she said. "I just want to give it to you."

She brought her hand nearer to his and they clasped hands, and she left the little ring on his palm. He took it clumsily and tried to fit it on his finger, but it was so small that it went only onto his little finger.

They both laughed.

Joe took the ring off his finger and deposited it carefully in his watch pocket. He felt something holy had happened between them.

"I want you to keep it," she said. "Don't ever lose it. Even if nothing happens between us, I want you to keep it."

"Dear," he said. He told himself if ever he had been unsure he was sure now. They were not like other kids. They were both wiser, grown for their age.

They kissed a light innocent fairy kiss. He got up. She went to the door with him and then they kissed long and more passionately than ever before.

Joe ran down the stairs, and she watched him, feeling purer than ever before in her life, feeling like a bride in white.

JADA JADA JIN JIN JON

Lately something had changed about the Big Ten. Naturally the fellows couldn't come around so much. Harry Perlin was down at Urbana, Mitch and Joe lived South, lots of the boys were studying law or working nights. But even the regular Friday meetings had changed.

At the start the idea had been to have a serious side to the club, and a social side too. At each meeting, one of the members was to give a talk. Rudy Stone had given that first talk on the microscope, then Harry Perlin had demonstrated radio, and Mitch Wilner had given a talk on "The History of Medicine." Joe had given a chalk talk that had gone over big.

The membership was limited to ten, but as some of the fellows went away to school the question came up as to whether they could have substitute members. Meyer Rosenberg and Chink Spingold got in, they were nice enough fellows, but nothing special. Once, when there was hardly a quorum present, the rule of ten was voted down, and more new members were admitted. Pretty soon a whole crowd of neighborhood kids got the habit of dropping around.

All that seemed to go on now was dancing and kibitzing. Sol Meisel had won that silver cup for bike racing, and brought it down to the place. A couple of pennants appeared on the walls. One night, for a social, they even strung yellow and green crape paper streamers across the ceiling. Joe Freedman, chairman of the decoration committee, was sore.

Then the question of a dance came up. The idea was to run a dance and make some money. Lou Green suggested that it be held during Christmas week.

Confusion began. Should it be a prom or should it be a hop? Could they make more money charging two bucks' tax for a swell affair in a hotel or selling dollar tickets for a hop in one of the park refectories? Runt Plotkin said he knew a politician and maybe could get the refectory free. Sam Eisen said he didn't see what the Big Ten needed to run a dance for anyway. What did they need money for? And the chances were they'd come out in the hole.

All that went on was business about the dance. Should the tickets be engraved or just printed. A long debate on whether to say Admission, or Tax, $1.00. A six-piece orch or a four-piece.

Sam Eisen was getting more and more disgusted. The Big Ten had started out to be something different but look at it now!

At the meeting a week before the dance, Lou Margolis took up the question of ticket sales.

"Well, so far we didn't do so good. It looks like the dance will be a kind of private affair," he cracked. The trouble was a few of the fellows were doing all of the work. If every member would do his share ... And he began calling each member by name for a report. When he came to Sam he said:

"I've got you down for five. Is that right?"

"Yep."

Lou wanted to know how many of those were actually sold.

"None," Sam said. There was an awkward laugh.

"How about a little co-operation, Sam?" Lou said. "We've got to sell these tickets or we'll be in the hole."

"The dance wasn't my idea," Sam said, controlling himself.

Lou kidded: "I know where you can sell a couple of bids right now. How about selling a couple to Sam Eisen?"

"I don't think I'll be there," Sam said.

There was a cold wait.

"Well, if that's the way you feel about it . . ."

Sam got up. He couldn't stand it any more. His big bustout was coming. "Listen," he said in a tight, low voice, "I don't know what's happened to this club but it isn't what it started out to be. It started out to be something worth while. We were going to get together a bunch of fellows who meant something. We had a purpose. Well, it just seems to me that it's changed, that's all. We're no better than the Aces and the Deuces and all those bums that hang around the sidewalks and whistle and shake a leg. I'm not against having a good time. You fellows know me too. I don't mean to ignore the social and the athletic side. But it just seems to me that the spirit here has changed. I'm not accusing anybody. Maybe I just don't get the idea. But look at us! A bunch of sheiks, come around and wisecrack and tell a couple of raw jokes and—aw, what's the use! I don't belong in this kind of a club, that's all. The best thing for me is to get out."

He was making a fool of himself. Now that he came to accuse—what was there to accuse? He became choked up with anger, rage at not being able to tell them, tell them . . .

He stood for a moment as if ready to answer any arguments. Then he moved past a row of knees toward the door. Maybe he had been hot-headed. But everything that was wrong in his life seemed to have brought him to that speech. The arguments at home, now the coat-makers were on strike again and his mother kept nipping, nipping at his father, other men went and *made* money during a strike; his dissatisfaction at the law school, his uncertainty; and his troubled, girl-wanting nights; everything seemed to converge into this explosion against the bunch.

The fellows took it strangely. There was a burning quiet. As Sam got to the door Lou Margolis said sharply:

"Are we to take this as a resignation from the club?"

"Yes," Sam barked out, but with a feeling of defeat.

Rudy Stone hurried over to the door.

"There is something in what you say, Sam." Rudy's calm smile reassured, and yet hurt him. He didn't mean to be against fellows like Rudy "Only you have to remember there is another side to the question. If the fellows want this to be a social club, that's their affair. There's nothing wrong with having a good time once in a while."

"Oh, that's all right," Sam stumbled. "I just figured I didn't belong here any more. It's nothing personal."

"Sure, no hard feelings, huh?" Rudy said, extending his hand. He was so understanding and friendly Sam felt a little ashamed of himself, and yet deep down he was sore at that too, because he knew he was basically in the right.

"Well," Rudy quoted, "if we can't be the same old sweethearts, we can still be the same old friends. Stop in at the store some time, you squidyalum!"

It was snowing. Large watery flakes melted on Sam's face like tears. He was still breathing hard. He felt sore at the whole world.

When Sam was gone, Lou Margolis said: "Any further business?" Runt Plotkin offered to take care of the checkroom at the dance. The meeting dribbled on for a while, and then was adjourned. It broke up into knots, while the fellows talked about Sam Eisen. Lou Green said the trouble with him was that unless he ran things he couldn't be satisfied.

Sol Meisel didn't know what Sam was bellyaching about. It was as if Sam had suddenly jumped up and started to punch everybody around him, for no reason.

"He'll end up with high blood pressure," Mitch said.

Of course the dance would go through as scheduled. Only after that things seemed vague. It was almost like Sam had said: the club had no purpose, any more.

In a couple of days, Harry Perlin came up from Urbana. He was sorry to hear about Sam Eisen. But he jumped right in to pull the dance out of the hole. Come on, fellows, we can still put this over. He went into every store on Roosevelt Road to get ads for the program. He got Rosen's barber shop and Kantor's delicatessen, and a half-page from Elfman's funeral parlor—from old man Elfman himself, who said: "You're a hustler all right!" Then he got a fellow in the Aces, and one in the Bluebirds, and one in the Y.M.H.A. to sell tickets to those clubs. He got Mort Abramson to sell tickets. Mort was very sympathetic and helpful when he heard the club was going in the hole. "Why don't you stick 'em with a wardrobe tax?" he suggested. "Once they've got there they have to pay it. The Bluebirds stuck everybody half a buck at their last affair." But Pearly thought a thing like that would give the club a bad rep. Besides, Runt Plotkin already had the checkroom concession.

Three weeks in advance, Harry had written up to ask Aline to the hop, but she hadn't answered his letter for two weeks and then she said she was sorry but she had promised to go with Rudy. So Pearly was stagging, and could take care of the door.

At eight o'clock Harry Perlin was on the spot. He began to worry would the orch come on time? Would the checkroom boys come on time? He made useless telephone calls. Nobody was home, nobody knew anything.

At last Runt's two brothers shambled in. They hadn't even brought checkroom tags. Harry Perlin nearly had a hemorrhage. Mygod, he had never seen an affair so mismanaged. He began tearing paper into slips and writing sets of numbers on them. The Polack janitor saw what he was doing and produced a set of numbered metal checks.

"Boss, you saved my life!" Harry cried. The boys started sliding on the floor, and that reminded Harry there was no floor-wax. The janitor appeared with a can of rosin, saving his life again.

He'd have to give that Polack a buck if it came out of his own pocket.

"I worry too much," Harry thought. "That's the trouble with me."

He could have picked up a tramp at the Dreamland. But this time Runt wanted a nice respectable girl. He wanted to get all duked up and bring some smart girl like Skinny Heller. Only she was such a giraffe. He didn't know anybody to ask. He even thought of taking his sister Clara, who was dying to meet some fellows in that swell bunch he hung out with. The boys at the garage were always pulling a big line about the swell bums they picked up in their hacks, or the broads that asked them to come upstairs and take their fare out in trade. As he cruised around he would think of some fine smart girl that would get into the hack and notice him reading law books or highbrow Haldeman-Julius booklets. She might turn out to be a judge's daughter. She would be peppy, little, and a snappy dresser. Boy, he'd like to shag in there with something that would knock their eyes out! Finally, since Sam Eisen had walked out on the club, Runt got the idea of calling Lil Klein. He had always had a yen for her and maybe with Sam out of the picture he would have a chance. But she told him she was already dated. He had a hunch it was a stall.

He stagged.

The idea! To be asked by Runt Plotkin! Lil trembled, and laughed at the thought. He had his crust, even to ask her! Why, he was driving a Yellow cab!

Sam certainly wouldn't come to the affair. And yet, if he should be there, let him see her walk in with somebody, oh, somebody that would make his eyes burn out—somebody like Alvin Fox, clever and handsome, a real sheik, home for the vacation from his university, and his father owned a factory!

Runt hung around the checkroom. He found a cigar-box under the counter, put a couple of quarters in it, and set it on the counter. "Take out the dimes and nickels," he instructed Hymie. "Just leave the quarters. Get the idea?" He figured everybody except himself in the family was dumb.

His kid brothers wouldn't dare hold out more than a couple of bones from the tips and even at that he should clear at least five bucks.

Lou Green was stagging too. He was kind of like a tail without a kite, as his sidekick, Lou Margolis, had given Rose Heller a break, taking her to the dance. So Lou stood with Runt Plotkin near the ballroom entrance, making sarcastic comments about Aline Freedman's bow legs, or tossing out knowing remarks to certain couples as they passed.

A lot of the Bluebirds were around, stagging, and Harry Perlin was a little scared that the Bluebirds might get funny. But Runt said he'd take care of things, he'd talk to the boys, and every few moments he scurried off and took someone aside and consulted, mysteriously, importantly.

> Sun shines east,
> Sun shines west . . .

Alvin Fox had a mustache! Call that a mustache, Lil Klein scorned, it's a misplaced eyebrow. And where did he get that girl!

Squiffs of laughter rippled through the Ladies' Restroom. But trust Alvin always to spring a sensation! The girl looked hardly fifteen. Her bony knees on stork-like legs stuck out under the scalloped hem of her girlish party dress. And with a cluster of Mary Pickford curls against the nape of her neck! She's putting on an act, was the opinion. Well, no matter how young she is, she's old enough to know better. It's a wonder she didn't wear a pink sash!

> But I know where
> The sun shines best.

In warmth, in wariness, the girls clustered in their bunch for the last whisper and reconnoiter, before entering the ballroom. The hastily exchanged last-minute bulletins on who had come with who. The shocks of relief and of agony, of friendship and betrayal—Aline said she was just going to wear her old blue sateen and look at her in that stunning silver thing with the swishing fringe around the tunic! It must be new! Celia just has on that rose thing she wore at the Sherman. All the girls affected a carelessness, a littleness toward this dance. They were careful to let each other know of the real affairs they were attending during the holidays—at the Edgewater, and the Del Roi, and the Blackstone! And still, there was a special air, a sort of hominess about this little hop, because it was the boys' dance, and it was sort of up to the girls to see that it went off all right. After all, they were their boys, trying to be social. . . . And whoever a fellow took here, there was a sort of meaning to it.

> In the land of Sandomingo . . .

Rose was scared. First she put makeup on her cheeks, then she rubbed it all off. She hardly ever used makeup and, when she tried to use it, she got flaring round red spots on her cheeks. "Oh, I look like a clown!" she cried in agony to Aline, who was lending her the rouge.

"Oh, take it easy!" Aline soothed. Poor Rose was just in a fit of excitement because Lou Margolis had finally given her a tumble. Why couldn't she take it easy? It was just Lou's system to go with the girls in turn, never going with anyone twice in succession. Oh, he was wise.

Lived a little oh by jingo . . .

But Rose, the poor kid, still had her crush on Lou, and she thought this was her real chance. "Oh, kid, what'll I do!" she finally broke down, pleading with her chum Aline. "What'll I talk to him about! I—I—"

Aline nearly had a fit. Why, Rose was the cleverest girl in the bunch, she had a tongue in her like nobody's business, she was always keeping the girls in stitches, and here she was afraid she wouldn't be able to keep a fellow interested. "Well, you know," Aline said, "there's nothing to it. No matter who the fellow is, you can always make him think you're the most interesting girl in the world by making him talk about himself. Just ask him what he's doing, and be interested in what he's doing, and he'll talk a streak. That's my system and it never fails."

Rose was staring at her like a drowning woman.

"Oh, don't be a blimp. Why, Rose, you can talk better than any of us." It was really simple. All you needed was a couple of catchwords, like Oh, yeah? and That's the cats, and Is that nice? or What makes you so quiet? and when in danger, you could always dance.

Oh by gee by gosh by joe by gee,
Oh by jiminy you're the girl for me . . .

She was the youngest and most brilliant student at Madison, Alvin let it get around. As if his bringing her were a sort of proof of his own brilliance. Her name was Nora Rosen and she was a North Side girl, no, no relation to Rosen's barber shop; in fact, her father was a policeman! Yep! a Jewish policeman! And she had won a scholarship prize at Wisconsin!

We'll raise a lot of little oh by gollies
And we'll put them in the Follies . . .

Lil Klein wandered a few steps into the ballroom. Quickly she scanned the crowd, while she held her hand up languidly fluffing the hair over her ear. Sam Eisen had not come.

She put on a smile as the dumb cousin she had conscripted to take her to the dance approached from the men's room. . . . Well, at least he hadn't come with anyone else.

He might still come.

It was really disgraceful. Disgusting. Solly Meisel and his redhead were shimmying like a pair of niggers.

"I think somebody ought to speak to them," Thelma Ryskind whispered to Aline.

Rudy Stone felt responsible. Perhaps after the dance he would get Lou Margolis to say something to Sol.

He had heard that certain of the fellows were carrying flasks, although it had been decided at a meeting that this was to be a respectable affair. Couples were going out on the balcony and swallowing gin.

"Oh, let them drink their rotgut." Mitch Wilner was scornfully liberal. "A little reverse peristalsis never hurt anybody."

—Did you see Estelle? After all there's a limit!

—Yeah? Not for her. I heard she and Sol have been—

—Don't be silly! Estelle isn't that kind of a girl!

Can she this and can she that?

You'd be surprised!

—I haven't got anything against her. That's what I heard, that's all!

And in the men's room, Lou Green heard: "Oh, boy, did you see Sol socking it in!"

I'll say she can!

But the scandal of Estelle was momentarily forgotten as Mort Abramson made a late entrance with Ev Goldberg.

The girls took one look and nearly passed out in a body.

Evelyn was wearing a full-length evening gown, straight to the floor, just the sort they had seen pictured on the society pages with the headline, "Paris brings back long evening gowns."

It was a blue chiffon covered with sequins, and with a wide studded girdle low on her hips, centered in an ornamental buckle. Around her shoulders was a gorgeous scarf-like creation of white tulle.

—Ev Goldberg! Well, no wonder! Her father has all those dress shops; that must be a Paris model he bought to copy.

—I admit it's stunning but I don't think it's good taste to wear it to an affair like this!

—I don't like those long skirts and it's a lot of bunk, they won't ever come back.

—They're just trying to change the style so everybody'll have to buy new dresses.

—I could have worn my yellow moiré, it's really stunning but I thought it was too—you know—for an affair like this.

—Oh, she's just a walking ad for the Evelyn Shoppes.

—I wouldn't wear a thing like that if you gave it to me.

"No wonder she wants to wear them long, she's knock-kneed," Aline said.

Happiness was in her like a tingle of two little silver bells in her heart, like the fluttering of Pavlowa's feathery toes. an endless tip tip toeing butterfly dance in her heart. She and Joe came late, from seeing Pavlowa, and the purity, the virginity, the happiness of being and feeling pure and idealistic and knowing that such things could exist in the world, this emotion flooded Sylvia, and she was pleased with everything tonight. Why, because, why, because of the blue of her dress, and even Mort was behaving tonight, Mort had brought none of his flashy girls, but a nice girl, Ev Goldberg, whose father owned the Evelyn Shoppes, see how nicely Mort was behaving, oh, Joeboy darling! And this strange wonderful feeling of unaccountable happiness, of all her friends being so fine, of her brother being so handsome, and her sweetheart being so sure, this flooded Sylvia, and there was an idiotic song whose words would not leave her, going across all the other songs that were played, and across the rhythm of dancing—

> Sun shines east,
> Sun shines west,
> But you're the one
> That I love best . . . !

At the end-swirl of the dance, Joe cocked his head and looked carefully, critically, at her face, and grinned. "If you will forgive a stranger's impertinence, miss, you have a very beautiful head. Might I ask you to pose for me?"

"Thank you, kind sir," she said, dropping a curtsy. And at the moment she loved all, everybody, the world, even Alvin with his silly new mustache. "I bet it tickles when it kisses," she said, and of course Alvin said: "You'd be surprised." And turning to Joe, said: "May I?" (Kiss your girl?)

> Jada! Jada!
> Jada jada jin jin jon!

Alvin stuck his head forward and actually made a peck at Sylvia; she withdrew, laughing, and barely felt his mustache brush her cheek. And, as she laughed: "I guess I'll have to wait till Joe grows one," Joe Freedman got an exultant scare. It was so final. Sylvia was Joe's girl, Joe was Sylvia's. He remembered that little ring she had given him that night when the Chicago opened. He reached for his watch pocket, though of course the ring was in the other suit. But he knew it wasn't there either. He had let it go to the cleaner's, get lost. He had a strange impulse to run home and look for that ring; it was an omen that everything so gay and good and sure-seeming, here, could carelessly be thrown away.

Never mind; love is young, there will be plenty of mementos.

> . . . of you
> The whole night through . . .

5. Foxtrot. Yours Truly.

6. Foxtrot. Mort.

7. Waltz. Mitch Wilner.

Aline studied the dance-trades Rudy was making. The same old crowd. "Oh, and Rudy," she relented, "give a dance to Harry Perlin." Poor kid, he still had a crush on her.

> . . . who you're calling sweetheart
> Now that you call me friend . . .

Lil Klein liked to be seen in the company of Celia Moscowitz because she believed they were contrasting types and sort of set each other off. You had to admit that Celia looked very nice when she fixed herself up. Not fat, but statuesque. That was the word, statuesque. The low waistline was really a godsend to heavy girls like Celia, Lil maintained, as it kept people from noticing they had no waist.

They watched Rose dancing with Lou Margolis; her face was rosy like a shining apple, she looked like she was on top of the world.

"You know, poor Skinny, she really has a crush on Lou," Lil volunteered. She laughed at the way Rose bent with her behind stuck out so she wouldn't show taller than Lou. "Can you imagine! what chance has she got!"

"She hasn't got a chance in the world!" Celia said. Her voice was firm, flat, and Lil was startled. Could Celia be after Lou herself? There was more to Celia than you thought.

> . . . I'll say she can . . .

You certainly couldn't call Lou a sheik, Celia Moscowitz thought, and this made her unhappy. Her secret passion was the sheik. Could it be with the other girls as it was with her? When Valentino's swarthy, warm face and that hot lush mouth trembled toward her from the screen, her body was all juices. "It's no use trying to resist!" his hot desert voice whipped her as he flung her onto a harem bed!

> . . . Jada jada jin jin jon . . .

Now she danced with Chink Spingold. His black hair glistened, and his side-hair was shaved level with his earlobes, like the sheik's. When a fellow first danced with her, he began with fast and jumpy jiggling, but after a few steps she had him dancing pasted against her. Maybe it was something mean in her, but she liked to make it happen and feel his embarrassment as he tried to hide it.

Lou Margolis was the only one to whom she never did that.

> Let me call you sweetheart,
> I'm in love with you . . .

"Don't tell me you guys don't take quant!" Mitch Wilner derided the premedic from Northwestern.

"We're supposed to be doctors, not chemists."

Mitch snorted.

"Everybody knows you Chicago medics can't even tell a case of measles without taking it to the lab," Schwartz countered hotly, looking to Rudy for aid. "All you guys ever learn is lab work. Northwestern turns out the best practitioners in the country."

"It's six of one and half a dozen of the other," Rudy said.

"You're crazy!" Mitch cried. "Northwestern is where they go when they can't make the grade at Rush."

"Ah, here you are!" Sylvia accused. "What's the matter, Mitch, are you trying to get out of your dance with me?" Listen to Mitch put it over that fellow! All her friends and Joe's friends were the smartest and nicest and wisest. They were a wonderful bunch.

"Hey, I got something more important to do than argue with you now!" Mitch gallantly told off the fellow from Northwestern. He grabbed Sylvia around the waist. "Shove off!" he said, and charged onto the floor.

She liked the way Mitch danced. He almost rushed you off your feet but he made you feel he knew just where he was going. Sometimes she loved dancing with Joey more than she could possibly ever love dancing with anyone, when they were in perfect accord, but sometimes it seemed to her he got confused, he would change step at every turn, two-step, waltz, foxtrot, toddle all to the same music!

Skinny Heller was a scream. So good-natured! Instead of taking it to heart that she was so tall and thin, she made fun of herself! Back in the corner behind the potted palms she was putting on her act. The way she stuck one finger alongside her nose, and sang in the most comical Yiddish accent:

"Papa has a bizness,
Strictly second hend,
Everything from toothpicks
To a bebbe grend!"

She wiggled her middle, so the fringe around her knees swished comically.

"I'm wearing
Second-hend hets
Second-hend cloes . . ."

She rolled her eyes dolefully *á la* Fanny Brice.

"I'm second-hend Rose
Of Second Avenue!"

And when she and Lou Margolis got together, were they a pair! The fellows got hold of Lou's arms and tried to drag him out to the middle of the floor but he shook loose, laughing.

"Hey, Lou, hey, Lou!" said Second-the-Motion. "Let's see an imitation of Eddie Cantor imitating Al Jolson!" That was the Sharpshooter's prize. He crouched down on his haunches, clapped his hands like Eddie Cantor, snapped his fingers like Al Jolson, rolled his eyes like Eddie Cantor, and sang:

"Maaaahmeh! Maaaahmeh!
Sun shines ist, sun shines vest . . ."

There was a burst of applause. Practically the whole crowd had collected at that end of the hall, trying to see over each other's heads. Lou pretended he hadn't known anyone was watching, and hid his face in mortification. Lou Green thought maybe now there would be a call for the two Lous to do Gallagher and Shean, but the orch took up the "Mammy" song, and Lou Margolis grabbed Rose Heller and they did the craziest imitation of a Bowery dance. Skinny's eyes were snapping and her cheeks were red, and did she look happy! And was she good-looking then!

Jada . . .

"Now," Harry Perlin whispered to the Polack, and off went the lights.

"Yay!" the yell rose from the floor. "Yay!" Like the kids on the street, Harry remembered with pleasure. "Yay!" When the lamplights bloomed.

. . . In the winter, in the summer,
Don't we have fun!

The couples danced in the dark, in the moonlight, with titters, with giggles, with shouts and smothered laughing screams, then the spotlight went on, sweeping and weaving over the dancers. Harry felt good. It made him feel good to see everybody enjoying themselves, the Big Ten hop was a success; he had checked up on the money and they had at least broken even, due to the large last-minute turnout. It was swell!

It's three o'clock in the morning,
We've danced the whole night through . . .

Sylvia, dancing with Mort, came moving down the spotlight swath. And as Sylvia, and then other girls, drifted across that white beam, X-rayed in silhouette, Joe felt a shock of their loveliness. It was the torso, the upward flow from the hips, whose form he seemed to notice for the first time. Woman, a vase, molding up from the hips! Seeing them dancing he wanted to place his hands against their sides, and feel the motion of their lines; the leg-movement flowing from the very center of the body.

. . . with you!

The drumstick whanged on the cymbals. Announcement. Thelma Ryskind . . . persuaded to render the *Moonlight Sonata*. She took her place. Of course, she whispered to Rose, the piano was out of tune. . . .

"I'm so warm," Syl said, and curled her fingers with Joe's, leading him out the French window. The snow was just like the whiteness of her heart. It was snowing and not cold. Moist lazy windless snow, with flakes coming down large, floating. They walked out a few steps, their hips moving in unison. They stood watching the snow come down. It felt like tonight was the real New Year.

Thelma's music, dimmed through the doors, sounded beautiful.

"It's like the sound of the snowflakes falling," Sylvia said reverently.

The snow already sat on the branches of trees, and the fresh snow on the pavement showed two clean, curving tire-tracks. They felt all their life together would be so smooth and so clean and so beautiful.

They walked a little further in that joined walk, as if their bodies were one being. Around the corner they nearly stumbled over a couple huddled on a deep ledge, necking. The kissers came up for air. It was Sol and Estelle of course. They all laughed.

"Don't let us disturb you," said Joe, and he and Syl walked on. A moment later a snowball hit Joe in the back of the neck. He scooped up snow, and shot one back at Sol.

It hit Estelle. She shrieked, ran out, and began flinging snow, with that awkward, elbowy girl's way of throwing.

Before they knew it a whole crowd was outside having a snowfight. Harry Perlin was one of the first; this was something a fellow could do, stagging. He made a snowball on the run, and threw it at Sol; Runt Plotkin was on Sol's side; a snowball hit the window of a parked car, a fellow who had been necking in the car dashed out and joined in the war; Harry Perlin threw and threw, laughing in his funny high excited giggle; Mort Abramson joined him and Joe; and before you knew it there was a gang entrenched behind a row of bushes, shooting at the army behind the row of parked cars. The Bluebirds came out in force, and suddenly there was a flock of girls running in their spike-heeled dance slippers, running across the snow. Alvin was standing behind the French windows of the refectory, and he saw them poised, and heard their mingled cries, titters, and screams like the pleasant tinkling of broken glass. He felt poetic seeing the young girls in the snow, their twinkling birdlike legs, their skimpy silks pressed against their outlines by the wind of their running, the scalloped bottoms of their dresses, the billowing frosty tulle against the snow, the red, green, mauve, and marigold fragments of them, colors glowing by moonlight seen against the snow. And the tender gawky attitudes of their figures, knobby elbows and bumpy knees, the arch of their throats and the perch of their heads as they poised momentarily scenting snowball danger, then screaming ran! The girls ran scattering across No Man's Land, shrieking and screaming with laughter. Estelle caught a snowball in the neck and it slid down inside, and Sol had to reach down a little, to wipe her, and they laughed and laughed. Harry Perlin tried to lead a charge against the cars and got a big wet soft snowball smack in the puss. Lil Klein stood there screaming: "Give it to them, give it to them!" Rudy Stone put on his coat before he went out but then he packed the balls hard and shot them with deadly accuracy!

"Come on, gang!" Harry Perlin yelled again, and led a brave charge, but when he and Sol Meisel and Joe and Mort got in the middle of the arena everybody turned on them and began peppering them from all angles.

"Yay! Yay!" Harry Perlin yelled as he sat down in the snow. "Yay!" like the kids yelled on St. Louis Avenue.

"Well, that's enough, that's enough," Rudy was saying, helping him up and brushing him off, and the kids, all weak with laughter, were stamping back into the building. The whole bunch was there in the hallway stamping and dripping and laughing and it was one of those bright grand moments when everybody was friends.

The dancing went on. The going home started. Little snowfights popped and burst. Not a couple could stick their noses out the door without getting a hail of snowballs.

> . . . But I know where
> The sun shines best . . .!

EARLY TO RISE

THE slide on the movie screen would say: Later. If it was a fancy slide it showed a procession of camels plodding across the desert, and the humps of the camels moved like slow pendulums, endlessly marking the passage of time.

Or, think of this time as of a pregnancy; and the mother, placid, waiting, seated with her knees spread, her hands folded over the slowly increasing girth.

The embryo thickens and spreads in the womb, carried warm, safe, smoothly suspended in its liquid bed. The mother-body may feel the January ice, the jar and prod of stairs, street-car bounce, the nag of nickels and dollars, the hostility of glass showcases behind which are snips of girls who speak such fine English; the father knows the hack-rip sound of the buttonhole-making machine, knows the slowtime hours of waiting in the doorway of the store for a customer, knows the long inward fear that the city may never want to build that school on the lots he has just picked up.

Arms conference in Washington, but ishkabibble, kiddo, the boys were too young to go to the last war, knock wood, and they'll be too old by the time there's another war. If ever. A lucky generation.

There's a famine in red Russia, and there's Bluebeard Landru in France, and the Giants just paid the record price of $75,000 for Slugger O'Connell. Sam Eisen's father is on strike again.

Should Uncle Bim marry the Widow Zander, that's the question!

At a quarter of three Runt Plotkin parked his hack on Randolph, and dashed into the law college. Through the glass door of 404 he could see the fellows still writing. The instructor, Leaky Donohue, was perched on the corner of the desk. Just then he looked toward the door. Runt ducked, but was afraid he had been spotted.

The first ones started coming out. There was Chick Martin with a Portia. Chick had played guard on the basketball team Plotsy managed.

"Hi, Chick." Runt grabbed his arm. "How was it?"

"A snap," Chick stated. "Say, Leaky is getting easy in his old age." He started to recount the questions. "The only tough one was recaption of personalty—"

"Yah, I know that one!" Plotsy said. "You can't use force. What else?"

Chick went down the list of questions, the Portia remembering those he missed. Runt made notes. Hurry up. He couldn't leave the hack out there forever. A spotter might pass.

"Oke. Think he'll give us the same quiz?"

"It's a cinch," Chick said. "Leaky is too lazy."

"Well, boys, I got the dope," Runt said, meeting the fellows in Raklios's. He spread his notes, like a conspirator plotting a safe-blowing.

Lou Margolis glanced at the questions and grinned. Pie.

But when they got inside Leaky handed them an entirely different quiz, and a stinger. The boys sweated through two hours. Fellows just sat staring at the paper and at each other, while Leaky Donohue perched on the desk, smirking, swinging his leg.

The results were up next evening. Twenty-four out of thirty had flunked. The craziest thing was to see who had passed. A couple of lunkheads that were the dumbest guys in the class, a Portia who showed plenty of leg. Even Lou Margolis had flunked, so it was no disgrace.

"Say, what is this?" Sam Eisen asked.

The quiz could be taken over. Fee, two dollars.

"Just a little graft," Lou Margolis said. "Twenty-four times two is forty-eight bucks."

The fellows stuck around the bulletin board. They didn't seem able to believe their eyes. "No exam is fair that can't be passed by the majority of the class," Sam Eisen declared.

"He gave the day class a snap!" Plotsy insisted. "He can't do this to me!"

Yah? Whatcha gonna do about it?

Do? He'd quit the damn holdup joint, that's what. He knew a better use for two bucks.

What was the sense of quitting? Bite off his nose to spite his face. "Might as well kick in," Lou Margolis advised.

"There are plenty of other schools," Runt said.

"Yeah? Where? The I.S.?"

The I.S. was a mill, but what the hell. "Well, what's the matter with the I.S.?" Runt shot back.

"You pays your money and you gets your degree," Lou quoted.

"Listen, Plotsy, those guys don't take your bar exam for you," Sam Eisen said.

Aw, what the hell, he could always take a quiz course and pass the bar. Nobody was going to rook him out of two bucks. Good-by, Leaky.

"Wait a minute. I don't like this any better than you do," Sam said. "We ought to talk to Leaky about it."

Finally it was decided that Runt and Sam could go but not quite as an official delegation from the class.

"Don't get hot-headed, now," Sam said. "Better let me do the talking."

"Don't worry about me," Runt said. "I just want to ask him one question. That's all."

But before Sam had said three words, Runt popped out: "I want to know why the day class was given a quiz they could pass. If we had their quiz we could have passed it too!"

"Maybe that's why you didn't get it," Donohue said, with his thin sneery smile.

Runt lost his head then and started to argue. If Donohue offered to give the quiz over, that was an admission it was unfair. And if the quiz was unfair, another one ought to be given at the school's expense.

"This school is run as a business," Donohue said.

Everybody took the second quiz and forked over two bucks. Except Plotsy. He took the quiz, wangled his credits out of an office girl, and lammed out of the school owing over a month's tuition. The I.S. was five bucks a month cheaper, too.

Another stunt Leaky Donohue had was to switch the textbook every couple of seasons so that the students wouldn't be able to buy seconds from their upperclassmen. One year it was Anson on contracts, and just when you bought an Anson for a buck you found Leaky had switched back to Ranson, and the stores were all out of second-hand Ransons. Five bucks new. Leaky got his rake-off.

Sam was sick of the whole cheap, twisting atmosphere of the school. Take men like you found on the Supreme Court bench. They didn't come out of places like this.

Sam had saved a hundred dollars. He wanted to get away from everything. He was bothered about himself, and girls too. He was afraid if he hurried through school and became a lawyer he would get married to someone like Lil Klein and that would be the end of him. In fact he was all mixed up. He had lost track of his main idea, his ultimate purpose. He wanted some time to look around. He wrote to Harry Perlin, down at Urbana.

Just about when he had decided to stay out of school, get some sleep, and earn some money during the next semester, Harry was surprised to get a letter from Sam Eisen. "What I want is the straight dope, Harry," Sam wrote. "You see the main part of my expenses will have to be earned on the premises—"

"You certainly can do it," Harry found himself writing. "You have to hump a little, but it's worth it in the end." Writing this, Harry reflected that in his own case the thing hadn't worked out so well because, well, because he was kind of slow at studying, needed more time than fellows like Sam. He himself was a bad mixer, he figured, but Sam would get something of the real life here, the fellowship, the girls. . . . "I would certainly be glad to show you the ropes if you come down, Sam."

And with Sam coming, Harry decided to stick it out. Grit and determination. And maybe, having a friend there, like Sam, things would open up more to him. He made himself a salami sandwich, biting chunks of it as he tried to think of what else to put in the letter, then wrapped the remaining bread and salami and put them in the dresser drawer.

Harry came straggling into his room, after military, to take off his uniform. Sam Eisen was sitting there.

The room suddenly appeared a hell hole, its gloom accentuated by the sickly strand of light coming through the dormer window; the blanketed cot-bed, the scarred Morris chair, the feeble, droopy banner of Illini on the wall conveying a sort of second-hand collegiate atmosphere. Pieces from a radio set were scattered on the cot, so Sam had had to lift aside some junk to find a clear place to sit.

Harry began to chatter. "Well gee hello, Sam! I didn't know you were coming so soon!" And he sort of slapped Sam on the back, while they wrung hands. "Just come from drill. Say, wait'll I clear some of this junk out, I dressed in such a hurry. She never gets up to clean up this room till it's just time to go to sleep. Can't blame her, I leave so much junk around. Hey, I fixed up this—see—gives me light wherever I want it." He demonstrated a complicated system of extension cords, and a contact he had fixed which turned on a light when the closet door was opened. "Nifty, huh? Seen the campus? Did you get set yet? She has some pretty nice rooms here, this is the cheapest one." He slung a wet towel into the closet, and then, abruptly, as there seemed utterly no reason for staying inside that room, herded Sam out onto the street; and now, marching Sam along the Boardwalk, pointing out the new auditorium with its white columns and its shiny tin roof, Pearly began to feel as though all this were his to show, to share with his friend.

"That's the co-op, get your books. Say, we want to register you in the employment office. I want to show you where they're building the new stadium. These are some swell frats along here. The Jews have got a couple of swell frats too. That swell new one over there is the S.A.M. house, the *goyim* call it the Synagogue. That new house must have cost them plenty."

"Yah," Sam said.

"They're not such a bad bunch though. The Z.B.T.'s, that's the bunch that puts on the dog."

"I wouldn't joint any frat," Sam declared.

"This is Meade's, I eat here sometimes."

"Uh huh," Sam said. He seemed to be taking it all in, carefully, as if he saw a lot more than the buildings, the kids on the streets, as if he were weighing it all.

At the end of the first week of the new semester, Pearly was wondering why he was going on with the struggle. Sam's coming along hadn't made so much difference after all, as he hardly ever had time to sit down, to jabber, to find those long cozy evenings before a fireplace, when fellows talked about everything under the sun: religion, politics, science; that was what a fellow sort of expected to find in college, friendships that would endure through life. . . .

So when the telegram came from his married sister, it was almost a relief to have an excuse to give up this struggle, pack up, and go home.

FATHER WORSE COME HOME AT ONCE.

Holding the telegram in his hand, he could already hear his mother's sorrowful singsong . . . but the doctor told him he shouldn't go back to work, standing all day on his feet, and with the smell from the furs so you can't even breathe the air. Dr. Meyerson *told* him! Stay, stay in the house, I said, but a man! the minute he gets up from his back, he has to go to the shop. . . .

Sam was at the Dusty Roads, eating.

"Say, Sam, you got a job yet?"

"Nope."

"Wanna take care of mine for a while?"

"Sure," Sam said, "what's the trouble?" and Harry showed him the telegram. "Say, that's tough. What's the matter with him?"

"Oh, he was getting weaker all the time," Harry said, one side of his face twitching while he felt a maturity coming into his voice, as though now he were older, wiser than his own father. "He had diabetes, and then he had some kidney trouble. He can't stand on his feet much, but he kept on working, like a fool. You know he's a furrier. They're on their feet all the time."

"Oh," Sam said. He had never known Pearly's old man was a furrier. His own father was a buttonhole maker. For a moment he wanted to bring that into the conversation, as though it would make a little bond between them, and help Pearly understand that he sympathized.

Fellows never thought of telling each other those things about their fathers. "I'm not ashamed of the old man," Sam thought. "He works for his living. Why should I be ashamed?" Maybe fellows never discussed their fathers, their families, because they knew their own lives were going to be entirely different. Their fathers were just wasted beginnings back there in the slime, in cheap jobs, in shops, in little stores, they had only been greenhorns, a wasted generation; but their sons would be something entirely different, growing to their full stature in America. Sam remembered, momentarily, scenes in movies where the big-chested old man, like Theodore Roberts, got up from behind his desk in his private office, and dropped his great paw on the shoulder of his stripling son; together they turned to the window, and stared out over the vast ship-building plant. Or, even here on campus, youngsters in plus fours standing on the running boards of roadsters, shaking hands with ruddy-faced men called "Dad."

"Say, anything you want, in Chicago?" Pearly asked.

"Yah, you can bring me back a hunk of wurst. Real hard salami, from Kantor's."

"Kayo, if I come back." They gripped hands.

From the train, Pearly saw the farms that seemed so isolated, prisoned in the snow, and wondered how people stood that kind of life.

In the *Trib*, he saw that a staff photographer was going around on the quiet, snapping people's pictures, and every day the paper gave away a hundred dollars for the best smile. Keep Smiling. Say, that certainly was a smart idea; everybody would keep smiling all the time because you never knew what minute that photographer might be snapping your picture.

The auto show broke all sales records on opening day. Anyway, going home, he could take in the auto show.

You are supposed to feel something and you don't know exactly how you feel. You get up. Why is the house so still? But it is so early, only five o'clock. You look at your kid brother Victor sleeping on the folding bed. Then you are afraid your look will wake him, so you turn away. Let the water run a few minutes till the hot water comes. Dress in the blue serge suit. Though it is so early, and you are home, you put on the vest and the coat, too.

She is awake, sitting in the kitchen. Splinters of coarse, grown-back gray hair stick out under the black orthodox wig she wears.

"Why did you get up so early, Harry?" she says in Yiddish. "I'll make you some coffee."

You look in the front room. It is there, spread on four chairs.

So that is my father, so that is my father, so that . . .

What is there to feel? He looks like one of those old-fashioned enlarged photographs, with the pale colors, and the whole thing yellowing. All the folds of flesh fall away from his large beak. That I have from him. Remember, when as a kid, when ma and pa were still jolly sometimes, they cracked a joke: "The nose he has from his father."

Eda is the first to arrive, and Harry, seeing everybody today with new eyes, sees this sister as a big, sniffling woman who is of the older generation, the generation that talks with a Yiddish accent.

"Nate got to get someone to stay in the store. He'll come over afters." And she sniffs. "Did you have any breakfast?" And she sniffs.

Aunts, cousins, neighbors . . . As the day grows, the flat crowds with people, all standing, all talking, until the hum of their hushed voices is like a growl. The men from the shop, and their wives; and then a delegation of lodge brothers, thick men, with gold teeth, who hold themselves stiffly until suddenly a word, an encounter with someone they know, relaxes them, and then they seem entirely at ease, sipping Eda's tea.

And it is only now, on this day of the old man's death, that Harry begins to find out about his father. The life the man lived, friends who recall smart words he said, helpful things he did: a person in the world.

A member of a lodge: the B'nai Asher. He bought a family lot in the cemetery, and the lodge brothers say: "Oh, that's a fine lot, you couldn't buy it today for five hundred dollars." And he was a member of a synagogue on the corner of Millard and Douglas Boulevard. Who would ever have thought of the old man as religious? The old lady was the religious one, keeping strictly kosher. But still, he belonged to a synagogue.

And to a union, too. There are men from the union, the same sort of men as the lodge brothers, but somehow different: you don't get them mixed up.

Now it is as if all those casual evening visits, when a few people would drop in and sit in the kitchen with his father and mother and have a glass of tea, those times now formed into an entire life, and that life was present here in the room.

A chunky fellow, with a section of striped shirt sticking out between vest and pants, claims him: "*Nu*, Harry. *Nu*. A sed day. A sed day, huh?" That is Laibish, his father's youngest brother, and Harry remembers himself as a child, when they lived in the four rooms, third floor back, on Loomis Street: then Laibish came, a greenhorn, fresh from Europe. And at that time the coming of Laibish changed the whole color of their life. The folks were always sitting around the table with him, relatives would come in, of an evening, and Laibish would be the talker, telling some awfully funny sort of jokes that would make the older people laugh until tears ran out of their eyes.

And, in the instant's flash, Harry remembers a few words from those jokes: always, at the climax, there was something like: "So he lies down, the priest, and he says, Well, what are you waiting for? Whip! Whip me! Quick!" . . . Why they must have been some sort of dirty jokes, some smacking, Yiddish kind of dirty joke, why, the old folks were human after all!

But now, like his older brother, who has just died, Laibish is a furrier, he has grown an alderman; and of course he has American children, and tells no more Yiddish yarns of the old country.

And in all this crowd of cousins, uncles, lodge brothers, neighbors, women who think they have to cry, Harry feels out of place; as if he and not they were the stranger in this house. There is no one who is his own kind, who knows just how he feels. If Vic were a bit older, if Eda were a couple of years younger. . . .

Naturally you couldn't expect any of the bunch to come over. He is glad no one came; he would have been embarrassed. To have them see this funeral, the people in the house, would be like being seen naked. After a couple of days he can stop in at the clubroom. But even that isn't exactly what he wants.

The funeral is by Elfman. Three hired limousines for the near relations. And there are about a dozen more cars. Elfman's new twelve-cylinder hearse would have cost ten dollars extra, but at the last minute Elfman shows he has a good heart and sends the de luxe hearse anyway, as it is not busy this afternoon. He remembers Harry Perlin as the nice boy who got an ad out of him for a dance program.

You drive straight out on Roosevelt Road, through Cicero, to the Jewish cemetery. My, those limousines are smooth riding jobs.

All Harry knew about "sitting *shiveh*" was that, when a Jew died, his family was supposed to sit in the house, and mourn, without leaving the house for seven days and nights, or how many days was it? And weren't you supposed to be barefoot? His mother didn't tell them what to do. It was as if she had withdrawn into her own world, doing things according to her strict religious ways; and leaving them to do as they wished.

They wanted to try to sit and mourn, for her sake.

The first day, Eda ran to the telephone every five minutes, to call up her husband in the store. "Did you get someone to stay when you have to go out? Call Joey Miller. Oh! T-t-t. Try that other kid, what's his name, Maxey—he'll want more money, but what can we do? How is the baby? . . ."

Harry and Vic were sitting in the frontroom, moping, when their mother led in a little Jew with a scratchy shred of beard, one of the synagogue Jews, who cocked his head at the two sons, twitched his mouth, and said: "So these are the *kaddish* sayers? So do you even know how to say a *kaddish*, my sons?" He pulled a prayerbook out of his pocket, and made them follow him in the *kaddish*, phrase by phrase.

"Can you lay *tfillin*? No?" he said almost hopefully.

At thirteen, Harry had learned how to wind on the phylacteries. Now his mother held in her hand the little embroidered bag, containing the phylacteries with which his parents had presented him at his confirmation.

The woman looked so small, so old, standing there against the leathery red embossed wallpaper.

"Let it go, let it go," the synagogue Jew said, shoving aside the phylacteries. "A *tsadik*, a sage, we won't make of him in a day. He's an *Amerikanisher bocher*, I can see. Well, at least you can mumble a *kaddish*."

On the second day Eda's husband came over, and Harry had a talk with his brother-in-law. The old man hadn't carried much insurance: only a thousand dollars, with his lodge. The two-story house had a big first mortgage. Still—no rent to pay. The best thing was to stay where they were. Things weren't so terrible. But naturally Harry was elected: he'd have to look for a job.

In a way it was a relief. He couldn't have gone on, working his way all the way through Illinois. Now, he'd go to night school. Armour's, or Lewis Institute. He'd be an engineer, give him time. To say, long afterward: "I went to night school," was even stronger than saying: "I worked my way through college."

Eda went home with her husband. He was alone in the store; what would be gained by her sitting here? She could mourn in her own house.

Victor was getting restless, sitting around the house all day; on the fourth morning his mother suddenly said: "Go, go to school, Victor. Enough. You are young."

Harry went down to look at the furnace. Since he was a college-trained expert in taking care of furnaces, they could save the ten dollars a month they had been paying the Polack janitor.

The basement had a good concrete floor. Up at the front of the house, under the two dungeon windows, was a lot of unused space. He could easily fix up a workshop down here. There was only one light, dangling over the washtubs, and Harry began planning extensions.

While he was standing there, his mother called from above, and he heard Runt Plotkin say: "That's all right, Mrs. Perlin, I'll go down."

Runt was the last guy, somehow, that Harry would have expected to come over.

"What's the matter, Pearly, hiding out from your creditors?" Runt kidded. He was wearing a huge box-cut overcoat of fuzzy novelty cloth. Snow melted from him. He pinched his chilled beak. "Say, you sure picked on the right weather for this, wadyacallit, sitting *shiveh*, hey! I didn't know you was such a *frummer* Yid, Pearly."

"Well, you know, my mother . . ."

"Sure, sure, I know how it is. Makes the old lady feel good. I'd do the same. Well, Pearly, you sure got a tough break." Runt squatted on a box.

Harry dragged up an old broken-backed kitchen chair. Gradually, as he talked of his old man's diabetes, he began to feel in Runt's presence something of what he had wanted all through these last days: a fellow to talk to.

"Well, say, howya fixed? You going to pull out all right?"

"Oh, I guess I'll get a job all right. I've got the kid brother to take care of."

"Yah. I know how it is. I got a couple of 'em, and sisters too. That's even worse. It sure keeps me hopping."

What kind of a job was he going after? "I thought maybe a garage, I'm pretty handy with cars."

Say, Runt knew a guy just opened a garage up near Columbus Park, on Harrison Street. Name of Bienstock. Might need somebody. Put it down, Bienstock. And he might hear of something else. He'd keep it in mind.

Runt gabbed for a while about the club, trying to get up a basketball team, about the Benny Leonard fight, say, he had a tip Benny had a bum stomach, he was going to put two bucks on Rocky Kansas; then suddenly he leaped up, "Got to get rolling," and was gone.

All the rest of the day, Harry felt steadier, clearer in his mind, more sure of himself in the world.

In the morning Harry would get up first and say the *kaddish:* "*Yisgadal veyiskadash*" Later he would ask the kid, Victor: "Did you say it?"

"Yah, yah, I said it."

They were ashamed to say it together.

Lucky the auto show hadn't closed while he was sitting *shiveh.* Now that he was out, and riding on a street car, the thoughts of all those days seemed to come together, to form a whole. His first thought was, how wise and how good, how sensible after all, were the old Jewish customs. Now, the sitting in mourning, for example, had slowed him down, and given him time to think of life and of death, and to feel about things and about people as he never before had felt. Just by sitting in the house quietly, and being alone, thinking of his father, of himself and of everything, of what he was going to do in life. It was as if he had made something, in the dark, by the feel of his hands, and now, coming into the light for the first time, could see what it was he had made.

Ask Dad, He Knows. (Sweet Caporal.)

Who were the people who called their fathers Dad? If he ever had any kids (Aline) would they call him Dad? Daddy? Dad?

The beams of light on the shiny cars made life glow inside of him. He gave himself into the current of the crowd. Boy, there were some smooth jobs. The cross-sections of engines running effortlessly under glass! A chassis, stripped like a bare sturdy runner. Look at that Reo, a heavy car, eats up plenty of gas but you can't beat it for endurance. Is Franklin still sticking to air cooling? Man, oh, man, look at that Paige roadster, just like a breath of wind.

Then Harry saw the stop-light. A new invention. When the driver put his foot on the brake, he automatically contacted this stop-light, mounted just over his tail-light.

That was his kind of thing! It was almost as if he remembered having had the same idea. Some little thing, like a stop-light, a windshield wiper, that could be put on every car! Some day he would invent something like that, and make a million dollars. He could sell his invention exclusively to Ford, or to General Motors, or else start a small company and make and sell his accessory independently, gradually building up until he had a huge plant making all kinds of accessories.

Harry saw Joe Freedman in the crowd around the Paige, and accidentally on purpose bumped into him. Sylvia and Mort Abramson were with Joe.

They sympathized about his father; and then Syl said: "Isn't this Paige a beaut?"

Joe Freedman raved about how the automobile was the real thing of beauty of this age, more beautiful than any picture or statue.

"Oh, Mort, can't you talk them into trading in that old junkpile of ours?" Sylvia said. "We really need a new car."

"You're telling me!" Mort said. "Why don't you help out a little? I've been working on the old man for a year now."

And suddenly their chatter seemed altogether strange to Harry. He was the one who would have to buy whatever was bought, in his family.

THERE IS ALL KINDS OF COMPETITION

Competition is the breath of life. Without competition, would Ford ever have perfected the assembly line? Would Columbus ever have discovered America? If a drug store starts on one side of the street, in a month there's a drug store on the other side of the street. Even in a game of casino one wins and one loses. In school, everybody got marks. In life, too, some will get high marks and some will get low marks, only in life the marks will be in dollars and cents.

A real man welcomes competition. It's no fun running unless you're running a race.

Everybody competes every minute of their life. There is competition when you try to get on a street car in a crowd, and there is competition when you take a girl to a dance. What would life be, Mort Abramson asks, without competition?

There is all kinds of competition.

Mitch Wilner kept a little whetstone in his locker, and stopped to give his scalpel a few strokes before going to work on his cat. Keep your mind keen, and your tools sharp.

"Hi, Mitch."

"Hi."

Mitch had to wait while Curly Seabury fished his cat out of the barrel . . . and wait some more while Seabury dug out, from under all the other cats, the specimen that belonged to the class beauty. She stood by, her hands dangling like the paws of a sitting-up rabbit. There was a helpless beauty in every class and fellows like Seabury could always be trusted to do their work for them. Seabury might have been a bright guy but she was dragging him down. Beware of women.

Finally, Mitch unwrapped his specimen. He propped his *Manual*, and set to work.

The Old Bunch

Seabury opened the window for the class beauty, who stood and drew a deep breath of spring. At the next table Wallace Costa was whistling to himself, "Oh, You Beautiful Baby."

But on the whole, everybody was humping. Already, this quarter, you could feel the process of selection in operation. The classes were still large, but you could begin to tell who would go. It was a beautiful day for a walk, and some of the droops hadn't even bothered to come to class, though the dissection of the semicircular canals of the ear was due for inspection tomorrow.

Within the bone of the skull, back of the ear, lay the three tiny canals, each for a different plane of balance, and in each canal, like a sac in a fountain pen, lay the liquid-filled tube that acted as a level. In humans, the same as in cats. The entire structure that Mitch sought to uncover was no larger than a fingernail. Go slow, now, go easy. He made ghost-thin shavings of the bone.

A howl went up from the table behind him. Mitch drew back his hand, and looked around. Art Schreiber had botched his dissection. "I've been scraping at this damn skull all week," he moaned. "Now look!"

"That's all right, a cat has two ears," Weintraub remarked.

Mitch strolled over and saw where Art Schreiber, after making minute shavings for hours, had become impatient and taken one thick cut. Of course that had to be the spot.

"You can still try the vertical," the lab assistant said. "If you keep even one of the tubes intact you'll be doing well for this outfit."

There was a myth that the assistant, in his day, had dissected out all three canals in half an hour.

Mitch bent over his specimen, his nose almost touching the cat. Instead of taking shavings, now, he began to scrape, stopping to blow away the powder after each stroke. He held the head against the light; there was a shadowy spot! Scarcely tickling the bone with his blade, he laid bare the horizontal canal. The tube was perfectly intact. With the needle-point like a sensitive extension of his own fingers, he touched the tube, and felt how it lay freely in its canal.

"Pretty!" he heard the assistant say, behind him. "See if you can get the other two."

Another hour, hunched over the table, and he straightened, only then becoming aware of the stiff cords in the back of his neck, of the crick in his spine. A low whistle went up from Wally Costa. Mitch had made a clean job of the three chambers.

And only then Mitch realized that half the class had grouped around his table, watching him work.

The assistant grinned and said: "If you keep on you'll be nearly as good as I was."

Mitch wrapped up his cat, and put it on top of the pile in the barrel.

It wasn't on top when he came to class the next day. He pulled out one cat after another, and finally found his own at the bottom of the heap. When he unwrapped the head, he saw that his perfect work of yesterday had been ruined. The bone was nicked, the canals were mashed.

His hands actually trembled with rage. That anyone could have it in himself to destroy so beautiful a piece of work!

The dirtiness of it, the unfairness!

"Hi, Mitch!"

"Hi, Hank."

"Hi, Mitch!"

"Hi, Art."

But now the chummy feeling was gone. Any one of these fellows might have done it. No, there were a couple he could be sure of, the top men didn't need to do a thing like this. Or, might not they be just the ones . . .?

The assistant came around. Mitch said, tightly: "I had a pretty fair dissection here, yesterday. . . ."

The assistant looked at the mess. A wry smile came onto his face. Out of a couple of hundred premedics, only about fifty could be admitted into medical school.

There is all kinds of competition; and Runt Plotkin is driving a Yellow cab. It is one of those swell early spring days that come in Chicago, sandwiched between an icy drizzle and a last week of snow. All of a sudden the streets are melted clear and dried. The sun is high, the air is fresh as a schoolgirl complexion, and nobody thinks of riding a hack. Everybody hikes. A fellow farts around the Loop all morning, grinding in low. Suburbanites come out of Northwestern station, stick their noses into the soft wind, kite up their tails, and walk to the office. The taxi stands are crammed with empties, moving up about as fast as the waiting line at the Chicago Theater on a Saturday night.

So Runt cruises.

On Clark Street there's an old fart of a hotel where the Checkers have a concession. Let them have it. The dump is full of farmers and dollar lays. But just as Plotkin is passing the entrance, a guy steps out and hails him. Some guy with a briefcase. There's a line of Checkers, but they've been waiting so long the front guy is snoozing. And this briefcase hails a Yellow. So naturally Runt swerves for the curb.

Do the Checkers wake up! Five horns go off like a pack of barking hounds. The front man steps on it and his jallopy takes one leap, squeezing in on Runt. There is a hit bang; their fenders have clashed, their bumpers are locked.

"All right," says Runt in a murderous low voice. "All right, you f—— Checker bastard. Back the hell out of there and go back to sleep. I got a fare."

The Checker opens his door and leans way out, inspecting the smash. He has a flat baboon face, unshaven. "You bastit! You bastit!" he screams. "That's my own cab! You pay for this!"

Runt rocks his cab, trying to shake the bumpers loose.

"Look out! Stop it, you bastit!"

"Pull your ass out of there!" Runt hollers.

By this time, two Checker drivers have emerged from their cabs. They see the damage is slight. "Go on beat it, you Yellow louse, where the f—— you think you're trying to horn in?"

"Beat it s——! I got a fare."

"Oh, yeah? Scram, you c—— ——, this is a Checker stand."

"That guy called a Yellow, didn't he, you sonsabitches, a guy has a right to call a Yellow any damn place he wants!"

"Who the f—— wants to ride in your robber hacks anyway! Pull outa there before I tear the wheels offa that crap wagon! Listen, you mother-f—— little runt, if you don't—"

"Oh, yeah? You and who else?"

"Come on outa that cab! Come on out and—"

"This is my pickup, see? All right, ask him. Ask him if he didn't call for a Yellow."

The guy with the briefcase, by this time, is gone.

"You made me lose my fare, you lousy baboon-faced s—— eater, you—"

"Where you tryna horn in, you got standsa your own—"

"This f—— Yellow cracks up his hack and—"

"Sure, what's it to a f—— Yellow? Listen, bozo, the Checkers are a bunch a respectable family men owning their own cabs. We don't want no trouble. Just pull out and tend to your own stands."

"Pull out, huh? Who the hell is gonna pay for this fender? I wanna know—"

By this time a cruising Yellow and another have hauled up across the street and the boys have sauntered over. By this time one of the older Checker drivers, a slugger-looking guy, is laying it down hard. "One more peep out of you, you sawed-off little runt, and I'll—"

"Any day. Any day—"

Somebody hauls off. Runt staggers clumsily against his radiator. He jumps back, head bobbing, feet prancing. Come on, you sonsabitches. There is a tangle of guys, howling, shoving, barking. "Yellow! Fulla s——!"

Runt ducks his head and squirms into the tangle, punching guys in the guts. Kick them in the nuts. A fist tears at his ear. He gets a sock in the eye.

It doesn't last a minute. A cop comes up from Van Buren, another from Jackson.

Run 'em all in! What the hell they think the streets are for? The Checkers started it. What's the Yellow doing here? Go on, run me in, whatya think we got lawyers for?

One by one, the men go back to their hacks. Runt cuts his wheels sharp, gives her the gas, and nearly tears off the Checker's bumper unhooking the cabs.

The Yellows drive off, and for a while a couple of Checkers follow them, ominously, nosing against them in every traffic jam. Oh, they want a scrap, huh? Runt steers past the big Yellow stand at the I.C. station, and gives the boys the horn. The lousy Checkers. We'll run them off the streets. Trying to give us competition, huh? He touches his blunt finger against his eye. Easy. Easy. It's a shiner all right.

Sol (Chesty) Meisel takes his sheba to the movies. "Florence Reed is playing at the Central, or, say, how about seeing Priscilla Dean in *Conflict?* She's my secret passion."

"Yeah?" says Estelle, with an arch look.

"Yeah, I'm nuts about redheads." And he squeezes her arm. "I read she's got red hair, like you."

After the movie Estelle asks: "Well, how did you like your girl friend?"

"Mmm-mm!" Sol rolls his eyes. "Is she the cat's nuts! Boy, I could go for her!"

"What are you trying to do," Estelle says, "give me some competition?"

Maybe she won't always want to keep Chesty Meisel lapping after her with his tongue hanging out. But a man is the same as a puppy, trotting off to sniff at every passing pair of legs. It isn't only the girls in your own crowd that your boy friend sees, heck, she doesn't have to worry about competition from fatface Celia Moscowitz or bow-legged Aline Freedman or even Ev Goldberg with all her swell clothes, or mama's angel Sylvia Abramson; but Gloria Swanson and Bebe Daniels and Mae Murray and that society girl Mary Baker, they all give men ideas. Being a woman was taking on the whole world, holding the man you wanted against all competition.

"Hey, kid, I'd take you for her any day," Sol said calfishly.

Mort passed up a couple of sure pickups on Sheridan Road. Business before pleasure. Though it certainly was a cinch to pick up the gash in the new Paige. The back seat was as good as a bed.

Maybe on the way home. If he made a deal in Milwaukee.

For he was going out like a knight after the grail. Only, the grail was the kale. First he would tackle the jobbers. And if he couldn't sell the jobbers, Mort had a plan. He would hit straight for the department stores! The old man would squawk if he knew Mort had such an idea, but he wouldn't know unless Mort brought back an order, and an order would make everything jake.

What use are jobbers in the world anyway? Middlemen. They stand in the middle, and collect from both ends. Do they produce anything? No. The manufacturer is necessary, to make the goods. The storekeeper is necessary, to sell the goods. But a jobber just stands in the way and gums things up.

Mort had been thinking about things, recently, refusing to accept what was handed him at face value. He had his ideas on socialism, too. He had an uncle who traveled all over the world, his job having something to do with Jewish charities. And this uncle with his tales of famine, and of the plight of the Jewish middlemen who had no place in the new order of life, had started Mort thinking along various lines.

Once, after an argument with a street-corner communist, Mort even got Karl Marx out of the library—he was slightly surprised to find they had the revolutionary book right there in the public library. Only, it was dull as ditch water. A few pages gave him a headache. This guy Marx took thousands of words to prove what any business man knew to begin with. That a dollar isn't a dollar, but what you can buy for it. It was as if somebody wrote a long book full of scientific words, the net result of which was to say, if you don't eat, you'll starve.

Mort gave it up after the first few chapters. But one thing he could tell Karl Marx. Laborers weren't the only necessary people. What would become of the goods in the shop if he didn't go out and sell?

For example, take the story in the *Saturday Evening Post*, by Booth Tarkington, that proved exactly the point he wanted to make. In Tarkington's story, there was an owner of a piano factory who suddenly got idealistic and decided to turn his plant over to his workmen. Just before he did this, he happened to turn down a deal for piano-wire because he knew where he could get the stuff cheaper. Soon after the workmen were in charge, the wire salesman happened to call back, saying: "We've lowered our prices." So the workmen gave him a big order. But the joker was that the new price was still much higher than the price at which the boss could have bought the wire from the other company.

A thing like that just went to show how necessary brains were, to the making of anything.

But what use was the middleman?

The Paige was running smooth as a Rolls. Mort waited until he was through Highland Park, where there was a speed trap. And then he stepped on the gas. Sixty! The segment lines of the concrete road slid under the wheels. He'd be in Milwaukee by two o'clock.

The town looked plenty peppy, even without the beer industry. He eyed the women's hats. Tams, everywhere! No money in tams, too much competition.

Schweitzer was so fat he couldn't turn sidewise in his chair. He wheeled the chair around, and faced Mort. "Well, maybe I did hear of the Glory brand. I can't keep all the little manufacturers in my head." His raggy chewed cigar wiggled up and down on his lips. His small eyes surveyed Mort amusedly. "What's the difference if I heard of you or not? What have you got?"

The old bluffer. Mort knew Schweitzer had picked up plenty of Glory hats from Frumkin, their Chicago jobber. Mort handed him the sample. "There's a nifty little number. I don't have to tell you, Mr. Schweitzer, the cloche model is going to be all the rage this season."

"You don't have to tell me anything," Schweitzer grunted, fingering the hat. "How do you know they will even wear these chamber pots? You are too young, you don't even know what it's for, but when I was on the road, this was under every bed." He held the hat, brim up. Way down in his guts, disdainful laughter gurgled. "Listen, Mr. Picker, I've been in this business forty-five years, and I can guess as good as the rest of them, and you know how many times I have been stuck?" The cigar pointed. "Every time I tell them what will be the rage next season."

Mort had come in all wound up like an alarm clock, but now he was beginning to slow down and get an idea of his adversary. One of these old geezers that thought they knew everything, and you were the dirt under their feet. All right. Old Schweitzer would sell himself, before Mort got through using psychology on him.

Schweitzer whirled around, pointing out the window. "You see what's going to be the rage? Those flappers are still wearing their tams and that is what you got to sell them."

"The tam is going out," Mort declared. "Why, I've got a sister that's been wearing those things and she's sick of them. The girls all want to wear real hats again."

Back and forth, back and forth; until Mort, battling his adversary every inch of the way, thought he had him to the point of talking prices.

And then Schweitzer pulled a big, kindly, toothy smile, as if to say, Well, boy, I only wanted to see how you would talk, and, turning back to his desk, in dismissal, said: "I'll tell you how it is, son. I get my regular line from Fleischman's in New York. When it comes to bread and butter hats, we got a big factory right here in Milwaukee."

"Why go to New York when you can get the same thing cheaper from us?" Mort cried. "We are not as big as Fleischman's—yet. But we can give you as good a deal, or better. We are looking for an outlet in Milwaukee—"

"What's the matter, you got stuck with this stuff?"

Mort grinned. "Oh, no. We're expanding. We're going outside of Chicago. We—"

But Schweitzer shook his head morosely, in complete dismissal. He was through amusing himself putting a kid salesman through his paces.

Mort felt sore at being pushed around. He took a bitter chance. "I'll tell you frankly, Mr. Schweitzer, we would rather deal with a jobber than with a store direct. But after all we're not a big house and if we can get one department store here as our outlet—"

Schweitzer's heavy, slow-breathing face seemed to swell, reddening, preparing to shoot out a stream of fire.

"Go to the stores, go! Go to the Boston Store, go to Paines's!" His voice cut off, sharp, like a steam whistle. "You think you can get along without the jobber, huh?"

In that moment there seemed a whole world of unknown, threatening disasters which he could hurl against Mort and his Glory hats. Mort sat quaking, wishing he could draw back his last words. Now he had ruined his chances in Milwaukee, probably ruined the whole idea of selling outside of Chicago.

"Go on, do your kike business. Sell direct. What do you need a jobber for? Carry your own warehouse full of stock. Get stuck with your own dead numbers. Pay yourself cash out of your own pocket! What use is a jobber!"

"I—uh—I didn't mean it like that," Mort hedged. "I meant, maybe we were too small for you to bother with."

Schweitzer stopped, mouth open. He looked at Mort for a long while, swinging his cigar from one side of his mouth to the other, rolling it in his lips, wagging it up and down. Finally he snapped: "Nine-fifty, and I'll see if I can handle it for you."

Mort straightened. Ten-fifty was the price; ten dollars a dozen was rock bottom. Schweitzer couldn't be getting this kind of stuff anywhere for less than ten.

"I'll have to make a call."

If the old man answered the phone, it would be all off. It was after four. His mother would have left the factory, to go home and fix supper. Maybe he had better call home. No, then the old man would feel hurt.

But it was Mrs. Abramson that answered the phone. "Mort? I thought maybe you would call, so I waited."

"So that old *Daitcher kopp* wants to chew you down, huh? Well, let him have the fifty cents. Tell him it is for luck, because it is a first sale. But he got to take at least fifty dozen, at this price."

"A new competitor always has to come in a little bit cheaper," Schweitzer stated, as he initialed the order.

The way Rudy saw it, this was a chance he couldn't afford to pass up. He was finishing his premed, and when he entered medical school he would need every dollar he could earn. The Standard Pharmaceutical's drummer tipped him off that the K.M. chain needed a night manager in their Madison Street store.

Rudy didn't know how to say good-by.

116

"Mrs. Kagen, you know I would rather work for you than for anyone else. You know I have passed up chances to make a little more money in other stores, but right now I need the money for school."

The old lady's eyes were watery, and he was beginning to feel weepy himself. It was like saying good-by to a mother. "Go, Rudy, with the best of my wishes," she said. "I wouldn't be the one to stand in your way like my own son! The store will get along, don't worry."

"Maybe I can come in on Sunday afternoons, and if there is any way I can help—"

"Listen, Rudy," she sighed philosophically. "In this world, everything is to the highest bidder. You are worth more money, and if someone can pay it to you then I can't afford to keep you, ain't that so? That's business. I am a business lady, so I know how it got to be. Come in sometimes, and have a soda," she ended, with quavering laughter, pushing him away from her, with her fingers on his chest. "Go, go!"

"Well! Take care of your lungs and liver!" he chirped. He started to take his white jacket, but instead left it in the closet. "I'll be seeing you. Don't take any wooden nickels."

Mingled with the regret of leaving, Rudy had the rising feeling in his heart of knowing he was wanted in more than one place. He would always be like this in life, leaving only fine memories of himself when he went from each place higher up.

Competition, that is the primary law of life; competition, get it into your heart; even when the two Lous stop into the Y for their daily handball game before supper, competition, kiddo—I'm three up on you. The little birdies are in competition for the worms, the stalks of corn are in competition for sunlight, Fords are in competition with Chevrolets, the Democrats are in competition with the Republicans, men are in competition and nations are in competition. But when you get to the top it is different. Who can compete with Dempsey? All right, who?

"Harry Wills," says Chesty Meisel. "They ought to give him a chance."

"Don't make me laugh!" boos Runt Plotkin. "That shine couldn't last two rounds."

"Carpentier, the Frenchman," says Mort Abramson.

"Yowee!" Runt waves his handkerchief.

"That Dempsey is built like a box car!" even Mitch Wilner says. "I'd like to dissect those muscles!"

No one can beat Jack Dempsey. Who can compete with Charley Erbstein in a divorce case, and who can compete with Clarence Darrow in a criminal court? Has Fritz Kreisler got any competition, or Galli-Curci? Why does Insull offer Mary Garden $250,000 to manage the opera? Why does Babe Ruth get $500 for every home run? Who can compete with America?

Throw away your hammer and get a horn, says Big Bill Thompson[1], Boost Chicago! Chicago will pass New York, and then who can compete

117

with Chicago? Who can compete with the United States? France was in competition with Germany, and they had a war; England is in competition with Japan, but the U.S.A. is at the top, we have all the dough, we make all the movies, we make all the automobiles, that is what everybody is striving for, in competition, to be like the U.S.A., to be at the top, to be beyond competition, to be the Human Flash of Lightning, the Joie Ray, the Benny Leonard, the Pavlowa, the Dempsey!

The beauty of competition is that it brings out the best of everybody, everybody works their hardest and shows their best quality to win a competition. For instance, if two girls are in competition for a fellow it is decided by their beauty, grace, and goodness. Rose Heller had a crush on Lou Margolis, but there was competition.

Estelle Green mentioned to Celia Moscowitz: "Kid, my brother Lou told me Lou Margolis is trying to get a job in a law office."

So Celia waited for Friday night, when the old man liked to listen, and do things for the family.

Friday night was family night, like in an old-fashioned Jewish home. Celia remembered the real Friday nights when her grandmother had been alive. All her uncles and her aunts and her cousins, complete to the latest baby, would be at the old folks' flat on Fifteenth Street. The table would have been elongated with wobbly extension boards. The old grandfather, Avrum Moscowitz, would sit there in his skull cap, sipping soup from the end of his spoon, with little smackings of his lips, and never getting his beard wet. Like a real old Jew from the Bible.

Now, since the grandmother was dead, Rube Moscowitz, being the eldest son, had to give the Friday night family suppers. To his wife they were a pain in the neck. She was stylish and didn't believe in old-fashioned foolishness.

But Rube would say: "What does it hurt, make the old boy feel good once a week!" The truth was Rube Moscowitz liked to have a lot of people eating at his table.

Besides, old Avrum still owned the business. When his sons demanded that he turn it over to them, he said: "I have not gone crazy yet. I have seen too many old men become beggars at the tables of their sons."

"You have to humor him," Rube said. He gave the old man a few thousand dollars for his Anshe Kneseth synagogue, and ran the business his own way. Once a year the patriarch insisted on seeing the banking accounts, and always squawked.

"Reuben, what is this, are we in the junk business, or in politics business? Who are you paying all this money? Five thousand here, two

---

[1] "Big Bill" Thompson, Republican Mayor of Chicago from 1915 to 1923, and again from 1927 to 1931.

thousand there, I know, I know what it is, to politicians. Have they got junk to sell?"

"Listen. Why bother your head about it? Look what I paid the car company for that load of scrap. They practically gave it to me!"

"Gave it to you. You paid them four times over, in the elections."

"That's all right, that's all right, that's the way we do business now, just keep out of it, will you, everything will be all right."

But around election time, when even on Friday nights Rube was interrupted every minute by telephone calls, by messengers who would stand at his elbow and wait for an answer, old Avrum would resume his mutterings.

"Politics. Politics. He ain't got time to eat. It's Sabbath eve in a Jewish house!"

And Celia's mother would chime in: "Sure, if it wasn't for politics, we could have moved up on Sheridan Road long ago. But here, I can't even move to the other side of Jackson Boulevard, it would be bad politics!"

"Sheridan Road! Aren't there people enough on the West Side?" Rube would roar.

"You know what kind of people there are here! It's nothing better than a ghetto."

"It ain't politics, it's business," Rube would insist. "If you want people to do business with you, you got to do them a favor once in a while."

"Why can't the street car company do their own dirty work, why do you have to do it for them?" Mrs. Moscowitz would demand.

When Rube was sprawled, stuffed, on the sofa near the grand piano, Celia could hear her mother having a kind of serious talk with her father.

"Listen, Rube, as far as I am concerned, mix in politics all you want, if you enjoy it. Only I don't like to hear people talk that my husband is a grafter."

"How can you be a politician without grafting a little?" Rube would say, leering, and begin to chuckle from the bottom of his belly.

Naturally, if a man is running the ward, he has to take care of everything in the ward, letting the bootleggers and the widows who run flats and the harmless gamblers contribute to the party funds. If you don't take their money, they'll go elsewhere for protection. You have to play ball, in politics. And the dough mounts up, too.

"Yah," the woman worried, "and look what happened to Len Small, governor or no governor."

"Aw, who told him to buck the *Tribune*!" And Rube's laughter would explode, his cheeks shaking like a fat woman's breasts. "Don't worry, you know I ain't in it from that end! I hand out more than I take in!" he would console her.

How could a woman understand the competition of politics? Republicans and Democrats! One of them gets into that pot of dough-re-me and he's so busy stuffing, cramming, and grabbing he only has time for an occasional back-kick at the other fellow who is on his tail, tearing and shoving to get inside the pot, howling and slinging great gobs of mud and rocks at his head to get him away from the pot. And so finally the pot-eater is shoved aside, and, wow! their positions are reversed. The second fellow hops into the pot, gorging and grabbing, and the first fellow is outside howling, slinging rocks.

Big Bill the Builder is in. Boy, is he in! No wonder he wants to build, and build! Pour the millions! Millions into the drainage canal and millions for a pier, build schools, tear up streets, show them something for their money, and, boy, how the money flows out! See that beautiful bridge, that Michigan Avenue bridge! (And three million smackers' "expert fees" alone, handed to the guys that were supposed to take a look at a few buildings near the bridge to assess their value.) Build Chicago, boys! Show them a bridge, a street for their money!

The Republicans were in, but the Democrats were hot on their tails. The Democrats still had a lot of judges in office, and how those judges could hand out indictments!

Indict Big Bill's grafting governor, boys. Indict Big Bill's grafting school board, boys! Sue Big Bill for those expert fees, smother him with indictments and he won't dare run again. That's giving them competition!

Governors? Mayors? Senators? It's a laugh! Everything goes in competition, boys. Sock them into jail, throw them in the can, they'd do the same to you—if they could—ha ha ha!

The Democrats have got those Republicans by the tail. Rube Moscowitz is a Democrat, and don't you worry, the Republicans can't even compete with him in his own bailiwick. When Big Bill took the town, he didn't take the Democratic Jewish ward.

For, every Passover, Rube Moscowitz would haul a fleet of trucks full of matzoth up Roosevelt Road. Across on Kedzie Avenue, down Sixteenth Street, they went, with Rube handing out the matzoth, personally, to poor Jews. Come and get your matzoths, boys, with noodles and chickens in the baskets.

"A new Moses in America!" his wife would kid him.

But Rube Moscowitz had that ward sewn up tight and it stayed Democratic. A stronghold of Democracy in a Republican town.

Now Big Bill Thompson's gang was on the run: Small, Lundin, and the rest, their tails afire with indictments, and when the Republicans were out and the Democrats were in again, Rube's power would be extended far beyond his ward, he would be a power to be reckoned with, all over the city.

So why shouldn't Insull[2] practically give Rube Moscowitz the scrap iron from the El and street car lines? Insull wanted new franchises from the city council, Insull wanted to extend the El lines into the new Columbus Park neighborhood that was building up fast, into other new fast-building neighborhoods, Chicago was outgrowing the El. Insull wanted that subway question settled; oh, how long, how long would Chicago talk about building a subway? If a subway was going to be built, he wanted control of that, too.

If Big Bill wouldn't play ball, then another mayor would play ball with Insull. Big Bill, talking big about the city owning its own subway! Why should the city try to compete with a business man!

Insull had a fund for the coming mayoralty campaign.

Republicans and Democrats, state your offers. You've got to compete for that little bag of gold.

Rube Moscowitz was passing out some of that Insull money; certain aldermen always needed a little help. Friendly aldermen could vote to extend the El lines, vote new franchises . . . !

The Thompson machine was cracking, sliding in every election. Why, the graft they had pulled on the school board alone was enough! And the contracts they had handed out for paving: the streets could have been paved with gold!

Sam Insull was going big. Did you see that stock market! A million shares a day, for seven days running! Why shouldn't Insull give Rube Moscowitz a few tips on the market? Good tips, too.

And Rube Moscowitz passed some of the tips on to Alderman Pete Grinnell, his sidekick, his *goyish* pal.

Celia was used to seeing Pete Grinnell in the house; my second home, the alderman called it, and he was always referred to, with big back-slaps by Rube, as "one of the family."

When Avrum Moscowitz had first located the junkyard on Ogden Avenue, this had been an Irish neighborhood. And the Irish alderman could do favors.

Gradually, it changed to a hundred-percent Jewish ward. Pete Grinnell, with his bulldog beefy Irish face, was still alderman. The opposition was always trying to win by running a Jew for alderman of the Jewish ward. But Rube Moscowitz, with the Jewish vote in his pocket, stuck by his Irish alderman.

Committees would come to whisper in his ear while he lay back in his chair in Rosen's barber shop, "Listen, Rube, after all, how long are you going to keep that mick in the council? After all, why shouldn't we have a Jew?"

"Say, he gets us everything we want, doesn't he? Say, that Irishman is a better Jew than a rabbi from Jerusalem."

---

[2] Samuel Insull was a powerful Chicago-based business magnate whose vast financial empire collapsed in the 1930's.

Pete Grinnell was like all those Gentiles who, even when on intimate terms in a Jewish household, never quite lose the sense of something mysterious about Jewish religion, imagining mystic secret meaning to whatever they witness.

He never failed to look with awe and wonder at the brass *menorah* that was taken from the sideboard, on Fridays, and set on the dining table. "Say, that's a fine candelabrum," he would hint. "Seven branches, huh? That's a holy number, seven."

"It's a family heirloom," Mrs. Moscowitz would reply. She allowed herself to forget that Rube had brought it home from the junkyard, in the early days. "It was brought over by the old grandfather, in the steerage." To admit that one's remote ancestors came in the steerage was okay. People could whisper: "Look where they are now!"

For all the years that he had known the family, if Pete stayed to dinner on a Friday evening, or on a Jewish holiday, he would act strained, standing behind his chair until Rube boomed: "Sit down, Pete! Wadaya think this is!"

It was as though the eating itself represented a tribal ceremony to the alderman, and to counteract his diffidence, he would act even more familiar than ever with the family, personally. He would put his arm around Celia and chuckle: "How's my sweetheart? When are we going to elope? Ha ha!"

You could be sure he told all the Gentiles: "Jews? Best people in the world! Why, I know the Moscowitz family like my own! A finer, more wholesome family you never saw!"

What if Rube Moscowitz wouldn't want him in his house, or in the city council? Where could he go, the old ward politician, with his tree-chopping voice, his over-ready laugh, with the deep lines of long-held smiles on his face? Start in another ward, at his age?

Grinnell would sit there, looking with a kind of boyish awe at old Avrum in his skull cap, waiting for Avrum to begin eating. A special, different food was always brought on different plates, old, thick porcelain, from his dead wife's household, for Avrum. And, long as he had been coming there, Grinnell did not know that this was the *joke* of the Friday night suppers; he thought it some sort of occult Jewish ceremony, the patriarch eating differently from the others, while the fact was that Avrum, suspecting that Mrs. Moscowitz kept only a lax half-kosher in her kitchen, insisted on bringing his own food and dishes for his meal, prepared by his own trusted housekeeper. "With a good heart, I don't want to insult you," he would say, bringing his package each Friday, "but we all know here in America Jewish wives are Yankees," and so, though the Friday night meal was really held for his benefit, he never ate a morsel of it!

"Well, Celia, when am I going to see a grandson-in-law in the business?" old Avrum squeaked, starting his usual Friday night subject. "Before I die, I should like to hold a great-grandchild in my arms." Why was it that as people grew old, all they could think of was propagating the family?

"Celia, sweetheart, you can't refuse an old man a wish like that!" Pete Grinnell kidded. "My, that's wonderful *gefillte fish*, Mrs. Moscowitz!"

"Oh, she's got lots of time," Mrs. Moscowitz said of Celia, and, of the fish: "Yah, the new girl finally learned. That's one terrible thing about trying to get a girl to cook for a Jewish family, you have to learn them everything."

Rube Moscowitz gobbled down two large pieces of fish, and kept eating from the side dishes, chopped liver, radishes, pickles, hurtling the stuff down his throat unchewed, never stopping between the courses. What he loved was pickles. He even ate pickles with his soup.

"Have some pickles, Pete," he yelled down the table. "Try some of those sour tomatoes. That's the real stuff. Kantor's."

In fact, Rube had loaned the delicatessen man ten thousand dollars to start a pickle and sour tomato cannery.

"All I get out of it is free pickles!" he sputtered.

"Say, if he has to supply you with free pickles, what has he got left to sell?" Rube's brother, Moe, snorted.

"Don't eat so fast!" Mrs. Moscowitz cautioned Rube. "Dr. Meyerson told you! You'll get high blood pressure."

This reminded Pincus Moscowitz, another brother, of something: "Hey! Did you see that in the paper where a doctor claimed he didn't have to pay his lawyer for losing a case, so the lawyer sues him, telling the judge, doesn't a doctor get paid even if the patient dies?"

"What would you rather marry, Celia, a doctor or a lawyer?" put in old Avrum.

"Huh?" said Celia.

One of Moe's three little girls, Rosalind, suddenly piped up: "I'd rather marry a lawyer, because doctors have to get up in the middle of the night!"

Pete Grinnell exploded, his laughter shooting morsels of food from his mouth. All the husbands and wives looked at one another, and then began to sputter, burble, and gulp with partly suppressed laughter. Rube Moscowitz swallowed his food and roared.

"Nowadays," said Hannah, Moe's wife, "you can't tell what kind of people your girls go out with. They do anything they want."

"I know all of my girl's friends," said Mrs. Moscowitz, icily. "They are the nicest smartest kids in the neighborhood. Now you take that boy Mitchell Wilner. Wasn't he the—what do you call it, Celia? At graduation?"

"The valedictorian."

"Wilner? . . ." old Avrum repeated. "There is a Wilner in my *shul*. He knows the Talmud backwards!"

Mrs. Moscowitz, watching Celia, tried again. "And who is that other one, Celia, you know, he was so brilliant . . . you know, the debater? . . ."

"What debater? There were lots of debaters," Celia evaded.

"Isn't he studying law or something . . . ?" Mrs. Moscowitz looked full at her, now.

"In the old country, Mistair Grinnell," Avrum put in, with the singsong that always started his old country reminiscences, "we would make a match already for a girl like Celia. A Talmud student—"

"This isn't the old country," Celia cried. And then, flushing, but needing to get it over with: "Hey, pop, that reminds me. A couple of the boys in the bunch are looking for jobs in a lawyer's office. Come on, be some use."

"Yeah? Who are they?" Rube said.

"Aha!" Pete Grinnell smacked his lips.

Celia realized how dumb she'd been. Why couldn't she have waited until she got the old man alone!

Still, she had to finish. "Oh, Estelle Green asked me for her brother, and he chums around with Lou Margolis—they've been here, the two Lous."

"Margolis! Oh, that's the one! The debater!" Mrs. Moscowitz piped. "Oh, Rube, you ought to do something for him. He's a brilliant boy!"

"So that's the one!" Pete Grinnell mimed, and giggled. "Well, Celia, I certainly am broken-hearted."

"Oh, I just told Estelle I'd ask," Celia muttered. Was her face red!

"What chance has age before youth?" the alderman went on. "That's too much competition for me. Just invite me to the wedding, Celia."

"Oh, leave her alone, Pete," Mrs. Moscowitz said.

"Say, I know just the place for your friend," Pete Grinnell suggested. "Rube, what about this fellow Preiss? Edelman, Preiss, and LeGrand. They handled the tax business for you, didn't they? A real high-class outfit. I bet they could take in a lad."

"I'll tell you, Celia, if they're friends of yours I'll see what I can do for them," Rube stated in the voice he always used when asked for political favors. "I'll call up Preiss myself, tomorrow. I don't know if I can get in two boys, but maybe one."

"Yah, which one do you want, Celia? Haw haw haw!" sang little Rosalind.

"Wait!"

Aline looked up and down State Street to make sure nobody they knew might be passing before she let Joe get out of the car in front of their father's dump, the Star Hotel.

As Joe came up the dented stairs, he was greeted by the Negro, John, whom all the storekeepers on the block called the *Shvartzer Yid*.

"*Vos macht a Yid?*" John delivered in a lip-smacking Yiddish. John was the street joke, claiming he was a member of a Negro tribe of Jews. He had picked up Yiddish and used each word like a mystic password. He also sang Yiddish songs. *"Eli, Eli"* was his favorite, and this he would sing with the soft melancholy of a sorrowing race, as he emptied the spittoons.

"Is Mike here yet?" Joe asked about the night man.

John put his hand to his cheek, in Yiddish woe. *"Oy, oy, shicker is a goy!"* he sang.

"Is he too drunk to work?"

"Aw, he'll be okay; you go on, take the old man home, to eat that *gefillte fish.*" Nigger John licked his teeth. "Mike's just laying in there mourning for all his pals that got shot up."

"Who?"

"You remember Shorty and that One-Eye crazy man? Lots of the regulars hang out here, they all got shot up. That's why there ain't hardly nobody around."

"Yeah? What's all the shootin' for?" Joe quoted.

"Ain't you read all that in the papers? That mine-shootin' down in Herrin, Illinois[3], that's where all these boys went. That fellow Shorty, he got shot dead, *olav hasholem*, but he ain't no loss to the world, that *ganef.*"

Joe remembered now reading about some shooting in a mine strike. So that's what the State Street bums did, went down there to work! For an instant he felt a strange, intimate contact with the world of things that happened. These bums who paid their half-dollars to his old man, who shot their streams of yellow tobacco juice into these very spittoons, they were in the papers. Often, watching the bums squatting on the flophouse chairs, he had been struck by the ordinary wonder, where had their lives begun, how would they end? Now it seemed he knew the end, and therefore the total of their lives.

"He have any folks?" he said.

"Yah, Shorty had some folks someplace," John said. "Used to curse 'em all the time."

There seemed no more to ask about Shorty.

"What'd they all want to go down there for and get into trouble?" Joe asked.

"Ten bucks a day, that's what! Man come along from the Quick Employment Agency, he sends them out all the time on those trouble jobs. Wants me to go along too. Not me. I don't want no trouble with strikers."

"What'd they shoot them for?" Joe asked.

The Shvartzer Yid stared at him. "They was down there strikebreakin'," he pointed the obvious.

"You mean they shoot them, for that?"

---

[3] The Herrin Massacre took place in June, 1922. Union members fought to block non-union miners; the final result was 3 union members killed and 20 (of 50) strikebreakers killed.

"Sure, man! You can't fuss with those striking boys! They don't want no competition!"

Joe found his father in the back-stair hole where Mike sat on a cot, fiery-faced, his eyes greenish, his tongue pushing around inside his chewed face.

"What's he been drinking, canned heat?" Joe said. "It's a wonder he don't poison himself."

"Nothing can poison him," said Freedman, as Mike wobbled to his legs, just like some old sick horse that finally, out of sheer loyalty to his master, has decided to get up.

A newspaper strewn on the floor had headlines about the coal miners' strike. The owners stated that if they raised wages they would be unable to meet the competition from Eastern coal fields.

Joe glanced at the name-list of strikebreakers who had been ambushed by the miners. Few had addresses—Joe wondered which name was Shorty's.

Aline was honking impatiently.

"*Gut shabbes!*" the Shvartzer Yid called as his boss got into the new Studebaker.

As they passed along South State Street, there were the familiar bums loitering in front of the beaneries and the *Join the Navy* posters. The bums had always seemed just freaks, drunks, derelicts, outcasts of life. But now Joe felt rotten about them; they were guys that would go anywhere, do anything for ten bucks, and yet you couldn't blame them, they were helpless, they took a job and then got popped at and died with surprised looks on their beery unshaven faces. They were helpless; they had been squeezed out by the competition of life. But who was safe, in this life? He too might end up a State Street bum!

"I hear you lost some customers," Joe said to his father, smirking uneasily.

Nathan Freedman didn't answer his son, about the bums. As they rode along in the Studebaker, Joe felt more and more uncomfortable. His father's silence this time seemed like the silence of a man who knows and feels a great deal, but realizes it is useless to try to make people understand. Let it be that those were just lousy bums, drunks who went out and got shot; their lives were worthless anyway.

Joe rang the Abramson bell and ran up the stairs. He walked plop into a mob of relatives. It wasn't just a Friday night gathering but some sort of special assembly. There was an uncle who had just come from Russia. "He travels all over the world," Sylvia whispered. "It's something to do with Jewish affairs. I think he's here to get a million dollars out of Julius Rosenwald, for Russian Jewry." She slipped away to perform those last-minute rites for which girls keep their callers waiting, and Joe found himself stuck among the relatives. They were having a terrific argument about the Jews. Even Mort was taking part in the discussion. Joe tried to sit there, just looking at them: an ordinary bunch of Jewish relatives, the women bursting their dresses, the men either pouchy or consumptive-looking. But their excitement got hold of him. Maybe because of the queer mood he had been thrown into by the death of Shorty, thinking where people came from and what became of them, maybe because of the personality of this Russian emissary.

Joe had never seen quite such a Jew. His English, while more heavily accented than that of the others, somehow had a distinguished flavor; he made none of the fat-smacking sounds of ghetto Yids; instead of *vot forr* he would say *how?* A European. He was short, stocky, with a solid face that seemed to have achieved its final, inflexible look and form. Parenthetic creases were at the sides of his settled, yet humorous mouth.

They were arguing at a great clip about those old Yids back in the old country. That had always seemed a laughable dead subject to Joe. All life that really mattered had come over here. But now, suddenly, he felt ignorant, and inferior.

Even Mr. Abramson who was usually sprawled out apathetic to the world was sitting erect, tense with argument.

Once Sylvia had told Joe how her father had become so skinny and worn-out-looking. As a boy he had smoked himself hollow, deliberately ruined his health in order to be exempt from the Tsar's military service. Then he had escaped from Russia. And similar stories echoed from Joe's own memory, tales heard in childhood of his own relatives' escapes from military service, of wild frightful rides down guard-infested roads, hidden under a load of hay . . . and how some guard jabbed a pitchfork through the hay, but luckily in the wrong spot, or you wouldn't be here, my son. . . .

The older generation was just full of those heroic yarns. Why had the parents so desperately needed to escape from Russia? Just to avoid military service? . . . As this crowd jabbered, astonishing things poured from them. Why, they had been full of ideas, ideals; they had even been socialists, freethinkers; they weren't dead to the world at all! Joe no longer saw them as mere hulks that had had to exist in order to produce Sylvia and himself, as greenhorns who had left that dumb country, Russia, to get to America, the land of gold, and raise smart children, geniuses.

In the intensity of their discussion, they seemed to have brushed aside Mort, himself, all the younger folk to whose importance they usually were so deferential. There appeared a greater concern for something vital, live, back there; and beside that issue, even their smart American sons and daughters were unimportant. They had dropped English, and were arguing in a Yiddish that was no longer a comical language, but the tongue of a self-respecting nation. Mort had to yammer along in a clumsy foreigner's Yiddish.

The fattest of the aunts argued: "Even Emma Goldman said that for the Jews, the Bolsheviki are as bad as the Tsar. Then there were pogroms, and now there are pogroms . . .!"

"Emma Goldman!" Bialystoker, the foreigner, sneered. "She too can talk! They kicked her out!"

"And why did they kick her out? Because she was telling the truth!" the fat aunt insisted.

"They kicked out Emma Goldman?" Mr. Abramson was startled. "But she was a *revolutzionistke!* a socialist, an anarchist!"

The bald-headed emissary laughed.

"And, Bialystoker," the fat aunt shot at him, "maybe there is no famine in Russia either?"

"Food there is not too much, and bread they need, I can tell you," Bialystoker admitted.

"And their Lenin is lying with a bullet through his head, and Trotsky will be next, and then an end to the whole Bolsheviki!" a fat uncle pursued the advantage.

"Like it said in the *Tribune*," Mort put in. "The Russians would trade all their Lenins and Trotskys for a Hoover. Say it with bread."

"Oh, the Tchicago *Tribune*" Bialystoker mocked. Then announced categorically: "Lenin is not dead, and nobody will shoot Trotsky, and the Bolsheviki are not making pogroms. Jews, how can you believe such *dreck!* Only a few Jews who were class enemies, capitalists helping the Whites— naturally they were arrested."

"White, red, a Jew is a Jew!"

"Listen, countrymen. In Russia, we Jews are now like everybody else. The workers will be protected and the capitalists will be destroyed. Why do we have to fool ourselves? The money-world has always been death to us Jews. We have been forced to live in this way and it has been death to us. What does a Jew really want? A chance to work, like other people. Haven't the Bolsheviki given us a whole territory of our own, in Crimea, the richest soil in all Russia? What more can we ask? At last we can go back to the land, work, live, develop our culture, our nation. We will be a nation within the great group of Soviets. How should the Jews be forgotten? Trotsky himself is a Jew."

"Trotsky shmotsky. Such a Jew, the devil himself is! Trotsky's own father disowned him! A *mamser* he must be! His own army makes pogroms!"

"Where do you get such nonsense?" Bialystoker cried indignantly. "From the Tchicago *Tribune*? The truth is, Trotsky gave guns to the Jews. Protect yourself, he said."

"Tea? More tea?" said Mrs. Abramson.

"Yah." Mr. Abramson was cynical. "It will be like in Poland and in Rumania and like with all those other heathen governments, a black year on them. Promises! Come, Jews, settle on the land, build houses! And we send money and the government takes it away from them. As the learned Rabbi of Bialystok said, a guarantee from a *goyish* government, begging your pardon, ladies, is useful to wipe the behind."

"But with the Bolsheviki it is different! . . ."

"Don't make me laugh!" the fat aunt screeched. "The Bolsheviki are different! My aunt had a little grocery in Berdichev, and now she begs for bread!"

"And Chaim Berman's silk factory in Odessa? The man was a millionaire. Now he eats offal! They won't even give him a food card! And what are they doing with the factory? It rots!"

Now a warty, consumptive-looking little man chimed in conclusively: "Aye, children! Why should we try to make a new life in Russia? We have our own land again, thank God! Let the refugees go to Palestine!"

"Palestine!" Bialystoker exploded. "Don't speak to me of Palestine! When a man is drowning, this is not the time to lie on the grass and dream dreams!"

"What kind of dream! The land is there! Rather than throw money in the ocean to a drowning man let us send him to our homeland, to settle in Palestine!"

"Yes! On the barren mountains! Jews are starving already in your precious Eretz Yisrael!"

"Better than starving in Russia!"

"Ut! there speaks your idealist!"

Pop-eyed, hot-faced, they were all screaming at each other like a bunch of—like a bunch of Jews. Each side accused the other of idealism. Then suddenly the Zionist cried: "Yes, it is an ideal! Why not? We Jews have always been idealists! And see, now, the ideal is coming true!"

"An ideal you call it!" Bialystoker snorted. "To turn back history two thousand years! To sit under your olive tree and have Arab slaves working for you, noble Jew! Good, so the Jews are idealists. And what is it that I am talking about? The great ideal of the human race . . . to build the new order of mankind! That is more important than to build another little colony for England!"

The idealists glared at each other, fuming. And now Joe saw what they were arguing for. The American Jew, the Rosenwald, had his hand in his pocket, and the idealists howled on each side of him—give money! Give for Jews and Zionism! Give for Jews and communism! It was a competition of ideals.

Mort jumped into the argument. "Idealistically communism is fine, but practically it will never work out!" he declared. "There was a swell story by Booth Tarkington in the *Saturday Evening Post* about a guy that gave his factory to his workmen, and when they tried to run it—oh, boy!"

"You will see, there will be pogroms in Palestine, too," Bialystoker was predicting. "Don't forget, the Arabs are there."

"Pogroms! Starvation!" Mr. Abramson cried. And they began worrying about Jewish refugees from Rumania, where should they go? It was this that confused, amused, and yet got hold of Joe. A houseful of relatives on a Friday night, a house on Avers Avenue, Chicago, and, by God, nothing escaped their worry; they worried about the Polish pogroms, the Lithuanian Jews, the Rumanian exiles, the Galicians . . . they never forgot one, not one.

Sylvia had come back; she was ready, but he wasn't eager to leave.

As they went to the door the whole scene imprinted itself on Joe's mind, like a scene glimpsed from a train, a place at once strange and familiar, to which a man knows he must return.

"Don't stay out late, Sylvie," Mrs. Abramson cautioned.

Like life, Sol thought. He said the words to himself, like life, the riding, the going around, it was a victrola record going around around, and the humming buzz of the wheels . . . like life. After the going around and the going around for half an hour for thirty-five minutes there was no end there was no time because time was the hands of the clock going around and you were going around yourself it was all the same thing, life. Like life. I figured it out for myself. I'm not dumb, a dumb athlete, Estelle, because here see I am thinking the same time I am riding. Like life. Around and around in a circle, does the old man do any better, does anybody do any better, I say everybody does the same thing, the old man pushing an iron up and back pressing pants. Around and around in a circle. I hang onto Bobby. Around three times and then he falls back and I hang onto the Dutchman. And I pass and someone passes me, and I pass again, and then we go for a long time the same, nobody passes anybody. Like life. It is a competition. You go for a long time and it is the same if you go to school or anything else. Come on, Estelle, come down early today. It is the long drag of the morning but maybe she will come and stand behind my pullman. Stand behind my pullman, Estelle, and like they say the earth goes around the sun I'll be going around you. That's a hot idea, see I am thinking, not so dumb, Estelle. You stand there and take your hat off, shake out your red hair like the sun blazing, and you will keep me going around and around keep me going.

The old lady was sore, what kind of a thing is it! A Jewish boy! A Jewish boy goes to school, to college, is a doctor, a lawyer; but a Jewish boy should do such a crazy thing! But ma, look at Benny Leonard, he is a Jewish athlete and he made a million dollars! Six days and nights on a bicycle! It is a *meshugass*! Crazy! Not my son, no, no, I will not let it! He will kill himself! (Boy oh boy did she put up a squawk! She nearly had Kabibble Cooperstein keeping me off the track. Keep that crazy mother of yours away from the front office, Pisano yelled, or Kabibble will scratch you, understan'!) But why is it crazier? Why is it crazier on a bike than a doctor gets up in the middle of the night, than the old man pushes the pressing iron, than a guy turns the pages of a book, the next page, the next page, like life!

See the blue and white flag on my pullman. What are you, Jewish? Kabibble Cooperstein says when the Wop drags me up the first time. You don't have to ask Kabibble if he's Jewish ha ha it sticks out all over his nose. You tell him, I stutter, says Pisano. . . . Listen, says Kabibble Cooperstein, What's your name? Solly? Well, Solly, don't expect to cop the first race, don't even expect to finish, don't kill yourself the first time. Let me give you a tip, Solly, in every race a couple of teams drop out before the finish. Maybe your team will drop out. Don't worry. It's the first time. I'll keep an eye on you. I just want to see how you can ride. It wouldn't be such a bad idea, if we could pick a couple of nice Jewish kids. . . . Like life. In America. The wops and the Greeks and the Germans, the dagos and the micks and the sheenies, all go around like when you stir the tea the leaves go around in the cup. Like life. Boy, was I shaking. Me lining up with Reggie MacNamara and Bobby Walthour and Carl Stockholm and those guys. Boy, was I shaking. You don't believe it when they say your knees shake but that's just what they do, like a pair of rattling bones.

That's all right you two kids ride together. Two Chicago kids. You two kids'll get along fine. Hey, Charley? Hey, Solly? Witczik had that green jersey and I had that blue and white jersey, that's the Jewish colors. So then we got red, white, and blue jerseys.

You never think you are a Jew until you sign up and then they say what are you? A Jew, and you see all the other bunks with Italian, German, French, Canuck flags and you go out and say where can I get a Jewish flag and you have to chase all over town but down on Halsted Street there is a place where they got all kinds of religious stuff, *talisses*, and Jewish flags three for a dime. Penny flags. Like life. I ain't riding under no sheeny flag, Charley yells, and it's nearly a scrap. All right, all right, the box has two ends, you put any flag you want on your end. I put my flag on this end. The American flag, Charley says, that's good enough for me!!

What do you know about the old lady, she gives in, on opening night she drags the old man down, and Aunt Gittel and uncle, the whole damn family. They come and stand behind the box. Estelle is there behind the box. So no use, they have to know each other. Meet a friend of mine. But the old lady gives her one look, and knows why she's there, standing behind my box. My girl.

So once you do something they brag about you. In the beginning they raise hell and won't let you do it but once you go out and do it they brag. See, that's my boy. That's my Solly.

And the whole bunch. I was the guy. The whole bunch came, Mort Abramson and his sister and Joe Freedman and Foxey and Dave Plotkin and Harry Perlin, and I was the guy. Hey, Solly, who sent the flowers? The girl friend? Don't blush, Solly! . . . And in the third sprint, fresh and new and afraid to step out in front of all those stars, in front of the Iron Man and Goulet, me, a kid, step out in front of them! But, jeez, the fellows and all the girls in the bunch yelling and screaming every time I passed where they were sitting together! So in the third sprint I had to give them something. Solly, keep your head, I said to myself, don't go showing off, you ain't no grandstand rider, but the fifth lap around Bobby dropped back and then just when we passed the field man holding up number six, the Dutchman dropped the lead and I was third in the chain. The sound of the wheels going around like the electric fan in the store, or like a faraway buzz right near, the sound even then the first couple of hours was getting to be something tagging after me and something pulling me on, but the Iron Man was in the lead. The way he looked back with his long face and the mouth hanging open and that hard look in his eyes, come on, you punks, you can't pass the Iron Man.

So you pull out of line wheeling high onto the track around the curve, passing right under the judge's nose on the ninth time around and as the bell begins to ding ding ding you shoot down ahead of the Iron Man pumping pumping pumping running away running away, your teeth on your tongue, head throwing from side to side ding ding ding ding ding bang! made it! and slow down and slow down slower slower last time around and Pisano running toward you while you lean your fingerless glove against the front wheel braking the front wheel and he catches you as you swing off in front of your bunk. Atsaboy! THIRD SPRINT WON BY SOLLY MEISEL OF THE CHICAGO JUNIORS TEAM! You see Estelle standing there right behind the box and as you roll for the bunk flash her the old smile. Not tired at all, but save it, take it easy, stretch.

Is that sonofagun never gonna wake up? Hey, am I supposed to be riding this race myself or have I got a partner? Hey, Lefty, my hour is up pull that guy outa the bunk before I fall off this wheel. That's what the old-timers say, the hour drag in the second morning is worse than the whole race. Well, I got through mine. I'm in.

Jesus Cuurist what a partner. I tear my guts out pumping up a lead to grab off a lap and then I have to hand it over to him and he loses it every time. What does he think this is, a picnic? This is a race, get it, a race, a competition.

You gotta have the right partner. Like life. Cuurist if I had the right partner.

Celia came down with Estelle. Estelle worried. His face was drawn, with purple under his eyes. But otherwise he looked all right. His legs looked fine, glistening, shaven and oiled, smooth, firm and endlessly strong. How meaty and solid they were, up above the knees, going into his trunks. For the next race, she was going to embroider a star on his trunks.

"He's got a terrible partner," she told Celia. "See, when they change off, he has to give him a shove, and he don't do it right. If Sol had a good partner he'd be right up at the lead. That Polack, he made them lose three laps."

"Yah?" said Celia, looking close at Estelle.

Then there was the first spill. Estelle's eyes were following only Sol, her head swiveling the track with him, but in the stretch of track that she couldn't see there was a crack, a jangle; a gasp went through the building, and the crowd in the pit flowed toward the point of spill, while the galleries rose, craning.

The bell clanged.

"It's Sol! It's Sol!" Estelle rushed to the other side of the track, boring through the crowd. Celia followed; she had never heard such a tone in Estelle's voice, oh, Estelle must have it bad.

They had already picked him up, and a brief clapping went up from the crowd, as he was led back to his bunk, limping. There was a long scratch on his left leg; blood was beginning to show.

"Is it bad? Is it bad?" Estelle followed along the inside of the track.

"Hey, Sol, your girl is talking to you," Pisano said.

Sol grinned weakly. Naw, just a little splinter. In a few minutes, a smear of mercurochrome on his thigh, Sol climbed onto his bike again. There was the usual scattered, limp cheer as the injured rider went back into the grind.

Estelle put her hand on Celia's forearm. "Feel how I'm shaking," she said, as though it were a joke on herself.

Their eyes met, and in that moment there was a delicious exchange between them, of girlhood, of confidence, of a sort of womanly confession on Estelle's part: oh, he's my weakness now.

Look at him riding now, riding like a fool, trying to win the sprint, to show the crowd he was game, after being hurt!

One part of her seemed to be trying to hold all the other riders back, and a part of herself seemed to be pulled along with Sol, being far from herself, taut, when he was at the other end of the track, coming warm, thrilling, when he shot by, close.

Now she was living. Now this was life.

She felt hot, and pulled off her monkey jacket.

This was the best time to tell her, Celia thought, because at this moment Estelle would surely understand and guard her secret.

"Listen, kid," she said. "My father knows a lawyer that has a job in his office, but kid! If—you know—ever found out I did it for him, I'd die. So, kiddo, have your brother tell him he heard of something. I'll give you the name of the firm."

"Leave it to me," Estelle said, taking her eyes off Sol for a moment, and looking at Celia's face. They felt like wives telling each other their secret ways of managing their husbands.

Lou Green had never got over feeling he owed Lou Margolis something for being his pal. So he would bring him praise he had heard, or inside dirt about the girls, or things he picked up having a sister around the house.

But bringing him this chance of a job was different. The Sharpshooter, so brilliant, would always be able to get a job. But how about himself?

And then he thought: I'm trying to hold out on a pal.

"Say, Lou, I heard they're taking on a clerk at Edelman and Preiss."

"Huh?" said Lou Margolis. "Say, let's the two of us go up there tomorrow."

"I wouldn't stand a chance," Second-the-Motion said.

"You got just as much chance as I got. Come on. You heard about it in the first place."

The offices were in the big new Conway Building. Preiss was a little guy with reddish-blond hair, thin on top. He made fun of Judge Donohue and all their instructors at school. "Well, I can take on one of you boys but I don't know which one." He left it to them, lying back in his chair and blinking at them shrewdly.

Lou Margolis said: "How about tossing up?"

That was what made Preiss decide on Lou Margolis. He said: "Call me up next week." When they were gone he phoned Rube Moscowitz: "Say, what was the name of the kid you wanted me to take in here? Two of them came up. . . . Oh. Yeah. Well, I'll see about it, Rube, as a favor to you. How's the wife?"

Harry Perlin got up at seven. "Why do you get up so early, take time, take time, nothing is burning," his mother sang, shuffling in her shapeless wrapper.

But the early bird catches the job.

He used to turn first to "Gasoline Alley" but now he always turned right to "Help Wanted." There seemed to be plenty to pick from but at least three columns were salesmen jobs, and he had already fallen for one of those house-to-house jobs and wasted a month; he knew better. When he read things like wanted, bushelman, welder, linotype operator, man experienced on power lathes, he got the feeling of knowing nothing. If he knew one thing solid, like electrician, steam fitter, he could go direct and say, I am your man.

Each morning he took his little box of brown shoe polish and went out on the back porch and gave his shoes a shine, and clipped his tie exactly into place with a bar-pin under the knot, because every little thing counts. But no matter how early he got to a place, there were always a couple of fellows there already, waiting for the door to be opened. There were all those vets still looking for jobs and naturally they got the preference. *Get the vets off the breadlines!* Though sometimes he got tired and discouraged and thought it was unfair to give a guy the job just because he had a service cap. Bet he had done as much military in the R.O.T.C. as most of those Camp Grant heroes!

You had to know somebody—you had to have pull.

Then he ran into Runt who said: "How's tricks? Say, did you go out to see my pal Bienstock yet?"

The Columbus Park Garage was way at the end of the Harrison Street car line. Here and there, a new building was stuck on the prairie.

Harry walked in. A big hundred-car garage, fine steel trussed roof, everything up to date. Empty, but for a few cars way off in a rear corner. Harry wandered down the long concrete floor, smelling the sharp odor of new cement, brick, the tangy smell of iron, and the stale smell of grease.

"Anybody here?" he called.

A grease-smeared face appeared over the hood of a car. It was some young kid, younger than himself.

"Where's the boss?" Harry said.

The kid motioned toward an open rear door.

A little man in a business suit was standing out in back of the garage and looking over the vacant blocks as if, in that moment, he expected houses to spring up, complete.

"Mr. Bienstock?"

"Yep. That's me."

Harry explained what he wanted.

"Are you a mechanic?"

"Well, I can do almost anything on a car."

"Aha. I got a boy, but he's a *klotz*. He can't do no repairs. He got wooden fingers. He gave me a hard-luck story, so I gave him a job!"

So he would have to take the job away from that kid.

Harry didn't have to talk. Mr. Bienstock marched him around the bare, concrete floor. See. Everything the latest. Press a button, bing, the doors open. Cost me plenty! Here, let me show you something. A toilet. With a shower. Where will you find another garage with a shower? But I believe in improvements. Cost me another hundred dollars, but I got something.

"You think this is no place to put up a garage, in a wilderness? Maybe you are right. Bienstock, they say, for the same money, you can put up a garage on Sixteenth Street! There you have people, customers! And what do I say? There they got garages. Listen, young man, I am a man that takes chances. Already Douglas Park is cheap and they go around Garfield Park. And where will they move when they move away from Garfield Park?"

He left the question, poised, like a bird in flight from Garfield Park.

"Columbus Park. In the next five years I am making a prophecy this neighborhood will be built up solid. And if they live this far out, they all got cars. And if they got cars, they need garages." He looked triumphantly at Harry.

What he needed was an all-around man. Take care of the office, do small repair jobs, be the manager. Right now, of course, he couldn't pay much, but as business grew, pay would increase. The hours would have to be kind of long. Start at $25 a week.

The kid had stopped work and was watching them apprehensively from behind that raised hood.

As Harry went out, he saw the boss approaching the kid.

Riding back, on the street car, he told himself, why should he feel sorry? If he was a better man, he was entitled to the job.

Sol and his partner hadn't spoken a word to each other for the last twenty-four hours, communicating only through Pisano.

Charley Witczik was giving out, Sol knew. He felt Charley like a weight around his neck. Why didn't the bastard admit he was the weaker? Why didn't he ask Sol to ride those extra laps, to ride the hardest sprints, instead of sneaking them over. Sol could actually feel the hot blood sweeping across his face every time he passed the bunk and saw the skinny, pooped figure of the Polack slung on the bed. The weakness of Charley was like weights on his neck, on his feet. Sol felt himself strong, able to keep up with all these stars, the Iron Man, anybody.

Then Willy Brauer, of the Dutch team, broke a rib and was carried out, and his partner was left. It was Sol's chance to team up with the Flying Dutchman and finish the race strong.

"Charley got to drop out!" he cried to Pisano. "He's dead on his feet anyway. He can't finish the race. Send him out. Lemme team up with the Dutchman."

Pisano talked to Witczik. "He won't go," he reported. "He says he can make it."

That skinny little bastard! Sol couldn't stand it any more. "Either he gets out or I get out," he screamed. "I won't get on a bike unless he drops outa the race."

"You're crazy!" Pisano cried. "Wanna get disqualified? Listen, I coached him and I coached you for this start, and you take orders from me, see?"

But under his blind anger, Sol knew, felt, that Pisano wouldn't let him go. He had shown up fine so far. Better than Witczik. In a competition, the strongest man wins. Between the two of them, he was the man. He lay in the bunk, refused to get out for his turn.

Pisano ran around in circles. He threatened, begged, swore. Finally he went and got Estelle. "You talk to him. He's gone crazy."

Estelle knelt by the bunk and said: "Listen, Solly, it's for your own future. Stick it out. The worse he rides, the better you show up. This isn't the last ride you'll be in. After this is over you're through with him."

"Say, the first thing I'll do after this race is over is beat the puss off of him!"

"But finish the race. Finish the race. The Dutchman got another partner already anyway."

He could listen to her. She had power over him. He admitted it to himself, wondered, and wasn't sorry. Pisano couldn't talk to him, nobody could talk to him: only his girl, Estelle. Grumbling, he crawled out of the bunk.

. . . A couple more laps, and his turn was over. How he could hit that bunk! Every fiber in his body seemed to be straining of its own will toward that mattress. His guts to lie down, a load against the wooden bed. He tried to shift his weight. If he could only find one spot on his ass that wasn't seat sore. Easy easy like pulling off a courtplaster, he shifted on the seat.

Twenty more hours. Spot the girl in the yellow dress. "Say, big boy, what do you do nights when you ain't riding?" her note said. Aw, girls like that were punks. He had Estelle. Coming around again he leaned forward to see if Charley was out of the bunk.

Charley was half sitting up, shaking his head like a dog trying to come awake. Lefty was feeding him some of that caffeine. "Come out of there, you bastard," Sol hissed. And just then the buggy Frenchman started a jam. Oh Cuurist that's all that was needed. All down the line riders began to pile out of their bunks and into the jam. Charley was riding like a dead one. Sol dropped behind, and leaned over to give his partner the shoveoff. At that instant, Charley's bike bobbled right into his front wheel and they went down together.

Falling, Sol pulled in his head, raised his arms. He knew how to take a fall now. OOOOooo, he heard the crowd, spill, spill! as if it wasn't for himself; at the same moment he thought: that bastard did it on purpose. Couldn't stand up with me in fair competition. So he tries to knock me out. Oh I'm going to sock him one! The burn of the wood against his skidding thighs. Ffff. Oh! That bastard louse had fallen right on top of him. Their feet strapped to their dragging, tangling bikes.

Just stay there. Rest. Stay a long time. Feel nothing.

Some jackasses were trying to untangle the bikes. A shot of pain in his ankle.

As they pulled him to his feet, he struggled, still with the bleary idea of socking Charley. Charley was up. Hobbling away, unhurt.

"You—!" Sol wrenched an arm loose, and swung. At the same time, he collapsed. All over. The framework of Charley's bike had crashed his ankle.

Moony and Horny

What is Love?

Winnie Winkle got engaged to marry Harry Tyler.

Uncle Bim bought a ring for the Widow Zander.

Walt was falling for Auntie Blossom.

Harold Teen and Lillums plotted to elope.

The inquiring reporter asked: "What do you think love is?"

Princess Mary, of England, had a wedding and there were two full pages of gifts that rivaled the riches of Arabia. Oh, she looked beautiful in her wedding gown, like a real princess.

But Lil Klein said: "Do you suppose it is really a love marriage?"

"Give me those rocks and I'll even marry a prince!" Estelle kidded.

"I wouldn't like to be a princess," Aline said. "They have no choice. They have to marry whoever they're told!"

MATHILDA McCORMICK, 16, TO WED RIDING MASTER, 60!

Even in the Yiddish *Forwards* that her mother still persisted in buying, Lil Klein saw the picture of Mathilda McCormick, 16, granddaughter of John D. Rockefeller, who sanctioned her marriage to Max Oser, 59.

—Imagine, girls! He's sixty, and she's sixteen!

—Y' can't kid me! There must be a reason!

—Say, that guy knew what he was after. A sixteen-year-old, and a couple of million dollars to boot!

—A guy as old as him, he ought to *pay* a couple of million dollars for it!

—Maybe this'll give old John D. Rockefeller some ideas. What is he, her great-grandfather or her great-great-grandfather? Look at that picture, he looks like the ghost of an ancient monkey, I hear he has a platinum stomach and they have to feed him through a tube. Next thing you know he'll be marrying a twelve-year-old!

—Oh, them days are gone forever, for him.

—I wouldn't be so sure. What does he live for anyway if he can't have any fun?

—He's trying to live to be a hundred.

—I bet he gets some monkey glands and starts all over, too.

Rose Heller kept imagining an old man, wrinkled, icy-skinned, putting his hands all over her body. Sixteen! Her kid sister's age! She got the sick feeling like that time all those things were in the papers about the Fatty Arbuckle trial.

Sixteen! Lil Klein kept saying. Why, we're a bunch of old maids. And secretly, by herself, she practiced writing on her new stationery:

Mrs. Lillian K. Eisen.

Then she dropped a blot over the words, and spread the blot with the point of her pen, until not a letter showed. But half hoping that in some magic way Sam Eisen would get hold of the sheet of paper and read the words under the blot.

What is love?

The Kaiser got married again.

138

Any woman who would marry the Kaiser—that is love.

A million dollars, that dancer said. A million dollars for her broken heart, when Vanderbilt left her cold.

Toot toot tootsie, good-by.

Celia saw Rudy Valentino in *Blood and Sand*. Oh, the hot love of the Toreador, the fling of his cape over his shoulder, and the look in his eyes, coming toward you!

Fifi Stillman went up there with that Indian guide.

Well, her husband was no better, he admitted having that affair with that chorus girl Flo Leeds.

Marriage! There is no love in marriage!

Love was like beautiful music, Thelma said. Like Mary Garden, in *Carmen.*

Alvin saw himself as Anatol, the Viennese lover, suave, debonair, sipping love lightly, tasting all varieties of women, sipping their love like a connoisseur in wines.

Nobody lied when they said that I cried over you. . . .

The *American* printed a picture of McCormick just after his monkey-gland operation[4]. It was said he was now going to marry an opera singer. Though Mitch Wilner told everybody monkey glands were a lot of hooey.

Just because you're you, that's why I love you. . . .

A fellow was found in a vacant lot on the South Side. He was bleeding, and his glands were gone[5]. Mort Abramson said if a thing like that happened to him he'd commit suicide.

And Harry Perlin, Rudy Stone, in tortured secret moments wondered if such a thing might not have its compensation, bringing relief from these night-time agonies of desire.

> She's so sweet,
> She's so dear,
> I go crazy
> When she's near.

---

[4] Harold Fowler McCormick was one of Chicago's richest citizens. Between divorcing wife Edith in December, 1921 and marrying opera singer Ganna Walska on August 11, 1922, McCormick became notorious by being operated on by a surgeon who specialized in transplanting animal glands into aging men, which supposedly could restore fading sexual potency. Juicy newspaper reports appeared in June, 1922, when McCormick was 50.

[5] This was a shocking news event of the day. At 3 A.M. on November 20, 1923, Charles Ream was walking home from his job as a cab driver when two men jumped from an automobile and abducted him and forced a chloroform-soaked rag onto his face. Three hours later he awoke lying in the grass, having been castrated.

Closed cars selling twice as fast as open cars, you know what closed cars are for![6] Texas Guinan at the Palace.

... Wanna?

Oh, do it again!

Alvin Fox took Sylvia Abramson to the opera at Ravinia, trying to impress her, and parking by the roadside said: "Have you any suppressed desires?"

That was his line. But it didn't work with her.

The sexy, the wildest generation, the kids who did bad things at country clubs—say, what's a country club? What is love? When a girl gives herself to a fella.

Would I give myself to him? That's how you tell.

Oh, there's just no place for love. No nice girl does it in a car. The first time has to be something beautiful, in a gorgeous hotel on a honeymoon, with the moon dissolving through the window. A sort of ceremony.

Two years, three, four years. The fellows have to get started in life. In the meantime, in between time . . . just wait and wait. Old-fashioned folks used to marry young and live on their parents.

Modern and independent!

Horny, always horny.

Rudy Stone worked it off by taking on extra jobs, keeping busy every waking moment, wearing himself out. They said cold showers helped. Lou Green fumbled with himself, worried somebody might catch him at it. The guys said girls did it too.

It's love that makes the world go round.

At Kelley's Stables they scratched their names on the wall, put their gin in ginger ale (fifty cents a glass), threw pennies at the singing waiter, and, dancing on the tiny square of floor, the girls rubbed bellies with the fellows. Those new dance sets, that leave the belly naked! They're wild!

And once Rose Heller let a fellow love her up; when she was half-faint he got as far as touching her bare thighs. She couldn't sleep, she wasn't sure, she didn't really know exactly what it was that men and women did together. Ashamed, worn to a frazzle with worry, she finally broke down, and asked her chum Aline. Was that it? Did he do it to me? Over and over she repeated the details. "Well, I don't know," Aline said. "I don't think that was it." Then what was it? What was it, exactly? "I don't know," Aline said, "but I think if it happened to me, I'd know."

---

[6] The rise of closed cars was a game-changer with respect to romantic liaisons; crowded living conditions and social mores of the day made private encounters in buildings difficult or awkward at best, but the new breed of cars became roving parlors.

Young, in the golden time! What is love?

Joe and Sylvia, is that love? When a boy is making a living and can establish a home, think how wonderful it is to know you've saved yourself for him!

A girl has to watch her reputation.

MARY PICKFORD WEDS DOUG FAIRBANKS!

That's perfect love!

There was a literary conversation between Mort Abramson and Alvin (the Duke) Fox:

MORT: Did you read the *God of Vengeance*? They suppressed it in New York.

ALVIN (*scornfully*): Say, that's about as modern as *Uncle Tom's Cabin*. I bet they paid the cops to suppress it for a publicity stunt. You want to read something good? Read *Jurgen*[7].

MORT (*excitedly*): Say, I heard of that! Can you get me a copy?

ALVIN: Well, a friend of mine up at the U had it but I don't know if I can get in touch with him.

MORT: It's pretty hot stuff, I heard.

ALVIN: Well, *Jurgen* is really literature. I can't get interested in a book just for its pornographic aspect but when it's got some literary merit that's different. Cabell is the greatest living author next to Anatole France.

MORT: I don't know about that. What about Jacob Wassermann. Did you read *World's Illusion*? That part where the guy gets the girl Ruth, in the basement, and tells her he's going to rape her?

ALVIN: Yes, that's one of the finest passages in literature, but on the whole I don't think Wassermann comes up to Cabell.

MORT: Say, I heard there was a place downtown where you could buy Frank Harris's *Life and Loves*.

ALVIN: He wants fifteen bucks for it but I know a guy that rents out a copy.

MORT: Yah? Have you read it?

ALVIN: I don't think so much of it from a literary standpoint but in some ways it's better than *Fanny Hill*, the classic.

MORT: How much does this guy charge?

ALVIN: A dollar a day.

MORT: That's not such a bad business.

---

[7] "Jurgen, A Comedy of Justice", by James Branch Cabell, is a 1919 fantasy classic that became notorious because of its suggestive (but not explicit) imagery and story line. It's a wonderful book, and worth checking out.

ALVIN: I was thinking of going into it myself up at the U. You ought to get it and read that part about the Negress. (*He smacks his lips.*) You'll learn something.

MORT: Say, Frank Harris'll have to be pretty good, to tell me something I don't know.

ALVIN: If you want it, I'm not sure I can get it for you this week, he has a waiting list, but I'll ask him. You can read it in a day. Frank Harris was an intimate friend of Oscar Wilde, you know. Say, Mort, did you ever see a copy of *Lysistrata*, with the Aubrey Beardsley illustrations? . . .

MORT (*to himself*): A buck a day. I wouldn't put it past the Duke to be getting a rake-off from this guy, whoever he is.

And, about 1 a.m., in bed, Mort was reading the part where this young Negro girl, who wanted to show her gratitude to Frank Harris for a favor, asked her mother what was the best thing a girl could do to give a man pleasure. After her mother told her, this beautiful young Negro girl came up to Frank Harris's place, and—

Mort sensed the door opening, tentatively. He just had time to slide the book under his pillow.

"I thought maybe you fell asleep with the light on," said his mother, glancing around the room. "Were you reading?" But she could see there was nothing to read.

"I—I was thinking," Mort said crossly. His blood was pounding. For a moment he had been afraid it was Sylvia.

Did she have to tuck him in? Couldn't he have any privacy?

"What do you have to think about, in the middle of the night?" his mother said, lightly.

"Can't you let me alone?" he snapped. "What do you think I am, a kid?"

She gave him a quick, hard look, shrugged, and went out.

When Sol awoke after sleeping for twenty-two hours, Estelle was by his bedside. His mother shuffled in and out of the room. It was all right for a girl to come into his bedroom because he was sick. And yet it gave Sol an excited feeling. The whole room seemed to smell of being in bed, this bed he had wanted her in, and part of him seemed still to be in the melted darkness of sleep, even way back into some infancy where there was a smell like the warm dew on a woman's breast all around him, the same but different scent he had caught upon Estelle's young breasts, sometimes when they were necking heavy; and part of him even seemed to be with his mother way back when she used to sing.

He wanted to lower himself back into sleep, and Estelle would be here all the time.

His mother pulled up the shade, and the alley-light came in and rested on the brass ends of the bed, making pencils of light on each post.

"You nitwit, you would go and crash when I wasn't even around to see it!" Estelle greeted him.

"Say, I could have lasted it but that lousy partner I had—"

"Sure, if you had a good partner you would have placed."

"Do me a favor, will you?" he mumbled. "Call up Nick Pisano."

"Say, he better not come near here or your mother'll bite his head off."

"Tell him I'm okay."

Even through his sleep he had felt his mother's ceaseless grumbling: "Fifty dollars a day! Fortunes he's making! That devil-tongued Italian, may his eyes be torn out of his head! A hundred dollars for a packing box to sleep in! And what has he left, my hero? Doctor bills, and a broken leg! Fine! Better he should be a cripple for life than a bicycle rider. . . ."

"Oh, she don't mean it, she's just glad you're all right," Estelle said.

"Did they bring my bikes home?"

"Pisano is taking care of them. She would have given them to the junk man."

The old lady was out of the room. Estelle gave him a long cool kiss, different from the kisses when they were necking; at the same time he felt her breasts against him almost as though she were in bed. Oh, this was gonna be good. Sick, with her around all the time. Oh, boy!

"Here, you wanna eat something." His mother came back, with a tray.

"I'll feed him," Estelle said.

This was the way you learned who were your friends, all right, when you were flat on your back in bed. The two Lous came, stood around, and kidded him, and Runt Plotkin came around and said it was a shame, he couldn't even get damages for a thing like that, and Harry Perlin came around, and a lot of girls called up, but Estelle was there almost all the time, answering the phone, and could she give them the ice!

On Sunday, Sol awoke with a suddenly fresh, rested feeling. He forgot his ankle. Then he knew why he felt so good. The folks were going riding with the old lady's brother. He and the redhead would have the place to themselves.

When Estelle came over, Ben was still around, the dope. "You don't have to hang around, Ben," Estelle said sweetly. "I'll take care of the invalid."

He gave them a look, and said he'd take in a show.

"Alone at last, huh?" Sol said. Even the little flat in back of the store had a Sunday cleanliness.

Estelle sat on the edge of the bed and fed him bits of fudge she had made. All the while they hardly spoke, and their touching of bodies was stiff, wary, as though they were strangers sizing each other up.

His hand fastened on her arm. "Hey, kid, lie down here for a while beside me."

"What for?" The shrillness of her own voice brought her back to herself. Why, she was acting like a baby. She knew Sol. He was so cute, the way he was angling for her. The way his body was kind of limp and yet she could feel the strength of his arms.

"Aw, it'll feel good. Come on," he urged, trying to make his voice sound innocent.

With a quick movement, she stretched on the outside of the covers. He began working his arm under her, and finally, while they were having a long gluey kiss, he pulled the sheet from between them, and let it fall over her, too.

Her dress would get wrinkled.

She kicked off her slippers.

What if she did let it happen? Ever since she had started going with fellows, she had been curious: what would the fellow be like? Hints, suggestions she had caught. Some men were good at it, and some no good at all. Oh, Sol would be good.

But she had never imagined they would do it like this. Not in a back bedroom with the shade raised and you could see the alley. She ought to get up and pull the shade but that would mean she intended to go the whole way. She wouldn't go the whole way, but just lie there peacefully as if they were sleeping together.

Oh, she couldn't let him do it. She was a nice girl even if she was kind of promiscuous about necking, her mother would go crazy if she did a thing like this.

So what? What had her mother got out of life? Her dopy mother, the way she had acted up that time she bobbed her hair.

What if it was here in the back bedroom, it was kind of honest and sweet, this was the way he lived, and was her own house so swell? Why make a pretense about everything? Why not be yourself?

And then, under his clumsily wily, groping hands, feeling the yearning and the torture and at the same time the worship and tenderness of his hands, and feeling herself knowing this kid so well, this kid that just wanted to ride a bike, be a great six-day bike rider and be a fine Jewish athlete who saved his dough, like Benny Leonard, make lots of dough and have girls send him mash notes—oh, she would take care of them—and feeling an intoxication of love sensations that swept up and down her body, she thought: maybe she would let him.

And then, he had lurched over, and there was a confusion of pain, and neither of them knowing quite how, and just as suddenly he lurched away from her.

Was that all? Had they done it?

And then, coupled with a kind of pity for him, she felt a low, sinking, deathly disappointment in herself: they had muffed it, and for this clumsy tangle she had lost—what? Aw, it's nothing, I'm no different! she thought. And yet, resist it as she would, the idea drove down upon her that now she was different, now she was like something that had been perfect but was scratched; she seemed to see her mother's reviling face looking down at her and looking away, looking down at her and looking away . . .

Aw, bushwah! she wanted to yell. Baloney! It's all a lot of baloney! And at the same time she thought of what the fellows said, a woman is like a car; a slightly used car that has been broken in by a good driver is better than a new car, any time. Then the other fellow always asked the first fellow: But would you marry a girl that had had it before? And the first fellow always hesitated.

And she wanted to laugh. Now she felt superior. Now she felt as though she could run her life to suit herself. And her mother looking down at her! Go on, look, what can you see?

Scared? She had been more scared that time after she got her hair bobbed. Anybody could see bobbed hair!

A Jewish girl! A Jewish girl doesn't do such things!

Oh me oh my ai ai ai! Poof.

My daughter should do such a thing! Raised in a good Jewish house, my daughter . . .

Estelle sat up in bed, and shook her hair hard, so she could feel the clusters swish against her neck and face. Well, she had never thought it would be like this, a brass bed, and bars of sunlight on the rods. So now she was started. It was kind of comical. And Solly was so sleepy, his head lolled heavily over the other way. So now she was a bad girl.

Ishkabibble!

He turned, and looked at her with moonish, loving eyes, that nevertheless carried, way down, a spark of belligerency.

"You're not sorry, are you?" he got out.

Estelle passed her hand over his face.

The poor sweet kid!

Everything Is Perfect

There is all kinds of perfection. Sometimes we speak of a perfect moment, when the surroundings, the company, the things being done, blend into a perfect whole, into something that seems to have a meaning beyond itself, expanding and multiplying until it is the way of life of the whole universe.

Like Harry Perlin said, watching the beautiful new Cadillac that a customer drove into the garage, a new car is perfect until the first scratch, and the first scratch hurts more than a smashed fender later.

To Mort Abramson a girl was something perfect, until she had been had.

A way of doing something may be perfect; all summer Alvin Fox raved about Louis Wolheim's acting in *The Hairy Ape*; that was perfect, he said!

Runt Plotkin told of a stunt pulled by Rube Moscowitz. After wrecking an old sewage plant, the city of Chicago had about fifty thousand dollars' worth of junk for sale. All the junkyards in town were hungry to bid on that stuff. This was one lot Rube Moscowitz wasn't going to get away from them, because there was a law that the city had to advertise for bids on any transaction over five hundred dollars. So how did Rube Moscowitz fix it with the politicians? They divided the fifty thousand dollars' worth of junk into lots worth a few hundred dollars each, and sold it all, lot by lot, to the Moscowitz junkyard! No other dealer had a lookin!

"That was perfect!" said Runt Plotkin.

It was a perfect summer.

Andy Gump running for Congress[8], that was perfect!

And Henry Ford for President.

Just because you're you, that's why I love you. . . .

Joe Freedman and Sylvia Abramson had perfect hours in the studio Joe had fixed in the basement the Big Ten had used as a clubroom. It was so cool there, and in the late afternoons Sylvia would sit reading poetry while Joe modeled her head. It was modern poetry: Carl Sandburg.

If both the Sox and the Cubs won their pennants, and that's what it looked like to Lou Green, that would be perfect! It hadn't happened since 1909.

Ev Goldberg was going steady with a full-fledged lawyer!

One day the girls felt that their unity was perfect. Their Sunshine Club was having a mah jong party at Celia's to raise their five-dollar monthly pledge for their Belgian war orphan. Skinny Heller hadn't showed up. Then, when it was nearly over, she burst in. And believe it or not, Skinny's hair was bobbed. The girls mobbed her, squealing and exclaiming. "At last! Skinny, how did you ever get up the gumption!"

And it was Lil Klein who noticed that now every one of them had a bob!

It gave them a funny, lumpy, perfect feeling of being together.

Skinny explained how she had finally got the bob. Just for something to do in summer, she had a filing job with S. W. Straus. And the company had two girls' baseball teams, long hairs and short hairs. They had just played a challenge game. The long hairs lost and had to bob their hair! Even though

---

[8] Andy Gump was a comic strip character in "The Gumps", which ran from 1917 to 1959. In 1922, the strip showed Andy running for Congress.

Skinny wasn't on the team, she had been swept along to the shop, and before she knew it—

"It's marvelous!" Aline exulted. "It's perfect!"

In the study of law you often get cases where a whole chain of whereases fit into each other as perfectly as a set of Chinese boxes and, at other times, there is a logical distinction that is beautiful.

Lou Margolis heard such a one, from his boss, Preiss. Lou asked, what is the difference between calling a man a Jew, and calling a man a bugger? It's like the difference between larceny and robbery, or between a civil and a criminal offense. You might insult a man by calling him a Jew, but you might injure him by calling him a bugger. Get it? He liked to tell it, for it was a perfect distinction.

It was a perfect summer. Sometimes Mitch took an hour off for a walk in Jackson Park with Joe, listening to Joe go into ecstasies about his favorite piece of architecture, the crumbling old Fine Arts building. He said it lay like a great bird with spread wings upon the ground. Joe was off the Gothic stuff now, only the classical stuff was perfect; in fact he was leaving the Midway studio and going down to the school of architecture at Urbana. Mitch kind of liked the decay of the crumbling walls, but Joe said it would be a crime if the city failed to rebuild the place.

They went up to Mitch's room. His life was really efficient this summer, in this cubicle of a dorm room, with the mission study table, the goosenecked lamp, the hard narrow bed, and the bare yellow walls. This was the life.

Joe sprawled on Mitch's cot, his head cupped in his interlocked fingers. Mitch was raving about a prof of his, that Russian, Vakhtanov, who had escaped from the Bolsheviki. "He was a big man in Russia," Mitch said. "These dopes here don't even listen to him, but he's got some wonderful theories. For instance, we don't know a damn thing about blood."

"Yah?" Joe didn't raise his head.

"Everybody's looking for germs," Mitch said scornfully. "Every day they've got serums for t.b. or they've discovered the cancer germ. But let me tell you, they don't even know what happens in the blood, and that's the whole secret of everything. It's in a lot of complicated chemical reactions . . ."

Joe half listened. He liked the earnest excited sound of Mitch, lecturing like a full-fledged medico.

". . . so look, you cluck, I'll put it simply. Maybe even you can understand. You're an architect. So the human body is a city. The veins and the arteries are the streets and alleys, and the bloodstream is the traffic bringing stuff to the cells, taking away waste."

"Ah, Venice!" said Joe.

"All right, Venice. Now in the body you have factories where certain necessary products are made, like the liver and the spleen and the different organs; then you have warehouses where stuff is stored—see, all this stuff travels along the arteries from factory to warehouse to consumer. Suppose your brain tissue needs a little more fat—"

Joe snorted.

"It's like an endless conveyor system, running through the streets, and into the houses, along the hallways, and every cell is a man in a room who pops open his door, grabs what he wants off the conveyor, and shuts the door. Only there isn't any man and there isn't any door. The cell has some way of dragging this stuff out of the bloodstream and pulling it right through the cell wall, yet keeping it inside so it can't get back out through that same wall. To make brains, to make bones, to make fingernails, each cell knows what compounds it needs, and gets them out of the bloodstream, see? How does it work? How come all that perfect organization? Where does the cell get that selectivity? How the heck, with the thousands of varieties of molecules floating along in the bloodstream, how does each individual cell, each particle of tissue, how does it *know* . . .?"

There was a pause, while the boys shared the same sense of being on the verge of something deep, something incredibly inapprehensible. Like that time last summer, walking together on the beach, under the country stars. . . .

And at the same time Joe was reminded of the feeling the city gave him, this same feeling Mitch was trying to express; sometimes the utterly inapprehensible complication of the city seized upon Joe: the wonder of street after street of houses, of people going in, coming out, carrying packages, of trucks going to stores, dumping goods to be pieced away by people who came to the stores on the street car, El, bus, from Devon Avenue, from Dorchester to Crawford, from Lawndale to Clark Street, who knew just where to buy victrola records, sacks of flour, Chinese lanterns; sometimes it seemed to him that if this maze of people on the way from one place to another and people eating and people pulling levers were suddenly to be stopped, arrested in motion, the whole thing would be seen to be an amazing, perfectly balanced pattern, every movement would be traceable from its source to its destination, and it would be obvious that the whole life of the city was at any one moment a different, but perfectly composed and balanced pattern of motions. Everything would be clear, and yet you wouldn't discover what you were looking for, but you would be choked with wonder at the perfection with which all these interrelated motifs came to balance. And maybe that was what Mitch meant.

Joe circled his arm along the bed, sat up, and for an instant stared straight into Mitchell's earnest brown eyes. They had a feeling of perfect friendship.

"What are these mattresses made of?" Joe said. "Wood?"

Be Yourself

That semester Sam Eisen couldn't arrange his courses any other way but that his gym hour came just before his drill hour. The gym was a mile away from the armory.

Once, as he was rushing out of the gym, a puttee came loose. "Balls!" He was late for drill already. He tried to tuck in the flapping cloth but finally had to rewind the whole thing. What was the use of running to drill only to get bawled out for being late by that stupid freckle-faced ag from downstate, his sergeant? Sam walked to his room, changed to a pair of baggy pants and a sweater, and sat down to study.

He began to feel good. This was really what he had come to school for. A little session with himself, the house quiet, his mind awake.

And on the next drill day, as Sam was walking toward the armory, gripy and discontented, he remembered that peaceful hour, when he had skipped R.O.T.C. Why go to drill? Eyes left, eyes right. Hup. Mark time, march. Mark time, march. Mark time.

Fix bayonets!

And what was there to this college life, for him, altogether?

Rushing to get through a pile of greasy dishes to get some food to shove down his throat and then rush over to a class on the Nineteenth-Century Poets. To sit around with a gang at the Mosi Over, eyes left when a pair of nifty ankles passed, eyes right when a couple of gigglers took the next table. Conversation out of the *Manual of Instruction*: Say, that redhead is kinda cute. Uh-huh, she's in my French Lit; lay offa her, she's got a Deke. Owo! Have those Dekes got an option on all the hot stuff? . . .

Once he had been fascinated by all that. A battered hat, a pullover sweater, a pair of tweed knickers; wished he could make himself over in that image. But lately he felt like a fool. Eyes left. Mark time. Mark time. Like that time with the fellows in the Big Ten. But he had busted out, then, given them hell. Maybe he had only made a fool of himself. He remembered the puzzled, vacant stares of Harry Perlin, Mitch Wilner. Yet, he had felt better, after that.

And suddenly, Sam thought: why do anything he didn't want to do? He would never fight in any war, so why should he learn to fix bayonets?

He turned back to his room.

And he had a wonderful feeling, a sense of rediscovering himself, the feeling that a fellow could get along, just being honest with himself; and he told himself that later, in serious life, he must remember this fact every time the crowd started to get him away from himself.

The dean of men had a square red face; he looked like a gentleman farmer.

Sam Eisen closed the door behind him, and walked to the desk. This was the dean famous all over the country for the way he handled fellows who got into scrapes.

"Mr. Eisen?"

"Yes."

The dean waved Sam to a heavy leather chair. The dean tilted against a windowsill, and took a frank, estimating look at Sam. He tapped a card against his palm.

"Well, I suppose you know what it's about?"

"R.O.T.C.?"

"Lieutenant Russell tells me you received several notices but you failed to show up."

"That's right," Sam said.

"Mmm hmm." The dean still watched him with mild good humor. "Then I take it your absence is deliberate?"

"Well, I guess so. Yes."

"Mmm hmmm. Well, Mr. Eisen, suppose you tell me just why you have decided to drop your military drill?"

"I don't believe in compulsory R.O.T.C.," Sam said promptly. And added: "I don't believe in war."

"I see." The dean slowly brought his chair down to the floor. His manner became friendlier than ever; he was like one of those fine modern parents who don't talk down to their children. "I guess nobody believes in war," the dean said. "I don't know how much faith we can put in treaties, but you know they're working on it in Washington right now. I expect great things from the Disarmament Conference. I think history will regard it as one of the turning points. Have you been following it?"

"Well, just a little in the papers," Sam said. Maybe he had been wrong in passing up the newspaper stories, figuring it was just another one of those political bunk parties.

"I think the leading statesmen of America and Europe feel just as you feel about war, and are sincere in their attempt to eliminate it, don't you?"

"That may be very true," Sam said, beginning to catch on, "but—"

"Was someone in your family in the war? An older brother?"

"No," said Sam. "Nobody."

"You arrived at this conviction yourself, then?"

"Yes," said Sam. While momentarily, into his mind, crowded pictures seen in the paper: ex-soldiers standing in breadlines; and signs: "Give a Soldier a Job"; and in a war movie the earth exploding, with arms, legs, helmets arching among the clods of flying dirt; and the futility, the destruction pictured in that book he had read: *Three Soldiers*. And it seemed to him that he was here, not because he had accidentally started skipping R.O.T.C., but as the end of a thought-out plan of revolt against the vile wrongs on earth.

"Well, now, I don't have to tell you the R.O.T.C. was not instituted as a militaristic measure," the dean said. "We could get into a long argument here about self-defense but that's really beside the point. The R.O.T.C. is here by government order, and there's no alternative. You see, Eisen, this thing is really not up to me. It's up to you. We believe when a man gets to the University he's old enough to think and act for himself. (Oh, yeah?) Now, the R.O.T.C. is a part of the state university. You knew it was here. What it amounts to is a gentleman's agreement—"

Uhuh. Springing the gentleman stuff.

"On the one hand, the state gives you an education. On the other hand, you sacrifice a few hours to military drill. It's healthful, why, most of the fellows enjoy it."

"It's not that," Sam said. "It's the idea—"

"Well, you could have gone to a school where R.O.T.C. is optional."

"I couldn't afford the tuition."

The dean pursed his lips. "Well, Eisen, in that case I should think you'd be willing to comply with the rules of the school that gives you free tuition. You know, ordinarily you would have been automatically expelled for this. But I thought I'd talk it over, see if we could straighten you out. I see you're going to study law. Shucks, you understand the very first idea of law, which makes us obey a lot of rules that might be a bit irksome, privately, but which are designed for the good of the community. You know, sometimes we just work up a resistance to doing what we are told we have to do."

Sam caught the special gleam in the dean's eye, as if the man knew he had touched on the right spot. Maybe all this was the result of his natural contrariness.

". . . But as I say the whole thing is a gentleman's agreement, which you undertook—"

Watch out! Sam felt a warning in his very guts. This beaming, broad, red, *goyish* face, was an enemy face. Here it came:

"I'll tell you, Eisen. There's one kind of fellow that I wouldn't hesitate to invite to my home for dinner, I wouldn't hesitate to introduce him to my daughters"—the dean chuckled openly, as man to understanding man— "I'm sure that's the kind of fellow you are, at bottom. But—"

Sam was blazing. Anyway, he now felt completely free.

"Think it over for a day or two," the dean said. "I'll try and hold up the ax. I don't like to see a fellow get started wrong. A thing like this might influence your entire life. And if you want to talk it over some more, come in and see me."

He offered his hand. Sam restrained an impulse to make a sarcastic remark. He took the hand, and received a firm, fellowy squeeze. In the dean's mind it was a certain thing that he was "straightened out."

"I don't think I'll change my mind," Sam blurted, as he went out.

"Well, we'll see," the dean said, with a friendly grin, for all life was a game.

As he walked down the steps of the building, Sam felt exactly that same wild inner exhilaration he had felt that night coming out of the Freedman basement, from the meeting where he had busted out of the Big Ten. It was a hollow, jerky feeling in his very guts. The same excitement a man might feel on walking out of a job; maybe he has lost something, yet there is an unquenchable singing in the heart, a feeling of lightness, of victory. He belongs to himself again.

Walking down Wright Street, he began to figure out what he would do next. Go back to the downtown law school. There was nothing for him here.

Just go home like that? Kicked out.

And in a flash it was clear to him: he must be the leader. That was the cause of this excited feeling within him, this almost drunken feeling of something big about to happen to him.

All his old passion for leadership, the passion that had driven him on to be the big man in high school, was awake. So far, there had been nothing for him to do, at Illinois. School activities had seemed like kid stuff, he had done all that in high school. The jellybeans and frat boys and sorority girls took care of that stuff, here.

But this was something real, something important, for him to do. He'd wake these college boys up to something serious! He'd call a meeting, he'd give them some talk! He'd knock out the R.O.T.C.!

There were plenty of returned soldiers on campus, they'd back him up all right.

"Don't be a nut," said Shappy, the while he gnawed at an end of a wurst Sam had got from home. "Do you think you can buck the whole caboodle? Why, do you know what you'll run up against? The United States Government."

"Yah," Joe Freedman kidded. "They'll probably send you to Atlanta."

"Oy veh!" Shappy rocked his head, imitating Yiddish woe.

"But even if we don't get anywhere," Sam cried, "at least we can wake up some of these dumbbells."

"Listen, Sam, why be a Bolshevik?" Shappy said, philosophically. "There's a lot of things, as you go through life, that you have to submit to. You can't have everything just the way you want it. So you go to drill a couple of times a week, so what? Is it going to kill you? When you're through you can tell them to kiss your ass."

"That isn't it!" Sam insisted. "The thing is, there are plenty of fellows that feel the way I do! They're just afraid to open their mouths, that's all. If we give them a start, they'll come out."

"Baloney," Shappy said, holding up the wurst.

Joe Freedman drew the pipe out of his mouth, and stuck out his lower lip. "The way I see it, Sam," he said, "your idea is that they have no right to tell us what to do. At the same time you want to go out and tell people what not to do—"

"No, no—" Sam interposed.

Joe continued: "As far as I am concerned, the ideal is letting people decide for themselves, without pushing them one way or the other—"

"That's just the point!" Sam yelled. He walked up and down, swinging his arms at them like a trial lawyer. "Make R.O.T.C. optional. Do you call it deciding for yourself, when you get canned if you don't decide the way they want you to?"

"That's quibbling," Shappy said. "There are other schools."

"Oh, is that so? Well, this is the state school, and I've got as much right here as any other citizen!" Sam declared. That was what he had forgot to tell the dean, damn it.

"Aw, why get so wrought up about it, Sam?" said Joe, scratching the bowl of his pipe. "R.O.T.C. is just a farce, take it as a joke. If it came to a war, and you wanted to be a pacifist, that would be the time to get excited about it."

"Anyway, if it came to a war you'd have to fight anyway," Shappy singsonged. "And at least, with R.O.T.C., you'd be an officer, and have it easy."

"Aw, for cry sake." Sam was disgusted.

"Listen, you got the wrong idea if you think the students would stick with you," Shappy said. "These farmer boys like the horsies, and the bayonet practice makes them remember good old pig-sticking time at home. Say, you raise your voice against the R.O.T.C. and those ags will run you off the campus, on a rail."

"All right, let them, let them!" Sam cried, testily.

"I don't like the idea of military," Joe said. "But at least they taught me how to ride a horse. That's the trouble with you, Sam. You ought to have signed up for the cavalry."

"Aw, what's the use of talking to you guys?" Sam said.

"Yeah, we're just a bunch of rubber stamps!" Shappy winked.

Walking across Wright Street, bitter-minded, absorbed, Sam heard a terrific honk right on top of him, and barely jumped aside in time to escape a Leaping Lena.

A caterwaul of laughter rose from the topless and fenderless flivver, which overflowed with arms and legs of fellows and girls.

"Missed him!" reported a jellybean perched on the rim of the rear seat, riding backwards.

Danger, 5,000,000 Jolts, Sam read, scrawled on the body. And, *Excuse my Back*. And, *Do It Again*. The flivver zigzagged along the street, aiming at pedestrians.

"There's one!" a girl screamed. And the others took up the cry: "Frosh! Frosh!" The car skeetered after a dazed freshman.

. . . Oh, what was the use?

It was Ev Goldberg's turn to entertain the Sunshine Club.

—Did you hear, Sam Eisen got canned from Illinois?

—No! What for?

—Oh, some sort of trouble.

—Girls! don't tell me that woman-hater has been cutting up!

—Naa. It was, he refused to take military training, wasn't that it, Aline?

—That's what Joe said.

—Well, of all things.

—What's he want to get kicked out for a thing like that for?

—Oh, you know Sam. He's so stubborn.

—What's he going to do now?

—How should I know? Haven't you seen him, Lil?

—Me? What have I got to do with Sam Eisen?

—Oh, nothing. I just thought—

—Kindly keep your thoughts to yourself.

—Well, what's got into you!

—You don't have to make any insinuations!

—Aw, be yourself!

"Well, anyway, girls!" said Rose Heller, "I think Sam is to be admired for his idealism. At least he sticks up for what he believes."

Dear Sam: I bet you can't guess who this is from but by now you have probably peeked at the signature so the surprise is over. I just had to write to you, Sam, as I never get a chance to see you any more and tell you I think it was very wonderful of you to stand up for your principles. I think war is a terrible thing and it was wonderful of you to quit the U because they make you take military training. I know you must think I am just a Dumb Dora because of the way I act up all the time but even dumbbells can appreciate a thing like that. I heard about it from the girls, as they were discussing it at a meeting of the Sunshine Club, and I was very proud that I knew the fellow who had done that. Well I used to know him anyway. That is the way with all great men when they get famous, you say I used to know them. Well, so long, Sam. I hope you will not always be a woman-hater. Your friend, Lil.

"He'll never get anywhere pulling that kind of stuff," was Lou Margolis's opinion.

Before his mother, Sam Eisen felt a little ashamed. He would eat, and rush away from the table. Why did she have to pity him? He had felt victorious, until she began watching him with her sad, patient eyes. As though she was afraid to interfere, but only hoped he wouldn't make another disastrous move.

So now she couldn't yammer to all the other wives in the butcher shop that she had a son in the university.

His father annoyed him too. To his father this was only another example of the evil of the world, proving why he, an honest man, could never get beyond a buttonhole maker's machine.

If the old lady bought a pot, and the enamel began to come off, Mr. Eisen glittered with happiness. "See! Swindlers in America! Even in the big downtown stores!" If the boss of the shop told the operators to make single instead of double seams, he was happy, triumphant. "Aha! I told you! Honest manufacturing!" When a strike was called and some of his own friends were caught scabbing: "There you have it! What can you expect in such a world! People are crooks, swindlers, thieves, robbers, and that's all!"

Now, his gold tooth flashing derisively, his eyes glittering behind his aristocratic half-moon glasses, Mr. Eisen declaimed: "Aha! America, a nation! So a boy won't carry a gun, so outside! Outside! You think it is different here than by the Tsar? We are supposed to be dumb. We are supposed we don't know anything. We can't tell them anything, our smart children, but they will find out, they will find out. . . ."

And he looked at Sam as though he were just a young simpleton who had needed this experience to learn what anyone with a grain of sense already knew.

Joe Freedman claimed that his case had nothing to do with Sam's. It was just a coincidence, he said, that out of all the things he could get into a ruckus about, he too should get mixed up with the military. Joe wrote his celebrated theme on military ticktacks because when the funny idea occurred to him, it was irresistible.

So he wrote, on the assignment, "Discuss the Order of the Day":

"There should be more routine and discipline in the daily life of a soldier. In the future recruits will sleep with radio earphones on their heads. At the sound of reveille the soldier will hear the voice of the sergeant booming:

" 'Left eyelid—hup!' At this command, he will open his left eye. The next command will be:

" 'Right eyelid—hup!' Both eyes are now open.

" 'Company—yawn!' commands the sergeant, and all mouths open as one. The mouths remain open until the command: 'Cease yawning!' But it is recommended that a special regulation be provided in case of a fly getting into the mouth of a yawning recruit. He may close his mouth upon the fly.

But in order to discourage malingering, he shall be required to produce the fly after so doing."

Joe snickered as he wrote. He could already hear the class roaring at this cleverness.

"The soldier now hears the command: 'Scratch heads! One, two, three, hup!' " and on and on, through the donning of underpants and pants, to the rolling of the puttees with provisions for swearing: " 'Companneeee—cuss; God damn! Sum bitch! Cease cussing—hup!' " Then came washing, shaving, and the big finale which had Joe actually laughing out loud as he wrote:

" 'To the latrines, march! Company, halt! Hands on flies, hup! Unbutton, hup! One, two, three, four! Snodgrass, this is the third day you have missed the fourth button, report to k.p. All right, men, snap into it. I mean out of it. Now, altogether, boys: Position! Ready! Aim! Fire! I mean water!' "

With that, Joe had to stop. It was too much. He would bust laughing.

One look at Lieutenant Goddard, and the fellows knew fireworks were coming. Goddard stood rigid beside the desk, but anger emanated from him like a phosphorescence. There seemed actually to be a smell of burning. The scar on his chin was glowing and fading with his pulse.

"Private Freedman!" he snapped.

Joe stood up.

"This your paper?" He held it up. Joe took a step forward as if to identify the paper.

"Why, I guess so, if my name's on it." He grinned.

"Wipe that off! Smart aleck! If you think you can get away with this kind of—of—"

"Why, I just meant it as a joke," Joe began.

"*A joke!* So you think the whole R.O.T.C. is just a joke, huh? Why, you, you lousy little—" Lieutenant Goddard checked himself, but with so terrific an effort that his veins bulged. "Get out!" he shrieked. "Get out before I—!"

Joe collected his books and, with an effort at seeming unhurried, unafraid, made his way out of the room.

Whew! He might have known that brass button would have no sense of humor.

And so Joe Freedman, in his turn, was called to confer with the kind-hearted dean. Joe liked to think that he looked at each new face with a sculptor's glance that cut into every crevice for detail, and at the same time organized the whole image into a unified design. "A square John Bull face," he said to himself, "the face of a gentleman farmer." He shambled toward the desk, smirking.

"I'm Joe Freedman."

The dean tilted back, and gave him a slanting look. Taking up the folded theme, the dean moved it against the flat of his hand.

"Freedman, I have to admit that in its way this is a clever little composition." The dean pulled one corner of his mouth into a pshaw smile. "I suppose you had a lot of fun writing it."

Joe's grin grew healthier.

"Well, we can write anything we please. But what we do with our writing is another matter. Now look, Freedman, I want you to try to think of this in another light. Lieutenant Goddard is a gentleman of the military profession. He has prepared himself for this profession just as you are preparing for . . ."

"Architecture."

"Exactly. Now, there is room for a great deal of difference of opinion in this world, but there are some things on which gentlemen agree. They don't insult one another's profession."

Joe's grin slid off his face. Ridiculously, he remembered the first time he had lunched with the group in the Midway studio, and had started to eat before everyone was served, then had seen his error.

So he was not a gentleman. Just a kike whose old man ran a flophouse. And the minute he came among gentlefolk, he showed his coarseness.

". . . naturally, in my job I come into contact with a great many instances of the—well, the thoughtlessness of youth. I suppose a thing like this can be blamed on high spirits. Not a bad thing, when controlled. So—well, Freedman, I guess I could persuade Lieutenant Goddard to accept your apology."

Yet, an impulse of defiance arose in Joe. So what if he was a boor? Why not be himself? The hell with all this pretense and bowing and scraping, and you first my dear Gaston.

"Suppose I don't feel I can apologize?" he heard himself saying in a brave squeak.

The dean didn't turn away, but it was as if he had. His voice tiptoed over offal. "I'll put it quite frankly, Mr. Freedman. If you apologize to Lieutenant Goddard I'll know you're the sort of person I could invite to dinner at my home. If you don't apologize, you're the other sort of person."

Joe tried to pull the grin back onto his face. Ha ha, I'll apologize and see if I get the invite; I hear he has two beauteous daughters. He tried to think: This is unfair! He's putting the whole issue on a personal plane.

He wondered if the dean had pulled the same thing on Sam Eisen. No. That was a simple case for expulsion—Sam had no imagination.

"Take a few days to think it over, if you like," said the dean, with a warm smile. "Meanwhile I'm afraid you'll have to consider yourself under suspension."

Every time Joe decided to apologize he would remember that Sam Eisen let himself be expelled rather than knuckle down to those tin soldiers.

Over and over he told himself that his case and Sam's were entirely different: his case involved the principle of free speech. If he stood up for his principles, and got canned, everybody at home would think he was just a Bolshevik like Sam.

If he went home the only idea the folks would have of it would be that he got canned. You couldn't explain a thing like this to them. They were proud of you and you had to do things to keep the damn fools from feeling disappointed in their smart son.

Sylvia would think he was a failure.

He'd show them! He'd send that theme to H. L. Mencken, with cartoons of Lieutenant Goddard and the dean! He'd go out in a blaze of glory, making Lieutenant Goddard the laughing stock of the school.

"I am still waiting," he would conclude his article, "for the dean's invitation to dinner!"

At the board next to Joe worked a laughing kid from Danville known as Blondy. One of those clean-cut, typically American-looking boys, with a right-angled jaw and cool blue eyes. The kind of guy who pulled practical jokes with thumbtacks but always had a buck to lend, cigarettes to pass around, an extra sheet of tracing paper.

He acted light-headed all the time, bubbling over his board with dirty songs, limericks. But Blondy could be serious, too. If any of the fellows got in a jam, he would grow calm and cool, like simmering water, when the heat is shut off.

A kind of taken-for-granted friendship existed between Joe and Blondy. What Blondy had, that Joe knew he could never have, was this complete acceptance of, and by, his environment. With him, Danville seemed exactly the right place to have come from, his house probably the rightest place in Danville. And now it occurred to Joe that Blondy was exactly the sort of person whom the dean would naturally ask home for dinner; Joe could picture Blondy taking out the dean's daughter, and loving her up, in a car. And the dean expecting him to do so.

"Hey! Where y' going with the T-square?" Blondy kidded as Joe packed his stuff.

"Blondy, I must bid you farewell." And Joe told him the trouble.

"So they want you to crayfish, huh?" Blondy said, his face still, and serious.

Even the expression sounded foreignly American. Small-townish, *goyish*. Joe guessed its meaning.

"Yah."

"Gonna do it?"

"I dunno." He wanted to ask: "Would you?" but the look of intent interest on Blondy's face prevented him.

He knew that Blondy would not have apologized; but at the same time, refracted through Blondy, his whole scheme for "revenge" by writing up the incident seemed cheap.

As he walked around campus, feeling that perhaps he was taking his farewell, Joe worried and struggled to make a decision; the incident seemed to augment in significance all the time. If he were home, talking it over with Rudy Stone, Rudy would tell him to apologize, and mean it. Mitch—well, Mitch would never have got into this kind of a scrape. Alvin would send the article to Mencken!

"Hey! What's the order of the day?" Shappy kidded, passing Joe on the campus.

"One, two, three—button up!" laughed Harry Josephs; the contents of Joe's theme had got around.

"What'd they do, can you?"

"They're sending for Pershing, for a court martial."

"Not yet; suspended. I'm supposed to apologize."

"Go on, apologize! What'll it cost you?" Shappy grinned, and the gang passed on.

In the late afternoon light the white mansion pillars of the Women's Building glowed like a row of smiling teeth; the brick of the building had a hearth-red warmth. This was the building partly designed by Stanford White, before his death. A man brought up in a house like this wouldn't have to be told how a gentleman behaves.

And Joe thought, hang it, there was something down here that he hadn't met before in his life. It was as though this were inner America. Sure, Chicago was America, but America made up of dagos, Irish, Poles, Jews, the bloody nineteenth ward, and back o' the yards, and Maxwell Street and Little Italy. You came down to a place like this, with space between the buildings, and things set at haphazard and yet with a certain style, this was like a homely living room assembled of odd pieces, but by people who couldn't be wrong. Here were these houses with their white-pillared porches, and they were right, and he was wrong.

Joe walked away from the campus, into Champaign. This was just an Illinois town, with houses set back from the streets, each on its lawn. And he suddenly had a complete idea of how he wanted his life to be, to live in some such house as one of these, with gables and cupolas, and a crazy little glass observatory on the roof; to have a garage fixed over into a studio with a big skylight; to walk back into the garage and work at sculpture all day, to walk up to the house and wash, and Sylvia would be waiting, dinner ready, maybe a kid with a snotty nose.

When you thought of the row on row of two-story graystone fronts on Central Park Avenue, Clifton Park Avenue, Lawndale Avenue, Sawyer Avenue, Millard Avenue, when you thought of the red-brick six-flat buildings wall to wall on Douglas Boulevard and on Independence Boulevard, you realized that this sometimes ugly heterogeny of the rural town, this styled stylelessness, these old houses built by some skilled carpenter with the missus telling him to stick out a baywindow there, stick on a bit of porch there, this was the thing, this was Blondy, this was America out of which true gentlemen came, gentlemen who knew enough not to insult their fellow-man's profession, gentlemen who asked each other to dinner.

He was about to push open the door of a tobacco shop, when he noticed the wooden Indian that stood by the stoop.

Ordinarily you took these things as part of the landscape, like fireplugs. Maybe it was the way the sunlight illuminated one side of the wooden face, as though the Indian stood by a campfire.

Life-size, and mounted on a two-foot pedestal, with paint so weatherworn that it seemed an integral part of the wood, with a large split up one of the legs, and a crack in the head.

Joe smiled. He could see some small-town carver chopping this image out of a log, spending days of patient and happy toil with a whittling knife probably, incising the long rows of markings on the feathers.

Why, this was American art. Why must he always go at things roundabout? Architecture was okay, but in his heart he knew it was just an idea of having a profession while he tried to become a sculptor. This was where he should start from. It would be better to be some small-town wood-carver, gravestone-carver than a fancy garret artist. To be part of a place, have a house to live in . . . He touched the cracked wood. Yah, them days are gone forever.

Joeboy Dear: . . . but I must try not to be selfish, because if you do get expelled you'll come back to Chicago and we will be near each other. . . . But, Joey, can't you treat the whole thing as if it were beneath you? I mean, I know you are impetuous and idealistic and I am glad of that, but why should we argue with people who are so narrow-minded? Would it be right for you to let your quarrel with them make you leave school? After all, architecture is the main thing, so why let those dizzy officers interfere? . . . Joe, I have been looking at nothing but cigar-store Indians since your thrilling description. . . .

Oh, and here is some gossip. Sam Eisen, the woman-hater, is falling for Lil Klein since he came back!

Sweetheart, I wish you were here. I hold your hand. And now, a kiss. Your girl, Sylvia.

P.S. Couldn't you just write a formal note of apology for those nitwits, and everybody would know you didn't mean it, and the laugh would be on them?

Joe smiled, and put the letter in his pocket.

Young Rabbi Waller was a recent graduate of the Cincinnati School, where rabbis could be as liberal, as reformed, as they pleased. And he had come to the B'nai Brith with the idea that they ought to get hold of the younger generation of Jews while they were still in the colleges. So the B'nai Brith had given him some money to try to establish a Jewish Foundation at a few universities. This Foundation was to be a sort of club, where Jewish boys could gather, play chess, and, the books being left around, maybe they would do a little reading in Jewish fields.

The dean, chatting with Rabbi Waller, said: "Lieutenant Goddard really feels quite badly about the whole thing, and I think Freedman ought to be brought around. I don't like to have to expel him over this, but the way he's acting, he's going to force me to do it."

"I have an idea," said Rabbi Waller. "But I don't want him to think I'm trying to influence him."

One night when Joe stopped in at Shappy's place, Waller was there.

"Pheh!" Shappy cried. "What are you burning in that chimney, horse manure?"

"The trouble is you pups are so used to smoking molasses and wrapping paper, you don't know real tobacco when you smell it," Joe advised him.

"That's Ploughboy, isn't it?" Waller remarked.

Joe nodded. He hadn't taken to Waller, because, first, he didn't see why the Jews had to go off in their own corner and have a Jewish Foundation, and secondly, he believed if a man was going to be a rabbi, then let him be a rabbi with a beard and heavy eyebrows. He was against the new breed of rabbis who looked like dentists, with their toothbrush mustaches and slick hair.

Waller had pulled out his tobacco pouch. He offered it. Joe sniffed. "Purty good," he assented.

"I mix my own," Waller said. "Want to try it?"

"Say, that's a noble pipe," Joe remarked, as the rabbi filled the bowl.

"Dunhill," Waller confessed. "I got it in London last year."

"How much are they over there?"

"Well, I paid a pound for this one. It's worth twice as much here."

Some day, Joe thought, he would go over, and bring back a Dunhill.

"Say, what happened with those *paskudnyaks*, are they going to shoot you at sunrise?" Shappy asked.

"That's one thing, a Jew can never get along in the army," Waller laughed. "They tell a story about how a couple of *Yidlach* missed a chance to win the war for Russia. It seems that there was a squad of real religious Jews on the Russian-German front, you know, Litvaks who carried *tfillin* in their knapsacks. When prayer time came they needed one more to make up a *minyan*. 'Come on,' says Chayim Traask, 'I know a place we'll maybe find a Jew.' So they crawl over to the enemy lines. There's a latrine, and there they wait. Well, it just happened that the Kaiser was visiting the Russian front, and he suddenly had to go. Sure enough, the two Yids see the Kaiser come in. They give him time to pull his pants down, but then they take one look, sigh, and beat it. Their pals jumped on them. 'Where's our *minyan*? Didn't you find anyone?' 'Yah, we caught one,' they admit, 'but the devil take him, it turned out to be the Kaiser, and he wasn't even a Jew, so we left him sitting there.' "

Joe was beginning to like the rabbi. Waller told another story, about a Russian Jew who was an orderly to a general, who beat and kicked him around. Every week, the little Jew's wife sent him a package of kosher food; one Saturday the general sees him eating it, grabs a piece of *kishke*, and gobbles it down. Fine! Wonderful cooking! After that, the poor little Jew is a goner. The general is nuts about kosher food, and eats up his whole package every week. Then the Jew decides to fix the general. He writes a letter to his wife. Next week, when the food comes as usual, the general gobbles it up, smacks his lips, rubs his belly. But the Jew runs outside and lies down on the ground and laughs till he nearly splits a gut. What are you laughing at, Yankel? That *poyr*, he says, that general, he likes kosher *kishkes*, he ate up the whole package, and do you know what they were? This time they were *treif!* From a pig!"

Shappy screamed with laughter. Waller went on. His store of Yiddish yarns was inexhaustible, and in each there was that characteristic Jewish twist, that humbled arrogance, that irony of the servant who secretly knows himself to be superior to his master. Gradually, as he talked, he threw in more serious touches, and he worked back to earlier wars, to stories of Jews who starved and maimed themselves to evade military service in Russia, and back further, to stories of Jews in times of the Inquisition, to stories of Kiddush ha Shem, when whole cities of Jews were burned by Crusaders, and back further, to stories of the false Messiahs, and of a Jew named Reubeni who sought to gather an army and recapture Palestine. . . .

And as Waller, a young fellow from New York, a smooth-faced rabbi who smoked a Dunhill, went on talking, Joe remembered some of the stories told by Sylvia's uncle Bialystoker, and got a kick out of contributing them to the session.

It was pretty late when they went out for coffee. By that time the question of the apology had been settled, somewhere far back in Joe's mind. The little lieutenant, with his posturing, his honor, was far beneath his contempt. You wrote something with a Yiddish twist. Something that apologized, and yet did not apologize. For instance: "Dear Lieutenant Goddard: I am sorry I turned in that paper making fun of the army. Had I known it would offend you, I would not have turned it in." See? And you thumbed your nose at his behind.

When Joe was back at work over his board, Blondy Walsh said, quietly: "So you crayfished, eh?"

"Huh?"

"You apologized to the loot."

"Oh, yah. It wasn't worth it. Wait'll I tell you what I wrote . . ." Joe began.

But Blondy, humming "The Bastard King of England" over his board, seemed hardly interested.

Sam Eisen heard from Shappy about Joe's case. Sam shrugged, wryly. Kids, was his opinion. They don't know what it's all about.

A Modern Marriage

Up to one moment Estelle was goofy about him. When he came back from New York in the tin lizzie he had bought with his earnings from the summer outdoor sprints, and on the very first night honked his horn in front of her house, Did you miss me kid, Oh boy I'll say I did, she was just goofy about Sol. It was something he did to her, his big good-natured face and his curly hair and his warm strong body. She felt like she would fly to him anywhere and do whatever he wanted.

It was swell all through the fall. Going out to the dunes with some of the bunch, driving the lizzie, and the two of them getting lost accidentally on purpose on some deep waste hollow of sand, and doing it there. Oh, do it again!

In the long evenings with the kids squatting around a fire, and Sol with his uke singing, "Do It Again," and none of the kids knew what the song meant to them, to each other. Do it again!

She got to feeling she was going wild with passion, letting herself go like this. The first fumbling time when he had been sick and she had crept into the brass bed they had been so bashful, the both of them so mixed up. But through the Indian summer Estelle began to feel, oh, it was wonderful, there was nothing like it, doing it with Sol! She would seize his hair in her hands and pull, harder, harder. Oh, ride me, big boy, ride me, ride me down!

In her house when her folks were out, with their ears awake for the sound of feet on the stairs; in the car, on a side road that ran off Ogden Avenue, she was hot, she was unashamed; she knew everybody was talking about her but she didn't care.

Just his coming near her made her want it. It was terrible.

None of the girls knew what it was like.

They! Just kids.

Then Estelle got a scare. She was a week overdue. She didn't want to say anything to Sol as yet, but after the first week he began acting kind of funny, as though he guessed something was wrong. Did he keep tab on her time? That was something mysterious and unclean they never mentioned to each other, but she guessed he knew what it was all about. Sometimes when she was about due, and they were necking, she would feel his big hand moving lower on her back, exploring, to discover whether she was wearing something extra under her clothes.

After two weeks, she could stand it no longer. She was jumpy and full of mean cracks, and that night when he took her to the College Inn after seeing *Merton of the Movies*, he said something about all the dough he was spending lately, and she remarked: "What's the matter, aren't you getting your money's worth?" So he got sore.

She waited all day for him to call. Oh, God, it was terrible. Maybe he was calling and the phone was out of order, if only a call came so she would know the phone was all right. Oh, God, it was terrible, in spite of being modern and unconventional, all a girl could do was sit and wait for the man to call.

A girl should never call a fellow. Even now, with what she had to tell him, she couldn't lower herself so much as to call him and give him the idea she was chasing.

But in the morning she couldn't stand it, and went to the drug store and phoned. Of course his mother had to answer.

"Who? Solly? Who is it please? . . . Oh, how are you, Estelle? So many girls are always calling up Solly, you know they go crazy for him when they see him riding the bicycle. So he tells me, don't even answer them. Wait, I'll tell him you are calling." Her voice hung for a moment. Estelle could almost feel it add: "What do you want him for?"

When Solly came over, his face was white and his lower lip hung. Estelle had never seen him look like that. Something went out of her.

"Aw, gee, kid," he mumbled, his eyes fishing away, "are you sure? Are you positive? I thought you were watching out." She couldn't help sensing the peevishness in his voice, now-you've-gone-and-done-it.

"I can't tell for sure," she explained. "But I've always been so regular."

"Listen. Cantcha do something?"

He didn't say, I'll stick by you, kid. He didn't say, If anything goes wrong, we'll get hitched. So she could have answered, Aw, don't worry, Solly.

"Can't you ask some of the girls what to do?" he blundered. "Can't you ask in a drug store?"

He got so shifty-eyed, so yellow-faced, that in her disgust she didn't want to spare him anything. "You'll have to take care of it. It wasn't my fault."

"Huh! How do I know it was me? I always used a safe!"

164

She went hot and cold. Her fingers curled to claws. So that was all she was to him! Chesty! With all kinds of girls calling him up. "Oh, I hope you choke!" she sputtered, inadequately. "I hope you choke!"

"Say, Plotsy, say, I know a fellow that—his girl got caught." Sol knew his face was a give-away. Anybody could tell it was about himself. But Runt was a good guy. Runt knew his way around.

Plotkin told him the name of some pills that cost fifty cents.

Sol avoided the drug store where Rudy worked, or any store in the neighborhood. He drove over to Madison and Kedzie. There were Christmas displays in the store windows. Merry Christmas. Yah, Marry Christmas, as the fellows said.

The drug-store guy got the stuff without a word, but soaked him a buck.

Estelle opened the box and read the ad inside the cover. *Safe and reliable. The kind your mother used.*

If that wasn't a scream, The kind your mother used! She laughed so hard you would think that would have done the trick, itself.

If only she could tell it to the girls!

The day after Christmas was a terribly cold day, with a blizzard swirling in the streets. Estelle lay around all day. The pain ground and ground. A half-dozen times her mother had asked her: "What's the matter, Estelle, don't you feel good?" The old lady could tell. But maybe she thought she was just being late.

Well, that bum was lucky.

Maybe she ought to call up the punk and relieve his anxiety. But she had no feelings about him, any more. What had it been, love, that had come and gone? Oh, she was getting to know so much, more than any of the girls.

Sol came over. The blizzard had stopped but it was bitter cold, and the wind shot along the streets. When he came in, his nose was red and his eyes were watery with cold. He looked so funny that for a moment she got a quiver of the old feeling for his cuteness, his boyishness.

Mrs. Green stood in the doorway saying: "Well, how are you, Solly, you are a stranger here lately," and finally backed out of the room, looking at them darkly, suspiciously.

Now they were alone, Estelle said: "Well I got a Christmas present for you. It was a false alarm."

"Gee, that's swell!" He was all changed. He was ready to act as though nothing had happened between them. He started to tell her how his car had frozen.

But she didn't respond, and after a minute there seemed nothing to talk about.

"How—how about New Year's, kid?" he said as he was leaving, sort of dutifully.

"We'll see. Call me tomorrow," she said, but she was already checking over who might call her up, for a New Year's date.

By, Sol.

She didn't feel sad, she didn't feel blue. She felt that from now on, she would know just how to handle men. Live and learn.

"Gee that's cute!" Estelle cried as Lil appeared at the edge of the Garfield Park rink, wearing a yellow and blue knitwear set of muffler, beret, and mittens. "Is it new?"

"Mandel's," Lil reported. "You'll never guess how much!"

"I'll bite."

"Five-fifty."

"Is that all!"

The girls squatted to strap on their skates.

"Look, we got an audience," Lil whispered. A couple of fellows were bending over pretending to fix their skates, trying to get a look up.

Estelle snorted. Maybe last year she would have got a kick out of it, like Lil, but now she knew what it was all about.

They climbed to their feet and skated right by the fellows, one of whom remarked: "Redheads are hot stuff."

Skating along, Estelle was beginning to feel herself coming to life, when out of a clear sky Lil piped: "Estelle, do you think a girl ought to give herself to the man she loves?"

Estelle nearly let out a hoot of laughter; but Lil looked so cute with her wind-reddened cheeks that she wanted to give her a big-sister hug.

"Of course everybody says a girl makes herself cheap if she gives herself to a man unless they're married," Lil went on. "They say after that he don't want her any more. But I don't know. Why shouldn't they love each other even more?"

"I guess it depends on the fella and the girl," Estelle said.

"That's just what I say! I think if they really love each other, they ought to go the whole way. I mean, what do you get being a virgin, anyway? I think it's dumb to be a virgin. If you really loved a fella, would you do it?" Lil said.

"I guess you do anything when you're in love."

"I mean, when people can't get married, and they may have to wait years and years, what's the sense of waiting?" Lil pleaded. "I don't mean just a cheap affair. I mean real love."

"Kiddo! Have you got it bad!" Estelle exclaimed.

The two fellows were clowning now, almost skating into the girls, then veering off with a haw haw and pretending to nearly fall.

"I hope they flop!" Lil said so they could hear. Then she couldn't help giggling as the taller of the two staggered on his skates, took a comical flop, and then pretended to count stars.

But immediately she grew aloof. "The thing is, it must be so *different*," she said to Estelle. "That's what scares me. It's—it's—something you can't take back. It must be like being born or something. If only I knew what it was like."

"There's only one way to find out," Estelle said.

"Wouldn't you be scared? I mean"—her tone became chummier than ever—"if you were in love with someone. Like Sol, for instance. Would you do it?"

"I'm not so crazy about Sol," Estelle said.

"Honest? I thought you were going steady."

Estelle snorted. It might as well get around that she and Sol had bust up. "I don't think I'll see him any more, altogether."

"WHAT!"

"Oh, I got kind of tired of him."

Her tone was final, closing the subject. The girls skated.

"They say fellas don't like it the first time with a girl," Lil resumed. Her voice was high, brittle, flappery again. "I don't think it's really worth while, being a virgin, do you, Estelle?"

Estelle replied in the same sophisticated tone: "Yah, think of what you miss!"

Arms around waists, they swooped over the pond, their heavy wool skirts deliciously blown against their legs. The two fellas chased them.

"My mother and father have gone out," Lil informed Sam. "Boy, are they swell tonight! They went to the Del Roi."

Sam hadn't yet decided where to go. Of course it was too late now to get tickets for the swell places, like Terrace Gardens or the College Inn.

"Shall we call up some of the kids and see what they're doing?" she said. "Syl Abramson is having a New Year's party."

He sat down on the couch. Naturally she sat on his lap and put her mouth ready for a hello kiss. There was no hurry about going any place.

They were necking fiercely, yet, in every movement that she made, there was a strangeness, abruptness, jerkiness, and sometimes her eyes stared wide at him with an expanding wonder.

"What's the matter, honey, is something wrong?" he said, at her long silence.

"No, no," her voice piped. She flung her arm around his neck, and gave him a long French kiss.

Sam remembered the time over a year ago when he had first had a crush on Lil, and had seen her necking in the car with Mort Abramson; but this was as if she were trying to erase everything she had ever done, and give herself to him.

As he picked her up, and carried her with fiercely tense muscles, her heart was filled with expanding sworls of fright—oh, what if the whole thing should go wrong?—but with a blind clenching little pride at her own recklessness; and beyond everything, her heart was filled with oh I love him I do love him oh I love him it's not wrong if you love.

When the bells began to ring and the whistles to blow, Lil couldn't help giggling. "That's for us, Sammy. Our New Year. Oh, aren't you glad we did it this way?" She slid the sheet from over her, and reveled, mischievously voluptuous, in the sight of her naked legs so nice and firmly formed, so young and sweet against the bed.

Sam got up and walked to the window. He looked so odd standing there naked, his hand against the brocade drape. Her eyes traveled slowly down his wide back. He was square-set, solid, and strong.

It had hurt a little, but she didn't feel any different.

"Sam!" she said, her triumph and happiness bubbling in her voice.

He turned and looked at her, so seriously. "Funny face!" she said.

"I love you, Lil," he said, awfully serious.

She skipped over and stood against him naked, and kissed him. Right there in the window, listening to the pistol shots and the auto horns and the factory whistles.

After a moment, she experienced a real womanly feeling of protection for his body against drafts and colds, and sickness and decay. It swept through her as something she had never felt before. "You better put something on, you'll catch cold, dear," she said, and knew she would make him wear rubbers when it rained.

"Wasn't this a swell way to have a New Year's party?" she giggled, feeling cute and clever again. "Was it a good party, my lover?" Tasting the strange word.

"Well, one thing about it, it certainly was a surprise," Aline Freedman said.

"Those kids are crazy!" Rose Heller insisted. "What will they live on?"

"I call it a gyp," put in Ev Goldberg. "The first one in the bunch to get married, and we don't even get a wedding."

"If you ask me," Thelma Ryskind said, "it looks kind of fishy. Lil wouldn't pass up the chance to have a big wedding, unless there was a reason."

"For my part, I don't think Sammy Eisen was in such a rush to get married either. Unless he had to," Aline offered.

"I wouldn't put it past Lil."

"She certainly worked fast. Why, when did he come back from Illinois?"

"Oh, that was months ago," Skinny Heller said. "It must be six months. That's time enough."

There was a shriek of concerted laughter; Skinny blushed.

Mrs. Heller came from the kitchen and stood grinning with pleasure at the enjoyment of the girls.

"Oh, I just noticed, Mrs. Heller," Celia Moscowitz said. "Isn't this a new rug?"

"Uh-huh," said Skinny. "Genuine oriental."

The girls all bent to examine the rug, chirping and marveling; is it real Persian or American Persian? How much? But of course the Hellers got their furniture wholesale through their store. No wonder they kept their flat so beautiful!

"I like to have a nice home for my children," Mrs. Heller said, as she retired to the kitchen.

"Well, I'll say one thing for Lil, she certainly got more out of it than Estelle," Thelma remarked.

"Meow!" from Rose Heller.

"As far as I am concerned, Sam Eisen is no loss."

Ev Goldberg remarked: "Some sheik."

"But why all the secrecy? Was she afraid we'd steal him away from her or something?"

"Oh, listen, girls, what's the idea of all this anyway!" Syl Abramson started to make a speech. "After all Lil is our friend and so is Sam and anyway I think it's disgraceful to run them down like this. Maybe it just didn't occur to you that they might happen to have got married because they love each other!" Her cheeks were burning.

"That's right," Aline Freedman voted. "We certainly are acting like a bunch of old hens."

"Oh, what does it hurt to dish a little dirt?"

"The trouble is," Skinny Heller observed, "her getting married makes us all feel like a bunch of old maids."

—Skinny, if you don't take the cake!

—Well, Lil was the youngest one of the bunch, wasn't she?

—That's right! Can you beat it!

—She's just your age, isn't she, Syl?

—Girls, we better get busy!

—But what's he going to do? How are they going to live?

—That's a heck of a way to get married.

—I wouldn't get married unless I had an apartment all fixed up and ready to move into.

—They'll probably live with her folks for a while.

—Listen, Sam isn't so dumb, don't forget old man Klein has plenty.

—Oh, Thelma, that's all you think about people.

—Girls. We ought to send Lil something.

—I don't see why. She certainly didn't act as if we were even friends of hers.

—Haven't you any romance in your soul? It was an elopement!

—Listen, how much have we got in the treasury?

—Maybe we could buy her a layette.

—Thelma! Will you cut that out!

"Oh, Mrs. Heller! You shouldn't have bothered!" Celia cried, as Mrs. Heller brought in a tray.

Mrs. Heller beamed on them. "Well, girls, what do you know about Lil Klein, she fooled you all, hah? She beat you to it! My my my, they are growing up and getting married already!" She surveyed them all, these lovely girls, so young, so fresh, so sweet, such fine young American girls.

We'll Build a Sweet Little Nest

Here is how things stood with Sam. Counting commissions he was pulling down thirty, thirty-five a week on the floor of the C. and J. Haberdashery Shop on State Street. He was good at selling. His intense manner pushed people, and the honesty in his face, due to his idealism, gave men confidence. He didn't look like such a kid, but could pass for twenty-three easily. His quick, heavy beard, always showing the shaving swath, gave him maturity.

He figured that in no time at all he should become a branch manager in the C. and J. chain. There was no competition. All the guys in the store were either middle-aged deadheads with dandruff dribbling onto their coats, or young pimply-faced smart alecks.

Sam figured he knew just what he was doing, getting married. He saw how all the rest of the fellows went around sniffing up girls' legs, went around with always dirty minds, like babies with dirty pants. His own body gave him no rest. When he was near Lil, all his guts were molten with love-desire. He needed her all the time.

And what could they do? Chances like that time New Year's night were rare. He had no car. He couldn't take a girl like Lil to a hotel, and anyway, that cost a lot, and besides, she couldn't stay all night. He wanted to be with her all night, at least once. The only way was to get married, and then he could have her like he wanted.

He resisted his conclusions as long as he could. After all he was so young, he might meet someone else, later. Then what would he do?

Other fellows wouldn't think of getting married till they were all set. But it gave him a kind of pleasure to feel he could take on the added burden of early marriage, and make good.

And sure, he really loved her. When he saw her cute and pert, waiting for him, ready to do whatever he wanted to do, a melting took place inside of him. He was crazy about her from that New Year's night, when she had stripped the sheet from her body and lain bare on the white bed, so brave, and yet so timid, so wise with her smooth sunny head and yet so bashful that she half turned away when his eyes went over her body. He was nuts about her. How she could make goo-goo eyes and be a kewpie doll, and in the next moment, before he himself knew he was tired of that line, could change to an intelligent modern girl, discussing serious things, their problems, their life! When he got near her he just went to pieces with having to have her.

So there was a Saturday that was just a little windy, and full of outdoor pep, yet with a warm sun; Lil met him at noon, she had her father's Dodge, and all of a sudden he wanted to go out to the country, to the dunes.

The dunes were deserted. They climbed, and stood on the highest sandhill and looked at the lake, so wide and clean, and even the Gary steel mills looked fine and clean in the spring air.

They passed a bunch of shacks, and, oh, if they could only stay all night, and all tomorrow. But Lil's mother would have conniption fits. "Tell her we had a whole gang out here." "She'll want to know who, and call them up." They started to drive back, but going through Gary there was an electric sign: Justice of the Peace. Legal Marriages Performed Here.

"What does he have to advertise it for?" Lil asked.

"Oh, Indiana is where couples from Chicago come, when they elope," Sam said.

So, on the spur of the moment, they did it. And went back to the dunes and rented a cottage for the night, and it had a real patchwork quilt. "Some honeymoon," Sam apologized. "I don't want a honeymoon, you're my honeymoon!" Lil sang, and squeezed him.

And she loved to tell the story of how she happened to get married: "We were driving home from the dunes, and there was the sign: Justice of the Peace; so convenient!" She loved to tell it like a harum scarum adventurous modern girl who would do anything on the spur of the moment. "In Gary! Imagine!"

But Sam knew all the time what he was doing.

As they got up from the table Sam realized he was a head taller than his father-in-law; this gave him an odd shock. Why, his father-in-law was just a little Jew. One week when he had had good luck on commissions, and earned more than his own father earned at the shop, Sam had experienced the same queer grown feeling.

Mr. Klein was one of those skinny little real estate men with sharp shoulders, a derby, suits with hard edges, and a cigar always in his mouth.

Sam had nothing against Mr. Klein, in fact he was anxious to like him, but it was a funny thing that Mr. Klein reminded him of their landlord, and of all the landlords they had ever had: the *allrightniks* to whom rent had to be paid.

Lil was helping her mother clear away the dishes, twittering: sit down, ma, rest, I'll do it; for Mrs. Klein was one of those sickly women who nevertheless insist on doing things around the house. She was always going to new doctors, trying chiropractors and electric treatments; at the table she had asked Sam: "What do you think, this Couey, do you think there is something to it?" And Lil teasingly told how she had caught her mother reciting: "Every day, in every way, I am growing better and better."

"You mean fetter and fetter!" Mr. Klein had jested, for that was Mrs. Klein's trouble, she kept putting on weight. "It ain't flesh, it's unhealthy," she insisted.

"Well, Sam, smoke?" said Mr. Klein, offering a cigar.

Sam mumbled: "Don't mind if I do."

"Well, my boy," Mr. Klein started out, in a bold, salesmanlike voice, "I guess I don't know what to say any more than you do; I only got one daughter, and I never had a son-in-law before." He cackle-chuckled.

"Well, you're the first father-in-law I ever had," Sam said.

"So we're even!" They both laughed, restrainedly. So far it was fine.

"Well, tell me, Sam," withdrawing his cigar with a sucking noise; "what is your ambition in life?"

Sam froze. Then he pitied Mr. Klein, all tight and creased like a real estate bond, and trying to talk to his son-in-law.

"This is the first chance we have had for a man-to-man talk," Mr. Klein said. "Sam, I won't conceal from you that if you had asked me, I would have said you should both be a little bit older before you—ah—sign up for a life term. But nowadays we old folks got to take a back seat. Youth will be youth, and what can we do about it?"

Sam squirmed.

"Oh, Sam, Lil didn't mention, what kind of business is your father in?"

"The clothing business," Sam said. But the next moment he corrected himself: "He isn't in any business, he's a buttonhole maker."

"Oh, ah. Well, Lil tells me you are going back to law school. That's a fine thing, Sam. You look to me like an ambitious feller and you know I got quite a bit of law business myself." He puffed. "I know people, I could help you get a start. How long do you have to go before you finish?"

"Nearly two more years."

"So long?"

"I missed out on a couple of semesters."

"Well, what is a year more or less?" The cigar waved. "Tell me, Sam, what kind of a job have you got? How much do you make? Haha, it don't hurt if I ask you this now, the worst is done already, haha."

Sam told him.

"Well that ain't so bad for a boy your age. That's doing pretty good! But listen, Sam, if I can help you out, don't hesitate to ask me."

Lil was wearing a ribbony negligee and as she came and curled on his lap it still felt shocking to see her combination undies and the gentle dent the garter made around her thigh. She braided his forelock and coaxed: "What'll it hurt you, honey? It's just to make them feel good, it'll only take a couple of hours and it'll be all over. You know you owe them something because if it wasn't for them there wouldn't be any me. Or would you be better off without me?"

"Now, Lil, baby, we agreed we weren't going to have any public wedding and make an exhibition of ourselves." He had to watch out; she was going to try to wind him around her little finger.

"It's only for mother's sake, you know a mother loves to see her daughter's wedding and here I didn't even give her a break. Honest, Sammy, she's really a sick woman and I'd feel so bad if anything happened to her and I knew I had disappointed—"

"Oh, everybody knows we're married already and why make fools of ourselves?"

"Well, it can be the Jewish wedding. Lots of times there's a couple of weeks in between."

"What do we want with a *chuppe* and all that junk?"

"It isn't for us, Sam." She moved subtly on his lap. "Honey, it's for them. After all we owe them some consideration . . ."

"Well, I'm not going to make a public exhibition of myself. All those kids in the bunch are gabbing about us already and if they think they're going to come and stare—"

"Oh, but we wouldn't have any of them! It'll be private, just for the two families. We can have it right here in the house."

Until they were in bed, and Sam was still saying: "But, Lil, you know I don't believe in weddings, all that stuff is the bunk . . ." when he heard her giggle. "What's so funny about it?"

"It's so," she giggled, "funny"—giggle—"talking about it—wedding— when we're"—giggle—"in bed like this!" and with a burst of laughter, she cuddled herself against him.

He had to laugh.

"Monkey!" he said.

"Bear!" she cried. "Grrr."

So Lil bought hand-made Italian lingerie in the Stevens shop, and the darlingest wedding dress of white satin, with a sweepy hemline high in front and low in back, suggesting a train, and with a trim of real ermine circling low on her hips.

Lil saw in the paper the picture of Gloria Morgan being wed to Reginald Vanderbilt, wearing her mother's bridal veil. And what was her surprise when her own mother dug a wedding veil out of an old bundle stowed away in the basement. As her mother, with a trembly diffidence, offered her the veil—for who knew how an American girl would react to old-fashioned customs?—Lil really cried. Why were the old folks so ashamed of themselves? When her family did things just like the Vanderbilts!

What a chance she had passed up, to have a swell wedding, and show the whole bunch how she had beat them to it! The house would really be too small, even for their relatives, so why not have the wedding in the Temple Judea? And just a small reception afterward, in the basement ballroom. They could get Husk O'Hare's Orchestra.

". . . But, Sammy, what's the difference? If we're going to have a wedding anyway we might as well have some fun out of it!"

"Fun! If that's your idea of fun—!"

". . . A wedding is the bride's affair anyway. The bride's family pays for the wedding so you have nothing to say about it!"

Her voice had risen to a shrill quavering note. They would be heard. That was the hell of living with her parents; Sam felt they were being watched, listened to, every moment. Well, that would be over in a few days, thank God, though how in hell he was going to buy a flat full of furniture he couldn't figure out. He hated the idea of installment buying.

"Listen, Lil, we've got to get this straight right now. So we'll understand each other, about things." He kept his voice calm, while he held her hand. "Now, if you wanted a fancy wedding, you should have asked for it in the first place, instead of trying to coax it out of me by bits. Let's always be square and open with each other. Now, it was in the back of your mind that you could gradually coax me into it, wasn't it?"

"Oh, Sam, how can you know all my thoughts!" Lil capitulated, filled with admiration for her husband, and figuring she'd better be more roundabout, after this.

In the afternoon, when the girls started coming over, Sam didn't know where to hide.

From the bedroom, where Lil was showing her things, he could hear their squeaks and exclamations. And Lil's constantly reiterated, "But you know Sam, he just wouldn't let me have a public wedding, it's so old-fashioned . . ."

Aline Freedman and Celia Moscowitz, Ev Goldberg and Thelma. He went out for a walk, but Rose Heller met him on the stairs. She took his hand and said: "Oh, I do wish you every happiness, Sam, oh, I do," and looked straight into his eyes.

She wasn't so bad.

Mainly, he didn't want to see any of the fellows. He was through with them all, with the whole bunch. He was going off by himself, to work hard, and to win out.

The flat was so crowded with people that Sam got kind of excited himself. And Lil looked so sweet in that white dress, with the roll of fur around her girl's hips circling as she moved, like a hoop floating on lapping water. He felt as though he had never known her naked.

Seeing her so pretty, Sam almost wished he had let her show off with a fancy wedding.

It was noisy, and everybody was eating tangerines and chocolates.

Strangers, who must be relatives on her side, grabbed his arm and stared at him. "So this is he? Good luck, young man!" And he thought he caught side glances licking over himself and Lil, as if there was something on them that showed they had been sleeping together before this ceremony.

Suddenly Sam found himself in Mr. and Mrs. Klein's bedroom, with Mr. Klein and his own father. The old man looked strangely stuck together, with his barber-shaven face, and the cleaned and pressed blue serge suit which he wore only on Yom Kippur and Passover. His yellow-dotted necktie was pulled into a small tight knot, lost in the arrow of his high collar. Those aristocratic half-moon glasses that he wore on a chain looked borrowed, in an attempt to put on the dog.

The three of them stood behind the bed, which was piled high with coats. Mr. Klein had secreted a bottle of vishniak, the real stuff. "Well, here is good luck!" he declared, and they drank the burning cherry brandy, and the two fathers stood and talked to each other like two men whose children are getting married.

Sam saw his father holding his head at a cocky, judicious angle; a mere buttonhole maker might be scared talking to a *real-estatenik*, but Mr. Eisen assumed the attitude of an intellectual, a philosopher, who could look around himself on any plane, as an equal, even as a sort of superior mind.

"Well, and how is business in your line?" Mr. Klein finally asked.

"Oh, we make a living. Right now it is slack season."

"You're in the clothing business, isn't it?"

"I am a buttonhole maker," Mr. Eisen asserted, so there should be no false pretense. Just then, in the word and look of his father, Sam realized that to his parents he was marrying above himself: a rich girl, an heiress! Lil! . . .

"I have a brother who is an operator," Mr. Klein hastened to say, as if to put himself in right with Sam's father. "He works for Hart Schaffner. Maybe you know him? Chayim Klein? He is here."

Mr. Eisen's whole attitude softened. He took another little glass of vishniak. "I worked for Hart Schaffner myself, for seven years . . ."

Rabbi Schor, from the Temple, was a puffily upholstered busybody with plump white hands. Though he was supposed to be a reform rabbi, he wore a *yarmalkeh*; it reminded Sam of a freshman's skull cap.

A chord sounded on the piano, and through the crowd of uncles, aunts, cousins of the Kleins and of the Eisens, Sam caught a glimpse of Thelma Ryskind playing the "Wedding March." Then he saw several of the girls scattered through the crowd; poor kid, she hadn't been able to resist asking them to her wedding.

A cousin and an uncle, holding his arm, propelled him through the mob toward the wedding canopy that was being held up near the front window.

"Hat! His hat!" Laughter burst among the younger element.

"He forgot his hat! That's the cat's nuts!" and from the older folk, a kind of scandalized murmuring.

Sam pushed his way back to the bedroom. Naturally, his hat was buried under the pile of clothes on the bed. Finally he dug it out. The soft crush hat looked like hell with the tux which he had worn only once before: at the Ogden senior prom. But he was keeping Lil waiting at the altar! He rushed back to the canopy, stumbling over his kid brother, Manny, who looked up at him with a scared, awed face.

Rabbi Schor made a little speech about the wise laws of Moses. Lil's grandmother, a big, toothless woman in a crinkly black silk dress, didn't understand the rabbi's swift English, and kept saying: "Hah? hah? What does he say? What does he mean?"

Suddenly Lil's hand clawed his. Sam saw that she had the giggles. Her mouth worked desperately as she tried to keep the laughter from popping out.

The rabbi burst into a quick mumble of Hebrew, which must be the marriage service itself. Lil's fingers relaxed; her palm lay against Sam's, warm and confiding. Now her face had become grave. She pressed against his side. He could feel her whole body vibrating, and as he looked at her he found her eyes speaking out to him, as though she were trying to look all of her love to him, through her eyes.

The rabbi was back to English. His voice was rolling and deep now, as a rabbi's voice should be.

". . . and I do take this woman for my wife, according to the laws of Moses, and of Israel."

Bunk. Moses and the city hall. Sam felt himself prodded. "I do," he said. He heard Lil pipe: "Yes. I mean, I do."

The rabbi handed him a wine glass. He sipped. Lil touched it with her lips; but as the rabbi was taking it away, she drew the glass back, and took a gulp of the wine.

Then the rabbi put something on the floor. Something wrapped in a napkin. Oh, sure, it was the glass the groom was supposed to break. Sam crushed it under the sole of his new shoe.

Mazeltov! Mazeltov! Good luck! the older folks cried, beaming, triumphant. And in the turmoil of red faces, wet mouths, Sam found himself momentarily embracing his mother. That moment pulled clear of the turmoil, like a word caught out of a jumble of sound. He felt her fingers pressing, clutching against his back, while her strained face, on which he seemed to see each separate grain of powder, pressed toward him. In that moment all the strangeness that a fellow felt about his mother: a mother always in the kitchen, or scrubbing the floors with her sloppy skirt tucked around her thick waist, a mother with straggly hair and a voice continually quarreling, complaining, ordering: all the strangeness vanished, and she was just a Jewish mama, tearful and joyful like the kind Vera Gordon portrayed in the movies, just a *Yiddishe mameh*. She was sniveling and at the same time laughing at him, *Hih hih, nu, mein zun, nu, Sam, zoll zein mit glick,* you should be happy! she sputtered, and then with a gush of feeling their faces pressed together, and Sam kissed his mother on the mouth, feeling her steamy, flabby lip trembling under his mouth, trying to press back, hard.

His father, too, not knowing just what gesture was right for this moment, put out his hand, to shake hands. "Well, good luck, Sam, good luck!" It was as if he were going off on some exploit, higher than his old man had ever dared. Mr. Eisen's squinty eyes blinked, and his free arm made a fumbly half-abashed gesture of embracing his son, which he changed to a kind of pat on the back. "Be happy."

Now his kid sister Fanny hung herself around his neck and pulled herself up for a kiss. All of a sudden the whole family felt together, and very dear to each other. Why, this kid sister, Sam felt, he had never known her at all. Fay was growing up husky and chubby, wide-hipped and big-bosomed like her mother. Her flesh was real pink, and her mouth tasted like fresh butter.

Platters of food stood everywhere: the dining room table was loaded, the library table, even the telephone table. Platters of chicken, and steaming corned beef, and *laks*—smoked salmon—and sour pickles, and hard salami, and sour tomatoes, and chunks of *gefillte fish*—eat whatever you want! Take, take! Layer cakes and cookies and bottles of sweet wine. Mrs. Klein's idea had been: a little of everything, so everyone can find what they like; for how could she serve a regular supper to such a mob in such a small flat?

For half an hour, they stood, a circle around each table, grabbing, cramming meat between slices of bread, Jews eating corned beef. Now the two groups of relatives, Sam's and Lil's, seemed to be stirred together, becoming more and more as one. His father had found her uncle who was an operator at Hart Schaffner's, and they were gabbing of foremen, piece-rates, strikes, bosses. Mrs. Eisen was in the kitchen with Mrs. Klein, who was telling her of her bodily ills, and repeating, with a kind of hopeful skepticism: " 'Every day, in every way, I get better and better.' Who knows? Maybe it helps." "Do you have to say it in English?" "Oh my! maybe. I was always saying it in Yiddish."

Then, out of the jumble of gabbing and gobbling, a voice arose like that of an auctioneer. "One thousand dollars!" it sang.

There was a hush, as the crowd pushed toward the front-room. An uncle stood on a chair, waving a check. "From the bride's father, for the young couple."

Sam found himself holding the check, while Lil patted his hand. "It's our wedding present, honeybunch."

He looked at the sum. Sure enough. A thousand bucks. "I—I—well, thanks," he said to Mr. Klein, as his father-in-law waved the sum away, with a self-conscious smile.

A thousand dollars. For furnishing a flat.

And getting a start in life.

The uncle on the chair was shouting off other minor gifts, as nothing beside that of Sam's rich father-in-law. Then he read a series of fake telegrams, with greetings to the bride and groom, and best wishes for early results; from John D. Rockefeller, and Gloria Swanson. "Lil, you have broken my heart!" from Rudy Valentino. Also a real telegram from Lil's brother in California, and one signed "The Bunch." That had been Rudy Stone's idea.

The old lady, Lil's grandmother, was holding forth in a high voice, in Yiddish:

". . . fleppers they are? Yenkees they are? Don't tell me fairy-tales. It's the same thing, here and in the old country! In Kovno the father would find his girl a husband, and send him to the *talmud torah* to be a rabbi. And in America he sends him to college to be a lawyer. So what's the difference? Ach, don't bother my head with their fleppers and their paint on their faces, they are the same children, I tell you, Jewish children, and when it comes to the end it is the same in Tchicago as in Kovno, they grow up, we marry them, and they have children, may they be healthy!"

The Sunshine Girls sent a beautiful set of electric polychrome torchères. "I saw the identical thing at Scholle's, for $12.50," Lil declared. "But I bet Rose Heller's father got it wholesale for them."

Harry Perlin sent a radio, with a double set of headphones.

Mort Abramson sent a rolling pin. "I'm sure this will come in handy!" he wrote on the card.

Lou Margolis sent a rattle. And also a nice bedroom clock. Lil suspected it came from his old man's pawnshop.

Runt Plotkin sent a set of Maupassant, bound in red leather.

Lil couldn't decide whether to buy a four-room outfit complete, like Revell's advertised for $425, or to shop for each piece separately.

And about the bed. It seemed dirty-minded to have a double bed. Even if people were married they had to have a certain amount of independence; that was the modern point of view.

Should the parlor set be mohair or velour tapestry?

"I'll go crazy trying to decide everything!" Lil said after the second week of going from Revell's to Fish's to Scholle's.

"So will the furniture salesmen!" Sam kidded, and had to kiss her.

BOOK TWO

Forever Blowing Bubbles

WEIGHT, COUNTERWEIGHT

As Mort passed the corner of Randolph and Clark, he saw Runt Plotkin standing in front of the cigar store, as usual. Mort parked the car and walked back. Runt was wearing a long, sporty spring overcoat tied by a snappy wide belt.

"Wadya know about Sam!" Runt said.

"Well, if a guy can't get it any other way," Mort responded.

"He didn't do so bad at that. I bet she's hot stuff when she gets started."

"I'll say she is!"

"Yeah? Talking from experience?"

Mort jiggled his eyebrows.

"Say, Mort, what's the lowdown? Is that a fact, was it a shotgun wedding?"

"And if it was?" Mort said. "She's a nice piece, and old man Klein has plenty of bucks."

They walked up to where Mort had parked the car, and Runt slipped the bottle out of his overcoat pocket and gave it to Mort.

"Don't mention this, will you, Mort?" Runt said, as usual. "This driver takes care of me just as a special favor; they'd take his hack away from him if they got wise."

Mort took the cap off and sniffed.

"That's good stuff," Runt said. "He gets it from a guy in the Fish Fan's Club. Can't get much. Just takes care of a few friends."

Mort handed over two dollars. "Say," Mort said, "what are you going to do when Dever[1] starts cleaning up on everything?"

Runt looked wise.

"You better hook up with Rube Moscowitz," Mort advised. "He's a big shot now they got the Thompson organization wiped out."

"Say, don't you worry," Runt said knowingly. "The old machine is right there. Don't worry." He looked up and down the street.

"What are you doing now?" Mort said.

"Oh, I'm handling a little cigar business. There's a cigar makers' strike on but I know where I can put my finger on a supply of goods."

Mort tried to match Runt's look with a wiser look of knowing, of being on the inside. "When they get through trying all those Lundin and Thompson guys for graft, they'll all be in jail."

---

[1] William Dever, Democratic Mayor of Chicago from 1923 to 1927.

"Yah?" Again Runt looked up and down the street. "Did you see who they got defending them? Darrow and Erbstein. Don't you worry. They can't pin a thing on them."

"Dever is an honest guy," Mort said, with a touch of pity. "He really means business. He's gonna clean up the town."

Runt looked at the sky, looked across the street, looked along the car tracks. "Nah," he said. "Let him be honest. He can't take care of every detail himself." Then, lowering his voice: "Every place that has a front door has a back door too." Runt nodded significantly, looked in the back seat of the car, looked up at the city hall, saluted his hand to a taxi driver, said Hi to a cop, looked back toward the cigar store, said: "There's a guy I gotta see," and hustled away.

St. Louis woman, with her diamond rings—

"Anything else?" the bellhop asked. He was a slovenly kid. Probably older than myself, Mort thought with satisfaction.

"No. I guess not," Mort said. It was a good thing he had bought that pint from Runt Plotkin instead of taking a chance on getting wood alcohol from a bellhop. And they stung you too.

"Anything you want, just gimme a call and I'll fix you up," the bellhop said, tapping toes on the carpet.

"Okay. I may want something later," Mort replied, showing he knew what was what.

St. Louis was supposed to be the town. St. Louis and New Orleans. I'se wild about my jellyroll. . . .

So Sam and Lil were married.

Nine-thirty. He'd take a walk around, maybe pick up something on his own. Dark women! But they all had syph. But a hotel like this would be careful about the girls they had on call.

So finally she came across with Sam. He remembered the feeling against his fingers of her bowl-round breasts, just right for the palm of his hand. They'd grow big. She'd be fat like her mother in a year.

Sam . . . if she didn't pass out on him too, ha ha.

Oh, de blacker de berry, de sweeter de juice . . .

He opened the satchel, took out the pint, set it on the dresser. Then he drew out his wallet. He had fifty dollars along. Mort separated out forty dollars. He might leave that with the clerk. Or would that seem inexperienced? In the dresser? She might look there. He opened the closet door and slipped the money under the shelf paper.

. . . So she would give it to Sam.

He would tackle Dorner, Sieffert & Co. in the morning and if he had no luck with them try Weisbrod next.

The strange thing was the feeling of having been betrayed, when really she had been nothing to him. The minute any girl he knows gets married, a man feels betrayed—how can any woman sign herself away while he is still around?

Tonight. In bed already now. Newlyweds. Bet Sam was a virgin, too. Somebody ought to give them a lesson.

Mort went out, walked. The street air seemed warm and enclosed, like bedroom air. All he did was look at women. Looking for a coffee-colored octoroon. They were supposed to be the best.

At eleven he was back in his room.

Oh, de blacker de berry, de sweeter de juice . . .

When he rang, a different boy came up. This fellow had a pimp face.

Mort ordered some ginger ale.

"Y'all want the fixin's?" They really talked Suthun.

Mort threw out, as one experienced: "Got any dark meat?"

He must have made a break. The fellow looked funny.

"Ain't no nigger guls let inside this hotel." But in the next breath he was friendly. "Just lemme call you suthin good. Just trust me and you'll be satisfied. She ain't gonna sting you either."

She came in without knocking. The first glance told him it was okay. She was wearing a slimy black dress that stuck to her like a wet bathing suit, her nipples tearing to get out. Her face was a strange color. Maybe because of the plucked eyebrows replaced by a thin pencil line, he couldn't tell what she was. She might have been anything from Chinese to Irish.

"Well, sheik, will I pass?" she said.

"You win the hand-painted bedpan," he sputtered.

When she pulled the dress over her head, he saw the warm yellowish tan of her skin, that the plaster of powder and rouge on her face had disguised. She raised her arms to take off the chain of big amber beads that hung around her neck.

"See that?" She held out the beads. "That's real amber. That ain't no imitation. You can tell by the heaviness of it. I got that a present from a traveling man was here las' week. He sells them."

Amber beads were all the rage. Mort hefted them, indulgently.

"You a traveling man?" she said. "What you travel in?"

"Hats," he admitted, with a large tolerance of her little game.

"Oh, yas?" She turned in his arms, her eyes mellow with childish greed. "Gimme see."

"No hurry."

She put the beads carefully on the chair where she had spread her dress.

Did they go to a hotel, Sam and Lil, alone in their honeymoon room? What more would Sam get than this?

"Say, you're good!" he heard the girl say.

"Yah. Every day I get better and better," he cracked.

Then the night became something he had never known before. Every thought, every impulse in the world seemed to stand before him, clear, divided into two component and counter-balancing parts. He thought, incongruously, of Runt Plotkin, and even the words Runt Plotkin had said about politics, this afternoon, seemed to have a component meaning here, so closely, so joyously was everything in the world interrelated; for a certain amount of good, there was an equal amount of bad, and the good depended on the bad, they cooperated; for every front door, there was a back door, and there were girls like Lil and there were girls like this, seesaw, and for black there is white, for in there is out, for up there is down—

His mind suddenly seemed to balance on edge, on a razor edge of pleasure, himself on one side, the woman on the other, both alive and awake to this balance, both giving and taking!

Now he knew what it all meant. He knew what a lot of fellows never got to know, what grown men who went sourly through life never knew, what people who thought buying it in a hotel was dirty and sad never knew, he knew life was easy, he had the password, life would always be wide open to him, front and back door, both! He laughed out loud.

Once she said: "Say, you Jewish?"

He laughed at that.

"I like Jews," she said. "Jews are pretty good."

Late Sunday morning, who should Mort meet in the lobby but Harry Turek, the drummer for Stein, Lerman. Turek was a chubby bastard, a thirty-third degree Mason who had been on the road all his life.

"Well, wipe my tail if it ain't Mort! Say!" His face suddenly fell, and he fixed watery, tragic eyes on Mort. "I was just gonna send you a telegram of condolences."

"Huh?" said Mort, cagily, suspecting a hoax.

"What? You ain't seen the paper?" Turek wobbled his head from side to side. "Not a one was saved. They all died in the fire."

"Yah? Who?"

"Why, your wife and six children!" Turek slapped him on the back; his laughter seemed hardly able to squeeze through the tunnels of fat, as his whole body shook. "You cockroach! Hasn't got his diapers off and crawls around stealing a man's business. What'd you leave for me?"

"Oh, I guess you can maybe dispose of two or three dozen to Dorner, Sieffert. But they're pretty well stocked up."

"My my my. I guess Edson Keith better close out the business. Abramson and Son is going to clean them out anyway."

So they ate together and talked business, Turek, the old father of the road, handing out tips to Mort.

"Say, had a good time?" he finally leered.

Mort leered back. "Boy, oh, boy, have they got stuff in this place."

"Yeah? Something special?" Turek squeaked.

"A No. 1," Mort said. "Ask for Lil—I mean Del."

"Say, what's the matter, you got so many you can't even remember their names?"

"That's me!" said Mort. "The answer to a maiden's prayer."

It was an ordinary case, trivial, a collection case, the kind that makes up nine-tenths of law business in spite of all the yapping about murder trials that gives the public the idea that's all that goes on in the courts. And it just happened that Lou Margolis was reviewing in law school at the time the same principle that was involved in this case-agency. After he saw what happened in court he knew there were a lot of lawyers who never in their whole lives got onto the law the way he was onto it now.

In the beginning a law clerk goes into the city hall on routine jobs, filing appearances, and it's like a strange poolroom. Always clusters of men talking out of the sides of their mouths, moving off when someone stops too near them; always the sour damp warm smell of talk, saliva, tobacco. Nobody looks natural. Or, they all look too natural: too much like cartoon types of ward-heelers, shysters, smalltime grafters. The chewed cigars, the spittoons, the derby hats, the air of mystery, everybody with a private little plot, everybody wise, everybody in on the know. Among all these people, never anyone that looks untouched by some dishonesty, or crudity, or lust.

Then, a fellow like Lou Margolis gets onto the ropes quickly. He gets to know all the bailiffs by name, and they know him by face and who he works for, he can pass the kidding word, he himself may pause near the elevator in a low-voiced conversation with a clerk from Sonnenschein & Barker, spilling a word of dirt about a certain judge who deserted the sinking Thompson ship. Or maybe it is only a dirty joke about what was found when they opened the grave of King Tut.

Oh, yes, he can explain now: these onhangers are politicians, lawyers, witnesses; but how can one penetrate all the opaque eyes, the knowingly tightened mouths, all the meanings of jerked heads, shrugged shoulders?

What happened was, a fellow never asked any more; he took it all for granted.

But this was a simple case. Lou's boss, Preiss, was supposed to defend Nate Stearns, who owned the Rosevale Rest Cemetery, against Mr. Cassell, who claimed a thousand dollars for working up some ads.

To begin with, Stearns owed the money. Every time the case was called Preiss would pull a toothache face and tell Lou: "Get it put over. Tell 'em— tell 'em a material witness is out of town. . . ."

Stearns was a big client. But on this piker case he was stubborn. "Sure that sucker made the ads," Stearns admitted to Preiss. "But I never used them so why should I pay for them?"

"You okayed them. He's got you cold."

"I don't care. Listen, this guy Cassell tried to put something over. In the first place he said he was a friend of Rube Moscowitz."

Aha! Now they were getting to it. Rube Moscowitz was a silent partner in the Rosevale Rest Cemetery development.

"So naturally I told him to go ahead with the ads. But Rube don't know this guy from Adam. Pete Grinnell sent him to Rube, so you know how Rube is, he says sure, go ahead, swell! So for that, I should get stuck for a thousand bucks!"

"Listen, Nate," Preiss would say. "You can't get around it. The ads were all right, weren't they?"

"Yah, but I decided not to advertise altogether. Advertising only cheapens the place. Every Mrs. Schmaltz would think she can get into Rosevale Rest! Why, we got people like Judge Schaeffer got family plots!"

The case was up again. It had already been stalled for over a year. "Let's get it over with," Preiss yawned. "Fix it for this afternoon. No use wasting a morning on that crap."

The corridor was already littered with dumpy women in shabby brownish coats and pot hats, puzzled little men who carried their hats in their hands. These were the early sheep unaccustomed to going to court, full of strange fears that their lawyers wouldn't meet them, that they had come to the wrong building, that they would miss out on some unknown legal stumbling block.

The bailiff was studying a full page ad for Piggly Wiggly stock, $55 a share.

"If you have any change you wanna grab off some of that," Vlacek said to Lou, tapping the sheet. "That guy Saunders was smart enough to beat Wall Street and Ford is the only other man ever did that."

"Yah," Lou said, "but he better watch out or these bulls and bears will get him yet. Say, I got a little case here, can you move it down?" Vlacek nodded and turned back to his paper.

"Around three o'clock," Lou said.

The sheep in the courtroom would wait all morning for their cases to be called.

"Did you talk to the judge?" Stearns gurgled as they hustled across Randolph Street. "Maybe he could use a little lot in Rosevale."

"What good is Rosevale to him?" Preiss sneered. "Think he wants to be buried with a bunch of Hebes?" They paused, near the elevators, while Preiss admonished his client. "Listen, chump, your only chance is to play dead. Say you never saw this guy. That dope in your office, Edelman, ordered the ads and Edelman wasn't even working for you, just rented space in your office. Judge Morris is a good friend of Rube's and he'll give us a break if he can."

Cassell's lawyer was a peppy kid whom Lou Margolis had seen around law school, must be just out. Probably got the case on contingency.

Judge Morris leaned back in his chair, his eyes closed.

It was all familiar now to Lou, a little mumbling from each lawyer, maybe a witness on the stand, and a judgment. The face of the judge, tired of looking at things day after day, for a moment reminded him of his own father; maybe because the two round globes on each side of the bench suggested the three-ball sign of the pawnbroker. Sure, his father behind his counter was like this judge, looking with the same dull eyes as people laid out their packages before him: heirlooms, wedding rings. Never anything new. That was a clever idea. Some time when he was a big lawyer he would pull it. He wouldn't have to say the pawnbroker was his father.

For the peppy young lawyer this was big stuff. He had a thick sheaf of evidence, letters on Rosevale Rest stationery, memos from Nate Stearns's private secretary, an open-and-shut case. On top of that he hauled out a volume of *Corpus Juris*, and a couple of volumes of *Northwestern Reports*, and even a recent Illinois Supreme Court decision.

"Volume 272, page 808 . . ." he barked.

The young lawyer finished, stood dignified and certain. Judge Morris leaned over and said to Preiss:

"As it stands now I can't do a thing but award them the judgment. The law is clear for the plaintiff in this case. I'll tell you what I'll do, though. I'll withhold entering the order for a few days, and if you can show me a law that applies, I'll be glad to reconsider."

The young lawyer's mouth opened, then shut. Lou himself had never seen the fix operate like this, in open court.

Back on the benches, in the courtroom, there was no sign that anything had happened. . . . Just another little legal tangle over some kind of suit for wages.

"Lou here can scratch up some kind of law," Preiss reassured his client. "He's a nice guy, Judge Morris, huh? A high-class judge too. He didn't want to give it to us without we show him the law. . . . Now I want you to look up some law," Preiss told Lou. "Anything will do."

Lou Margolis was, in fact, listening to his instructor. But his mind spun around the instructor's sentences, as a dog running circles around his master.

Sure, everybody knew fixing went on. But the incident today had created a new kind of balance in his mind.

On one side was all this law: Torts, Contracts, Corporations, tomes, libraries, endless files, affidavits, transcripts. A structure elaborate and fine. Once he had been blinded by the perfection, the security of law. But now he saw clearly the meaning of the old saying that there is another side to every question. Even when there was no other side. Even in an open-and-shut case. Now he saw the balance.

On one side was the law, on the other side was the lawyer.

It was a perfect state of balance.

The result was the same as if there were no law and no lawyers, and Nate Stearns could pay his employees or not, just as he wished.

Way back, almost in the first day of law school, remember how Sam Eisen had argued about the justification of defending a client you knew was guilty? Lou Margolis felt he could really answer Sam now.

To Lou Margolis, law appeared now as even more perfect than in his previous conception. Before, law had seemed a high tower: Justice, founded upon ethics, morality. What he saw now was a two-part structure emblemized in the scales held by blind Justice. There were two weights, either one of which could nullify the other. In life, if he didn't have one in his grasp, he could always have the other.

And it seemed to him that humanity had deliberately developed this balance between law and other-than-law. Everywhere in life. People passed Prohibition, and then devised a vast system of bootleg drinking that balanced the law of Prohibition. In some obscure way there was a general, recognized right on both sides.

In the hallway, they ran into Sam Eisen.

Lou Green snaked his books from under his arm. Sam, a year behind, was still on Contracts.

"How's the married life?" Lou Margolis said.

"Oh, fine. How's the law business?"

Lou Margolis told about the Rosevale Rest case.

"Did the advertising guy recover?" Sam asked.

"You're just taking Agency," Lou Margolis said. "What's the rule?"

"Well, he should have, unless this fellow in the office who gave him the order was acting as an independent contractor."

"Aha!" Lou Margolis said. That was the angle.

Judge Morris reached down for Preiss's brief.

"We have cited several cases under the rule of independent contractor," Preiss began.

That was enough. The judge glanced at the brief and handed it back. "Absolutely. That's right. Independent contractor. I'll dismiss the case."

"But, judge!" the opposing young lawyer began.

"Kleinschmidt vs. Sokol," the bailiff called.

Lou thought he could tell, if needed, the exact reason for the presence of every person there: the oily fellow with the face sharp as a hatchet, the thick Greek with porcupine whiskers, Preiss, himself, and the out-of-place peanut who ran the elevator; Lou felt that now he could balance the entire equation. He felt wised up. Smart. He was on.

"There ain't a box in the world that can't be cracked," the vociferous but mysterious stranger announced, and Runt thought: this time he was in contact with the real McCoy. This time he was in a regular hangout of heisters.

"This stuff is needled," he offered his opinion, as he called for another glass of beer.

The stranger tasted his beer. "Damn right. I can smell the ether."

"What is this, Spike O'Donnell's stuff?" Runt said knowingly to the bartender. "Or is Diamond Joe coming into the Loop?"

The bartender shrugged. "That's good beer," he said flatly.

"What man can make, man can break," the stranger continued his discourse. Take a simple combination box, it was no trick at all to hear the tumblers. Well, they fixed that, but the burglar went right along, step for step with the manufacturers. He drilled around the lock. They put in drill-proof plates. He made a sandpack and souped the whole door. Now they got these vaults with five-ton doors. To hell with the doors, he says, and chips through the concrete in back of the vault. "They invent a time lock, and think they got him beat, but lemme tell you, there are a couple of tricks for beating a time lock . . ."

The fellow looked around the speakeasy. Runt, too, looked around. Every man there might be a Tommy O'Connor, Runt reminded himself.

The fellow decided to keep his professional secrets to himself.

"But lemme tell you," he emphasized his point, balancing one palm upward, and the other palm upward, as though he were hefting a couple of gold watches, "you can trust this principle, you can bank on it. Whatever man can make, man can break."

Runt nodded, solemnly.

Pearly laid his hand against the rear axle and shoved, sending the dolly scooting from under the Ford. He rolled over and scrambled to his feet. Sumbitch, his elbow was sore. That lousy bolt must have been put on in the days of King Tut. If he only had a snug-fitting socket. He had been under the car so long his knees were wobbly when he tried to walk.

Couldn't find the missing socket. Half a dozen sets around the place but that goddam Henry Ford machined his bolts just a trifle out of size so you had to have a special set of tools for his cars, or send the jobs to a Ford agency. That guy never missed an angle!

Harry took a bolt-cutter and a long-handled wrench, and got back under the car. He didn't like to cut off bolts. The idea was to make the nut come off natural. He swung his body over, with his free hand gripping the front axle for counter-resistance. He tugged until his guts ached. The nut was frozen fast.

He hammered around the nut with a small sledge, put the wrench on again, and hammered the end of the wrench. Twice the wrench slipped off. Grease fell into his eye. He screwed his head around, trying to wipe his eye against the shoulder of his coverall. With one eye closed, he went after it again. He tried a straight hold, bracing his feet and tugging at the end of the wrench until he could feel the strength going out of his knuckles. There was a squeak. The nut had begun to give.

The damp, rainy air gave Mitch a feeling of cool clarity. Nyquist's lecture beckoned. Even the dopes woke up with a spark in their hearts before the bluff cracks and raw jokes of Nyquist, the traditional grand old man of medicine. Though you approached him through the haze of his reputation with a fear that no one could really be so grand, you found in the end that nothing could do justice to Nyquist, and through it all he was such a human guy; like only the other day he had repeated his annual joke of gazing through a co-ed's microscope, when she was analyzing her own urine sample, and asking in a loud, startled voice how sperm happened to be present.

The old man was already in the room, preparing some sort of solution, while his assistant laid out the dog. Mitch went up to the table and looked at the animal. Already drugged, it lay with heaving sides. One leg was shaven for injections.

"Observe!" Nyquist commanded. The class stared at his brick-rough face, then down at his huge red hands, holding a syringe and a test-tube.

"We have here a de-pancreatized dog," he proclaimed. "We take a blood sample." About his least movement there was a theatricality that might have fitted a stage magician. He injected the needle, and drew back the plunger, rotating it as he pulled steadily and evenly. Mitch could never take his eyes off Nyquist when the prof was working. Even in the smallest things, his superb, controlled technique showed.

Nyquist tilted the blood sample into the tube, adding citrate against clotting. Then he strode over to the centrifuge, inserted the tube, clamped down the lid, and returned to the platform.

"Today we will discuss the functions uff the pancreas," he announced.

Behind him the centrifuge hummed.

After about ten minutes, in which he informed them that "until recently, most uff all that we knew about the pancreas was that we can't get along without it," he marched back to the centrifuge, removed the tube, poured its whitish serum into an ordinary test-tube, and, back at his desk, added a dash of colorless, and a dash of blue Fehling's solution to the serum. He waved the test-tube through a Bunsen flame, shaking it a bit as he did so. Then he held it out for them to see. Below the blue mixture was a red precipitate.

The class sank back, disappointed. After all, they perfectly well knew the test for sugar in the blood.

"Aha!" Nyquist said, just like a magician who lets you catch him at his trick. "So nobody is fooled? Perhaps Professor Nyquist needs another lesson from Houdini. Now, please observe, we make the same test again."

But this time he preceded the test by picking up a prepared syringe and injecting half its contents into the dog.

He talked for about fifteen minutes, letting the mysterious stuff work in the dog. Then Nyquist drew a fresh blood sample. With the ascending buzz of the centrifuge, Mitch could feel his very heart beating stronger. What had old Nyquist injected into the dog, before taking that second blood sample? It seemed that when the lid would be unclamped from the centrifuge, something like the very source of life might be revealed.

Then, all at once, Mitch knew. He caught the eye of Nyquist's assistant and whispered: "Insulin?" That was the magic word, the amazing new discovery that would change prolonged agony, and death, to normal life for hundreds of thousands of diabetics.

The assistant nodded.

But the knowledge of what was happening before his eyes only heightened Mitch Wilner's excitement. How would it work? What was it? How was it found? How was it made?

"One good way to find out what something means to you is to try and get along without it. In this way you can find out the function uff a bankroll, or uff a sweetheart, gentlemen, or uff the pancreas. In 1889 there were some experiments by von Mehring and Minkowski, to find out what is the function uff this mysterious pancreas. So they did not remove it from themselves, but began by removing the pancreas from dogs. The dogs did not die so soon, but they became very thirsty, they became voracious, and at the same time their food did them no good, they wasted away, became feeble, and in the end they passed into a coma and died. Perhaps you bright young doctors will recognize these symptoms. Well . . ."

Sure. Remember Harry Perlin talking about his father? "He eats all the time, he's crazy for candy, but the food doesn't do him any good. The doctor says lots of Jews got diabetes." Now, only a year later, Harry's father could have been saved!

". . . and most often, why, we do not know, among the Jewish peoples," Nyquist was saying, as he walked over to the centrifuge, opened it, and took out the second serum sample. He repeated the sugar test, and held the tube up before them.

There was no precipitate!

Within fifteen minutes, the blood of the de-pancreatized, diabetic dog had changed from a plus to a normal sugar content!

". . . so we have insulin! And it is not because a few young men went into the lab one fine morning and shook up a few test-tubes. . . . For twenty years we have known that the problem is to isolate this substance, to determine the chemical nature uff the pancreatic hormone. In Berlin, in Chicago, in Boston, in Toronto, all over the world men have labored on this problem, and do not think any uff their work is lost because someone else has made the final discovery. Each step is used by the following worker; without the analysis uff Langerhans, the work uff Minkowski does not come, without Minkowski, the work uff Lusk is not begun, without Lusk, without Schafer, this famous discovery uff Banting and Best would not be in our hands today!" He wiped his face.

"But, gentlemen, if you believe research is always going forward as fast as it can go, let me tell you uff what has happened here in this very department." There was a barely perceptible change in Professor Nyquist's tone as he went on. The combative vitality seemed to turn upon himself, rather than upon some dread disease, and also there appeared, Mitch thought, a much older man, a man who has weighed the plus against the minus, seen failure as well as brilliant success.

"Ten years ago, in this department here, I had a student working on the possibility uff a pancreatic extract. One day this young man came to me in my office, and he was excited. 'Dr. Nyquist,' he said, 'I believe I have found the stuff!' . . . Well, gentlemen, today I confess to you. Ten years ago this student brought me an extract that was pretty close to this insulin which has just been discovered. Ten years ago in this laboratory we conducted a series uff experiments on depancreatized animals, and there was a very strong indication that, with refinement and experiment, this material would serve. But, gentlemen, I thought to myself: Here is a material which has to be injected intravenously three, four times a day to be uff use to a patient. How can people make use uff it? Remember, this was some time ago, our techniques were not so good as now, and I thought that people would not be able to inject themselves so frequently without infection. And for a patient to run three times a day to a doctor for injection would not be practical. So I have to report, gentlemen, that ten years ago I did not encourage the development uff this material for use in diabetes." He stopped. There was a heavy silence. "It only goes to show what damn fools we can be, sometimes, any uff us," he said.

Why had he told them this? Among them there were fellows like Mitch who felt it would take a long time, and a lot of experience, for them to understand the full implication of Nyquist's confession. A warning against themselves? Against chance? Against daring too little?

He concluded: "Well, now we have insulin, even little children are able to inject themselves quite safely, and perhaps the only people who do not like it are the ladies who have to wear naked evening gowns."

His joke lacked his usual zest.

Mitch was among several students who were up around the desk, with questions. Nyquist had stepped into his office to get them some material on the method of insulin preparation. As they hung around waiting, Gans, the cockeyed fool, picked up the syringe Nyquist had used and leaned over the dog.

"Let's give him another shot," Gans proposed, as he found the vein. "If a kid can inject it, I can."

"Yeah? I'm not so sure about that!" Weintraub exclaimed.

"Hey! What the heck!" Seabury interposed, too late. Gans had shot the rest of the mixture into the dog.

"How's that for technique?" he observed, wiping the needle.

"Hey!" Mitch was watching the dog. It began to tremble. Then the whole body of the animal jerked, as if to shake off sleep and death; the mouth fell open, and the tied legs pulled spasmodically; the animal heaved with the contraction of every muscle, while a strange, smothered noise came from its throat.

The fellows watched, scared.

Nyquist had returned. He took in the situation at a glance. "Glucose!" he howled, grabbing and injecting the sugar mixture that he had prepared in case of an overdose of insulin. Almost instantaneously, the convulsions ceased.

When the dangerous moment had passed, the professor looked up. His face was clotted with fury. His cold eyes looked them over, one after another. "Well, Mr. Gans? Did you have a good time in kindergarten today? Did you play with all the toys?"

"I—I didn't know—" Gans began.

"You didn't *know!*" Nyquist roared. "You have only to remember that if someone tried to inject more than a minimum dose uff brains into your head it would probably have the same fatal effect! You are supposed to be preparing for the study uff medicine. . . ."

Mitch was scarcely listening to Nyquist's blistering reprimand of the unfortunate Gans. More important than Nyquist's oration about accuracy and exactitude and certainty in science was the realization of the strange beauty of this that had happened with the dog. The proposition was becoming clear, in his mind, blazing in hard outline. The veins of the living dog had responded to these substances as perfectly and as beautifully as the two pans of a balance react to added weights. Insulin on one side, glucose on the other. If the animal was loaded with sugar, give him a dose of insulin. If there was an overdose of insulin, give him sugar. Back and forth till they balanced. The conditions of hyperglycæmia and hypoglycæmia were regulated as delicately and as accurately as the balancing arms of a tightrope walker.

Then Mitch felt his mind soaring beyond and beyond, on the wings of this proposition. The perfect state of nature was the state of equilibrium, when all the forces rested, checked, held one against the other. Here he had seen it in the blood again, in the mysterious stream of a myriad combinations and instant actions, that stream that was like a vast calculating machine in which innumerable different equations were being formed and dissolved simultaneously, while their total sum always balanced. Man's place was to find out, to measure all the forces, physical, chemical, psychological, affecting the changes in that stream. To find the gaps in those equations of which only scattered factors were known. To contain, within his mind, the balance and the harmony of the entire human mechanism!

Should she be a good little wifey and jump out of bed before her hubby and get his brekky ready so that by the time he shaved his scratchy whiskers the toast would go pop out of the automatic electric toaster (a present from Aunt Stella) or should she be a modern woman, not a household slave, and sleep her beauty sleep and let him grab some coffee downtown?

Marriage is a partnership, and how could she stay in bed when poor Sam had to get up and work so hard and go to school nights all for her for them!

He liked raspberry jam. When she had bought strawberry he hadn't eaten it at all, strawberries were too gooey and sweet, he said, he liked raspberry, and see, she had a new jar! She knew this about her Sam. He liked raspberry jam.

Lil remembered sometimes hearing her mother and a neighbor woman go into long discussions. . . . Well, mine, he don't like anything comes out of a can. . . . Well, mine, he eats canned stuff all right but one thing he won't stand is a ketchup bottle on the table. . . . Mine, he . . . those confabulations went, always he; and the other day, when the grocer had started to hand her a jar of strawberry jam, she had said: "Oh, no, he doesn't like it!" and had heard herself, and laughed at herself with private joy.

How does it feel to be married? everybody asked; and the answer to the girls was: Oh, it's wonderful, or, with a giggle: Try it and find out; and the answer to her mother was a shy and slightly angry evasion, and the answer to fellows was a wise and flirting look.

But what happened in bed wasn't really the important thing. Lil still felt naughty when on getting up in the morning she saw the other twin bed undisturbed. But really the thing itself wasn't what it was cracked up to be. If she had a chum close to her heart, she would tell her that in some ways she really had got more of a kick out of necking. Sam was terribly passionate, and one of them had to have some sense or honest he might hurt himself. And she would lie as though she were alone, and her patient eyes would look up at the ceiling, and afters when he was weak that was a good feeling, having let her boy have what he wanted.

"I bet you can't say this," Lil challenged, giving Sam the part of the paper with the prize-winning daily tongue-twister. "Go on, say it."

"Seething seas sweep sandy shores shifting siny—"

"Eeee!" she screamed triumphantly.

"One hundred berries for that!" Sam said.

"I bet you could make up a better one, easy," she said.

"A minister won this one," Sam reported. "I suppose he'll use it in his sermon."

"Oh, Sam, I bet you could win a hundred dollars. Why don't you try?"

He didn't pay any attention. She poured him more coffee. If she were as clever as Sam, so smart with words, she would send in a tongue-twister every day, till she won a hundred dollars!

"Oh, Sammy," she said, "did you write that letter to Mrs. Lubov about raising the rent?"

"No," he said. "I don't think she can afford to pay any more. Her husband works in the Post Office and you know they have a limited income."

"Oh, so she was handing you that line? She gives me a pain. You'd better write to the Millers and to that Mr. Whitehead too while you're at it, their leases are up in October too."

"You know the girl is the only one working since Mr. Miller got sick," Sam said.

"Well, we could get fifty dollars for these flats any day, rents are going up all over the North Side."

"The building is paying your father all right, I don't see any sense in making a fuss trying to raise the rent," he insisted.

He was such an idealist! Why, on Parkside there was one place where the rent five years ago was forty dollars and now it was eighty and the landlord was asking a hundred and twenty!

"I want to show my father he isn't losing a thing by having us manage the building; I want him to see what a good business man you are," she said.

"Listen, I didn't want to take this flat in the first place, Lil, I told you we could rent a place of our own. If I have to start raising the rent and being a landlord and kicking people out I won't do it!"

She laughed at him. "Oh, Sammy!" The crazy idea he had of landlords. Well, his family was always so poor; some tenants they must have been!

"Mygod, I'll be late." Sam plunked down his cup.

"Oh gee, Sam," she pouted, "you could get a position where you don't have to punch a clock."

"Yah, where do you get jobs like that?"

"Oh, people who know you . . ." she hinted. As he was grabbing his hat, she thought of reminding him about the phone bill. But it would only make him sore to think of money again. Some time she would work it so he would say: "Here, honey, you take care of the money." In her mind she had it all figured out. She would say: "Well, you need carfare, that's fourteen cents a day, and lunch, a quarter is enough for lunch, and . . ." Oh, she would get him systematized, straightened out! See, marrying her had helped him already. He had taken up law again and was full of ambition.

"Don't forget I'm meeting you downtown to go to the folks' tonight," she said.

"Oh, God. Do we have to eat there?"

"Didn't you marry me for my mother's cooking?" she kidded.

She figured on giving her father and Sam plenty of chances of getting together, on business.

Alone, Lil looked through the paper to see if Walt had proposed to Miss Blossom today. Rudy Valentino was coming to the Trianon. She couldn't see why so many girls were crazy about him with his greasy yellow face. She checked up on the furniture ads. There was a bedroom set exactly like hers at Lane's for eighty-nine dollars, fifteen dollars more than she had paid.

She went to the desk and got out the list of tenants, with the dates when their leases were up. All right! She would write the letters, and raise the rents herself!

Between her and Sam. She could feel it, not exactly a struggle, but they had to find each other out, get to know each other; certain things had to be made clear: who was going to do what, so that the one who could do certain things best should handle those things for both of them. Together they would be a team, her practical nature balancing his impulsive idealism.

Coming home for summer, Joe brought Sylvia one of those amber bead necklaces. Mort took a strange dislike to the thing, insisting that the beads made her look cheap and common, so Sylvia put them on only when she went out with Joe.

Joe was waiting on the steps of the Art Institute. "Those beads look nice on you," he noticed. "The color is nice against your skin, it gives you a gypsy look."

She decided that Joe was smoother and more sophisticated.

He even noticed her hat. "Say, is that an Abramson creation?" he kidded, and she admitted: "Mort got this idea for a King Tut model and he insists that I wear it. He has become a regular Babbitt. All he talks about is grosses and sales and how he put over the King Tut!"

There was an exhibition of sculptures by Mrs. Harry Payne Whitney: soldiers going over the top, and soldiers dragging wounded comrades; Joe got very sarcastically critical, pointing out how unbalanced some of them were. "A man eternally falling," he said. "Is that art?"

And he explained: "See the way this figure is arrested in a motion in which it couldn't be arrested? You stand here waiting for him to fall. It's just wrong, it pains your sense of balance." He became animated, showing her how much he knew about art. "Look at Rodin's *Man of the Bronze Age*, see how he is in a pose of balance, his weight is distributed so that you feel the whole thing is solid, permanent. I mean, that is the basis of art . . . the formation of a design in which the weights check off one against the other. . . . That's what she can't get, but what do you expect of a woman, they never can be really great artists, they can't grasp the fundamental truths."

And just then Sylvia turned, with a face laughing at his prejudice, and he caught her movement, caught the girl scent of her; a man might spend a lifetime trying to imprison, in stone, the impression of a moment such as this: of her turning to him, mobile.

It made a lie of everything he was saying; or maybe it indicated the deeper truth, that life-motion was at every instant balanced, and to express that liquid equilibrium, an artist would have to dig, dig to the final sources.

He thought of this woman, this Vanderbilt woman, working away at the job, no matter how shallow her surfaces. There would never be time enough; why couldn't he be at it! That woman could be in a studio piling up all this sculpture, while he fussed away his time at school.

Joe had a premonition that there would always be some shadowy frustration upon him, that the world would always be off balance for him; he would never arrange his life, work, produce a roomful of sculptures, so much better than these.

"Dear," Sylvia reminded him, "the kids will all be waiting for us, to go to the beach."

The big sensation was when Alvin came home for the summer announcing that instead of going back to Madison in the fall he was going to Cincinnati to study to become a rabbi. A modern rabbi, of course. He had got the idea from young Rabbi Waller of Illinois, who had been up to lecture at Madison.

"I thought you were an atheist," Sylvia twitted him, reminding him of the time he had made a soap-box speech.

"Oh, that! Why bring up the sins of my adolescence?" Alvin retorted. "Anyway, religion has nothing to do with it. Some of the best atheists are rabbis and ministers. In fact, that's the best way to become an atheist. The main idea is that the rabbinate is a high-paying profession, easy work, and they need smart young fellows like me!"

His folks were supposed to be secretly tickled with his new plan, but they didn't dare let on or he'd drop it. So during the vacation his old man made Alvin put in some time in the chair factory, as if he expected Alvin to carry on the business.

The Duke used all his wages to buy clothes and he positively slew everybody, those days, with his array of silk shirts, twelve-dollar sport shoes, and imported linen plus-fours.

Alvin was all set in the front seat of Rudy's new Ford, blazing in a fancy beach-robe, when Rudy stopped in front of the Freedman house and blew his horn. Mort's car was already there.

"Oh, look, Rudy's got a new tin lizzie!" Aline screeched from the sunparlor window, and in a moment the whole mob was looking over his flivver, while he sat at the wheel with a grin of ownership.

"Say Rudy, didja know Ford bought a new factory?" Lou Margolis remarked.

"He ought to, now that he has my five bucks," Rudy bit, innocently.

"Yep!" said Lou. "The American Can Company sold him their factory!"

Rose Heller remembered reading the same joke in the "Line."

"Ja get rich all of a sudden, Rudy?" demanded Lou Green.

"I bet a mysterious stranger has been leaving five hundred dollars on his doorstep," Aline suggested, referring to the mysterious stranger who left five hundred dollars for Andy Gump every day; this morning it was a packing box full of 1,626,642 rubles. As she climbed into the car, her slicker parted, revealing her legs, the thighs faintly downy.

Rudy was explaining to Mort that, on Ford's installment plan, the car practically paid for itself, as it would easily save him five dollars' worth of time a week.

"Did you hear what Ford is going to do when he gets elected President?" Lou Margolis asked. "Give away a flivver with every postage stamp."

"Just because he can make automobiles is no sign he can run a government," Joe Freedman argued.

"What the government needs is efficiency," Rudy said. "That's Henry Ford's middle name!"

"I'm burning up!" Rose moaned, shifting her feet on the hot pavement, which she could feel through her bathing slippers. "Let's get going."

"The way he licked Wall Street," Mort affirmed. "I'd bank on Ford any time."

"What! That Antisemite!" the Duke cried in kidding-serious tones. "Say, you're a fine one, Rudy, patronizing a Jew-hater like that, why didn't you buy a Chevvie?"

"Wadyou mean Antisemite, what's Henry Ford got against the Jews?" Joe Freedman asked.

"Why, everybody knows he hates the Jews," Alvin said.

"Baloney. I bet it's a story some competitors started to get the Jews to buy other cars."

"I heard Ford won't hire any Jews," Rose contributed.

But Lou Green testified that he had a cousin in Detroit who worked for Ford.

"He's been printing stuff in a magazine he owns[2]," Alvin said, from the superior height of a prospective modern rabbi. "The fake *Protocols of the Elders of Zion*."

---

[2] Henry Ford published a newspaper, *The Dearborn Independent* (also known as *The Ford International Weekly*), from 1919 to 1927. It promoted strongly anti-Semitic propaganda, such as the fraudulent *Procols of Zion*. After 1927, Ford apologized and closed the paper.

"Say, are we going to the beach or not," Aline demanded, bored.

"The what?"

"The *Protocols of the Elders of Zion*," Alvin repeated with satisfaction. "It's some kind of a forged document that's supposed to prove there's a bunch of rich Jews that meets secretly somewhere and runs the world, they started the war and everything."

"Aw for cry sake. Just some dizzy fairy-tale, in a magazine."

"Do you have to stand here all day arguing about it? I'm roasting!" Aline said. The gang piled into the two cars. "Skinny, you sit on Lou's lap," Aline ordered. "Maybe that'll make him stop arguing."

Aline must think she still had that high-school crush on Lou.

"Even if Ford is an Antisemite," Lou kept at Alvin, "what has that got to do with buying his cars? The car isn't Antisemitic!"

"A Jew-hater should get my money!" Sylvia Abramson sneered.

The motor spattered into life.

"Huh, self-starter and everything!" Joe admired.

"You have to admit that some Jews give them plenty of reason," Lou Margolis said confidentially.

"Well, anyway, some of my best friends are Jews," Rose cracked.

"The trouble is"—Alvin dropped wise words through glistening teeth—"the Jews have a racial inferiority complex."

The other car drew alongside and there was a brief argument about going to the Wilson Avenue beach.

"All the *shlumpers* go up there!" Aline complained. "It's a regular ghetto."

"Oh, it won't contaminate you! Come on, we're blocking the traffic!"

"Leopold and Loeb[3] didn't help it any either," Alvin said. "They did more harm to the Jews than Ford can ever do."

"It's a darn good thing they didn't pick on a gentile kid," Sylvia said.

"Yah. They kept it in the family," Lou Margolis jested.

How could he joke about such things! Rose Heller felt like getting off, away from him, from the contact of his body. All summer, the headlines, the whispered details of Leopold and Loeb murdering that little boy had haunted her. Like when that terrible Fatty Arbuckle murder took place, the sick feeling that her own body had somehow taken part in the horrible

---

[3] On May 21, 1924, Nathan Leopold and Richard Loeb, a pair of brilliant Jewish law students at the University of Chicago, murdered Bobby Franks, a young local boy. The murder was apparently motivated by the philosophical notion that the boys could prove themselves Nietzschean supermen, beyond the rules by which ordinary humans are limited. The pair were arrested a week later. The story (and its follow-up) was a national sensation. Meyer Levin, who was the same age as Loeb and was also attending U. of C., knew of the pair. He later novelized their story in his book, "Compulsion."

scenes described in the papers. (And now Fatty Arbuckle was at the Marigold Gardens making a comeback.)

"You know what they really intended to do?" Alvin confided. "They intended to pick up a young girl, of fourteen, and rape her. At least that young so they'd be sure she was a virgin."

"Oh, shut up!" Sylvia cried. "Can't you talk about something else!"

In the other car, Aline was telling them that she knew a girl on campus, who had gone out with Dickie just a week before the murder! Of course her name was being kept out of the papers.

"Those South Side Jews," Mort snorted. "They've got too much money, that's what's the matter with those kids. They had everything in the world, money, and they just didn't know what to do next."

And when they got on the beach, the subject of the Leopold-Loeb case kept popping up among them, like lava forever boiling under their conscious thoughts. To Mort, it was just a sign of the decay of that rich South Side crowd of German Jews. Their crowd was used up, and the West Side Jews were coming on! Those German Jews, with their exclusive Prima Club, where no son of a Russian Jew might enter!

But Alvin perversely championed the murderers.

"The only crime those boys committed was getting caught," he argued now, digging his big toe into the sand, the while he looked at Sylvia's girlish breasts, clearly printed against her wet bathing suit. "If Babe Leopold hadn't dropped his glasses, then their crime would have been a perfect creative piece of work."

"You don't mean you think there is any excuse for them!" Aline Freedman cried.

"According to Nietzsche," Alvin went on, "whatever a superman does is perfect, and if they had done this thing perfectly, that would have been enough excuse."

"A lot you know about Nietzsche," Sylvia twitted. "I bet you never even read him."

"Their act was no more wrong than a hunter killing a rabbit. In proportion to their intelligence, that kid was a rabbit," Alvin said. The girls shuddered.

"That's a fine way for a prospective rabbi to talk," Aline snapped.

Alvin positively glowed.

"Do you believe a person has a right to kill anyone they want to?" Mort challenged.

"I'm only trying to show you their point of view," Alvin said. "Everybody has a right to live according to their own point of view. Just like Cellini"—he could go on now, to talk of Aretino, of Huysmans's *Là-Bas*, of *Dorian Gray*, of the beauty of evil, fascinating them with the black luster of his thoughts, amazing them with his brilliance.

While Alvin talked, Sam Eisen and Lil appeared. Rose Heller, letting out a little cry, called them over.

Lil looked very sweet in a yellow bathing suit; her upper arms were soft and rounded, womanly rather than girlish, and her thighs had an almost puffy appearance. She was apparently pregnant.

The girls made a great screeching and whispering around her; and Sam, flushing, entered loudly into the argument about Leopold and Loeb.

"Any jury in the world would have hung them!" he declared, passionately. "Don't you worry about Darrow. That was the smartest thing he did, waiving jury."

"I don't believe in capital punishment," Rudy concluded. "But in this case, I think they deserve it."

Mort Abramson, never taking his eyes off Lil's pregnancy, said: "After what they did to that kid, it would be a crime against society to let them live." He hinted about the secret testimony before the judge. Runt Plotkin had got some of it from a newspaperman. There were certain mutilations. . . .

Rose Heller got up and walked off, sisterly, with Lil Klein. Rose knew she looked terrible in a bathing suit from behind. Someone whistled: "Lank and leany Chile beanie—" and she heard Lou actually laugh. This was the end, she felt sadly, of her girlhood crush.

". . . Well, if they're insane, everybody that commits a crime is insane!" Aline said.

"What's the difference between insanity and genius? None!" Alvin cried. "How do we know our laws are right? Why can't it be that just the opposite is right?"

"Is that what you're going to preach when you're a rabbi?" Sylvia said, mischievously.

Alvin looked directly into her eyes and smiled. She smiled back. He was fighting them all, Joe and Mort and the whole crowd, fencing with his wits, dancing his intellect before her.

"If I want to be a rabbi it's because there's good money in it and I can lie as well as any other rabbi," he declared. And in that instant he saw himself as a rabbi, preaching morality to a swanky congregation, and going around and seducing their wives; a suave Jekyll-Hyde personality, in whom those forces that tend toward the poles which for want of better terms we call good and evil, were always tenuously balanced, so that his soul forever quivered like a ball suspended between two magnets.

"What good would it possibly do to hang them?" he said. "What is the sense of destroying such brilliant minds?"

"Think of their families!" Aline said. "If they're executed!"

"Really everyone admires Leopold and Loeb," Alvin maintained. "Everyone wishes they had their nerve, to do exactly what they want to do."

"Oh, you don't believe any of that junk," Sylvia said. In her heart, she was thinking of the girl who loved Babe Leopold. What if Joe, in one of his moods, did something wild! But no, Joe had his work, his art, in which to release his talent, Joe was better balanced than those boys. Oh, it was better to have work to do, to have to struggle; work was healthy and clean, like the sun-baked sand, and the water. Idly, she had clasped Joe's fingers, and now they were heaping a hill of sand over their joined hands. . . . "You're just trying to show off!" Sylvia said to Alvin. "You just talk like that because it sounds smart."

"How do you know what I believe?" Alvin challenged.

"Well, underneath, I think you have more sense," she said. "You're just young."

He glared at her, while icy, supercilious remarks rose to his mind. But her face was yet so guileless, so girlishly pure, so unworried in the sun, with its perfect heart shape, that Alvin began to smile, and then she broke into a friendly, smooth rill of laughter. Somehow the instant seemed to be entirely between the two of them. Joe was out of it, at last. Alvin had an exhilarating sense of touching the truth between good and evil; she was a part of this discovery, she was the good, just the good, the goodness of a girl, the pure-hearted. She was with him now.

"Want to go in?" He jumped to his feet, pulled her up, and then they were standing on the faint indentation made by the last wave.

Alvin thought of this as the fine balance-line between good and evil; the good, as man knew it, was the sun-warmed land; the sea was the evil sphere, with inhabitants of its own, and it was constantly washing up on the land. Man could not remain long in the sea.

He felt clear-brained and capable; he felt much wiser and healthier than Leopold and Loeb, who had got drowned in the sea. He felt that being a rabbi, guiding other people in their sense of right and wrong—in a modern way—was exactly the work for which he was fitted.

Sylvia screeched as Alvin galloped into the lake, pulling her after him.

Mrs. Abramson and Mort had been at the shop all evening, wrestling with the books. The old man walked around the shop, picking up ends of trimmings that the cleaning women might throw away, and sorting them into boxes. He wouldn't bother with the accounts. "What we have, we have, and what we spent, we spent," was his philosophy.

Around ten o'clock, he shuffled back to the office, where those two had the books spread out.

"*Nu? Nu?*"

"I got it balanced, except for a dollar thirty-five cents," Mort said.

"Too much or too little?"

"Too little."

The old man drew some change from his pocket, counted out the money, and smacked it on the table. "*Na*. And an end. So it balances!"

CONQUERING HEROES COME

ON the way home from that beach party, Alvin had watched Joe and Sylvia cuddling in the back of the car, and had felt generous, giving them the free full rein of their puppy romance.

Each time he took Sylvia out, his destiny seemed larger, brighter to him. He saw himself in a fancy temple, delivering brilliant orations, while she sat in the front row, listening. The third time, he came all set to propose. He was wearing white flannels and a blue double-breasted jacket with a fancy silk handkerchief in the pocket. He had a new wrist-watch.

From the empty lot opposite, he could see their back porch. It was lighted. He approached through the lot. He could identify their voices—Mrs. Abramson, firm and loud—maybe soon his mother-in-law. And Mort! They were playing poker. Meanwhile a conversation went on about the Prince of Wales, in Chicago on his tour.

"You know who he looks a little like, Mort?" Mrs. Abramson was saying.

"Aw, come on, ma, admit you've got a crush on him!"

"I!" Mrs. Abramson giggled.

"What's the matter, ma, are you tired of Rudy Valentino?"

"Come, are you playing poker or not? Mort! Give two cards!" the old man snapped.

"Three for me," Sylvia said.

For an instant Alvin was disappointed at the way Sylvia fitted into the picture, a smug, ordinary home. But just then she rose, he saw her in something summery, and he knew he would take her with him to things above all this.

Mort opened the door to him, grinned wisely, and went to call Syl from the back porch.

"What's the idea, giving Joe some competition?" he heard Mort say.

He saw Sylvia smooth herself, for him, and make a face at Mort as she came out.

"My, you look like the Prince of Wales!" she said.

"All except the horse," he bantered, nervously.

"Maybe you just fell off the horse!"

"Well, it all depends who I'm falling for." He colored, dismayed at his flat persiflage.

"You'll never believe it but I saw him today! He was right on campus!" Sylvia recounted.

"No! Can I touch you?" He touched her arm, with an extended finger. But his movement was jerky, instead of light.

"Did he give the girls a thrill! You should have seen them flocking after him!"

They went into the frontroom.

He was smirking at her, and yet his face was white.

"Why, what's the matter?" she asked.

"Listen, Sylvia, I have to talk seriously to you." His words came in a sudden, confident rush. He thought he would be eloquent. "I know there is Joe, but listen, this is different. I love you, Sylvia." Now banal words, not clever at all, flew from his lips, and in the very agony of knowing their commonness, Alvin felt a kind of glow at their truth. He was being just like everybody else, saying the same words everybody said, they must be the right words. "I can't live without you, Sylvia. Will you marry me?"

His confusion was so obvious that Sylvia felt herself almost drawn to yield by his sincere want.

At the same time she thought: I bet he had a clever way to propose, all fixed up, poor goof.

And underneath everything was the glowing thought that this was the first time a man had really proposed to her; with Joe it was just an understanding.

He went on, in her silence: "Listen, Sylvia, I know about Joe but I think if you give me a chance you will see this is different. I want you to agree to give me a chance to show you what I really am, that's all!"

She put out her hand. "You're all right, Alvin," she said. Oh, men were so simple! Just because she had made fun of him he had to decide she understood him, and fall in love with her. "But you really don't understand about me and Joe," she said. "It's more than you think. It's—I don't like to talk about it, but there can't be anything else. I'm sorry if I've got to be the one to hurt you. I—I really feel honored that you think you want me that way, Alvin, that you think I could mean so much to you."

But now Alvin seemed actually to go to pieces. His voice shot off pitch, and she was afraid he was going to cry. "Sylvia, I don't know what's happened to me! I'm crazy about you! Honest, I—I'm—I'm like a man out of his senses. I go around saying your name over and over. Sylvia, you don't know what it is. I—I'll never love anyone else. You've got to give me a chance—"

Actually, he was going to fall on his knees! Why, what was the matter with him!

"Alvin, you mustn't take it that way! I never imagined you would act like this. It isn't that I don't like you. I could be your friend, and—"

At that word, a kind of moan burst out of him.

Oh, words were so useless. How could he make her understand the certainty he had felt, and the sense of power it had given him? He couldn't exist, without that certainty. He begged: "Listen, Sylvia, don't decide now.

Don't make it final. I just want you to know that I'm serious. That I mean to win you—"

She smiled her most womanly smile. She smoothed his hand.

He jerked himself erect. "I'd better go," he said dramatically. It was as though he saw himself from two sides. He laughed at his own posturing, and he was sorry for himself. "You think this is just a passing fancy. You think I'm putting it on," he said.

"Oh, no, no, Alvin. Only—don't you understand . . .?"

"All right." He clamped his lips tight. "I won't say anything more about it." He heard Mort coming toward them whistling:

"Oh, last night, on the back porch . . ."

and suddenly felt in perfect control of himself.

The Sixteenth Street Savings Bank was a cheesy little neighborhood bank where a lot of old Jews, actually old Yids with beards, kept their few dollars; and when it went bust, of course Droopy Meisel had to have his total savings there. It was only about eighteen dollars in an Xmas Savings Account, but he felt as if the whole thing had been done against him.

What was the use of scroining away his lunch and carfare money when the bank lost it for him? He could just as well lose it for himself.

So he was feeling sore, and reckless.

He answered the phone. It was a squeaky, tinkly voice that asked the usual question: "Is Solly there?"

"Solly isn't home," he said. And suddenly added the words he had often imagined himself adding: "Won't I do?"

"Huh?"

"How about me? I'm Solly's brother."

"Yah? And I'm Gloria Swanson!"

"Wadya want Solly for? Won't I do? My name is Ben. How are you, kiddo?"

And before he knew it he had dated her up. "Sure, I'll be there with bells on. Wednesday night. By, Grace."

Now Ben was a pretty sloppy-looking fellow, but like a lot of guys who wear the same greasy tie from winter to summer, and never shine their shoes, he had a hankering buried way behind his ears to be a sheik, too. When a suit was so badly damaged in cleaning that the customer had to be paid off, he got it. Usually the coat fitted him like a burst potato skin, while his wrists dangled out below the cuffs.

Now he hardly had nerve enough to go through with this date. What if the girl should tell Sol?

But, gee, the kind of a girl that called fellows up would probably let him go the whole way with her. Wait till he saw those wise guys, Mort, Runt, and his brother Sol, he'd hint around—oh, boy, some sweet mama I've got,

I'll say she can! Where does she live? Uh-uh. What's her name? Well—Gladys. A good *shikseh* name.

So there was Ben Meisel on Wednesday after school, furtively hauling out his good suit, a brown one, uncalled for when nearly new. Approaching the pressing machine, he laid the pants on the board. "Here, wait, let me," the old man said after a moment of watching him, and pressed his suit for him.

He had two dollars in his pocket. Maybe have to take her to a movie.

The address was on Buena Terrace. Boy, wasn't that the Wilson Avenue district? Were the broads hot around there!

The hallway was dirty imitation marble. One of the mailboxes hung open, busted.

Besides her name, there were three other names scribbled on a card over that box. Maybelle Schreiber. Kallen. Aline Taylor. Grace Norlander.

On the third-floor landing, a door was being held slightly ajar. "What is it?" a voice piped, in a tone that could get mad any minute.

"Uh. I'm Ben Meisel," he said.

"Who?"

"Uh, is this where—is Gracie—Miss Norlander home?"

The door opened halfway. He could see her now; she was blond, and she had on a lot of make-up. She was wearing a waist that showed her valley. Plenty there. Mmm-mm!

She certainly gave him the once-over.

"Gracie isn't here," she said.

"Huh?"

"Gracie went out."

He stood, blinking at her.

"Was she expecting you?" the girl, woman, broad, whatever she was, asked coolly. And that was the first moment he got the idea she was laughing at him.

"Why, uh, I guess so, uh, did she say when she was coming home?" he blundered.

"I think she went out for the evening," the woman said, as though she were having a laugh, inside. She put her hand to hair, in a ritzy gesture. "Shall I tell her you called?"

"Why, uh, yes, I mean, don't bother, it's all right . . ." All he wanted was the stairs. Down, down. Quick!

Did he hear a titter? Laughter, following him?

He stopped, and crept back halfway up the stairs, his blood beating. He heard nothing. He went down and into the street.

Only then did Ben begin to feel certain that the girl he had been talking to was Gracie. She had looked him over and decided he was nothing like Sol.

She was all set, but when she took one look at him . . .

He passed a movie but it was a Rudy Valentino picture. He bought an *American* and got on the El and read about the Love Cult in the House of David[1].

PASS: GRANGE[2] TO LINDY[3]

During the first months, Lil had acted as though she wouldn't admit what was happening to her. She acted as if, in her case, the belly would stay flat under the wide patent-leather belt she wore with her plaid skirt.

Then she compromised by letting out her clothes a little, secretly, as though hiding the fact even from herself. Finally, when the little circles at the base of her nipples came alive, changed from a dried-leaf color to a delicate, transparent purple, when she felt her rising and swelling breasts all the time, she went to Lane Bryant's and bought some maternity clothes.

Before she got really big she was all the time wanting Sam to take her out. She wanted to go to dine-and-dance places, to Kelley's Stables on Saturday night, to see the *Covered Wagon*, everywhere, as though she were storing up her last pleasures.

Sam had to put in his evenings at law school, and at studying; besides he got no kick out of going to cabarets where a lot of couples shuffled around in one spot, in the dark, to the tune of the "St. Louis Blues," and then having to pay a dollar for a glass with some ice in it. And he dreaded the chance of meeting people, kids from the bunch in places like the Stables, or the Dill Pickle Club on Sunday nights.

Then Lil came to another phase of her pregnancy. She was always standing up and turning around before the girls, or before relatives. "Well, can you notice it yet? Aw, you don't have to kid me. I'm ashamed to be seen in the streets!" She was like a two-year-old who has done something nasty in the back yard, and insists on leading everybody to it, and pointing it out.

Whenever Sam caught himself thinking in that way of Lil, he would be surprised at himself, and pained, because after all she was being such a good sport about everything.

---

[1] The Israelite House of David was a small but industrious and prominent Christian sect founded in 1903. It became notorious in the 1920's when allegations surfaced that the organization was a sex cult. This was probably untrue, but the scandal sheets promoted the stories, and legal charges against the leader followed.
[2] "Red" Grange was a football hero of the 1920's and 1930's.
[3] On May 20-21, 1927, Charles ("Lindy") Lindbergh became the first aviator to cross the Atlantic non-stop. Previous attempts had ended in failure and, in some cases, death.

But there were moments, when he was overworked, tired of abstracting cases, weary of the unceasing daily grind from job to school to bed to job, when she got on his nerves.

It seemed to him then that Lil had abandoned her own self and moved into him, and that she wouldn't let him have a thought or a breath to himself. If he so much as got up from his reading, for a glass of water, she would call from the bedroom: "Sam, what are you doing?"

"Nothing. I went to the kitchen for a glass of water."

When he came home from working in her father's office, she wanted to know everything that had happened, who was there, what deals were going on, were the floors being laid in those houses her father was building on Congress Street?

Her latest campaign was to get her folks to go to Florida for the winter. "Sam could take care of the business," she kept saying. "Pa has high blood pressure, and Florida would be the best thing for him."

Knowing Mr. Klein, one knew that the last thing he could do was leave his business and go off to Florida. Yet lately Lil was even talking about it as of something settled. "You can leave as soon as Skeezix arrives," she would say.

One night when Sam was all in, and had just answered the phone and had to report to Lil that it was a wrong number, he thought: "I didn't want to take this flat from her father, but we took it. I didn't want to work for her father, but I'm working for him. It wasn't my idea to raise the rents, but we raised them. . . ." He stopped himself from analyzing how they happened to get married.

And anyway what was wrong about all those things? They were working out okay.

Then, a few months before her time, things were quieter. The prenatal calm that one heard about seemed to have settled over Lil, and she was content to sit for hours with her hands folded upon her pregnancy, with her legs, that now seemed puny and short, resting on a hassock. In those long evenings there was a restfulness, a sense of order and of the calm unfolding of life, that Sam had never known before.

He felt himself to be so much older, more mature, than the fellows around law school who talked of nothing but Dempsey beating Firpo and Zev beating Papyrus and Chicago beating Northwestern, and did she have It?

He got a laugh out of good old Illini. Somehow his name seemed to have got on the mailing list of alumni. He kept getting pep letters asking him to buy a brick in the magnificent new stadium. And now: your Alma Mater calls you! The homecoming! The big game opening the new stadium, Chicago vs. Illini.

His Alma Mater! Even though he had been kicked out!

He saw himself when a middle-aged man, maybe a judge, leaning back in his chair, telling this joke on the university that kicked him out.

On a Harrison Street car, going out to the new buildings with a message for Mr. Klein, Sam met Harry Perlin.

"Hello, Harry, what are you doing in this neck of the woods?"

"Oh, I work out here. Say, Sam, I haven't seen you in a dog's age. What are you doing these days?"

"Oh, I've got a job," Sam said, not caring to mention that it was with his father-in-law.

"Still going to law school?"

"Yep."

"I was going to Armour nights, but I'm staying out this semester," Harry informed him. "My mother has gallstones and I've got to send her to Rochester for an operation, so I took on some extra night work at the garage."

If he wasn't the original hard-luck Harry, Sam thought.

"Going down for the game?" Harry asked. "I certainly would like to see that Red Grange, he must be a wonder. That's going to be some game, one man against a team!"

A lot of the bunch were driving down for the game, Harry had heard. Gee, it would be a great homecoming. The best he could do would be to get it over the radio.

"I'd like to see that new stadium," Harry said with wistful humor. "I've got a brick in there someplace."

Red Grange was the fellow that carried the ball, alone, slipping and dodging through a whole opposition team, and streaking for the goal.

That was one kind of player Sam would like to watch. A single player, running the gantlet of the entire opposition, and reaching the point for which he set out!

That Saturday morning while Sam was making coffee for himself and toast for Lil, he noticed that the cover on the milk bottle was damp, and he wondered if this foggy chill day would give Red Grange the added handicap of a muddy field, and if Red Grange could make it, even through mud!

Sam was usually alone at the office on Saturday mornings, as Miss Nathan had religious parents. The office consisted of two cheesy little rooms over Mrs. Kagen's drug store on St. Louis and Roosevelt. *Real Estate, Loans, and Insurance* was printed on the pebbly frosted glass, with the words, *Notary Public* in a lower corner. Mr. Klein had a sort of partner, a fat geezer named Shiffrin, who went out peddling insurance. Klein and Shiffrin, sometimes together, sometimes separately, dealt in second and even in third mortgages. Besides, they were loan sharks. Loans from fifty to a few hundred dollars at interest up to three percent a month, plus commission. Besides general office work, Sam had to collect rents in buildings which they owned in complicated partnerships; here, and on the Northwest Side, and a Thirteenth Street slum where he hated to take money. On the North Side building in which Sam and Lil lived, Klein had raised a second mortgage in order to finance the construction of four buildings way out on Congress Street, as that new Columbus Park district was certain to boom. The deal on those buildings was typical: Klein owned two of the lots, Shiffrin one, they owned the fourth together. They had borrowed some money from the West Side Bank and, Sam thought, had practically borrowed from each other. The contractor was always hounding the office, threatening to quit the job unless he got some cash, and yet always accepting more notes.

Klein was a little sensitive about his loan business. Only lately he had cut out the twenty-five dollar loans. Sam remembered how as a child he had often heard talk at home of commissions, notes due: once his mother had needed two hundred dollars desperately, in a hurry, to bring over a young brother and save him from military service in the old country. Sam liked to imagine how many times each hundred dollars of Klein's had gone back and forth, bringing a Jew to America.

Many of the customers would start talking Yiddish, but Mr. Klein would respond in a cold staccato English. Occasionally, when a client really knew no English, Mr. Klein would unloose a fluent *mama-loshen*, the mother-tongue, but the words would be dropped from his lips as though they had an unclean taste.

Sam found, gradually, that part of his job was keeping tabs on Mr. Shiffrin, and on Miss Nathan, who was a relative of Mr. Shiffrin, and was trying to keep tabs on Klein.

Each dollar was loaned, borrowed, loaned, till it served a dozen ways; on every deal that was made there had to be a rakeoff; if Klein ordered coal, it was: "Yah, I know, but what's the price for me? Don't I get a rakeoff?" and if the contractor showed Klein some bills for lumber, Klein wondered how much the contractor actually paid.

Sam had always known a little about this kind of Jewish business; but now he began to feel the ceaselessness, the relentlessness, of this incessant squirming, gnawing, bickering. And it was a lust with them! They enjoyed it, lived for it, couldn't be otherwise. Occasionally, with a kind of awed respect, they remarked about some large company: "That's a one-price place."

Borrowing on borrowed money and lending that out to be borrowed again. And each time the sum left an increasing part of itself as interest, and yet was whole.

Klein, and his friends, and Miss Nathan, and the dentist down the hall—everyone trying to guess how much the other fellow was really worth. . . . "What's a hundred bucks to a millionaire like you, Klein?" "Yah, millionaire! Say, if I had your dough . . ."

Well, how much *was* Klein really worth? If, at any one instant, the whole involved turning of wheel within wheel could be stopped, what number would be up? As far as Sam could figure out, his father-in-law, Marcus Klein, was on the way to becoming a millionaire. He must be worth at least fifty thousand dollars in his own right.

Klein came in a few moments after Sam. The greeting would go: "How's Lil?" "She's fine." "That's fine. Say, Sam, did that old *kaker* Davidson bring in that ten-dollar payment yesterday?"

This morning there was a kind of Sabbath calm about the office, about the whole building. It was as if everybody had actually gone off to synagogues, or football games. Marcus Klein came over and sat near Sam.

"Listen Sam, uhh, about Lil, when the time comes . . . I believe in taking advantage of all the latest things in civilization. She ought to have a room in a hospital, and they've got this twilight sleep now, a woman hardly feels the pains of childbirth. You don't know what it is, Sam, to have to listen to it!"

His father-in-law was only trying to help him. Yet Sam felt as though he were being treated like a kid.

"I heard that stuff wasn't all it's cracked up to be," Sam argued.

"Listen, better not take any chances. Let her have a private room in the Israel Hospital. I'll—hh—I'll take care of it. . . ."

"It's up to her," Sam said. "But if my wife needs anything to have her baby, why, whatever it is we'll want to take care of it ourselves"; he was unable to keep a note of belligerence out of his voice. "I mean, you've done a lot for us getting us started but you know a fellow likes to feel, a thing like this, he can take care of it himself."

"You know, Sam, we can't take any chances. Girls, these modern girls, they won't have it so easy. Their mothers used to scrub floors on their knees and having a kid was nothing for them. But a girl like Lil never raised a finger all her life. You know how it was with us fellows too, we came green to this country, and we had to do the best we could, without any education, without any connections. So we want our children to have it easier."

He fingered his cigar. Sam was silent.

"Sam, what's the difference, if it has to cost something you can pay me back, I'll make it a loan." And, with his familiar rigid smile, he joked: "You can even pay me interest if you want."

Half meaning it, Sam thought. Three percent a month.

"That's all right, but I don't think I'll need it this time," Sam said. "Of course I want to do the best for Lil, anything she wants . . ."

"In a couple of years you'll be a lawyer, you'll be making plenty of bucks, Sam, this little help don't mean a thing."

"It isn't the money," Sam said. "You know I wouldn't take any chances with Lil because of money, Mr. Klein. But you know a fellow likes to feel— well, independent . . ."

Hitching his leg over the table, Mr. Klein began to talk, as though deciding to say something he had had in his mind for a long time.

"Listen, Sam, why do you go around with a chip on your shoulder? You know what I mean, even in business I noticed it, you talk to people as if they were against you all the time. Believe me, Sam, my boy, this is from my heart. When it comes to being friends, Sam, this is my experience: people want to be friends with people." All the while he spoke of friendship, Sam noticed, Marcus Klein's face wore his usual half-pained expression, that expression of waiting for small change. "You take life too seriously, Sam. Don't worry, everything will be all right, a young fellow like you ought to enjoy life!" His tone changed to that of a person relieved of a duty. "Hh, hh. Why, any day you'll be passing out cigars, and I'll be a proud granpa! Getting old! Time to retire, and sit in Florida, with my rheumatism, huh! Say, what are you going to name him?"

Their eyes met, and they both felt embarrassed, estranged, wanting to be intimate and unable. Sam went to the window, and noticed it was drizzling, and thought of Red Grange, and thought maybe the real thing his father-in-law had been getting at was that he didn't fit so well into this business, he didn't seem to get the hang of kibitzing and finagling, he couldn't chortle and slap on the shoulder with the rest of them, oh, maybe he was just too young, had let himself in for things too soon.

He wondered about this twilight sleep, and decided, if he saw Rudy Stone, to ask his opinion.

Excuse my dust! was scrawled on the back of the flivver, and *So's your old man!* Illini banners flew from the braces.

"Yeah! Chicago!" the kids shrieked challengingly, as Mort whipped the Paige out of line, snaked between the flivver and an oncoming truck, and zammed down the clear road.

A derisive scream arose from the flivver. It was an overflowing kettle of sheepskin boys and raccoon girls, the red-blobbed cheeks of the girls glistening in the milky drizzle.

The driver of the flivver yelled and stepped on the gas. Galloping with limbs all out of joint, the Leaping Lena jumped up alongside the Paige, and kept pace.

"Well, I'll be!" Mort banged his foot to the floor.

"Mort! Have a heart!" Aline cried from the back seat.

"Mort! We'll skid!" Sylvia admonished.

"Mort, we aim to see this game from the grandstand, not from the morgue," Mitch Wilner protested.

The girls in the flivver were singing:

"We've got string beans and honions
And all kinds of fruit—"
The Paige cut in front of them.
"But, YES, we have no bananas—!"

Mort just missed another truck that came banging out of the fog. He couldn't bear to ride behind anything. He was Red Grange, and the cars that cluttered the road were the clumsy opponents, blocking his way. "I want to get there before the final whistle," Mort said. "I want to see that guy walk all over the Maroons!"

And Mitch and Syl, suddenly full of school spirit, argued wildly with him; they didn't even know the names of the players on their team, except the Thomas brothers, but now in the rising morning, going where everybody was going, being carefree and collegiate, they cried: Huh, what is one man against a TEAM, it's TEAMWORK that counts, and they were the center of America, the core of the crowds headlined in the papers: GOING TO THE BIG GAME!

The sometimes endlessness of still being in school, the sometimes fear of never really meeting life, was wiped out, vanished; in a time like this they knew that they were inside and the world was outside trying to come in, trying to be like them; even Mort somewhat hung along, somewhat borrowed from their contact; and prophetically they knew that their entire lives might be a centering back to the certainty of this fine cool rain-splashed morning on the road, when they were real college kids.

Joe had been necking a girl on campus but of course she was just a pastime, compared to Sylvia. This Myra Roth wore soft woolly skirts and wide-sleeved blouses and a real Spanish comb in her hair. Very exotic. They had met through an argument over Shelley in the Lit course, each addressing the instructor, while in truth they were shouting at each other as if the class didn't exist. The girl had called Shelley a sentimental romantic, too soft for this world, and Joe had defended Shelley, crying: "Why, he was even a socialist!" "Well, if that isn't sentimental romance, I'd like to know what is!" the girl retorted, and the whole class roared. So they continued the argument after class; and when she lent him *The Dance of Life* he had to start walking her around the cemetery at night. She came from a wealthy family, was sort of a distant cousin to Leopold or Loeb, and she left a vague mystery there, as though she was burying herself down at the State U, hiding from her own crowd.

The bunch came running up the stairs, filling the room. Sylvia entered last, and Joe could sense how she stood just within the door to catch the first true feeling of the room, and of him toward her again.

"Hail! So you actually got here in time!" he greeted them.

"The way Mort drove it's a wonder we didn't get here yesterday!" Aline said. "Hey, where's the Theta house?" and pretty soon Mitch Wilner had shagged off to find his fraternity, and Aline had dragged Mort off ("Give hon and dearie a break," they heard Aline say on the stairs).

For a moment they stood just as they had been when the others went out, and in that moment Joe funnily remembered the little ring Sylvia had once given him, on that night when they had been to the opening of the Chicago.

She was looking at the board where he was doing a joist problem, tiresome stuff.

"Gee, I've missed you," he said, feeling far away from college romances, and permanent with her.

Sylvia looked into his eyes, like a woman who takes a man back.

All twisted their necks to see the airplane. "Know what the stadium must look like to him?" Joe remarked. "Like a horseshoe magnet, and all the people and the cars like iron filings drawn to the magnet."

"Say, that's just it!" Mitch said, admiring Joe's imagination.

"This mud isn't going to do Red Grange any good," Mort observed.

"Say, don't worry about him!" Joe cried, with a sudden surge of school pride.

"You know what happened when they opened the Yale bowl," Mort said expertly. "The home team always loses when they open a new stadium!"

Emerging out of the stairhatch, they saw the filled stadium.

The two legs of the horseshoe stretched far into the mist, two streams of speckled color. Like the dots on a pointillist canvas, Joe saw the picture, innumerable dots of primary colors fitted side by side, until they made a wholeness.

The Illini band! Largest college band in the world! In perfect ranks, marching!

The Chicago band! Wheeling the biggest drum in the world!

Oh, they could yell for both sides, for everybody, for the whole thing together, for the crowd, and Chicago and Illinois, for the planes zooming and crisscrossing above them, and the giant new stadium beneath them, for everybody and for themselves.

The mob on the Illini side had all their wills bent upon that one fellow, that new star, that soph Red Grange: that he might get away, bust loose, run! The spectators on the Chicago side had come to see him stopped. But even from Chicago there was the desire to see this man thwart their own resistance, thwart the mud, the threatening rain, thwart the sky that hung heavy ready to pounce on him; he must break loose from all, get free, run, win! He was the sun against all the clouds in the sky! Sixty thousand wills bent upon him! Break free! Run! Win!

All eyes turned following the arc of the kicked ball; a man waited, shifting under it; destined, it came into his waiting arms. He slipped, lost the ball.

Who recovered?

Chicago's ball! On the Illini fifteen-yard line!

Touchdown Chicago! Touchdown Chicago! and Syl cried: Pooh pooh, your Red Grange!

But this is only the device of fate, to put man at the furthest point from his goal, to crush him under the heaviest odds; then he must rise, the man alone, against that opposing machine, that smooth eleven-headed hammer all aimed for him; through the mud that sucks at his heels, through the wall ever re-forming before him, tearing and dodging, he must triumph.

The Staggmen thrust the ball right through the Illini line. Made it? Run out with the tape!

Watch. First, the orderly arrangement of the players: two parallel lines, and behind each line, men placed in balanced arrangement. Hike. A new pattern, and one line shifts with the other, as though purely following the laws of design, of symmetry. Then impact, and confusion. What happened? What's his number? I think it was an end run. No, a line buck.

All the names they know are end run, forward pass, hit the line. Behind them two expert collegians sit and call the plays: "He's going to try it through Ferguson, watch"; "This is a fake"; "It's a crisscross." Joe, Mitch, Mort, too would foretell, they too would be quarterbacks. Watch! A forward pass! Sure enough, the ball is in the air!

The whole mass of humanity arose, as if the stadium by one breath had extended itself, and one great throat howled: "He's away!"

Then Mort, Mitch, Joe, Sylvia, Aline, Art, Butch, Nell, Bella, Ethel, Whitey, saw him streaking. . . . It's Red Grange, it can't be any other, only he could do it! Can you see his number? That's him! That must be him! The whole field streaking after.

One man cut across, a tangent arrow, aiming straight for the runner. Oh, he'll get him!

No! A break in rhythm, a half skip, and the runner slipped wide of the tackler. They could see the tackle's empty grasping hands as he fell.

He's free!

Oh, a beauty! A beauty!

But they'll get him! Those two, waiting for him.

Near the twenty-yard line, two men brought him down.

Slowly in a rumbling wave the mass of people bowed to their seats. Slowly, the screaming, the hysteria, faded. This too had to be as it was. Man, in sight of his goal, halted. He must rise again, and make it.

It began to rain now. Darkness, mud; the final obstacles were being flung around determined man.

Now, as they settled to watch the game furthering itself, Joe began to feel, and wanted to communicate, that sense of perfect design that comes fleetingly in football games. Momentarily one sees the players arranged as in a frieze, here a man fallen to one knee, just above him a runner with straight-arm thrust out, a tackler half launched through the air. Sometimes an action newspaper camera catches such an instant: the rise and fall of vari-posed figures breaking the spaces of the picture, composing into a single harmonious unit. It is as if one had taken a cross-section of time, a microscopic slice so fine and thin as to halt the fluctuating pattern that is at every moment perfect, but whose continuity may sometimes seem unbalanced.

Some time, Joe thought, he must compose a frieze like that; an American sculpture, of college football. Oh, all the things that he had yet to do!

The rain was steady now, an ever-falling curtain, a damp gauze being let down, unceasingly fresh on their faces. They could hear the smack of bodies falling in the mud.

And in the third quarter, perfectly in the appointed time, like the rise and climax of a symphony, the moment came. Illini got the ball. All knew the ball would go to Grange. All aimed for him. A sidestep, a circle, a dance, a turn, and through for a gain. Down. Again. And down. And the third time, following the known and inevitable crescendo, the man, the hero, Red Grange, the hero, with the ball tucked close, eluding fate, eluding the rain, shaking the mud off his hoofs, knocking aside all opponents, Red Grange is away! He's away! Skirting the field, streaking along the sidelines, and,

He's done it! he's done it!

veering in and planting the ball.

In that moment, all arisen, all reaching to their fullest heights on their toes, with their arms upflung, with their greatest voice, all are with him, and all are as one. In that moment the crowd, America, is one will of achievement, one shared triumph, in that moment love surges in the throat, for beauty and unconquerability, and the proven way of life! Love, love for these raccoon- and mink- and squirrel-coated backs, these red, yellow, green, blue felts, these black, brown, yellow curls peeking out over pink ears, these glistening and shining girl faces and young men faces; there is a gush of love, a sweeping sense of unity, of the goodness of life, the fullness of coming life!

Under his yelling joy, Mort knows that he has witnessed truth, seen man, seen himself conquer, buck the line, dodge, twist, vault, run, make that touchdown! Mitch Wilner sees himself after repulse and rebuff planting his beautifully carried out work of research square behind the goals of human knowledge: here, I have brought this, torn it away from the first adversary, ignorance, doggedly fought it through the stages of doubt, finally run with it alone clear to the final conclusion. Joe Freedman sees his statue high on some proud white skyscraper; Aline sees herself the hostess at her door on Sheridan Road; all, sixty thousand, are lifted in triumph to their various goals.

But suddenly a doubt quells them. The referee has the ball tucked in the crook of his elbow. He is stepping back. Always some sneaking trick of fate, to take away what man has rightfully achieved. They say Red Grange stepped out of bounds as he ran. On the seven-yard line.

Like that, some force will always try to drag you. back after you have won. But never mind. He'll make it again. There was a false-alarm Armistice but it was immediately followed by the real Armistice. Clarence Saunders made a fortune with Piggly Wiggly, had it taken away, and made it again. Just so, Red Grange will double-prove his right.

The Maroon wall hardens. A player bangs his head against the wall. Give it to Red! Give it to Red! It's his job, it's his right! The two teams are in one heap. He squirms, twists, worms the last inch, and he's over the line.

His face in the mud. The ball parenthesized in his solid palms. Done. All obstacles overcome.

Slowly the wild shaken spirits subside. They have seen what they came to see.

Faces in the mud and faces upturned to the rain. Nothing can stop a man.

Selecting his tiniest screwdriver from the neat tool rack, Harry Perlin bent over his workbench. He drove the little brass screws of the new condenser into place, and returned the tool to its groove. Eagerly, he tested the sound: ". . . Chicago tries a desperate aerial attack . . ." The sound came through the tubes sweet as the purr of a new motor: ". . . and now the Staggmen are driving down the field, desperate, hungry for the touchdown that will even the score . . ." Some day like Red Grange he would suddenly burst out of the backfield and show them what was what.

The gray weepy outdoors heightened his feeling of peaceful security among these basement walls that he himself had whitewashed; behind him, far back in the basement, was the dry warmth of the furnace he himself had tended, burning the coal his wages paid for. Lately, maybe because of his mother, Harry had begun to feel something different about the Sabbath. As a kid she had commanded him: never ride on a street car on Saturday, never even carry a penny in your pockets, it's a sin. Of course he had dropped all that silly stuff. Yet even now, merely by changing the tablecloth on Friday night to one of thick white linen, by lighting the brass candlesticks, his mother seemed to bring a transformation upon the whole flat, until it glowed with an inner warm glow, like the heart of a candleflame.

Now, since his father had died, his old mother had become more religious than ever; she was always changing butchers and grocers because she suspected what they sold her was not strictly kosher. Another thing, she seemed to have forgotten all the English she had ever known, and now spoke to her boys only in Yiddish, while they answered in English.

But on Saturdays, the peaceful Sabbath spell seemed to reach down like a crack of sunlight into the very basement where he worked on his hobbies.

". . . He's away! The crowd is on its feet again! But that mud is treacherous . . ."

Right now he would have been a junior, sitting in the stands with his own collegiate crowd. The first hundred years are the hardest, and after that first lonely semester he would probably have got to know more people, even fellows like Red Grange; things would have been jollier, easier.

The crack of the gun; the vague wild jumble of jubilant cries sounded in his ears, and something welled in his throat: We won! We won! Aline! Joe! Ha ha ha! We won!

As Harry passed up the rear stairs to get himself a glass of milk and a hunk of the rich yellow Sabbath cake the old lady always had on the table for him, he heard the garage door banging. A dozen times he had told Victor, next time he left the door open he'd never get the car again. That kid took things too easy. He'd graduate from high next semester and Harry was thinking of sending him to Illinois but he'd have to work part of his way, Harry determined.

It was while closing the door that he thought of his million-dollar invention.

All the houses were lit tonight, girls and fellows in gay laughing crowds flitted from frat house to sorority, the fellows with their crushed felt campus hats perched over their tuxedoes, the girls with shimmering formals wisping out under the sheepskin jackets they had borrowed from the boys; from a veranda came a clear snatch of song, throaty:

"I've got a cross-eyed papa, but he looks straight to me . . ."

And Bradley's was jammed; in two far corners rival gangs were trying to outsing each other with Maroon and Illini songs, but someone started "Yes, We Have No Bananas," and both gangs chimed in, with a united roar.

Myra Roth was there, scintillating in a gang of campus intellectuals. "Oh, hello," Joe said, and, with the knowledge that girls have, Sylvia drew within herself, cold, at the introduction. Later, in the shuffle, there was a moment when Sylvia was dancing with Mitch Wilner, and Joe found himself near Myra. "So that's the little girl you're going to marry some day?" Myra said.

"Sure, I guess so," Joe replied. And suddenly the sense of doom, of limitation, came down upon him.

"She's sweet," Myra said with a slow parting of her red ribbon lips.

"Uh huh," Joe murmured. As she moved away, it seemed as though all adventure were moving out of his life; why, he was an artist, one who should have a life thronged with women, with deeds.

"So that's your campus crush?" Sylvia said intimately, squeezing his fingers with womanly knowing, and forgiveness.

They went out and drove, and sat in the car. Joe was moody again.

"What's the matter, Joe?" she said.

"I'm sick of all this. Oh, why do I fool around, wasting my time?"

"You're not wasting your time . . ."

"Oh, I'll chuck all this and come to Chicago, I can get a drafting job, there is so much building going on, and we can get settled, and I can really start to work."

"Why, Joe, is this a proposal?" she said.

"No, honest, I'm sick of it all . . ."

She patted his hand. "Oh, Joeboy, we have to wait. We don't want to be like Sam Eisen and Lil . . ."

He agreed, silently, hopelessly; and yet he thought, what was wrong with Sam and Lil? At least they were set. No tortured nights.

But sure, first thing a kid, and tied down. . . .

A Child Is Born

The seven wise virgins got together in Ev Goldberg's ritzy house and proceeded to dish the dirt.

"Kiddo," Aline inquired, "how long have they been married?"

"Was it March, or was it April?" asked Rose Heller's kid sister, Mae, who was so suddenly grown up this year.

"I could have sworn she was five months gone that time we saw them on the beach, but I didn't want to—well, you know, insinuate."

Evelyn counted the months on her fingers.

"It's a pretty close shave, I'll say!" Aline cracked. Thelma snickered.

"What I don't understand is what the heck they expect to raise a child on," Sylvia remarked, somewhat tartly.

—Oh, don't worry, her folks'll take care of them.

—Why, Sam's working for her father now.

—Working. Ha ha.

—Don't kid yourself, he's earning whatever he gets from Lil's old man. We used to rent an apartment from him once. He wouldn't even buy a window shade.

—Well, when is the big event, anyway?

Rose Heller was the only one who had seen Lil lately. "Oh, girls, she looks terrible," Rose said.

They pounced on Rose for details.

The room was warm, snug with the juiciness of them, bright-eyed, avid, big girls now, developed in the last couple of years to the verge, and some over the verge of womanhood. Celia had large, creamy thighs whose candor sometimes startled her, and Thelma's figure had definitely become that of a waddly woman with a bump behind and a bump in front. When they got together there was a warm group female smell; and the room, the chairs after they left, seemed to bear an acrid, powdery humidity. Here even the sweet girls like Sylvia, the cool girls like Rose, were the same as all the girls; here, when they got together in a room, was unleashed a ferocious naturalness, clawing, catty, vulgar in screeching laughter, ruthless, and just as suddenly, dainty, reticent, tender as a summer blush.

—Believe me, I wouldn't go and have a kid like that. Say, I want to have some fun while I'm still young.

—Well maybe she got caught.

Horse-laughs.

—Page Margaret Sanger.

Shriek.

—People haven't got a right to bring children into the world unless they are all set to take care of them.

—Well, bulieve me, when I get hitched, it's going to be some guy my folks don't have to support.

—Oh, Lil roped him in.

—He'd never have married her of his own choice, you can bet your last brassiere on that.

—I bet she had the kid on purpose.

—What of it? She's got her man and she's entitled to keep him.

—GIRLS! you'll die when I tell you who I saw. I was with Charley Lazar and we were sitting in the Chez and who should be sitting right at the next table—

—Who?

—Estelle! . . . And you'll never guess what with!

—I know. A marathon dancer. They keep on for two months instead of six days.

—Rose, you'll kill me!

—A *sheigetz?*

—Howja guess? And is he a sheik!

—What's he like? Is he a good dancer? Has he got any mazuma? Is she going out with him, or . . .?

"Girls, he's positively devastating," Evelyn announced. "Oh, I could fall for him myself. He's got the swellest line. I danced with him. He said he only goes out with Jewish girls, by preference."

—Yah! knowingly.

"He's real blond, like butter. Tall, like Rod La Roque, and he's an engineer or something for the telephone company."

—Yah, I bet he's a nickel collector.

—Well, I wouldn't go out with a Gentile if he was a Rockefeller McCormick in person.

That started the old argument.

—Listen, those *shkotzim* are after only one thing.

"You don't have to give it to them do you?" Aline cracked.

—You can trust a Jewish fellow but you can never trust a *sheigetz*.

—But suppose it was a fellow you really liked. Suppose you were in love with him.

—You wouldn't marry a gentile, would you?

—I certainly would if I wanted to.

—Aline, your mother would die.

—She'd get over it.

—Well, it never works out.

—I'd go out with a *goy* but I wouldn't marry one.

"My cousin married a gentile and they're perfectly happy!" Ev Goldberg contributed.

"How do they bring up their children? That's the problem," Sylvia said sensibly.

"Oh, they haven't got any."

Only yesterday, two doctors conquered scarlet fever. Today, a doctor announced the cure for cancer. Every day medicine was making such terrific strides. So why should women still suffer in childbirth?

To suffer was indecent, it was putting modern woman back in the class of the squaw, Lil thought. Surely there was a clever bobbed-hair way of having a kid without all those ugly old-fashioned pains.

Night after night, as Sam sat at the table, studying: "I don't think it's really dangerous, Sam, do you?"

"What? Oh. No, I guess they wouldn't give it to people if it was dangerous."

"Mrs. Malkin was up here today, she says the natural way is the best, but I think when such marvelous discoveries are made people ought to use them. . . ."

Sometimes Sam had a peculiar, annoyed feeling that it was indecent for a woman to talk so much about how she would have her child. ". . . But Mrs. Barnett told me her first three deliveries she suffered terribly, she's so small. But the fourth one she had twilight sleep and she hardly felt it."

And she was small, too. Maybe she was a terrible fool to be doing all this, so young. Why had she wanted to be the first? To show all the girls? Why should they all benefit by her experience?

In another couple of years doctors would have perfected a way to make it absolutely painless. She just had to be a fool and be in a hurry. The last time she had been to the doctor he had seemed absolutely coldhearted. "He didn't even make any more urine tests," she complained to Sam.

She was wondering if it would be dangerous to switch doctors at this last minute.

"Sam . . ." she said. . . .

Rudy was putting in his free Sunday at Mrs. Kagen's, when Sam dropped in to ask about twilight sleep. Old Doc Meyerson was there, and Mitch Wilner was gassing with Rudy.

"Waaal, I'll taal you," Rudy drawled, "my idea is, let nature take its course."

Old Doc Meyerson suddenly burst out: "What pain, what shame! Listen, my young man, pains they've got, and pains they will have! All they know now in the hospitals is twilight sleep and forceps. If the labor takes five and a half minutes, doctor, the forceps! It's only a wonder they don't go in with a pick and shovel!"

They all laughed. "The doc's getting pretty old," Mitch murmured to Sam.

"Who's taking care of Lil?" Rudy asked. "Dr. Kroger? Well, you can leave it to him." Professionally: "He's a good man."

When the pain came, Lil was lifting a cup of tea (her mother said tea was good). She felt the pain like a fist clenching within her, holding, slowly opening.

So she dropped the cup. It seemed the cup was in her hand just for that purpose.

Sam was studying for a quiz. He rushed to the phone and of course there were no nickels in the house.

The moment the nurse pulled the tight nunlike white cap on her head, and that long awful moment while the nurse raised her stone-heavy legs and pulled the rumply white stockings up on them, Lil felt a chill despair in the very center of her heart. In a hospital. Operations. Death.

And as she lay there awhile alone, Lil felt tragically old, and able to judge herself of the past; how worthless and silly she had been, oh, she did everything wrong, even now, scaring everybody with a false alarm, and why did she need a private room when Sam took it so bad about money, oh, and it would even have been better in a ward, among other women, or at home, but not alone in this little prison room; and oh, Sam, I haven't been much use to you I even go and have a false alarm just when you have a quiz and need to study; and suddenly she felt an awe of Sam, and a terrible widening love, something so immense that it would rend her soul apart as this childbirth might rend apart her body.

And she thought to herself, now, at the very moment of the end, she knew everything; for the first time she understood her mother and her father, and how they had torn their needs from the wall of life, shred by shred, to build a safe life for her; it seemed to her that she even saw the whole life of her child spread before her, and because everything was all at once so clear, Lil was sure that her end had come. You could not see life, know life, and live. It was like a dread secret: those who knew it must die.

Just then the door opened, and it was her husband, Sam.

She reached her hand, small, squashy-fingered, damp, out from under the bedclothes.

"Sam, Sam," she quavered, "promise me, if anything happens—"

"Why, Lil!" he said strongly. "Nothing is going to happen. Don't be a sil!"

Oh, how tired he looked. And he had a quiz tomorrow. She saw in a flash Sam taking his quiz, tired, nodding, falling asleep over a schooldesk, Sam never a lawyer, all on account of her.

Her chin was trembling. Oh, how horrible she must look, her face all sweaty and blotchy, with those pimples along her nose, and her hair pulled back under that white cap better to show off her horrible face. She clutched his fingers; he pressed back, lovingly.

"Sam, if anything happens," she heard herself saying, "you're young. You must forget me. I want you to—I want you to marry again."

"Why, Lil, why, darling . . ."

"No. Please, Sam, you must promise me. Promise."

"But, Lil, honey. Don't talk like that. Nothing is going to happen."

A strange deep smile of wisdom flicked across her mouth. She wet her lips with her tongue. "Sammy. My Sammy. Oh, I know I've been a silly little girl . . ."

"Lil, darling. Don't." His face had become soft and his eyes started with pain from under his thick brows. The lemon-pale electric light struck one side of his face, and she could see the tight muscles and veins from his ears to his forehead.

In a low voice, feeling as if at last they two had arrived at the true togetherness, she said: "You're not sorry, about everything, Sam, are you?"

"Why, why, Lil, dear, of course not. I love you."

She let her hand relax.

"And, and promise, will you?"

"All right, honey, I promise." For a moment after these words he was silent as if the chill thought had at last reached his heart. "You sil," he said.

Suddenly her mouth contracted. Her pointed little nails dug into his palm.

It passed. She lay deep in the cradle of exhaustion. She felt now she had done all a real woman must do.

After her mother had come, Lil began to whimper for the doctor. And the nurse went away and let her suffer. Jealous old maid. Oh, where was Dr. Kroger?

He held her hand while a pain came and went, and then he was gone. She would die. She or the child. If it has to be a choice, let my child live. I don't want to live! What is there in life?

The pain was coming, she knew it was coming, she opened her mouth and screamed out of sheer impatience, screamed to bring on the pain, let it come, let it kill her—there!

"Give me something, oh, doctor, can't you give me something? Make it stop! Oh, doctor."

He was frowning. He didn't like her. Nobody liked her. Something was wrong. Oh, she would die.

The doctor's pink-fleshed fingers reached for her arm, turned it a little. The nurse handed the doctor the thing with the needle. Lil closed her eyes so as not to see it go in. She would show them she was a modern girl and could bear pain. She would not cry out when it pierced her. There.

It didn't help at all. The pain was coming on again.

"Lilly, Lilly, darling, push down, push, inside," her mother kept saying.

What did her mother know! It was different in her time, it was easier for them, they were made different!

"Now be good. Be a good girl. You aren't being good at all!" the nurse said, with pressed mouth.

And then Lil felt the change coming over her. She had been holding on tight, tight with her hands till she felt the knuckles would burst; now slowly all the strength in her hands seemed to seep away. Her hands felt numb. And gradually this helplessness invaded her body. Twilight, yes, like twilight, when everything, rocks and trees and houses, seems wrapped in a haze of softness and yet you know they are there, hard. Everything wrapped in cushions of space so you walk and walk and can't get at things, can't touch them, and yet you know they are there, hard.

The pain came, distantly, and yet sharply, within herself. But she could no longer do anything. She had lost all control of herself. What was happening to her was happening painfully and terribly; she could feel the pain sharp as though she were her own twin and felt every twinge and piercing, but could not touch the hurting spot on her other self. Over her eyes was an endless leaden weariness.

And distantly Lil knew this was the way it belonged with her. She was the kind who would reach out for things, but in some way, all her life, a twilight sleep would be between her and the real real things that she wanted to touch.

It was a protracted and difficult delivery. Dr. Kroger got very nervous before it was over. The twilight sleep didn't help any. "Well, she didn't help any, either," the nurse said cryptically, in one of their hasty exchanges, in the doorway.

Afterwards, Lil said to the nurse: "Was I good?"

"Well, as good as could be expected," the nurse sighed.

. . . No, no, nobody knows . . .

The street car crossed a set of tracks. Bounce bounce bounce and ride. Sam shrunk against the corner of the seat. Through the soles of his shoes he felt the stinging warmth of the heater. Yet, whether of cold, or of nerves, a shiver went down his spine.

The chill was fear. It had begun to come over him as he looked at the blob of flesh held out toward him by the nurse. Surely he had been too weary, with the surging of anxiety all night, to feel any joy of recognition at the child. He had only felt: this is it. Afterwards, afterwards I'll love him like a son. He had stared for a whole moment into that blob of face, trying to awaken a response in himself, and had thought he felt it coming, like a word one tries to remember. Then the nurse had marched out.

And he looked at Lil. Her face perfectly round, and strange to him. For a while he had not known what it was that made the strangeness of her face; then he had remembered: her bangs: they were hidden under the hospital cap. Her face, pale and clear now, had looked up to him with the strangest look he had ever seen, a look that was an utter invasion of him. It frightened him.

"Did you pass your quiz?" she murmured.

And her mother, at the door, looked at him too, brimming. "Aha, Sem, aha. You see, what a woman has to go tru?" Her eyes were leaking. She was a sick woman. He felt a gust of anger, and pity at what this woman had done with her life.

Now the fear was in him. It was as though he had just been handed the ball: go, see what you can do! Only, it was a live child, and he had to be very careful how he stepped with it, where he landed the child.

Sure, now he knew a lot more than the other fellows. They were just kids, horsing around, taking girls out on dates, feeling them up. He knew what a woman was. In flashes, at rare moments, a man understood. His mind reached back to a time when they had been going out. Lil had stood at the door. "Ready?" he had said. And just then he had *seen* her, this small womanly figure, a short-legged creature like Schopenhauer said, but altogether not like Schopenhauer thought, a woman standing there looking over her house to make sure the back door is shut, the gas is off. Just in that moment, in the shape of her coat, widening downward, in the way her two short legs were planted, he had seen Lil, and understood womankind.

Sam looked up and about him at the people in the car. It had always been his habit to look at faces, to try to imagine what people did for a living, where they were going; and now in this street car full of tired-looking people, mostly workingmen, he sensed a sameness to his life that almost overcame his fear. Why, just after a man's wife had a kid, he was supposed to tell his pals, who would slap his back, make wisecracks. Whom would he tell? Smirking Lou Margolis and snickering Lou Green? Suppose he were to tap the man in front of him, who would turn an unshaven tired face, and say: "My wife just had a boy . . ."

Why did he have this wish to talk to people, get nearer to them, and yet find it impossible to do so? The street car bounced. He picked up a newspaper. Teapot Dome scandal. Now they hinted dead Harding was in it too. The President. Everything was dirty. A boggy muddy world. Oh, kid, what I brought you into. Up there in front with the motorman (Please Do Not Talk to the Motorman) a bunch of skinny kids with unshaven downy faces were shoving and cuffing each other around, laughing loud horse-laughs. One of them was trying to sing:

"Old-fashioned tomaato,
Long Island potaato—
But, YES—"

while the others shrieked him down, put their hands over his mouth; triumphantly he glubbed the final words through cracks between their fingers.

". . . we have no bananas—today!"

What's in a Name

Rose Heller got Aline Freedman off into the bedroom, clutched her hand, and gasped: "Oh, kid! He wants to take me home!"

Aline stared into her eyes with a look that said: Kiddo, I know how it begins. "Oh, Rose! That's scrumptious!" she squeaked.

"But he came here with Thelma. She'll have a fit!"

"Well, let her! Anyway they all came together in a bunch."

Rose couldn't give up this chance of getting a fellow tall enough for her. He was at least six feet tall with a long face and slick brilliantined hair. His name was Manny Kassell and he was a dentist. Not as good as a lawyer or a doctor, but he was already graduated and practicing. He had a sense of humor too and he was answering everything with the statement: Yes, we have no bananas. When Aline asked him would he like a piece of cake he answered solemnly: Yes, we have no banaan', and when Rose asked him if he had seen the Moscow Art Theatre he said: Yes, we have no bananinsky! That line got to be a scream.

There were hardly any Jewish fellows that tall; and if a girl didn't grab what she could she'd be out of luck.

He took her home on the bus.

"I see where they gave that prize for naming that new magazine," he remarked. "Twenty thousand smackers for a name!" and whistled.

"What did they name it?"

"Liberty. A Magazine for Everybody. Imagine! Twenty thousand berries!"

"They must have got in a million names."

"It was more than a million. I even took a shot at it."

"Yah? What was yours? I bet it was good."

He nipped out a pencil and pulled a scrap of paper from his pocket. "You have to see this to appreciate it." He printed: U S.

"Get it? US. A Magazine for Americans."

"Say, that's cute," she appreciated. "You know a friend of mine just had a baby. I wonder what they'll name it. . . . Sam Eisen, do you know him?"

"Eisen? Is he a short fellow?"

"Yah. He's kind of heavy-set."

"Brown hair?"

"Yah, that's the one."

"Then I don't know him!" he guffawed.

"An aunt of mine just had a kid and they named him Isidore," Rose confided. "Isn't that terrible? Izzy! Imagine what a kid has to go through with a name like that!"

"Know a name I always liked? Vincent. That's a nice name."

"Mygod, the names some people give their kids! I was to a *briss* downstairs of us and they're old-fashioned Jews and they named the kid Mattashmayas or Shmatenyuh or some Bible name, it certainly sounded terrible. I don't see why people should persist in giving their children Jewish names. After all, we're Americans."

"Well you know the old folks came from the old country and didn't know any better. You know what my Jewish name is?" he confessed. "Manasheh." He snickered.

"Ich!" she squealed. "Bet you'll never guess mine?"

"Rochel?" Manny Kassell submitted. "Rifka?"

She shook her head. Her eyes popped with laughter. "Chayah-Shaynah!" Rose exploded.

"A rose by any other name is just as sweet," he said.

"When I started to school I changed it to Rose. Once I changed it to Rosalind but everybody kept on calling me Rose."

"Some of those Jewish names aren't so bad," he said. "But imagine being called Yankel or Shmool or some of those terrible Bible names like Mordecai!"

"Say, I'll bet that used to be Mort Abramson's name. You know what Sylvia Abramson's name was? Shulamith!" They roared. "And Aline Freedman's name used to be Lena. Her mother still persists in calling her that. Honest! Aline has a fit, every time."

"That's nothing. I got a kid sister named Ethel, and my mother calls her Gittel!"

"Some people just have no consideration," Rose said. "If I ever have a kid, I'll give him a decent name."

"What would you call him?" He dropped his arm around her.

"I like a name like Ronald. That's a nice name. Or Peter."

"Y' know a name I like? Clarence," he said.

"Me too." It was thrilling, the way they agreed on things! "Clarence is a doggy name."

Lil's folks wanted them to call the kid Jacob, after Mrs. Klein's dead father, Yankel Silverman.

"Let's humor them," Lil said. "Afters, we can change it to James."

Alone at home, Sam thought of looking in the Bible to refresh his mind about Jacob, after whom he was naming his son. He found the Bible that he had swiped out of a Y.M.C.A. that time when the crazy old coot who made speeches trying to convert the Jews on Roosevelt Road had got him curious about the New Testament.

And as he read the story of Jacob, Sam thought: What a clever rascal, what a crook! No, not really a crook! Everything Jacob did was within the law. Sure, he knew people like Jacob. Lou Margolis, and his own father-in-law, Marcus Klein.

See, Jacob doesn't steal his brother's birthright, he buys it with a mess of pottage. And is it Jacob who fools his father with the hairy goatskin? No, he lets the old woman be responsible for the scheme. And later, what of the flocks that he steals from his father-in-law? Does he paint them with rings and spots? Oh, no, technically he is innocent. He merely breeds them that way, and lets nature load the dice for him.

A smart Jew, Sam thought, and a physical coward too, hiding behind the skirts of his wives when he met the brother he had wronged.

And yet, even as he saw the narrow, slippery qualities of this patriarch, Sam could not feel that it would be a shame to name his son after Jacob. For Jacob was only using his cleverness to strike back at fate for making him a second son, at Laban for giving him cow-eyed Leah instead of the girl he loved, and for whom he had slaved seven years.

It was as though some cord of Sam's own body and mind grew way back into those times, reaching Jacob, and Sam remembered, and understood the faking and lying that a Jew sometimes had to do, against his own best conscience, to make his way in the world. This imperfect creature, this Jacob, now stood to Sam as a kind of archetype of the Jew, embracing all the good and bad qualities of the race, and lovable because he was so humanly and truly the father of all the stanch and slippery, lying, idealistic, smart, bragging, cowardly, boot-licking, and swaggering little gleamy-eyed Jews who now inhabited the earth. He could call his son Jacob. That was what Jews came from, and that was what Jews were like.

Sitting alone, reading, Sam sensed himself at last an adult who could judge his own elders; he was a man who had come upon an old family record, for the first time seeing his ancestors as humans and sometimes rascals, instead of as the mythically perfect beings presented to him in childhood.

He read on, of Joseph, the son of that wily old Jacob, and here he saw the cleverness of the father skillfully used to good ends, benefiting whole peoples, Egyptians as well as the Jews; and in Joseph, Sam recognized the wish of himself. He too must rise from nothing to be a power in the land, showing people how to conserve and divide their wealth; and wasn't America, after all, a kind of Egypt to the Jews?

Look, he had made his own son into Jacob, and himself into Joseph, the son of his own son.

Was he afraid to have his son a better man than himself?

Or, was this the way in which the Jewish strain eternally renewed itself, going back and forth from Isaac to Jacob to Joseph, mixing their qualities of loyalty and cunning and subtlety.

Sam sat there, smiling with himself.

And Sam Eisen did all right for himself. There was this year when the warm wet baby smell continuously filled the flat, and diapers hung on all the chairs, and Lil was a mother, and Sam felt himself driving, driving, like a throbbing power eating up the law, pushing toward the top.

In mock court was where he shone. He had something the other boys didn't have. It wasn't oratory, it wasn't superior knowledge of the law. He had a powerful sense of conviction. There was something almost hypnotic about Sam when he quoted a case, questioned a witness. He was positive. Where the other fellows mumbled their citations he shot them out like bombs.

Lou Margolis stopped in once and listened to Sam. "He's good," another kid near the doorway said. Lou shrugged and made a wise face. "He'll antagonize the judges," Lou said.

Lawyers

The two Lous were taking Harrison's fifty-buck one-month quiz for the bar exam.

Runt Plotkin was in a special $100 course given by John Hines, the quiz-master who was nearly disbarred because he "guaranteed" his students would pass the bar. Runt was cramming sixteen hours a day. He was so stuffed with agent, contract, corporation, that there were long blank moments when all the words lost their sense to him. His cheeks were hollow and his eyes were red.

Lou Green was scared. All week before the exam he had been off his feed. "It's a cinch," Lou Margolis said. "We just have to get forty-nine out of the seventy questions."

"Heh heh, they can't run those exams without me. I flunked three times already," a skinny greenish guy remarked.

"Where ancestors a freehold take, the words 'their heirs' a limitation make" was all Lou Green could think of. It went on and on, over and over in his head.

"Lo, Plotsy," Lou Margolis said, "where's your pony?"

"In the stable." Runt patted his vest pocket.

They filed into the large lecture amphitheater of the Illinois Medical School, borrowed for the law exams.

"Smell the stiffs," Runt whispered, hoarsely.

"Where ancestors a freehold take . . ." was all Lou Green could think of. The words rang in his head. And this once, that old standby had been left out of the questions. He couldn't get rid of the rhyme.

There was a hollow clunk. All turned. A Portia had passed out. Two monitors were lifting the heavy girl, whose middle sagged ridiculously as they carted her by arms and legs.

Lou stared at the unconscious girl. His mouth began to taste funny. He jumped up, and went for the toilet.

Runt Plotkin also went to the can. He settled down in one of the compartments, took a couple of cigarettes out of a package, unrolled the flimsy notes he had concealed in the cigarettes. He felt kind of cheated because actually he could answer most of those questions without his pony. He took a look just to check up, flushed his papers down the toilet, and emerged.

There he saw Lou Green leaning against the wall, yellow at the gills.

"What's the matter, Lou?"

"I'm stuck!" and he began to bawl.

"Jeez. If I'd 'a' known a minute ago. I just threw away my pony. Listen. What are you stumped on?"

"I'm stuck. I can't answer a one."

Runt dragged Lou behind a toilet door and began to prime him. Lou stared at him, vacantly, jumping every time they heard a door open. Runt could see it wasn't helping much, still . . .

"Jeez. Thanks, Plotsy. We better go in now. You don't wanna get caught—I don't know if I can make it, but jeez, you saved my life!"

"That's all right, pal. Meet me here tomorrow and I'll slip you the next installment."

As Lou preceded him out of the can, Runt gave him a heartening slap on the back.

The next day there was a monitor in the Men's Room.

"Well, look who's here!" Lou Margolis exclaimed, halting dramatically just inside the office door and staring at Celia, who was sitting at the switchboard, reading Moon Mullins, as though she had been in the office all her life.

"If it isn't Lou Margolis!" she said with feigned surprise. "Don't tell me you work in this office!"

"I wouldn't exactly call it work!" Lou cracked.

"What happened to Rae?" asked Lou Green.

"Oh, she's gonna get married. Didny' know?"

"Better watch out, Celia. This is a dangerous job. You're next!" Attorney Preiss said, coming through the office just then.

Celia laughed good-naturedly. "I'm not the one that has to watch out, if that's the case!" She turned the paper. "Did you see where Walt finally proposed to Miss Blossom?" she said, handing it to Lou Margolis.

Lou Green took the *Daily Law Bulletin* and retreated to Lou Margolis's old desk; since failing the bar exam, he was on Lou's old job. The Sharpshooter now had a big glass-topped desk in an office he shared with Preiss's son, who had passed the bar last year.

The Kind of a Girl Men Marry

"What makes her so popular?" the other girls said.

—Well you have to admit Sylvia is good-looking.

—I wouldn't exactly call her a raving beauty.

—She's got brains too. Fellows like an intelligent girl.

—That rare combination, beauty and brains . . .

Haw haw haw.

—Well, I bet she makes Phi Beta Kappa.

—I'd rather make Zeta Beta Tau.

—Ev, you'll slay me!

—If you ask me, if there's one thing Syl hasn't got, it's It.

—Well, evidently she has another kind of it.

—She doesn't use much make-up.

—Well, who does?

—With her dark complexion she doesn't need it.

—If you ask me, she looks as if she never washed her face, with her dark complexion.

—Who said she's so popular anyway? You can call her up any time without getting a busy signal.

—Oh, sure, the fellows are crazy about Syl.

—Yah, who for instance?

—Well, naturally Joe's her steady.

—Well, Alvin was so crazy about her he proposed to her.

—No!

—She can have him!

—He threatened to kill himself. He said his heart was broken.

—When?

—Last summer.

—Uf. Ancient history.

—Rudy Stone is gone on her too.

—RUDY STONE!

—Aline, is that a fact?

—How should I know? I don't keep tabs on him.

—Just because he took her to his frat dance . . .

—She isn't exactly what I'd call a snappy dresser.

—Well, she never gave me any competition.

"If you ask me, she gives me a pain in the neck sometimes!" Aline snapped.

—I think she's all right for a certain type of fella, but she isn't my idea of a popular girl.

Alvin read *Sanine* by Michael Artzibashev and was convinced that he too was a wild fatalistic character, with a streak of Russian pessimism, bored with the futility of life.

He read in the papers of the college boys who had shot themselves, tired of living because life was so futile, and he understood them.

"The only reason I don't do it is because I get a kick out of the idiotic and asinine attitudinizing of the human race," he wrote to Sylvia. "Puffed up with their little egos . . ."

He also wrote that he had completely got over his momentary infatuation for her.

"The only thing that was hurt was my ego," he declared. "I was used to getting what I want. But even that may become boresome so I ought to thank you for breaking the monotony."

Just to show how unconventional he was he suggested that Joe accompany him on a cattleboat trip to Europe for the summer vacation. . . . "Have you seen Emil Jannings in *The Last Laugh*? It is a real work of art even if it is a movie. Of course it was made in Germany, not Hollywood. . . . So long, as it is time for one of my classes and this is my only chance to visit the prof's wife."

"Who does he think he is, Frank Harris?" Mort said when Sylvia read him the last part of the letter, but refused to explain the allusion.

No more futzing around being a schoolboy, Joe swore. Look what others were getting away with! That goofy equestrian statue of Sherman by a guy named Gutzon Borglum, stuck up at the end of Lincoln Park—an acrobatic warrior on a toe-dancing horse! He'd go back to the Midway studio and knock out a big figure. He'd put it in the Art Institute show, cop the fifteen-hundred-dollar first prize, and go to Europe.

The work was not going right. Some basic knowledge was lacking. He didn't know a damn thing about anatomy.

What Joe was trying to make was the figure of a typical State Street bum, sitting on a flophouse chair, gaunt and yet tough, aimless and yet omnipresent, dead-eyed and yet alert with that stubborn, accusatory, inward awareness of the bum. This was to be the composite portrait of the drifter, the bum, the hobo, the failure; since childhood he had seen them sitting their days out in his father's flophouse, smelled their butts swimming in spittoons; and who could tell but that he might some day be such a relic of a man?

It was as though, by creating this figure, he would exorcise his own fears.

But as he worked, the figure kept shifting, assuming different meanings, seeming never to be exactly what he wanted it to be. At times the bum was a stronger person than himself, a contemptuous and ineradicable fellow, coming out of a canned-heat stupor with a dangerous flicker in his eye; the man who went west and harvested, the man who was in the Herrin mine riots.

Joe wanted to get into that statue a kind of lean, hard, enduring beauty of flesh, to show the residue, the thing that nothing could kill in man. Like that time in his old man's flophouse when they had found Mike asleep with his shirt off, seen the bitten and wasted form, and yet the remaining powerful muscles of the arm, the wide wrist, and the hand that lay curled as if ready to grasp an implement. In these men who had been through the dregs, in their bodies that had thrown off cold, and sores, the bite of bugs, and the clap, in them was the truth and reassurance he sought; through their flesh the strange indestructible beauty of the human form still showed; their faces told the final few truths: warm food and sleep. They had the surprising knowledge that they were still alive, after every destructive force in life had had a crack at them.

All this Joe wanted to get into his statue: an old bum sitting in his chair, his bony, knotty hands ready for anything.

But it seemed he couldn't do the simplest things! When he wanted to shift the position of a knee, his armature was in the way; then when he dug into the clay and fixed the armature, he found he had shifted the weight of the entire figure; a shift of the leg meant a shift of the rump, a different balance of the torso; nothing could be faked; and he was trying to take short cuts.

Sylvia walked in a semicircle, looking at the roughed-out form, not yet speaking. But Joe could feel: she didn't like his work.

"Well?" he said, over-anxious.

"Oh, it's strong, Joe, but there's something about it that scares me, for you."

She had caught it, then. The meaning that this was himself, this was the end of every man.

"Dear, I know I am going to sound like a Babbitt and I don't mean to lecture you about isn't there enough sadness in life without making statues of it. I mean, oh, Joe, there is something ugly about this." The toothless jaws, she meant, the lipless sunken mouth. "I mean, Joe—I know how you feel about your father's place and maybe you had to get this out, but, oh, I know you can do something beautiful . . ."

Then he had failed. He hadn't captured that feeling of beauty ground down, but enduring, or Sylvia would have known.

He looked at the clay again, and it seemed only a stringy, cadaverous caricature of decay. He wanted to tear it to pieces.

He simply did not know enough, yet, to carry out his ideas. It wasn't that he knew less, or had less talent than the other fellows in the studio, though that crazy Indiana was a hell of a talented kid; it was simply that his ideas were greater, deeper, than theirs, and the means that were sufficient to them were not enough for him. He felt a need to crawl into the very interior of the muscles, to make the clay express the laxity or tenseness of the cells, to feel the bones within the flesh, the hang of skin over lean cavities, to know the path of each tendon in the hand.

Instead of the bum, Joe sent a little bust of Sylvia to the Institute, it was accepted, and won a hundred-and-fifty-dollar prize. He couldn't feel elated. He had been unequal to the job he had attacked. Damn it, he was going to Europe anyway, to get the real stuff.

The car shot over the stretch of straight concrete, over the water-patched marshes, before Gary. They breathed the sulphurous air of the steel and oil plants; the flame-topped smokestacks of the steel mills were like torches to their ending youth, to their parting.

Joe watched her, in her blue bathing suit, running before him up the dune, remembering how last year, on the beach with the kids, talking of Leopold and Loeb, he had noticed the hollows of her girlish thighs. With a sculptor's knowledge he had realized how a woman's thigh-bones are pointed slightly inwards, prepared to balance the added weight of child-bearing. And now, he saw, the forms were fuller, the suggestion of awkwardness, of knock-knee, in the filly was gone, the girl had the shape of a woman.

They were settled, with a sandhill all to themselves. Sylvia had a going-away present for Joe.

It was a gift edition of Walt Whitman's *Leaves of Grass*.

"Oh, this is swell."

"Do you really like him?"

"I'm nuts about him."

They lay belly to the sand, feeling their sides touching, while Joe turned the pages. With the sun flowing down upon their backs, seeming to flow into their blood, one, then the other, read:

"The love of the Body of man or woman balks account—the body itself
    balks account;

That of the male is perfect, and that of the female is perfect. . . ."

It was this, Joe knew, that was lacking in his monument. The dignity, the American vigor. . . .

The poem seemed, like the sun itself, to enter their blood. They pressed closer, in the sand. Surely, now, she understood.
"Be not ashamed, women . . .
You are the gates of the body, and you are the gates of the soul."

Sylvia took up the reading, in her clear, open voice:
"O my Body! . . .
Head, neck, hair, ears, drop and tympan of the ears,
Eyes, eye-fringes, iris of the eye, eyebrows, and the waking or sleeping of the lids . . .
Hips, hip-sockets, hip-strength, inward and outward round, man-balls, man-root . . ."

She went on, yet with a slight tightening in her voice:
"All attitudes, all the shapeliness, all the belongings of my or your body or of any one's body, male or female . . .
The womb, the teats, nipples, breast-milk . . ."

He put his mouth to hers, and turned her, until they lay on their sides, pressed against each other, his fingers begging her to draw her arm out of the suit.

"No, no, please, darling, not that . . ."

"But, sweetheart—"

"Oh, I know, I know we should. Joe, I'm afraid. Not now. When you come back . . ."

He did not understand, and yet felt he understood, she was still afraid he might just be an artist, a bohemian, who loved them and left them.

ODYSSEY OF ALVIN AND JOE

The time was for all young men of artistic sensibilities to go to Paris. On a cattleboat.

Alvin said he was going over just to buy a copy of James Joyce's *Ulysses*. He promised to buy one for Mort, too.

And yet each fellow had a sort of secret quest. A fellow didn't know exactly what it was that he sought, but he knew it was over there, and he would recognize it when he came upon it. Every instant of the journey, he would have to be awake, alive, watching out that he didn't pass it by.

And maybe it was something that could never be brought back to America, the land of Babbitts. Maybe he would have to remain over there, with his find.

The cattleboat agency had a mile-long waiting list of college boys, and after hanging around for a month trying to get on a boat, Joe and Alvin finally got wise, paid twenty dollars each for the privilege of working their way across, and sailed with the next load of cattle.

Alvin knew he was the weak link in the bucket brigade. With each relay, Scotty, a little bastard as tough as a hunk of knotted oak, had to come a couple of steps further into Alvin's stretch. He'd smack down the two full pails so that the water sloshed over into the crappy muck underfoot. Then he'd glance at Alvin, with a disgusted stoicism that was a complete commentary on fancy-pants college boys on cattle crews.

With the wire handles cutting into his open-blistered palms, Alvin staggered sidewise along the narrow passageway, the pails bumping his ankles, the water sloshing down his best golf pants. Joe was already waiting, his empties on the floor. The Duke bit his lip, tried to come ahead faster. Damn it, he was acting like a baby, trying to prove himself "as good a man" as Joe.

Joe came up and relieved him of the full buckets. "You should have practiced lugging around tubs of clay, it's good training for this," he said lightly.

Alvin heard the whoosh of some damned steer sucking up his bucket of water in less time than it took to turn on a faucet.

He staggered out for the afternoon trick, barely reached the hatchway, and slumped against the wall. "Sick," he gasped. And had to spend the rest of the voyage lying in his bunk. Well, anyway, he was no laborer.

In the cattle crew was a Harvard guy who was working his way to Russia. He was nuts on the subject of communism and the holiness of labor. Every evening he held forth, until the boys drowned him out singing "Hinky Dinky Parlez-Vous." But Alvin was the only one who could really hold up an argument against him. Half the crew were bums, and all they could think of was to give Garnett the raspberry, asking him if he would like to have his sister nationalized, like in Russia. "See, there is your intelligent proletariat," Alvin would crow.

And yet, when the fellows came in sweating, dog-tired, and somehow victorious from their labor, he always felt kind of ashamed. He noticed that Curtis Garnett never took advantage of those moments, to argue with him.

"See you in Moscow," Garnett laughed, when they left the boat.

In future memoirs, perhaps to be called *The Confessions of an American in Search of Civilization*, Alvin mused, he might out-frank Frank Harris in telling of the appropriate act with which he saluted Paris. He would tell how he had had it for the first time the first night in Paris. After they had dutifully strolled up and down the Boul' Mich' eying all the women at the café tables, trying to guess whether they all were tarts, and gone emptily back to the dinky hotel which had to be on the rue Saint-Jacques, Alvin went out again by himself. He found the café des Noctambules; a guy with a blond satyr beard told him to drink Pernod, so he gulped Pernod, feeling as though a hand were squeezing his heart, then he listened to a skinny whore brag to an old whore how many times she had gone already tonight, *neuf fois, neuf, un doo trwa cat*—then he was blasé and superior to baby Joe asleep in his pure white bed probably frigging the pillow, and the hell with Sylvia, whore, you are Sylvia; then Alvin told himself he felt the Paris night like cool sequestered fingers on his brow; and he was stumbling along the rue Saint-Jacques with that cadaverous c——; then he hit the bed, but she pulled and squirmed at him and he knew she was calling him filthy names; then it happened quickly; it was nauseating; then somewhere toward dawn she was squatting beside the bed over a chamber pot and he was crying no, no, pas ici, hall closet, and she looked at him with a wild contemptuous look; then in the morning she wasn't there and neither was his hundred francs, lucky he hadn't cashed another check.

But later Alvin stood in Joe's doorway, grinning a cat-grin, and said: "Well, the damn bitch cost me a hundred francs but she was worth it."

They sat beside the Dôme, and inside the Select, and at the Deux Magots, where the guy at the next table might be James Joyce, at the Closerie, at the Rotonde, and they stared and made little sarcastic comments about the tourists, who stared at them. They picked up pals, who hailed them with a loud Ça va? from across the café. They sometimes were in a bunch around a café table, passionately discussing expressionism far into the night. And maybe that was Man Ray, at the next table, with Kiki.

And yet it was like coming to a party that is in full swing, and never getting caught up.

Joe had to get contrary, and oppose modernism. It was crap, he said. Cocteau was crap. Picasso was crap. Everybody had a little hammer and was taking the machinery apart, leaving the entrails strewn around like a kid with a busted watch. Nobody was trying to put anything together.

Alvin carried a sword-cane. He could distinguish at a glance between a Manet and a Monet, he could even tell a Picasso guitar abstraction from a Braque guitar abstraction. Then he bought a sketchbook with spiral binding, a watercolor outfit, and a pocket full of disks admitting him to the Grande Chaumière. At first he hid his distorted croquis from Joe, but when a little Russian in the class made a fuss about their primitivism, Alvin wondered if he might not yet beat Joe at his own game. He developed an individual style, which consisted of making a fetish of the sexual parts, drawing breasts as perfect hemispheres, with nipples like the spikes on German helmets. Then he began to make abstractions out of sexual symbols, circles, triangles, spear-forms, and in this way, combined with a series of sexual exploits, he felt he was freeing himself from the quaint biological slavery that had impelled his fixation on a pure girl. His latest, picked up at the Chaumière, was an American girl, who, he said, completely freed his libido. She was a nice girl, came from a good family, but when she got into bed she was even more shameless than himself, thinking up the wildest experiments. Yet to look at her she might be any one of the girls in the bunch back home, except that she wasn't Jewish.

"I really was her first, too," Alvin told Joe. "She used to monkey around with girls, but a psychoanalyst told her that what she needed was a man. So—"

"Did she need a psychoanalyst to tell her?"

Joe could make the proper responses, hand out the Paris line, but all the time he felt Paris must have something more than this, and they weren't getting the real thing. There must be some secret, hidden core, where the real meaning of art, of life, was known, something beneath this seething oil of Montparnasse.

And Alvin, too, felt he hadn't found his goal. There was a world beyond the sophisticate cafés. There was a cabal, which he had to penetrate. Every once in a while one ran into hints, subtle leaders toward this cabal. It was whispered that Jean Cocteau conducted a Black Mass, such as Huysmans described in *Là-Bas*. A couple of Germans he had met, one a painter, one a dancer, and whom he suspected of being homos, suddenly went off and became monks. And every once in a while the Dadaists would confound you with a quotation from Thomas Aquinas.

Sometimes Alvin fancied that nearly the whole human race lived within a world of limited dimensions, while the remaining, secret few were spiritually fourth-dimensional beings. At rare intervals one encountered these people who "seemed to live in another world," people for whom everyday sayings and doings seemed to have a transparent vacancy; it was as though they lived in and through and all around mere existing humanity. One might live in the same house with them, eat the same food, handle the same money, yet all the while those others possessed some essential secret that made this same life something entirely different, to them.

It was at this time that Joe and Alvin went to see Aaron Polansky; Rabbi Waller at the University had given Joe a letter to Polansky and said: "Be sure to look him up. I think he may mean a lot to you."

There was no light in the courtyard or in the hallway where the Polanskys lived, yet even through the dark there came an impression of poverty and obscurity, decaying stairs, peeling walls. Above, a door opened, and a woman's voice swooped to meet them:

"Attendez! J' porte la lumière."

Both had the sense of something symbolic, of an apparition in the blurred form above them, the glowing hand shielding the candleflame that thrust a flare of light around the grave face of the woman descending the stairs toward them. As she came nearer, they saw that her black, luxurious hair, parted dead center, fell almost loose behind her shoulders; only the tip ends were braided.

"Ah, you are the young men from Chicago," she murmured, welcoming them.

The man, Polansky, was standing in the doorway of the little apartment. There were two other guests, a man named Hippolyte, birdlike, with glowing eyes, and his wife, who— like her husband and the Polanskys— emanated a peculiar, excited intensity.

Joe felt uncomfortable. As though he had walked in on something.

Alvin felt stirred, alert.

The people seemed to accept them completely as fully known friends; Rabbi Waller had already written of them, and it was as though this alone made them intimates.

Joe had known vaguely that Polansky too was an artist. Now the man took him into his workshop, below. In the middle was a sort of cobbler's bench. An assortment of hammers, mallets, chisels, was laid out neatly. Polansky's medium was hammered copper.

Sheets of copper, hammered into bas-relief, stood around the walls, glowed in the lamplight.

They were all biblical subjects: Abraham sacrificing Isaac, Samson bursting the pillars, Moses smashing the stone tablets as Jews worshiped a golden calf. But these were not the conventional biblical patriarchs. These were squat, stumpy little men and women, Jews with long, narrow noses, elliptical faces; instead of biblical robes they wore the knee breeches and short coats of old-country talmudists.

Alvin and Joe had seen such as these, old bearded Yids with ear-curls, who persisted in wearing their flat fur-rimmed hats and tight black coats even in America; there were still some moth-eaten old Yids like that around Maxwell Street and Sangamon Street. They were a joke.

But here, hammered out of dull reddish copper, they possessed a grave dignity.

"This metal is like the Jews," Polansky explained, "hard, and stiff, but enduring. With a little rubbing"—he smiled—"see how it glows!"

He set up before them a plaque showing Jacob, a winsome, slightly dandy little man in a tight suit, asleep, head pillowed on a rock. Above him, a ladder, and a flight of fat cherubs playing violins.

"Aha!" Alvin glistened. "*Cholam shel Yaakov.*" He spoke the Hebrew words, showing off his rabbinical learning.

Polansky, pleased, brought out a huge Hebrew Bible. He leafed the pages, showing them the precise passages[4] which he had illustrated.

---

[4] Jacob's Ladder, described in Genesis 28. Genesis 28:12: "And he dreamed, and behold a ladder set up on the earth, and the top of it reached to heaven: and behold the angels of God ascending and descending on it."

> . . . and he took of the stones of that
> place, and put them for his pillows, and
> lay down in that place to sleep. And he
> dreamed, and behold a ladder set up on
> the earth . . .

Aaron Polansky placed his hand on the text. "I believe in this," he said, candidly.

Joe heard the words as a statement strangely out of time, and yet true.

While they had been reading, Joe had been looking at a plaque that showed the large, bearded head of an old Jew, whose two hands were raised toward his face in a sacramental gesture. This was evidently a portrait. In sculpture, one sometimes sees a figure cast with a solid rod to its support. So now Joe had a queer sensation as of some linking arm growing from his very spine, reaching into the earth, imbedded far back, in time. He remembered how as a child, when strangers came to visit his family, there was always a questioning: Where does a Jew come from? From Odessa? Vilna? Kovno? Berdichev? Lodz? Ah, a *landsman*! That question had always seemed ludicrous to him. What matter where they came from? Their children were American born.

Now, as Polansky asked where he came from, Joe knew it wasn't Chicago that was meant, but some source in eastern Europe. That was the place of origin.

"I think my folks came from Kovno," he said. "I used to hear them talking about it."

"Oh, then I would not know them. I come from Bialystok."

But the name Bialystok struck some chord in Joe's mind; why, Sylvia's uncle was named Bialystoker.

"Is there an Abramson family there?" he asked.

"Looking for Sylvia's *landslait*?" Alvin kidded.

"They have a relative named Bialystoker," Joe prompted. "He travels around, for some Jewish charity organization."

"Ah. Meisheh Bialystoker! Then I know him!" Polansky glistened. He pointed to the portrait of the old man, which Joe had been studying. "But this is his grandfather, the Bialystoker Rov!"

Just a crazy coincidence, Joe thought. All Jews are cousins.

In the conversation that night, between those four people and Alvin, Joe was completely out of his depth. The Frenchman Hippolyte and his wife were devout Catholics, Joe gathered, and the discussion was all about the cabbala, and apocryphal writings, and branches of mysticism where the Catholic and Jewish religions seemed to converge. Alvin, through his rabbinical training, kept up with the conversation.

Now the three men were hunched toward each other, and at one moment they all, even slick-faced Alvin, seemed to be figures out of Aaron

Polansky's plaques, dark coppery faces glistening with some inner light, hands arrested in backward gestures, Jews, intense, disputing over the law, religious!

"Antichrist must appear first!" Hippolyte was saying. "He must appear in the flesh. After the appearance of Antichrist, your Moshiach, or Messiah, as we call him, will come."

"No! No! Messiah and Antichrist must appear at once, together!" Hippolyte's wife put in fervently. "It is written, the two will struggle hand to hand, and Messiah will overthrow Antichrist! This must happen literally, as it is written! We have been told the signs of their coming. The Jews will return to their land, in great numbers, and when a sufficient host of them have gathered in Jerusalem, the ten lost tribes will appear! And that will be the time for the appearance of Antichrist. It is known! It is written!"

"My father, who is a learned man, believes that the Great War was what was meant in Scriptures by the appearance of the Evil One; and see, the Jews are returning to their land, ever since that time, as though by the work of Messiah!" Madame Polansky said with naïve faith.

"Ah, what are you speaking of, my dear? Zionism is only a political movement, how can we see it as the answer to prophecy?" Polansky cried, annoyed.

Joe was puzzled. Were religious-minded Jews, like Polansky, opposed to Zionism? He had always thought Zionists were the most religious of Jews[5].

Hippolyte remarked disparagingly: "The leader of the Zionists, Herzl himself, denied that he was Messiah," and laughed.

"But no," Chaveh Polansky insisted, "as my father puts it, Messiah does not come as a man, in the flesh, but as the whole Jewish people; in returning to the land and fulfilling the prophecy the people itself is Messiah! I wish I could explain it to you, as he puts it. He is a scholar."

Hippolyte answered Madame Polansky dogmatically: "Messiah is the name of the Holy Ghost, who, third in the Trinity, has yet to appear to mankind. Antichrist comes before Messiah as Simon Magus came before Jesus."

Alvin had a sudden idea. "Can't these two legends represent the same being?" he ventured. "Can't Antichrist and Messiah be the spiritual and

---

[5] Zionism was originally a secular movement that grew out of fierce European anti-Semitism, and the vision of an ancient homeland that was at the time mostly a wasteland. Religious Jews tended to oppose the Man-driven reformation of Israel, believing this task belonged to the Messiah to come. An assimilated American Jew like Joe would not know this. After the subsequent Holocaust and the Arab attacks on Jews, the practical necessity of a secure Jewish homeland overwhelmed the idealistic notion of religious opposition to the modern secular state.

material aspects of the same idea, and can't they be united?" Almost at random, he added: "As in Russia."

The word made a terrific sensation. Hippolyte's eyes turned yellow. "Russia! Yes, there the Antichrist has truly appeared! Bolshevism! Ah, my boy, how can you speak in such great error? How can the spiritual be united with the material?"

"As the mind is with the body," Alvin persisted.

"They are slaughtering holy priests in Russia!" Hippolyte cried. "And as for your Jews, they too have abandoned their religion!"

Alvin started to argue that religion and spirituality were not the same thing. Suddenly, eloquently, he found himself the champion of Russia. Why, Bolshevism itself could be understood only as a religion. And wasn't its aim the same as that of all religions: to bring people a happier, more joyous life?

"Oh, no no no!" Polansky said painedly. "True joy is the joy of purity, of humility, while the joy of Antichrist is the joy of licentiousness, the joy of the golden calf. These two conflicting impulses have always been in the story of our race; the Messiah teaches poverty, the Antichrist teaches material riches, arrogance, lust. That is your Bolshevik joy. And it is for the very reason that we fall into this fallacy that we are given, from time to time, a great teacher who reminds us of the joy of humility."

Joe had not been terribly interested in the dispute about Russia, but now, as Polansky went on to another tack, he found himself drawn in, fascinated; here at last came a hint of a way of life to which he responded.

"Not so long ago there was a great teacher among the Jews of Galicia," Polansky said, "and his followers—the Chassidim—they alone understand the Jewish way of life, today. Your friend's grandfather, the Bialystoker Rov, was such a one." He leaned toward Joe as if this incident brought Joe truly into their circle. "He was a follower of the Baal Shem. It was the Baal Shem who taught us again the joy of working with our hands. For, like Hillel, he practiced the behest that every learned man must earn his bread by his handicraft. The Baal Shem was a charcoal burner; thus his learning was given to God, and not sold as is the learning of modern religious men."

Joe happened to look at Polansky's hands. They were powerful, the fingers scarred and hardened—a metal worker's hands.

"The Baal Shem taught us that the only true way to worship God is in being always happy, in celebrating before God the joy that we take in every act of living on his earth, in breathing, in eating, in labor, in talking to one another, in walking on his earth, in singing and in dancing."

Could it be that the old ear-curled Yids of Maxwell Street had something of this in them?

Later, Aaron Polansky told a Chassidic story showing how human joy was the delight of God. A pious old Jew had a little son who simply couldn't learn anything, and was set to tending sheep. On Yom Kippur, the Jew took the boy to the city, to hear the great rabbi. "You know how it is with Jews in the synagogue on the Day of Atonement, they beat their breasts, they beat their heads against the wall! But at the very height of the service, the little boy suddenly took his reed out of his pocket and began to fife. The entire congregation turned, as if to annihilate the child. But the Baal Shem reached out his hands and cried: 'Let the child play! His song is more welcome to God than all your pious lamentation!' "

"Ah, the Baal Shem, the Chassidim," Hippolyte said. "They were such souls as God delights in. But they are few, and look what has happened on earth. Men have banished joy from the earth. People live violently, they hurl food into themselves, they get rich, they run all night after pleasure, they pay fabulous sums to whoever can make them laugh, and there is no joy."

"But whose fault is that? Their own! There is still life on earth! What is there but joy? In everything!" Polansky insisted. "I will show you how the Chassidim dance!" he cried and, rising, he began to hum. The melody was small, it rolled around and around itself, rhythmic as the sway of a scholar over the scrolls, and it seemed to Joe that he had heard it somewhere, long ago. In that small space, Polansky began an angular, self-absorbed dance: a suddenly bent knee, an arm flung out, a palm flicked upward and sideward; head cocked, his eyes small, pointed, ecstatically smiling; then his body turning around and around with quick sharp steps, and his hands flung one way and another, acutely angled on the wrists, all the while his humming continued, self-absorbed, absorbed in God, queerly and intoxicatedly joyous.

"What was all this crap about the Messiah and the Land of Israel?" Joe asked Alvin, as they strolled back, down the rue de Maine. "Aren't these religious Jews in favor of Zionism?"

"No, no," Alvin explained. "Don't you see? They don't want the Jews to go back there unless it's according to prophecy."

If that wasn't like the Jews! Give them what they cried for, and they said no.

"Then if the religious Jews are against it, who are all these Zionists?" Joe persisted.

"Oh, just Jews," Alvin said.

"Oh."

"But you know, there was something in what Madame Polansky said— why shouldn't it be that a whole people is Messiah? . . ."

"Say, are you getting religion or something?" Joe cracked. "It really would be unbecoming in a future rabbi."

Now Alvin had something to juggle. He was all set to start a movement, an intellectual neo-Judaism that would cause more talk than the fancy neo-Catholicism of T. S. Eliot and all the literati.

Now over café tables, he involved Joe in long, furious arguments about everything from Chassidism to Jewish art. Passing co-eds might easily mistake them for a couple of young Ezra Pounds.

Joe maintained it was all a lot of bushwah. "There isn't any Jewish art because there never was any Jewish art," he argued. He too was getting skilled in biblical repartee, and pointed out: "It's right in the ten commandments! Thou shalt not make graven images. So how can you have a Jewish art when to begin with a Jew can't be an artist and remain a good Jew? In fact, I'm a sinner, and Polansky is a sinner, no matter if he does illustrate the Bible. In fact that damns him completely! There are no Jewish artists, as Jews."

But Alvin said there was a Jewish temper, it was in the blood, it had to show in a man's work. "What about Soutine?" he yelled. "And Pascin is Jewish. And what about Chagall? And even Polansky!"

"Aw, that stuff looks Jewish because Jews are in the pictures, that's all. You can't tell me there's an abstract Jewish quality in art, and that just because a man has Jewish blood he works a certain way. Baloney! Sculpture is sculpture, and I owe more to Athens than to Kovno." Still, Alvin noticed, this was the one argument which Joe was always ready to resume.

"My great-grandfather," Mort mentioned to Jim Wilson, a department store man in Fort Wayne who had turned the conversation on ancestry, "was a celebrated rabbi in the old country. I come from a line of rabbis."

"That so?" Jim Wilson looked at him respectfully. The order was clinched.

"Where in heck is he now?" Aline pulled the map out of the pocket in back of the *Encyclopædia Britannica*, and fought with its complication of creases and folds. She spread the map on the floor.

"Ulm," Sylvia referred to her letter. "He went crazy over the cathedral there, he says it's the best one in Europe." She squatted near Aline.

"Ulm?" Aline scratched her head with the pencil.

Mrs. Freedman came into the frontroom and stood over the two girls. "Well? Where is my *tachshid*?" She beamed on Sylvia as upon one of the family.

"He says his health is wonderful, Mrs. Freedman." Sylvia turned the page, read on.

"Well, what else does he say?" Mrs. Freedman asked.

"Nothing."

"In all that letter?" Mrs. Freedman cried naïvely.

Aline hooted. Sylvia blushed sweetly.

"One thing, before he ever decides to come back, I'll be an expert on the map of Europe," Aline remarked.

"Does he say anything about coming back?" Mrs. Freedman wanted to know. "First they were only going for the summer, and now it is over half a year already. Is he giving up his university? Is he at least getting something out of it? My husband don't begrudge him to send the money, so long as this is really useful to him, so long as he is getting something that he needs there, but tell me, Sylvia, to you he is more honest than with us, is he really getting something out of it?"

"Oh, yes!" Sylvia said. "It's very important for him!" and through her mind flowed the whole content of all Joe's letters, but how could she explain to his mother the alternate exultation and despondency of his moods, as he tried to swallow at one gulp the entire art tradition of Europe, and how could she explain that other theme of his letters, the sense of a quest for he knew not what, only that his instinct would tell him when he found it? How pitiful it seemed to Sylvia in that moment, that Joe was already so far away from his simple mother that it was impossible to explain to his parents the complicated motives, about art, and tradition, and styles, that were actuating his journey. And at the same moment Sylvia felt a compression of fear for herself, for wasn't he gradually working himself away from her, too? Wouldn't he be another person, a foreigner, when he returned?

"But tell me, what is he looking for?" the mother said. And then, intuitively: "I don't know if it is so good for him."

And in this last letter, Sylvia read: ". . . All these anonymous sculptors of the cathedrals, they knew what they were doing, they were telling of their gods, and the great Greek artists were telling of their gods, and all that stuff in Italy was church stuff, and maybe that was why I was so sore at Michelangelo, because he swiped my Moses, this sounds like I was getting religion, doesn't it? But I mean even Polansky has that serenity and that purposive quality in his work, and it has made me think: what am I driving at? And I don't find anything at all. So you see, I've got to knock around some more, try to find my way. So you see, kid, I'm not the smart guy you thought I was, and it may be a long time before we can come together, you ought to have a whole man, and I feel as though I'll be kind of wobbly for a long, long time. Sylvia—"

She stopped reading, for fear she would cry, before Mrs. Freedman.

"You know, Sylvie, my husband has a funny idea," Mrs. Freedman offered timorously, "he says if Joe is already going so far, he wants he should go to Kovno, the place where we come from, my husband still has some relatives there, and say hello." She laughed uneasily. "I guess my husband wants to show off what a son he has! . . . I told him it was a crazy idea," she hastened to add. "What would Joe want to drag himself there to see those crazy old people in the old country, he wouldn't want to bother."

She waited, ready to belittle the whole thing.

"Why, I think that's a wonderful idea!" Sylvia said. "Why, Joe said he was thinking of visiting that friend of his, Mr. Polansky. He goes back from Paris to the old country every year and asked Joe to come there and visit him. That must be near where you came from, too."

"But if he goes there, it will only take longer till he comes home," Mrs. Freedman said, watching Sylvia. "What will he see there? Near Kovno, it is only a little village, farms. Ah. Tell me, don't you want Joe should come home, Sylvie?" she asked, blushing and grinning herself.

The bell rang. "I think that's for me," Sylvia said. "Rudy Stone was going to meet me here, we're going to a show."

Aline scrambled the map together, and rose.

Mrs. Freedman looked at Rudy and Sylvia almost tragically, and went back to the kitchen.

"Rudy, did you hear that new song, 'My Old Pal Stole My Gal'?" Aline kidded. "I think I'll send Joe a copy."

If Rudy took a girl to the theater, it had to be to the greatest show ever staged, the *Miracle*, and he had to have main floor seats, and take her in a cab though she wouldn't have minded the El; he was so sweetly dignified, she sometimes wanted to muss his hair.

"What do you hear from Joe?" he said.

"Oh, I don't know if he'll ever come home! After Vienna, he wants to go to Greece. I suppose it would be a wonderful experience for him."

"Is Alvin going with him to Greece, too?"

"No, Alvin has gotten communistic all of a sudden and wants to visit Russia! The last I heard, his folks won't send him any more money except to come home on."

"That's what he ought to do," was Rudy's opinion. "From what I hear he's been running pretty wild all over Europe."

"Oh, yes," said Sylvia. "I guess he's been trying to live up to expectations."

"I thought he had some brains," Rudy said regretfully. "What he needs is a little will power, something to snap him out of it. You know, a nice girl would be a wonderful influence on a fellow like that."

"Oh, he thought he was in love with me for a while," Sylvia said, "but I cured him of that."

She felt Rudy draw away, on the cab seat. Poor fellow. She put her hand near his.

"It isn't much of a compliment for a fellow like that to be in love with a girl," Rudy said.

"I can't believe men really are like that," Sylvia cried. "Though with the horrible example my own brother is setting it's a wonder I don't get disillusioned like everyone else."

"Men aren't all like that," said Rudy. He was glad with a high inner gladness that so far he had been able to save himself.

Sometimes Rudy felt perhaps even Joe didn't understand the purity and beauty of a girl like Sylvia, the way he knew it. At moments like that in the theater, when he had thought of Sylvia as the Virgin becoming the nun, the illuminated purity that flooded his heart was so overwhelmingly beautiful that he could not imagine anyone else experiencing this emotion.

Rudy saw in Sylvia the transfigured being in white, the eternal nun who was nevertheless a mother, a wife; in her was the finest expression of humanity, a womanly purity that endured and would endure in spite of all the filth in the world and all the unhappiness and injustice, disease and death.

Would he ever find anyone like her?

"What's the matter, Rudy?" she said.

"Nothing." And then, as though she would know his thoughts if he didn't say something, he mumbled awkwardly: "Do you think Aline really meant that about sending Joe that song?"

Sylvia burst into a peal of laughter.

"Well, you know how Aline is. That would be just her idea of a joke," Rudy said confusedly.

"Do you think she has any cause to . . . ?" Archly. Oh, he was such a serious darling.

"Well," Rudy considered. "Certainly not on your part."

"Oh?" Her surprised, questioning note trailed down into sympathy. She put her hand on his. If there was only something she could do, something of the purest friendliness, to show a man like Rudy how worthy he was. And in some way she wanted to keep Rudy close to her, and Joe, all their lives.

"You know, Aline is really a lot more sensible than she lets on, she just puts on an act," Sylvia said. "You know, Rudy, she's really awfully good-hearted. Why don't you take her out more?"

Rudy looked at her solemnly, as though to discern her true meaning.

Joe sat by the oven, and hoped they would let him alone long enough to read the letters which Shmayra had just brought from the railroad twenty miles away. But Chayim the Pest glided down beside him. "Well? Letters from home? Did you tell your father—remember Chayim? We used to pee in the same hole together!"

"Chayim! What do you drill at the boy's head for? Let him read his letters!" Mama Dveira, pushing across the floor, screamed at Chayim the Pest. She stationed herself over Joe. "*Nu, Nu?* Read your letters! Does he remember me, your father? I rocked his cradle, and sang him the *tsigale mitn vigale.*"

The pilgrimage was a failure. He had finally pursued his way, on lousy trains and broken-down Ford trucks turned into buses, through sleet and snowdrifts, to this godforsaken village, his source. Here a brother of his grandfather still kept the village inn. The inn was nothing more than an earthen hovel, where the *goyim* came and got drunk. Though old Lazar had spent his eighty years among them, they still cast taunts and insults at the Jew.

Out of this muddy wagon-stop in the province of Kovno, Nathan Freedman had gone to Chicago, America; there too he set up in the hotel business—a flophouse on South State Street.

Every night since Joe's arrival, the village cobbler and tailor and baker, and a few raggle-taggles of the Jewish congregation, had gathered in the kitchen to stare at him, making remarks about him to each other. One by one, every young person in the village had managed to pull him aside, and beg—did he know how they could get away? Get to America? A few looked at him with silent scorn, as Joe himself might look upon some pampered brat in a chauffeured car.

One young fellow was a Zionist. He was vaguely related to Joe, being related by marriage to old Lazar the innkeeper, and he alone seemed bearable, talking to Joe neither from above, nor from below, but as an independent fellow-man. "To America? What for? What do I want to go there for? To sweat over a sewing machine? Ah, they don't fool me with their tales of diamonds in the streets. To Eretz Yisrael, that is different. There I would sweat, but I would know I am in my own land."

The rest of them gave Joe a pain. Mama Dveira was constantly screaming at the old man Lazar, threatening to leave him in his old age because he let the peasants cheat him.

Joe had no point of contact with them. They would sit staring at him, smiling with their eyes, as though, any instant, a flame of true communication would spring between him and them, and finally they would break the silence with a question about some other Jew who had emigrated years ago, and of whom he had never heard.

Why had he come this far?

He went and stood in the doorway of their little wooden synagogue, but it was useless to try to imagine a contact there; religion was meaningless to him.

Even the few days he had spent with Polansky in Bialystok had not shown him what he sought. Polansky's family, too, had embarrassed him with overwhelming hospitality (why couldn't Jews learn to let a fellow alone!) though they had been less crude than these villagers. Polansky himself had hovered over him, as though anxious that he find, find, find. With the eagerness of a little boy inducting a member into a secret club, Polansky had steered him into a back-room hovel of a synagogue to see the real thing, real Chassidim, and he had seen them, a few moth-eaten old ones who looked up at him angrily, a few lean-cheeked young ones who swayed back and forth over their Talmuds like the scholars in the *Dybbuk*, and he had heard the rhythmic hum of their learning. "A pity," Polansky had said, "you did not see them in Simchas Torah, when they get a little brandy in them, when they dance, ah, that is something to see! Only wait, I will show you, on a Sabbath eve . . ."

That had been better. For a day it had reminded Joe of his childhood, when Sabbath had been a different kind of day even at home in Chicago.

Before the folks got ashamed of their greenhorn ways, with their American children. That was home, home, but as unretrievable as childhood itself.

All through the day, members of the family came and went, congregating in the huge whitewashed kitchen of the Polansky home. Married brothers, branch-relatives; the women gossiping amongst themselves; there was the sporadic sound of teeth cracking almonds, a little quiet drinking of sweet home-made wine. Afterwards Aaron Polansky had slipped out with Joe, to the little synagogue. This time they had found the talmudists in their long shiny black coats. Aaron had brought a little bottle of brandy and soon they had begun to sing, the endless, spinning melodies of Jewry, di di dada dee dee di, and soon a hand clapped and a hop, a cry, a stamped foot, then another was dancing, then all; and one began a wistful, slightly comic song that children sang:

> "When Messiah comes,
> All of us shall feast upon
> Raisins and almonds . . ."

And when that was done, Aaron called the name of a song, "When the Rabbi Sleeps." Ah, this, he whispered to Joe, was a real bit of Chassidic humor, showing the lightness, the joy of their way of life. A skinny, comic-eyed old one got up to lead the song. He intoned the first line:

> "When the rabbi sleeps . . ."

and snored a great snore. All responded:

> "Then all his Chassidim
> Also sleep!"

and they snored hugely. The leader sang:

> "When the rabbi sneezes—
> Kaachoo!"

And they responded:

> "Then all his Chassidim
> Also sneeze—
> Kaachoo!"

The leader sang:

> "When the rabbi dances . . ."

He shook a leg.

> "Then all his Chassidim
> Dance with him!"

They leapt up, and began dancing again, flinging their feet, turning their palms, singing as they danced.

But it was already a thing of the past, a show; on the streets of the town the young Jews wore suits ready-made from America.

One thing more Joe had had to do: visit the Bialystoker Rov.

The importance of this synagogue had diminished a great deal since the death of the Great Bialystoker Rov, and in a way Joe was relieved to learn that the present rabbi was related to the Abramsons only in the complicated, distant way of Jewry.

Polansky conducted Joe to the house of the rabbi. It was a large house, filled with people, whispering, haggling: "When will he see us?" "Did you ask him for the decision in Meyer's case?" "They say Meyer has slipped the *shamas* a few zloty . . ." A house with a strange air of intrigue, of kotowing, of fear, and of power.

"I must tell you," Aaron Polansky whispered apologetically, "among the Chassidim too things have changed; the true, humble Chassidim are very few. As you see, the rabbis now live in riches, they accept gifts for every piece of advice, for every favor . . . it is not as it was." Now Joe saw that all this pained Aaron, the apostle of Chassidism. Perhaps he had been living in a memory, and the coming of a guest was forcing him to see things as they were. Joe felt somewhat guilty, at having brought this disturbance into the artist's life.

Finally, the holy man, attended by several stout Chassidim with glittering, voracious eyes, passed into the room where he gave audience. He spied Polansky and leaned patronizingly toward him: "Ah?"

"A friend, a young man from America," Polansky presented Joe. It was an absurd moment; could it be that he had come all this way for this? And suddenly Joe knew what this man, what this crowd was like. It was like the crowd around Rube Moscowitz.

The rabbi of Bialystok breathed in his face, patted his cheek. "They are not so pious in America, I have heard," he observed. "The young folk, especially."

"No. But I have a friend who is studying to be a rabbi," Joe managed.

The rabbi waggled his head. "Yes? Then perhaps America is not yet lost," he jested, patting Joe's cheeks again as he passed on to settle a dispute about the sale of a lace factory.

That was where Syl had come from.

And here in this squalid, earthen-floored hovel of an inn, was where he had come from, himself.

Alvin was in Berlin when his folks cabled: "Mother having operation come home." He figured it was just a trick to keep him from going to Russia, but still it might be true. His mother was always chasing around to specialists, fearing she had a cancer. The last letter had contained a hysterical warning from her, he could just see her dictating it to his father's secretary, over the phone: Tell him he shouldn't go to the Bolsheviki, it is a famine, it is a plague, it is a fever there, what is there to see in Russia, we all ran away from there! And they had sent no more money, only a ticket home.

Well, if he had guts he could still go. You didn't need money in Russia.

If he went, it would have to be entirely on his own.

Alvin puffed at the Dunhill he had bought in Paris. He studied the cable. Maybe his mother really was going to have a critical operation. . . .

Joe stood on the rim of the hillside. He was utterly alone, with these stones. And here, perhaps, he was home. Surges and surges of elation coursed through his heart. For here was the miracle of complete harmony, the work of man mated to nature, singing with the tranquility, the eternity, of time. The coursing of the stones along the hollow hillside was sweet to him, and the velvet grass, softening each edge and crevice, was intended so to be, and the ancestral olive trees were true. He walked down the slope of the amphitheater, to the pedestal that still stood in the center of the circle. Dionysian—the word came to him—godlike! Oh, these were people! He thought of the sculptures that adorned and were part of their temples, the tranquil, eternal smile of all their gods and goddesses! and these were the people who had truly known joy, a constant, harmonized joy, in every act of living: in breathing, walking, eating, and making love. And this was why he had so worshiped that classic building in Jackson Park, in Chicago; it had been his first hint of this truth that was here.

What more could there be than this?

For an instant Joe hesitated, with a vague, uneasy feeling that perhaps he was avoiding destiny. Perhaps he should go on: Palestine was just a day, directly across the sea. A Jewish sculptor, in the Jewish land.

He walked down a lane of trees. Here had been a group of buildings devoted to the cure of the ailing, and here a temple to the god of health, Æsculapius. Joe could almost see the patients in their white garments strolling among the white buildings, breathing this health-giving air. Through the grove they walked to the amphitheater and watched the dancing that was like sculpture.

Some sculptures still remained in Epidaurus, and in the excited clarity that had come over his mind, Joe saw, and wondered why he had never realized before, that here in Greece the two things that he had wanted to do were one, sculpture and architecture were a part of each other.

As he was standing there, a gray and stubble-headed native came along, perhaps the caretaker of this place.

"You American?"

"Yes."

The native's eyes lit up. "You know Chicago?"

"I come from Chicago."

"That so! I was live in Chicago! Thirty year!" He stared at Joe with strange, unblinking eyes; as though a deep community had been established.

"You know—Halsted Street?"

"Yah."

"You know—Harrison Street?"

"Yah."

The Greek seemed flooded with happiness. "You know— Blue Island Avenue?"

"Sure," Joe said. "I was born and raised in Chicago."

"Blue Island Avenue," the Greek repeated tenderly. "I usta have my candy store, nine eighteen Blue Island Avenue, that's thirty year." He confided: "I was save a little money, so I come back to the old country to see my people; I am retire."

He peered at Joe. "What place you live?"

"I used to live on Independence Boulevard, that's near Roosevelt Road."

"Roosavelt Road?"

"It used to be called Twelfth Street."

"Oh, sure, Twelve Street, sure, sure," nodding and nodding, happily. "Blue Island Avenue, that hit Twelve Street, not far from where I have my store. Blue Island Avenue," he murmured, "well, good luck!" and, as two Americans meeting, he offered his gnarled hand.

"Blue Island Avenue," Joe repeated, smiling, as the old Greek pattered away. He would make American sculptures, to go on modern skyscrapers.

Stopping in Athens, Joe thought perhaps after all he'd go across for a look at Palestine, before leaving for home.

But in a hotel in Athens he found an old rotogravure from the Chicago *Sunday Tribune,* and on the front page was a colorphoto of the co-eds in the U. of C. graduating class. Precisely in the center of the front row, as if placed there by the photographer to light up his picture, stood Sylvia. She wore a yellow dress, and was smiling.

A fellow thought he was deeply changed. He had been half around the world. But when he got on the Garfield Park El, there was the same ad for Sloan's Liniment. He might have just gone downtown on the El this morning and be coming back now.

And because of these same sidewalks, houses, stores with the white scrawled prices on their windows, Joe had his first misgiving. What had he brought back after all? Oh, he had deeper, broader ideas, about Judaism, classicism, but wasn't he like someone who had rushed to a store and bought the wrong things? How would they help him in this life, in Chicago?

There she was, coming out the door as always, waiting for him at the landing as he ran up the same old flight of stairs.

"Miss me?"

"Uh huh."

They sat in a glowing stupor. Was this all, the end of life, Ulysses come home from his wandering?

"Look what I brought."

He had unwrapped the copper portrait of the Bialystoker Rov, a gift from Aaron Polansky.

The folks all came in; they stood the plaque on the piano, and admired it. Joe felt awkwardly half included in the family.

"Did he really look like that?" Syl kidded her father.

"To tell you the truth, he was dead before I was born, I never saw him."

"I bet there never was a Bialystoker Rov!" Syl joked.

"Oh, yah?" said Mort. "Say, he was one of the most famous rabbis in the old country."

"My, is Mort getting religious! You ought to see him, Joe, he goes all over the West Side hunting for real Chassidim, with beards!"

"Yah, I give a quarter a piece for them," Mort said.

"How about growing some *payess*?" Sylvia suggested, pointing to the orthodox ear-curls on the portrait.

Mrs. Abramson brought the brass candlesticks and placed them near the plaque.

"The family shrine," Mort remarked.

The folks left them alone again.

Joe caught the sound of Mort and Mrs. Abramson talking in the dining room. There was a wary, disturbed note in Mrs. Abramson's voice. He caught the words: "What's he going to do now?"

The first thing he had to do, Joe decided, was make money. Everything hinged on that. Everybody was watching him, expecting something of him. Now they regarded him as all set, graduated, back from a European training. It had been bad enough to have to live on the folks until now, but now it might be years before he could come through as a sculptor and he wouldn't let himself be hounded by dependence on them, by the thought of their worrying about their poor artist son. What he needed was a way to make a stake that would give him a couple of years of clear independence.

He slouched on the sofa, brooding. One of Aline's flapper dolls, enflounced in an elaborate taffeta dress, sat upon a frilled silk pillow. He flicked his thumb against the face of the doll. Silk and glue.

He thought: why not make novelty dolls, with caricature heads of famous people, Charlie Chaplin, Red Grange, Gloria Swanson, Pola Negri, to take the place of these vapid flapper faces?

Why, they were easy to make. Just a couple of long seams and a little cotton stuffing. Why, there must be a fortune in this stuff. Every home had a couple of dolls sitting on the davenport, the piano, the radiators, the beds. All with these vacant, pretty faces, puckered mouths, reminding him somewhat of Aline.

A line of dolls with some pep in them ought to cop all the business. He would clean up on the idea! And then he'd be able to do whatever he wanted.

"What is he making, is he making anything on those dolls?" Mr. Abramson said uninterestedly, stretching out on the couch.

"Maybe he will make a little something. Sylvie said he got an order from Field's," Mrs. Abramson said, her tone showing she hoped more than she believed.

"A couple of dozen," Mort specified. "He'll never get anywhere with that stuff."

"They are cute dolls," Mrs. Abramson said. "Maybe if he gets a start . . ."

"Ah, he don't know how to go about it," Mort said. "He makes them too expensive. He's got some crazy idea he has to make them all himself, by hand. . . ."

"He even had Sylvia sewing on them," Mrs. Abramson said, dubiously.

"*Kindershpiel!*" Mr. Abramson snorted. "What is he going to do, that boy? She could have plenty of fine boys, doctors. That Rudy is a fine boy!"

"Well, Joe may be a famous sculptor some day." Mort was respectful. A great artist in the family.

"He is very talented," Mrs. Abramson agreed. "But who knows . . . ?" Then she added: "They love each other."

Mort remarked: "Anyway, people cleaned up on those boudoir dolls, and Joe's got a new idea on it."

"It's a fad, it's finished already," Mr. Abramson said. "I was talking to Sam Weiss, he's in the novelty business. He says they can get them twenty-five dollars a gross."

"I told him he ought to hire a couple of *shiksehs* for thirty cents an hour, then he'd have some time to go around and get orders." Mort made a face. "He don't understand business."

"I don't understand him," Mrs. Abramson said. "Why didn't he finish architecture?"

Mort made a Jewish shrug: "He has to be a sculptor."

"Is this his sculpture, to make dolls?"

"Well, I guess he wants a business to fall back on. What do you expect him to do, take over his old man's flophouse?"

They were silent, thinking of Sylvia's future.

"Wait, wait," Mort said, "we'll have him in the family yet, designing hats."

"Sylvia don't say anything," Mrs. Abramson complained. "I don't even know, are they engaged, or what?"

"She don't know herself," Mort surmised.

Sylvia came in. There was a hush. Mrs. Abramson picked up the *News*. "Look, they're fainting like flies at Rudy Valentino's funeral[6]! Pola Negri fainted!"

"Why shouldn't she faint?" Mort said. "It's good publicity."

"Mort, why do you have to be so cynical?" Sylvia complained. "Maybe Pola Negri was really in love with him. Some people have feelings, Mort."

There were times like this late November day.

Joe was working in the little frame house he had rented on Erie Street. He had dubbed it the Doll's House.

Now he had a fire going in the old-fashioned nickel-plated parlor stove; the panes in the front of the stove glowed orange.

The floor was littered with kapok. Heads of dolls, in all stages of drying and painting, were on the long table, and set around the stove.

Sylvia sat by the window, stuffing kapok into the long snaky limbs of the dolls. Bits of silver cloth, oilcloth, leatherette, and the various other fabrics which Joe couldn't resist buying, on the chance they would make up into modernistic dolls, were scattered around her.

Joe caught a sweet, slow breath of home.

Maybe it was the glowing stove, touching far back into his childhood, when there had been such a stove in the frontroom. Maybe it was because Sylvia sat in the position so utterly suggestive of home, and peace: a woman sewing.

He pried the little mask out of its mold, and sat on a stool, touching up the face with fine sandpaper, sharpening the features with a carving tool. As he sat there working with his hands, earning his living, he understood the happiness Polansky got out of having found a medium that was a craft as well as an art; and though this was scarcely an art, the work gave him a sense of being one with a whole line of people, with a fine and traditional way of life.

He was getting a dollar apiece for the dolls, which the store was selling for two dollars, undressed.

He had thought that once he got all the molds set and the work systematized he could turn out maybe fifty a day, just himself and a helper, but what with running to the hardware store for plaster, and downtown for special glue, what with finishing and polishing and wigs and this and that, he averaged about fifty a week, and out of that went expenses.

"Is this the way you want it? Have I stuffed it too hard?" Sylvia said, holding the sample toward him.

He felt it. "It's a little too hard," he said expertly, and then they laughed at each other.

He dropped a kiss on her hair.

---

[6] Movie star Rudolph Valentino died on August 23, 1926, aged 31. An estimated 10,000 people lined the streets of New York City to pay respects at his funeral, and the crowds rioted all day on August 24.

It was too perfect, too sweet to be working like this together, and he thought: I am really an old-fashioned guy, I am trying to revive a way of life that is gone.

Sylvia went to the kitchen, to see about fixing some lunch. Joe followed her there. They were kissing, leaning against the old tin sink.

"Dear, what are we waiting for?" he begged. Nearly five years they had been sweethearts. "I suppose we'd better get married," he said, defeated.

"I don't know," she said. "How would it change things?"

That was it. This silly Doll's House, the whole crazy idea of trying to make a living this way. It was nothing to marry on.

"Listen, Syl, I could get a drafting job with an architect, and we could get married."

"I don't want you to do something you don't want to do, just to get married."

But what was he doing now, with these dolls? Oh, it was just a crazy system, but if he could once get a start, and be financially independent, they'd be all right.

"How much do you think we would need?" he asked, feeling sad, lost.

"I don't know." She too was sad, perplexed; not happy the way girls were supposed to be when for the first time they actually discussed the means of marriage with the loved one.

"Think we could do it on fifty a week?"

"Why, I guess so," she said. They both seemed so defeated. It was such an awful place for their love to stop. It would never go beyond this.

They were still tender toward each other, brushing against each other, kissing, while she made French pancakes.

Sylvia sat across the table, watching Joe eat. She wasn't hungry any more.

"This is how it would be," both thought, "married."

ARTS AND SCIENCES

A little chain of laboratory incidents, of the sort that sometimes lead to discovery, happened to Mitch Wilner. While injecting his rabbit, in Bacty, he became aware of Beautiful standing behind him, being helpless.

She had broken her needle and wanted to use his.

Why they ever let such Dumb Doras into the medical courses was beyond him. Tromping around on their spiked heels, squealing daintily when a rabbit messed their tables, stopping their work to watch the cunning play of a couple of guinea pigs they were supposed to be injecting.

"Oh, I don't see how you ever find those veins so cleverly," she gurgled as Mitch handed her his syringe.

Mitch watched the girl jabbing at the ear of her rabbit. Finally, disgusted, he took the syringe. She had practically ruined the vein, but, going down lower, he found a possible entrance. He had scarcely emptied the syringe when the rabbit's head began to jerk. Then it made a circular motion, exactly like that of a drunkard.

Puzzled, Mitch lifted the animal out of the box. It wobbled on the table.

"Tish tish. He's pie-eyed," Beautiful remarked. "I bet you had gin in your syringe."

The eyes of the rabbit were bloodshot. It made a few furtive, crawling steps; small whistling sounds came as it struggled to breathe.

"Say, is this your regular rabbit?" Mitch demanded of the girl. He looked for the number clip on the ear. There was none.

"Oh, I left that off," Beautiful said. "I don't think it's necessary to stick holes in their ears, to identify them. He has a little yellow spot . . . why, say, this isn't Squeaky at all! It's another rabbit!"

"Know what's the matter with him?" Curly Seabury said, approaching.

"Is this anaphylaxis?" Mitch ventured.

"Yeah. Ever see it before?"

"No."

Professor Titus stood behind them, fussing, frowning.

"Where did you get that rabbit?" he snapped. "That rabbit is in use. He was injected last week. Where did you—?"

Beautiful had taken him out of the wrong cage; it was her partner, absent today, who usually went down to the basement for their animals.

The rabbit slowly settled to the table.

"Aw!" moaned Beautiful. "He's dead."

"Dames!" Mitch said to Art Weintraub.

Professor Titus clicked his tongue, and walked away.

Mitch went after him. "Could I open him up?" he requested.

The prof gave him an abrupt glance, as if uncertain whether he could even trust his favorite pupil. Then he shrugged. "Go on, do as you please."

After class, Mitch spread the rabbit, and made a long ventral slit, opening the fur. He had not yet got over, and thought he never would lose, the moment of excitement when the inside of a creature was disclosed. There, compactly arranged within the sheet of transparent tissue, lay all the organs, bright and alive as a holiday basket of fruit.

Instantly, Mitch saw how the rabbit had died. The lungs were expanded enormously, filling every cranny of the pleural cavity. Evidently the involuntary muscles had been paralyzed, so that the animal had been unable to expel his breath.

"So that was the gasping!" Larry Gans said.

"Sure. Anaphylaxis," Curly repeated.

"I don't understand it," Mitch murmured.

Gans, with the eagerness of a dumbbell for once explaining something to a superior student, began: "Well, he had a dose of horse serum last week. So he developed a sensitivity to horse serum. When he gets this second shot of horse serum, he gets an anaphylactic shock."

"Yah!" cried Mitch impatiently. "And two and two is four."

"Well, what else dya wanta know?" Ganzy groused.

"I don't understand it," Mitch repeated to himself.

"*You* don't understand it!" Curly Seabury snickered. "Say, even Einstein can't tell you why two and two makes four."

But why should the same stuff which an animal readily absorbed one week kill him the following week? Suppose a child were inoculated with diphtheria antitoxin, prepared in horse serum. He would become sensitized to horse serum. Suppose, later, he were given tetanus antitoxin, also prepared in horse serum. He would get this shock.

And that which man had prepared to cure, might kill!

"It don't affect humans that way," Gans said.

"Why not?"

"Well, you don't hear of anybody dying from it."

"Do y' think they're going to broadcast it?" Curly Seabury's father was a doctor.

For one thing, Mitch reasoned, the principal antitoxins used on humans are prepared in different animals. Sheep's blood, chickens, cows. And you only got the serum shock if you repeated with blood from the same kind of animal.

"There have been a few cases," Curly said. "Of course it doesn't amount to anything, compared to the number of people saved by serums."

Professor Nyquist leaned back in his swivel chair. His face glowed brick-red, angry at man's insufficiency. "Well, I'll tell you, Mr. Wilner. Anaphylaxis is one uff those baffling and apparently contradictory phenomena that man has run into, as a result uff sticking his nose in things. Sometimes I believe that nature is perverse, and every time we think we find something out, she puts one uff these peculiar stumbling blocks in our way, she sticks out her tongue in our face. Just when we think we know how to fool her with immune serums, we have this anaphylactic shock."

"Well, is it a reaction in the blood?" Mitch asked.

"You mean, does the anaphylactic reaction take place in the bloodstream?"

"Yes."

"Suppose you answer this for yourself."

Mitch thought back. The cause of death had been the freezing of the smooth muscles.

In the cells of the muscles, then?

In the involuntary nervous system?

"Some very fine work has been done on this point," said Professor Nyquist. "Look. You take a dog which is sensitized to horse serum, and you transfer his blood to a non-sensitized dog. Then you inject horse serum into the second dog. Will he have a shock?"

Mitch puzzled. If the reaction took place only in the blood, then the sensitivity should be transferred, with the blood, to the second dog. But instinct, or a whole submerged process of reason, made him answer: "No. The sensitivity won't be transferred."

Nyquist beamed. "The blood itself is innocent," he repeated.

Then how did it happen?

Perhaps the first injection of a serum sensitized certain cells. And when there was another injection, a reaction took place between blood and cells?

Again the blood, the problems of the bloodstream, which he had studied so intently, held in fascination since his first glimpse of a smear on a slide, absorbed since that introductory course by Professor Vakhtanov. But here was the broadening of his fascination, here was the instantaneous reaction between the blood and the cells of the body, here was the chemistry of life.

"Maybe you would like to repeat that experiment, some time?" Professor Nyquist suggested.

"So he keeled over, kaplunk?" Rudy Stone said.

Dr. Meyerson rolled the lower muscles of his face. "You got to watch out for that," he said. "Boys, with all these toxins and shmoxins and schmearums that all you young Arrowsmiths are popping out with every day, it's a wonder they don't put everybody in bed with serum shock. They got a serum for cancer and an antitoxin for t.b. and an injection for the wart on your behind."

"Don't you believe in them, Dr. Meyerson?" Mitch asked, to lead on the old fossil.

"What are you, another one of those Arrowsmiths that's going to discover a bug that will eat up every germ in the world?" Dr. Meyerson fairly shouted. "They're in such a hurry to beat each other it's a wonder they even wait to make up a sample. Let me tell you, nine-tenths, no, ninety-nine percent of these discoveries they are announcing every day are plain baloney. You want to know what happened to me with their serums?" He began to speak in the lower, confidential, and informal voice that doctors had for doctors. It happened when he had scarcely begun to practice. He was inoculating a little girl against tetanus. "Right under my hands, that child began to go. I tell you I nearly went crazy. I remember it today! I can show you the house, on Troy Street. I picked up the kid and started to run to Sinai Hospital. I was running on the street like a crazy man. I thought maybe there, at the hospital, they knew something to do for this. I felt the child die on my arms, as I ran." His eyes were fixed on them with a kind of confessional pleading. Now they were nearly doctors, they could know.

The boys looked at him, silently.

"We are no better than medieval magicians; with our little circle of knowledge around us, we are safe," Dr. Meyerson said. "But everything outside this circle is dark and hostile."

"Did you try digitalis on that child, doctor?" Mitch said.

Dr. Meyerson stared at the upstart. Gradually the anger went out of his eyes; he even snorted a short laugh, and patted Mitch on the arm.

"It is true," he admitted, "gradually, this circle is being expanded. But it is by millimeters, *boychik*, by millimeters, and not by miles."

A few weeks later, anaphylaxis came up in the course. Professor Titus was using a sensitized guinea pig for demonstration. With incredibly neat, swift technique he slit the neck-fur, fished out the threadlike jugular vein, injected it, clipped the skin together, and let the pig loose. It died of anaphylaxis.

Each student had to repeat the process.

Here, in demonstration it seemed a routine phenomenon produced at will, under control. Mitch realized that, if he had first come upon it this way, he would not have been fascinated by this subject. But it had happened to him, with that rabbit, as it must have happened to Dr. Meyerson with that child, wildly, out of the dark, beyond control.

Coming into the lab to do some extra work after class, Mitch caught a whiff of ether, and went over to see what was going on. Beautiful held a dab of cotton to the snout of her guinea pig. "Oh, I couldn't bear to cut them open while they're conscious!" she whined. "I don't think the professor ought to do it either! There!"

"I never saw such a perverse set of animals!" her partner growled. "This is the fourth, and we can't seem to produce the shock."

"When the rabbit wasn't supposed to die, he died, and now these are supposed to die, and they won't!" Beautiful objected.

Mitch laughed, and walked off. They probably were missing the vein, he thought.

On Saturday afternoon, Joe and Syl drove over to pick up Mitch, for some tennis. Syl waited while Joe went up to the lab.

"Wanta see?" Mitch said. They watched one of the guinea pigs die of shock, then Mitch slit it open. Together, they leaned for a moment over the animal. Joe touched the marbled, yellow intestine, touched the bright red scarf of the liver that lay against the butter-white flesh.

"Beautiful, isn't it?" Mitch said, feeling that it was in moments like these that Joe's path and his ran together.

"No wonder Rembrandt hung around butcher shops," Joe said.

Mitch explained about anaphylaxis.

When Sylvia came in, sniffing and delicately holding her nose, Mitch had only one more guinea pig to inject. "Can I watch?" she asked.

"Sure." But remembering Beautiful, he went and got a bottle of ether. "Want to play nurse?" he said, giving Sylvia a dab of cotton-waste.

She watched, coolly, as he made the slick incision, prodded out the dainty vein. He slipped in the needle.

The pig showed no sign of shock.

"Well, is the operation a success?" she asked.

"Not unless the patient dies," he said, puzzled.

Suddenly he knew. It was the ether. Ether had something to do with anaphylactic shock. Held it back, submerged it perhaps. . . .

"What's the matter, Mitch, is anything wrong?"

"I don't know. It may be—it may be all right! I got a hunch!" He was excited.

Sylvia was smiling at him as though she knew exactly what was in his mind.

Rudy was taking his first real vacation in years. He called up Mitch Wilner and said: "Say, how would you like to take in the Mayo Clinic?"

"Boy, that's one thing I wouldn't like to do nothing else but!" Mitch said, already wondering if Professor Nyquist would give him a letter to Dr. Durand, the big blood specialist at Rochester.

Rudy said it was no use wasting the back seat, and had the bright idea that Syl and Joe might like to come along for the ride. Joe said okay, he wasn't doing anything these days anyway.

It was slack season in millinery, and Mort decided he was due for a vacation, so would anyone object to his company?

"Okay with me," said Mitch. "So long as you don't drive."

They figured to drive slow and easy, taking in the countryside, especially as Rudy was breaking in his new trade-in Ford.

"How come you bought another Ford?" Mort, the new guardian of Judaism, criticized.

"Well, I was going to make it a Chevvy this time," Rudy said, "but after all Ford apologized, didn't he?"

"Damn tootin'. He was losing too much business!" Mort said, climbing into the front seat, as he figured to spell Rudy at the wheel.

Sylvia settled gayly among all those boys.

"Well, Nina, how does it feel to have all your men at the same time," Alvin kidded, seeing them off.

"Humph! Nina had nothing on me!" She proved herself up on the latest literature. "Three was her limit!"

They figured to drive easy, but once they got outside the city, there was Mort with the road map tangled out, jutting into everybody's face. "We could make it by Wednesday morning," he figured. "Say, we could make it by Tuesday afternoon."

From the start, Joe was grouchy. It griped him that Rudy could go along working his way through medical school and even buy himself a new car for good measure. Everything seemed to fit, for such fellows. Here he had put in months trying to establish himself, worked like the devil too, and never done a lick of sculpture—what did he have to show for it? . . . And he was griped by their gayety. Rudy and Mitch surprised everybody, acting like puppies, making up songs about the signs along the road, especially Pluto water; and then, because they were four boys with one girl, developing the most comical, elaborate gallantry toward Sylvia. They stopped at every stand and fought over whose turn it was to buy her Baby Ruths. They sang songs of unrequited love. Mitch recited: "Who is Sylvia, what is she?" They challenged each other to duels with beanblowers at six paces.

Sylvia entered into the game, conferring upon one or the other the favor of sitting next to him, or suddenly begging Mort for protection.

Joe got more and more annoyed. He ground into his corner of the car. The rear seat was crowded, with bags underfoot. The gasoline smell gave him a headache. Sylvia objected to his pipe.

Or then, Rudy and Mitch would get into a serious discussion about medicine, Rudy upholding surgery, Mitch emphasizing research, and Mort and Sylvia would hang onto their words as though they were oracles.

In this crowd, there was nothing he could talk to Syl about. Even the scenery was flat.

There was only one time in the ride when Joe stopped feeling out of place. Chugging up a high embankment, they first saw the big lazy Mississippi. Rudy stopped the car and the five of them sat there looking at the river flowing wide and easy, spreading easily around a few islands, lying soft along the marshy shores. For a short while, they were five separate beings, each taking in the beauty all alone.

—Like a big nigger woman in bed, Mort thought, her great arms embracing all lovers.

—A man needs to get out and really see the size of the country, Rudy thought. You never realized how big was America, a big country with big rivers. Gee, this trip was doing wonders for him, after those hard grinding years closed in the backrooms of pharmacies, closed in the classrooms and labs, smelling only sickness; gee, this was clean, this washed away the city. Some time he would drive all the way to California.

—They should have made this trip alone together, Joe told himself. Sitting alone with Sylvia, looking out over this river, the final communication would have been established, the tearing at each other, the periods of not seeing each other, then the rushing together, then the separations again—all that would be over. A man living in a house out around here, even on this hill, could find some real expression of America, oh, some full Walt Whitman expression. This would be the spot for a great bronze figure of an Indian, simply patterned as those native, primitive cigar-store carvings he had once been so crazy about. Remember, Syl?

"This is the most beautiful sight I have ever seen," Mitch stated. "Has Europe got anything to beat this?" he asked deferentially of Joe.

"Well, what are we waiting for?" Syl kidded hurry-up Mort. "We want to get to Schmaltz Creek by four o'clock! Drive on! Drive on! Ain't you ever seen a river before?"

The gabled homes and the ordinary small-town buildings of Rochester looked like servants crouching at the feet of the massive hospitals. What had once been a small-town general store was filled with wheelchairs, trusses, crutches, and complicated artificial limbs. Restaurant walls were covered with lists of diets, and with the vitamin and calorie content of every dish. Menus were arranged according to vitamins and calories.

"Hey, Mitch; what do I have to order to get some ham and eggs?" Mort jested.

As they walked down the street, they saw, everywhere, convalescent half-cadavers sitting around on verandas, greedily absorbing the sun, and the eyes of wheelchair patients glittered at them with a triumph that cried: "I am here! You young sprouts are no better than I, I too am alive! I have not died! The Mayo brothers have saved me!"

Every house was converted into a rooming house. When they stepped into theirs, eyes on all sides devoured them, as if to pierce the sham of their healthy husks, to guess what horrible decay was in their bodies, what would be cut out of these young people with knives. On the porch, a wan stranger confronted Mitch and Joe hopefully. "Have you been examined yet? Which one of you is it? Or both?"

"Medic students!" he repeated with awe, at Mitch Wilner's explanation. And it seemed to Joe that the man was ready to grovel on the floor. All day Joe had noticed this reverence for the medical profession; it was as if a halo sat upon every white-coated doctor, interne, nurse, that crossed a street. People actually stepped aside for them.

The invalid's eyes gleamed acquisitively as he leaned toward them. "Tell me now, doctor—oh, I know, you gentlemen don't like to speak outside of the profession, but just sort of tip us off—which is the better man now, Charley Mayo or his brother?"

Mitch tried to sidetrack the question, but the patient persisted fanatically. Not that he would ever be operated on by either of the Mayos; his interest was idealistic, almost religious: who was the true Pope?

The landlady appeared, offering expert evidence on either side: Charley had performed a miraculous operation on a man's heart, but Willie had operated on a man's brain. Charley was a wonderful administrator but Willie was the one that got the money.

"They're both wonderful men," Mitch said. "And they have some great men working with them."

"They are the greatest doctors in the world," the invalid affirmed.

"Think of what those two have done here!" the landlady said. "Why, I can remember when I was a girl and this was just an ordinary sleepy town. But now, why, there are people from all over the world here this minute, coming on the pilgrimage to have their lives saved; they have operated on royalty and on presidents, and at the same time, money is no consideration, the rich pays for the poor; if you are a poor man you have as much chance for the best care as the King of England. And believe me, nobody fools them, everyone that comes here is investigated so they know if they are lying when they say they can't pay. You know there are some people that try to make themselves look poor. Sometimes Jewish people—" but keeping her eye on them, she caught herself up. "Why, they made this town, and they made it famous all over the world, there are special trains running here, and it is all the work of those two men, just by their skill, and nothing else!"

An awed silence greeted the end of her speech.

"Just goes to show—what is that saying?—if you can make a better mousetrap, the world will beat its way to your door," the invalid concluded.

Joe could almost feel the ambition surging in Mitch Wilner, to rise, to be as famous and as great as the Mayos, to be the biggest thing in his line, to have hospitals built upon the fruits of his work alone.

They walked to the curb, meeting Rudy.

"They had a place in Greece," Joe said, looking across at the nondescript hospital buildings. "Epidaurus." He was angry at himself for needing to show off, and spoke half ironically: "They believed that the contemplation of beauty gave people health."

In his mind Joe was trying to populate that dreamy hillside where he had been so moved, so inspired. When it was crowded with patients, were they like these? Surely people are the same in all ages. He had brought away an idea of stately sanatoria, of a dignified people strolling on the grass, letting the sun and clean, sparse foods work upon them, people repairing to the hillside theater and sitting there in the sun, or slowly circling the temple of Æsculapius, going within the temple, and worshiping the sculptured image of that god of benevolent nature, to whom physicians were mere aids.

But perhaps Epidaurus, living, had been like this—a madhouse of stunted humans, voracious for life. People were never equal to the beauty of their own works; even this Rochester, visited in ruins, might seem as ideal and as beautiful as Epidaurus.

"They weren't so dumb," Rudy said. "Nature is the doctor's best medicine."

"Give me an X-ray machine and you can keep all the ruins in Greece!" said Mitch.

What got him was that medicine was here, and nothing else. All the other things that cluttered up life—business, and junk—had been cleared out. This was the pure one hundred percent thing! Oh, to work in a place like this!

"Old efficiency himself," Rudy proclaimed, showing them the visiting cards he had already procured, signing them all up as medic students. Even Sylvia. He had a list of tomorrow's schedule of operations, and he and Mitch went into a huddle about which were the best ones to watch.

Mort growled from the bed: "If I want to see butchery I can go to the stockyards at home," and turned over, and slept.

Mitch laughed.

Rudy led them among the buildings, he already knew the ropes. Syl had never seen Rudy so animated. Here, he was in charge of everything, even Mitch seemed to concede to him. "Hurry up, Dr. Haendel is operating first thing, I don't want to miss that!"

They were given white gowns, and filed into the narrow gallery of the operating room. The swathed figure already lay on the table. The gallery was filled with serious-faced men, many half-bald country doctors, young medics taking the dreamed-of trip to Rochester.

What began now was like a dumb-show seen through glass, every movement of the surgeon anticipated by the assistants, the whole operation proceeding like a rehearsed pantomime, a thousand finger movements following each other like the playing of a memorized piece on the piano. Sylvia tried to catch the few whispered words that the surgeon uttered, as one tries, sometimes in a theater, to interpret the half-sounds which a magician directs toward his assistant.

—They dress up for it, Joe was thinking. A ritual, in white. And now he realized the idea he had only half grasped yesterday. In Greece, medicine had been an art subordinated to the power of the gods, and the doctors had humbly aided, in their small way, the cures effected by the sculptured gods; but here, in America, the surgeons were the gods, and religion was the handmaiden, indeed some of these nurses were actually nuns, humbly aiding the power of science. This operating room was the church and the synagogue of the American people; the surgeon was the high priest. And the operation was a ritual; the white robes, the hush, the stationed assistants and the reverent watchers, the patterned movements, each according to rote. The beauty of the room, square, chaste, with the fewest necessary tables bearing instruments; the grouping of the nurses, in their shaped white uniforms, the pattern even of the little blood clamps as the surgeon laid them swiftly in a fringe around the incision.

The entire scene was composed for white plaster. Some time, Joe thought, to make a bas-relief embodying this religion, to express the holy antiseptic reverence of America, to express the American idea of perfection here: perfection of manual skill, coupled with memory; what else was a surgeon's task? Deft hands, and remembering anatomy.

And further, Joe thought: it is all materialist, all a worship of the gross forms of life, of the body; but not of the beauty of human form. It is merely a worship of success, in the form of health, of victory over disease, of cheating death.

—What a man! Rudy whispered. What a technique! He crouched down in his seat, leaning forward, to get an angle through the crook of an interne's elbow, to see right into the open flesh. The surgeon had exposed the tumor now.

"Do you think they really had to operate?" Mitch questioned.

"Of course," Rudy whispered. "Look at the color of it." How simple things were after all. In a shut world, evil, rot might be growing, and how could you tell? Open it up, and there was your lump of corruption. Take a knife and cut it out. Here in this superb operating room, where the art of antisepsis was at last complete, surgery came home to Rudy. What could a doctor do, but help the body do things for itself? And when it was too late for that, for people mostly came to you too late, there was this beautifully clean and simple aid, the knife, to cut the enemy growth out of the body. Hundreds of clinics he had attended in school, but he had never known this so clearly as now: the body was a case of perishable goods that could always be safely opened—with proper care.

Rudy, Joe, and Sylvia waited while Mitch went in with his letter to the great blood specialist, Dr. Durand.

"Didn't Mitch make a discovery? About that blood shock?" Sylvia asked. "Was it important?"

"Well, he published a paper on it, in the *Courier*," Rudy said admiringly. "For a fellow his age that's damn unusual."

"Didn't he discover how to prevent that shock, by giving ether? I was there—remember, Joe?"

"He did some swell work on the ether effect," Rudy said. "Lots of men have been claiming ether is a stop for anaphylaxis and Mitch really did a swell set of experiments on animals. Mitch has got the stuff!" Rudy said. "He's going to be an outstanding man."

Mitch came out glowing. "There's a prince of a man!" he said.

"Oh, Mitch, Rudy has been telling us how you discovered that taking ether prevented that blood shock. I'm in on it, remember I helped you make the discovery!" she laughed.

Mitch joked about his trifling contribution. But he admitted Dr. Durand had read his article in the *Courier*. There really was an ether effect, he had found, in guinea pigs and dogs; it sort of slowed up, submerged the shock. But he still was not sure whether ether could prevent fatal anaphylaxis. Anyway, the thing might work altogether differently in humans. Maybe ether merely submerged the symptoms without really preventing the shock. That was what he wanted to work on next.

Many physicians were in fact advocating the use of ether, before administering serum, as a precaution against anaphylaxis.

If he could ever work with a man like Dr. Durand! "What he doesn't know about blood! And say, he has a complete system of blood groupings worked out, by the use of anaphylactic reactions." Mitch explained. The closer together the species of the animals, the slighter the shock they could get from each other's blood. Thus the serum-shock tests verified the evolutionary relationships of sheep and goats, apes and humans. Through bloods, a whole chart of evolution had been constructed!

"It's a beautiful job!" Mitch said. "And say, do you know who came in while I was there?"

"Who?" Sylvia gasped.

"Dr. Charley, in person!"

"Let me touch you!" She touched his sleeve, mockingly, but awed.

"Did you talk to him?" Rudy said.

"A little, just a few words," Mitch said. "He asked me when I was going to be through, and I told him. Then Dr. Durand said for me to get in touch with him when I was out."

They all gasped.

Why, that made it practically certain Mitch could come to Rochester after graduation!

Mitch and Rudy went off to another operation. As Sylvia watched them go, Joe said, with a sudden sense of completion: "Mitch is the kind of a fellow you ought to marry. You probably will."

COMMERCE AND ADMINISTRATION

> Blue skies smiling at me,
> Nothing but blue skies
> Do I see.

A hand grabbed Harry's shoulder, and a familiar voice growled in his ear: "So you had to go to your granma's funeral, huh!"

Harry turned. "Plotsy! I haven't seen you in a dog's age! Whatya doing these days?"

"Oh, I'm giving Darrow a little competition." Runt pulled out his wallet and handed Harry an embossed card. "Still working in that garage?"

"I'm the manager now," Harry said. "That neighborhood is developing fast, and Bienstock doubled the size of the place."

"Say, you must be dragging in the shekels."

"Oh, I don't make so much, and I've got to help out my kid brother down at Illinois, he's on the football squad."

"What is he, another Benny Friedman? Did you see where Red Grange just signed up for a half a million buck movie contract? It's a good investment, Harry, it's a good investment!"

"Oh, he's only a sub," Harry said.

"I just had to get a couple of my brothers started, set them up in business," Runt sympathized.

Just then Babe Ruth came up to bat. Harry turned back to the game. The King of Swat missed one. Cheers and yowls and cat-calls rose. "You stink!" "He's getting old!" "He swings like a beer sign!"

"A dollar he knocks a homer!" Runt offered.

"Strike two," the umpire called. Harry felt scared. Babe Ruth was getting fat, fat as a beer barrel, wobbling on those skinny ankles.

"You still betting?" a guy next to Runt haw-hawed.

"There's your money!" Runt waved a bill.

Cubs' Park echoed with jeering laughter.

Suddenly the King of Swat turned on the crowd, angrily waving his arms. He stretched out his bat, pointing to the furthest corner of the field. That's where the ball was going.

A stunned silence fell at his audacity. The ball was pitched. The hit was a pebble in the silence. They saw the ball, a speck rising against the windows of the apartment houses, on that far side of the Park. The Babe had done it just like he said![7] A homer!

Runt was jumping on his chair, pounding, hugging Harry. "That's showing 'em! That's calling 'em! Anybody wanna bet?"

"Boy, they got wonderful pastrami here, good as Kantor's delicatessen." Runt hustled Harry into the place.

That ball was still sailing, sailing in his mind, and Harry mentioned to Runt:

"I've got a little invention I've been working on the last year or so; I think I've got it perfected now."

"Say! What's the invention?"

"It's got something to do with cars," Harry admitted.

"Boy! there's millions in it if you got something they have to put on a car!" Runt snapped. "Lemme handle it for you!"

"Well, it don't exactly go on a car. It's for private garages."

"What is it, a burglar alarm?" Runt ventured.

---

[7] Babe Ruth's legendary "Called Shot" was at Game 3 of the World Series, played at Wrigley Field on October 1, 1932. This may be a fictionalized variant, set at an earlier date?

The main thing an inventor had to remember was to keep his idea secret. But Harry couldn't resist testing it out.

"It's an automatic door-closer, so you don't have to go back and close the garage door from the inside."

"Uh huh," Runt said, and tapped the porcelain table with a gilt Eversharp. "Say, that's a pretty smart idea, at that."

"I've got it now so it will fit on any type of door," Harry said. "Every home garage owner ought to be in the market for it."

"First thing you want to do," Runt advised, "is get a search made for a patent, to see if anyone else had the same idea. That's got to be done in the patent office, in Washington."

"Does that cost a lot of dough?"

"I've got connections in Washington," Runt said largely, remembering the ads of various patent law firms. "I'll get it done for you at what it would cost me. Maybe twenty bucks. You don't have to worry. I can put up the dough if you're short."

"Oh, that's all right, I can take care of it," Harry said in a thoughtful voice.

"What are you going to do, are you going to try to put this thing on the market yourself?" Runt said.

"Well, I figured after I got it protected, I'd try to sell it to a big company, like Prentiss Hardware, or Sears," Harry said, imagining himself walking out of an office with a million-dollar check, like the young Russian who invented the photomaton.

"Why let someone else have all the gravy?" Runt said. "What you want is to get some backers and start your own company. Listen, I know some parties."

Harry saw himself cracking out one invention after another, saw a factory growing, spreading, with a thousand machines stamping out parts for his devices.

"Look, this is how it works," he began enthusiastically, taking Runt's pencil—why, someone had made millions on a simple idea like the Eversharp—and drawing a diagram on the table-top.

"Say, what do you think I am, Einstein?" Runt put his hand to his head. "Listen, you bring the plans up to my office"—he reached for Harry's check, brushing aside Harry's protestations.

"Wait a minute," Runt said, as Harry got up, "you never can tell who might come along." Runt rubbed out the diagram on the table-top.

Harry had really intended going to Lou Margolis for the patent. But now he saw Runt was okay.

I Got Ambition

"Was I right, or was I wrong!" Mort shouted. "I told you if we didn't go after Monkey Ward's[8], Sugarman would crawl in there! Why stand on etiquette! Why sit on our tails and wait for the jobber to go after them! What use is the jobber to us! How is it that Sugarman can start in business, and Willis Cohen can start in business, and half a dozen more new shops open, and they all get business? It's supply and demand! There's plenty of business and if we won't go after it someone else will! I could have sold Kresge if you had let me go to New York. This class of business is bound to come to Chicago, pop! They got union labor all over New York now and we can beat them ten cents on the dollar! Wake up, will you!"

"All right, all right, Mr. Supply and Demand, so there is enough for Sugarman, and for Villis Cohen, and for the jobber, and for us too. We are doing good enough, knock wood, and don't try to bite off more than you can swallow," said Abramson, senior.

Mort walked back and forth, fuming. "Listen, pop, I'm out on the road and I see what is happening. The whole jobber system is too slow. It used to be a winter hat and a summer hat, and finish. But now, like Morris Heilman said at the convention, it's a hat for every minute, a hat for every mood. You can sell them not one winter hat, but five. Ask Sylvie how many hats have the girls got! The latest thing is ensembles; we can sell them the idea they got to have a hat for every dress! We've got to put out a new model every day, and the next day it's got to be in the stores, not in the jobber's warehouse."

"But what do you want?" Abramson yawned, while Mrs. Abramson remained neutral. "We just put in ten new machines. We couldn't squeeze in another girl with a shoehorn. The fire inspector was even here and gave me hell. We can't handle more business if we get it."

Mort sighed, exasperated. For months he had been screaming: Let's move! And is there a law that all millinery shops have to be in the crummy fire-traps around Wabash and Lake?

"Listen! On Milwaukee Avenue we can get a modern, daylight floor at half the price. It will even pay to keep a showroom in the Loop, for you to play pinochle with your boy chums," he kidded his father.

"Aha, you want to get me out of the shop altogether?"

"Listen! We could have a model factory, plenty of room, the girls will be more efficient without the El hammering around their heads, we can give them restrooms—"

"Right away, Mort's worrying about the girls," Mrs. Abramson jested.

"But the main thing is, we'll have room to expand! In a couple of years, why shouldn't we have our own building—!"

"Oho! Oho! He's getting started."

"Why not? Why not? We've got a good brand! Didn't we cop all the prizes in our class at the convention? I met that old *kaker* Harry Turek in Madison and, honest to God, he told me every once in a while he gets a request for Glory brand. We ought to have another man on the road! We

---

[8] Montgomery Ward was commonly referred to as "Monkey Ward."

ought to advertise! What's the matter with advertising? We got a fine slogan . . ."

He could see himself on the road, whizzing by a flaming poster—a beautiful McClelland Barclay girl, snappy, modern, *zaftig*, her bobbed locks curling out from under a Glory tricorn model. And just one line—his slogan:

THE CROWNING

GLORY

(Glory Hats, Inc., Chicago)

"Why not advertise?"

"Ah, don't be foolish; to who are we advertising? The customer don't know the name of the hat. The wholesaler buys it."

"That's just it, when the customer knows the name, he'll make his store order our brand. Why shouldn't we have our own stores, too! Look at Thom McAn, with his chain of shoe stores! Look at Sears Roebuck opening a chain of retail stores! Everybody is expanding! Trying something new! In a couple of years we could build up a chain—"

"Wait, hold your horses!" Mrs. Abramson was chuckling. "My, has he got ambition! He's as big as Sears Roebuck already! . . . But one thing he is right, we've got to move to a bigger factory."

. . . 'cause I'm sitting
on top of
the worruld . . .

He had gone around to the judges and offered himself as free defense counsel, and finally he had drawn a real case, robbery with a gun, and the accused was a repeater; conviction meant life.

Sam made his case by confusing and ridiculing the state's witnesses and by proving an alibi, just as that bastard Donohue had taught.

When the defendant shook his hand, after the victory, Sam felt all mixed up between elation and confusion. The guy had tears in his eyes and yet a crooked leer on his lips. "You get a present for this, Sam, you get a present for this if I have to go out and do a stickup!" he joked. And seeing Sam's look: "Naw I'm off that stuff. I got some sense. Next time I get the book. What's the use of taking chances?"

Sam felt a little dubious; but Lil greeted him like a conquering hero, and after all he had saved an underdog.

He was getting experience and building up a practice this way, pretty soon he could leave his father-in-law's business. The case was talked about up and down the County Building, and everybody slapped him on the back. "How's the defender of the people?" Even Lou Margolis grinned, meeting him in the County Building elevator.

They call it black bottom
And, oh, sister, it's sure got 'em. . . .

His belly shaking like a dish of Jello, Alderman Pete Grinnell sank onto the davenport and heeheed and heeheed.

Rube Moscowitz strode to the Chinese lacquered cabinet and took out a flagon of wine.

"I told you that bum was putting on an act!" he howled, as the wine poured over the brim of the glass.

Still half choked with laughter, Grinnell made a sanctimonious face, and mimed: " 'If Mr. Insull wants a subway, why doesn't he go and dig it himself! Why should the city dig him one, to the chune of two hundred millions!' "

"Yah, why, that's what I wanna know," Rube yelled, and hawhawed. He overflowed another glass, and offered it to Grinnell.

"It's the best sacramental wine," Rube Moscowitz bragged. "I got a new fellow that keeps me supplied."

"You know who it is, Lou," Celia said. "Remember Runt Plotkin?"

"Is he peddling liquor? He better watch out he'll get disbarred."

"He has his brothers do it," Celia said.

"Honest Oscar!" Rube howled, scornfully, still recalling their exploit.

The subway question was in the air again and this time it looked like something would really be done. Mayor Dever had promised Chicago that subway! London has a subway, New York, Paris, Berlin, even Boston has a subway, what's the matter with Chicago! And it looked like this time Insull and the city would get together on a deal.

The city was to spend a couple of hundred million dollars on a subway and also eventually to buy out Insull's El and the street car lines for a few hundred million, and this whole shooting match, subway, El, car lines, composing the Unified Traction System, owned by the city, was to be turned over to Insull to run.

The only question now was how much Insull was to get for his El and street car interests. Insull had helped elect Dever mayor and now, by God, Dever and his crowd were developing a conscience and offering a paltry hundred and fifty million for Insull's traction holdings! So Rube had to see a few aldermen about the traction business. The aldermen could vote down this proposition, and if Dever wouldn't play ball, there was always another election.

"So are you going to put his son through college?" Lou prompted, curious as to the deal they had made with Alderman Oscar Hoaglum.

"Naw, I gave him a little campaign fund. It's going to be a tough election," Rube laughed, making a note in his little book.

"Well, that sews up the council," Alderman Grinnell said, with satisfaction. "Here's to the next mayor? Gonna run yourself, Rube?"

"Me?" Rube roared with laughter. "Moscowitz for mayor! Can you picture it? Aw, we'll get somebody."

"Say, you better not leave that book lying around. You want to start another Teapot Dome?" Pete murmured, nervously.

Rube gave him a good-natured shove on the shoulder. "So what? What did they do to those guys in the Teapot Dome? Beans and bugs!"

> Clap hands and do a
> Ta da ta
> It's hot!

In spite of working his way through, Rudy Stone was among the top ten, and practically had his choice of hospitals.

"I think you ought to go to the Israel," Aline advised sensibly. "Of course, as you say, you see more kinds of cases at County, but what use will that junk ever be to you? At Israel you get the class of people that are going to be your patients."

> I love you so,
> Sonny Boy!

"Listen, Solly," Mrs. Meisel coaxed, after waiting till he had devoured half a roast chicken, "what are you doing with all your money? On girls you can't spend it all!"

Sol hummed "Ramona."

"Are you giving it to that dago? Is he your banker too?" she pressed him.

"Aw, he's all right, I'd trust him with my last shirt!" Sol said. "Say, if it wasn't for Pisano, I'd never even of got started."

"How much are you making now, Solly?"

"Well, y' gotta figure, there's plenty of expenses, and I don't ride all the time."

"Three hundred a day, do they give you?"

How did she know?

"In the last year, with all your expenses, you should have had left over ten thousand dollars, easy," she said.

"Well, I know what money is, I don't throw away money," he hedged.

"I am talking for your own good. How long can you be a rider? The best thing is to put your money in a business that will support you when you give up the game."

His father broke in anxiously: "What do you know, maybe that dago is playing the stock market with your money."

Sol laughed. "Well, what's wrong with the stock market? Say, some big shots come to the Garden in New York, and I cleaned up on a couple of tips."

"Listen, Sol"—his mother came out with it—"I want you should put your money in a business."

"Huh?"

"You could be partners with Ben, and he would take care of the business while you were away."

Ben kept on eating.

"What's the matter, isn't schoolteaching good enough for him?" Sol said.

Mrs. Meisel disregarded this. "You know Epstein the cleaner?" Sol knew. Plenty of times he had chased out to Epstein's crummy plant, on Wentworth Avenue, with a hurry-up job. "Epstein has a couple of lots in Cicero, and he wants to put up a new cleaning factory, the latest machinery, everything up to date. Sol, it is a fine chance for you to be a partner. Epstein knows the business through and through, and we know the stores, and we could work up the biggest cleaning plant in Chicago."

The scheme didn't sound so crazy at that. Come to think of it, the great Chicago rider, Carl Stockholm, was in the cleaning business too!

> Blue skies smiling at me,
> Nothing but blue skies
> Do I see.

"Turn here," Runt said mysteriously, and Mort turned off Blue Island Avenue onto Twenty-Second Street. Polack neighborhood.

"Better park along here. They don't like cars too close to the joint."

The three of them walked back to the alley.

"Hey, maybe I should have brought my blackjack for protection," Sol jested lamely.

Down the alley, a small bulb glowed over a door. Runt knocked. A peephole slid open.

"Hi," Runt said. "Just some of the boys."

A face glowered through the aperture, then the door opened. "Just act natural," Runt whispered.

The place had a swell old-fashioned mirror-backed bar. Mounted elkheads and mounted fish were on the walls. A three-piece orchestra was playing the "Blue Danube."

The dining room was fairly well filled with ordinary-looking men and women. Beer was served openly.

"They sling up some great goulash here," Runt said. "They get fish up from New Orleans. These boys are particular what they scoff. Wadaya wanna drink, Mort?"

The waiter stood over the table. "Hey, what's good tonight, Gus?" Runt inquired, like a habitué.

Mort ordered the celebrated pompano from New Orleans. They got wine in coffee cups.

Runt, meanwhile, was cautiously looking over the customers. "No big shots here yet," he confided.

Just then a squat man ambled over to their table. "Hi, Chris," Runt said, jumping up. "I want you to meet a couple of the boys, Sol Meisel, the famous six-day bike rider, and Mort Abramson." They shook hands with Chris, owner of the place.

When the boss had ambled away, Runt showed two fingers held together, and said: "He and Al are like this."

Runt tasted the wine. "Too sour. Hey, Mort, how was that stuff I got you? That's real wine."

"Say, where do you get that stuff?" Mort inquired, with a knowing look. "What have you got, a racket?"

"Naw, I got it fixed up for my kid brothers to handle a little of it, that's all," Runt said, largely. "That's real sacramental stuff, with a government okay."

"Yeah? Don't you have to be a rabbi to get it?"

Runt pulled a wise face. "My old man belongs to a little *shul*. I got the list of members, see. The government allows so much for each member. I just send Rube Moscowitz a couple of gallons and it's all fixed."

Mort laughed, appreciatively. "What do you do when you use up all the members?"

"Say"—Runt winked—"that *shul* got a list of every Yid that's died in the last fifty years. The law don't say the members have to be alive, does it?"

"I've got to hand it to you!" Mort said. "Gogol the second!" But Runt didn't get his literary reference.

"I wouldn't get mixed up in this stuff on a big scale," Runt said. "But I've got a lead on a racket that'll roll in the big money."

"Yeah?"

"This is straight. It's an invention. The biggest thing since traffic lights were invented and you know how they're cleaning up on them! Listen, Mort, do you keep your car in a public or private garage? Okay! How do you lock the garage door?"

. . . Handling the patents . . . mechanical genius . . . keeping it on the q.t. . . . big companies after the rights, but why give them all the gravy? . . . ground floor . . .

"Gee," said Sol Meisel, "and I just put all my dough in a cleaning factory!"

Mort said he'd think about it.

Two men went up to the bar. Runt tensed. He whispered hoarsely, keeping his eyes on the tablecloth, "The guy on the other end . . . that's Killer Mac. He's Al's chief executioner. Toughest mug in Chicago!" Mort and Sol hushed their breath in the presence of the great.

> They call it black bottom,
> A new twister,

> And, oh, sister,
> It's sure got 'em—
> It's hot . . .

"Oh, kid, he's a dream!" Estelle confided as she ordered the Paul Ash sundae. "The thing about a Gentile fellow is you never know what he's going to do next. And can he dance!" With awe she added: "He's a Catholic!"

"But, kid, you wanna watch your step," Celia advised. "You know those fellows think they can get away with anything with a Jewish girl."

"Didn't Irving Berlin just marry a Gentile? She was a Catholic, too!"

"Yah, but when it's the girl that's Jewish it's different."

"Say, listen—Dickie isn't that kind of a guy. He's a college graduate!"

> I hear the mission bells above
> Ringing out our song of love . . .

A red arm of steel stuck out over the sidewalk; on this the big electric sign would hang: *SPEEDY CLEANING AND DYEING CO.* The framework of the sign welded right into the steel structure of the building.

Chesty Meisel sat in his Cadillac roadster and looked at the yellow brick walls.

> I press you, caress you . . .

They certainly had slung up the walls in a hurry. That was the ticket! Speed! Between his last Chicago race and this Chicago race—the walls flew up!

A chicken passed, and he blew his three-note horn. She turned, but he didn't like her face.

> . . . care . . .
> . . . rambling rose in your hair,
> . . . Ramona . . . !

He leaned back, watching the workmen swarm into the place, they were laying the concrete floor, now, and in his mind he began to count over all the girls he had laid.

Starting with Estelle, because she was the first real lay in a bed. Estelle, and next was Mitzi Callahan that sent the letter to the track, and should he count that old girl he only laid once, what was her name, Genevieve, phoo, and Betty Isaacs, and in New York, Mae the blonde, and Tillie Cohen, boy, she was a wonder, and Grace Norlander, and her roommate, what was her name—Rose, and, in Philly, the society jane . . .

He counted forty-three, but was sure he had left out several. Forty-three, and never paid for it once! Bet he could make a different girl every night, up to a hundred!

> Oh, de sweeter de berry, de blacker de juice!

"Shoot it all!" Mort said, shoving forward his whole stack of chips.

His father closed his fan of cards and tossed them on the table.

Harry Turek's eyes glittered like diamonds set in curls of fat. He met Mort's bet.

Mort laid down three kings and two deuces. "You got to be good when you play with the Abramsons!"

Harry Turek sadly joked: "At least when I worked for Stein, Lerman, when I got paid, they didn't take it away from me."

"Listen, we got to pay for our new shop, don't we?" Mort raked in the mazuma.

Oh, de sweeter de berry, de blacker de juice!

Ev Goldberg got engaged!

Aline and Rudy announced their engagement!

Lou Margolis picked off Celia Moscowitz!

Blue birds singing a song,
Nothing but blue birds all day long . . .

At a bridge of the Sunshine Club, now a branch of the Junior Hadassah, Rose Heller wailed: "Girls, I'm going broke! Nothing but showers and weddings!"

Even her kid sister had just become engaged.

"Don't worry, kid, you'll get it all back with interest; what about you and Manny Kassell?"

But what was Manny Kassell, a dentist, to the kind of fellows the rest of the girls were grabbing off!

—He's a graduate of Harvard.

—Trust Ev Goldberg!

—Well, Celia got a lawyer too, didn't she?

"Uph! how can you compare! Lou only went to night school, and as Ev said, half of the Presidents have been graduates from Harvard Law School!" Thelma declared so loudly that Rose feared Celia would hear her in the bathroom.

—What's Ev trying to pull? I knew Faivel Warshavsky when they lived on Morgan Street and his old man peddled brooms.

—So now he's Philip Ware.

—Did you see the rock?

—Honest, it's so big it looks like glass!

Celia Moscowitz won the bridge prize, a cigarette box of inlaid wood, made in Palestine, and Rose announced the club had earned two dollars and sixty cents on the affair, to be used in the support of a hospital in Jerusalem. (Not counting the four dollars she had spent for refreshments and prizes.)

Thelma put *The Rhapsody in Blue* on the Hellers' new orthophonic victrola. "I don't like jazz music," she said, "but this is really classical!"

Singing in the rain, I'm singing in the rain . . .

Mitch Wilner was elected to the Sigma Xi, honorary scientific society!
The *America* stood ready to fly from New York to Paris!

Ah, sweet mystery of life,
At last I've found you!

"You wouldn't dare do it!" that fellow Howie cried.
"Wouldn't I! You supply the wine!" Estelle responded.
She was the sensation of the party.
"Me and Earl Carroll!" Howie bragged.
"And I don't mean dago red! I mean champagne!" cried Estelle.
"Champagne! Whadaya take me for?"
"A big butter and egg man from Peoria!" was her snappy comeback.
"Oh, yeah? I'll give you your wine-bath!" and Howie emptied his gin glass down her dress.
"Owo!" she yelled and jumped a mile, pulling her dress away from her body.
"Some babe!" Howie said, lamping her bosom.
"She can be had," his friend Dickie hinted.
She was the sensation of the party!

. . . on top of the worruld . . .

"Where were you all night?" Mrs. Greenstein demanded, blocking the doorway.
"At Jeanette's." Her mother didn't move. "Oh, be yourself, ma, get out of the way. I've stayed with Jeanette before."
"If you want to stay by Jeanette, go and stay by Jeanette, you *nafkeh!*" her mother cried, slamming the door in her face.
"All right, all right!" Estelle screamed at the closed door. "You'll see if I ever come back! You're the one that's to blame! Even if I did anything, you'd be the one that made me!
"Ishkabibble." She shrugged, as she walked down the stairs.

Hallelujah! Bum again!

Wall Street offered Ford a billion for his business and he said not for two billion would he sell!
Debs died in Chicago.
Dempsey-Tunney comeback fight, the battle of the century, for Soldiers' Field, Chicago.
Krishnamurti came to Chicago.
Queen Marie came to Chicago.

> When my baby
> Smiles at me!

Queen Marie visited the Rumanian Jewish synagogue on Douglas Boulevard and Rube Moscowitz made the speech of greeting. Standing on the stairs, in a high silk hat.

Celia was presented to Princess Ileana!

Ev Goldberg outdid them all with her shower for Celia Moscowitz. You never saw such originality! It was given according to the exact etiquette of a royal reception and all the girls bought things in Rumanian peasant style. Naturally you couldn't give Celia Moscowitz anything cheap and there was a hand-woven linen table service that cost forty dollars, alone.

Everything was monogrammed, with a crest copied from Rumanian royalty.

> You're the cream in my coffee,
> You're the salt in my stew . . .

The Freedmans moved into an apartment in their brand-new eighteen-flat building near Columbus Park. It had the latest improvements, even a Frigidaire in every apartment!

Two and a half million shares of stocks in one day!

> Blue birds singing a song,
> Nothing but blue birds all day long . . .

The new Stevens Hotel, bigger than the Palmer House, the biggest hotel in the world. Three thousand rooms. You could sleep in a different room every night, till 1935, without duplicating.

"Gimme a different woman in every room, and I'll try it!" Mort said.

Another super-plane stood ready to race the *America* from New York to Paris!

> You're the starch in my collar,
> You're the lace in my shoe!

Who said brides had to be in white! "Brides of originality," wrote the Chaperon, "are appearing in shell-pink and cerulean blue, this season."

The bridesmaids were in shell-pink, and Ev, in cerulean blue, was a dream.

The wedding was in the grand ballroom of the Edgewater, and the place was simply turned into a conservatory; Thelma Ryskind said the flowers alone cost a thousand dollars! The orchestra was the Collegians! They were so hard to get, Ev had changed the wedding date three times before they could be booked. And then, for the wedding march, Thelma

Ryskind had helped Ev select a classical quartet. They got two hundred dollars, just to come and play the Wedding March.

Rabbi Sherman, of the swanky North Shore Temple, officiated. It was a modern service, without the old-fashioned wedding canopy.

It took half an hour to read all the telegrams of congratulations, and none of them were faked.

"Celia will have a hard time beating this," everybody agreed.

BOOST CHICAGO
A world's fair for 1933!

'Cause I'm wild about my jelly-roll!

"Where have you been all my life?" the sophisticated straw-blonde cried, flinging her arms around his neck.

"Let's get married!" Alvin responded, and doubled her back in a kiss.

"I want to know only one thing first," she cried. "Do you like *The Sun Also Rises*?"

"It's the great unAmerican novel!" Alvin cracked.

"My soul-mate!" she succumbed. "Let's go!"

"What the hell, why not! What's love?" said Alvin. A gamble where the careful lose.

So they drove to Crown Point.

Ah, sweet mystery of life . . .

Big Bill Thompson, back in the ring.

Big Bill Thompson, his loose lips lurching up in a grin, shuffled onto the stage. He held his arms stiffly out before him. From each paw dangled a wire rat cage. In each cage a white rat scrambled, scratching at the tin floor. Big Bill set the cages down upon a table. He addressed the rat in one of them:

"Don't hang your head now, Fred."

The theater shook with roared laughter. They knew whom he meant! At the first lull, Big Bill remarked: "I had four more of them last night, had them all in one cage, but I guess Fred and Doc ate up the other four. They were smaller."

They screamed, they wept with laughter. They knew everybody he meant, all right.

"This one is Doc," Big Bill continued. "I can tell him because he hadn't had a bath for twenty years until we washed him yesterday—"

Lil giggled till the tears came out of her eyes. "He's funny! He's a scream!" she insisted.

Sam Eisen leaned forward, intent. He looked at all the faces in the theater. Mouths agape, excited. Big Bill knew how to bring them to life! What matter, how you did it!

The biggest, wildest, loudest election ever held in Chicago. Processions of honking cars, banners slung across the street, America First, Big Bill the Builder, steam calliopes!

"Why not, what's wrong with Thompson?" Sam Eisen demanded of Mort. "At least you have to admit he's honest! He believes in a wide-open town and that's what he's telling them.

"Look at Dever! So we had a reform administration! There was more gang war and killing than any time Thompson was in! And look at the graft! Terry Druggan with nights off from jail to throw parties in his Lake Shore Drive apartment!

"Thompson may be as big a grafter as the rest of them but at least he leaves something to show for the money. Look at the Municipal Pier he built; look at Michigan Avenue, Wacker Drive! And he was the only guy that had guts enough to tell the truth in the war! Pro-German! He was honest, that's all! The hell with these bluenoses and the *Tribune* running Chicago! Thompson at least does something for the people!"

"Yah! he cleans them out, and four years later he's back yelling poke King George in the snoot, and he'll clean out their pockets again!" Mort Abramson sneered.

". . . coming back because the people, the plain folks of this city, you and I and your brother-in-law and my uncle, we all *want* William Hale Thompson to come back and be mayor. Chicago is sick of Sunday School government!" Sam Eisen yelled from the back of the truck. "You haven't even got any rights in your home any more! You can't stop the cops from busting into your house and fanning your mattress for a bottle of home brew! Is that Chicago?"

"No!" a roar responded.

"Chicago is no sissy city! Chicago is a man's town! Those bluenoses are taking away your rights as an American citizen! Why, if anybody tried to search my bedroom I'd break the bottle over his head, except it might be a waste of good beer!" He waited for the roar to subside.

He felt that glow of power that always came to him when he knew he had the crowd.

"Great stuff, Sambo!" One of the red fat faces leered over him, a paw patted his back. "They ought to use you at the big meetings!" Hal Noonan cried.

Now he was getting in! Play the game their way, then beat them at it, when the time comes!

My baby smiles . . .

"Runt showed me this place," Mort said, opening the alley door for the bunch. "He knows all these gangsters."

"My, he's getting up in the world," Aline said, scraping mud off her slipper-sole.

"Wait till Thompson is elected, then we can go in the front way," Mort promised.

"Thompson has a good chance to win," Rudy said judiciously.

"He might at that. I understand Insull is behind him this time," Mort informed them.

"What's all this crazy stuff about punching the King of England in the nose?" Aline asked.

They all roared.

"The Prince of Wales ought to come back to Chicago and take him up on it, I understand he's a boxer," Rudy said.

"It's just a campaign slogan—attracts a lot of attention and doesn't mean anything!" Sylvia explained.

"It's going to be a hot election," Mort said. "There'll be a lot of scraps."

"How can Thompson win, if everybody knows he's a crook?" Aline asked.

"Organization," Mort said. "They fill up all the flophouses on State Street and every bum votes at least twenty times."

Aline looked as if she knew nothing about flophouses. "Celia's ring is twice as big as Ev's!" she remarked. "I never saw such a rock in my life. Honest, I think it's vulgar to wear such a big diamond."

"Well, Celia's a big girl."

"When bigger girls are made, Lou Margolis will make them," Mort cracked.

"Oh, Mort!"

"She said he got it at Peacock's but I'm willing to bet my last stepin he got it at his father's pawnshop," Aline hinted.

"Look," Mort whispered. "The guy at the bar. That's Al Capone!"

The girls shivered deliriously.

> . . . nothing but blue skies
> Do I see . . .

The ward committeeman gave the boys final instructions. "And if they try any rough stuff, fellows, just call us up. We'll shoot over some assistance."

Sam looked at the crew of toughs grinning behind the committee-man. No wonder a repeater could always get his alderman to fix him up with a parole. In times like this, the boys were needed.

Sam got to the polling place at 6 a.m.; Bill Dillon, the Democratic precinct captain, was already on the job. Sam stuck out his hand. "Let's play the game square, Bill. No funny stuff on either side."

Bill looked him clean in the eye. "Okay!" he said, and gripped hands.

An honest election for the seventy-ninth precinct, forty-sixth ward, Chicago!

A few moments after they had opened the polling place, Slim Greeley, Sam's watcher, pulled him outside and proudly showed him a blank ballot.

"Where'd you get that!"

Slim gasped at his innocence. "I get my vote, don't I?" Naturally, he had dumped a scrap of paper into the box, instead. He had his ballot all marked ready for their first voter, who could leave them his ballot in return. The old chain-voting stunt so they could be sure their voters weren't double-crossing them. "It's a cinch."

"Nix," said Honest Sam.

Nine o'clock, Slim Greeley grabbed Sam aside. "Hey, Sam! They're voting 'em. I just saw Dillon slip one to a guy."

"Go on if you have to, but I don't know anything about it," Sam said. Play the game, man, play the game.

They had their coats off and their shirts open. Empty pop bottles and sandwich rinds littered the backroom of the cleaning shop.

Sam had carried the precinct for Big Bill, 112 to 74; and 28 Socialist votes, lots of Germans around here.

"Hey, Sambo," Bill Dillon said, taking defeat like a man, "let's split these Socialist votes. I got to make a better showing."

"Huh," Sam said. "We can't do that."

"Awright, leave 'em a few. Leave 'em the eight, you take ten and me ten."

"Nothing doing!" says Honest Sam. "They get their full vote!"

. . . Sonny Boy!

A fellow came flying out of the West. Beside the two super-planes he set his silver ship. Now there were three, ready to race across the Atlantic. His name was Lindbergh.

Drink, drink, drink to the—

"Every Tom, Dick, and Harry that moves to the North Side gets married in the Edgewater!" Mrs. Moscowitz insisted. "At least the Drake is exclusive."

When they found out that the Drake ballroom was more expensive, the question was settled.

Sure, Rube Moscowitz lost a pile of money in Florida, a fortune, over a million! But so did everybody, even Al Capone! Lose a million today, make two million tomorrow! Rube had a fistful of these General Motors stocks, that went up a hundred points at one crack.

Judge Schaeffer's son, Nate Schaeffer, shared a case with the Preiss office. Lou worked with him on the case.

"I bet Nate Schaeffer would do it, why don't you ask him?" Celia suggested, though Lou had been figuring he'd have to have his shadow, Lou Green, for best man. "You know what, kid? I bet he could get us into the Prima Club, too."

Lou met her eyes, and raised his brows. Right with the Loebs and Rosenwalds.

Oh, Lindy flies over the ocean . . .

Alvin spread his sketches of modernistic chairs all over the old man's desk. "Listen, pop," he said, dead serious. "You wanted me to come into the business. All right. I tell you the only thing I'm interested in is doing something new. I'm not going to sit here and check off your lousy funeral parlor folding chairs. Only let me start out with a couple of models, a small modern line, and if it don't go we can drop it."

"Mygod, it's nothing but a lot of gaspipes!" the old man squawked, looking at the designs. "Do you think people are going to buy this junk?"

"I tell you it'll be a rage! In Europe it's already the biggest sensation—"

"Ah, don't bother my head any more with this junk. I told you we haven't got the machinery for it," his father said.

"Then get it!"

"Ho ho! Get it!" Laughing, in dismissal, the old man picked up his newspaper. "Look at that, Alvin! He started! He left them all sitting there on the field, and he jumped off by himself! Tck!" Sol Fox clicked admiringly.

"Sure he started!" Alvin argued. "That's just what I'm trying to tell you! Jump off! Let the bigger fellows wait!"

Fish gotta swim,
Birds gotta fly . . .

And on that bridal day, in the midst of the furor in the Moscowitz household, of flowers, of telegrams, of wedding gifts arriving, and the cleaner ringing the bell, there came a moment when Rose and Celia were together in the bedroom, and no one else was around.

They looked at each other, and "Oh, kid!" Rose said, her voice on the verge of tears.

It seemed to Celia then that Rose had always been her best chum, closer than anybody in the bunch, especially since Estelle had sort of dropped out of things. Celia squeezed Rose to her body, and they quivered, and blubbered a little.

"Kid, I hope you'll be very, very happy," Rose said. And Celia answered: "Oh, Rose, I hope the same for you, soon, soon."

Then they both broke out giggling.

"You know," Rose laughed, "I had a crush on Lou myself, once! Honest! You'll die!"

287

"Did he kiss you?" Celia said. "Come on, out with the worst!"

"Oh, mygod, no, he never suspected!" Rose still giggled. "You know the biggest thrill I got out of Lou? He was working at Rossman's, remember, that summer, so Aline and I went in there, and he waited on me!"

"He'll die when I tell him!"

"Don't you dare!" Rose was nearly convulsed. "Because, I remember, did he gyp me on those shoes!"

They both screamed.

"One was a half-size smaller than the other!"

They wept with laughter.

"Well, it's a good thing you got over it," Celia said, "or you'd have given me some competition."

"No danger. Who wants a beanpole?"

Celia ventured: "What's the matter with Manny Kassell?"

Rose blushed.

"After all you've been going together for over a year."

"Two years."

"Is it that long?"

"Oh, we had a sort of understanding. Kid, I don't know. I don't think we were meant for each other."

"Has he asked you?"

"Oh, he sort of takes it for granted. That's what gets me. I mean, he's kind of conceited."

"Listen, kiddo, do you think Lou is perfect? Do you think anyone is perfect? What I say is, people that think each other perfect ought to be the last ones to get married because when they get disillusioned, oh, boy! Naturally I think Lou is pretty good or I wouldn't be marrying him, but I mean, Rose, to really love a person you have to know all about them, their faults and everything."

"If that's the case," Rose said, "I certainly ought to know Manny because he certainly has plenty of faults."

"What's the matter with him?"

"Oh, you know how he is, if he tips a cab-driver he wants everybody to know it, and—"

"Oh, listen, kid, what are such little things compared to the main thing? Oh, honest, Rose, two years is a lot to throw away!"

"Well, I don't want to do anything unless I'm certain," Rose said. Who could tell? She might yet meet someone. . . .

An extra was shouted in the streets.

"Oh, I wonder if he made it!" Rose rushed to the window. . . . That Lindbergh was so tall!

A ship had seen him, flying toward Ireland.

"Do you think he'll make it?" Celia said. And to herself, she said: "If he makes it, it's a sign. It's a sign for me and Lou."

Oh, Lindy flies over the ocean . . .

Sol mounted. The Paris crowd never let you alone. Any other city, you could expect a dead hour. But here, all night! No chance to rest a blistered can.

"Hey, Chicago, you think he will make it?"

"Sure he'll make it, peanut!" Sol affirmed.

Duprès, from one of the French teams, pulled alongside and bet him a hundred francs the American flyer wouldn't land in Paris.

"Any more suckers?" Sol cried.

Verhaeven, a nice Belgian who had ridden the last New York race, pulled alongside, worried. "You really think he will make it, Chicago? Hey? Old man?"

"Bien sure, mon veeyay!" Sol popped. "He's a guy, what he starts out to do, he does!"

"You know him?"

"Sure! Me and him—" he held up two fingers.

Through the night, hour after hour, they called to Sol: "Hey! What is the news? He is still flying?" as though Sol were in personal touch with the flyer. And he answered them: "Sure! A ship just saw him! He signaled!"

Through the night he felt no fatigue. The hiss of the wheels going slowly around the concrete, so different from the sound on the wooden tracks of America, the hiss followed him around, but it couldn't get him tonight, he wasn't tired. During the long quiet circling around the track, he imagined himself riding in the cold, dark blue upper air, the hiss was the steady drone of his motors, he was coming ahead, coming ahead, in a beeline for the Eiffel!

"Come on, Lindy boy, come on, Lindy boy," Sol prayed.

I gotta love one man till I die . . .

Harry had attached the loudspeaker over the open door as a crowd was collecting.

Seen over Ireland.

"Right on his course!" Harry marveled. "Right on time! On the dot! He'll make it!"

Oh, blue skies . . .

Joe Freedman climbed down from his ladder. For the third time that afternoon, he went out for a look at the headlines. He walked to the corner of State and Ohio Streets. He could tell before he got to the newsstand. Everybody that passed the stand walked off with a different rhythm.

"Made it!"

A shivery welling up of tears, as at some utterly crazily beautiful piece of music, or at scenes of crowds cheering, in the newsreels. He took the paper back to the studio.

Entering, Joe saw his colossus as for the first time, freshly. Big, something tremendous that he had attempted; he too could hurl big achievements at the world; this would stand out, wherever it was shown. It would bring him prizes, a Guggenheim! Why, its very faults, its very awkwardness, and the clash of styles in its modeling, added to the life of the thing! Even in this unfinished state it had the main thing, Power!

Ribs, belly, backbone, joints of the backbone,
Hips, hip-sockets, hip-strength, inward and outward round, man-balls, man-
      root . . .

His fingers closed, as if to close upon her hand, as if they two were standing and looking at his work.

Now she would see.

> Fish gotta swim
> Birds gotta fly . . .!

And the wind was in their legs. "Ils sont fous, les Américains!" the Frenchies called, and Sol and Bert streaked away, unwearying, madmen, all day long, pouring the laps out of themselves, clocking them up, like clocks set to run fast, and no stopping them! Seven laps behind in the morning, four in the afternoon sprints, even, by the evening sprints, and third in points.

They were working together like sweethearts, Olson from New Jersey, Sol Meisel of Chicago. "Whadya say, Sol, shall we give 'em a rest?" "Naw, let's jam 'em again!" "Nice going, Solly!" "You're sure showing 'em, Bert!" "Swell riding, Solly!" "That's wheeling it, Bert, old boy, old boy!" Beefsteak rare, and ride the legs off the world!

Ten aldermen, and Judge Schaeffer of course, and Judge Russo, and Judge Horowitz, Judge Rorty of the Superior Court, and a couple of county commissioners. They say old man Insull, in person, will be here. They say George Jessel, appearing downtown, will stop in after the show.

> Oh, Lindy flies over the ocean!

"What's going on upstairs?" the doorman asks the starter.

"Some sort of Jewish wedding. I think it's a West Side politician!"

"Hum. I guessed it was something like that," the doorman said.

Ev Goldberg in a gorgeous creation of silver chiffon, a copy of the latest Lanvin model! Estelle Green in a dress of that daring new transparent velvet, as red as her hair, and "Say, listen," whispers Ev Goldberg, "I know dresses, and if she paid for that herself, she's making an awful lot for a steno!" That *sheigetz* with her wears a tux as though his people came over on the *Mayflower*.

The bride in close-fitting white satin. "Oh, she looks like a queen! She looks just like Queen Marie, only younger," says Thelma Ryskind.

Rube Moscowitz, and all the Moscowitz brothers, and all their wives, and all their children, and old Avrum Moscowitz with his white hair; seen all together, there is a family resemblance, a chunkiness, all solid, the kids all husky with fat legs, the men all big-chested with short necks; and in their tuxedoes they don't look fat, but powerful, muscular, strong.

And Alderman Pete Grinnell, red as a beet, slamming everybody on the back. "Where's the bride? Hah, Celie, so you gave me the gate!"

The Margolises, Lou's mother kind of dazed, and splashing tears of happiness all over everybody; and old man Margolis, shrewd and sleepy-eyed.

—What did he give?

—He's giving them the honeymoon, I heard. Two thousand.

—What did Rube give?

—Ten thousand dollars worth of Insull stocks!

—And they're worth twelve grand already! You know Rube Moscowitz is on Insull's secret list—only a hundred names! Oh, it's got the Ryersons and the McCormicks and Galli-Curci, and when he's going to put out a new stock he sells them some before the public gets it and the price goes up!

Celia sits among her bridesmaids. Aline, Rose, Sylvia, and her cousins, Rosalind, Ruth, and May. Suddenly it seems to her that she wants to stay only with the kids in the bunch, she wants her wedding to be only for them. "Stick to me, girls! Oh, Rose! Oh, Aline!"

> . . . Nothing but bluebirds
> Singing a song!

"Is it a political rally or a wedding?" cracks Mort Abramson, shining handsome over the wing collar.

"Hey, Mort," says Runt, "didja see the private testimony in Charlie Chaplin's divorce? It's better'n Peaches Browning!"

"Yeah? Wouldn't she play woof woof?"

> Oh, it ain't gonna rain no more, no more . . .

"Stagging it?" Harry Perlin said to Runt. "So'm I."

"Twenty-five thousand berries," Runt said. "For one night's work."

"Say, he earned it!" Harry said. "That was a perfect job!"

> It ain't gonna rain no more!

"Well, what are they waiting for? The bride is ready."

"Is the rabbi here yet?"

He's here. Dr. Rosenston, of the exclusive South Side Temple.

"Wait!" says Rube Moscowitz. An usher darts off on a mysterious errand.

Sylvia Abramson was dancing with Mitch when Joe came in. As they danced by, Syl gave him a smile.

"Hya, stranger," Rudy said, coming up to him. "How's your lungs and liver?"

Drink, drink, drink to the days of our youth—

"How have you been, Joe?"

"All right." He kept staring at her, standing so naturally next to Mitch, smiling the way she had always smiled, when out with him.

"Want to dance?"

"I've got the next one," she said, with ordinary regret. The music began, and Joe walked away. As he turned, he caught the fragrance of her, clearly, overwhelmingly, the scent that had always seemed so mysteriously personal to him.

> Black bottom,
> It's sure got 'em . . .

—Oh, there they are!

—Is that her? Well, she is sort of pretty, for a blonde.

—It doesn't look natural to me.

—Why shouldn't it be natural, for a *shikseh*?

—I heard Alvin picked her up on a drunken spree.

—Well, anyhow he's settled down and working in his father's factory.

"Hello, Alvin! How's the married life?"

"Oh, miserable! Miserable!" Alvin says, and Eunice echoes: "Miserable."

—What are they waiting for?

—Everybody is ready! They shouldn't keep the bride waiting.

The usher runs up to Rube Moscowitz. Rube beams, and strides toward the entrance. A distinguished-looking little man, in full dress, is just arriving. Rube escorts him into the ballroom. A thrilled hush lies upon the room.

Samuel Insull, in person!

Cymbals.

Now the wedding can go on!

And then the low, soulful, Jewish sound of the solo violin.

> Here comes the bride,
> All dressed in white . . .

And Celia Moscowitz walked down the long white carpet to where her bridegroom and her people waited.

"It's very impressive," Thelma Ryskind said.

The bride halted beside the groom. The violin hushed.

The voice of Moishe Pearlman, the sensational young cantor, rose sweet and touching to every heart, singing "*Eli, Eli.*"

"It's like Al Jolson in *The Jazz Singer!*" voices whispered all over the hall. "It's beautiful."

Joe Freedman was standing far back in the crowd, and looking for Sylvia. Just then he saw her. She was pressed close to Mitch.

The bride and groom mounted a few steps to the low orchestra platform. Rabbi Dr. Joseph Rosenston, of the exclusive South Side Temple, wearing a full dress suit, with tails, read the ceremony, making the words sound like a poem. The loudspeakers carried his voice clearly over the entire hall.

When he had finished, there came a surprise. Rabbi Nathan Solowitz, of the great Russian Jewish Orthodox Synagogue on Douglas Boulevard, stepped under the canopy. His beard spread over his entire shirtfront. In a heavy singsong, he chanted the Hebrew ceremony.

And thus, under the blessings of the two most important rabbis of Chicago, Lou Margolis and Celia Moscowitz were wed.

"The wedding of the pawnbroker's son to the junkman's daughter," Alvin the Duke remarked cynically to his *goyish* wife. Thelma Ryskind, chancing to hear, had to put her hand to her mouth to keep from exploding.

All kinds of liquor appeared, pocket flasks, a big bowl of spiked punch; and in the men's room a row of cheerful Negroes, behind a long table, were shaking up drinks and handing out whatever was called for.

Rudy Stone took two drinks and lost his dignity and tried to do the black bottom!

Runt Plotkin met up with a girl, he didn't know who she was, and she was a head taller than him, but could she shake a mean leg! "What's your number, baby, when'm I gonna see you again?"

A judge sang in the washroom.

Sophie Tucker showed up, and sang: "I'm a red-hot mama and my papa's doing me wrong!"

Estelle Green got high, and she and her *sheigetz* did a step that cleared the floor, everybody watching and clapping them on.

Lou Green drank gin, then whisky, and puked. He sat for a long time by himself on a toilet until finally Mort and Runt found him. When they pulled up his head, he said, dizzily: "He was my best friend."

> Ah, sweet mystery of life,
> At last I've found you!

Joe Freedman walked home. He turned on a full blaze of light in his studio, and stared at his work; suddenly it seemed to him hopeless, mawkish, out of proportion, the head too small, the muscles of the legs sticking out like coiled snakes; the whole feeling of frustration welled up in him, enraged him, and he seized a stool and started to swing at the clay colossus, fish gotta swim, birds gotta fly, I gotta love you till I die, the silly archaic face smiling at him, oh, what a dope he was! His arm fell. He sat there trying to laugh at himself.

Nothing but blue birds all day long.

"Les Américains! Les Américains!" The crowd screamed, and Chesty rode with fire on his tail. The last hour of sprints was a wild non-stop, and he and Ollie were taking everything, Meisel, first, Olson, first, Meisel, first, Olson, first; they took the sprints with laughing regularity, they led in points, they led the field by a lap, the race was in the bag, and Sol felt young, fine, fresh, his muscles easy and tough as rubber. "Vive Lindbergh!" the crowd yelled. "Vive les Américains!"

He cut down from the bank and swept into the lead again for the last sprint, cutting by the Flying Dutchman so close he could feel the breath of him, and he was away, winning, winning the race, his first time tops in a six-day, four times third, once second, but this time tops, and in Paris, only one place he would like it better, tops in the old home town of Chicago, like that first time he raced, with the old bunch yelling from the grandstand, and redhead Estelle behind his bunk.

The gun popped, crazy French little pistol.

The band was crazily playing maybe the only American song they knew, they were still playing it over here: "Yes, we have no bananas! We have no bananas today!"

"They must think that's the 'Star-Spangled Banner'!" Ollie laughed to him, as they circled arms around shoulders, as the judges hung the wreaths around their necks, and Sol Meisel, the Chicago Kid, pedaled slowly, victorious, around the track, bobbing his head and grinning happily to the screaming cheering world.

BOOK THREE

Anything but Love

POLITICAL ECONOMY

A MAN gets on an El train to go to an unfamiliar part of the city. He isn't sure he is on the right line, but it seems to be going in the right direction. He is afraid that any moment the train may turn and carry him out of his way. But then he can always hop off at the next stop, and go back to the turning point.

Suddenly he gets the idea he is on the wrong train altogether, for he should have come to the place already. He looks out anxiously for signs, street names. "It's far enough, it must be about here!" he thinks, and tries to get out. "Here! Here! This is my station! Off! Off!" but the car is jammed, he bombs himself against rocklike, indifferent men who stand braced in the middle of the aisle reading the sports pages; he is squeezed between the large solid behinds of corseted women, like pulp between rollers; corners of bundles that people are carrying nick against his face; young women stare at him indignantly while he sputters: "Off! Off!"

The train starts away from the station. Then it is an express, and there is no other stop for miles.

"Sam, I certainly don't understand how you can even consider letting a cheap crook like that come into your office!" Lil stated flatly. "I certainly wouldn't have a thing to do with him!" She leaned over to cut little Jacob's meat into small squares, her bent head underlining her faint double chin, so that her full throat suggested a pouring of cream, overlapping itself.

"Who's talking about taking him into the office!" Sam said. "He wouldn't be coming in as one of us. It's just temporary. He needs a place to meet a few people, and a telephone number, till he gets set again. He wouldn't be there more than a month."

"Sure! Before you knew it he'd be settled there with his name on the door and those gangsters he deals with would scare away all your clients."

Sam chuckled. "Baloney. Runt just likes to put on an act."

"Yah? Then what kind of business does he handle?"

"I don't think he has much business," Sam said sympathetically. "He never had any decent connections. He used to hang around the South Clark Street station and the bondsmen would put him onto a case once in a while. Say, if he gets a hundred-dollar damage suit against the gas company it's a big case."

"Well! Marvelous contacts you'd be making through the people that come to see Runt Plotkin! Don't you realize, Sam, that everyone that walked in there would be putting you in the same class with him? Do you want people to think you're a shyster!"

Sam gave her an appeasing smile, and lapsed into silence. He would never have mentioned the matter, except that she might have walked into the office some time and found Runt settled there, and raised a stink.

The maid brought in a glass of milk and set it before Jacob; immediately the kid began rattling a toy bank which he had brought to the table.

"Now I'll tell you what I'll do, Skeezix[1]," Sam said sportingly, as he drew a nickel out of his pocket and held it up; "I'll give you the nickel if you can guess which hand it's in. But you have to drink the milk first."

The child looked at him with bright-eyed suspicion, and then broke into an excited laugh, shaking his head vigorously all the while.

"Na, na, gimme."

"Come on, be a sport," Sam persisted, putting his hands behind his back. "You can guess first, or after."

"He'll never do it," Lil said. "He knows he's supposed to get his nickel for drinking the milk."

Over the boy's head, Sam gave her a don't-interfere scowl. But it was too late.

"It's mine! You owe it to me!" Jacob cried, leaning way over and trying to snatch the coin from his father, and still laughing, nervously.

By finally offering two nickels, Sam induced his son to play the game.

The kid solemnly studied Sam's fists. Then he pointed midway between the two hands, and said: "This one."

"The little devil!" Lil laughed.

"Oh, no, you don't! Come on, choose. Which one?" Sam persisted.

The kid chose. Sam opened the palm. It was empty.

"Lemme see the other one! Lemme see!"

Sam opened the other palm and showed the coins.

The kid glowered.

"Come on, drink it up, you're not going to be a bad loser, are you?"

Lil sighed a now-look-what-you've-done sigh.

"Jacob! You know what they do to bad losers? They take 'em for a ride!"

"Drink it," Lil conciliated, "maybe daddy will give you your nickel anyway."

Looking slantwise at his father, Jacob drank half the milk.

Sam leaned back, relieved. He had achieved something. He reached over, ruffled the kid's hair, and dropped one coin, then the other, into the bank.

Lil resumed: "All Runt is looking for is a month's free rent. He probably never paid where he was. That's why they're kicking him out!"

"Oh, he offered to pay his share of the rent."

"Yah, and what about the office girl and the phone?"

"His share of the expenses, I mean."

---

[1] Skeezix was the name of a baby in the popular *Gasoline Alley* comic strip.

"Sure! And he's just moving in for a month! You let him in there and you'll be stuck with him! Sam, don't be crazy!"

"I just said he'd asked," Sam retreated. "The other fellows have something to say about it too."

Lil's eyes followed his fork to his mouth. Then, quickly, she tasted from her own dish. She looked off anxiously into space, concentrating all of her attention on the taste. "You like it spicier, don't you, dear?"

Now he noticed the roast tasted kind of wooden.

"Myrtle!" Lil called. The girl shuffled in. "Myrtle, try to remember, put a little garlic in the meat. That's the way Mr. Eisen likes it."

Myrtle glumly retreated.

"You have to watch her all the time!" Lil sighed. "She can't remember from one day to the next. Want some ketchup?"

Sam grinned, to himself. Only lately she had ruled the ketchup bottle off the table.

"Myrtle, you can bring some ketchup in that little sauce-boat," Lil ordered.

When the child reached for the ketchup, Lil shook her head. Jacob drew back his hand. "I don't want him to get the habit of drowning everything in ketchup," Lil remarked.

Sam poured a red pond of the stuff onto his plate. Jackie sneaked a spoonful from his father's plate, and licked it. Lil caught him.

"Sam!" she cried.

"Oh, what does it hurt?"

"You don't have to be with him all day! How do you think I am going to get any obedience out of him when you teach him to disregard my authority!"

The kid dropped his spoon, spattering ketchup everywhere.

"T! I knew it! Myrtle! Get a towel and a damp cloth!" Lil shrieked, as Myrtle ran in clumsily with the coffee-pot.

"I'll get it." Sam rose. Lil gave him the let-her-do-it look, but he went to the kitchen anyway and got the spots off his pants.

There was the maid's meal laid out bleakly on the edge of the kitchen table. "Why can't she eat with us?" he had argued many times. He never could get used to having a servant hand him things in the house. Being waited on in a restaurant was different.

As he came back, Myrtle was leading the child to the bathroom.

"He's getting terrible!" Lil complained. "Today he even asked the elevator man for a nickel. I was never so mortified in my life."

"Did he give it to him?"

"I made him give it back. Everybody would think our kid had to beg! And the minute I let him out of my sight, he's got some dirty alley gang he plays with."

"Living cooped up like this isn't so good for the kid," Sam said. "He hasn't got anywhere to play!"

"I take him to play school, don't I!"

No use resuming that old argument. Lil felt they simply had to live in an apartment hotel. She settled back to her meal. "And what do the other fellows think about it?"

Sam oozed hopelessly down in his chair. "They sort of left it up to me. After all, I'm the one that knows Plotsy."

"Sure! And you're the one whose office he'll be camping in! You'd certainly let people walk all over you, Sam, if somebody didn't stop you. What's he in such a rush for anyway? I bet he pulled something funny wherever he was!"

"He says Novak pulled something on him, and it's a matter of principle."

Lil exploded. "Runt Plotkin, a matter of principle!"

But she really didn't know the poor sucker, Sam wanted to say. That was the funny thing about Runt: in his queer, subterranean way, he had principles. "What's the difference, anyway, the guy is in a jam and—"

"I notice he doesn't bother Lou Margolis or any of those other boys he went to school with. Oh, no. You're the one."

"All right, all right."

"Of all the chances you have to get in with decent people, you have to pick on such chumps. Your Milt Gold! He's practically nothing but an ambulance chaser."

"What's the difference!" Sam snapped. "They're not my partners, are they! What's the difference who I share the suite with! It's each one for himself!"

He got up.

"Wait, your dessert."

He looked at his wrist-watch. "I have to see Gus Lund before the meeting."

She sagged.

"You know it gets like this toward the end of a campaign," he said, conciliatory, going for his coat.

"I told Ev we'd be over tonight," she said in a strained voice.

"You knew I had to be there tonight, I've got to speak." He tried to keep from being exasperated.

"Well, anyway you can wait a minute and eat your dessert," she wailed, her voice high-pitched, as she scuttled into the kitchenette and came out with a plate of applecake. He knew she had made this herself; it was his favorite dessert. The cake gleamed rich, golden. He was being unfair to her.

"Ev told me Phil saw you in court the other day," Lil hinted. "He said you have an excellent courtroom manner. I think Phil intends to quit the firm and open offices for himself, and is looking for a partner."

"Yuh." He knew all about that idea. Not for him. Just as she slid a second helping onto his plate, the buzzer sounded.

It was Paul Laparetti, a skinny, goggling fellow who was helping Sam in the precinct. He was supposed to meet Sam at the ward headquarters, but whenever he wanted money he found some cataclysmic excuse for coming to the apartment. He wasn't so dumb, Sam realized. It was hard for a man trapped in the munificence of a Sherwin Arms home to make out that he couldn't spare five bucks. But Paul had four brothers and three sisters of voting age, several with their mates and in-laws, and besides he was a persistent bell-pusher. Sam dug into his pocket, and Paul departed.

"How much did you give him?" Lil said.

"Oh, just a few dollars. A sister that's living with them just had a kid, and her husband is out of a job."

"Of all—"

"Well, it's another vote, in a couple of years," he tried to kid her out of it.

"Why you should have to buy their damn votes and pay for the precinct work in addition to giving them all your time and energy is something I can't understand! How much have you handed out of your own pocket in this election? I bet it's two hundred dollars."

"Oh, not that much."

"It's over a hundred and fifty, I know, and—"

"Well, Lil, I've got to deliver the precinct, and I can't go around punching doorbells myself."

"And another thing"—she pressed her advantage—"if you're going to keep on in that dirty politics, I don't see why you can't get something out of it. My father is paying all those taxes and you know all you have to do is talk to somebody—"

"Listen, Lil," Sam said, "I'm not going to ask them for favors. Somebody is liable to investigate those crooked tax evaluations and then there'll be trouble."

"Right away, you're an angel! If the rest of them can get away with it, you can get away with it. My father did enough for you so you can do him a little favor, does it cost you anything!"

"I haven't asked those fellows for any favors and I'm not going to."

"Well, what are you in politics for, for the love of it? Next thing you know you'll be blown up someplace with those bombs they're throwing around! Why don't you at least get one of those lawyers' jobs that are being handed out to every dumb boob in the Thompson gang? We could use fifty dollars a day, too!"

"Listen, Lil, is there anything special you need?" Sam said icily.

"Huh?"

"I mean, you're not starving or going naked are you?"

"Sam, you can't talk to me like that! I'm only thinking of your own good! I want to see you get someplace!" She controlled her rage. That would be just what he wanted, for her to go off screaming, leaving him with the argument won. "Sam, will you please explain one thing to me?" She was cool, cool. "If you won't even take favors, what are you wasting your time for? I sit home, by myself, every night. I stood for it for a whole year, but I see it doesn't lead to anything. I'm not trying to tell you how to run your affairs, Sam . . ."

While she talked, he put on his overcoat. But as she went on, coming and standing right near him, there was something so liquid, so utterly womanish in her talking to him that it cut through all his anger. It was like very early in their marriage, when the simple scent of her, the mere physical nearness, touched him profoundly.

"I know, I know, kid," he said. "But—"

"Everything I want is for you. Just to help you *be* something. But you're so good-natured, Sam. You let people use you!"

"It's all right, kid. I know what I'm after," he said. "You know I was never interested in these cheap grafts and things a fellow can get out of politics. You know what I want. It's something bigger. And maybe in another year . . ."

"What do you mean in another year? Are they going to make you something?"

"Oh, it's nothing definite, you know how these things go, kid, right now, I'm pretty near the top among the young lawyers in the organization, and I suppose in a couple of years I could even get on the ticket, if I wanted . . ."

But why hadn't he told her? That he might be a judge? The youngest judge in the city, she'd bet!

"No, no, I'm not even sure I want anything like that, but . . ." It was too difficult to tell her exactly what he wanted. Even in the naming of the possibilities, his desire faded; even as he told her he knew where he was going, his doubts became more insistent.

But now she seemed suddenly docile, content with this much confidence. It was strange how they got to these points of opposition; as she said, they both wanted the same thing: his success; yet they were like two factions of the same party: Deneen against Thompson, both Republicans, fighting each other viciously with everything from mud to bombs, because each had his own ambitions for, and with, the Republican Party.

"I'll get through as early as I can," he said, putting his arm around her, "and maybe we'll still have time to go out."

It was a lousy night. A wind cold-slapped his face the instant he pushed out of the door. The sidewalk had icy streaks. He didn't feel like talking. It was a night to spend before a fireplace, with people who were real friends.

Friends, yah, who? Well, anything, even something dopy like playing bridge, to take his mind off this lousy game of politics. The "reformers" were out after Big Bill's candidates with every gun in the arsenal. The primary was going to be tough.

Turning on Broadway, Sam stopped in a little store that sold magazines and cigars.

"Well, whatya know?" The proprietor, an elderly man wearing a brown sweater, came from behind the counter.

"Not a thing. How's it going?" Sam bought a couple of packages of cigarettes.

"All right, I guess. Say, Sam, you ain't throwing them bombs at Judge Swanson, are you?" the old man kidded, his face remaining woodenly serious.

"Well, you got me," Sam said. "I guess I better confess."

"I bet he had those bombs planted himself," remarked a lounger, showing he was a loyal Thompsonite who knew how he was supposed to interpret the mysterious assault. "It's just a trick to attract sympathy."

"I notice they didn't hurt anybody," the proprietor said.

"Well, he's got only one way to win the election," Sam said. "He's got all the churches praying for him on Sunday. Maybe that'll help him."

"In that case you better get some of your rabbis to pray for Thompson's gang," the proprietor returned the jest. "You know what Napoleon said: 'God is on the side with the heaviest artillery.' "

"Well, it won't be long now."

"Say, Sammy, I want to talk to you." Pop drew him aside and reminded him that a nephew of his, recently come from Indianapolis, needed work.

"Maybe after the election," Sam said. "You know, if anything comes to this precinct, you'll get it. I'm not holding anything for myself."

He pushed out into the wind again. The thing was, it was such a filthy campaign. Oh, he was not the kid that he had been a year ago when he had got up at a rally and made a speech about why do we have to sling mud, why can't we conduct this campaign like gentlemen? and Alderman Kinney had dropped an arm on his shoulder and mouthed: "Sure, you're right, kid, that's what I believe myself, but you know how it is . . ." And it wasn't even the bombs that were exploding under the front porches of the opposition candidates. It was the whole cumulative atmosphere of power and contempt, a sort of galloping consumption that had been screaming through the organization until now it was as though the rats that Big Bill used to exhibit in the little cage had grown to the size of elephants and were clawing and biting all through the city streets.

And what was it all leading him to? Way back, he had had a sort of program. To work with the strong party, even though he had to do a lot of things he didn't believe in, so that he might learn the tricks, and get a certain amount of starting power. But what could he ever do that counted, within the rotten structure of this life?

The windows of the store were littered with placards bearing the photographs and names of candidates. A large canvas sign, its lettering streaked and blurred by rain, named this Ward Headquarters. AMERICA FIRST. And then the list of candidates, Sam wryly noticed, from Giuseppe Paolino to Vladimir Vlacek.

Inside, the yellow walls of the vacant store had been strung with signs: *Big Bill the Builder; Boost Chicago; He Kicked King George Out of the Chicago Schools; AMERICA FIRST.* A large American flag covered the rear wall. Sam went through to the backroom, hearing Gus Lund making his usual speech.

He was always struck afresh with the amazing typicality of the ward committeeman's voice and appearance. Even from outside, anyone hearing the strident twang would know a ward politician was talking. Gus was small, wiry, with a creased leathery face, a wart on his long nose, and with wrinkled pouches under animal-cautious eyes.

"And you fellows know, I'm not the one that gets the votes, you're the ones, and you're entitled to the benefits. I'm going downtown and I'm gonna tell them, okay, my boys delivered for you, now you deliver to the boys. Now fellows"—lowering his voice—"no use kidding ourselves. We got a fight on our hands. And when I say fight I mean fight with everything in the bag. But they ain't got a thing we haven't got and we've got something they ain't got. We've got the jobs. You've got men in jobs and they want to keep those jobs and they're going to deliver the votes if they have to knock 'em down and drag 'em in . . ."

On the fringe, the boys greeted him: "Hi, Sam"; "Lo, Sambo"; "Sam, you ain't going around putting bombs under front porches, are you?" "Say, I hear Swanson is trying to get pineapple insurance at the next church he's gonna speak at." "Haw haw haw, even Lloyd's won't insure a Deneen man in Chicago!"

Gus Lund had completed his exhortation, and was going off in corners with guys for private little conferences; presently he dropped a hand on Sam's shoulder. "How's it going?"

"Okay."

"Say, Sambo, I may have a little business for you if things go right." He pulled his features downward, a grimace equivalent to a wink.

"Anything good?" Sam said, with the proper inflection.

"Well, I guess a smart lawyer could make something good out of a few receivership cases, huh?"

"Any day," Sam said.

"Know that building on the corner, Broadway and Winona?"

"That new building with the stores?"

"Yah, they had a $225,000 bond issue, it's quite a building, only they never got it rented." Gus made the face again. "If we elect a few judges, Sambo, I might get hold of a few receiverships. And you're entitled to as much of the legal end as any of the boys."

Sam made a smile to express appreciation. Did Gus suspect he was wavering?

He got on first and was through by nine o'clock. He gave them the comical blue-law speech.—Why, Swanson would make people take their drinking water to court to be tested for alcoholic content before they could swallow a drop. Why, by the time they got through paying taxes for all those reforms, Chicago would be the home of the fee and the land of behave, he cracked, and got a laugh from the sparse crowd as he stepped off the platform.

"Attaboy, Sambo." Some Hal Noonan slapped him familiarly on the shoulder, and Gus Lund gave him the face-twitch as he passed, as if to say: "Check." He felt touchy. The habitual over-friendliness of a political crowd, expressed in kiddish pokes and shoves and arms on your shoulder, irritated him more than ever. Each face was a mask over a pair of chopping fangs. His speech had been pretty lousy. He needed more of an audience. Or maybe he was just fed up.

As he got home, they were calling an extra. Diamond Joe Esposito, lord of the bloody nineteenth ward, had been murdered. Ambushed in front of his home. Maybe it was alky war, maybe blackhand. But Diamond Joe was an anti-Thompson man.

Lil was wearing her new ensemble. The Nile-green spring coat, with felt helmet to match, tan gloves, tan purse.

"It's freezing out," Sam said.

But she simply had to wear her new outfit to Ev's.

The Rex Shore was just north of the Edgewater Beach. "They must pay at least a hundred and fifty for two rooms here," Lil murmured every time she and Sam stepped into the Spanish patio foyer. "He certainly doesn't make that much with Keeney, Patterson, and Shore."

"Well, he has some practice of his own, too."

"We are expected," she said to the elevator man, and his supercilious glare turned into a toothpaste smile.

Ev opened the door. She was wearing one of those new sensational evening dresses that looked like a skirt but could be seen to be trousers when she walked.

"Oh, how stunning!" Lil cried before she was through the door.

"I simply couldn't resist dressing up," Ev said. "It's a Patou model and you know moiré is all the rage." She turned around, letting them see the slick fit over her handsome flanks.

"Pants!" Lil declared. "Isn't that cute!"

A scotty pup rushed at them and danced around Sam's legs, slavering over his trousers.

"Thirty-two fifty, wholesale," Ev went on. "And I saw the identical thing at Saks's, marked eighty-five dollars! . . . Oh, Lil, what a beautiful ensemble! It's new, isn't it?"

"I got it at the Avenue Shop," Lil mentioned, to let Ev understand that after all she didn't have to go on buying her things at such places as Goldberg's Evelyn Shoppes. "You know, the Avenue is really not much more expensive than Field's."

Sam tried to get the pup away without kicking him.

"How much," Ev generously estimated Lil's coat, "around a hundred?"

"A little more," Lil said modestly.

"Why didn't you let me get it for you wholesale?" Evelyn sweetly reproved her. "You could have got it for half."

The scotty jumped and playfully snapped at Sam's hand.

"Down, Rocky, down!" Ev cried. "You know, Phil named him John D. Rockefeller, isn't that appropriate!"

"It's awful cute," Lil said.

The husband rose as they entered, and Sam knew Lil was thinking that he would not have arisen.

Lil's brows went up, for, sitting with Thelma Ryskind, who was dressed to kill, was Manny Kassell, the fellow who had always gone with Rose Heller.

Thelma was raving about the wonderful tone of the new combination radio-victrola, in an Italian-style hand-carved cabinet, which the Wares had just acquired.

"You know I've always been against canned music," Thelma declared. "I positively couldn't stand it! But when they make them with a tone like this, I have to give up the fight. I'd fall for one myself."

"Two twenty-three," Ev said. "We got it from the warehouse. They're three hundred everywhere."

> "Did you mean it when you said I love you,
> Did you mean it when you said I care . . .?"

"Isn't that Paul Whiteman's band?" Thelma said. "They're the only ones I can listen to, playing jazz. They're as good as a symphony orchestra."

"Wait, you must hear how the victrola works," Ev said, turning off the radio. Selecting a record, she said mischievously: "This is for the married folks only."

Manny leered, and licked his chops. A husky voice moaned:

> "When you get good lovin', don't ever spread the news,
> When you get good lovin', don't spread the news,
> The other gals will steal him
> And leave you with the empty bed blues."

Ev listened, with the air that sex was a delicious naughtiness.

"It's orthophonic," Thelma said with respectful finality, as the wailing croon ended.

Rocky had parked himself in front of the instrument, just like the dog in the old trade-mark of *His Master's Voice*.

"Did you ever see anything so cute?" Ev demanded.

He became the sole subject of conversation. "Scotties are the most intelligent dogs, you know . . ." "Sometimes I think they are just as smart as people . . ."

"Smarter than some people I know, heh heh!" Manny Kassell cracked.

Sam couldn't understand why it was, but every time this bunch got together they sat around watching and talking about the dog. As usual, Ev made Phil demonstrate the dog's specialty, which consisted in "conversing" with his master. "Aarf arf?" the lawyer would inquire, and the dog would answer expressively: "Owarf!"

"Just like Judge Rorty!" Phil appealed to Sam. "Isn't he?" Showing he practiced only in the Superior Court.

But now the dog seemed exhausted of tricks, and the six of them sat in silence, staring at the scotty, as if expecting him to bring up a new subject of conversation.

Ev passed some chocolates around, but Lil refused, "I'm dieting," and accepted an English cigarette from Phil.

"Reach for a Lucky instead of a sweet!" Manny Kassell quoted. At the same moment, he and the host sprang their lighters at Lil. "Ha! It works!" Manny cried with comical astonishment. But she was using Phil's, so he said: "Coises! Beaten to the draw."

Just as the dullness was getting noticeable, the host dragged out a bridge table. Seeing there were too many for the game, Manny pleaded: "Let me kibitz. I'm the world's champion kibitzer."

"Sam doesn't play," Lil confessed. "He simply refuses to learn."

"Don't you?" Phil inquired, with his Harvard-Oxford inflection. "Of coss auction is a woman's game; the real game is contract. We used to tear off a session of contract occasionally in the law library at Haavad. Oh, you don't have to be afraid of me, I'm really not much good at cards . . ."

"Yeah, what are you good at?" Manny cracked.

"Wouldn't you like to know?" Ev smirked, her ring glistening as she glided her hand down her husband's side.

Sam fingered the new books on the table.

"How is this?" he asked, picking up *The Bridge of San Luis Rey*.

"Oh, it's very deep," Ev said. "It's about five different people who get killed when the bridge falls down, and the idea is, the reason each one had to die just then."

"That's cute," was Lil's opinion.

"Only there isn't any reason to it," Phil said, shuffling.

"That's just the point," Ev remarked. "Life is like that. We just go along and all of a sudden we fall off a bridge, so why not have a good time while you're alive, that's my idea."

"Yah, don't fall off your bridges till you come to them!" said Manny.

"I should like to do an article on the situation here for the *Haavad Law Review*" Phil remarked to Sam. "This city probably offers the classic example of graft and corruption in all its glory."

"Oh, the Thompson gang isn't any worse than any other, they're just more efficient," Sam said.

"Say, they're all gangsters, all those politicians," Ev said.

"Did you see they killed that Diamond Joe Esposito, that dago politician?" Thelma remarked.

"I bet it'll be a wonderful funeral; the last gang funeral, I had to wait an hour before I could get through the traffic," Lil said.

"Oh, I was real sorry they bumped him off," said Ev. "He was so cute. He was real fat and he wore a diamond horse-shoe stickpin, remember, honey, we had spaghetti in his restaurant once, on Halsted Street. He had marvelous spaghetti."

"Say, all those West Side politicians are like that; do you think Rube Moscowitz is any better? It wouldn't surprise me if he got taken for a ride some day, in spite of all the dog they put on," Thelma put in.

"Lil, I don't see how you can let Sam go in for politics."

"Oh, you don't have to be crooked to be in politics." Lil flushed. "And if a fellow has the ability he can get to be something. If you want to get to be a judge," she hinted, "you have to play politics, on one side or the other." They all stared at Sam. He felt sore.

"Your bid," Phil reminded Manny.

"I do not choose to run." Manny passed.

"What have they got against Thompson? What are they throwing bombs about anyway?" Ev asked.

"Oh, it's something about a ten cent El fare," Lil explained.

"I don't see what all the fuss is about raising the El fare," Ev said. "Most everybody has a car nowadays."

"Well, no, dear, to the people who have to use the El, those few cents matter," Phil conceded. "And it mounts up to millions . . . Sam, you ought to appreciate the company's strategy." And he explained how the city's own corporation counsel, who was supposed to prove for the taxpayers that Insull was not justified in raising the El fares, was himself a former member of a law firm that handled Insull's affairs. "That's playing the game, isn't it, Sam?" he grimaced.

"It's certainly a cute trick!" Ev exclaimed.

> You've got the cutest little baby face,
> No one else can take your place,

Baby face . . .

"You know, that's what I'm more interested in, the theoretical side of the law," Phil said, edging confidentially toward Sam. "Of coss I don't get much time for the sort of thing I want to do; and I'm afraid I'm not rilly cut out to be a courtroom lawyer."

Sam noticed that Lil was listening, watching the approach.

"Naturally, Keeney, Patterson is a big firm and they're doing big things, but you know how it is, I've been thinking perhaps I ought to set up for myself, in combination with someone who could take care of the general practice, while I specialize on corporate law . . ."

"Uh huh," Sam said. "You can't get anywhere in someone else's office."

"Of coss it's difficult to find someone really suited to one's temperament. I tell Ev, it's almost as difficult as finding a wife . . ."

Suddenly the fellow appeared to Sam pitiable, bare, and small; the whole nature of this bluff of the fancy apartment was apparent; why, this Warshavsky kid was off by himself in a corner, didn't even know how to scare up a law partner but had to have his wife fix it up for him; he probably got thirty a week as a junior in that law firm, and picked up twenty, thirty more on the Evelyn Shoppe cases. . . .

"I've got an idea!" Lil cried, as if just having heard the end of their conversation. "I bet you two would make a wonderful team. Wouldn't they, Ev?" As if this was all that they needed to perfect a deep friendship.

"Phil and Sam?" Ev said. "That is an idea."

Phil puffed, sort of smiling at Sam.

"I—uh—well, we can talk about it some time," Sam said, acting embarrassed.

Waiting, Sam heard the girls in the bedroom:

"Well, she wasn't married to him, was she!" Thelma cried.

"Three years, wasn't it?" Ev said. "I thought they were engaged."

"No, they never were formally engaged. I'm certainly not trying to take him away from her, but if a fella calls a girl up . . . And anyway I introduced him to her in the first place!" Thelma pointed out. "To tell you the truth, I don't think she appreciated him. Manny is awfully clever, don't you think so?"

"He's a scream," Lil concurred. "He's real cute."

"She was always running him down, and a fella can't stand that, especially if he's sensitive, like Manny. A girl ought to show her appreciation for a fella."

"Well, she should have hung onto him if she wanted him!" Lil proclaimed. "It's every girl for herself!"

They emerged; Lil's lip rouge was on crooked.

"Why, he practically asked you to team up with him!" she exclaimed, aghast at his attitude.

"All right, so what if he did?"

"I don't understand you, Sam! Here I break my neck to get you a chance like that and all the thanks I get—"

"All right, all right, what do you think I'd be getting out of it? Corporation law. I bet all the corporation law he practices is the shoplifter cases he gets from her old man!"

"Well, you don't have to be so critical, there was a time when you were glad enough to accept help from my father–"

He jammed on the brake, just in time to avoid passing through a stop light, and the car skidded slightly.

"You don't have to kill me while you're at it!"

Sam controlled himself.

She resumed: "Phil has got wonderful connections."

He could see life stretching out before him: a cute hotel apartment, and bridge with the Wares twice a week.

"Well, I suppose you'd rather hook up with a cheap shyster like Runt Plotkin . . ."

"I'd rather be like him than like those fourflushing—"

The car skidded slightly on a turn, and she grabbed for the wheel. "Listen, Lil," exasperatedly, "at least let me drive if I'm driving! Do you have to run my business and drive for me too?"

"If you're so dumb!" she shrieked.

"Leave me alone! Leave me alone, will you!" Both trembled with rage.

Lil kept her silence in the elevator, tight, hard. The night elevator man, a kindly, used-up old fellow, gave them a slow, wondering look.

"I see they electrocuted that Ruth Snyder[2] after all," he observed to Sam. "Wasn't that an awful picture of her in the electric chair? They oughtn't to print such things. They oughtn't to have women electrocuted either. I don't think so."

"Well, she was just as guilty as the man, wasn't she?" Sam said as the elevator stopped at their floor.

"Well, it don't seem right, to do it to a woman," the old soul said. "Good night."

Lil kept her silence as they undressed and went to their separate beds. Then just as she was about to get into bed, she flopped, her knees on the floor, her head buried in the quilt, sobbing broken-heartedly.

Sam started toward her, but checked himself. He felt utterly cold-blooded.

---

[2] Ruth Snyder was executed on January 12, 1928 for killing her husband.

The Streets of Chicago

Sol Meisel was riding in Toronto when he read in the paper that a Speedy Cleaning Company truck had been burned in the street, in Chicago's latest gang war. Racketeers were invading the cleaning industry, it said.

"Lemme see that truck! That's all! I wanna see it!" Sol rushed through the plant, almost too sore to notice all the girls turning from their ironing boards to look after his broad-muscled back. His mother clumped behind him, her hair flying. Ben hung back.

"Well, mushmouth, are you coming?" Sol yelled.

There was an almost inaudible titter, look at the boss catching hell, as Ben obeyed.

Sol yanked at the garage door. "Wait, wait, Solly. We got to keep everything locked, now!" Mrs. Meisel explained. Ben's hand actually trembled, but he managed to unlock the door.

The first thing Sol thought of in spite of his boiling excitement, was: "Good place to take one of those girls for a hump!" Then he noticed three trucks standing idle, and he was mad as hell.

"What's the matter with these! Why ain't they out on the job! Nobody burned them, did they!"

"Wait, wait, Solly, you just got home, you don't understand what's the trouble yet—"

"There ain't enough work to send them out," Ben said flatly.

Sol turned on him, just as little Epstein came pussyfooting into the garage.

"We got a late spring, Solly," he murmured. "The slack season is still on by everybody."

"You double-crossing little fart!" Sol wanted to spit at Epstein. But even from way long ago, when he used to chase to Epstein's plant to try and find undelivered pieces of garments, he knew it was useless arguing with Epstein. That fart would always have a tricky excuse. No use beating up a guy like that unless you are going to kill him; if you leave him alive he will find some way to spill you, so the best thing is to try and get along with him.

Three trucks standing idle, and one out of commission: four out of his ten.

And why didn't they tell a fellow what was going on? No! Letting him ride his ass off in Toronto, in Paris, in Philly, always squeezing him for more dough, all the boys thinking him a miser while he stayed in cheap hotels to sink more dough in this lousy hole; always the same story, "It ain't on its feet yet, Solly, it takes time to get the business, send another couple of thousand, pretty soon we'll be sending you money instead of you sending money here."

Yah. In a pig's ass. Why the hell didn't they tell a guy the truth, instead of waiting till he saw it in the papers?

Sol inspected the wrecked truck.

"Our luck only that he didn't have a whole load!" his mother singsonged as he strode around the blackened, mutilated car. The windows were frames of jagged glass; the body paint was blistered like burnt skin, and the red, white, and blue trade-mark, *Speedy*, had peeled off in chunks so that only a few letters remained. The cab of the truck was completely wrecked, raw ends of wires trailing like guts out of the dashboard.

"He left it standing for a while, it was on Western Avenue, near Taylor Street. In a minute he looks out of the store and the truck is burning—"

"The trucks was all insured for fire," Epstein said glibly, as though he had put something over. "We'll get paid for the truck." He added: "Now I got a boy sitting in every truck, so when the driver goes in the store, the truck is not standing alone. A boy can holler. Schoolboys, a few dollars a week."

"Yeah," Sol said, staring at the wreck. He pulled open the rear doors. The inside was just a black hole. The stink of burnt cloth was still there.

"Sure, now every *yenteh* that had a dress from Klein's, it was a latest hundred-dollar model from the Stevens Shops, and every cheap two-pants suit was a Hart Sheffner and Mocks," his mother went on. "But they got to prove it! They think whatever they ask for, they'll get!"

"They will settle, they will settle," Epstein cried disdainfully. "It won't pay them to get a lawyer to sue for a thirty-dollar damage, the most. The whole business won't cost a thousand dollars. If they think they are going to put me out of business with a little thing like this . . ."

Sol turned on him, sputtering. Just a thousand bucks, huh! Go on, click it off! You try pumping up every cent of that dough with your legs. You pull it out of your guts, roll it out on a wheel, you greasy little chinless louse! Just a thousand berries, huh! Oh, Currist, I told them not to go into business with this guy in the first place!

Instead, he heard himself saying: "Why should anybody want to do a thing like this to me! I got no enemies! Did I ever do anything to anybody!"

"Who says they done it to you?" Epstein smiled through his tight lips, like an adult who, even at a tragic funeral, can't help being amused by the naïve remarks of a child. "This ain't anything personal. It's business!"

Call this business! Burning up trucks!

"It's gangsters!" his mother cried. "A black year on them."

"What do the gangsters want with the cleaning business, ain't they got enough bootlegging?"

"When we take the business away from the other fellers, do you expect them to thank us for it?" Epstein said.

"This is their thanks," said his mother.

"This is a free country! If we can get the business, we got a right to take it away!" Sol asserted.

"Sure." Epstein ducked his head in assent. "So we got to protect ourself, that's all."

"You know why they did this? I'll tell you why they did this!" Ben burbled, suddenly pushing himself between Sol and the others, talking a mile a minute, his voice steadily mounting in pitch, until it was a girlish squeal. "They did it because he's trying to charge cheaper than anybody else, that's why, he's trying to cut the prices, that's why. We don't belong to the Cleaners' Association, see; you don't know a thing about it, Sol, they don't tell you anything, but you think this is finished, this is only the beginning, they'll burn up all the trucks, they'll blow up the plant, they are a hundred against one, and they got a tough gang in the Association, they got all the same prices and if we try to do it cheaper this is what we get; watch out, I tell you, watch out!"

Epstein was staring at Ben as at a foolish boy afraid of dark closets.

"They won't listen to me! I got nothing to say about anything! I'm supposed to be a manager here!" Ben wailed despairingly. "I say we've got to join the Association, we've got to be like everybody else, charge the same as the rest of them, then they'll let us alone. It's your dough, Sol, I tell you they're gonna run us out of business, you'll lose every cent!"

Sol stared at his mother. "Is that a fact?"

"Association smussociation," she said. "Do you think we are the only ones that don't belong! The Columbus, and the Rainbow, they are even cheaper than we are, the Columbus advertises retail a dollar and a quarter a suit, he is five times as big as us, and what do they do to him, nothing!"

"Nothing?"

"They started with him too," Epstein grinned. "But he gave them back pineapples with interest."

"Listen, Sol," his brother pleaded, "what do you want to get, in a gang war! You know what that Columbus Company did, he got gangsters in his business! He took in Bugs Hogan for a partner! He gives him half of everything, and they've got a gangster with a gun on every truck!"

Sol looked at them, dazed. What kind of business was this?

"You don't know what's going on here!" Ben continued. "This last year it's terrible. Those gangsters are muscling in on all the businesses. That old Korshak took in Al Capone for a partner in the Rainbow cleaners, that's why Columbus got in Bugs Hogan. Big Tim Murphy is running the laundry drivers' union and he is going to get in the cleaners' union too, and they will hold us up for whatever they want. Everybody that owns a garage has to pay eighteen bucks a month to another bunch of gangsters, Harry Perlin told me his boss has to pay—"

"What for?"

"For protection, that's what they call it. How do we know it was even the Cleaners' Association that did this! Maybe it was some mob around here trying to muscle in on us, maybe it was even Capone's gang, they'll burn up a couple of trucks and then they'll come around and ask us if we want protection. How do we know who it was? Maybe it was the union. . . . They came in here from the inside workers' union but he wouldn't make a union shop—".

"Ach, *bobeh maises!*" Epstein cried. "We got no trouble with the union. By me is an open shop! I know who did it. It was Wolper, and that's all. That son of a bitch, excuse me, Mrs. Meisel, has been trying to do me harm all his life. Wolper, from the Association. When I was small, he didn't care so much, if I joined the Association, if I didn't join. I paid dues, sometimes I couldn't pay dues—two hundred dollars a year, and special assessments every Monday and Thursday—for what? To keep up an apartment on Lake Shore Drive and a Packard with a chauffeur for Mrs. Wolper!"

"What's that got to do with me?" Sol said.

"Ah, sure, so now, when I put up a big factory, Wolper is after me. I should have to ask from him permission to enlarge my business! You think you can put up a cleaning factory in Chicago! Try! The building department is like this with Wolper! You want to put up a factory with your own money, on your own lot, you got to ask Wolper so he should tell the building department to okay it! So what did I do? I built across the street, in Cicero!" Epstein glittered. "Who is he, a tsar in America, he has to tell me what I can do and what I can't do?"

"Well, what if I want to join? The Association got nothing against me, have they?" Sol insisted.

Epstein gave him the same patient elderly look. "We got three trucks standing in the garage now. Do you want they should all be standing here? Join Wolper's Association."

"Their trucks are out, aren't they? They're doing business."

"Sure, they are doing business."

"Well, what's the matter with me? Listen, I want to run this business on the up and up! I got something to say about it!"

Epstein put his hand over his heart. "You think I ain't honest?" He deepened his voice, appealing to Mrs. Meisel. "For fifteen years I did business with your family! Was I ever a penny off? What do you think I am, young man, a racketeer?"

"Epstein is honest, that I will swear!" Mrs. Meisel declared. "Anything else, you can accuse him, but not this!"

"How much are we charging a suit?" Sol asked.

"Aha! That's it, Sol! That's the whole thing!" Ben cried.

"How much are we charging? Like everyone else!" Epstein asserted. "Wolper claims I am running down prices. Am I crazy? Can I go in a price war with the Association? Solly, you could ride five bicycles a day, and you couldn't keep up with them! They are charging, retail, a dollar and a half a suit. So our price is the same. I am not ruining the industry, pulling down prices!"

"Sure the retail price is the same," Ben accused Epstein, "but what about the tailors? He gives it cheaper to the tailors. He gets away the tailor shops from the other cleaners, and the Association don't allow you to take away a tailor unless you pay for him."

At this, Sol was completely dumfounded. What if a cleaner did lousy work, couldn't the tailor go to another company? No, his mother explained, everything was closed tight. Then, for cry sake, how could he ever build up a business? Sol demanded. What had they gotten him into? Well, his mother said, if you wanted more business, so when another cleaning company decided to sell a route, you could buy the tailors from them for maybe five, six hundred dollars apiece.

Epstein shrugged. "It ain't so bad. If a tailor wants, he can find a way to come to us. What is it anybody's business what price we make with the tailor shop? If we can give a tailor a little cheaper price, he should make a nickel for himself, is it a sin? Let the tailors make a living too! Your mother and father had dealings with me for fifteen years, Sol. Why? Because I gave them a little cheaper."

Now Sol got the picture. So this was what the Association was sore about.

"You think they're going to let you get away with it?" Ben quavered. "Listen, Solly! What do we have to be kikes for! Charge the tailors the regular prices! Those customers we got will stick with us anyway, they ain't going to find anybody else to do it cheaper."

Epstein looked at Ben pityingly. "Listen, my boy, don't be afraid of any threats. Nobody will kill you. I been in business all my life, and I understand how they try to scare you out. In America, business is a war, that's all. Sol! You are a sport! You understand what it is! A fight!"

Now Sol was beginning to get the feel of this business world. He had thought a business was a business: you sold something, and made a profit. But now he saw it as a deadly battle. You weren't even sure who was knifing you, in the dark! Maybe it was this Wolper of the Association, maybe it was Bugs Hogan's mob, or Capone's mob, or some Cicero gang trying to chisel in on his business; this was like fighting your way through a dark room, filled with unknown enemies wildly flailing their knives! It was like cutting your way through when a whole bunch of riders tried to gang up and box you in! Sol looked scornfully at Ben's scared, sleep-haunted face.

"Sol! They'll blow up the place!" his brother whined.

"Shut up!" he barked at Ben. "What the hell do you know about anything!"

Ben backed away from them. Hot, shameful tears welled up uncontrollably; he turned his face so they couldn't see. Let the whole damn plant be wrecked! Why should he try to save the business for that dumb bicycle rider of a brother! All year he had stood up for Sol's rights. Fine appreciation! Oh, why the hell was he so wrongly made that when he was angry, and wanted to yell and be hard, tears leaked out of his eyes? He'd be tough! After this, he'd be only for himself! Hell with the business! Ben rushed out of the garage.

Going back through the plant, Sol passed the row of Hoffman pressing machines, at the first of which his father worked. The old man wouldn't take anything from his son but a presser's job. Sol caught an odd look on his father's face, half sarcastic, half sympathetic, a Yiddish look.

All that ever happened between him and the old man when he came back to Chi, even if he had been gone for a year, was a grave little handshake, and maybe a word about how much raise was in his new contract.

"*Nu?*" the old man said.

"Jeez, they certainly burned up that truck."

The old man gave himself a little bounce on the foot-lever and swung off, letting up the pressing lid. "And the acit?"

"What acid?"

"Once in a while, is a little acit on a suit."

"Huh? Where?"

A shrug. "In the shop."

"Huh? Who does it? Cantcha tell who does it?"

The old man slipped his foot onto a second lever, that let up a hiss of air under the pants-leg. Sol noticed that Mendel Liebowitz, a spotter, and a crony of his father's ever since he could remember, was listening to the conversation with a kind of wry smile, as though he were taking part.

"Who does it? Anybody can do it," the old man said. "The clothes goes through lots of hands. Only last week, was a woman's dress—"

"But—but—" Sol sputtered, and realized it was no use asking. Then, maybe because of the knowing half-sneer on little Mendel's face, he faltered: "Would it be better if there was a union in the shop? Is the union doing this?"

The old man jerked his head toward the office. "He don't want a closed shop. He got a lot of his relations on the payroll, they don't belong to no union."

"They make you pay higher wages, don't they?" Sol inquired.

"Well, for good inside men, you have to pay wages anyhow." The old man called to his crony: "Mendel, come here a minute." Mendel deliberately laid aside his work, and came over. "You know my boy Solly."

"Shuer," Mendel said, "the bicycle rider, hah. Well, how is the bicycle riding business?" with his amused, sarcastic look. These guys always made Sol feel that what he was doing was child's play. Didn't he make forty times as much dough as they did, sweating out their lives over a pressing machine? And yet, this little fart that he paid fifty bucks a week to take the grease spots out of lousy clothes could make him feel ashamed of himself. "So! He is a big sport now, eh, your boy!" Mendel observed to the old man.

For cry sake! Sol wanted to assert himself. It's my dough that built this place! I'm even your boss, see!

"Mendel, the union had a little trouble with Epstein?" the old man prompted.

"What? No trouble. Our union don't make trouble," Mendel said, inscrutably.

"Well, gee," Sol said, "I come back here and I fnd the whole place is being bust up, they burn the trucks, throw acid on the clothes, what for? Who is after me?"

"He got enemies," Mendel said wisely.

"Well, what about this acid, right in the shop? If there was a union shop, would it be any different?"

"If they was all union people," Mendel said sagely, "why should there be any trouble?"

"I don't know about these unions," Sol said. "All I hear is they're all in the control of the gangsters."

"No." Mendel promptly shook his head. "There is good unions and bad unions. In the drivers' union, you got maybe some toughs. That's why he let the drivers' union come in, he is afraid of them. Lots of unions, now, the gangsters got. The janitors they grabbed, and the teamsters' union, but in our union they tried to come in, this same Big Tim Murphy, but we wouldn't let them in."

"Whadaya mean, come in, how can they come in? They have to be members, don't they?"

Mendel smiled with gentle pain. "Only last month they tried to come in on our union. Bob Frische, the secretary, was just stepping out from the office. You know, on 686 Ashland Avenue. He gets in his car and two boys push inside, with guns on him, and they tell him: Drive. And while he is driving they tell him: Don't come back to the union office. Stay out. We are now the union. Those are the boys, from Big Tim Murphy. They come inside and they take over the books and the treasury, and they are the boss."

"So what did he do?" Sol asked, in suspense.

"What did he do? Bob Frische they can't scare so easy. He says the hell with them, and he goes back to the office, and stays there. We passed a motion, five hundred dollars for a bullet-proof door."

Mendel glittered at Sol. "You think they didn't shoot at him? They shot at him too. But they can't scare him. 'Over my dead body,' Bob Frische says, 'will the gangsters come in our union.' "

Sol said: "But can't you call in the cops?"

Again the patient smile. "The gangsters are stronger as the cops. They got their own organization, just like the police."

"Then how can you fight against them?"

And once more Mendel descended into inscrutability.

"For you, the best thing would be you should talk to Bob Frische, and settle with the union."

Unions! Associations! Sol was going dizzy. From every side, he was surrounded. "Do I have to join the bosses' association too?" he asked.

"The bosses' association? What has that got to do with me?" And, with his slightly amused smile, Mendel shuffled back to his work.

A couple of days later, Sol was right in the plant when one of Epstein's relatives named Shmoos, a consumptive-looking washer, came into the office and whispered to Epstein. Sol followed them out to the machine room. The hood was lifted off one of the large washing machines. Purple-dyed garments pulled out of that wash littered the cement floor.

Epstein's eyes reddened. "Oh, if I could put my hands on them! Oh, the dog that sent it in!" Then, screaming: "Who checked in this stuff! Why didn't they look in the pockets! They could send in a ton of dynamite in the clothes and it would go into the benzine!" He rushed into the plant, waving a purpled coat, dripping, stinking of benzine. "You checked in this lot!" he screamed at Ben. "Why don't you look in the pockets? . . ."

First, Sol went to Rube Moscowitz. "What can I do, Solly?" Rube declared, expansively. "I can't send a cop along with every one of your trucks. . . . It's those racketeers in the city hall! They're letting the gangsters get away with murder! If my bunch was in, I could do something for you, Sol. That's what we're fighting for, in this election. If we get in we're going to clean up this city!" he boomed. "Why, they're making a no man's land out of Chicago!"

"Jeez, I know," Sol said. "But I worked like hell and I sunk all my dough in this and I just want to run a business, on the up and up. I got a right to run my own business, ain't I?"

Rube said: "Listen, Sol, if I was you, I wouldn't try to buck anybody. Play ball, whoever it is, play ball. And anyway, what can I do, your factory isn't even in my ward!"

Sol gave him a complimentary box to the next races.

"Unions! Don't talk to me of the unions!" Epstein was yelling, jumping out of his chair and almost dancing up and down with rage. "A hundred and ten dollars I paid a driver last week! A driver! I should get so much out of the business, I would be satisfied! Why? He has a union!" He spat.

"Phoo. Let a union inside, and you know what they will want? Try and lay anybody off in the slack season! All year you will have to keep the whole force, and pay them full wages, for what? For sitting on their *tochas*, excuse me, Mrs. Meisel!"

"Well, this way we lose anyhow," Sol said.

"Unions!" Epstein fumed. "Who gets the money? The men, do you think? The gangsters! They collect it all, and they live like kings, that's what the unions are for, for the union agents! And we got to pay for it! I am independent. No unions! No associations! All my life I was an independent business man!"

"Yah, that's all right for you to fight them—with my dough!" Sol cried, finally. "You think I'm going to sit around and let them burn up my trucks, and pay bills for all the clothes that gets spoiled! How do I know what's gonna happen next! You can't even get no insurance! A swell business!"

The next thing was an explosion. Sol was telephoning when he heard a dull hollow sound from the drying room, but thought it was nothing. Why jump every time a mouse squeaks? Then Jake Weiss came rushing out, fire on his tail. His eyebrows were gone, his face was smutty, and he smelled of burnt hair. Some of the girls laughed, hysterically.

A billow of very white smoke streamed up toward the ceiling. The stench of burnt cloth crept through the plant.

Jake, having recovered coherence, was explaining: "Xplussion podder. Podder. They sew it in the lining of the gahment. In a lady's coat, maybe. In the shoulder. Look, like this!"

"Yah, Wolper sent us a present," Epstein said.

"Well! Go on back to work! Go on back to work!" Mrs. Meisel yelled at the girls who had crowded around.

Sol turned on Ben, who was standing behind him, white, trembling like jelly. "Jeezus Cuurist, I hope they put dynamite in your asshole!" he roared. "You goddam lummox, you're supposed to examine this stuff when it comes in! They could send a pineapple in a coat pocket and you'd pass it through! What the hell good are you?"

"Why is everything my fault! I—I—" Ben screamed. Tears squirted from his eyes, but he didn't even try to hide them. His voice was like a pig's angry squeak. "Go to hell! I'm through! I'm through with your crooks and gangsters! Did I ask you to take me in? Everybody jumps on me! You made me quit my job! Let me alone now! I'm through, I'm through!"

He grabbed his coat and rushed out of the plant. Sol saw him, a scurrying spineless figure, saw him no longer as a kid, but just a little Jewman with a worried face.

"Aw, what good is he? No guts. Let him go back to school-teaching!" Sol said.

Runt Plotkin had a little case, trying to collect damages for some clothes burned up in a cleaner's truck, when he noticed it was against his old pal, Speedy Meisel. So he went out to see him.

"Quite a place, quite a place you got here, Solly."

"Yah, headaches, that's all I got."

"Say." Runt patted his arm. "I didn't realize at first it was you. Say, clients or no clients, I ain't gonna help them hold up an old pal of mine. Huh?" He made a knowing face.

"Well, say, that'll be swell if you make them settle reasonable, Plotsy," Sol said. "Honest, since I came back I had nothing but headaches from this business." He recounted his troubles.

Runt patted him on the arm, leaned closer. "Listen, Sol. The way I look at it, this partner is no asset to you."

"You said it." Sol warmed to Runt's wisdom.

"Well, listen. Lemme handle this for you. In the first place, you don't have to worry about sending out your trucks." He grimaced. "I know somebody, see? He's pretty close to Al. I'll mention it, see? and they won't bother your boys any more. But lemme give you some advice. You want to put some guys on your trucks that can take care of themselves, see? Lemme get you a couple boys. And then, you need a little political protection, see? Rube Moscowitz couldn't do you any good, I could of told you that. But I got an in with the right crowd. Why, you remember Sam Eisen . . ."

"Sure."

"Sam is right in my office now. We got a suite together. Sam is in the political game, and he knows all the boys, I'll have him put in a word to the State's Attorney. They'll leave you alone after that."

"Well, jeez, if you can do anything, Plotsy, go ahead and try it. The thing is, I can't do nothing with Epstein."

Runt looked at him shrewdly. Then, confidentially: "You could make it so hot for him he'd be glad to get out."

Sol hesitated. Not enough to fight unions, associations, competitors. You had to fight your partner, too.

"Business is a struggle for existence. It's dog eat dog. You gotta be tough, Solly," said Runt.

Runt hustled into the office. Maybe the girl would guess he had just landed a big new client.

"Oh, Mr. Plotkin, there was a personal call for you. She called twice." Her look included scorn for any girl who would chase a man, phoning him twice a day.

"Oh, David, you must think it awful of me to call you like this, but there is something I want to ask you. Will you meet me somewhere?" Gwenda whispered in her mysterious throaty voice. As though he hadn't been splitting a gut trying to date her up every night last week. But this was his lucky day. He would make her today, too.

"Sure, lady. How about dinner?"

"All right," she consented, her voice already retreating, making him feel as though it was he who was getting the favor.

With these military-heel shoes he had bought recently, he was an inch taller; if Gwenda happened to be wearing low heels, they wouldn't look at all bad together. Maybe after he got going with her she would catch on, and wear only low-heeled shoes. The shine's radio blared:

"Did you mean it when you said I love you,
Did you mean it when you said I care . . .?"

Shines were happy bastards. The way he slapped the cloth over the toes.

"You gonna see mama tonight?" Runt asked.

"Yaaas-suh, suweet mama," the shine sang, drumming the cloth, ta-da-tum, ta-ta.

"Is she coming across?" Runt said, friendly. The shine looked up and wriggled his brows. One thing about shines, they never had trouble getting it from their women.

"They don't come across, I make 'em come across, I say: Sa-ay, what do you think I come here for, just to play bean-ball? Hayh yah hah!" the shine laughed.

What about lining up the shines? Runt thought. Say, a dollar a month. Naw. He didn't want it to get around that Runt Plotkin had to take it away from the shines. If he could swing that Cigar Store Protective Association, he'd be satisfied. See, boys, we got to get together and fight the United! That was the line to give them. If he could line up five hundred stores in Chicago alone, say at two bucks a month, that was a thousand a month. That was a racket! It was a wonder the big shots hadn't grabbed it yet.

There was a real Windy City wind; he bucked his way up the street. Feeling himself strong. Let the wind whip his coat, cut his cheeks. He had a hunch she would come across tonight.

The trouble was he had started wrong with her. Putting on the act. Opera. Main floor seats for the *Desert Song*. He must have blown five C's on her already. If he hadn't met her at that doggy Moscowitz wedding at the Drake he would have acted plain and probably made her a year ago.

In the restaurant, he walked a little behind Gwenda, so that people wouldn't notice their heights, side by side. Once they were seated there was scarcely any difference between them. It was her beautiful long jambs that made the difference.

She pushed a lump of her taffy-colored hair back from her cheeks, clearing her face of the long Garbo bob. Her fingers were all yellow-ended. Then she relaxed in the chair, letting him search her bored, anaemic face, with its lipstick mouth like a tearing smear on tissue paper.

She ordered from the dollar and a half dinner, so he had to do likewise.

Then she lapsed into her habitual silence; as though she hadn't called him, as though she hadn't mentioned something urgent that she wanted to tell.

Runt went for his food.

"Look, there's a man with a face like a frog," she mentioned. Watching the man mouth his food, Gwenda actually emitted a small, shaking laugh.

It was by moments like these that she held him. Just like a strange kid.

When they had finished eating, she leaned forward, put two fingers on his wrist, and said: "David, I was going to ask you to do me a favor."

"Shoot."

She leaned back, relaxed, and said in her usual bored tone: "I guess I need a little operation."

Runt nearly jumped out of his chair. The whole idea of her swung around in his mind like a flash-o change-o photolight in a store window. So all this time she had been putting it out to some bastard! The bitch!

But there she sat, relaxed, contemptuous, sleepy-eyed, as though she had just asked him for a cigarette.

The way she looked at him, he couldn't even ask her: Who's the guy? Who's gonna pay for it? How far are you gone? The way she looked at him would make him a cheap louse if he asked her a single question.

"Say, listen," he said. "That's kind of tough right now. They just handed this Dr. Rongetti a death sentence. Nobody is taking any chances."

She lit another cigarette. "I thought you might help me out," she said unconcernedly. "As a friend."

He could have grabbed her by the neck and flung her on the table and ripped her dress off, right there, the damn bitch. Putting on the frigid act while all the time she was—

"What about the guy? What's the matter with him?" he flung at her, trying to keep his voice down.

She puffed, turned her eyes away, shrugged. "David, I didn't think you'd want to cross-examine me."

He gasped, wondering at himself for taking that from her. Then he compressed his lips. He had her where he wanted her now. Put on the lily act, baby, but you'll come across now!

"Let's go up to the office," he said. "I'll make a couple of calls."

He signed them into the nightbook, and gave an answering smirk to the elevator man.

All he hoped was that the goddam scrubbing women would stay away. As he switched on the light, he remembered times he had looked at office buildings at night, seeing occasional lighted windows, wondering if someone was having a good time up there.

He didn't want to grab her while she was standing, because of their heights, but waited until she settled onto a chair. She let him get a few feels, and then casually reminded him: "Weren't you going to make some calls?"

So she too wanted to collect, first?

She didn't even know how to plug a line into the switchboard; finally he managed to get a line himself.

He knew Doc Tamas, who took care of the girls in Becky Halperin's flat on Fifteenth Street, but Doc would be scared stiff right now as the cops were supposed to be watching the regulars.

. . . Mitch Wilner must be a doctor now. But, naw. That guy was a cold fish. And he hadn't been in contact with Mitch for years—not since that vacation at Benton Harbor. Then he remembered meeting Rudy Stone, interning at Israel Hospital, on an accident case.

"Listen, Rudy," Runt pleaded, "this is something that I wouldn't ask unless it was terribly important, y' understand. It's for a close friend of mine, and I don't want this girl to take any chances. With a fellow like you on the job . . ."

She sat smoking, with a wanly amused look on her face.

"Sure, I know how it is," Rudy said sympathetically. "But even if it was one chance in a million of something going wrong, I couldn't take it, Plotsy. I'll tell you though, I know a good man, he happened to get into some trouble so he hasn't got a regular practice."

Runt winked at Gwenda, and made another call.

"He wants two hundred simoleons," he said to Gwenda as he hung up.

She shrugged.

Runt decided that in the morning he'd fix it up with Dr. Tamas who would do it for fifty. Gwenda would think it was the two-hundred guy. Maybe Tamas would even do it gratis, as he'd shoved quite a lot of change the doc's way for expert testimony on injuries.

"I'll take care of it," Runt said.

"Thanks," she said, ironically.

He walked over and locked the door.

Then he took hold of her, pulled her sidewise on the chair, and bent her backwards.

"What is this, do I have to pay in advance?" she said, still with that bored superiority to everything that could happen to her.

"Whadaya think, you're going to get away with it?" he said viciously, this time, without pretense.

She was still cool. "Isn't it customary to use a bed?"

Half crazed, he pushed her onto the floor.

As she adjusted her clothes she still had her bored, acquiescent air of superiority, and he tried to shake off the feeling that she had won. "You ——— ———," he said, "if I ever catch you two-timing me I'll tear you to pieces."

As they went out, she gave him one of her wan, fleeting smiles, and touched her hand to his wrist. This touch was the one intimate, yielding gesture she had made.

You Gotta Be Tough

Runt Plotkin picked up Mike Cone in Jake's place and took him over to the Speedy Cleaning Company.

"Mike is a real scrapper," he told Sol. "Put him on a truck and you won't have to worry."

"The other guys'll have to worry," Mike blurted.

It cost Sol two hundred bucks to get Mike into the drivers' union, before he could put him on the job.

Then, one morning, Max Glick, a driver with a North Side route, drove back into the yard with his full delivery load in the car. He sat trembling like a girl.

Three guys in a sedan had forced him to the curb, and warned him to keep out of the territory as it was now taken care of.

"Did they have guns?"

"Sure they had guns. They had a machine gun in the car."

Maxie was a family man with three kids.

"Listen, the streets are free, they ain't gonna keep my trucks off the streets!" Sol yelled. "Go on back and deliver the stuff. I'll go with you!"

No, no, with that route, Maxie was through.

"All right, then you're through! I want drivers that ain't gonna jump off the trucks if somebody gives them a look!"

"Gangsters you want, not drivers!"

"All right, that's all! That's all!"

Sol climbed on the running board.

"Solly! Don't go!" his mother screeched. Finally they prevailed on him to wait for Mike Cone. Let Mike drive. And he should follow in his car, that would be a better scheme.

"Y' got a gun?" Mike said.

"I don't need nothin'. I ain't gonna shoot anybody."

"Yah? I know who done that, Bugs Hogan is closing up the North Side. Y' can't argue with those guys with your mitts."

"This ain't the Wild West, this is the streets of Chicago," Sol said. "This ain't no beer truck, it's a cleaning truck, and I got a right on the streets. Go ahead, drive."

"Here." Mike handed him a pistol. "I'll stop and get my brother's."

Sol got into his yellow Moon roadster. If something really happened, what could he do? If they really had a machine gun—he imagined the arc of bullets, and himself against the pavement, and Estelle reading about it in a newspaper.

The truck turned on Roosevelt, and he followed. Mike stopped in front of Jake's place. "Listen, I know a coupla guys, you better take 'em along. Say, whyncha put on these guys for drivers, instead of those shits like Maxie Glick?"

It was decided to have the two guys hidden inside the truck. Mike pulled off. Sol got into the Moon and followed. Mike raced north on Crawford as though he was driving a Stutz speedster.

They made half a dozen deliveries and Sol was feeling easier. The whole thing was a bluff.

It was a nice spring day. Sol noticed that Mike brought out bigger bundles than he delivered. At last the spring rush was opening up.

They stopped on Crawford near Montrose. There was fairly busy shopping around here, and lots of cars were parked along the street.

Sol realized afterward that he had actually seen the sedan come along the other side of the street. But it was so unbelievable that anything like this should really happen right on a busy street-car street that, though he was watching for trouble, he wasn't really expecting it. He saw the sedan head in toward the curb, and park in front of his truck. Then, as he heard the sedan door slam, he jumped out of his car.

Three ordinary-looking men were coming along the sidewalk.

Mike emerged from the shop, both arms clasped around a fat bundle of clothing. Two of the men grabbed him. The third went around in back of the truck and reached for the door-handle.

A strange guttural shriek ripped out of Sol's throat. He completely forgot about the gun. He jumped on the two guys. He got a kick in the shin, struck out wildly with his fists, stumbled over clothes, heard Mike yell: "Look out, look out!" and heard a shot.

There was a woman's scream, like a signal for a whole chorus of shrieks; Mike said afterwards a woman wet her pants. "Get the sons of bitches, get the sons of bitches," was Sol's only thought, but the two had wrenched themselves loose and were running toward their sedan. Sol saw the open rear of his truck, and the surprised face of the third hoodlum as the two guards confronted him. The hoodlum ran.

Sol lunged after him; but with a dodging, scurrying movement the fellow made the sedan, which was already drawing away from the curb.

"Get 'em, get 'em!" Sol yelled, and hopped onto the truck. But before it could pull out, that sedan had swerved around a corner, and he knew the chase was useless.

The dropped clothes lay in a heap on the sidewalk; one orange-colored jersey, separated in the scuffle, looked like a pool of blood.

—Anybody shot?

—They got one!

—They got away.

—Gang war . . .

A confused babbling and running together of people was beginning, the more daring approaching the truck. Mike sourly gathered up the heap of clothes.

The tailor had run out and was yelling: "I saw it, I saw it all!"

"I know one of those guys," Mike said to Sol. "That's Bugs Hogan's mob all right!"

Sol went back to his car, and nearly had to run over people to get away. He followed the truck, to Jake's place.

"They won't bother us any more," Mike said, once they were inside. "They got an idea we got a gun inside every truck and a car following behind!" He laughed, triumphantly.

Sol felt shaky, victorious, scared, and queerly unhappy.

He reached to his back pocket for a handkerchief, felt the gun, and saw himself, a man with a gun, taking his living off the streets of Chicago.

Anybody that wanted to get tough with him!

Runt Plotkin rushed into Sam's office and reported the wild gang attack on Speedy Meisel, on Crawford Avenue. Sam was in politics, wasn't he? Sam could get the S.A. right on the wire and put up a big howl. About how his friends couldn't even conduct their business in peace.

"I know, I know," Sam said. And what would happen? A promise: "Sure, sure, we'll take care of it," and that would be all.

They were too busy with the primary, fighting for their own lives.

And even if it wasn't election time, it came to Sam, nothing would be done. Nobody cared. Big Bill's bunch wasn't interested.

For the first time it struck Sam what a wild place the city had become. The streets were wild.

Not that he was a reformer; he hated the stuffed-shirt reform crowd. He had had a real feeling for Big Bill as somebody alive, somebody that was raw and bold, noisy, American, but who way down understood what the people wanted. Big Bill was easy, he'd say yes to anything. You want to build something, make something, run a business, run a racket, sure, sure, go right ahead, sure! Just see that the boys are taken care of and from then on the town's yours. Big Bill was easy, he believed in everybody going ahead, getting what he wanted.

And they were getting it. The town was running away.

Why bother with actual details of government? Let the people scrap it out in the streets, let the toughest have their will.

Political Economy

Evenings, when he was supposed to go and talk at rallies, Sam got to walking around by himself, puzzling, trying to figure out where he stood.

And when the Wilson killing happened on election day, he knew he was through. The killing happened in a polling place on Lake Street, where Judge Horowitz was ward committeeman. Wilson, a frock-coated Negro reformer who had the nerve to make speeches against Judge Horowitz in his own bailiwick, was shot while acting as a poll watcher. Sam knew the ward. He had used to collect rent in those slums, for old man Klein. Lately Negroes were moving into the neighborhood.

Of course Horowitz claimed the killing had nothing to do with politics. Why should he be held responsible for those guardians of good government? Could he help it if a goo-goo stuck his black nose into a tough polling place and got bumped? Anyway, it was probably some private feud, among the colored folks, the reformer must have been borrowing some black mama.

When Diamond Joe had been knocked off, it somehow hadn't mattered. But the idea of that poor, dignified shine, in his frock coat . . .

And that wasn't all that had happened. As a great hue and cry of ballot-stuffing had been raised by the reformers, hundreds of volunteer poll watchers had been enrolled and sent to the polling places. In another ward, a closed truck, the size of a police wagon, had pulled up in front of a polling place and a bunch of armed hoodlums had forced all of the poll watchers to get into the truck. Then they had been taken to a room, somewhere, and locked up for the day.

Sam knew what that feeling was like. A couple of years ago, before getting into politics, he had volunteered to the Bar Association as a poll watcher, and had been sent out to that lousy ward. The black looks he had got, from both Democratic and Republican precinct workers! But he had stuck it out, to the bitter hour when the votes were counted, with guns lying on the table.

Sure, his own ward was fairly clean, a respectable residential neighborhood. But wasn't it all the same racket? How had he ever expected to do anything, in this racket?

And yet, what else could he do, in this world? There seemed nothing for him but the humdrum practice of law.

Lil came into the office to show Sam a beautifully framed engraving of "Trees" which she was giving her mother for her birthday, and though Runt was obviously ensconced there, taking phone calls, she kept her peace.

But the minute Sam got home, the storm broke. "Either he gets out of your office, or I get out of your house! That's all!"

"But, honey—"

"Don't honey me! If that's all my wishes mean to you, okay!"

"He's only there temporarily," Sam insisted. "He hasn't even got his name on the door."

327

"I don't give a damn! It's me or him! It's—" The kid was watching them fighting but she didn't even care.

Sam trembled with the effort of keeping calm. "I'll stay at the Morrison tonight," he said, and went out, quietly. He remembered her look, astonished, frightened, yet undefeated.

The next day she called him at the office. She made no reference to their quarrel. Just at the sound of her voice, calm and nice again, he sagged with relief, and knew what a strain he had gone through.

"Gus Lund called you last night, Sam, said he's thinking of taking out his golf bags if Sunday is nice. He wants you to come along. He said for you to call him."

"All right," Sam said. "Thanks." He waited.

"Are you coming home to dinner?" she capitulated.

It was a fine dinner, and they were nice to each other, but scarcely talking, afraid they might set off that fire again.

Finally Lil asked: "Did you call Gus Lund?"

"No. I don't think I will."

"Are you sore at him or something?"

"No. I'm just not having anything more to do with that crowd."

"What?"

"I'm through with politics."

She stared at him. Then it burst out again: "Honest to God, Sam Eisen, it would take a genius to understand you. First you drive me crazy, never home, chasing around, giving your time for nothing, why, you even spent two hundred dollars on the last campaign out of your own pocket! And all of a sudden, just when he gets where it can do him some good, he's through!"

"Well, I know it may look funny, Lil, but certain things made me see I was on the wrong track."

"What?"

"Well, it's hard to say exactly, but it's a feeling that's been growing on me, and here recently with all these election shootings—"

"So they shot a nigger! They just cleared Judge Horowitz, didn't they? And it wasn't in your ward! I don't say it's right, but you must admit something has to be done, those niggers think they own the city. My father has some property over on Thirteenth Street, and it's no joke. Those niggers are coming in, and ruining the neighborhood. Anyway what's it got to do with you?"

"Nothing. It wasn't that. Only, that's just an example. I mean, I decided I was on the wrong track."

He tried to talk honestly with her, maybe she would understand. "I could never change anything, all that would happen would be that it would change me, make me like the rest of them. I can't play ball with those guys and be myself, so I'm getting out."

She seemed to understand. "Well, the least you can do is talk to Gus, Sam. You can't just walk out on him leaving everything up in the air."

Sam dubbed along. Gus was silent till they reached the third hole.

"You haven't been coming around," he observed.

"No," said Sam. "Not lately."

"The fellows noticed it."

"Yah?"

"Uh-huh. That was a lousy thing, that Wilson shooting," Lund commented.

Sam was surprised at his intuition.

"That louse Horowitz never knows when to stop. Bill Thompson should have dropped him long ago. Bill don't like that kind of stuff himself and it gives the party a black eye."

"Yah, especially when the whole gang is freed," Sam said.

"Well, you know how it is, they had to give the boys a whitewash."

They tramped after a ball.

"Sam," Gus opened again. "You're a good kid, and I'll tell you straight, you've got possibilities. You've got more stuff than any of those punks that hang around. That's why I'm taking the trouble to talk to you. Maybe I can help you get straightened out. You could go a long way in this game, Sam."

"Thanks," Sam said. He felt touched, warmed. "But I guess I'm dropping out of politics."

"Yeah, I've been disgusted myself sometimes," Gus Lund said. "But it's all in the game. If you go in for it, you've got to play the game."

"I know it. But it's not for me," Sam decided.

Gus Lund gave him a long look. "Okay, Sam. Any time I can do you a favor . . ."

Sam was wondering, trying to shape in his mind what he wanted to ask. Maybe Gus, in his long experience, knew the answer to this empty, bleak disgust. If you couldn't even get started doing what you wanted in life, what did you have left to do? But Gus would think he was soft.

Mr. Liebling, a friend of Lil's father, came into the office and explained his case. A worker whom he had fired was suing for two months' wages.

"You haven't got much chance," Sam told him frankly. "You really owe this fellow the money."

"Listen," Liebling breathed bubbly into his face. "I wouldn't pay that dirty snake if I have to fight him to the Supreme Court of the United States. You know what he did to me? He came into the shop with a gangster from the union and tried to organize the whole shop on me!"

"Sure, I understand," Sam said. "But legally he worked for you and you owe him those last two months' wages."

Liebling half arose. "So you don't want to take the case, Mr. Eisen?"

Sam felt phlegm in his throat. For once, he wanted to spit out at that slobby, squint-eyed sweatshop boss: No, I don't want the case.

He said: "I'm just telling you this so you won't blame me if we lose. Naturally, I'll try my best. . . . Has he got anything to prove he worked for you, those last two months?"

Liebling's eyes lighted with appreciative understanding. "What do you mean, he worked for me?" He grinned. "He wasn't even there!"

They had to draw Judge Horowitz.

"How's the young feller!" Horowitz said, dropping his arm around Sam's shoulder, when they met in the city hall corridor.

"Say, I've got a case coming up with you."

"Yah? What is it?"

Sam explained.

"Anything for you, Sam, anything I can do!" Horowitz said expansively, his fat lips puckered obscenely. "You understand, I get a lot of support from the unions but—well"—he winked—"got to make an exception once in a while." He winked again. "What the hell, we can't let those buttonhole makers get away with everything, huh?"

There was nothing to it, in court. Liebling and his partner swore that they had discharged the man in January, and now he had the nerve to claim salary for February and March!

Judge Horowitz sat in his characteristic judicial attitude, his nose on his desk, his pink eyes peering up. Only, since he had been exonerated of the election killing conspiracy charges, Sam thought there was something even more cruelly and farcically dignified about his manner.

The plaintiff got on the stand. As Sam moved near, to cross-examine, he noticed the man for the first time: a little buttonhole maker, dry-skinned, with a paunch from sitting on a chair all his life . . . thinning hair . . . it might have been his own father. None of the other workers in Liebling's shop had dared to come and testify for him.

"No questions," Sam said, suddenly utterly disgusted with himself.

Horowitz peered at the buttonhole maker, and remarked, friendly: "You are a union man and I know union men are reliable. But I have to go by the law. The law says there has to be proof. You haven't brought any proof into court, that you worked those two months, so my judgment has to be for the defendant. Case dismissed." The judge frowned heavily at Sam, as if angry that he had to give him the victory.

It was plain robbery.

"Ah, that was smart! No questions!" Liebling foamed over Sam. "That was smart, Sam! You didn't give him a chance to talk! Klein told me he had a smart son-in-law but now I believe him!"

Sam managed to shake them at the city hall door. He felt like washing his mouth. He wished he knew how to get drunk.

"I heard you tried a case for that crook Liebling," Sam's father remarked, that Friday night.

"Yah."

"That buttonhole maker, I used to work with him in the same shop. He was on the next machine. Berel Pasternak. So he lost two months' wages, from Liebling?"

"Yah," Sam admitted, looking the other way.

The last straw was the argument about Passover. Lil's folks were in Rochester, where her mother was being treated, so Sam thought they would go to his folks' for the *seder*. Instead Lil wanted to go to Ev Goldberg's.

"I don't understand what makes you so religious all of a sudden!" Lil exclaimed sarcastically. "Why don't you grow a beard and go to *shul* while you're at it!"

"Religion has nothing to do with it," he responded patiently. "You know perfectly well, all that stuff means nothing to me. It's just the—the social side of it. I mean—"

"That's the whole point! Socially, it means something to us to go to Ev's."

"Listen, Lil," he said with hopeless restraint. "You know perfectly well that, if your own mother was having a *seder*, we would have to go there. But since your mother and father are in Rochester, my folks naturally expect us to come to them. It would be like a slap in the face not to come."

"Oh, mygod, do I have to sit like a prisoner till twelve o'clock while your grandfather mumbles the whatyacall it through his beard? We were there year before last and that ought to hold them for a while!"

"It was three years ago."

"Whenever it was, once was enough. Mygod, you'd think that, with all your uncles and aunts, your family would have enough customers for their *seder* without dragging me into it!"

"That isn't the point," Sam said. "It doesn't hurt us, and it makes them feel good to see their son and their grandchild at the table."

"Listen, Sam. We're young, we're modern. For three years we were tied down to the house with the kid and everything, but now at least we can begin to go out and see people, so why do we have to get stuck with a bunch of old dodoes? I think Ev's idea is wonderful. Why not have a *seder* for young couples only! I wish I had thought of the idea myself! A *seder* is supposed to be a celebration, isn't it! Why not have a good time!"

"If you're so keen on going there, go on," Sam said. "I'll take Jackie to my folks."

Lil gave him a burning look; her hand went to her mouth, stifling a sob. "Oh, so that's it! So you want to show them what a terrible mother he's got!" She rushed into the bedroom.

Sam sank into a chair and clutched the arms, tight. Gradually, his anger eased. He decided to laugh the whole thing off. That he should quarrel about religion—he, the agnostic!

He found her lying face down on the bed, sobbing.

"I'm sorry, Lil." He stroked her hair. "I don't know what's the matter with me lately, I'm getting so nervous I get contrary on the slightest provocation." He wanted to tell her, to tell someone, about the times in court or in his office when he felt himself getting all tense in knots, as though he were a rope being twisted tighter and tighter; to tell her of the disgust and loss he felt in his daily work, in his getting out of politics, in having to curry favors from a louse like Judge Horowitz.

"It was my fault, Sammy. I aggravate you when you're tired," she said, sitting up and drawing his head to her. "I shouldn't even have mentioned Ev. We ought to go to your family this year. It's only right."

"Oh, it doesn't matter, they probably won't even notice we're missing. We can go there for the second night, anyway. They're used to having us come then."

"Of course!" she exclaimed. The second night was a *seder*, too!

"C-o-n-
S-t-a-n-t-i-n . . ."

the radio was going, as they entered. Thelma was dancing with Manny Kassell, and there was a strange couple dancing. Ev, who looked ravishing in a flowing white gown that completely concealed her condition—though there was nothing as yet to conceal—came rushing toward them.

"Oh, darling, look at me! Does it show?" she whispered quite audibly, to Lil.

"It doesn't show a bit!" Lil whispered back.

"She just wanted an excuse to wear that gown," Phil remarked, with a loving proud sophisticated kidding glance at his wife.

"Oh, it's cute," Lil said. "It's darling."

"Oh, Jackie! Isn't he cute!" Ev swooped.

"Say hello to Aunt Ev, Jackie."

"Hi, toots," Jackie said, and they all roared.

Phil introduced them to the strangers, Mr. and Mrs. McIlwain, who were dying to see a Jewish Passover ceremony.

The maid passed around cocktails, and little caviar canapés on matzoth.

"Aren't they wonderful!" Mrs. McIlwain cried, examining the canapés. "Passover or no Passover, I think that's an awfully smart way to serve caviar."

"They're awfully cute," Lil agreed.

"Darling, you must tell me where to buy this—what do you call it?" Mrs. McIlwain said.

"Matt-zote," Ev carefully mispronounced the word, and giggled.

"Say, this don't taste like bathtub gin to me," Manny comically complained of his drink.

"That's real prescription stuff," Phil admitted. "I'm afraid you'll have to put up with it, as Ev has been using our bathtub lately."

They laughed.

"One of the saddest things about Prohibition," McIlwain said, "is we don't know good liquor when we get it. I always used my old man as a tester-in-chief. Boy, he used to sozzle the real stuff!"

They looked at him, envious of his being the son of a real drunken Irishman.

"Well, Sam, I hear you have deserted the sinking ship," Phil remarked.

"Yah, with the rest of the rats," Sam caught him up.

"Oh," Phil laughed appreciatively. "Well, I guess Big Bill is through, in this town."

"I don't know," Sam said. "He's still mayor."

"He must be kind of lonesome, in the city hall these days." McIlwain referred to the defeat of Thompson's candidates.

"Anyway, he might as well get out," Phil said. "His pals've grabbed everything there was to be grabbed."

"I guess that's so," Sam agreed. "They've about scraped the bottom of the till."

"I hear he has presidential aspirations," McIlwain remarked.

"With him, it's a case of I do choose to run," Manny cracked.

"Will you men stop talking politics!" Ev laughed, and steered them into the dining room.

"Oh, Ev, it's just too cute for words!" Lil screamed, seeing the table. In the center was a layer cake, and atop it was a doll in a flowing robe, with a long white cotton batting beard stuck to its cherubic chin. Moses!

"Do you get it?" Thelma tittered. "What's it supposed to be?"

"Moses on the Mountain?" Mrs. McIlwain ventured.

"Uh-uh."

"I got it! If you can't eat bread, eat cake!" Manny roared.

"No fair, you knew!" Ev cried.

They all laughed, and Ev modestly said: "It was Phil's idea."

The place cards were the cleverest things! Each card was a cut-out of a biblical character, only Ev had fixed devilish little short skirts over the long gowns of the women characters, and put derby hats on the men. But the most comical thing she had done was to get pictures of movie stars and paste their faces on the biblical figures.

"Who is this supposed to be?" Lil screeched, and they all piled around a picture of Adolphe Menjou, in a silk hat, on the body of an Egyptian taskmaster who wielded a whip.

First they thought it was McIlwain because he was a gentile (get it, Egyptian) and, besides, he was an engineer; but it turned out to be Manny Kassell on account of his Menjou mustache, and the whip was because he was a dentist. Next to him was a picture of Lillian Gish as Queen Esther playing a harp, and naturally that was Thelma, on account of the harp. Phil and Ev were Doug Fairbanks and Mary Pickford, the perfect couple, as Samson and Delilah! Sam was Groucho Marx as Adam, and Lil was Vilma Banky as Eve, and Jackie was Jackie Cooper as David. Immediately, he yelled: "Mother, I wanna slingshot!"

"Hush, Jackie, mother will buy you one tomorrow."

"Naw, I wan' it now!"

"Where on earth did you get all those pictures of the movie stars?" Lil said, trying to ignore him.

"Oh, Phil has a friend in Lubliner and Trinz," Ev said, "and he got them out of their advertising department, special."

"Wanna!" Jackie tugged at Lil.

"Look, Jackie," Phil said, and picked up the favor on Jackie's plate. It unfolded into an Indian headdress. "Nize beby," he quoted Milt Gross.

Jackie stopped bawling and put the paper feathers on his head. "Yay, I'm an Indian!" he yelled, happily.

"You know, Phil really has a way with children," Ev said. "I guess he'll make a good papa after all."

The others were discovering their favors. On each plate was a comical hat of the sort worn at New Year's parties.

"You see, good Jews always wear skull caps or some kind of hat at the table on Passover," Ev explained to the Gentiles.

"Don't get the idea this is a real service," Phil said. "We just decided to do this our own way for a change."

The McIlwains put on their hats. Mr. McIlwain had drawn a red-white-and-blue fez with a tassel on the top. His young, round, pink-massaged face beamed good will. Sam's hat was yellow and green, and shaped like an overseas cap. Manny had a dunce cap! The girls had hats, too.

"You know who would appreciate this? Alvin Fox!" Thelma exclaimed. "Remember he trained to be a rabbi and gave it up."

"I was going to ask him," Ev said, "but they just went to Europe on a late honeymoon."

"He married a Gentile girl," Thelma said to the McIlwains, beaming.

"He was ruining the business putting out those modernistic chairs," Phil laughed, "so the old man said it was cheaper to send him to Europe."

They all laughed good-naturedly.

Now the wine went around. Phil had secured some real Chianti, with the straw basket around the bottle.

"Just like a regular *seder!*" Lil cried as the maid served the first dish, consisting of hardboiled eggs cut up in salt water.

"What do you call this?" Mrs. McIlwain inquired.

"*Charokis*," Ev promptly responded, anglicizing the word beyond recognition.

"How did you ever know about all this stuff?" Lil said, awed. "My mother used to make a kind of a *seder* but I would never dream of trying it myself!"

"Kid, you'll never guess where I got the directions," Ev said. "There was a complete Passover menu in Prudence Penny's column!"

"No!"

"I'll prove it to you!" And Ev produced the clipping. "I just gave it to the girl and told her to follow it religiously."

"Religiously, that's good," Manny repeated.

"What kind of bread would you like, rye or white?" Phil jested, passing the plate of matzoth.

"I'm really going to eat this, it's good for you, I'm on a diet!" Ev said. "My gynecologist said it was the best thing."

The maid brought in a plate of hot biscuits, which most of them accepted, though the McIlwains insisted on eating matzoth.

"Isn't there supposed to be a glass of wine for somebody?" Lil prompted.

"Oh, yah! *Eli hanoveh!*" Thelma supplied.

"What's that?"

"Elijah," Phil translated.

"Yah. That's cute," Lil said. "You're supposed to fill a glass with wine, and Elijah comes and drinks it up."

"How about giving Elijah a real treat, for a change?" Phil said, and filled a glass with gin. "There you are, old boy old boy! Open the door for Elijah!"

"Who is Elijah?" Jackie said.

"He comes and drinks it up," Lil explained.

"When?"

"Right away. You can't see him. He's invisible."

"Aw." Jackie watched her face. "You're kidding me."

"It's a fact," Lil said. "He goes into every house, and drinks the wine."

"Yah? Then I bet he gets pie-eyed!" Jackie piped.

They roared.

"Isn't he the cutest thing!"

Ev leaned intimately to Phil.

"Oh, Lil, make him ask the four questions!" suggested Thelma.

"That's right, that's what he's here for!"

Philip explained to the McIlwains. "Of course we're not doing this in proper order or anything, but at a real *seder* they follow the *Haggada*, that's a sort of book of procedure, and the youngest son of the house asks the traditional four questions, and the head of the household, usually the grandfather, reads the responses."

"Surprise!" Ev said, and produced a *Haggada*, printed in both Hebrew and English. This curiosity was passed around, everybody explaining to the McIlwains that the Hebrew was read backwards instead of up and down, like Chinese. They studied the booklet respectfully.

"Oh, you know what I want to sing!" Thelma cried. "*Chad gad yo!* We always used to sing that when I was a kid!" She turned the pages. "One kid, one kid for two *zusim!*" she began. The wine was affecting her noticeably, her cheeks were flaming. "*Chad gad yo! Chad gad yo!*"

"Doesn't that come at the end of the meal?" Ev said.

"What's the difference!"

Manny began to sing with her: "*Chad gad yo! Chad gad yo!*"

The maid brought in an immense, sugar-baked ham.

Squeals and titters.

Manny picked up a curled streamer that lay near his plate and blew noisily. The red crape paper shot across the table, and dropped over Sam's ear.

"The four questions, the four questions!" Lil insisted.

"All right, you read them for Jackie, and Phil will answer them!" Ev said.

"Now, Jackie, look." Lil showed him the lines in the book. "You say what I say—ready?"

Jackie nodded eagerly.

"Why . . ."

"Why."

"Is this night . . ."

"Is 'is night."

"Different . . ."

"Diffrunt."

Sam heard his son piping and, glancing across at the book in Lil's hand, suddenly remembered the Hebrew words: "*Mah nishtanoh halaylah hazeh . . . ?*" as he had used to say them, awed, and the grave answering intonation of his grandfather.

"From all other nights?"

"Fmallothnights." Jackie stuck out his hand, for a reward.

"Because this is April 4," Phil answered, "and every other night is another night."

Their guffaws rattled the glassware.

Sam got up.

"You'll have to excuse me," he managed to mumble, as he made for the door.

Lil rushed after him. "What's the matter, are you sick?" Her first look at him was worried. Then: "Are you crazy? Disgracing me before my best friends!"

Ev rushed up to them.

"This is the end!" Lil sputtered hotly, collapsing in tears into Evelyn's arms.

In Sam's mind, these words were flashing, as though he were reading them on an electric sign, on and off, on and off: "This is where I get off. This is where I get off."

> Ah gits weary an' sick of tryin',
> Ahm tired of livin' an' feard of dyin',
> But ol' man river,
> He jes keeps rollin' along . . .

Since that street war, life was hell; any minute a bomb might smash through the plate glass and blow up the plant. Every driver went out in fear. Every worker in the place talked in whispers. Even Epstein was scared, and ran from his own shadow.

Runt Plotkin advised Sol: "Say, Sol, this is the psychological moment to get rid of your partner. See? After you get rid of him, you can square yourself all around. That's my strategy."

Runt had a swell girl with him, tall, a head taller than himself. Sol could tell: there was the kind that did, and the kind that didn't. She did. She smiled across the table, a bored yet fascinated smile, while he described his gun battle. This tired weak-looking kind of dame could turn it on plenty hot, too.

"See?" Runt said, and conspiratorially shoved a bit of paper under Sol's nose. It had a dot with a circle around it. "Boy, when he gets this he'll give you his share for nothing." Runt laughed.

And in fact, next day, Epstein's face was blacker. He was afraid to come to the factory and he was afraid to stay away. "All my life I been in business, but I never saw anything like this! It's no more law in America!" He hired the Pinkerton Agency and paid two hundred dollars in two weeks, but they couldn't trace the threats.

Then something happened that clinched the business. On the South Side, an independent cleaner was shot to death. It was Morris Rosenblum, who had put out a leaflet charging that the Association and the unions were in cahoots, all in the control of one gang strangling the industry. The

Association claimed that Rosenblum had been killed in a private fight with a small-time mobster who was moving in on the South Side cleaning racket.

Epstein locked himself at home.

Sol gave him notes for ten thousand dollars, and five thousand in cash.

Epstein said he had his eye on a small plant in Elkhart, where he would have peace.

Sol wondered: maybe he himself was the sucker.

"Have I got a headache with that factory!" Sol moaned to Bert Olson, with whom he had teamed ever since the Paris race.

"Yah? Jeez, I sunk all my dough in a chicken farm and I ain't through paying yet."

Pisano came around. He was starting a couple of new kids in this race, and had little time for Sol. But he shook his head and clucked: "Boy, you sure look lousy. Watcha been doin', laying the whole West Side?"

"Aw, f—— you," Sol responded. "They're driving me nuts with that cleaning racket. Hey, Wop, maybe you know a couple of good hoods I can put on my trucks."

"Wadya think, every dago has to be in a mob?" Pisano actually seemed touchy on the subject. But he added, friendly: "What's a matter, kid, they really got you in a jam?"

"Christ, unions, partners, protection! Now I need five grand, cash, to buy out my partner."

"Ttt, that's tough," Pisano said. "Well, I told you, a man got to stick to what he knows. I know bikes, and I stick to them, see?"

Sol sat on his bunk, next to Bert; they watched the amateur sprints that preceded the six-day starting gun. "I wouldn't give a nickel for the bunch of them. Kids don't learn how to ride any more. They ain't got what it takes."

He felt old, of another generation.

The old Coliseum was filling up. Some guy was megaphoning a song, with the band:

> "I can't give you anything but love, baby,
> That's the only thing I've plenty of, baby."

Sol was riding a lousy race right from the start, and he knew it.

Used to be he rode a race and all he thought about was janes or what to eat or sometimes he had the trick of riding off the long drags by making each lap the name of a girl he had laid, always starting with Estelle.—Jeez, there was a good kid, he had never really finished with her. But now all he had on his mind was headaches with unions and insurance and trouble. He would think of that little spotter Mendel, his old man's pal, and Mendel would be riding alongside of him with the sarcastic look on his face like, no matter what you do, in the end I will win. If the bosses had a right to make an association, then the workmen in the shop had a right to make a union.

338

That was square. If he let the drivers have a union, then it was square to let the inside workers have their union. I always played fair and square.

He was riding a lousy race and Bert was sore and he could see Bert wished he would break a leg so they would break up the team. In the slow hours of early morning some of the boys rode around reading a newspaper and looking over Tommy Cramer's shoulder he saw the headlines BIG TIM MURPHY SLAIN, WAS TRYING TO MUSCLE IN ON CLEANERS' UNION.

"Say, that mobster had a swell-looking wife," Tommy said as Sol drew closer to see the story. "Look." There was a picture of her, a cute number all right, but for once Sol was more interested in the news. He could see little Mendel's face, with a kind of quiet victory. We can take care of ourselves too.

Chick came back from the drug store and slipped Sol the little bottle. The Wop would be sore to see him hopping up so early as the third day. But they were trailing the race and Sol was so pooped out he was ready to take a good spill and let himself be carried away on a stretcher.

Sol drank two mouthfuls of the caffeine mixture and lay back. When he was scratching bottom like this he could feel his strength returning as though his muscles were violin strings and someone was tightening the squeaky keys. Around his heart, especially, he got this tightening tonic feeling of strength. He ate a swell steak, nearly raw. Bert found the bottle in the bunk and gave him one of those looks with a stuck-out underlip.

The announcer sang out the premium for the next sprint. A hundred bucks from Alderman Monahan, that old racing sport. "Okay, here goes for lousy Epstein," Sol muttered to himself, and climbed onto his bike.

LOVE AND MARRIAGE

AT last it was her turn on the copy of *The President's Daughter*[1] and Estelle was beautifully settled on the couch, reading, and the radio hummed low, and from the bathroom where she was washing stockings Muriel joined in the refrain:

"Life is just a bowl of cherries . . ."

The bell rang.

"You expecting someone, Red?" Muriel sang out, dashing for a robe.

Estelle looked up stupidly. "Oh. I bet that's my brother. He wanted to come up and have a confabulation about the family."

"I didn't know you had a brother," remarked Muriel, getting interested.

"Oh, he's just a cluck."

Nevertheless Muriel fixed her face.

"Gee, this is hot stuff," Estelle said. "I guess it's all true, too. Imagine, the President! They're all the same!"

"Some dump," Lou said, appreciatively taking in the classy reproduction of Mona Lisa on the gesso wall, and the fancy brackets with imitation candle-drip. Over the couch was a drawing of a naked man in the prow of a boat, which he didn't know was by Rockwell Kent. There was also a framed picture of Lindy standing beside his *Spirit of St. Louis*. The picture was labeled "We."

It was a room-and-a-half dinette on Barry Avenue, in a place with carved chairs in the lobby, and an automatic elevator. He figured it for seventy a month.

This was certainly a respectable place, Lou was glad to see; and with another girl living in the same room there couldn't be much funny stuff going on.

"My brother Lou; Muriel Dillon, my roommate," Estelle said gracefully. The girl wore a dark woolen dress, and looked like she didn't monkey around much.

She went over and picked up a book. "Don't mind me," she said, in a musical voice.

Thirty-five bucks apiece for rent, he figured. Estelle had told him she was making twenty-five a week, but girls didn't eat much, and fellows were always taking them out to dinner.

---

[1] "The President's Daughter" was a scandalous 1927 book about Warren G. Harding, president from 1921-1923. The author, Nan Britton, claimed that Harding had fathered her illegitimate daughter in 1919 while Harding was a Senator.

Estelle looked different here than when she came home on Sundays, looked like another kind of person, surer of herself, an adult. Why not? She was twenty-five. Twenty-five used to mean an old maid. Looking at her and her roommate, Lou couldn't figure out whether they did or didn't, yet he had an idea they knew what it was all about. Yah, bet they could tell him a few, living home all his life.

"Gosh, Lou, you're getting fat," Estelle said. It was a fact. He had to leave his top shirt-button open, under the tie.

"It's about ma," he said bluntly, though he felt he ought to be roundabout. "Honest, I think she's going nuts."

Muriel put down the book and walked across the room. "I think I'll run over and see Del," she said. "So long. Be good."

Estelle looked at her gratefully. "I'll tell Rodge to get you there if he calls."

When the roommate was gone, the embarrassment between brother and sister was even greater.

". . . and men, if you want the latest scientific discovery in razor blades . . ."

Estelle snapped off the radio. "Well?"

"Yesterday she tried to kill herself," Lou blurted.

Estelle's eyes popped.

"I tried to call you up but there was nobody home. Then it was all over, so I thought it was no use getting you."

"But what did she do? Why didn't you—why—?"

He floundered, ashamed to tell even her of their rotten home life, for she was now outside of it.

"I came home and found her on the bed. She took some poison."

"What did she take? Maybe it was an accident."

"She took some sleeping tablets. She took six, that was all there was, a couple more would've killed her."

"Oh."

"I called Rudy Stone and he fixed her up; he gave her something. He said to keep all that kind of stuff, iodine and everything, locked up."

"What did pa do?"

"He came home when it was all over. She wouldn't talk to him."

"Oh, for cry sake!" Estelle paced the room. "What's wrong with her life! She has it easy enough now! What does she want to do things like that for!"

"She's going nuts," Lou said. "She's got all kinds of ideas about pa. She makes it hell for him. You know he's always stayed late working and now he's got that little shop he stays there all the time, he just likes to sit there I guess, he hates to come home. He don't even come home to eat. She's got nothing to do."

"Well, why doesn't she go out and enjoy herself, go to the movies, play bridge . . . ?" but Estelle knew the answer, and almost emitted a bitter laugh at the picture of her mother "becoming a Yankee in her old age" and playing bridge!

"She doesn't even talk to anybody around there," Lou continued glumly; "she sits by herself all the time. She got an idea the old man is running around with chickens."

Estelle snorted.

"She's liable to poison him too."

Estelle looked at her brother's lumpy, serious face, the bloodless lips open. "You know what it is?" she said. "I bet she's having her change of life."

"Huh?"

"Are you dumb!"

"Oh," Lou smirked, catching on it was something about females. "She wasn't so bad last summer when you lived home, it gave her something to do," he said. "The main trouble is she sits around with nothing to do."

"Listen, I'm not going to sacrifice myself to give her a vicarious kick out of life," Estelle said, even then noticing how impressed he was with the fancy word she had caught from the crowd she hung out with. "So far as I'm concerned, I'm through with her. She thought she was going to run my life and tell me who to go with, she was so narrow-minded I couldn't even bring a decent fellow home if he happened to be a *sheigetz*, and I'm through. If she hasn't got enough gumption to get along with herself, I can't help it!"

"Yah," he said. "Sure. Only I don't know. I'm scared. Y' can't tell what she's gonna do."

There seemed to be nothing more for them to say to each other.

Lou stared at a photograph on the desk.

"Is that the new boy friend?"

"New! I've been going with him over a year. Isn't he cute?"

"Yah, he looks all right. Say, your old boy friend is getting his name in the papers. Did you see all about that shooting he had in the street? It was on the front page."

"Oh, you mean Solly Meisel. All he needed was to get mixed up with gangs. That dumbbell will get himself bumped off yet, and it won't be any loss to humanity, either."

"I saw him in the last six-day bike race," Lou said. "He didn't come out so good. He had to quit on the fifth day."

Estelle didn't seem at all interested. "Well, I gotta be going, I got to bone up for the bar exam," he said.

"What's the matter, can't they give that bar exam without you taking it?" she rasped.

"Aw, I didn't even take it last year. I dunno if I wanna pass anyway. I'm doing all right the way it is."

She gave him an exasperated glare. "Go on, be a process server all your life!" Suddenly she went at him. "Why don't you do something! Laying around year after year! Why don't you move out and live your own life?"

"Aw!" he said.

"I bet you haven't even got a girl!"

"Aw," he squirmed, "she makes me sick, if I move out she'll go crazy, sure, all by herself!"

Estelle took a deep puff, and exhaled, giving up the case. She reached over and turned on the radio.

"... love, baby ..."

Weekends, Muriel went home to Wheaton. On Saturday nights there was always a party with Howie's crowd, they were a broad-minded bunch, very sophisticated, practically all college graduates except herself, but there wasn't much got past her now. They always assembled in the studio apartment of Mac Hurst, a bond salesman who liked to act like a drunken reporter. As soon as he got tight he would crush a soft hat aslant over one eye, grab the telephone, and call up numbers picked at random out of the phone book. The whole party would gather around him while he imitated the reporter in *Front Page* and asked: "Lady, is it true that you have just been raped by a Peeping Tom?" Mac had a swell collection of dirty records and they would play them all, everybody waiting to hear Bessie Smith singing "Empty Bed Blues." Then everybody would yell for Estelle and Howie to sing "Frankie and Johnny"; they had it down so it was a scream. Especially when he flopped on the floor and she put her foot on his head and growled: "He was mah maaaan, but he du-hun me wrrrrrrong!"

And when the party was real hot they would take turns singing dirty limericks, and all join in the refrain. She always contributed the one about the Young Girl from Detroit who was so very adroit.

Then after the party she and Howie would come home here, having the place all to themselves. And what she loved was making those big Sunday morning breakfasts for the two of them, invariably ham and eggs, after playing around in bed till one o'clock. Then the sleepy Sunday afternoons, while they slowly read both Sunday papers, Howie always grabbing Moon Mullins first, and moaning because there was no more Old Doc Yak.

Muriel would come home from Wheaton and find them cozy, like that. She was broad-minded.

Once Howie said: "Say, Muriel ain't so bad-looking when she takes her glasses off," and they put their heads together scheming to get a boy friend for Muriel. Finally Howie brought around a pal of his, Clarence Akers, known as Akey, and from then on they went out on foursomes. It was like growing closer together with Howie, getting away from the noisy Saturday night crowd.

Muriel never wore her glasses when she went out. She rarely went home to Wheaton now. The four of them went out often, eating dinner in A Bit of Sweden, where the appetizers were all on a big table and you filled your plate so high you couldn't eat the dinner when it came, and other cute places to eat, and they all went to see a sexy actress, Mae West, that was put in jail in New York, she was acting in *Diamond Lil*, and the boys threw pennies on the stage. Howie and Muriel were always getting into side discussions about when they were kids, comparing their towns and having the same jokes about ministers and churches, which Estelle could never quite appreciate.

And then you couldn't tell exactly which fellow was with which girl.

Oh, Estelle saw it from the beginning, and had to laugh at herself in the old tragedy: her roommate stealing her man.

Then there was the party where they got into a discussion of different nationalities, and how strict they were with their girls.

"One thing you never want to get mixed up with is a Polack," Mac Hurst said. "Boy, I tried to make a Polish girl in the office once, and honest to Pete if the old man didn't come down with a shotgun . . ." He had them rolling on the floor.

"Well, give me the Irish," Akey said. "They're broad-minded."

The Irish girls present roared with laughter.

"But not the Catholics," Mac reminded him. "If she's Catholic, watch out, boy, or you'll be standing before the priest in jigtime."

"How about Jewish girls?" someone said.

"Jewish girls are the hardest to make," Howie piped up, "but once you make them, oh, boy!"

Estelle knew he didn't mean a thing. It was all in conversation. But a little silence had fallen on the room. It was the other girls who were creating the feeling, she knew. Cats.

Why, by this time she had practically forgotten she was the only Jewish girl in the crowd, and so had everybody else.

Howie gave her a reassuring squeeze under the breast.

"Oh, she was just a farmer's daughter . . ." Mac tactfully began to sing.

Then there was the Saturday when Muriel said she was going to Wheaton, and Howie didn't call. Estelle sat and waited, didn't go out to eat, just ate a few chocolates for supper. And the blasted radio, every time she tried it, had some deep blues singer groaning:

> "For like caressing
> An empty glove . . ."

Looking in Muriel's dresser drawer she found Muriel's glasses, and had a fit. Wheaton, huh! Then she grabbed Howie's picture and was going to tear it up but couldn't get it out of the frame.

She decided she would pack up and move. She would put some nasty note under the glasses. Like: "Next time you go out with my boy friend, dearie, don't forget your glasses." She actually pulled out a suitcase and threw open the lid.

But the sight of the empty, waiting suitcase broke her down. It was just like her heart, she thought, so empty. Two years, and what had it all amounted to? Just two years crossed out of her life, for a few Saturday night brawls. Oh, didn't we have fun! Here she was, twenty-five, and all the girls she had gone with were married, some even had babies. . . .

Alone, aging, an old maid; for a wild moment she thought of drinking iodine. Then she remembered about her mother, and gasped at herself, seeing herself becoming just like her mother.

She stuck her face close to the mirror, and thought she made out wrinkles forming around her eyes, that was where they came first. She pulled on her cheeks, to see if they were sagging, if they still had resilience, but this made her look so comical she had to laugh. She sat on the edge of the bathtub and laughed out loud. So he wanted to go back to his *shikseh*! Let him, the bum! Let him go and lay dishrag Muriel! Ishkabibble!

> When you get good lovin'
> Don't ever spread the news,
> The other gals will steal him
> And leave you with the empty bed blues.

She flopped on the bed.

The phone rang. It was Akey. Wanting to come over.

And now Estelle began to see the thing clearly. Before Howie, there had been that fellow Dickie. And hadn't Dickie introduced her to Howie? Just before he got married, too.

So that was what she was.

Let him come, that Akey. She'd show him about Jewish girls.

A Pillow of Stone[2]

When Estelle heard Sol's voice on the phone it made her feel as though no years had gone by at all. Here she was living at home again and her old boy friend on the line.

"Bet you can't tell who this is!" Sol taunted.

"Oh, how could I ever forget you!" Estelle responded.

They made a date.

---

[2] A reference to the patriarch Jacob's Pillow of Stone. See Genesis 28. Jacob flees the wrath of his brother Esau, and, as darkness falls, gathers stones as pillows. He dreams of Jacob's Ladder, and awakens to declare the sanctity of God and heaven. The site, Bet-El ("House of God"), becomes a symbol of national and religious schism.

Coming home from work, Estelle found that her mother had taken out her new long-in-back Nile-green formal, ironed it, and laid it on the bed. All silently, without a word. The crazy.

Lately, she had taken the role of servant altogether upon herself. She spent her whole time alone in the kitchen, coming out only to work for them. She had even placed a cot in the kitchen, and there she slept. At meals, she would bring their food to the table, and retreat.

When there was something of which she had to speak, Mrs. Green addressed them impersonally, in Yiddish. This evening she spoke.

"That Sol Meisel is turning out to be a worthy young man. He gives his mother and father everything of the best. She sits like a queen in a big flat on Independence Boulevard, that Mrs. Meisel from Sixteenth Street! He did well with his bicycle riding in spite of what everyone predicted, and now, like a sensible man, he has put his money into a business. He owns a fine cleaning factory. What more could a girl want in a man for a husband? I wouldn't wish my own daughter worse. They say he ran around with loose women, but here in America what can one expect of the best men? Only the worst. It is better that a man should appease his appetite for such filth when he is young than, instead of like some men, when he creaks so that he can hardly lift himself onto the bed of debauchery."

Mr. Green bent to his food.

"One knows, one knows what is going on!" she insinuated. Then, softer: "By now this Sol Meisel has learned that the tricks of one whore are no better than the tricks of another, and most likely he is ready to marry. A girl who knew what she was doing could get married to him. For my daughter I would like to see a life better than I had myself, though she doesn't deserve it. Let her at least marry someone with money, that she may not drag out her days in a dark rear flat, haggling with butchers." Again she turned her scathing words upon her husband. "Though he has a shop of his own now and both children are working, God knows what he does with his money; he spends it on whores!"

Lou giggled nervously. Estelle put down her fork. "All right, all right, ma. For a long time it has been quiet here. You know by now I can take care of myself."

"He isn't a millionaire yet," Mr. Green remarked. "Sol Meisel is having a lot of trouble with gangsters in his racket."

"Do you think I blame them, the gangsters!" Mrs. Green cried, continuing in Yiddish against their English. "In America, all are gangsters. I would a thousand times rather deal with a gangster, with his gun. What can he do, shoot me? What is death! It would be welcome! Better than to live my life with an innocent-faced sneak who would stick a knife in your back!"

Mr. Green's spoon splashed as he dropped it in his soup. "What do you want of me!" he cried, returning to Yiddish. "What insanities have you got in your head! I slaved all my life, I raised children for you, I brought every nickel to the house, denying myself a package of cigarettes! Why are you embittering my last years! How do you expect a man to come home to a cursing spout that throws hot coals on his head day and night!" he screeched, waving his trembling hands. They had never seen their father like this.

"He complains! He is the one to complain!" the mother screamed.

"Yes! I! Who else! Look at yourself! What is lacking to you! A home! Your children grown! Nothing to do but sit all day! Look at yourself!"

The children stared at their mother, seeing her with the discovery of the too familiar. Her hair, gray-clotted, stuck out in irregular clumps from a careless knot, a sloppy edge of petticoat showed under her housedress, one stocking was half down, wrinkled; she shuffled about in ragged house slippers. Her skin was pallid, dry; her figure had shrunken to that of an old woman.

"Yes! look at me! This is what you have done to me! Is the old scarecrow lacking in beauty for you? My greenhorn Yiddish is not stylish enough for you! Go, go to the parlors, my beau, perhaps you will find your own daughter there, for a dollar!"

"Oh, ma, oh, that's enough!" Estelle cried.

"Stop it, for cry eye, for cry eye," Lou burbled incoherently.

"A herd of wild pigs! Go wallow in the slime together, wallow!" Mrs. Green rushed into the kitchen.

"Stop her, she'll do something!" Lou shouted.

The father stood biting his lips, preventing himself from saying that he hoped she would. Then he took his hat, sadly, and went to the door.

"He is going! Going!" Mrs. Green shrieked, rushing out of the kitchen. "Go, devil! Go to your bitches!" She stepped to the table and seized the breadknife.

All three seemed paralyzed. The yellowish shine of her eyes held them, more than the flat gray streak of the blade.

Estelle jumped up and caught her mother's arm.

"Well, so you think I am insane?" Mrs. Green said calmly, letting go of the knife.

Mr. Green, with a squeaky, hopeless sound, slid out of the house.

Lou came morosely into Estelle's room, while she was dressing. "Dya think she ought to be sent away?" he said.

Estelle shrugged. "How could we do it, even if she needed it?"

"Yah, I guess those joints are expensive."

"I can't understand how she got that way," Estelle said. And yet she could understand. It went all the way back. But all women of poor families didn't go crazy. Who knew how many, or how close they got, sometimes? "We weren't so poor," she thought. And then: "Well, the trouble was we were always running with a crowd that was better off than we." And of her mother: "She never fitted in. She never even learned English."

To her brother, Estelle said: "I think she's got an inferiority complex," feeling the feebleness of the glib term.

"Yah," Lou said. "Maybe the old man ought to stay somewhere else? For a while?"

"That's an idea," Estelle said. She wanted to get out of it all, be safe, get married maybe.

Yah, marriage . . .!

"Gee, kiddo, you look swell, say, you ain't changed a bit," Sol said.

"What did you expect me to look like?" she challenged.

"Well, I thought maybe you was a peroxide blonde by now, hah hah."

"Think that'd be an improvement?" She gave him an opening.

"Well, you know, gentlemen prefer blondes," he hawed. "But I'm no gentleman!"

The dope seemed really glad to see her. He was actually blushing, and he squeezed her hand.

"Well, you haven't changed much either," Estelle said. "You look about the same, only a little heavier."

"Say, I'm way out of training. All I do is eat. I got so many business headaches I figure at least one thing, I can eat all I want, and I eat."

He held the car door open for her, like a gentleman.

So he probably figured she would fall in love with him all over again, as girls are supposed to love their first sweethearts. Lovers, she corrected her thought.

"Well, how they been treating you? Jeez, I thought you'd be married and everything by now, everybody got married," he said. He kept staring at her with sparkling eyes. Estelle was pleased at his surprise in finding her still so desirable. Mygod, she was only twenty-five!

"Aw, Jeez, a guy doesn't know when he's well off." All through the drive to the Stevens, he kept spilling a long harangue at her about his big gun-fight, yah, right on Crawford Avenue.

"So now I'm paying this Pinkerton Agency to catch those hoodlums that tried to hijack my truck, see, if I ever nab them! Oh, boy! Cost me five hundred already . . ."

She cupped her chin on her hands and stared at him across the table. He certainly would be easy to take.

As they danced, Estelle could feel him sniffing at her; almost immediately he pressed his body intimately against her. So he thought she was going to be a pushover? By what rules did a fellow think that once he had slept with a girl he could have her any time he wanted! She drew slightly away.

"Hey, Estelle," he blurted, "you're not sore at me or anything, are you?"

"Why should I be sore at you?"

"Aw, you know, I guess I was a dumb kid, huh? Let bygones be bygones, huh?"

"Sure." She restrained herself from laughing. "As Howie, a friend of mine, says, what's a past or two between friends?"

"Say! Who is this Howie!" he bit. Was he dumb!

"Oh, a friend of mine."

"A particular friend?"

She shrugged. "I'm particular of all my friends."

So finally he had talked himself out. And it was one o'clock. Estelle waited, with an inward smile, for his proposition. There was always this delicious pause, waiting for a fellow to play his tricks. Would he try to get her to a hotel, or did he have a place all laid out in advance, confident he could make her? And a girl knowing her own answer all the time, saw every move of the fellow's as comical.

His arm around her, he drove down Jackson and stopped at the Graemere.

"Uh uh," she said.

"Aw, come on up for a minute. I wanna show you, I got a doggy little apartment here. Say, this place is just as swell as the Edgewater."

"Uh uh." She put her hand on the shift lever.

"Say, Estelle, I thought we were gonna be friends again . . ."

"Sure, but you got big ideas."

He looked into her face, with doggish eyes. "What's the matter, don't you like me any more?"

"Sure, I like you." She felt his body, chunky and appetizing, appealing to her. "But what kind of a girl do you think I am?" she said.

She watched bewilderment flooding his face. That was one swell thing about being a girl. You did anything you pleased, and the next day, if you pleased, you were a virgin again. The nitwits that were afraid of their "reputations"!

"Well, gee, Estelle," he said. "We both been around. I mean, we know what it's all about, you and me." Suddenly he enveloped her and gave her a biting kiss. She came out of it, smiling at him with a cool, womanly smile.

"We don't want it to be like this," she said, touching his hand. "Take me home now, Speedy."

He was beginning to look at her with that different look. Obediently, he drove her home.

The fourth date, she went up to his place and had a drink, but made him take her home.

The next time, she could tell he was hardly even hoping. They went to Agostino's and had a big spaghetti dinner, and the wine spread through her body giving her a swell lazy feeling, and she thought: it's months and months.

"Hey, I'm celebrating." Sol told her some endless story about fixing it up with the union.

So they went up to his place, and she stretched on the couch, feeling so warm in her belly, and sleepily sexy; and when his arm went around her she guided his fingers to the snaps of her dress.

Sol got all excited, clumsy, nearly tearing her dress apart. Lucky she was only wearing that rayon underwear, as he might have ruined her best Italian silk.

"Gee, Estelle, I'm nuts about you, you were always the one for me," he blurted.

She was curious to discover that she had no feeling for him at all. That idea about the first man had been crawling into her lately, but now she was rid of that too.

He was getting kind of squashy around the waist, but his legs were still tough and swell. She studied them, tracing her fingers along the scars where track-splinters had been extracted. There was one awfully long gash above his left knee. And he made her feel where his collar-bone had been broken, in a spill in Detroit.

"Aw, gee, what's the rush, honey?" he pleaded as she got up. "Aw."

"I'm tired," she said. "I don't want to fall asleep here, mister."

"Aw, babe, that's just what you ought to do. Gee, I'd like to wake up next to you in the morning. Aw, I mean it serious, Estelle, I was a punk before and I gummed up the whole business, I guess, but I mean it now, let's do it right. I don't want to gum it up again, I mean, you make me feel different, you make me feel like you're the real woman for me."

Poor kid, he seemed so terribly lonesome and aching to come home, just like herself sometimes.

She brushed her hand over his hair. He quivered toward her.

"I mean, the way it is I've got to have someone," he said. "We ain't kids any more. You know, Estelle, a guy goes on and on and then he wakes up and he ain't a kid, and he's out all by himself. Gosh, Estelle, sometimes I feel terrible all by myself. Say, how about it, you and me, huh?"

She felt sorry now that she had started the whole thing, that she had let it go so far. He was so sweet and helpless. "Is this a proposal?" she said.

"Well, you know, sure, why not? That's what I mean. We could even get hitched."

She brushed his hair again. "No," she said slowly.

"Aw, what's the matter? I'll do anything for you! I'll give you anything. I've got to have you, Estelle."

"Oh, we wouldn't get along any more, Sol. We're different kinds of people now."

"Don't you care for me? Don't I mean anything to you? What we did just now?"

"I was just curious, that's all," she said.

The poor kid seemed to shrink into himself, bewildered. He didn't even try to say any more. He got up and dressed to take her home.

Maybe way back and for a long time she had wanted a kind of revenge on Sol, for the way he had knocked her up and walked out on her that time. Or maybe she had started this affair with an idea of marriage; but if he was dumb he wasn't dumb enough. He was too real a guy. And she couldn't see herself married to him with his headaches about his cleaning business and his endless bragging about that time on Crawford Avenue. All of a sudden there, when he was wolfishly repossessing her, she had found her honesty again. What the heck, let the old man and old lady figure out their lives for themselves. No use ruining a couple more lives to help them into their graves.

At the door, she pressed Sol's hand in a friendly, nice-girl farewell. "So long," he said. He grabbed her and kissed her but seemed to realize that didn't work with her any more.

"Well, I'll be suing you," he said.

"Yah. Call me up some time," she responded.

Maybe she would be sorry as hell for passing up a chance like this, some day.

In a Land of Love It Seems

The day began like any other day, with Mort honking impatiently while the old man hunted all over the frontroom for his cigarettes, and when they finally got started, with Mrs. Abramson cautioning Mort to "have a heart, if you have to read the newspaper, driving, wait at least until there is a stoplight." And Sylvia, soothing her mother with "oh, look, this is so cute, Skeezix bought a top for his new baby brother. And Walt says, the baby's too young for a top. So Skeezix says, I know it, I'll use it for him till he's big enough! Isn't that cute!"

"Say, did she have the baby already?" Mort said.

"Sure, you're behind the times. It's almost a week old. It weighed eight and a half pounds," Sylvia informed him.

"Some racketeers broke a dentist's finger because he wouldn't join a dentists' association," Mr. Abramson reported from the paper.

"It's getting terrible!" Mrs. Abramson said. "What those gangsters did to the Meisels, they had a fight, with pistols, in the street, and now they have to pay drivers double to go out on their wagons."

"They should only keep away from the millinery business," Mrs. Abramson prayed.

"Whataya think, there aren't enough racketeers in it already?" Mort grinned, sliding through a light on the yellow.

"Even my shoemaker told me he has to pay three dollars a month or they break his windows! A poor shoemaker!" Mrs. Abramson complained.

Mr. Abramson remarked: "It was better by the tsar. There you knew you have to pay the government graft, you *schmeered* the police, and you were finished. But here, *eey* the government, *eey* taxes, *eey* police, and then you only have to begin to pay out to the gangsters!"

They dropped Sylvia at the social service bureau on Wood Street, Mrs. Abramson remarking, as usual, that she didn't like the idea of Sylvia working in such a neighborhood.

"Well, why don't she get married, so she'll have enough to do?" Mr. Abramson said.

"Why? She don't tell me anything," Mrs. Abramson worried. "Ever since she broke up with Joe. I don't even know for sure if she broke up with him. I think maybe she is still in love with him."

"They broke up," Mort said tersely. "Mitch is the better guy for her any day."

"I got nothing against Joe," Mrs. Abramson said. "Only I have to admit, Mitch is a person that seems more human. More like somebody you could have in the family."

"Well, he's still got to finish interne," Mort said.

"We could help them get started," Mrs. Abramson said. "I hear he is the smartest boy in his class."

"This neighborhood certainly has gone to the dogs," Mort observed as they continued down Taylor Street and passed the decaying buildings of the old Jewish People's Institute. Great patches of concrete shell had fallen off the wall of the gymnasium that he, as a kid, had always spoken of as "the new building."

"Ach, those Italians, how they ruined this neighborhood," Mrs. Abramson complained, looking out at the streets littered with empty boxes and rotten vegetables. "They are so dirty, so poor, phew!" she commented on the odor of their streets.

"The J.P.I. is moving to that new building on Douglas Boulevard," Mort said. He was thinking of joining the dramatic club there. The J.P.I. had always won the city dramatic club tournaments.

"What do you think, Lawndale won't be like this in a couple of years?" Abramson predicted. "Dagoes are moving in already, on Grenshaw and on California Avenue. And after them comes the niggers. Ach, it will be the same thing."

And, as on every morning, they fell to discussing the wisdom of selling the house and buying on the North Side, where the better class of people were moving. As they neared the shop, Mort mentioned that Schweitzer, the Milwaukee jobber, wanted a lot of stuff and Turek had heard he wasn't such a good credit risk any more. "What! Schweitzer! He is the biggest house in Milwaukee!" "He was, you mean. What does anybody need jobbers for? Everybody sells direct to the stores now. The turnover is too quick." "Well, don't worry, Schweitzer is good for it." Mort dropped them at the factory, and started downtown. With inner satisfaction Mort remembered that first time he had sold Schweitzer, in Milwaukee, and how that pig had bulldozed him. He fell to humming:

"Gee, I like to see you looking swell, baby . . ."

and turned down Lake Street, where there were fewer stoplights.—Have to take Syl to see *Good News*.

From the time when he rushed out of the Celia Moscowitz wedding feeling broken-hearted, things began to pick up for Joe Freedman. There was the day when he was visiting the Midway studios gassing with Indiana, and happened to answer the phone. It was a long-distance call from Flint, Michigan.

"I wanna talk to Professor Norcross," a voice boomed.

"Sorry, he's away on a lecture tour," Joe said.

"Well, this is Sewell Rider of the Viking Motor Car Company!"

"Can I do anything for you?" Joe modulated his voice.

"Any other sculptors there? You a sculptor?"

"Yes, I'm a sculptor."

Joe heard a mumbled conference. Then: "Look here, we're after a gadget to go on a radiator cap. Gotta look speedy, and plenty of class. Like some of those foreign cars got."

"Oh, I see," Joe responded quickly. "Why don't you use a Viking? Or one of those stylized birds, like they had on the prows of their boats?"

He heard Mr. Rider say: "Yah, this guy is full of ideas." And to him: "Say, could you hop on a train . . .?"

Joe got five hundred bucks for two days of work and five days of conference, which produced a Viking in a breech clout and a sort of winged football helmet, posed like a shot-putter. It had a nice horizontal line, and a Rockwell Kentish smoothness, and it looked okay springing nickelplated from the radiator of a Viking car.

"Pretty good for answering the phone," he said.

Indiana had just got himself a job carving decorative panels for the elevators of the Palmolive Building, that was going up near the Drake Hotel. "Go see those guys, they're lousy with dough," Indiana said, and Joe landed a job making twelve-inch figurines to grace the shop-doors.

One thousand berries.

He wondered if Sylvia heard he was making money now. If he had got this start last year . . . No, it wasn't exactly money that had failed them.

Joe moved to a studio above an old coachhouse, off Michigan Avenue.

Joe and Indiana gave wild open-house studio parties on Saturday nights, at which everybody got drunk on gin and Italian wine, and sang dirty limericks to "Sweet Violets," and Joe wondered if Sylvia was hearing about his parties; he made a couple of girls, and lived with a girl named Edna, and bust up when it got too serious. And one of the party hounds worked for a stockbroker, and made Joe six hundred dollars on margin on General Motors. He set up a big figure again, so people wouldn't always be asking him if he was doing any sculpture; struggle as he would, the figure seemed to retain an inherent slickness; he even gave it a broken surface *à la* Epstein, but it still looked like a colossal radiator cap.

Then one morning Joe got a letter advising him that he had received a Guggenheim fellowship. It was on the basis of that figure he had wanted to smash, last year.

Joe sat at the phone. He had not called that number for months, and he had used to call it almost every day. When the new phone book had come out, like an idiot he had looked to see if her number was still there. But if it was news of his success that brought her back, he would only despise her.

The hell with Chicago, he was through. What was there here anyway? If he ever came back to the States, he'd be an established artist, and live in New York.

Indiana came in and jumped all over him, and a big celebration party was set.

All day, all evening, Joe expected some token from Sylvia, expected someone to come in and mention that she was engaged, married. Some touch of her always came on big days for him. A crazy superstition! Yet when people started coming to the party, strangers, anybody, Joe expected every time the door opened to see Sylvia and Mitch with some gang, not knowing to whose place they were coming.

Leaving the party, he walked down Michigan, paused to look at the art books on display in Kroch's window—he would buy a swell collection in Europe—and all the time he knew he might pass Orchestra Hall just as the symphony let out. The bunch all went there on Saturday nights.

Joe was on the corner of State and Jackson when he saw Mitch Wilner and Sylvia crossing the street, coming toward him. They were laughing about something.

He felt his heart actually leap. "That's what it does, it leaps," he said to himself. Like a caught fish.

They were coming right toward him. His muscles were constricted across his chest, and he felt a little dizzy. He walked toward the newsstand, as if he had been about to get a Sunday paper. He would let them say the first "hello."

Then they had passed, within touching distance. So completely absorbed in each other that they hadn't even seen him!

Joe stared after them. They began a game, Sylvia running ahead, and Mitch catching her.

A bus came along, and they let it pass. On the other side of Jackson, Joe walked along, keeping them in sight. "Me, the disappointed lover, lurking in the shadows," he kidded himself, and yet why did such a meeting have to happen on this day?

As the couple passed the dark block of the post office they stopped and leaned against each other. Good subject for a figure, he thought, call it *The Neckers*; not like Paris lovers frankly kissing in the street, but still with that hiding quality, that furtive uncertainty of Americans in everything.

Joe followed them to Wells Street. There, they finally got on a bus. He thought of grabbing a taxi, pursuing—what for? To see how long they necked in the hallway?

He came to the bridge, and laughed at himself, broken-hearted lover jumps in the river. Adolescent frustration, that's all it was. . . . But why did he have to see her like that today? Why today?

Aw, pick up a punk on the bridge and get it out of your system.

He leaned on the rail and looked at the Daily News Building, a swell monumental setback job, and at the Opera Building across the river, racing to completion; he studied a few barge lights in the river. He told himself he had known he would get this.

A guy had to rid himself of the idea of woman, sweet woman, as the reward for deserving man. Sure, it was a magazine-story idea, a Sunday-school idea—where had he ever gone to Sunday school? And yet those ideas crawled into you, they permeated American life: The better the man, the more beautiful, the sweeter the woman, his reward.

You're a better man than I am, Gunga Din!

Gazing down now, into the Chicago River, Joe saw himself and Mitch as two swimmers in this mucky stream of life, and oddly remembered that time long ago when they were kids and had gone to Benton Harbor for a vacation, and how scared and impressed he had been with Mitch Wilner's feat of swimming a mile.

A doctor. That was a Sunday-school idea too, only in this case the Sunday school was the Jewish home; from childhood, the propaganda was there. A Jew's highest vocation was to become a learned doctor.

Why, right in his own home, now, that virtue was in bloom. His sister was marrying a doctor. And the family, and Aline, exuded satisfaction; she had done the best that any Jewish girl could do.

Were Rudy and Aline in love? Here were his sister and a fellow whom he had known since a kid, and yet Joe felt he didn't know the first thing about them.

Were Syl and Mitch the same as Rudy and Aline?

Mitch was on duty in pediatrics when Joe came around to say good-by. "Gee, you old Turk, haven't seen you in a dog's age!" He wrung Joe's hand.

Joe's face was strained, he noticed. Must be the excitement; a twenty-five hundred dollar fellowship was nothing to sneeze at. Boy, who wouldn't be excited! "Say, I'm glad to hear about that Guggenheim, Joe, old boy, I knew you'd make it some day!" he said warmly.

"Thanks," Joe said.

Mitch looked into the examining room, for a place to talk. Curly Seabury was there, phoning a date. "You remember Curly, don't you? He was at school," Mitch reminded Joe. "Say, Curly, this bum has just copped a Guggenheim fellowship!"

"Hayah! Congratulations!" Curly gripped Joe's palm.

Mitch sat on the metal examining table. "Gee, I'd like to be able to get over there!" he said. "Vienna."

"Why don't you come over for a year? You'll be through here soon, what are your plans?" Joe asked. His voice seemed oddly strident.

Well, who wouldn't be excited? Mitch imagined being along with Joe in gay Vienna. "But I couldn't ask my old man for another year," he concluded. "Have to start earning a living some time."

The way Joe was staring at him Mitch couldn't think of anything else to say. "I bet Sylvia was tickled to hear the news," he ventured.

"I haven't told her," Joe said.

Mitch couldn't understand that. He thought Sylvia and Joe had intelligently decided they were not in love, but surely they were still friends. Joe always had been a complicated, emotional cuss, an artist. "When are you planning to go?" Mitch asked.

"In a couple of days."

Joe's stare began to bother him.

Funny, he and Joe had always been such pals, and still were, really, but for the moment things seemed to have gone dead. Maybe it was because it was a parting, and a stranger was in the room.

"Where you taking her, Curly?"

"See Gulloria Svenson in *Sadie Thompson*."

"That ought to get her hotted up."

Curly winked a wicked eye, and went off to dress.

"Don't do anything I wouldn't do," Mitch said.

"Aw, can't I at least hold her hand?" Curly shot back.

"Who's he going out with, a nurse?" asked Joe.

"No, this is some girl he's been going with since he was a kid. He wants to get hitched."

"Well, what's wrong with that?" Joe seemed belligerent.

Mitch shrugged. "Oh, I guess it's all right for him, his old man has a practice to turn over to him."

"Well, is a fellow expected to wait forever 'cause he's a medico?" Joe said. "How about yourself?"

"Say, women mean nothing in my life, I got things to do!" He filled in: "They got the right idea where you're going. Paris. Oh, boy!"

"What about all these nurses?" Joe smirked.

"Aw, that's just a lot of bull," Mitch laughed. "Of course there are a couple of fellows that monkey around but most of the time we're too busy and tired. Anyway, who wants a dose?"

"From a nurse?"

Mitch still couldn't figure what Joe was getting at. So he told a funny one about a new interne, Swaboda. How the boys fixed him up with one of the easy nurses, and gave him a terrible scare the next morning. "Curly told him, try some iodine, maybe it's not too late. So Swaby rushes into the can and sticks it in a bath of iodine! God, he was howling for a week! He's still walking bow-legged!" Mitch laughed.

"Aren't some of the internes married?" Joe persisted. Why was he so curious all of a sudden? "That's the best way for a doc to wreck his career, early marriage," Mitch replied. "Unless the girl has dough. Anyway I got a couple of years to go before I get set and begin to think of such foolishness."

"A couple of years, huh?" Joe repeated, with a peculiar smile, adding: "Say, did you ever take them up about going to Rochester?"

"That's a pretty hard joint to get into," Mitch said. "One thing, they take very few Hebes. But if you're a top man they just about can't refuse you and if I can get just a few more breaks . . ."

"That sounds swell," Joe said. "Though it would mean another couple of years, wouldn't it?"

"Yep," Mitch said cheerfully.

He saw a cockroach skittering across the floor, and squashed it. "You ought to see the rats," he laughed. "We never have a shortage of lab animals." He kept on talking. "I'll be glad to get out of this dump. Though one thing I can say for it. When you've interned here you've seen everything. The other day they had a case up in the men's contagious, amœbic dysentery, that's a tropical disease, I'd probably never have been able to recognize it if I'd interned anywhere else."

Joe still eyed him, measured him with that funny look. Only at that moment, Mitch got the idea that Joe might be jealous because he was seeing a lot of Sylvia. But, heck, Syl was just his night-off date! It would be years before he could think of marriage.

It was a relief just then to have to take care of a patient.

A woman's blubbering could be heard as the nurse opened the door. It was a small Negro woman lugging a child almost as large as herself. Swaboda shepherded her into the room.

"Put him down, he can still walk," Swaboda said, with a patiently exasperated expression.

The woman continued to hold the kid, who looked ten years old. Her eyes were a frightened animal's.

Mitch slid off the table. Swaboda handed him the case history, as the Negro woman spluttered: "Oh, I seen this comin'! He's just my first-born boy! He ain't gonna pass away! He ain't no call to pass away!"

"That's all right, we'll do the best we can," Mitch was trying to say calmly, as the woman finally yielded the boy to the nurse. He glanced through the history. Fever, and the shakes.

"Looks funny to me," Swaboda offered. "Maybe you better get out the old needle."

Mitch noticed a piece of adhesive on the child's left hand. "Tetanus?" he ventured dubiously.

"One cigar," Swaboda said.

Mitch took hold of the hand. The child raised terrified eyes and let out a gasping grunt as the adhesive was pulled off. There was a livid new scar across the palm.

"How did this happen?" he asked.

A hit-and-run driver had knocked the kid down, when he was on his way to school. "He's been all right, docta, they stitched up his little hand and he's been fine, he's been in good health till las' Monday, docta."

And then she told her pitiable tale. The child got feverish, and she had brought him to the hospital. But in the admission room downstairs they had asked her: " 'Who you vote for?' 'Vote for? I dunno,' I says. They told me take my chile home and put him to bed, ain't nothing wrong with him, he jest got a cold. 'Next time you come here, bring a letter from the boss,' they says downstairs. 'What boss, I dunno no boss . . .!' "

"If it's not a serious case, they make them bring a letter from their ward boss, showing they voted right, before they give them a bed," Mitch remarked to Joe.

The woman sang her grief: "I took him home and that poor chile gets worse and worse. This morning he got the shivers bad. I don't know no boss. You goin' take care of my chile, docta, you ain't goin' let him die?"

The nurse was undressing the child. Under his coat was a sweater, all holes. The mother made a little rush as if to stop them from stripping him to his torn underwear.

"Tetanus, all right," Mitch said to Joe. "Those lugs downstairs should have sent him up last Monday; but it's pretty hard to recognize in the early stages. Well, we may still be in time."

The kid had a stringy sort of body, the color of coffee with milk.

"How much you going to give him?" Swaboda said, handling the squat bottle of antitoxin.

They sat the kid up on the table. Suddenly his body seemed to tighten into itself, and vibrate, as though every muscle was pulling against its balancing muscle. It was like the shaking of a bolted-down engine.

"Oh, see him now! Oh, sweet Jesus!" the mother cried.

Her hands involuntarily moved toward the child; you could see the great effort with which she controlled herself, forcing herself to let the doctors and the nurses do their will.

Wieniewski, a resident, came in.

As Swaboda handed him the needle, Mitch hesitated, disturbed by a hunch. "I don't know about this. A dose like this will knock him cold if he's sensitive to horse serum," he said dubiously.

"Old Anaphylaxis Wilner," Wieniewski kidded.

"Well, I don't want to take any chances," Mitch said. "I think we better give him ether."

Wieniewski gave him the professional look which doctors reserve for the colleague who has to show off his specialty at every opportunity. "What's the difference?" Wieniewski said. "Come on, let's shoot this into him."

"Listen, I did a lot of work on this stuff once. What's the sense of taking a chance on a shock when the ether may stop it?"

"Does it?" Swaboda asked respectfully.

"It usually does in guinea pigs," Mitch said.

"Haven't you read Dr. Wilner's paper on the subject in the *Courier*?" Wieniewski remarked, with affected amazement.

"Well, but how do we know this kid is sensitive to horse serum?" the younger interne asked.

"How do we know he isn't?" Mitch countered.

"Say, lady," Wieniewski addressed the mother, "is your husband a jockey? Or was this kid born in a stable?"

"What's that, docta?" She stared, afraid that some lack of understanding in her might mean hurt to her child.

Mitch brushed over the joke. "Can you tell me if your child ever had an injection against scarlet fever, or diphtheria?"

"No, docta. He ain't never had none of them," she responded, still apprehensive. "His sister Elmira she had scarlet fever two years ago."

"He catch it?"

"No, sir! He ain't never had scarlet fever."

"Did the doctor give him something so he wouldn't catch it?"

She stared at him, helpless. "What's he got, docta? That ain't scarlet fever . . . !"

"Listen, Bud," Mitch said to the kid. "Did a doctor ever give you a shot of something in your arm?"

"At school, they did," the kid answered.

Damn it! How was one to *know!*

"Probably diphtheria toxoid," Wieniewski guessed. "That wouldn't sensitize him."

"More probably an antitoxin."

"Oh, for cry sake, Mitch," Wieniewski said. "You're bugs on this subject. Come on, show us a little of that fancy U. of C. needle technique!"

"Say, even a Northwestern man can stick in a needle." Mitch picked up the rival school banter that went on at every consultation in Chicago. "I'm not taking any chances."

"That ether is a cockeyed U. of C. idea anyway. When he's under, you won't have any way of telling whether he's got a shock or not."

"Say, if this kid is sensitive and we shoot that much horse serum into him he'll shock higher than a kite. Come on, Miss Graham," Mitch ordered. "Let's have the cone."

Seeing the child stretched on the table, the ether cone held over his face, the mother backed away, frightened, yet pathetically hopeful.

Mitch nodded to the nurse. The drip began.

Wieniewski stood by, looking bored, holding the syringe full of antitoxin.

The kid went under smoothly. Mitch took hold of his arm and washed a spot with alcohol.

"Better take her out." He motioned to the mother.

A nurse took her out of the room. She went, docile.

Mitch grooved the needle into the vein, and moved the plunger imperceptibly.

"Pulse is a hundred and ten," the nurse said. She had the habitually worried look of the anæsthetist.

There was a long silence. Mitch moved the plunger a bit further, and waited.

From outside the room they heard the warm, trembling praying of the Negro woman. "Oh, sweet Jesus, don't let him pass away. He's just my first-born boy. Sweet Jesus, don't let him pass away. Oh, sweet Jesus . . ."

"A hundred and thirty," the nurse said.

Wieniewski leaned over the mouth of the child.

"Why in hell do they prepare everything in horses!" Mitch cried.

"You know you couldn't get a decent tetanus antitoxin in any other animal," Wieniewski said seriously. And had to add: "The horse is the friend of man."

The child's chest began to jerk, stiffly, and the muscles of the throat tautened, as in the throat of a fighter.

"Looks like shock to me," Mitch said.

"Can't tell unless the face gets purple," remarked Wieniewski. "Fat chance, in a dinge."

With a decisive movement, Mitch withdrew the needle.

"Caffeine!" he snapped.

A nurse fluttered to a cupboard behind them. Another hurried out of the room.

They heard the mother's voice as she caught at the nurse, in the instant of the door's opening and closing.

The stringy body, like a spatter of coffee poured out under the blazing reflector, jerked noticeably. It seemed to be trying to come awake.

"Adrenaline, then! Isn't there anything here!" Mitch snapped.

At last, the second nurse returned with a small bottle, and a prepared syringe.

Mitch shot in the heart stimulant.

Wieniewski was shaking his head, ticking his tongue.

The body began to make throttled gasping movements.

"What's the use, Mitch?" Wieniewski said. "The tetanus will get him if the shock doesn't. It'll only take longer."

"Yah, it would inevitably have got him," Mitch agreed, his hands in a half-open gesture, as if reaching for the next thing to do, finding nothing. "If they'd have sent him up here the first time she brought him in, we might have stopped it."

It was up to the organism, now.

"For all that, the ether may have checked the shock some," Wieniewski consoled Mitch.

"Naw, I guess that's not the way around it," Mitch said.

They waited.

Joe moved forward. Though he had caught Mitch in a moment of helplessness and even of defeat, he could not help feeling that the individual patient, here the little Negro boy, was actually negligible in the great cool detective game that the mind must play against the still unknown. Even though they were watching actual death, Joe sensed that something had come alive for Mitch Wilner—a problem, an idea. Joe reflected on what had brought him here. He wanted to see, to know Mitch, to understand why a woman should choose this fellow instead of himself. Well, then, it was because no woman, nothing, could ever matter to Mitch Wilner, no love could ever touch him, he was entirely engaged in this work. It was an obstinate, single will, scornful of pain and death and love, as against its own immediate purpose. And a woman had to worship that because even though it scorned her too, it was the essence of man, the source of racial progress.

Outside, the praying of the woman had changed to an incoherent sputtering, in which she talked to herself, to God, to her child, alternately, or, after moments of silence, sang snatches of spirituals, and then checked herself, remembering where she was.

"Might as well get the dead box," Wieniewski remarked.

An interne and a nurse wheeled over the mounted stretcher that stood against the wall. It had a metal cover, like a cover over a hot plate.

"I want an autopsy," Mitch said.

Wieniewski shrugged. "Now for the fun," he remarked, going out to the mother.

"Go on up, I'll meet you later," Mitch said to Joe.

Finding the internes' dreary quarters, Joe dropped into a Morris chair. The death had seemed a matter of course. Yet it was the first human death he had ever seen.

A Negro kid. Well, what would he get out of life?

Negroes were sort of happy. They enjoyed living. Look at that shine in his old man's flophouse. Always happy.

From the showers, somebody was singing:

> "Rainbow round my shoulder,
> Skies of blue above,
> The sun shines bright,
> The world's all right . . ."

Joe thought of the book *Rainbow Round My Shoulder*, and saw that dead kid as a grownup carefree Negro, footloose over the United States.

Rainbow round my shoulder. Just the first line was Negro. And the rest was tripe. Whites made tripe out of everything. Love, life.

Mitch came in, walked to the door of the bathroom, and slammed it shut.

". . . 'Cause I'm in love!" Curly sang, defiantly.

"I wouldn't have been so long only she raised such a howl about the autopsy," Mitch said.

"What killed him?" Joe asked. "The tetanus, or the delay, or the serum shock?"

"All of them," Mitch said.

> "The sun shines bright,
> The world's all blllluscolll . . ."

came Curly's voice, stuffed as he toweled himself.

> " 'Cause I'm in love!"

He danced into the room, flicking his towel.

"Say, you should have seen this, Curly. Fatal anaphylaxis. A beaut!"

"Don't bother me, can't you see I'm busy?" Curly sang, putting stuff on his hair.

"You know, I've got an idea," Mitch said excitedly. "You remember I did some work on anaphylaxis a couple of years ago?"

"Yah, you mean the ether effect. Try it today?"

Mitch nodded. "But that was the wrong end to go at. Why try to counteract the effect of the blood serum? The thing is, not to give them any blood serum."

Curly wiggled his brows. "Pasteur the second."

Joe didn't understand.

"The thing is," Mitch explained, "to separate the antitoxin from the blood serum in which it is prepared! If we could give them the pure antitoxin, there wouldn't be any danger of blood-shock. See?"

Joe grasped the idea.

"Boy, if I had another couple of years in a lab . . ."

"Why don't you do it?" Joe said, wondering how big, how important, the thing might be. Would it make Mitch a great man?

"The whole thing is chemistry," Mitch said. "God, how much we don't know!"

In a room in the fancy Straus Memorial section of the Israel Hospital, where he was taking an extra year as a resident in surgery in order to round out his training, Dr. Rudolph Stone stood behind the fashionable surgeon, Dr. Feldner, who was examining a post-operative.

The patient was Maximillian Weber, Sr., owner of the Weber shoe factory. He was a pretty sick man. In addition to gastric complications, Weber had a bad heart; Rudy had seen plenty more of these purple-veined, tight-muscled, aging manufacturers, with a life-consuming impatience in their eyes. It was obvious that Maximillian Weber wouldn't last very long, in any case. With luck, maybe another year.

Rudy had assisted at the operation when Dr. Feldner removed a piloric obstruction. Now the patient was complaining of abdominal pains.

"I think there are bad adhesions," Dr. Feldner said. "We'll have to go in again."

For a moment, Rudy thought Dr. Feldner had forgotten himself. "But, doctor," he reminded him, "doesn't the patient's heart condition—?"

Dr. Feldner gave him a cold stare. "I've considered it," he said, brusquely.

Even the nurse seemed to understand; she exchanged a knowing look with Rudy.

He had seen plenty of things at hospitals, but this incident stuck in his craw. Weber was a two-to-one bet to fail during the second operation. And the operation wasn't necessarily indicated, at all. The abdominal pains of which the old man complained were hardly more than usual. There was no persistent vomiting.

In the ward, Rudy ran into Dr. Matthews, a young staff surgeon, and the only man around the place, he sometimes felt, who had his own attitude about things. He had often wished he could get closer to Matthews, but Matt, though not in the least high-hat, was after all the son of a sort of *Mayflower* family full of professors and brokers. Matt was kind of idealistic, with his head usually in the clouds, and you didn't feel he could come right down and discuss the price of beans with you.

Still, Rudy was so disturbed that he got Matthews aside and told him about the Feldner incident. "Weber is almost certain to have a circulatory failure," he said. "There's no point in the operation at all."

"Except to collect another five-thousand-dollar fee," Dr. Matthews said bitterly.

"I don't know what to do," said Rudy. If he made a fuss about the case and demanded a staff consultation over Dr. Feldner's patient, his goose would be cooked. Here he was just about ready to go out on his own. Planning to get married, too, when he finished this year as a resident. How could he ever hope to get a start, if he was in bad with the big men at half a dozen hospitals where Feldner operated?

"It gets you, it gets you," Matthews said in his nervous quick way of talking. "Actually, Stone, what do we care if an old hog like Weber dies a month sooner? He'll die anyway. But that's not the way of doing things."

"I suppose Feldner has to pile it on wherever he can," Rudy found himself temporizing. After all the surgeon gave most of his time to charity. "He did three operations this morning that he won't get a cent for. I guess Weber will have to pay for them," he ended ironically.

"That's not the way, that's not the way," Matthews kept repeating, deeply disturbed. He put his arm on Rudy's shoulder. "Stone, this whole damn business we're in is cockeyed. It's run absolutely cockeyed. It shouldn't be this way."

Rudy felt Matthews's doubt spreading from the Weber case, to include the whole practice of medicine. The case was becoming general in his mind now, too—the patients in the free wards, and the patients in the Straus Memorial—drag a five-thousand-dollar appendix out of a Mrs. Vanderplatz so you can run downstairs and take care of a dozen anæmic West Side kids.

At this moment he felt an apprehension about his whole training; here the house was complete, and he doubted its foundation.

He shook off the fear. After all, he wasn't the only one.

When the news came of her mother's death, Lil felt utterly deserted. She stood near the door, gushing tears, and nobody to see or hear, nobody to care. She thought: This will bring him back. Surely he would hear of it, and come to console her.

The play school delivered Jackie, and he came clambering over her.

"Jackie," she said. "I have something very sad to tell you."

"What's the matter?"

"You won't see granma any more."

"Huh?" He looked into her face. "What happened? Did somebody take her for a ride?"

"Jackie!" she gasped, and yet thought of the effect on Ev, when she would quote that cute remark.

"Hey, where's my old man anyway, he ain't been home in a dog's age. Did he get taken for a ride too?" Jackie demanded.

"No! no! Jackie, don't say such awful things! Your father is out of town for a while, on business."

"Oh, yeah?" He cocked his eye on her, knowingly. "Hey, kin I go to the funeral?"

The calls of condolence began to come, but Sam didn't call.

Lil sat at the phone and repeated over and over to relatives and friends: "Well, she looked big and strong but she was a sick woman. You know how she suffered all those years. Perhaps it was for the best." But Sam didn't call.

She couldn't touch food, but she made Jackie eat his spinach.

Now, this was the hour when Sam used to come home from those terrible political meetings. Ten o'clock. Lil turned on the radio, low. Someone was singing "Life Is Just a Bowl of Cherries."

Oh, now she was utterly deserted. Her mother was gone, and her husband had left her, all, all at the same time. She lay curled on the couch, sobbing, and wishing he would come in at this minute and see what he had done to her.

"Oh, ma!" she wept, feeling the spirit of her mother looking sorrowfully down at her. "Oh, ma! He insulted me before my best friends, he's ruined my life, and I don't even know where he is, oh, ma! I'm afraid to be alone, I'm afraid . . ." and she began to shiver with hysteria. Then it seemed as though the dead body was there, locked in that little box of an apartment with her, instead of being on the train, coming from Rochester. "Oh, I'll scream. I'm going insane! I can't stand it alone!" Amazed, she heard herself screaming.

Jackie came running out of bed, in his pajamas, his face distorted with fright. "Oh, ma! Ma!" he cried, and hurled himself against her, and she locked him in her arms and sat there sobbing, rocking back and forth, the two of them sobbing cheek to cheek.

> Oh, I wish I had someone to love me,
> Someone to call me their own.
> Oh, I wish I had someone to live with
> 'Cause I'm tired of living alone,
> Cold prison bars all around me
> And my head on a pillow of stone.

When he had walked out on Lil it had been with the excited rage of righteousness, with the vibrating exhilaration in his mind that he had felt only a few times before in his life. That time when as a kid he had walked out on the meeting of the Big Ten; and that other time at Illinois when he had walked out on military drill.

Just as in those previous times, Sam had a happy sense of the amazing simplicity of his gesture: like taking off your coat when you're hot.

The joke was that the whole thing had happened over a religious question. He, the freethinker, getting excited because people were making fun of religion!

Then why had he done it?

He needed a long time by himself to get things clear, and time for being alone and thinking spread luxuriously before him. He walked around a lot in the evenings, thinking, and it began to seem to Sam that things had been wrong between himself and Lil from the very start. He remembered and reshaped little incidents, even to that first yielding of hers, on New Year's Eve, he put things together into a pattern by which she seemed to be trying to dominate him, to shoehorn him into her way of life. The flat in her father's place, the job with her father, the friends she made . . .

For a few days, this isolation was fine. Eating supper alone bothered him a little, but he read the paper between courses. He ate fast anyway, too fast. Always had.

Without Lil to bother him, he even passed one evening reading Shakespeare's *Macbeth*, feeling it odd that he hadn't read any of Shakespeare since high school, when the forced study had made him hate the stuff. Now he was mature, and could appreciate Shakespeare, now he would get back to a lot of reading.

All his senses, reactions, seemed to be awakened, and perceptions sprang from himself as never before.

As he came up on the El platform, he tossed a quarter to the cashier and said: "Tickets."

"Sorry, but we are only selling single fares, the ticket rate has been discontinued," she parroted.

Sam saw himself one of an endless row of customers, just the people of the city, each having to drag another nickel out of his pocket for every three rides on the El. Just as a few days ago he had gagged and puked at his domestic way of life, he felt, at this moment, a catharsis of his whole experience of the public way of life, a revulsion against the system. That delusion, that he would ever fit into such a scheme of things, was part of his life with Lil, too. He grabbed his change and passed on to the platform, knowing he would never again try to play this game. Maybe he was destined to be a lonely and angry watcher at the saturnalia of Chicago, of America, but at least he would be clear with himself.

He opened his *Trib*. Walt and Skeezix were figuring out a name for the new kid. Sam felt homesick.

Informed of Mrs. Klein's death, Sam thought: Why should I let this interfere with the way I really feel about Lil? This is special pleading.

But later in the day, Mr. Klein himself phoned. His voice was small, weary, and yet unyielding. "Sam, I don't know what happened between you two kids, and the way I feel now, you can understand. But I want to ask one thing of you. Come out to the house, and only for the funeral act like nothing happened. In a time like this, you know how Lil will feel, facing all her relatives, you understand. Sam, do me this favor."

When a man put it that way, what could a fellow do?

People were streaming in and out of the house, and it was easy for him to keep away from Lil. There was plenty for him to do, too. Mr. Klein owned a family lot in the Rosevale Cemetery, "completely paid up," but now he couldn't get a burial permit without paying a twenty-five dollar "special assessment." He burned with indignation. "To make a graft out of a thing like that! Have they no shame? Is there no limit?" He wouldn't pay, he cried, with a tense, tragic rage. It was his ground. Nobody had a right to assess it. He would go to the law!

Sam went to see the officers of the cemetery association. Oh, they had a neat little racket, legal too. The assessment had been "voted." He paid it out of his own pocket, got a burial permit, and told Klein that he had secured it merely by threatening the fat slobs with suit and exposure.

Then there was another headache. The undertakers, in cahoots with the drivers, had fixed it with the drivers' union to forbid private automobiles at funerals! The men would not drive unless all the cars in the procession were the undertaker's limousines! It was outrageous, it was ghoulish, but two or three funerals had recently been broken up. Sam had a personal talk with the squat, double-chinned undertaker Elfman. A heavy watch chain, dangling a Masonic emblem, spanned his chest. Oh, sure, he was a lodge brother of Sol Klein, and he would talk to his men, in person. Finally he secured a compromise. If fifteen limousines would be hired, the drivers would allow an equal number of private cars. "Klein has plenty of bucks, it won't break him to give his wife a decent funeral!"

All morning Sam had busied himself with these haggling errands, but now the procession began, and Lil sat stiffly erect, her handkerchief to her nose, her face turned away from him. Mr. Klein sat on the other side of Lil, looking sad and righteously indignant; two red spots flared on his cheeks; oh, if they hadn't got him by the nuts because it was his wife's funeral, he would have given it to the lousy racketeers! But they had him gagged, he couldn't even raise his voice and kick, it wouldn't seem nice.

Not a word was spoken, all through the ride.

At the burial, standing near Lil, Sam was moved by his love for her; even the womanish selfishness in her was lovable. He saw a little woman, round-faced, butter-fleshed, still young and attractive, but on the whole a woman who could recede easily into the thousands one daily passed, unnoticing, as they streamed into Mandel's, into the Davis Store, Field's, as they hurried, or loitered, or gossiped. And now she was sobbing at her mother's funeral.

Jackie grasped his hand. "Hi, pop," he whispered. "Hey, it's a big funeral, ain't it?"

"Shhh."

"I bet it's biggern any gangster's funeral. I bet she had a solid silver coffin."

"Shhh."

"Hey, ma bawls all the time you ain't home."

367

"Listen, Jacob. I'll play you a game. See who can keep still longer, you or me."

"Oke. Gimme a dime if I win?"

"Okay."

Riding back Mr. Klein went with his sisters, and Sam and Lil were alone in the limousine. After they had gone some time in silence, Lil exclaimed: "Oh, is your heart made of stone!"

"I can't help it," Sam said sincerely. "This is the way I am."

"Hey, I win, pop! Gimme the dime!" Jacob cried. And Sam had to laugh. Lil laughed too, and Sam shelled out. She caught herself laughing, and subdued her laughter, ending it in a sigh. Sam looked at her, and her underlip quivered appealingly and defeatedly, she swayed against him, and he held her.

"Oh, Sam, I've been so lonesome," she said.

He admitted: "So have I."

"Oh, why do we act so foolish?" she said. "Nobody is worth that much! To let us quarrel over them."

He saw clearly how he was letting himself slide, slide into this again. But, oh, it wasn't so easy to break a marriage, and habit, and the habit of love, and leave the growing child. And now, riding, they felt so sweet to each other that all else seemed secondary.

In the elevator, a scented and fast-looking blonde was with them. "Know who that is?" Lil whispered as the blonde got off. "Judge Russo is keeping her."

"I didn't know they'd allow it in this building," Sam remarked.

"Oh, but he gives her a magnificent apartment!" Lil said, with a kind of respect.

Sam wanted to fondle her and laugh. The little idiot.

But, after they had been together again, the old battle of wills began. He could see her, like a little cat sidling toward a forbidden dish, making covert approaches to having him apologize to the Wares.

"I told them you had been working so hard, it was just your nerves . . . and you were brought up Orthodox . . ."

"I wish you hadn't said anything. It wasn't necessary."

"Well, since you wouldn't apologize, I thought I'd do it for you. After all," she said lightly, "you did act disgustingly."

"Why shouldn't I, before disgusting people?"

"They're among my best friends."

"Well, they're no friends of mine!"

"Oh, Sammy, let's not start it all over again just when we—"

"I'm not starting! . . ."

They caught themselves that time. But there was the time when she demanded he evict a woman in her father's apartment building on Montrose Avenue, because the woman was running a flat, and would cheapen the building. "But you don't mind about Judge Russo's girl friend, right in this building," Sam twitted her. "Oh, but that's different!" Lil cried indignantly. And when Sam laughed at her, she got sore, and then he got sore, and then . . .

The last straw was when Mr. Liebling, her father's friend, came to Sam with another case, trying to gyp a presser out of compensation for an injury, and Sam practically threw him out of the office. Lil heard about it.

"I suppose next thing you'll be throwing my father out of your office! I might have known! As soon as he helped you get your nose out of the gutter you're too swell for his kind of business!"

That ended it.

At least this time it wasn't religion, Sam reflected bitterly. It was the real trouble, at the bottom of everything. Call it what side you were on.

Phil Ware handled the case for Lil. Thelma Ryskind testified that she had seen Sam strike his wife at a bridge game, and again at the Passover service. Thelma had to be reined in a few times by Attorney Ware, as she got over-enthusiastic and wanted to re-enact the scene before Judge Russo.

Sam found himself listening to this routine case as though it were any one of a number of routine divorce cases he had himself conducted. The grounds established. The perfunctory effort of the judge to have them kiss and make up. Lucky they hadn't drawn Judge Sabbath, who'd have taken them into his chambers, given them a Y.M.C.A. lecture, and wept over them for half an hour to raise his quota of miraculous divorce court reconciliations.

Now came the real function of the divorce court. The climax of the case. The wrangle about how much.

He had known it was no use fighting about the child; and anyway, he agreed: Let Lil take the child. Visit, one day a week.

But the wrangle about how much. The furniture is mine; don't you remember the parlor set was a gift from my father? The car—the hell with it all. Let her have it all. And at least in this case they would be spared the final haggling in which the judge set the lawyer's fees. Only this morning Sam had been through it for a poor sap who worked for Western Electric. "How much do you make? Thirty a week?" The judge calmly apportions: "You can get along on fifteen, that leaves fifteen. Ten a week for the little woman and five on the lawyer's bills." The wife's lawyer kicks, but finally accepts, on condition he be paid first. It's always assumed the poor man will scrape up the dough to pay his own lawyer somewhere. . . .

Sam caught himself—his mind wandering at his own divorce!

Lil didn't want anything for herself, she announced hotly. She accepted twelve dollars a week for the child.

It had been, Sam had to admit from a professional point of view, a decent case.

BUSINESS PSYCHOLOGY

For the life of him, Harry couldn't figure out business men. They were supposed to be live wires, quick to jump for anything new, and yet, so far as his experience went, they wouldn't see a fortune when you dumped it into their lap.

Time and again while he was running the garage for Mr. Bienstock, the boss would remark: "Harry, you're a fine mechanic but you're a hell of a business man." Once, it was because he had cashed a check for a fellow who only came in there occasionally. But the check had turned out to be okay. Again, there was a case when Harry's torch broke, on a welding job. He could have done something else while a part he needed was sent out, but with his usual persistence, he spent a whole morning monkeying around improvising that part, and got the torch working. In making out the bill for the welding job, he refused to charge the customer for the time he had spent fixing his tool.

So he was no business man. As far as he could see, business was just a proposition of buying as cheaply as you could and selling as high as you could.

What was driving him crazy was the way business men acted about his invention. He had imagined that all he had to do was demonstrate it to any company in that line of business, and walk out with a contract.

"Say, I hear the Warren-McNulty Company is looking for some new ideas in garage hardware," he would get a tip from a salesman. "They've got piles of dough and if they get behind a thing they'll put it over."

So he would rush over to the Warren-McNulty Company and after wasting a couple of weeks seeing stenographers and college boys he would finally get to somebody in a private office. "Yes, we're open for new ideas." Then Harry would show his automatic door-locker. "Hm" and "Hm" and "Well," the official would say. And finally: "Well, that's kind of a radical departure. Nothing like it on the market." "That's just it!" Harry would beam, seeing the thing clinched. "Hm. Sometimes gadgets like that catch on, sometimes they don't. Now we had an experience with a similar idea . . ." Harry's heart would sink. But the similar idea would prove to have been a garage-door burglar alarm. It didn't take, and the company lost ten, twenty thousand dollars. So, hm. And, hm. And, well, I'll tell you. Just now our plans are full up. We're not in a position to open up a new line just now. But if you have any other ideas . . .

Harry was beginning to suspect that big business men were nuts. They had no vision. But if they had no vision, how had they become big business men?

And he would try another firm.

Runt Plotkin had stalled him along with the idea of getting capital and setting up a company of their own. After all, Runt had been sincere. He just hadn't been able to connect. But the big business outfits were driving him crazy. Each one took about six months to consider his invention, and after it had passed every imaginable test, they would send it back. Years had gone by!

Every time a hardware salesman came into the garage with a new gadget he was certain it was going to be a swipe of his invention. People were always saying: "Seems to me I saw something like that on a new garage a friend of mine just put up." But each time the rumor turned out to be a false alarm. Anyway, he felt safe, with his patent. Or, could Runt have left some loopholes in that patent?

Then there was a put-it-away-and-forget-about-it period, while he worked on an idea for a cigarette lighter. But someone was always noticing the gadget on Harry's own garage door, and saying: "Where did you get that, Harry? I never saw one like that." "Made it myself." "You don't say! Why, an invention like that ought to be worth a lot of dough! . . ." and the chase would start again.

When he took the thing up to the W. J. Ryan Manufacturing Company, Harry vowed this was his final attempt. He got an interview with W. J. Ryan, himself.

"Not a bad little idea," Mr. Ryan said, smiling indulgently. He was a friendly, pudgy, elderly man, with a hot-towel face. "Tell you, though. Every new garage that goes up these days has a sliding type of door."

Harry knew the answer to that one. "Yes, but there are millions of old-style garages that would be prospects for this article."

"Well, there is something in that," Mr. Ryan said. "But to get to them you'd have to sell from house to house, or alley to alley. Yes, this would be an alley canvassing proposition. And I'll tell you, son, we ourselves manufacture a type of sliding door. And naturally every one of these that's sold takes away a sliding-door prospect."

"Well, then why not buy this and eliminate the competition?" Harry smiled.

"This wouldn't be any competition for us," Mr. Ryan said, sternly.

That seemed a little contradictory to Harry, but by now he had learned to take it easy with big business men.

"Tell me, how much did you figure this would sell for?" Mr. Ryan said, offhand, his fatherly smile broadening.

"Ten dollars, about."

"Well, young fellow, it's four times as easy to sell a five-dollar article as a ten-dollar article. Now, how much do you figure as your manufacturing cost?"

"In mass production, about four dollars."

Mr. Ryan rocked his chin. "You could never sell that for ten dollars. You've got to give it to your retailer for, say, six dollars. What about your distributor? What about advertising? Why, that would have to sell around fifteen dollars, at least. And people aren't going to buy it at such a price."

Harry shrank back, defeated. It was true. Hadn't he himself figured out that the materials in a hundred-dollar radio were worth only about fifteen bucks?

It always amazed him that things should have to sell at four, five times what they cost to make. The actual manufacture of an article was the least important thing. It was the guys that rode around and talked and filled out slips of paper that accounted for three-fourths of the cost. But the thing was already made. Funny.

"I'll tell you what I would do if I were you, young man," Mr. Ryan advised. "Put it out yourself. Start on a small scale. Oh, fix it up a little, put a fancier casing on it, so all those bolts don't stick out. Then get yourself a little machine shop and take a crack at the business. Turn out a couple of hundred. Sell 'em yourself on Sunday or get some kid to go in with you and handle the sales end. See? That way, you've got only one profit to make. See? A thing like this, if you handle it yourself, in a small way, you might do better than a big fellow who has to figure on advertising and all that stuff. Then, if it gets going, you can enlarge. Heck, Henry Ford started with a little machine shop in his backyard!"

He beamed at Harry as though he envied him this opportunity. Being young! Starting for himself! "Yep! that's what I would do if I were you!"

The feeling of scare, and yet of liberation, at quitting a job. Walking out of a prison, but into a jungle! And the feeling of power, and scare, drawing half of the six hundred dollars out of the bank. The feeling of scare as the hundreds shoot away in a couple of days, rent for that slant-walled shack on Harrison Street, rent for a couple of machines, cash for tubing, bolts, springs. The feeling of power and yet the shamefulness, putting in an order with the big Continental Castings Company, but probably the smallest order they ever handled.

Knowing you are your own boss, you can sleep till ten if you want to, but rushing to the shop at seven-thirty to get going. On your own. Starting for yourself. Sixteen hours a day. Just to get started.

—Did you know Aline and Rudy are marrying in June? And then they're going to Europe.

—Well, okay. So he's a doctor now. Rudy's a swell guy. He worked his way through. Well, I had some tough breaks. Soon as I get this business going, I'll take a year off and finish up my engineering course. Heck, I'm not too old.

Working for yourself. Discovering little time-saving tricks. Got a regular little one-man factory, with the Ford conveyor system. Only I'm the conveyor. First make batches of the various parts, then lay them out on the whole length of the shop, and, in assembling, walk from one end of the shop to the other, the thing growing in your hand as you go along.

"Who's the boss here?" says a salesman at the door.

"I am."

It takes six weeks to get going. That six hundred has skidooed.

And it's getting hot. No ventilation. A bake-hot tar roof. And hot work inside.

Hurry it up, though, to get some money coming in. Everybody has a tough time at the start.

The Saturday night when he was invited to Aline and Rudy's wedding at the Temple, Harry worked until two o'clock, to get his first batch of door-closers off his production line. After all he hadn't seen those kids for years. He sent an electric clock as a present. Nobody would notice that he wasn't there.

He simply had to get the stuff ready tonight, as Vic was coming out with him on Sunday, to try and start selling. That was the big test.

At 2 a.m. Harry stacked up twenty of his models, all set, wiped, polished, the attachment bolts in place. If they ever sold that many in one day, it would be plenty!

Vic had a golf date in the morning. Harry couldn't help feeling as though he were crawling after Vic, pestering him with this cheap alley business. Christ, why didn't he have the guts to go out himself and sell! But he waited.

"Well, big shot!" Vic stood grinning, still in golf togs. "Where's the pushcart?"

They drove over to Harry's works.

"This the junk?" Vic looked at the pile, and frowned. "Got any boxes?"

Harry's heart sank. "I didn't think I needed boxes," he said. "We're gonna put them right on the doors if they buy them."

"Jeez, Harry, you can't sell them this way," Vic said, gingerly lifting one of the contraptions, but holding it off to avoid greasing his clothes. "This looks like it came out of a junkyard. You gotta have a box, with the name on it—what is the name, anyway?"

"Well, I hadn't decided. The Garage Door-Closer, I thought."

"Yah, isn't that snappy!"

"Maybe by next week I can get some boxes with a name," Harry pleaded. "If we just go out today and see how they sell . . ."

With a cluck of put-upon patience, Vic grabbed the device, and made for the car. "Well, you picked your territory?"

"I thought we could just try around here."

"Nix. I got a few customers around here."

Finally Vic suggested Oak Park as a nice residential suburb where people would have old-fashioned garages.

They drove out.

Harry felt his pulse racing. If the things wouldn't sell, he was dead broke and out of a job. But as they passed the alleys, Harry saw, with tweaks of gladness, that lots of double-garage doors were spread open. "Looks like Gasoline Alley itself," Vic commented, seeing a few men tinkering with their cars. Harry stopped. Vic got out, and sauntered up to the first tinkerer. "How do." A fine friendly grin was on his face; Harry hardly recognized his brother. "Just thought you'd like to see a little gadget we have, the Close-A-Door, for your garage," Vic said.

"Nope, not interested," the man said, in a routine voice.

Harry, feeling already dejected and defeated, approached with the device. Vic went on with his sales talk. The man straightened up, looked at the mechanism, inquired the price, said a final "Nope," and went to cleaning spark plugs.

Harry nudged Vic to come away. Vic shrugged, and walked off. "You got to keep after these guys," he said, as they got into the car. "He might have bought."

The second prospect only rented his garage and wouldn't spend a nickel on improving it. The fourth was a jolly fellow in golf togs. "I'm a sucker for gadgets," he bragged. "Looka that car." It bristled with mirrors, lighters, had double windshield wipers, and two driving lights mounted on the windshield frame. "Close-A-Door, huh?" He shelled out ten bucks before Vic even started his spiel.

The world turned sunburst bright for Harry.

Harry stood on a rickety box, mounting the device. He had to work with his arms tiringly upward. All the while, he heard Vic and the purchaser conversing about business. Vic led into the subject of gold bonds, revealing that his main interest was in the financial field; this invention was "just a little stunt" that he was trying out, before sinking capital into the thing. The Oak Parker turned out to be "close to the stock market," and gave Vic a tip that General Electric was going to cut a melon pretty soon.

"How you getting along there, partner?" Vic called to Harry, once.

"Be through in a minute," Harry reported, apologetically. How at ease they were, in the heat, in their natty golf-pants, exchanging dope on stocks and bonds. He himself was just a mechanic.

"That's all there is to it," Vic said when they drove off.

Harry's hands were greasy, his sleeves and cuffs were spotted, his underwear was stuck to his back and biting his crotch, he looked hot, and he was sort of ashamed of bothering people. After all he was the inventor and yet he couldn't help feeling inferior to his brother.

"That's all there is to it," Vic said. "Get yourself a salesman, kid, you may make out all right."

Harry felt grateful. The main thing had been proven: Close-A-Door would sell!

COMPARATIVE RELIGIONS

WITH the rest of the worshipers, the four knelt on the ancient flagstone of the chapel. The priest's benediction came down upon them, winged on the angelic voices of the nuns, whose singing the visitors had come to hear. Alvin did not bow his head, but watched the line of devout sisters passing behind the grille that separated the church from the nunnery.

Each nun, upon nearing the priest, knelt, and opened her mouth like a starling. The priest reached through the iron foliage and placed a wafer on her tongue. She arose and moved on; another sister knelt.

Polansky arose, went down the aisle, and knelt at the altar rail, among the waiting communicants.

At first Alvin thought Polansky was only curious, like himself, to taste the holy wafer upon his tongue.

But Eunice whispered: "Your friend is Catholic."

Alvin looked to Madame Polansky. Her eyelids moved slowly downward, in devout affirmation. She leaned over to them, as if imparting a precious mystery, and whispered: "This priest was born Jewish, too." Aaron Polansky rejoined them, with a look of simple admission toward Alvin, and they left the church.

Now it seemed odd to Alvin that he had not understood sooner. Even last time he and Joe had been in Paris, they were present at long ecclesiastic discussions between Polansky and his Catholic friends. Alvin remembered the arguments about Christ, the Messiah, and Zionism.

He should have known, then. Now that they had fully admitted him into their confidence, it was a sign that even these Europeans felt he was come of age, intellectually.

Hippolyte, himself a gentile, was the center of their little group of converts. Alvin guessed they would work on him, now. He lent himself to the game, reading Thomas Aquinas and the scholastics, sampling masses in various churches in the town, quoting T. S. Eliot to them, as his own contribution.

Eunice seemed to be watching his progress with faint amusement.

They never discussed the subject with each other, but when they were seated at a café table with an American crowd, it was easy to cross-analyze. "Alvin has never gotten over his racial guilt at marrying a gentile," Eunice would say, "so he's trying to overcome it by going Catholic. You know, like killing one germ with a deadlier germ."

"That's quite plausible," Alvin would say. "But it doesn't happen to be true. I have no tribal emotions. And anyway there is nothing incompatible between Catholicism and Judaism. I need hardly point out that Jesus was merely an excellent rabbi. And take Aaron Polansky. Even now you have to admit he is a really sincere Jew, his art happens to be the most truly Jewish art we have. Catholicism is an extension of his Jewishness. What really draws me to Catholicism is the doctrine of humility. . . ."

That would always bring a cynical laugh, and a call for another round of Pernods. And Alvin would pay for the drinks, calling that his penance.

He was sick of himself and felt he had made a glib failure of life, living a planned planlessness. Instead of the one girl, a man suddenly realized he could marry anybody; instead of living in a certain place, he could live anywhere. There were these two schemes of life: the strictly unified, and the heterogeneous. To live a unified life, a man had to believe awfully in his own importance, attach importance to everything that he did. Like some artist who believed his every stroke was a work of genius. But in living a heterogeneous life, a man admitted he wasn't much, he was dust to be blown by any wind. That was a kind of humility, a negation of self.

And as for Catholicism, why, it was a way of losing one's self. And at the same time gaining the illusion of living a unified life, according to a rigid plan, a dogma. Communism was the same. Oh, he had his eyes open.

The model stepped down from the stand and flexed his muscles. He stretched out an arm and solemnly turned it, palm up, palm down, while he inspected his skin. "Ça marche?"[1] he said perfunctorily, flashing his teeth at Joe. He glanced at the work, like a mechanic who is satisfied that he has done his own part well, and shoves the job over to the next department for completion.

Joe walked away from the thing. "Marche pas[2]," he said.

"Ah, even for the masters there are days of discouragement," the model said sagely, as one who had posed for such as Maillol, Despiau. He was a short man, but triangularly developed, with fine, apparent musculature. He was like some of the stocky wops proudly cavorting on Clarendon Beach, back in Chicago.

Joe rapped his pipe against the base of the statue. He tried to believe that he had accomplished something in this session, turning the right foot so that it more firmly supported the weight of the figure. He had changed it perhaps a quarter of an inch.

"Patience, that is what is needed, patience," the model said cheerfully. He dressed.

Why have I got so damn finicky? Joe thought, staring at the damned foot, wondering if it oughtn't to go back a trifle. The cursed thing about sculpture was its permanence. No other art so obviously stood before its creator as a final statement, made for all time. Stone or bronze. And it was this cursed responsibility to eternity that gave a man the obsession of perfection. Never to be able to alter the slightest detail. . . .

---

[1] "It works?"
[2] "It does not work."

The model was waiting, an ordinary-looking little man in his clothes. This was the end of a fortnight, Joe realized, and went for the man's wages. The model checked the amount against a record he kept in a notebook.

"Exactement," he said. "Merci. Au revoir."

Joe remained standing, staring at his contraption. His wrists felt powerless. Across the court, Gus Hardy was beginning his all-afternoon repetition of Bach records, whistling to them as he painted.

"Art art art shit!" Joe exploded.

Now that he had time, money, a swell studio, a good model, he couldn't produce.

"Well, let's see the opus," Alvin offered.

"Oh, it's pretty lousy."

Still, a fellow wants a friend to say: "It isn't as bad as you make out, in fact it isn't bad at all, I like it." Joe unwound the damp sheet from the figure and stood off, himself, to have a look. For a moment, he imagined it wasn't hopeless.

Alvin turned away, uninterested.

"So it's lousy, huh?"

"It doesn't mean anything. All great art has to have religious feeling," Alvin declared.

With the second Pernod, Joe began to talk nervously, fast. He didn't get drunk, but seemed, literally, quickened. "I know it's crap," he said. "I know there's something missing. But what am I going to do? Sit and wait for the revelation?"

"The trouble is modern artists believe in themselves instead of in something beyond themselves," Alvin said. "They don't know the meaning of humility."

"Bushwah. Don't feed me that religious crap. What about Rodin? What about Epstein?"

"Listen, Joe. You admit there's something lacking in your work. . . . You respect Polansky, don't you?"

"Sure," Joe said. "But I'm not Polansky. What do you want me to do, go Orthodox?"

"Go anything," Alvin said, with a slyly ambiguous smile. "But go!"

Approaching across the courtyard, they heard the rhythmic metallic tapping of hammer on copper. It was comforting, workmanlike.

"Ça marche?" Polansky greeted Joe.

"Marche pas," said Joe, and blurted: "I think I ought to get out of Paris. I'm not getting anywhere."

"Ah." Polansky laid aside his hammer, and fixed him with a sad, friendly look.

"The trouble is," Alvin said, "he doesn't know what he wants to do."

Polansky bent toward Joe, and said, in a tone more inquiring, more intimate than ever before: "But what is it that you want to be, Joseph?"

Joe shrugged uncertainly. He hated all this atmosphere of introspection that Alvin had brought around. Pretty soon Alvin would be springing that neo-Catholic crap on him. Everything seemed phony. Even Polansky seemed odd, with his questions. He had thought he would answer: "A good sculptor," but he found himself saying: "A good Jew."

"A good Jew," Polansky repeated. "And what is that?"

Polansky continued to stare at him, with a kind of pity, Joe thought. Perhaps for his being an American. Then the older artist got up and lifted out a copper plaque from behind some stuff against the wall.

It was a Descent from the Cross. It was done with the same naïve, peculiarly Jewish awkwardness that gave so human a quality to all of Polansky's work. And yet it sounded a deep chord of reverence. The weight of the sparse, bruised body of Christ could be felt, coming down into the waiting arms of Mary. The reddish golden metal glowed with the eternal enduring of that pain, fleshly and spiritual.

First Joe looked at the work only as at a new design, shown by one artist to another. Gradually, he realized that Polansky was trying to tell him something.

"I believe in this too," Polansky said.

It seemed to Joe that he had been stupid not to know this sooner. All those trips to hear fancily sung masses. It was bizarre, and childish, and sad. A kind of sickness was growing in Joe. Not at the fraud, but at the hopelessness of finding one simple truth, in a world so involved. Alvin was no true believer, he was sure. Alvin couldn't believe in anything.

Joe couldn't feel the revulsion that a Jew is supposed to feel, confronting an apostate. Looking directly in Aaron's face, he saw only a beautiful, painful sincerity. "I believe in this," Polansky said. And Joe had an infinite feeling of pity, as for a friend whom one discovers suffering.

God, this sick Paris, this Paris of distortion, of the cult of the bizarre, the Paris where everyone was driven out of emptiness to seek something ultimate, something beyond.

"I—I didn't know," he said to Polansky. "I can see that you feel this deeply. But to me, well, it wouldn't be my way."

"We are friends, as before?" Polansky said.

"Of course! Why not?" Americans don't give a hang about a man's religion, Joe reflected, ironically. Why did everyone get sidetracked with some shred of truth, with religion or love, politics or surrealism, but so few seemed to keep themselves open for the whole bitter and nourishing truth of the human race?

Afterwards Joe remembered that night as one of those crazily intense Paris nights, when everything said and done seems to have a whole set of symbolic meanings, but, taken apart, to be compounded of nothing but inanity.

People winding their emotions tighter and tighter, trying to arrive at some sensation sharp enough to cut through the rot of their lives.

Joe and Alvin were at the Coupole when the whisper went through that Pascin had been found in his room, a suicide[3].

Pascin was a Jew, a Frenchified painter of flesh.

A lightning-streaked gloom pervaded Montparnasse. Few had known Pascin, yet now every café-sitter felt him as an intimate, and recognized his suicide as the inevitable personal answer to the futility of modern life. One story went around that he had had syphilis. Another, that he had gone mad. Famous, known to all Montparnasse; and his body had lain for days in his room. Alone. Away from the café, everyone was alone. And the end of this emptiness was suicide.

"Feen," Alvin would order. And again: "Feen," shoving his empty glass. Joe nursed his drinks.

Gradually, the thought of Palestine had been taking possession of him, an open place, in the clean and healing sunlight. He had gone everywhere else last time, except there. He had made a long journey, and turned back just within reach of his goal. What had stopped him? Hadn't it been a letter from Sylvia, and loneliness?

"I should have gone to Russia," Alvin said.

Between the two of them, now, was a queer sense of union, of being the same person. For once, it was tacitly admitted that they had even wanted the same girl, and, because neither of them had attained what he wanted, they felt even closer together.

"You could go now," Joe pointed out.

"Aw," Alvin said. "I bitched up everything." What did they need him for, in Russia?

The Coupole was closing, and they went across the street to the Select. At one table was a bunch of Montparnassians, among them a woman weeping drunkenly and broken-heartedly that she had slept with Pascin.

Eunice found them there. "Father, dear father, come home to me now," she said. She was kind of high herself.

"Joe's going to Palestine," Alvin announced, as though it were a mission.

"Why don't we go along?" Eunice said. "I'd love to go there."

"Sure, why don't you take her?" Joe kidded.

"I'll wrap a scarf around my head and be a what do you call it, *kalutza*," she persisted, laughing.

---

[3] The artist known as Pascin (Julius Mordecai Pincas) committed suicide in Paris on June 5, 1930. Meyer Levin has apparently taken a dramatic liberty here, because the book's timeline is still in 1929.

"Chalutza," Alvin corrected savagely; why could a *shikseh* never learn the *ch* sound!

"Well, I guess Joe will have to take me," she said, and their eyes met with the flirtation that skirts possibility. Alvin caught the glance. He was suddenly, wildly jealous. He grabbed his wife. "Come on the hell out of here."

Joe remained. This far toward morning, his mind was almost painfully awake, his eyes were lidless. He stared through this night, as through a sea that must yield the desired shore.

In a crowd that came along, there was Myra Roth. They went toward each other, falling on each other's necks, like long-lost sweethearts.

Suddenly fate seemed clear to Joe. He would marry a rich girl. They would live in Palestine, visit Europe and America every few years; he would do big works.

"I'm going to Palestine tomorrow, come with me," he said.

The girl was white-faced, sick-looking, burned up with nerves. She was drinking Pernods. "You're sweet," she said regretfully, and stroked his cheek once. She had the deep-down blues; her despondency became suicidal. "Oh, God, oh, God, I'm going crazy!" She hung onto him. Joe pulled her out and walked her around the block; her weight was heavy, dead on his arm. All her tight-wound horrors unraveled. Analyzed in Vienna. No use. Even fell in love with analyst. No use. She had a fixation. She was distantly related to Dickie Loeb, had been in love with him as a kid. She'd never get over it. Oh, why had Dickie done it, he could have had anything he wanted in the world, and done anything, he was so brilliant! Years . . . and the horror wouldn't release her.

"I had a fixation, too," Joe babbled. "A girl, purity. It's all nonsense. There's nothing to it."

Leopold and Loeb, now, tonight, after years, he could see them as the prophetic symbol of their time. Now the generation was grown and their time was claiming them.

The air had cooled, with the damp, bracing freshness that came before dawn. Joe could feel his skin relaxing under his clothes, losing that all-night dryness and tension, becoming alive again. They were still young. He saw the two of them as bitter, scarred souls who nevertheless could escape their generation, still having the resilience of youth.

"You meet me tomorrow, we'll go to Palestine," he insisted.

He should not wait; they should start right away, act on this impulse; the hell with Sylvia's knowing eyes: "So you married a rich girl, Joe, after all."

Joe got home alone. "This is where I live," he said out loud, as though he were gesturing Sylvia into the building, into the silly little ascenseur. "Some class, huh? a Guggenheimer."

The word echoed to him. Live? Here? Why in this strange house, in this strange city, what the hell was he doing here?

In this dawn, Joe thought, he was really alone. All by myself in the morning, all by myself in the night. Ann probably had the curse; that was when she pulled those unexplained three-day absences, staying in her room on rue Vaugirard, going modest, and forgetting her character of a Hemingway heroine.

There was an anæmic dawn, greenish upon the panes of the immense studio window. With stoical anticipation, Joe pulled the cloth off his figure. The hopeless lifelessness of his work was almost a satisfaction to him.

He had to go, to find. Like kids playing ball, he had to go back to the base he had failed to tag, before touching home.

He looked at his work, this pale imitation Greek. This would be no frenzied night of emotion, as on that night of the Moscowitz wedding, when seeing Sylvia and Mitch had driven him nuts. He picked up a gouge and ran it crisscross upon the clay. Then, grinning at his act, he put his hand on the clay penis and balls, wrenched them off, and threw them into the waste-tub.

Ann was sitting on a low stool, her hands clasped around her ankles, hugging her brown wool skirt around herself, making herself into a small pathetic being. When he came in, she didn't move.

"So we are off in search of the soul?" she said in a small brave voice.

"Yes, I've got to go," he said.

"Kiss and farewell," she said. Then, breaking a little: "Oh, Joeboy, let's go out and get tight."

Where had she got that name for him?

The mere idea of drink brought to his mouth the taste of Paris futility, oh, this whole crowd, even Ann, with their Pernod, fine, cassis, encore, garçon, garçon, garçon, shit.

She had begun, quietly, to cry.

Why the hell didn't he marry her and at least make one person happy?

"I hope you find your beautiful olive-skinned Jewess," Ann said, "with kinky hair, and doe's eyes."

On Saturday afternoons things were sweet in the lab. There was the sense that the strangers were gone, and only a family remained, those with the common blood of wonder.

Mitch had a dialysis going under each tap. But it was slow work. The alkalinity tests were an hour apart; in between time there was not much he could do but sit on his can. In fact, he was taking it easy, reading *All Quiet on the Western Front.*

Six months on his problem and nothing to show for it. All he seemed to be doing was crossing off the possibilities, narrowing down the field.

In fact, he had run into every snag in the normal course of research. Delays in getting materials, a period of false hope when a precipitate behaved strangely, a sudden shock when Luke D'Angela walked into the lab and pointed to an article in the British *Journal* saying: "Looks like someone beat you to it, Mitch."

The feverish reading of the article, and the slow relief: the job was only partly done. Oddly enough, the report concerned some work at the Hebrew University, in Jerusalem; but the process used had been extremely complicated, and the yield of serum-free antitoxin had been so low that it was impractical. Only about fourteen percent. But they *had* proven that his hunch was right. Antitoxin was separable from blood serum.

Then the jump back into the job, with a sense that others, in obscure laboratories dotted all over the world, were competing.

If he had had his own way, he could have gone faster. But as in a great many of the practical research problems at the university, there was a tie-up with a commercial firm. The Gorham Pharmaceutical Company maintained several five-hundred-dollar research fellowships in the department of chemistry. Any patentable results secured by a student on a Gorham fellowship belonged to the firm.

When he had proposed his problem to the chemistry department, Professor Vakhtanov had immediately suggested that he work on a Gorham fellowship. Adding that, of course, if Mitch discovered a method of preparing serum-free antitoxin, it would belong exclusively to Gorham Pharmaceutical. Mitch had been a little startled by this new wrinkle in "free research." It looked like a nice cheap way for Gorham and other chemical firms to get laboratory work that otherwise would run them ten times the cost. But after all, as Professor Vakhtanov pointed out, scientists were only interested in getting an opportunity to work on their ideas, and these fellowships gave them such opportunities. If practical results appeared, why shouldn't they be assigned to a friendly, reputable firm?

The only trouble was, the commercial connection slowed him up. As the Gorham Company supplied the antitoxin upon which he experimented, there were sometimes week-long lapses, while he waited for material to be sent from Battle Creek. Once, a whole month of work went to pot because they had sent stale antitoxin.

His approach to the problem was completely different from that of the Hebrew University. The first thing Mitch did was to wash the serum in water, a slow, week-long process called dialyzing; the Hebrew University process omitted this.

The antitoxin hung in a little rubber bag, and water seeped through, carrying out whatever was soluble. What remained in the bag was subjected to various precipitating agents, and the precipitates were injected into guinea pigs, which were then given tetanus.

So far, negative.

Even the horror of *All Quiet* failed to hold Mitch Wilner's attention. All he seemed to see across the page was rows of dead guinea pigs. In fact, the more he refined the stuff, the longer he dialyzed, the worse the results.

Aside from his chemical researches at the lab, Mitch was working in allergy at the brand-new Billings Hospital, across the street.

Luke D'Angela came in to give him a laugh at an article in the *Trib*, about the Chicago Woman's Club passing a resolution for a Sneezeless World's Fair, with the slogan *Make Chicago Ragweed-Free by 1933*.

"Maybe we can get them to pass a few more resolutions," Mitch said. "How about passing a law against arteriosclerosis?"

"I think maybe a couple of fellows around here are using the same system in banishing diseases," Luke said, gossiping about Schaeffer, the young biologist who had announced that he had isolated the flu germ and was hopeful of finding an antitoxin. Only, half the department of biology was down with the flu as a result of his researches.

"What becomes of all those epoch-making discoveries anyway?" Mitch said. "I remember when I was a premed there was some sensational announcement every day. They had everything licked. One day some guy in Vienna had knocked out the tubercle, and the next day some gink in England had found the cancer germ! All bona-fide, recognized scientists. I was so scared they would have everything cleaned up before I got through, honest, I nearly dropped medicine and went into law. How old is Schaeffer anyway? What's his hurry?"

"Just about thirty."

He was twenty-seven. Two spears of baldness were gradually working their way up from his temples. By the time he was thirty, would he have solved this problem? No rushing into print with half-baked results.

"Yep, a good man takes his time," Luke quoted with double meaning, as he fished a couple of rubbers out of Mitch Wilner's supply box. "Mitch, I could use some of these."

"Yah? What for?" Mitch said disparagingly.

"What for! Holy Mary!"

"Uh huh. Just about your speed."

"Well, I wouldn't be wasting them on a goddam dialysis. Say, are you sure that's all you use 'em for?"

Mitch leered.

"That's a hot one! Getting the university to supply you with Merry Widows! That's one for the book!" Luke pulled a dialyzing sack out of the water. "Say, I always had an idea these things were waterproof."

Mitch envisioned the tiny molecules of water sliding out between the molecules of rubber, while larger bodies, such as sperm, were stopped. "Dope!" he laughed.

Sylvia arrived; Luke gave her a knowing look, and took himself off.

Mitch stood red-faced holding that suggestively loaded, damp little sack. He was sick of being kidded about the rubbers anyway, and made a mental note to find some other type of bag for the dialyses. Besides, if he got a material with larger pores, there might be better results.

"Look out, dear," she said as he was about to set her hat on the lab table. "That's genuine Italian straw. It was fifteen dollars at Saks's and Mort is having it copied for our two-dollar line."

He couldn't even keep her in hats.

"Come on," she said, playfully pulling him by the hand. "I'm going to drag you out, it's simply wonderful outdoors."

"Wait. I'll polish off this last test, and we'll have an hour till the next one."

"A whole hour! Mister, you overwhelm me!"

He lifted out the test-tube, and matched it against the color chart.

"Oh, let me!" They bent together, studying the tube against the tinted squares.

Mitch said: "I got a letter from Joe today. It was a pretty wild letter."

"Yes?" She studied the chart, intently.

"He's in Palestine."

"I knew."

"Syl, the fellow must be going nuts. It was a long rave about why don't we get married, because that will break the spell you have over him."

"I know," Sylvia said. "He's developed an awful fixation."

"He seems to be in a terrible hurry for us to get hitched," Mitch said. "Half of his letter is that he still loves you and always will, and the rest of it is why don't we get married so he'll know where he stands."

"He knows where he stands," Sylvia said softly.

And what if he were to walk into her house tonight; wouldn't she feel that same old intolerable thrill at his nearness? Oh, that wasn't love.

"Did you answer him?"

"I told him he had just as much right to try to win you as I have. If he wants to come back here I'm not going to try to stop him," Mitch said. "I told him it's none of his business, but I can't see my way clear to getting married for another year, maybe, and—well, I can't always be asking you to wait . . ." He looked firm, yet ashamed.

"Oh, Mitch, can't we get married now, and get done with all this?" she begged. "Dear, I'm twenty-five. Just a repressed old social worker, like that old maid in *Street Scene*. Oh, another year and another year! What's the difference about money?" she cried. "You know my folks would be glad to help us along for a year or so. We could even go to Vienna, if you want . . ."

He let go her hand. "You know how I feel about that, Syl. I've accepted a lot from my father, but he can't go on selling insurance forever, and I don't want to be dependent."

384

"Oh, what's the difference! Must we waste our lives because . . .?"

But they had gone over those arguments, again and again.

Why was Mitch afraid, just as Joe had been afraid? Why were they so unsure, and so insecure in life? Why did they have to spend their best years in working toward that security, while she waited, wasting her life too? Other people, even poorer people, went right ahead! It was just in their own class that men had to be so proud.

She had taken out a pack of cigarettes, and was fumbling at the cellophane, unable to find a free edge. He took it from her.

"Oh, why do they have to wrap everything in this junk?" she said, exasperatedly. "Camels started it and now they're all doing it."

As he tore the cellophane, Sylvia said: "Mitch, crossing the campus just now, I felt so old. I hardly recognized the place. They've got new buildings up all over Sleepy Hollow, even this building wasn't here when I was here, and that great big hospital, it all makes me feel as if I belonged to another generation. Why, they even let women smoke in the buildings now," she laughed bitterly, "and here I am, nothing has happened to me . . ."

He was listening to her, feeling sorry for her, feeling an awful inadequacy in himself, that he couldn't give his woman the marriage she wanted, and at the same time weighing the evidence and acquitting himself, he was working as hard and as well as a man could, this was the system. And simultaneously, crinkling the cellophane in his palm, it occurred to Mitch that this material ought to make an excellent bag for the dialysis. Even while Sylvia was finishing her complaint, he was reshaping the cellophane in his fingers, wondering whether it would show different results than the rubber.

"Mitch," she said, "all I do is go about all day among those wretched people, and there is so little I can do for them, everything seems so hopeless, and I'm so lonely . . . I can't stand this sort of life any more! I thought maybe if I went away for a while, things would be changed when I came back. Maybe I could go abroad . . ."

And she had wished that her first time abroad would be together with him, on a honeymoon.

"I've got seven hundred dollars saved up," she said. "One of the girls at the agency is going, asked me to go with her. You know, Janet Leavitt. But, Mitch, I thought—we could use the same money to get married on and I could keep on working."

She found herself smiling and crying.

He shook his head, while he pressed her tenderly. "You know I wouldn't do it that way."

It was so funny too, that a girl could waste her money on a trip abroad, but a man couldn't let her use that same money for their marriage.

"Janet is a secretary or something of Hadassah," Sylvia said, a bit archly. "Maybe we'll go to Palestine, too."

"Why don't you marry Joe, he's got a Guggenheim, he's all set!" Mitch said, half kidding, half jealous. "You wouldn't have to wait for him!"

They looked at each other with confidence.

Suddenly she felt lighter, gayer. The trip to Europe seemed attractive. When she returned, Mitch would be ready, life would open.

"Aren't you worried, dear, if I go to Palestine?"

He chuckled. "You might bring me back some of that clay those guys in the Hebrew University used on this experiment."

"Oh, you!" she said, and loved him.

Slipping up to the net with two of his long darting strides, Mitch waited with smiling relentlessness for the ball. He cut-smashed. She straightened, smiling at Mitch, feeling beautifully civilized as tennis always made her feel, glorying in the summer sun sweet on her cheek, knowing she must look nice in this white skirt and girlish middy, with the dark blue velvet band of ribbon around her head.

Mitch swirled up on his toes, going into his serve. It suddenly occurred to her that medics played a special kind of tennis, a violent, even cruel slamming game.

Mitch was a swell player. It was all she could do to give him a game.

"It's a wonder that didn't go right through," she laughed as his cannonball serve hit the net.

At that instant, Mitch Wilner's research problem was solved in his mind. Suppose the tennis ball were an antitoxin molecule, and the net was the rubber sack-wall. If the holes were a little larger, the molecule might pass through.

No wonder he had got worse results, the longer he dialyzed! Some of the antitoxin was going right through the rubber! Down the drain! He could get pure antitoxin out of that waste water! And then he would just have to find a material with bigger molecular spaces than rubber, and he would get a larger, a practical yield of pure antitoxin! Maybe that cellophane? He hurried back to the lab.

Up above Safed, they said, there was marble to be found. A New York Jew had even tried to open a quarry there, oh, it was fine stone, better than Italian marble! But the expense of hauling to Haifa defeated the business. The stone lay way up almost to the Syrian border; it was even a little beyond Cfar Giladi, the last outpost of the *chalutz* communes. A mountainous region, gray, and yellow, spotted with the deep green of olive groves.

Joe was in shorts, brown-legged, and brown deep below his throat. He carried a knapsack containing a few clothes and his carving tools. Coming up toward Giladi, he saw a young Jew with a shepherd's crook tending the commune's flocks. Sheep, and black, silken-haired goats.

In this land, biblical phrases were as native and as fresh as the songs of Walt Whitman to America.

"Behold, thou art fair, my love . . . thy hair is as a flock of goats, that appear from Mount Gilead . . ."

Even at this moment Mitch Wilner's letter burned in Joe's mind. "I sat down and had a good laugh. To think that we should ever quarrel over a girl . . ." Was that the fellow Sylvia loved, and was going to marry? "I've seen plenty of fellows, especially in my profession, wreck their careers because of a wife hanging around their necks. That's one thing I'm not going to do. I'll get married when I'm good and ready, Joeboy, no matter how impatient it makes you . . ." Only one sentence in Mitch Wilner's letter stopped him from turning back to America. After joshing for pages, Mitch said: "But one thing is certain, Sylvia and I will end our days together."

Joe had formed the habit of imagining that Sylvia was with him, especially in moments on this voyage when the high, emotional beauty of the country quickened him, made him feel as though he were living within a prophecy that was coming toward fulfillment[4].

Surely Sylvia must see with him the mountain-grown quality of this group of stone houses, must share his fearful sense of coming home among the settlers here.

They were stony, silent, tall, as if in harmony with these wild surroundings. Their faces were strong, stubborn, sudden. They rode horses like bedouin; their moods of laughter and of anger were sudden and fierce and childlike, like the Arabs'. These were like an old tribe of Hebrew people, Habirim out of the wilderness.

During Joe's first days among them, he was contemptuously left to himself; none asked questions about his world, for unlike the valley *chalutzim*, these were incurious. They had their place. Let the American see what he wanted, and go away.

It was a walk of two hours up a further hill, to the abandoned marble quarry. There, too, Joe exulted with the emotion of discovery. "Look, Syl, look what we have found!" The stone was even-grained, silky, and reddish tan in color. There was a rudimentary chute, for getting it down to the cutting-shack. Crude machinery for blocking the marble was still intact.

Joe clambered around the slope. He saw where the last break had been made, and outlined a great stone that could be loosed; if he could get it down! Eight foot of it!

In the courtyard of the commune was a smithy's shed; Joe prowled excitedly through a pile of scrap iron, and found a long iron bar. Shlomo, the smith, fixed a chisel edge on the bar. Then Joe asked Chayim Ben Yehuda, one of the leaders: "Could I get a man to help me for a day? I want to bring down a stone."

---

[4] The reformation of Israel was prophesized by Ezekiel; see Ezekiel 37 (the Valley of Dry Bones). The Zionist movement was largely secular, but nevertheless the confluence of modern human events and ancient Biblical prophecy is intriguing...

Shlomo went with him the next day. When they went to work quarrying the stone, Joe noticed Shlomo's huge hands, red hair sprouting from the knuckles.

Now they were changed toward him, treating him as one of themselves, a worker, who knew his own craft.

Coming back from the quarry, Shlomo took him by the small cemetery on a hillock, perhaps half a mile from the commune. Three graves were together in a center mound.

"You know who died here?" Shlomo asked.

Joe knew the legend of the three graves.

Years back, in the first flush of Zionist immigration, when this commune had been founded, there had been trouble here. A sheikh, known and thought to be friendly to the settlers, had galloped up to the gate of this isolated, lonely colony. He had declared himself to be hunting a personal enemy, who might have taken refuge here. They had opened the gates to him, let him search for his enemy.

The sheikh and his followers had gone into the barn. A moment later, shots were heard.

In that barn, the leader of the commune, Trumpeldor, a one-armed veteran, had held off the band of attacking Arabs. Trumpeldor and two young women had lost their lives.

Who knew why the Arabs had begun to shoot? The Arab is a creature of dark motives, of sudden fury; know him, and he is treacherous too.

Through the years, this incident had grown into legend, as typical of all the dangers and hardships of settlement, of the treachery of Arabs, of the struggle against isolation, disease, malaria, homesickness; all were included in the memory of the hero, Trumpeldor, who had fought in the barn, single-handed, wounded, against the whole party of attacking Arabs, and held them until the colonists could gather and save their settlement.

"Why don't you make a stone to his memory?" Shlomo said.

Why not? Already Joe felt in his blood something of the wild deep hatred of the enemy, call him Arab, call him some universal adversary: all that was against Jewish settlement in this land. You had to be here to know it, to feel this primitive stubborn urge, born in these stones. He had already schemed the rugged figure of a man, a monument to the settlers of these hills; now he saw him as a hero, too; as Trumpeldor, the national hero.

A crew of men turned out; with a tractor and a sledge they brought the stone and set it up where it would be a monument. There, Joe went to work.

He remembered the gaping crowd that had watched the stone-carvers on the Straus Building on Michigan and Jackson, until the artisans had to be screened from the curious watchers. He remembered the flocks of awed and timid visitors who had been shepherded periodically through the Midway studios, remembered their inane remarks.

Here, he worked in the sun. Occasionally, the comrades came by and spoke with him. He was one of themselves, a man who toiled. He used mallet and chisels, sweated at his labor, and was skilled.

On Sabbath, the comrades would stroll about the farm, and many of them made the cemetery the goal of their walk. Chayim Ben Yehuda and his wife, Shulamith, came by. She was a girl born in Palestine, the first Joe had known. She was a purely Semitic type, far different from the short-legged, short-necked women of Russian-Jewish stock who filled the communes. Had there, then, been Jews in Palestine before this Zionist movement? Ah, but what kind of Jews! Huddled together in settlements in the ancient holy cities—Jerusalem, Safed, Hebron—entire communities of mothy alms-eaters. Colonies of orthodox prayer-sayers, thin sap of generations of talmudists, who busied themselves these hundreds of years in writing begging letters to the Jews scattered throughout the world, for were they not performing a mission for the entire race by the mere fact of living in the holy land? Generation after generation, they had compiled and guarded the addresses of Jews throughout the world who might respond to a begging letter sent out around Yom Kippur or Passover. The entire community lived on the proceeds of these letters. Cooped in their holy ghettos, they loathed the influx of young settlers, godless, beardless, who smoked on Sabbath and worked for a living. But among their own sons and daughters, a few stuck out their heads, whiffed the new life, and abandoned the orthodox slums for labor in the colonies. Shulamith had been one of these, and in a *chalutz* commune she had met her husband, Chayim Ben Yehuda.

Here she is, Ann, with her doe's eyes, olive skin, and her two black crinkly braids; should I seek out her sister, and remain here, breeding native Jews?

Shulamith walked around the forming monument. "Trumpeldor was a cripple, with only one arm," she said, "but it is good you are giving him two. It is not necessary that this should be the image of the man, but it must be in his memory, the image of a hero, a pioneer."

Could you say it better, at the Select, Ann?

Joe smoked his pipe. Tobacco grown in the colony.

The figure was emerging, a wiry and powerful Hebrew, with large hands, and a hawklike dreamy Semitic face. Here, more than at any time before, except for those few months in Chicago when he thought he was getting ready to marry Sylvia, Joe felt he was working well.

The trouble came vaguely, first a rumor to be treated lightly, of riots at the Wailing Wall. Who cares for the Wailing Wall where the dying graybeards mumble and spit, in that passageway damp with the piss of Arab donkeys! The *chalutzim* have other things in mind, in Palestine, than crying at a stinking old wall!

And yet, haven't Jews been praying there since the time of Solomon? If the graybeards want to pray there, they have a right to pray.

389

Then came a swift visit by two authoritative comrades in an auto. They held a sudden council with Ben Yehuda and the other leaders, left a small box, and were gone. In the evening, a general meeting of the commune. Comrades, how many have pistols? And then the order: Wear dark clothes only, white shines at night.

Shulamith saw Joe in his white shirt. "Have you no other? I'll lend you one of Chayim's." In the morning: "Comrade, better not go up the hill to work, it's dangerous for you to be there alone." Joe hung around the yard. At noon, another general meeting, and then each man was assigned his post, in case of trouble. The women and children were to go to the barn. That night, doubled guards. Every hour, a rider clattered into the yard. "All quiet."

None knew how the news came. The commune was cut off, without telephone, the roads were closed: several Arab villages lay between Giladi and the next Jewish settlement. Yet all over the yard there was whispering of the massacre at Hebron[5]. Many American students in the Yeshiva there had been butchered, too.

Here in the clear mountain air, the rumor of insane strife seemed unreal to Joe. He was clumsy when Chayim showed him how to put a magazine of cartridges into an automatic, and remembered wryly how he had walked out on military drill at Illinois. There was no pistol for him anyway. "Arm yourself as best you can, comrade." Joe picked up the immense crowbar he had used in the quarry. His post, if trouble came, was at the door of the dairy.

"But why should they attack us? Why? We have been on good terms with the Arabs. What is all this about Arab nationalism?"

"Nationalism!" Chayim snorted. "What does the Arab fellah know about nationalism! He sees a chance to raid and steal our livestock. The bedouin will drive the horses and cattle over the border and sell them in Syria. Even Sheikh Salich, our friend from the village down the road, might take an opportunity such as this."

That night Joe stood a turn on watch. For this hour he had been given a pistol. Chayim, who seemed endlessly on duty, was mounted and wore an Arab abayeh. At a suspicion of movement, he would dash down the road, leaving Joe alone, sitting on the doorstep of the *cheder ochel*. It would seem hours before his return.

Once, while Chayim was gone, Joe thought he heard a distant shot. He stood trembling, wondering—to wake the others? It might have been a rock, falling. He stood, waiting, and in that space of time the thought came

---

[5] The "Hebron massacre" refers to the killing of 67 Jews and wounding 58 others (out of a population of about 500 Jews) in Hebron on August 24, 1929 by Arabs incited to violence by false rumors that Jews were slaughtering Arabs in Jerusalem and seizing control of the al-Aqsa Mosque.

to him that perhaps he was near death. It would be so strange to meet it here on a lonely mountainside in Israel, Joe Freedman from Chicago. Would Sylvia come to his grave, up there next to Trumpledor's? And Sylvia's name was Shulamith; Shulamith must be her true Hebrew name.

Behold, thou art fair, my love, thou art fair, thou hast doves' eyes, thy hair is as a flock of goats, that appear from Mount Gilead.

Surely, wherever she was, she knew he was standing here alone, and needed, at last.

And if he should die now, what would his young life have been but a failure? He had failed with Sylvia, he had failed with his work, only here perhaps the thing he had made, rugged and as yet roughly finished, could stand.

How strange that the thought of death was in no way alarming; something cool, like this night, and vaguely elating, like this whole mountain region. Perhaps the saddest thing about his life was that he had found nothing so far to which he felt he had to cling; all of his life had been a severing, trying to rid himself of the fixation on Sylvia, trying to rid himself of his background of the West Side of Chicago, of the ugliness of his father's flophouse; and death would be the final, the perfect riddance. The most tragic thing of all, Joe thought, was that at this moment, scarcely having lived, he felt ready and willing to die, for no cause, with no heroism as these others might die, but through having little will to live.

Then laughingly, like a sudden breeze against his cheeks, he realized that he had no need to rid himself of anything. He could possess, embrace, be big! Why so mournful! He wanted to end, when he was just beginning.

There were hoofbeats. Joe waited, the whistle at his lips. Now he made out the rider.

Chayim slid off the horse. "They tried to pull me down, there, on the mountain. There are bedouin."

As if by intuition men had begun to emerge from the cottages; then women came.

—What? What is it? An attack?

—No, nothing, be still, hush. Only, to be safe, let the outpost men go to their places.

Eight men crept off, radiating toward different corners of the farm. Little groups gathered, whispering.

—The English have a warship at Haifa, it will soon be quiet now.

—Bedouin have attacked Tul Kerem. Two comrades are dead.

Joe handed his pistol over to Shlomo, took his crowbar again, and went to his post. With him was Ben Maimon, a comrade whom he scarcely knew.

"Women, go back to sleep," Chayim said. Still they prowled nervously around the yard. "Better go into the barn then." The children, as a precaution, had already been taken to sleep there.

Awaited, and yet unbelievably, there came a rapid succession of shots from above, on the mountainside.

—Theirs, or ours?

The women fell absolutely silent.

Five horsemen burst across the yard, riding toward the shooting. Several men began to run in the same direction.

Chayim halted his horse, wheeled. "Wait here! Shmarya, you are in charge. Wait till you are called. All others keep to your posts."

There were more shots. Joe stood still, his hands clamped around the bar of iron, chill as the night. What use would it be? If bedouin rode into the courtyard, shooting and cutting, could he swing at them, strike them from their horses? He had heard tales, too, of what they did to men. Cut off the genitals, and stuck them in the mouth.

From a distance, a wild war scream, ludicrously like a yodel, spiraled into the night. He had heard Arab horsemen yelling like that as they rode around immense fires on distant hills, in their games called *fantasia*.

The women closed around Shulamith. How is it? Are they many? The vermin. . . .

And now, completely, Joe felt what they felt. It was an inexpressible hatred. The word, the thought, of Arab aroused in him only the wish to kill, to see them fall, dead; he had not dreamed that it was within himself to wish to gloat on killing.

The firing began again, and endured. From two sides.

Shulamith cried: "They must need ammunition!" Then, incredibly, Joe saw her run out, and toward the battle. She was carrying the box. He started after her, took hold of one handle. It was mad. If the men had need, they would have sent a message. But with the panic of intuition, the girl ran.

Voices called them back, but they ran.

The firing had died again. A crack, and then an answering shot.

They ran together, over the stones, sure-footed, toward the olive grove blotting the hill. They had reached the first trees, and could make out the forms of white Arab horses, turning, clambering up the hill, fleeing.

They ran harder, feeling the power of triumph.

Just then, Shulamith was struck. She stopped, waited as if to know, then folded to the ground.

In the commune they sensed that the skirmish was over, and rushed forward to meet the defenders.

One of the men had a flesh wound in the shoulder; not serious, the comrade nurse could take care of him. But further, a group formed out of the darkness, carrying Shulamith.

In the morning her fever was 103. Utter quiet lay upon the commune. The people seemed to Joe to have become like some mute creatures of the mountains, moving silently, silently breathing the air. Small groups collected, with their faces toward each other, but didn't speak. They were like melancholy cattle gathered under a tree.

The doubled sentries went out to the edges of the farm, those they relieved came in, sat in the kitchen drinking tea. None could sleep.

At last Joe saw the mechanic, Maishe Levin, binding down the canvas sides of the farm truck. Then he filled the body of the truck deep with straw.

Chayim Ben Yehuda came out of the barn where his wife lay, and approached Joe.

"Listen, Yosef," he said. "Lower down, the road is already closed by the English. They may not let us pass. Someone will have to talk English to them."

"Will you take me along?" Joe said.

"Good."

Two comrades carried the girl out of the barn and placed her on the bed of straw. Her husband climbed into the truck; her eyes were open; she reached out her hand and clasped his tightly. Joe sat with the driver.

The comrades followed the truck to the gate.

The road was narrow, steep, and wound insanely around blind corners. They would have to pass two Arab villages.

As they neared the first, they saw a few Arabs with donkeys coming towards them. Joe looked back into the truck; the girl had her lover's hand close against her cheek. Maishe Levin stepped on the gas. The truck hit the bumps wildly, and slewed past the group of Arabs.

Two shots followed, in a shower of stones.

"We should not have come in daylight," Maishe said.

It was only when they were well past, spun around a curve, the first village out of sight, that Joe realized: he had been shot at. Last night had not seemed personal, but this was aimed at himself. Why? Why this? Coupled to his abhorrence of violence was an idealistic feeling that plain people, the real people of earth, were not bloodthirsty, but peaceable. Why had the Arabs risen, gone berserk, hacking to pieces the talmudists of Hebron, besieging the isolated colonies?

Were the Jews harming the Arabs?

Maishe Levin pointed his chin toward two bedouin tents, black upon the gray mountain rubble.

What can Jews take away from them?

Outside of Palestine, Joe knew, there was much talk about Arab fellahin being forced off their ancestral lands by the hordes of incoming Jews. But the attack last night had not been that of vengeful natives, driving out an invader. It had only been a furtive, sneaking raid, an attempt to steal the stock of an isolated farm.

And he had seen these fellahin. What had they to lose by the Jewish immigration? Treading out their meager harvest of grain under the hooves of camels, giving a third and a half over to their feudal sheikh, to whom they were perpetually in debt for seed. It would take the wild imagination of a political economist living in London to prove that the Jews had deprived them of their ancestral land, for, on the spot, anybody could see that the Jews had bought and developed waste lands, marshes, and land left idle by absentee owners, fat sheikhs who lived in Syria. Then why were the fellahin slaughtering Jews, who had brought them no harm, but a raised price for labor? What had let loose the bloodlust of this submerged people?

Riding beside him, Maishe Levin seemed to divine his perplexity.

"They have been told that the Mosque in Jerusalem has been sold to the Jews," he said, simply.

For a moment Joe couldn't grasp his meaning. The Mosque? But how could anyone believe such a story? And to slaughter human beings on the strength of it!

"They believe it," Maishe said. "In each village, there is a mukhtar, who reads them this news out of the Arab papers. What has happened in Hebron, and in the old city of Jerusalem—these were holy wars."

"But why should these mukhtars spread such lies?"

The truck, progressing slowly with the wounded girl, made a turn, and below them, with jewel-cut clarity, lay the valley; the olive trees of distant orchards stood leaf-clear, as in primitive painting. Everything was believable here; Joe felt that he knew why religions had arisen here.

"Why should they spread such lies?" the driver repeated, and answered: "To raise the price of the land."

"Who?"

Maishe looked at him, wondering at the simple-mindedness of the American. "Who? The sheikhs. The Arab landowners. They caused this thing to be printed in the Arab newspapers, to be spread by the mukhtars in the villages—that a great council of Jews, meeting in Europe, had bought the Mosque of Jerusalem. That is why the talmudists were the first to be attacked."

"But how will this raise the price of land? I should think it would lower it."

Maishe smiled wryly. "We Jews are a stubborn people, and this the Arabs know. Trouble only makes the Jews more anxious to buy up land, to bring their villages close together. And, as the Jews are anxious to buy, the sheikhs are reluctant to sell."

Maishe Levin concluded sadly. "You see, it is all a question of property, of money. But they who kill, don't know."

And yet, out of the confused pressure of these multiple forces, it seemed to Joe that some truth must come. It was in the tender beauty of this strange country, in the intimate mystery of this land. This trouble was like the seething of the world at its center. And his imagination, quickened in this stress, pictured this trouble between the Arabs and Jews as the intimation, the first small thematic sound, of a world turbulence, out of which peace and truth might finally prevail. For wasn't the world in tension again, for the final struggle between east and west, between a spiritual and a material approach to life? When the next war came, it would be the uprising of all the oppressed peoples of Africa and Asia, and Palestine would be the bridge between Europe and her possessions, here again would be the center of conflict, and the Jews would play their prophetic and historic role.

The buildings of Salich's village were plainly visible now; a group of squat, muddy hovels groveling under the sheikh's two-story house. Ordinarily this was a friendly village; the sheikh had built his new house with Jewish money. But now they saw Arabs drifting toward the road.

The truck, making a hairpin turn, was confronted with a blockade.

A swarm of Arabs, on foot, on donkeys, gesticulated and screamed.

Maishe Levin drew his gun. Chayim scrambled to the cab of the truck, his face between them.

Now it would happen. Joe, too, held a gun. It felt meaningless against his palm.

"Dash through," Chayim muttered.

Impossible. They had placed rocks in the road. "I'll try to talk to them," Maishe murmured, at the final moment, applying the brake.

Chayim laughed bitterly.

It was at this instant, when they had reached the impasse, that a car appeared from below.

It isn't true! Joe said to himself. Things don't happen like this!

Yet their rescue was before them; the immense touring car halted not ten feet away, and half a dozen British marines, carrying bayoneted rifles, piled out.

The Arabs spread to the side of the road, muttering.

The marines were kids, none looked over seventeen, all were stunted by wartime childhood, all with a sadly vicious air of indifference, of hatred for the bloody Arabs and the bloody Jews.

A sergeant got out of the car. "Road's shut off!" he yelled at Maishe Levin. And then, with the irritated speed of a man who knows his language isn't being understood, swore: "The bloody fuckn goddamn Jew bastards! Stick their bloody fuckn heads out, and then they squeal bloody murder 'cause they don't get protection! Get back to your holes!" he shouted, waving at the truck. "Turn around, man! Back! *Yalla!*" He dropped his voice, and spoke to a civilian who had remained in the car. "How the devil does a man make these Jews understand. I say, you talk their Chinese Hebrew, don't you? Come on, tell these fat-headed blighters to go home!"

A civilian, stoutish, bald-headed, emerged from the tonneau. At once Joe knew he had seen the man before.

"Our beloved benefactors, the British," said the civilian, "have closed the road, and this military genius is angry with you for venturing forth. He orders you to turn back."

"We have a wounded woman here, we're taking her to a hospital," Joe said to the sergeant.

For a moment, hearing English spoken, the sergeant seemed appeased. Then he snarled: "Sick woman, is it? Now what's the game? You ain't out hunting a few Arabs by any chance?"

"Look for yourself."

The British closed around the truck. The Arabs crowded in from the road-edges, angry, gesticulating, yet afraid of the half-dozen tin-helmeted lads with rifles, who remained utterly contemptuous of the danger of their position.

The sergeant hoisted himself up onto the truck. "How do I know she's sick? What's under that straw?"

"She's very sick! She's running a high fever! We were attacked last night and she was wounded!" Joe screamed. "I'm an American citizen . . ."

He realized Bialystoker had recognized him, too.

"Trust these bloody fuckn Americans to make a mess!" the sergeant swore. "Now, you, fellow, I'll take no responsibility for you! You're a Jew same as the rest of these, and your bloody American passport won't do you any fuckn good when a couple of Arabs pulls out what's in your breeches."

"This woman has to be taken to a hospital at once. What possible reason could we have for risking our necks if this wasn't true!" Joe persisted.

Shulamith had closed her eyes. The sergeant climbed down from the truck. Bialystoker spoke to him quietly.

"Come ahead," the officer said to his men. "We'll have to escort these blasted Hebrews to town." He turned on the Arabs and shouted angrily: "Go on! Scatter! Vamoose!"

Bialystoker climbed onto the truck. "Yes, we have met before," he said, putting out his hand to Joe.

"In Chicago, at the Abramsons'?"

"Yes. Several years ago." Bialystoker chuckled. "What am I doing here? I am now a correspondent for the *Wiener Zeitung*. So. I was here to write articles of Palestine, when the trouble happened."

That seemed simple enough. A coincidence. The British had allowed the journalist to accompany the patrol. But why was it always happening, so? As though she still had some meaning in his life.

"I have seen your friend in Vienna, only last month," Bialystoker said.

"Who?"

"But my niece, Miss Abramson. She is traveling in Europe."

"Oh. Oh, yes." Joe pretended to have known.

"She spoke also of visiting Palestine, but now, with this trouble, I imagine she will not come."

"No. Probably not. It would be foolish."

Safed was hushed, the streets deserted. The car drove up to a house that had been taken over as the Hadassah Hospital. A nurse, an American girl, perhaps visiting Palestine to see what all the Hadassah bridge parties had accomplished, spoke to them in the doorway. "I don't know where we'll put her, we can't possibly take care of her," she murmured distractedly. Seeing Joe, an American, she seized onto him, at last to talk her heart out. "We haven't the room, we haven't the funds—oh, what do they expect of us!"

Maishe Levin and Chayim were carrying Shulamith up the stairs, and as the American girl saw the wounded Palestinian[6], she shuddered, with fear, hysteria. Joe thought of his sister and her friends, Rose Heller, Thelma, and even of Sylvia— dutifully arranging their annual dances for Hadassah, and the millions like them all over America, the turmoil and the fuss they made. Well, after all, they were here in the emergency; without them there might have been nothing.

"Do you want to see? I can show you," Bialystoker said, with his narrow smile.

They went into a room crowded with wounded. Mostly bearded Jews from the old city, synagogue Jews, alms-livers of Safed. They had not been able to defend themselves, as had the new breed of settler. There had been a massacre in the ancient part of Safed. Joe walked among these wounded, Jews with orthodox ear-curls limp against their yellowish cheeks.

There was one younger man, whose bandaged stump lay upon the sheet. His hand had been hacked off.

In all the room, in the faces of the nurses, in the faces of the visitors, and of the wounded, was an unearthly despair. The riots had reminded them: this land was not theirs.

For the first time, Joe really felt the ominous message of the pogrom. He had not been like those other comrades, given over permanently to this homeland, to Eretz Yisrael. During the last month, love of the homeland had been growing within him, and he had glimpsed the possibility of a clear, unified, purposeful life in remaining here.

Now it was a twig nipped off. Nothing would grow there any more. And for these others, a whole flowering had been cut down.

Eunice came into the studio with the Paris *Tribune* and, showing him the headline, said: "Joe Freedman is still there, isn't he?"

---

[6] Note that the use of the term "Palestinian," in this era, refers to Jews that have migrated to British-controlled Palestine. There was no independent Palestinian ethnicity, there were only native Jews and Arabs.

Alvin experienced the crazy impulse to run into the streets shouting: "Jews! Jews! To arms!" To charter a boat, to fight!

In the cafés, in the streets, there was life as usual. His rage could only beat, beat the air.

He went to Polansky's.

Hippolyte was there, already deep in an involved, mystical discussion of the crisis in Palestine.

"No, this is not the time," Hippolyte concluded. "It is absurd to see in this event the advent of Messiah. . . ."

Alvin paced the workshop. . . . Damn that Joe, he kept seeing him lying on a road, bleeding. . . .

Aaron Polansky came toward him, rested a hand on his shoulder. "Arabs and Jews are killing each other over the possession of land," Polansky said. "No spiritual truth can be uncovered there. . . . Besides, Joe is an American. He will be safe."

Alvin stared at Polansky. All this mysticism with which he had been flirting, this Christ and Messiah stuff, these masses chorused by virgin nuns. . . . God, what an ass he had been!

He walked until he was very tired, then he sat in a corner of a workman's bistro, alone.

What were they fighting about, in Palestine? About praying at the Wailing Wall?

Then started a feverish siege of reading; he got every book, every paper he could find, for the first time he read the Balfour Declaration[7], how slimy and slippery a document, promising everything and nothing to the Jews, because a Jewish chemist had helped them win the World War. For the first time he read Colonel Lawrence's fiery adventure, and of how England had promised everything and nothing to the Arabs for aid in the World War.

Gradually, as he read, Alvin saw himself tending to make excuses for the Arabs, saw himself looking for reasons on their side. It was his own contrariness, he knew. It was his desire to beat his conscience, to convert his sense of guilt into a sense of justice.

Lately, when he had been toying with Catholicism, he had even tried turning ascetic. The basis of their marriage thus far had been a bright mutual pleasure in sex, a kind of childish delight in the perversities and sometimes amusing intricacies of technique. The partner who heard of or invented a variation which they had not yet tried brought it to bed

---

[7] The "Balfour Declartion" was a letter from United Kingdom's Foreign Secretary dated November 2, 1917, indicating Britain's favorable attitude toward establishing Palestine as a Jewish homeland if Britain should prevail in the Great War and get control of the territory that was then controlled by the Ottoman Empire. This helped tilt wartime Zionist support to Britain; however in the aftermath of the War, an official Jewish homeland remained elusive.

triumphantly. In two years, they had naturally exhausted the novelties recommended in *The Perfumed Garden* and other such guides, but the combinations were plentiful, and they still had appetite.

Now, when Eunice turned into bed and waited, her husband continued to read. When he came to bed he sometimes lay rigid, tight, tight with his own inner conflicts, and as his mind picked over the arguments between Arab, Jew, communist, capitalist, imperialist, nationalist, he would dream that beneath the shouting and the turmoil of these forces, he heard the ceaseless, yearning call that the great Chassidic rabbis had heard, the home-calling from those ancient lands.

And as his wife touched him, he would twitch with anger, and guilt.

Eunice tried to control the resentment that gorged her. After all, her husband was a sort of sick character, a maladjusted Jew, complex, intense without outlet, and she was willing to draw off some of his life-horror.

She touched him. "What's eating you, Al, can't you tell me?"

There was a scarcely audible rumbling within him.

"I'll go away if you want me to, for a while."

His body shrugged.

"I know what you think," Eunice said. And before he could stop her with some withering witticism, she went on: "You think those massacres in Palestine are a sort of punishment on the Jewish race, for backsliding, for marrying Gentiles. Oh, yes, inside you feel guilty, you've always felt you did something wrong . . ."

"Have you been reading Ludwig Lewisohn?" he said sarcastically.

"The trouble is you really have a religious mind, Alvin," she continued. "Perhaps it was that rabbinical training. In any case, I refuse to be the sacrificial goat."

"What do you mean?" He pretended blankness.

"You know darn well what I mean."

"Let me alone, can't you!" He had missed out on everything, missed his calling when he had a chance to become a rabbi. Yes, the old Messiah illusion, but every man had it, why shouldn't he? And why couldn't he have become a leader, a bringer of peace to the modern Jews? Instead, here he was at twenty-six, adrift, a parasite, getting checks from home, playing around with arty furniture designs when what people wanted was folding bridge tables.

And he was even no good to his wife. Torturing the poor kid. Why take it out on her? He tried to make himself embrace Eunice, soothe her, prove to her that his miseries were all his own, admit that they were due to his rotten sense of inferiority. But he was too conceited, he couldn't humiliate himself before his wife.

—That's my defense mechanism, he thought.

And he said: "All right! Move out if you want to!"

They went together to find her a room, Alvin insisting that it contain a fancy bidet for her possible infidelities. He even listed the suitable candidates. No matter how your mind loathed your actions, the cheap attitudes of sophistication retained you. "Don't sleep with that nigger that's dancing at the Maudit, babe," Alvin said. "He may be a swell jazz, but he has the clap."

The cable was from Mort. Sylvia understood why Mitchell had not cabled. He did not want to influence her decision. The thought of his scrupulous fairness brought her love welling upward, drowning all the doubt she felt, and for a while even drowning her heartache and her worry for Joe.

She must not let herself be influenced by the drama of Joe's plight, by the sentimental urge to go to her lover because he was in danger.

And what could she do? By the time she got there it would be all over. Perhaps Joe had changed, too.

They were refunding fares to Palestine. She could return her ticket. All this was destiny, keeping her for Mitch. She might have done something foolish, meeting Joe there, everybody said it was such a glorious, beautiful country, affecting you strangely. Sylvia studied the tickets. Arrive the twenty-first. Joe's birthday!

"In honor of your visit, my wife has put in an appearance," Alvin remarked, when Eunice greeted them. "Who knows, she may even sleep with me tonight!"

Sylvia surveyed the studio, which contained an immense couch covered with a white fleece, and some chromium-pipe chairs.

"Well, it's quite modernistic," she said, wondering if Joe had lived in this elegance. "How much do you pay for this?"

"About thirty bucks a month."

"A place like this would cost at least a hundred fifty, home," Sylvia estimated.

Eunice poured wine. Alvin picked up the modernistic goblet and passed the wine under his nose. "Here's to Joe," he toasted. "May the Arabs cut his balls off."

Eunice returned Sylvia's look, as if to say: "He's hopeless tonight."

"Why shouldn't they?" Alvin went on. "The Arabs are in the right, anyway; and it would be a good thing for him. Which reminds me, *dear*, have you seen Ann lately?"

"Ann?"

"You know, Joe's last mistress."

"Oh. No. I heard she went back to Kansas."

"A very fine place. As I was saying, all balls do is get people into trouble. Joe would probably get a lot more work done, without them."

"You know what's the trouble with you?" Sylvia said, unable to keep the high, shrewish note out of her voice. "You probably have chronic indigestion."

"A very keen diagnosis. Sylvia, you will make a perfect doctor's wife," he said. "And how is Doctor Wilner?"

"Oh, Mitch is fine. I just heard from him. He's made an important discovery."

"No doubt. And have you heard from Joe?"

"No. Why should I? Have you?"

"No."

They were quiet.

"I don't believe anything could have happened to him. The trouble is all over now," Eunice said. "There wasn't a thing about Palestine in the Paris *Tribune* today. It was all full of some stock-market crash in New York."[8]

After dinner, they went to a tiny backroom theater on Raspail, to see an art film[9]. "It's surrealistic," Alvin explained. "You want to watch for the scene where they slice open a man's eye."

They saw the closeup of the knife deliberately drawn across the staring eyeball, and juice spurting.

"Oh!" Sylvia gasped. The whole world as it was became symbolized in that deliberate, dripping cruelty. "Blood, blood, how senseless!" She saw the Arabs, and Joe, suffering, and Alvin's refined narrow face, and his cruel intellectual knife, prying within her heart.

"It's only a pig's eye," Alvin said. "They used a pig's eye. Blood is a religious symbol, you know. The Catholics drink blood at mass. The decadents are getting religion these days. Jean Cocteau is a neo-Catholic."

"Is he?" Eunice said. "I thought he was a dope fiend."

"Well, religion is the opium of the people, *dear*," Alvin repeated, smacking his lips.

They took Sylvia to her hotel. "So you're not going to Palestine?" Alvin mentioned as she got out of the cab, knowing she would go up to her room and cry.

Tonight, he felt forever free of Sylvia and all her kind. Just a good girl who wouldn't have a lover even in Paris.

"I think you were mean to the girl," Eunice said.

A half-dozen of the girls had brought the clipping which contained Joe's name in the list of Chicago Jews in Palestine.

---

[8] The Wall Street Crash began in late October, 1929, and the years of the Great Depression followed. It was not widely anticipated at the start that people other than stockholders would be affected by the stock collapse.

[9] The "art film" is Luis Buñuel's "An Andalusian Dog", released in 1929.

"Oh, I'm sure he must be all right, though why he doesn't cable I don't know," Aline said. "You'd think he'd have that much sense, but you know Joe, he's so irresponsible. . . ."

And again she related how her mother made her call up the British consul every half-hour and how the British consul's office said everything possible was being done.

To her special chum, Rose, she confided how sweet Rudy was being these days, coming over every evening and soothing her mother. "You know he and Joe were such friends."

And everybody was chattering: "Isn't Sylvia Abramson in Paris? Wasn't she going to Palestine?" And there were all kinds of hints and conjectures. Had the big love really broken up? Are Syl and Mitch officially engaged? Was Sylvia traveling in Europe to mend a broken heart or had Joe gone to Palestine to mend a broken heart? Wouldn't it be romantic if they should meet again there and . . .

"It was just a misunderstanding," Aline hinted, intimating that anything might happen.

They dived into the bridge tournament with fervor. And they planned a really big affair for Junior Hadassah, a dance that would raise several hundred dollars.

They could see Joe Freedman, lying wounded in a hospital, being saved through their efforts.

Now they could feel themselves truly the "daughters of the people," as their motto signified. This was an emergency, and they could be relied upon.

Rose Heller spent practically her whole salary on tickets for the benefit raffle.

The prize was to be a beautiful bust of a prophet, with a long flowing beard. It was by Boris Schatz, the great Jewish sculptor of the Bezalel, in Jerusalem. His work had recently been exhibited at the Covenant Club. Mort Abramson called it the Covetant Club.

Mrs. Freedman served the girls strudel for refreshments. She apologized for not having made a salad; she was so worried about Joe.

Harry noticed that his mother seemed even more shrunken, like a drying kernel. She read her Yiddish newspaper, over and over, every day. "Harry!" she said, "they are making a pogrom on the Jews, even in Palestine." She was slowly weeping. Sometimes, just as a figure of speech, she talked of the time when she would lay down her old bones in Jerusalem. "The Arabs are killing Jews in Palestine," she repeated, as though he couldn't know of it.

"I know," he said. "It's in the English papers too."

She was surprised. "It's in the English papers too?" She adjusted her *shaitel*. Her voice was so old, and plaintive, and patient. "Why? Why do they make pogroms? If an old Jew wants to lay down his bones in the Holy Land . . . Oh, a world."

A man who has once risked his life has a new sense of himself; he has outfaced doom. And a melancholy, like one who emerges from ether, after a perilous operation.

Joe flung himself onto the golden glowing sand of Tel Aviv.

The sea and sky cried aloud with the clarity and simplicity of life; the beach blazed with open confidence and beauty.

But it seemed that people would never speak with their full voices again.

Yes, Palestine would remain, and the settlement would go on . . . but the glow of the miracle was gone.

It was the same as in his own life. He was always awaiting, expecting the miracle.

—She won't come. Her folks would never let her come. She would have had to sail in the midst of the riots.

—But she knows I'm here. She knows I've been through this. She really loves me, and will have to come. It's my birthday.

A boat from Marseilles was arriving at Jaffa. She would have to be on that. She might come walking along the sand, at any moment, and they would meet casually, as though this were Clarendon Beach.

Joe stepped into the water. He started swimming outward, using the breast stroke that he had learned when a kid, going to the J.P.I.

He had gone out beyond the usual beach crowd, but a few ambitious heads still bobbed beyond him.

—I wonder how far it really was that Mitch swam, that time in Benton Harbor. It couldn't have been more than a mile, you know how immense distances seem to kids, and I was really only a kid then.

He would swim way out, further than Mitch, and when he came back, she would be waiting for him on the shore, on the beach of Tel Aviv, saying Happy Birthday to you.

—Oh, unendingly romantic, incurable I, he was aware of himself, and his head ducked under again, in the long hypnotic monotony of swimming. He passed the bobbing head of the farthest swimmer, noting the swirl of the wet hair, and he waved to show his strength and capability. He got a mouthful.

How far would a mile be? Joe turned on his back, and lifted himself, treading water, and saw with a shock that he had come far enough away so that the view toward the beach was a new one; he could see Jaffa, extending its point into the water, and could realize the configuration of the port.

Maybe this was half a mile; going back would make it a mile. But he wasn't really tired, he had his second wind and could go on like this indefinitely, thrusting out into the sea.

He turned, and pushed on.

Far out alone in the water, beyond the reach of help if he should shout, for his voice would probably be drowned in the small noise of the beach, the shrill squeaks of girls; beyond the line where small boats went, he was alone.

Her name had always been Shulamith.

Joe turned over on his back, floated. The city of Tel Aviv was now visible as a small, gentle-breasted hill, the hill of springtime, by its name; and the Arab city of Jaffa was a sharper, more clustered hill.

Now was he cleaned of all his childish doubts, fears, wishes; was he free?

Only now he recognized the true love they had all felt for each other, back there on Mount Gilead. Now, with the calm Mediterranean lapping over his body, lying on the waters swelling and lowering with a gentle breast-breathing, Joe remembered and recognized the true love that had been in them all on that night when Chayim had quietly said: Comrades, go to your places.

They had walked off, spreading into the dark; and the reluctance in their hearts had not been the reluctance to face danger, but the mere sweet unhappiness of separating for a while, from loved friends.

And yet if he were to go back up there on Mount Gilead, he would not find that feeling again. That love had given way, had been fused in a white arc of emotion; the comrades were united now by hatred.

It was commonplace to say how love had turned to hatred, and yet it seemed to Joe that this was the test of real truth: it was commonplace. It had been seen and recognized by all humanity.

And in the same way it was commonplace to say that the bringers of peace, the Jews forever in the world, brought only bloodshed.

There, visible, was the strange mechanism of polarity, by which creation continued.

Joe Freedman began to swim back toward shore; and then he realized that he was very tired. He felt no panic, no rush of fear: calm as at that moment when he had stood by the dairy, a ridiculous stretch of crowbar in his hand, waiting for the attack.

He was calm, he took it easy. He held his breath long and smooth as he let his leg stroke propel him under the water; his legs were not tired, only his arms were somewhat weary.

He thought of a book he had read and considered marvelous when he was a kid: *Martin Eden*, by Jack London. In the end of the book, the hero, who had struggled through to fame as a writer, and was disgusted because all the good things of life came to him too late, wriggled out of a porthole and swam down, down under water until he was so far down that he could never come up alive. Now, thrusting wearily through the water, Joe wondered what was the point of such death? What was the point of any death? Amusing and romantic notions people had, as though dying were noble in itself, but even death for a cause said nothing, absolutely nothing. If the world was rotten, was it made any better because a noble person died?

He could see the small Arab fishing boats now, and felt sure he could make it that far, at least. Would they take in a Jew, a spent swimmer?

When he pulled himself up on the shore, no one there could have any idea what he had just done, how far he had been, what he had proved to himself. He found a clear stretch of sand, and flopped on his belly, and let the sun beat into his spine.

Joe tumbled into the tender, his suitcases were tossed after him, miraculously missing the sea. *Yalla!* the Arabs began their rowing chant. As they reached the liner, Joe saw Bialystoker hanging over the rail, laughing.

In the evening they stood together watching the ship's wake.

Sometimes there were long silences between their remarks, while they simply looked at the unending sameness, the liquidity that formed ceaselessly into small hills of waves.

"So we are through with the *chalutz* adventure? Finished. *Chalas!*" Bialystoker said, passing one palm slowly over the other; Joe felt his smile glint through the dark.

"Maybe I'll go back and live there some time. Just now, my money's run out," he said.

"Ah." Bialystoker smacked his lips. "The Guggenheim does not provide for a whole life?"

Joe was about to say: "Why should it?" But if it was recognized that one year in an artist's life had to be provided for, what of the rest of his life?

"Well, we're lucky to get what we can, the way things are," he said.

After a while, Bialystoker remarked: "What do those others do, who go on living there when their moneys run out?"

"Oh, sure, I could dig ditches," Joe said. "But I'm supposed to be a sculptor."

"Yes. In that you are right." Joe still felt Bialystoker smiling at him. "And in America you can be a sculptor?"

Joe shrugged. "When you get right down to it, it might be easier in Palestine. If I could get myself a racket, like that Boris Schatz, the official Jewish sculptor, and make prophets with beards."

Bialystoker chortled sympathetically.

"That isn't really the reason why I'm leaving—money," Joe said. "If I wanted to stay, I'd stay. I mean, well, I guess I got what I wanted for the present."

Yes, he meant that what Palestine stood for existed within him now. That part of him, the Jewishness, was quiet. He could carry it along, anywhere.

"You are not a Zionist?"

"I'm not against Palestine. I really believe in the whole thing, but . . ." Joe tamped his pipe. He offered some of his tobacco to Bialystoker, who tried the mixture. "Palestinian tobacco is good," the journalist said. And added: "You do not believe in political Zionism."

"No," Joe said. "But how can there be a Jewish settlement without it?" The man had a strange way of getting around you until he taught you something by making you say it yourself. "Weren't you interested in Russia?" Joe asked. "I remember long ago, that time I met you at the Abramsons', weren't you getting money from Julius Rosenwald for the Jewish colony in Russia?"

"Ah, then . . ." He spoke as though things had changed.

"You're still—interested in Russia?"

Bialystoker smacked his lips. "Yes, in Russia I believe. But—since that time there have been some changes, my friend. Trotsky is in exile . . .[10]"

"Is that so?" Joe was astonished. He didn't follow those things.

"Yes, it is so for more than a year." Bialystoker seemed ironically amused.

They puffed and watched the sea.

Joe was thinking, if Bialystoker was a communist, as he must be, then why didn't he speak of communism, try to make a convert? Communists like this Bialystoker, Joe decided, took it for granted that the world would come around to their way; they waited, smilingly watching, never bothering to urge.

"But don't you approve of the communes in Palestine?" Joe resumed.

"Ah, they are all right," the journalist said, idly.

"But I thought, as a communist . . ."

"There were many experiments of this sort early in the century. Fourier, and a number of such little agricultural communities; in America you had a good many of them. I believe a few still survive."

Joe thought of the House of David, in Benton Harbor. A fad, a joke. But in Palestine the communes were different. "They are the real thing," Joe asserted. "I lived in one, in Giladi."

"Vegetarians," Bialystoker dismissed the subject. "Communists, shooting Arabs for His Imperial Majesty."

Joe said: "If people are just allowed to live and do their work and go on making love and making wine, what difference does it make who collects the taxes?"

"Ah. If they were just allowed to live."

---

[10] Leon Trotsky was deported from the Soviet Union in February 1929 as Stalin solidified his leadership. Trotsky, although ethnically Jewish, was not religious. His background as a Communist revolutionary leader made for some awkward controversy, both inside and outside the Jewish community.

"Well, I suppose you believe England was behind all that trouble?"

Bialystoker shrugged. "In this case you can believe everything. England did it, and the Arabs did it, and the Jews did it. It is an impossible situation."

"Well," Joe exhibited his knowledge, "naturally England has to keep the Jews and Arabs on edge. Divide and rule."

"So what difference does politics make to lives of the people?" Bialystoker slyly repeated.

"Well, I mean the thing can go on, it is going on, it isn't only a dream— it does exist. Why, there is a whole generation born and raised there already, they live a real Hebrew life. What's wrong with that?"

"Nothing. Did I say that was wrong?"

"But you don't think anything will ever come of it?"

"A few more Jews will come there and live off the orange groves and perhaps off the potash deposits of the Dead Sea. What does it matter, eh?"

"But even if the whole country were communistic, would it make any difference?" Joe blurted. "The Arabs would still be there."

"Ah. And Arabs are not people."

"Oh, sure, but you know, actually, I mean they're a backward race, they're just like serfs in the Middle Ages, scratching the earth for a rag of cloth and a bit of bread, that's all they live on. While the Jews are really developing the country, developing a culture . . ."

"Doubtless. But what is more important, then: to raise the cultural level of the cultured Jews, or to free the Arabs from serfdom?"

The Arabs would always be there. And "next time we will be ready for them," the boys had said.

Joe was silent, and the boat carried them, and he watched the little line of smoke left behind them by their pipes.

"Do you know that even your Jewish friends in Chicago nearly tore down the offices of a newspaper—yes, a Jewish newspaper—that dares to print that the Arabs had some right on their side?" Bialystoker snorted. "The comrades were sitting with shotguns on their knees, in the newspaper office in Chicago."

"I don't mean that the Jews are more important than any other people," Joe said. "But somehow I feel, as everyone who comes there feels, that there is a destiny in that land. I'm not religious, but you know that the premonitions get into you, they seem to be in the very air of Palestine . . ." He felt his ideas becoming beautifully clear now, and flowing out of him with a rhythm as sure as the pulse of the ship upon the sea. "Perhaps I really believe as you believe, perhaps in the long run everyone believes alike, and wants the same thing— peace, and a kind of communism. And in Palestine, you get to feel that the world has always converged on that spot, and that, oh, maybe because it's the Jews, and the Jews have always been the bringers of every big idea, of religions, and communism is like a religion, you get to feel that the next movement of the world may again come through Palestine, it may be communism brought to the world through the Jews perfecting it, living by it in Palestine."

Bialystoker was smiling warmly and pityingly. "Yes, that is a dream of love, my friend. And how do you feel toward the Arabs?"

The word alone was enough to bring back that blind loathing.

But Joe said: "I know. It isn't ready yet. It will take a long time. There may be a great struggle, first." It whirled in his mind, some great struggle of the future, and he could almost divine the conflict shaping in the entire world.

"Yes, it is a country of love," Bialystoker said. "And do you know, Joe Freedman, why the British have given the Balfour Declaration to the Jews? For love?"

Joe raised his head.

"For T.N.T., which Dr. Weizmann gave the British, in the war."

"Still," Joe said, "the Jews are safe as long as England has to hang onto the mandate."

Bialystoker recapitulated: "And why must Great Britain hang onto the mandate? To keep the Suez Canal. And why must she keep the canal, Mr. Joe Freedman?"

"Why, to get to her colonies."

"And why must she keep her colonies?"

"Why? Foreign trade, I guess."

"And if another profit-nation had to sell stuff to the same markets? And if the natives began to manufacture?"

"They can't. As long as the world has the same system," Joe said.

And he saw—that was where Bialystoker had led him.

After a moment Joe said regretfully, to show how he stood: "The British are too smart. They know how to keep the system going. Look how they handled Gandhi."

"And if an Arab Gandhi should arise? And simultaneously—"

"Well, sure," Joe said. "That may be coming. That may be the next thing. . . . But Palestine alone isn't endangered by that. And not only the Jews. The whole world is involved."

"Yes, it is a common fate," Bialystoker agreed, with his same small smile, as though his pupil had completed a lesson. And added: "The British have begun to build a military port, in Haifa."

They were silent for a long time. It was a cold, starless night. The boat seemed to be going faster, rushing.

CAPITAL AND LABOR

HARRY PERLIN had a helper in the shop now; not that he was making a lot of dough, but he found by experience that even if he sold all the Close-A-Doors he turned out by himself, he couldn't pay his overhead. So he got Mack Petella from Bienstock's garage, paying him fifty bucks a week. Which was a lot more than Harry was taking out for himself, but naturally, he owned the business.

Another thing he had to do was borrow a thousand dollars from his brother, to invest in machinery.

Harry liked to pay bills on the dot, but he had discovered that it is okay to owe money in business, in fact the more credit you had, the bigger business man you were. So he had over a thousand dollars of credit on castings and hardware.

Vic said naturally he would go into debt while he was building up the business. That would all take care of itself later.

The selling end had hit a couple of snags after that Sunday when Vic had sold Close-A-Doors like hotcakes. Harry had sent two fellows out with cars, guaranteeing them twenty dollars a week, plus commission. He lost money on them. Vic razzed the pants off of him and Harry learned to send the men out on straight commission.

They beefed that sales couldn't be made on weekdays as housewives were not interested in buying gadgets for the garage. Sunday was the day.

Vic gave Harry the bright idea of advertising. Spare-time work, earn fifty to a hundred dollars on your day off.

So from then on there was an average force of ten fellows selling two or three Close-A-Doors apiece on Sunday. After a few of them had taken his stock and failed to return with the money for the articles, Harry required a deposit. He said: "I, personally, trust you, but the owners of the firm require a deposit. You understand."

At the end of every week when he saw the Close-A-Doors with their long arms of rust-proof silvery steel lying in platoon formation on the floor of the shop, he felt fine. He delayed boxing them until the last moment.

Harry was thinking of looking around for a wife.

At noon, he and Mack, whom he jestingly called his force, padlocked the shop and went to a lunch wagon together. Mack had always been a baseball fan; and now that the Cubs were playing a world series, the first world series in Chicago since the Sox won the pennant in 1919, Harry felt his interest in the sport reawakening.

"Who is McCarthy starting today?" he asked, sliding over the stool.

"Maloney. Man, I'd like to see that game. It's going to be a classic," was Mack's opinion. "Sling me the goulash, Pete."

"Same," Harry ordered.

Pete, the usual Greek counterman with a one-day growth of beard, yelled: "Tu plate," and turned up the radio.

"If they only had one more pitcher," Mack said. "It's Bush and Root and Maloney, and I wouldn't give a nickel for Maloney against . . ."

". . . tape is now twenty-two minutes behind," the radio announced, "and it looks like another record run on the market. Two billion dollars in profits were wiped out yesterday when six million shares . . ."

The Greek boredly went over and whirled the dials, getting "I Can't Give You Anything but Love, Baby."

"Those Wall Street boys are certainly taking it on the chin," a customer observed.

"Whatever goes up must come down," Harry Perlin said. "I certainly wouldn't ever gamble on the stock market."

"This is the time to buy," Mack said sagely. "The trouble with Maloney, get him in a pinch and he blows up like a firecracker."

"A buck Chicago cops the series," Harry offered.

He had to walk from the end of the shop to answer the phone. It was Vic. "Say, Harry, can you rustle up some of that dough you owe me, I need it by tomorrow morning!"

"Huh? Tomorrow? Can't you borrow it someplace else Vic, it may take me a couple of days to—"

"Get whatever you can right away," Vic snapped. "I may need the whole thousand."

Harry tried not to feel sore. After all Vic had a right to ask for his money whenever he needed it. "Mack, you got any dough?" he approached his helper.

"Coupla bucks." Mack reached into his pocket.

"No, I mean dough."

"How much you need?"

"All I can get up to a grand."

"All I got is about forty bucks in the bank and I—"

"That's all right," Harry said. "Never mind." Then he explained: "I guess my brother got caught on the stock market. He's in the bond business, you know."

"What'd he have?"

"I think he had some General Electric."

"That's a good stock," Mack said. "He ought to hang onto it. He have it on margin?"

"Why, I guess so."

"Say, why don't you try the Morris Plan; my old man borrowed some money there."

From the Morris Plan to his old boss, Mr. Bienstock, to the Liberty Bank, and after waiting another hour and a half because the Loan Department was jammed with customers, all Harry got was advice to try the West Side Mortgage and Loan Association.

Three old worried-looking Jews, and one aged woman wearing a *shaitel* such as his mother wore, sat opposite the door. Their heads swung together, following him, like clockwork.

"Yes?" said an office voice. And then: "Why, Harry Perlin!"

It was Lil Klein, or rather Lil Eisen, behind the desk. She was wearing a bright orange smock, the latest fad.

"Well! What are you doing here?" he asked.

"Oh, I'm just helping my father, you know this is his business. I've got nothing else to do." She lifted her hand to her hair. "I guess you know I'm divorced, Harry?"

"No! Is that so!" He was uncertain whether one was supposed to take such news sadly, like news of death. And at the same time it felt odd that important things like divorce could have happened to people he had known so well, and not even come to his hearing. He'd gotten so far away from things.

"Oh, we just agreed to disagree," she said. "So we separated. So here I am, back in circulation."

"Didn't—didn't you have a baby?"

She laughed. "A baby! Why, he started school this year!" And then her face fell, at the realization of age. "Oh, yes, I have the cheeild. . . . So here I am just an old lady with a past," she said, her look challenging him to deny this classification of herself. And in fact, from her appearance you would never guess she was a divorcee with a kid. Her hair was blonder than it used to be. "Well, Harry, what have you been up to all these years?" she inquired.

"Oh, nothing much."

"You're not getting married or anything, are you?" she blinked at him, archly.

"Oh, no. Where did you get that idea?" He blushed.

"Well, that's what people usually need money for. See, I know all about it," she jested.

"No, the fact is I need a little cash for my business," he said. "It's going fine, but you know, sometimes you need money to turn around with."

"Oh, sure. What sort of business is it, Harry?"

"Oh, it's just a little invention of mine." And before he knew it he had told her all about his affairs.

"Well, Harry, that sounds awfully exciting! I just knew you would do something some day! An inventor! I'm sure my father can take care of you." And lowering her voice she added: "I'll make him see you next, so you won't have to wait for all these dopes."

But they were already leaning back resignedly. Evidently they had divined that he would cut in on their turns.

"Well, we have a little two-story building," Harry admitted, when Mr. Klein spoke of surety. "But it really belongs to my mother, and there's a little mortgage on it anyway." That had been to send Vic through college.

Mr. Klein suggested that, instead of cramping himself by borrowing a hundred here and a hundred there, at exorbitant interest, Harry ought to take out a second mortgage on the house, say for fifteen hundred dollars.

"I'll have to talk it over with my mother," Harry said. "I guess it'll be all right."

He could put on more salesmen, work nights, and pay it off in no time.

When Harry came out, a skinny bright-eyed child was talking to Lil.

Lil's voice was a trifle sharp. "Oh, Harry, here is my kid. Skeezix, this is an old friend of your mother's, Harry Perlin." She had her arm around the child.

As the kid went, she said: "He's so cute. You know we've always called him Skeezix, 'cause he's the same age. So the other day, when he saw that Colonel Coda had left all that money to Skeezix in his will, he said: 'Mama, I'm going to make them give me that money, 'cause my name is Skeezix.' "

Harry laughed, appreciatively. "Why don't you come around and see us, Harry?" she said. "We still live right here in the building, you know. My father has to stay near his business."

She gave him a bright, uncertain look.

Mort felt crabby. He always felt lousy after sleeping alone; there was no letter from Sylvia in the box and he was afraid she had gone to Palestine after all, though she could hardly have had enough money; driving down Madison Street he noticed another new Wylie Hat Store opening, all hats $1.88, and this made him sore as the devil because the folks had never let him try out his chain-store idea direct from maker to wearer and now someone else was cashing in on the same idea; he could have been the biggest man in the business if they hadn't held him back! And they would have been independent of these damned little slumps when the stores quit trying to sell hats. The Cubs had lost the series so he owed Harry Turek ten bucks, but it wasn't the ten so much as the satisfaction he had expected at seeing Chicago cop the world's title, for once; and on top of everything he had dropped two hundred bucks on Sears stock, but he figured that made him even as he had made over three hundred in a previous little flyer on the market. The thing was, like in poker, to know when to quit.

"Aha, here it comes," Mort thought as, through the glassed wall of the office, he saw Birdie Volpi veer off the course to the ladies' room and make for him. The forelady, down at the other end of the shop, made a gesture of exasperated frustration. Mort gave her a forgiving nod and waited for Birdie.

Why the heck couldn't they take it like men! The same crying at the end of every season.

"It isn't for me, Mr. Abramson," Birdie Volpi breathed the instant she got inside the door.

"You didn't get laid off, did you?" he said. A few of the older hands had been included in the layoff this time, as the winter stuff was unusually slow getting started, and he was not going to show a deficit when the old man and the old lady came back from Saratoga, where they were taking mineral baths. Birdie was one of the older girls, having been in the shop six years, though she only looked about twenty-one now, with her two bombs bursting against her green blouse, and her mouth a wide bright red smear *à la* Joan Crawford.

She was about the liveliest number in the place, singing over the buzz of the machines, and she worked so fast that if they could have set the piece-rate by her they'd have saved twenty percent on wages.

Birdie was okay, and occasionally in passing, Mort would give her a slap on the behind, or cop a feel of those bombs of hers. But he never pushed it any further. Never played the shop girls.

"It's for Mrs. Steniewski," Birdie said. "I wanna ask you."

"Who?"

"You know, she's the one with that burn on her neck. She's only been here a couple of months."

He couldn't be expected to know all the girls. "What's the matter, she get laid off?"

"Yah. She's got a husband out of work and three kids and—"

Mort scrunched his shoulders. "Listen, Birdie, I've got nothing to say about it. The newest hands get laid off. We'll call her back as soon as the season starts."

"Yah, but Mr. Abramson, she needs it more than anybody. That's all her family got to live on," Birdie pleaded. "Honest, I been watching her, she hardly ever even eats any lunch. There's a lot of other girls could stand it better than her." In her excitement, her bombs fluttered her dress.

"We can't play favorites. We've got to go according to the list," Mort said. "Or do you want to go in her place?"

She gasped, and colored.

He smiled back reassuringly.

She became self-conscious, and moved her legs to hide a stocking-run.

"Honest, Mr. Abramson, I wouldn't ask you to do this for me, but she's too scared to ask you, she's scared of you."

"But you aren't scared of me, huh?"

They laughed intimately.

413

Now the sense of the two of them as a man and a woman was awake, and the female scent came to him as it did sometimes in July when he passed through the shop of warm half-uncovered women. But it was really pretty coarse stuff. The idea of coupling with the shop girls was a little like going after some kind of animal.

She had lifted her lip over her large teeth, half expectantly. She was laid out for him to grab; nobody home these nights, he could even take her to the house and have some party. But, naw, Lew Nathanson got one of his *shiksehs* into trouble and look at him now, couldn't raise his voice in his own shop, couldn't hire or fire without her say-so.

"No, I can't do anything, Birdie. Honest, I can't. If we start making exceptions, you know how it is."

A few minutes later he heard someone bawl, and saw the forelady and Birdie huddling a woman toward the ladies' room. Then he saw Birdie talking to that blocker, George Frazier, whom he suspected of being a trouble-maker.

Going through the flat, Mort put a light on in each room, until reaching the kitchen and looking back, he saw the series of lights emphasizing the emptiness and loneliness of the apartment. A perfect setup wasted.

He drifted back into Sylvia's room and stood by the dresser. In the second drawer, he knew, was the box containing Joe Freedman's letters. He lifted off the white silk slips under which Sylvia hid the box, drew out a few letters, and glanced through them again. Those kids had been in love all right. How young, how idealistic, the letters were! In some of them he had found mention of himself, of his "behavior," and he smiled. He had nothing against Joe.

Sometimes he wished for a love like that, the real thing, with a virginal girl.

He was broad-minded, and yet deep down he felt any girl he married would have to be a virgin. . . . Just once in his life to know that it wasn't some punk he was with, but a pure girl, giving herself to him.

What the devil was Joe doing there in Palestine anyway, trying to make a martyr of himself? For a moment Mort wished he had an opportunity like Joe's, to be free, to follow out the truth of himself, to find some meaning in life. He found himself longing for some sort of expression of his Jewishness. Maybe he too should be there fighting Arabs. He could almost feel the physical dread of a lonely mountain road, and himself a night-rider on a camel. An ambush. And in the morning his bleeding body found with his member stuck in his mouth. Like that time they found a U. of C. student in a vacant lot, his glands stolen. Mort shuddered. He would rather be dead.

And anyway the whole idea of Palestine was impractical. You couldn't grow anything in that country. And what if a few thousand Jews could make a living in the orange groves, would that provide a Jewish life for all the millions of Jews in the rest of the world—Jews like himself, who felt a sincere longing for something, a Jewish culture, perhaps? Lately, he had been attending a lecture series at the Sinai Temple, hearing Stephen Wise and Count Keyserling. He had also joined the Players' Club of the J.P.I., and now he had a real idea: why shouldn't they put on plays about Jewish life, like the *Dybbuk*, or Sholom Asch's *God of Vengeance*?

Mort could already see himself, wearing a thick black beard, playing the stern father, the brothel-owner. He thought over all the girls in the club and what jokes he could make about casting one for the virgin daughter. And casting the brothel girls.

Mort's proposal started a battle. "Just because this is a Jewish club, do we have to flaunt our nationality?" a beak nose argued. "Why not put on something worth while, that has to do with modern life? Like *R.U.R.*!"

But Mort received support from a new member, who pointed out that *The Golem* had been a great success at the Goodman Theater. She was dark, and wore her hair in a trick way, leaving a cluster of short curls rattling against the back of her neck. She looked too sophisticated to be a virgin; and yet, you could never tell.

They were voted down for *R.U.R.*, and drew together in the sympathy of defeat.

"Yes, we've met."

Her voice was low, with a kind of glow in it, and with carefully studied enunciation. "It was years ago, at a dance. Oh, I was just a kid then."

Her name was Sorka Rosen. "Only then, I think I called myself Nora," she jested.

Why it had been at that silly Big Ten dance, and she was the girl Alvin Fox had brought around! She had been a prodigy at the U. And wasn't her father something strange? A Jewish policeman?

"Alvin Fox! Whatever became of him?"

"Didn't you hear? He married a *shikseh*."

"No. I've lost track of everybody. Been in New York trying to get on the stage."

The man she would give her soul to work with, she said, was Sergei Samsovetsky, who treated the actor like a piece of furniture.

"He was with the Habima," she said, awesomely.

"Oh, the Habima!" Mort was thrilled at their mutual enthusiasm. "You know they started as just a bunch of amateurs, too, in Moscow."

They stumbled on a pair of neckers, braided together on a prop couch, and exchanged a knowing glance, as if to say, that's all these kids come here for.

"Why not come up to my house for a while, I'm a bachelor these days," he said.

"Going to show me your etchings?"

"No, my first editions." It was a thrill to be so perfectly attuned.

She gave him that Norma Shearer look and said: "Don't forget, I'm a policeman's daughter."

Mort got out some of the old man's prized vishniak, and then showed her his copy of *Lysistrata*, with the Aubrey Beardsley illustrations. He perched on the arm of the chair, and together they laughed over the huge organs of Beardsley's gnomes.

He put on a dirty record he had bought since the folks were away.

The Negro voice throbbed:

"He bought my first cabbage and made it awful hot,
He bought my first cabbage and made it awful hot,
Then he shoved in the bacon and soon overflowed the pot."

He slipped down beside her, their mouths glued, their legs entwined.

"Uh uh, Mort," she said sympathetically, coming out of the clinch. "Let's get to be friends, first."

Maybe he was falling in love, Mort thought. No one had ever given him that feeling of being anticipated, met at every turn.

Only, one thing bothered him. Sure, he was sophisticated enough to say that virginity was just a joke. But now, feeling himself getting serious about Sorka, he had a disappointed feeling too, as though he was about to be cheated out of something he had waited for all his life.

He was even wondering how she would fit in with Syl and Mitch and the rest of the bunch when Syl came home. Her father was no ordinary copper, but was an expert on racketeers, almost as important as Make Mills, the celebrated chief of the bomb squad. Yet when she asked him to dinner, Mort sensed that Sorka was, in the modern scornful way, ashamed of her family.

They lived in an eight-room flat on Flournoy Street. It didn't look very swell. He must be an honest copper, Mort thought, noticing the ancient upright piano. "I can't get them to do anything with the dump, I've given up trying," Sorka apologized.

She fenced Mort off at her end of the table and had dinner with him in complete disregard of the others. But her father, and the eldest son, Ed, tossed a few bits of conversation at Mort.

"Hear you're in the millinery business, how goes it?" Ed yelled.

"The season is late," Mort said. "And if all the girls keep on wearing berets it never will get started."

Mort asked Sergeant Rosen if the clean-up campaign was on the level. Did Swanson really mean it? Were they really going after the racketeers?

Rosen stuck a huge hunk of meat into his mouth.

"Well, you know, State Street is getting pretty sore," Ed said. "The big State Street boys put their foot down. It's hurting business. And you know all the new hotels, the Stevens and the Bismarck and the Palmer House.

They want the town cleaned up for the Fair, or they're afraid no one will come here. It's hurting business, the hotels are empty, so this time they mean it."

"If they ever have the Fair," Sorka said skeptically.

"Oh, they'll have it," Mort said. "Why, Rosenwald and a couple of other big guys just subscribed five million dollars. Don't you kid yourself, a guy like Dawes wouldn't monkey around unless they meant business. He says the other five million is already subscribed, too."

"I bought a coupla bonds myself," Ed said. "It's worth it, even if I'm giving 'em the money, for the business it'll bring into town!"

"That's right!" Mort said. He liked Ed. He kind of liked the whole family. Though he could tell that Sorka thought they were boorish. It gave him an advantage. Maybe tonight was the night.

After seeing the four Marx brothers in *Animal Crackers*, they went to his house again. He took her into Sylvia's room.

Business got worse. It passed the stage where you pretended to your rivals that things were okay. Around the cigar stand in the lobby of the Milliners' Building, all you heard was beefing.

—People ain't buying, that's all. They won't pay the price.

—Well, y' can't blame them at that, look at our prices.

—Yah? Who gets the dough? I don't see a nickel of it. Look at the wages I got to pay.

—Blockers, getting sixty dollars a week!

—Girls, getting thirty dollars a week. What do they need it for? Come to work in silk stockings, two bucks a pair.

Everybody was talking wage cuts.

And at the same time, the help was getting funny. Every time a shop had to lay off a couple more girls, they threatened strikes.

Whoever heard of girls in a union? Maybe fifteen, twenty percent of the cutters and blockers belonged to a union. But girls! Next month, next year, they figured on getting married. So why bother with unions?

Only now you could feel the unions growing in the shops. Mort knew it was that guy George Frazier, the blocker, who was probably laying Birdie Volpi and getting her to organize the girls.

Around the cigar stand the discussion grew serious. Look what happened to the laundry business, to the cleaners, to the movie operators, to the building trades, they are in the grip of union gangsters! Now is the time to wipe out this union, before it even gets started, or we'll be in the soup!

Unions? All gangsters, bombing, murdering each other on the streets of Chicago, worse than bootleggers.

Wasn't Swanson conducting a big crusade against union racketeers, cleaning them out of Chicago?

And Mort had the idea—sure! Hitch right onto Swanson's crusade! Show up the union racketeers, who would prey upon the poor working girls, take away their hard-earned wages to buy bullet-proof limousines.

The winter season didn't start at all. Nobody was buying. Business kept getting worse and for Mort it was actually a relief to have the folks come home. Every week when he had to make out the payroll it looked like he'd have to go into the reserve funds. And when it came to making out checks for Saratoga Springs and for Sylvia, on top of the payroll, it was tough. He was even going to ask Syl to come home tourist instead of second class, but seeing as this was the end of her trip, he didn't want to alarm her, and managed the extra hundred bucks.

The old lady came home peppy and full of energy; with her new bob she looked like a girl.

She caught onto the situation at once. You didn't have to tell her anything. "George Frazier," she said, "he is the trouble-maker. A radical too, a socialist, a communist, a I-don't-know-what."

It turned out, if you tried to fire George Frazier, all of the blockers and cutters and many of the girls would walk out. Was the old lady burned up! They are telling me who we can hire and fire! But she controlled herself. She kept him on a while longer. In the meantime she got hold of one of the girls and inside of a week she knew who were union members, in the shop.

At a meeting of the shop-owners, she got right up and talked. "What is the use of kidding ourselves? Business is terrible. Prices are cut in half and we are still paying high wages. So the cutters and blockers want to have a union, all right! We will give them a wage scale!" From sixty dollars cut to thirty dollars, from forty dollars to twenty-five dollars, she proposed.

You could see those shop-owners sparking to her talk. There was a woman!

The unions laughed at the offer.

The shop-owners voted a lockout, to destroy the unions, once and for all. Now is the time to wipe them out, what have we got to lose, there is no work in the shops anyway!

The union called a counter-strike.

Mort laughed. "You can't fire me, I quit!" he jested, at the cigar counter.

There was only one way to make sure that those who were taken back to work were not union members. Have them sign contracts. The shop-owners' organization got them printed.

In the morning, Mort took the Studebaker and rounded up several of the foreladies, bringing them to the shop. George Frazier and his gang were already out, blocking the sidewalk, lined up with their signs:

Capital and Labor

THIS PLACE IS

UNFAIR

TO ORGANIZED LABOR

The first minute, it looked comical to Mort—in front of their own shop. Then, as the hooting and booing rose, he felt sore. He bust out of the car and shoved his way through, with the foreladies.

"Mort Abramson and his harem!" Birdie Volpi cried from the picket line.

"Scabs!"

"Girls! stay out of there!"

"Girls, don't sign the yellow-dog contract!"

"Ay, ay, ay!" George Frazier mimicked the sheeny bosses.

From the window Mrs. Abramson called: "Birdie, I'm surprised at you, so long you worked for us didn't we always treat you right!"

Birdie made a fart-noise.

"You just try to get another job in any shop in Chicago!" Mort cried.

Mrs. Abramson was at the telephone calling up relatives, friends, former hands who were now married. All day, Mort rushed around bringing people to work. Each time, he had to pass through that booing crowd, listen to the new filthy names they had for him. It was good Syl hadn't got back to Chicago yet.

Hardly any of the girls showed up for work. They didn't belong to the union but they were afraid of trouble. When the foreladies got them on the phone, they said their mothers made them stay home. A few agreed to come, if called for. But even when brought, some were afraid to cross the sidewalk into the shop.

The manufacturers had already got an injunction against picketing. Downtown, it was easy to enforce as almost all of the shops were located in a few buildings around Wabash and Lake Streets, and a couple of cops on the corner could take care of the whole strike. But as the Glory Shop was out by itself, a crowd of pickets hung around.

In spite of everything, Mrs. Abramson got the shop going by the end of the week. The old man himself worked as a cutter, and a couple of cousins worked the blocking machines. The foreladies had dragged all their relatives to work, and now some of the regular girls began to return.

A lieutenant from the district police station came in and Mrs. Abramson slipped him an envelope containing twenty-five dollars, and pretty soon a cop was on duty in front of the shop. Two days later he didn't show up in the morning; the lieutenant came, got another envelope, and the cop returned.

It was costing a lot, and didn't do much good.

That George Frazier hung around across the street, and at opening and closing time a couple of carfuls of strikers would circle the block, catcalling

419

the scabs, and following them, threatening to beat them up. The police arrested George twice, but a union lawyer sprung him on bail and he was back in front of the place in an hour, each time.

"Say, I'll get rid of that bastard!" Mort said. Why, he was a personal friend of Sergeant Rosen.

The next morning, Mort and Mrs. Abramson stood at the window, watching. Most of the girls came to work themselves now, coming in bunches, and as they neared the shop, the strikers would try to block their way, would jeer at them, or try to get them into arguments. There was an icy wind, and the strikers were struggling to keep their placards from blowing off the sticks.

"It's cold out there," Mrs. Abramson remarked, watching the red-faced girls fighting the wind.

"We'll make it hot for them pretty soon," Mort said.

Just as George Frazier and Birdie Volpi went up to four girls, the squad car shot around the corner. Two dicks got out and grabbed George. He could be seen pulling away, resisting. His mouth worked, shouting, but it was funny because, indoors, they couldn't hear the sounds.

The four girls had run into the building. Another squad car drew up and several uniformed cops got out. People scattered. George Frazier was still trying to argue, and Birdie Volpi was struggling in the arms of two grinning dicks.

Then Mort saw a club rise and arc, and descend to a perfect hit on George Frazier's head. There was a slow, waiting moment while Mort and his mother waited to hear the sound of the club hitting the skull. It was unreal, not hearing any sound. The strike-leader had already been bundled into the car.

This time George Frazier didn't come back.

After a couple of weeks, the strike was over as far as the shops were concerned. You could get plenty of girls at any wages, and plenty of cutters were coming back, too, at half-price. The union dragged on with desultory picketing for months, but it was just a laugh, their union was broken and the strike was broken.

Mort heard of Birdie Volpi trying to get a job in a downtown shop. "Next time she shows up, send her back to me," Mrs. Abramson said. "Maybe she learned a lesson."

In the cleaning industry, too, there was a lockout.

After he got rid of his partner, the first thing that Sol did was to call on Wolper, of the Association, and explain that he had squeezed that louse, Epstein, out of his business, and was now anxious to join and be one of them.

It cost a little, well a few hundred dollars for membership, not to mention dues that came up to about a century a month.

One thing Sol prided himself upon was his relationship with the people working for him. He was just one of the boys. Mike Cone came into the office and said: "Hey, boss, wanna get in on the pool?" and he shelled out a buck on the world's series pool. When one of the girls got married and he saw an office girl going the rounds making a collection for a present, he said: "Hey! Don't I count around here!" and put in ten bucks.

In spite of everything, business was okay during the summer, because at a dollar seventy-five a suit and six bucks for cleaning an accordion-pleated skirt, you can stand a lot of losses. Now the slack winter season began and it was pretty slack. Half the help stalled around with nothing to do, hastily grabbing some garment and unfolding it and refolding it when the boss walked through the plant. Everybody said things would pick up around the holidays. Sol passed up a couple of good offers for the races, as he was so worried about his business.

That was when the word went around of an important meeting of the Association.

He was easily the youngest one there, Sol figured. The youngest owner of a plant. The rest of them had scratched around for twenty, thirty years before they could get as far as he was already.

The big shots were all there in person, this time. Old man Alex Weiner, the owner of a million-dollar plant, and a chain of stores, was there with Alex Weiner, Jr., a man forty years old. The Kantrowitz brothers were there in person, sniffing around like a pair of spaniels. Big men dropped their arms around Sol's shoulder, saying: "Hello, Solly! How's business?"

He answered: "Can't complain!" having learned that the idea is never to let your competitor know how badly off you are.

"And how's it by you?" Sol would ask, and get the same answer.

Maybe business was really not so bad for the others, perhaps it was he alone who was slipping, since he had lost his partner.

Sol drifted from the fringes of one group to another. Hearing them talk, he was surprised they were such a lot of kikes. . . . All Epsteins, only worse. Such a cheap, suspicious bunch he had never seen. Everybody was a rat and a crook to everybody else. Three words and they were screaming and swearing at each other. Now everybody was talking lockout! It was as though they had already had a meeting which he had missed. "Now is the time to break the sonofabitch!" They were talking about Bob Frische, the union boss whom he had seen on Ashland Avenue, when he signed up to have a union shop.

"I would ten times better deal with a gangster any day. At least with a gangster you can make a deal."

"And he isn't a gangster?"

"The man is getting wild. He thinks he is a king! I had to let go a couple of deadheads. He comes into my plant and tells me, no, I can't do it!"

The main thing they were scared of was that the union was threatening to put up a huge model cleaning plant. "First they tell us how to run our business, then they don't even need us, they'll run us out of business! With our own money—where did they get it all if not from us!"

"Sure. I got a brother-in-law right in their union. They're going to put up a plant, he tells me, the biggest in Chicago. They already paid for a whole block on Laramie."

"Say, listen, by the time we get through with them, if they have a dime left, they'll buy hamburgers, not real estate."

Once and for all, they cried, lock them out, break the union! And what about the drivers! Would they stick with the other union or with the bosses?

"Don't worry. Wolper made a deal with the drivers."

"What do the drivers care for the inside workers, to the drivers they are *dreck*."

The gilt chairs that had been set in orderly rows, for the meeting, were brushed into clumps, and the men milled around, testifying to each other.

"A hundred and twenty-five dollars I paid him! To a spotter! I can show you the check! It is more than I cleared myself in the whole month!"

"That's nothing. I got a nigger in my place I been paying sixty bucks a week, regular. To a nigger! Can I cut him? No! A union man!"

"*Shiksehs!* They come to work in silk dresses! Forty, fifty dollars a week. My girl is a university graduate and don't make so much as they with their pressing iron!"

The gavel rapped. Wolper, Sam Kantrowitz, Weiner, were sitting behind the table. Looking at the three big shots, Sol had the feeling that everything was already settled.

"We're going out for open shop," Wolper announced flatly. "Maybe some of you fellows can stick to this crazy union agreement, but I am all washed up with them. Nine months a year a guarantee. Does anyone guarantee us nine months of business a year?"

There was a pained laugh.

"What about their plant!" a terrified voice howled from the floor.

"They'll never open that plant," Wolper promised.

In the shop nothing but black looks. Whispering, which broke up when he neared.

He knew they knew, but he had to tell them. He rang the gong. It sounded louder than ever before. Sol swung himself up onto the sorting counter.

"Listen, everybody, heh, I guess you all know you got to take a little vacation." His joke didn't go over, and Sol suddenly felt ashamed of himself. "You know me," he pleaded. "I always got along with everybody working for me." He waited for some sign, but there was only a sullen silence. "The Association is calling a lockout against the union. I got nothing to say about it. I've got to go along with them. All I can do is take back anybody that wants to come back under the new conditions. . . ."

There was a laugh.

Here he was trying to be friendly, decent to them, and they were tough. Already they were turning away from him, buzzing amongst themselves.

"Come on, let's get out of this stinkhole. . . ."

"They'll charge us rent for standing here, the kikes. . . ."

"Listen, Sol," his father put in breathlessly. "Take my advice and close up the shop altogether. How long will it last, a week, two weeks. Close. It will be better."

Even the old lady was scared. "With those gangsters, don't make a fight." She trembled for Sol's body. But Sol growled: "In two weeks we'll lose all our customers!"

He telephoned home and ordered Ben to come down to the plant.

Ben squawked. If the school board found out the reason he was absent, he'd lose his job.

"So you'll lose it! Some job! They don't pay you anyway!"

"Aw, we'll get paid! It's only a couple of weeks. The city is good for it," Ben asserted. "I'll come down every day after school. That's all I can do."

"All right," Sol growled. Not even his brother stuck by him in a pinch.

Sol drove up with his mother and father and a couple of relatives. As the old man crept out of the car, his spotter friend, Mendel Liebowitz, called: "Hey, Chayim, are you scabbing on us too?"

"A fine son, makes his father a scab!"

The old man turned to Mendel and said with comical earnestness: "Believe me, if I could, I would be outside with you."

There was a laugh, not entirely unfriendly.

"You should live so!" Mendel retorted.

The Meisels piled into the shop.

Sol himself took charge of the washing machines and the extractor. As the hours passed, his head began to ache, and he felt himself saturated with acrid fumes of naphtha. There was a heavy load in the extractor, and the huge pot whirled, rocking slightly on its springs, rocking the way his heavy head was rocking. His chest felt constricted, his lungs full of gasoline. He went to the doorway and breathed cold air.

What a lousy job!

Ben came down and tried to be a spotter. He flung a suit onto the table, reached for the alcohol bottle and dabbed at a grease spot. In a moment a hole was eaten through the suit. Mendel, the spotter, had substituted sulphuric acid for all the chemicals.

At night Sol and Mike Cone guarded the plant. With a couple of scabs who were afraid to go home, and slept on piles of dirty clothes, they played poker. Sol lost twenty dollars to Mike.

"The drivers wanna walk out," Mike said. "I dunno if they're gonna stick."

"They promised!" Sol said. "They made a deal, before the lockout."

"Yah, the union made the deal but the boys are getting sore. Bob Frische is getting to them. Y' know they got a lot of dough invested in that plant. Lots of the boys bought stock."

And in fact, instead of picketing, the workers all hung around Laramie Street, watching their plant go up. It was being rushed. Bricklayers chased the structural workers. Streets were torn up for feed lines. It was going to be a model plant, and the biggest in Chicago.

Huge ads appeared in the newspapers: *Send Us Your Clothes by Parcel Post.*

Epstein, in Elkhart, was one of the first to advertise a parcel-post cleaning and dyeing service for Chicago. Cleaners in Gary, Elgin, Peoria, jumped for the business. Even while paying the cost of parcel post, they could afford to give the customer a cheaper rate than the Chicago firms charged.

An immense amount of business was going out through the post. And maybe it would stay out even after the lockout was settled.

On Thursday night Ben Meisel left the cleaning plant, alone. Sol, who usually drove him home, was at a meeting. Ben took the Roosevelt Road car, and got off at Independence Boulevard. As he passed under the viaduct, near Grenshaw, a man started walking on each side of him. They walked him into an alley.

"Son of a bitch, mind your own business. Keep away from that plant. Understand?" An open palm rasped across his cheek. His head snapped sideward, and met a fist.

He began to squeal, closed his eyes, and struck out blindly.

When he woke up he was sitting in the alley, propped against a fence. His face was wet with snow.

As he wobbled into the house, the old lady screamed.

"Why do they pick on me!" he whined, and he howled as she washed his tender flesh.

He lay in the dark, aching, and trying to figure out where he fit into the picture. He was no boss. Why should a fellow get beat up for trying to help out his brother?

The truck drivers went out on a sympathy strike and that shut up the industry. Sol closed his plant. The big six-day was starting in Madison Square Garden and for two cents he would throw away this whole lousy business and go where he belonged. Meanwhile the holiday season with its promise of a rush of business was approaching, and the cleaners were hysterical. They jumped around Wolper nearly tearing him to pieces. "A thousand dollars a day I am losing!" "They will open their union plant and we will be left with nothing!"

One group split off from the Association, and was for settling with the unions, and opening their shops.

Another bunch cried: Bring in Korshak. He knows how to run his business, he never has any trouble, let Korshak run the whole industry. He has Al Capone to take care of the unions, yes, let Al Capone take care of the whole industry, and we'll have order in the business!

And why not? Cry gangster at Al Capone. But at least you had to admit he ran his big business with an iron hand.

That was what was needed, an iron hand!

Until at last the State's Attorney's office had to try to save the tortured, bleeding cleaners' industry of Chicago.

Sol heard what was going on. They were getting together. The tough guys from the teamsters' union, now on the bosses' side, now on the workers' side, were getting together with the smart guys from the cleaners' union, that smart Bob Frische with his union-owned plant, and Korshak, the big independent, was coming in, and the Association was coming in, they were all going to get together and find a way to run the industry. No longer each one trying to strangle, blackjack, murder, control all the others, but from now on, co-operation!

They had found some guy—Dr. Hart. It was rumored that wily Korshak had engineered this Dr. Hart into the deal. But he was an honest guy, a university professor. Dr. Hart for an umpire, just as Judge Landis was the big boss umpire of the baseball business.

"What about the unions running a plant!" the owners shrieked. "That's unfair! A union can't operate a plant!"

Dr. Hart agreed. The line had to be established. Workers were workers. Bosses were bosses. Only fair.

So there was a deal. The million-dollar plant would never open. On the other hand, the guarantee of nine months' work a year, and the wage scale, had to be renewed.

The help came back into the shop. The trucks whizzed out just in time for the Christmas rush. It was not as large as had been expected but it was something.

The first few days, no one spoke directly to Sol, unless spoken to. Then with the coming of the Christmas spirit, the strained feeling began to wear off.

Something in himself had changed. He didn't like to hang around the plant so much as he had used to.

He wanted to feel friendly toward everybody, so, for Christmas, since he had to make a loan at the West Side Bank in order to meet the payroll anyway, he went in a few hundred deeper and got five-dollar gold pieces—one for every employee.

When the envelopes were opened, he could hear a pleased buzzing spread through the shop. A couple of the girls came in and said: "Thanks, Mr. Meisel. Merry Christmas."

But it was different from when he used to subscribe to all the little shop collections. After the first few, he got embarrassed, and wished no more would come in. A young kid, a sorter, said: "Thanks, boss." All at once Sol felt sore. Like sometimes when a shine knelt slavishly over his shoes, he had the feeling to kick out. And he felt even sorer at those that didn't thank him at all, but turned away, with a kind of sly, ironic glimmer, those like Mendel Liebowitz.

It was different than when he had felt himself one of them, a kid that had grown up on Sixteenth Street with them and their kids, played baseball in the same empty lots, gone to the J.P.I. together, and to school, gone to the Central Park, and the Gold Theater, eaten corned beef sandwiches at Kantor's. Then he was just one of the boys who had good luck and made a pile. But now, they were all his enemies.

He wished to hell he had a home to go to, someone sensible to talk to, like Estelle, instead of going out helling around. He wished he had a friend who knew the business game, like Wop Pisano knew bikes.

Sol Meisel ran into Mort Abramson.

Soon they had exchanged their business experiences.

"So you had it too?" Sol said. "How did you come out?"

"We beat them. We smashed the lousy union."

Sol marveled; and Mort told him how it had been accomplished. "The thing is, never let them get a good start," he analyzed. "That's the mistake that was made in your industry, they let the unions get too strong."

Even so, Mort said he wished he had known about Sol's trouble. "I'd have called up Sergeant Rosen and he'd have fixed you up. He's a personal friend of mine."

"Yah?" Sol said. Mort Abramson had always been a smart fellow. Sol figured he ought to hang around with Mort, and maybe learn something about business.

"You aren't through yet," Mort said, ominously. "I don't know about this Dr. Hart you got for a czar. How is he going to make the bosses and the unions work together?" He had a flash of insight. "It's like the Jews and the Arabs in Palestine. You can make them keep quiet for a while, by force, but when you have hatred like that something is always going to break out. In business, it's a war with the unions. It's either them or us."

Sam Eisen's father sent George Frazier to him. The millinery union's lawyer didn't want to press Frazier's case: he had to play ball with the police.

"The Abramsons, huh?" Sam didn't bother to mention that he had known them. "Well, I don't see how we can make a case against the Abramsons," Sam said, "though they certainly put the cops up to it." The only chance for a suit was against the cops.

As Sam listened to Frazier's detailed story, he felt his scalp tightening. He had, in his time, seen plenty of evidence of police rough stuff. Years ago when he had defended criminals. But every once in a while a case came along that got hold of you as if it were your first encounter with injustice.

Frazier was nervous as a minnow. Once when a door slammed he swayed sidewise as though dodging a blow. "I been that way since," he confided apologetically, with a feeble smile. Sam noticed the gaping space of missing teeth.

"The car stopped and they got out. Two, see? I didn't know it was police. I was figuring, Abramson is hiring gangsters. Right away, before I knew it, bim!" He bent his head, showing Sam the bald spot left from the blow.

"They didn't tell you they were the law?"

"I said: 'Who are you?' He says: 'We'll show you who we are.' Bam!"

"Did they show you their star?"

"Naw. Bam. I seen plenty of stars after that," Frazier jested wanly.

"Did you resist them?" Sam said, routinely.

Frazier stared at Sam as though this lawyer was not so smart. Then he repeated patiently: "Am I crazy? I was trying to get away, I was on the sidewalk, trying to crawl away. . . ."

He had been taken upstairs to a locker-room. As he went through the door, "I got a hard kick and I fell over on my face. 'What's the matter, can't you walk?' the bigger one says, and I said: 'He kicked me.' He grabs me, tearing the coat, and yells: 'Who kicked you? What do you mean, kicked you?' Then he pushed me so hard I bumped my head on the wall, and fell down again. The big guy, Schmidt, I think it was, came up to me and kicked me right in the crotch. . . ."

They had taken him from one station to another, never booking him.

". . . my shirt was torn all the way down the back and my mouth was all blood. I could feel with my tongue a couple of loose teeth. See, I lost them." He showed his mouth. "They pushed me out on the stairs and the big guy yelled: 'Hey, stop the dirty red sonofabitch, he's trying to get away!' and then he kicked me right in the nuts, so I fell down the stairs.

"I was in the hospital unconscious twenty-six hours. Say, when I come to, I was all bandages." He gestured, head to foot. "I was like a mummy, like King Tut, yah, I thought I was dead and buried, sure."

"They never told you you were under arrest?" Sam persisted.

"Maybe they told me when I was unconscious," Frazier mournfully jested.

Sam glanced through the record. Frazier had been booked on good old 4211, disorderly conduct, and fined one and one, obviously so he couldn't charge false arrest. Still, with so flagrant a case of brutality, it might be possible to get into court again.

The poor guy didn't even have the cost of entering suit. Sam considered the Civil Liberties.

At that time, he had already handled a few cases for the committee, through Joe Shapiro, a socialist whom he had met in the last election campaign. If he called them in, he'd have to do it their way. So, first, he took a crack at it himself.

As the best bet to issue a warrant against the cops, Sam picked Judge Vories, an anti-administration judge who, he heard, was sore because he was being shunted around to the lousiest police courts. The Maxwell Street court smelled of jail antiseptic and dried spit. Judge Vories crouched behind the desk hearing motions.

"Listen, Eisen, what's the use of wasting your time and my time and the court's time? Suppose I give you a warrant. You'll never get a conviction and you know it. We're having a lot of trouble with these union racketeers. We're trying to clean them out."

"Sure, but why pick on the wrong guys?" Sam said. "Swanson may want to make a show of cleaning the gangsters out of town, but what does he go after? This is an honest union."

Vories yawned. "Say, you know what they are. A bunch of reds. They're worse than the gangsters. You ain't fooling me, Eisen." He winked.

Sam persisted: "This man was beaten half to death in a police station, without even being booked. You know as well as I do, judge, that Rosen's squad has been overstepping the limits, and we want a warrant in this case."

"All right, all right, so he got a little rough handling. He's able to come into court, isn't he? He isn't in a wheelchair, is he? Listen, Eisen. I can't issue any warrant. I don't want Rosen to think I'm riding his men over nothing at all. You bring a real case in here and I'll tell Rosen where he gets off at. But I can't do anything with this. Whatya think I am, a Bolshevik?" He looked at Sam cagily, and handed back the papers.

As Sam brushed through the hallway someone caught his arm, and squeezed.

"Where's the fire, Sambo?" Runt greeted him.

"Hi, Plotsy. What's new by you?"

"Can't complain. Can't complain. They're keeping me hopping," Runt sparkled, and Sam realized that with Swanson jugging thousands of gun-toters, Plotkin must be in his heyday. "Anything I can do for you, Sam? Vories is a friend of mine," Runt mentioned, pulling Sam aside.

"Just trying to get a warrant," Sam said, explaining the case. Runt listened sympathetically, clucking his tongue. "Yah. 'Sa shame, the way they give 'em the hose. So Mort Abramson had a strike in his shop? Say, was it Rosen's boys?" He eyed Sam. "You missed the angle, Sambo! No wonder they murdered your pal! Mort practically sleeps in the same bed with Rosen. Or at least with his daughter." He smirked. "Some babe, too. I've seen Mort with her at the Chez, a couple of times. Catch on?"

Sam nodded. That didn't make it any easier. Still, if he could ever get that interesting tie-up before a jury.

Runt looked at him solemnly. "I appreciate what you're doing, Sam," he said. "I wish I could handle some of those cases myself for the C.L.U. But right now I got my hands full. Yep, I've got more than I can handle. But listen, Sam, why don't you get Alderman Kinney to fix it for you."

"Well, you know I don't go around with that crowd any more. I sort of dropped connections," Sam said.

Runt eyed him still more earnestly. "I've got some pretty good connections now," he said. "Come on across the street, I know where we can get a drink while I call up."

"I'll go along," Sam said, "but you know I don't drink."

Runt grasped his arm. "You know, maybe it's a good thing you dropped out of politics, Sam," he said. "You had a lot of stuff, you certainly could hold a crowd, but, Sam, to be frank with you, I don't think you know how to really get along with the boys. I mean, now, you don't drink. Well, you know, in politics you have to take a drink with the boys, and be one of them."

Sam smiled.

"I admire you, Sam, I think you're doing a great thing. Somebody ought to take a sock at Rosen's squad. You know Rosen is all right himself, he doesn't tell them to pull any rough stuff . . ."

"But he doesn't tell them not to," Sam said.

"But you take Maserow, he's the worst of them. He enjoys it. You know that fellow is a sadist," Runt declaimed.

"I don't doubt it."

They went into a black-windowed speakeasy across the street from the police station.

"Hi, boys," Runt said, and took a table. "You know, Sam," he said conspiratorially, "I'm sympathetic to your views. I've been doing some reading lately, take Bernard Shaw, he's got a lot of radical ideas, it's all straight stuff. Only, human nature being what it is, there'll always be some guys riding on the backs of the multitude, and I want to cash in while I can." He spoke somewhat apologetically, as though ashamed of himself in the face of Sam's idealism. "Now take this crime drive. They mean it, Sam. Why, they've got every cell in town packed, they pulled in a thousand hoods last month. They're telling the boys to lam it out of town and they're lamming. You know why? The stock market." He paused significantly.

"Well, it's deeper than that," Sam said.

"Sure. It's just the big gangsters, the McCormicks and the Rothschilds and the Melvin Traylors cracking down on the gangsters like Al Capone and Spike O'Donnell. When the going was good, the big guys didn't care if the mobs scooped up some loose change. There was plenty of mazuma and they let everybody grab. But now it's getting tough, so what do they do? They clamp down the lid. They have a crime drive and clean out the little crooks."

"There are some pretty big holdings among those little crooks, too," Sam observed. "I thought Al Capone was pretty powerful."

"Yah, and where is he? Taking the rap in a jail in Philly. They told him to pick his jail and he went. Listen, the big rackets are taking in the little rackets, that's all. Why, Al lost a fortune in the crash. I got it from the inside. All he has left is some real estate. His mob is even short-changing on beer, trying to scrape up some cush. Yah. Every beer barrel is part empty. The State Street boys are even calling the federal government to clean up the rackets. They got a new one they're pulling on Terry Druggan. They couldn't pin anything on him so they got the federal courts after him to send him to Leavenworth for omitting to mention his brewery profits in his income tax! The big rackets are tightening up, see? They want everything for themselves now, see? There isn't enough to throw around."

Sam nodded.

"So why shouldn't I help these hoods out?" Runt persisted. "They're no worse criminals than the big shots on the stock market, only these fellows are more honest about it, they commit their crimes in the open, with a gun."

"Plotsy, you're okay," Sam said, feeling the same amused friendliness toward Runt that he used to feel when he had let Runt share his office. At heart, Runt Plotkin was so sincere, so crazily honest.

To get to Vincent Belden, you passed through a long library stacked with law books from floor to ceiling. It was the largest law-office library Sam had ever seen. Maybe in the distant future he could attain something like this, secure and scholarly. Peace, without yielding one's principles.

In Belden's private office, Sam noticed a large photograph of Lincoln, and on the same wall a small autographed photo of Eugene V. Debs.

Belden glanced through the story. He missed nothing. And when he discussed the case, Sam saw that he hadn't missed any of the unmentioned angles, either. He caught on that George Frazier was perhaps a left-winger, not in any too strong with his own union. "So Judge Vories refused a warrant?" He put his finger-tips together. "Frankly, Sam, I doubt very much if we could get to first base with a criminal charge."

"They've got to give us a warrant!" Sam declared. "If we have to go to the chief justice!"

Belden advised a civil suit.

Sam had known that was coming. "But this was a criminal assault!" he insisted.

Belden lit a cigarette from a monogrammed lighter. He explained. Experience had proven it was utterly impossible to get a criminal conviction against a cop in this type of case. Even an award in a civil suit would be a miracle.

Sam knew Belden was right, and yet this was already a compromise. Well, at least he would get the case before a court. He would put that flatfoot Maserow on the stand. He saw himself taunting him with sarcasm. "How much do you weigh, officer? . . . T-t-t, only two hundred and ten?" and the jury would laugh as they looked from Maserow to little George Frazier, beaten up for resisting. He would add up the weights of the entire squad, against warped, consumptive-looking George Frazier, who weighed a hundred and thirty-two. The jury would howl.

On the morning of the hearing, Sam felt tense, eager as he had not felt for months. His stomach was tight; he could hardly sip his breakfast coffee.

Judge Horowitz, who had managed to get re-elected to the bench, was up there.

Maserow and Beal sauntered into the enclosure and joined their counsel. Sam recognized one of their lawyers—Hal Noonan, who had electioneered for Thompson with him, a couple of years ago. Hal had collected the fruits—a berth in the corporation counsel's office. He was stouter, redder, more assured. He greeted Sam with a wide grimace, that allowed Sam to come in on this joke or not, as he wished.

Opposite the jury box sat Sergeant Rosen and the rest of his squad. All fastened their eyes on Sam and his client with a derisive fixity.

Sam had subpœna'd Mort Abramson, and now he saw him come into court. It was the first time they had seen each other in several years; Mort hadn't changed, except that his face seemed healthier, his whole bearing was well greased.

He raised his brows at Sam, in a look much the same as Noonan's. As though, deep down, he thought Sam must share this joke. Only, in the contraction of his eyes there was a shade of doubt. Maybe Sam Eisen was really nuts.

Judge Horowitz leaned toward Sam. "Since when are you mixed up with these socialist sissies?" he remarked, just loud enough for the court to hear.

Sam flushed, but controlled himself. At least he would have a jury.

From his first glimpse of the jury panel, Sam knew, inwardly, that he was beaten. He felt a quiver of rage, frustration, and in the same moment tightened his grip on himself. He would fight it out anyway. He would show

431

this thing up so strong that even this jury would be ashamed to go through with the fix.

He pounded at them, one after another: "Have you any relatives on the police force?" And one after another they blandly admitted a brother, three brothers, a couple of cousins, seeming to enjoy the farce.

Judge Horowitz, too, smiled at the coincidence, attempting the dignified amusement of a jurist. "But come on to the case, Eisen, we can't waste the whole day picking one little jury for one little claim."

Sam speeded up his selection. He had weeded out most of the obvious plants but he was sure at least a couple of the accepted jurors were in the gang.

"How much do you weigh, officer?" he began, in examining Maserow.

The judge leaned away, bored.

When Sam made the point about the combined weights, a baldish man in the jury tittered, but was silenced by a glare from the fellow next to him.

The cops swore that Frazier had set upon them with an iron pipe, and that he had to be subdued. Sam cross-examined until they gave contradictory descriptions of the weapon, but it was no use. Hal Noonan put up a doctor who testified that the plaintiff's injuries might have been due to a fall down a flight of stairs.

Sam got Mort on the stand.

"Isn't it true that you are a personal friend of Sergeant Rosen, one might even say a family friend?" Sam asked.

Noonan leaped up and towered belligerently over Sam while he shouted his objections. The whole atmosphere of the court turned completely against Sam. Mort looked enraged—as if he were about to ask Sam to have it out in the alley.

Judge Horowitz glared at Sam as at some boor who had violated the gentlemanly air of his court.

Sam squared his shoulders. "I can prove that this was a conspiracy to destroy the leadership—"

"Objection sustained," Judge Horowitz rapped. "Do you want to be held in contempt!"

Noonan moved that the case be thrown out of court for want of evidence.

"Granted," Judge Horowitz said.

Sam remained standing, mouth open.

Mort strode past him, as though they could never even have been in the same world.

The others were shoving their way out, their glances at him now more contemptuous than amused. He realized that Judge Horowitz was lecturing him, in a castor-oil friendly voice. "What's the medder with you, Eisen? I used to think you had a head on your shoulders. You don't want to get mixed up with this kind of stuff—trying to shake down a couple of coppers that were just doing their job. You better watch your step. . . ."

The more enraged he grew, the more impotent he felt. Belden's patient, stroking voice only made him angrier. As Belden pointed out, an appeal would be costly, and sure to fail, and there were stronger cases for which to save the limited ammunition of the committee.

And yet Sam felt, if he had only made it a criminal charge in the first place. He at least would not have compromised.

Lil had never been able quite to figure out how much her father was worth, and one of the things she still held against Sam was that, when he had had the opportunity, he had neglected to do so. She sensed that her father was out to double his fortune in a hurry, and after that there would be no stopping him.

One thing, she knew he was trying to make a big deal with Rube Moscowitz. She'd be able to go around and say: "My father is the partner of Rube Moscowitz."

Lately, business was rushing. There was always a row of people on the waiting bench, and sometimes a few were standing. Her father was calling in all the money he could get his hands on because he could loan it out at high rates. He had her prepare bills a week in advance on all the notes, and send them out the minute they were due. She caught talk in the office about a "beautiful new building, a honey," that was all finished except for the glass in the windows. A couple of times, she knew, her father had been sore because he had had to turn down fine propositions for lack of capital. Listening in on a few telephone conversations, she gathered that he was trying to get Rube Moscowitz to put two hundred thousand dollars into the business. Then her father, also, must be worth two hundred thousand.

A millionaire's daughter.

The day he expected to close the deal with Rube Moscowitz her father was so nervous he nearly drove her crazy. She had been planning to get a marcel, as Harry Perlin was coming to dinner, but she couldn't leave the desk for a moment.

Just before one o'clock Rube Moscowitz himself marched into the place. "My father is expecting you, Mr. Moscowitz, go right in," she chirped, noticing how the mourner's bench gaped after the big man.

When she got the buzzer, Lil flew into the private office.

"Forty apartments, and a honey," her father was saying. "They are practically giving it to us! The thing is, Mr. Moscowitz, that in real estate you see what you are getting. Take all these people that lost money on the stock market lately. Why? They didn't see what they were buying."

"You're telling me!" Rube Moscowitz boomed, good-naturedly. "Listen, the minute there's a little pickup"—confidentially: "you know there's gonna be a little pickup—and then I'm pulling out of the market so fast they won't be able to see me for dust. You know, I've got certain tie-ups, and when they tell me to buy, I've got to help them out, I've got to buy. Support the market," he said largely. Then, chuckling: "But if I got all my dough in real estate, I can't buy any more stocks, eh?" he winked, appreciating his own maneuver.

"It's the smartest thing," Mr. Klein said. "Look, just look at this stuff." Lil handed him the sheaf of notes, among them, Harry Perlin's notes. "The only real security is real estate, and here it is! Now is the time to do business. I never saw such an opportunity in my life!"

Her father gave her a look, so she had to leave.

She set out the candlesticks which she had used in her own apartment, with Sam. She used her own beautiful goblets. But, the last moment, she noticed that the foot-buzzer was out of commission. That Jackie! That devil!

"Make yourself to home, Harry," she said. Then, with an inspiration: "This do-jigger just went out of commission and I was trying to fix it."

"That's just in my line!" said Harry, and as they squatted down under the table she felt she had really rid him of his bashfulness.

"Somebody disconnected one of the wires," he said, and had it fixed in a moment.

"Harry, you're a positive genius," she declared. "Oh, for a handy man around the house!"

It was just a simple, good meal, and she was tickled at the way her father and Harry were getting along.

"Well, how's business?" Mr. Klein said.

"Oh, I can't kick."

"Did you get your financing problem all straightened out?"

"Oh, that was to help my brother, and he lost it all on the market anyway," Harry said cheerfully. "He had some General Electric stock and it went down a hundred and twenty points! So he got cleaned out. Now I guess it'll go up again!"

"I don't believe in playing the market," Mr. Klein announced.

"Neither do I. I believe in sticking to what I know about."

"I had a man in today," Mr. Klein said. "A big man, too. He's trying to pull out of the market now, and put his money where it'll do some good."

Lil thrilled. So Moscowitz was coming in with her father!

"I guess stocks will go up again now that they shook out all the suckers," Harry predicted. "I noticed John D. Rockefeller bought stocks today."

"Is he still alive!" Lil said. "Mygod, he must be a hundred and ninety years old!"

Pretty soon she had Harry talking about his inventions. He had a new idea for an emergency brake that would be on the dashboard instead of on the floor. Not only would it be handy, and save accidents, but it would enable three people to use the front seat of a car more comfortably.

"That's fascinating!" Lil said.

She saw herself as the wife of a millionaire inventor and manufacturer. He would be a bigger man than Sam, any day. That crazy fool, she had heard he was actually trying to get a cop sent to jail for beating up a radical, and he was trying to drag the Abramsons into the case. Why, they could buy him and sell him a dozen times over. He was just banging his head against a stone wall.

"When you get some money, put it in real estate, that's the only thing," Mr. Klein advised Harry. "Now this man I know gets his stock market tips straight from Insull. But even Insull lost money in this crash."

"Oh, he's got plenty," Lil said. "Look at the new opera he's putting up. Oh, would I like to go opening night! I bet all society will be there!" She gave Harry the eye.

"I understand they're not going to have any boxes for society, like in the old Auditorium," Harry said.

"No?" Lil was disappointed.

"Nope. They're just going to sit among the ordinary hoi polloi, on the main floor."

The glitter returned to Lil's eyes. "Just imagine, you might get seats, and turn out to be right next to Mrs. Rockefeller McCormick!"

Harry missed the hint, but she bet with herself that she would get him to take her to the opening.

"Ev has a cyst," Aline informed Rudy. Her tone carried the whole story of the wife who realizes her wealthier friends can't be expected to patronize a young doctor, especially for a serious operation, but who nevertheless can't help feeling they have somehow slighted her husband.

"That so? Who's she going to?" Rudy asked.

"Dr. Hargraves. He'll probably soak her a thousand dollars."

"Well, he's a good man," Rudy said with professional courtesy, maintained even at home.

Oh, and Aline had a suspicion that Thelma Kassell was pregnant. "If she dares to go to someone else, after the job Manny did on my mother's teeth . . . ! And, honey, if she calls, have her come to your downtown office. Manny is doing very well, he's always very busy."

Rudy, too, was very busy; but with the difference that a very busy doctor isn't necessarily doing very well. Still, he was getting by, which was considered good for the first year of practice. He shared the office and was taking over some of the practice of old Dr. Meyerson; and in the afternoons he usually assisted Dr. Matthews, a brilliant young surgeon who had taken a shine to him when he was interning at Israel. Dr. Matthews was one of the few gentiles on the staff there. For his fancier practice, Rudy used Dr. Matthews's downtown office.

He was giving eight hours a week to the clinics at Israel, and was always taking extra courses at the Post Graduate School of County.

When he had been working as a druggist, the more work he took on, the more money he made, but now the reverse seemed to be true. Still, there were hundreds of men who would give their eyeteeth to work with Dr. Matthews; and by giving eight hours instead of the usual four to the clinic, Rudy had hopes of being made a staff adjunct next year.

"What'll that get you?" Aline pointed out. "The privilege of leaving your paying patients to rush down there to take care of some emergency case for nothing!" But she too knew how she would get the word around: "Why, Rudy has just been taken onto the staff of Israel Hospital! and you know how hard it is to get in there!"

He had Lou Green's operation set for this morning. One swell thing about helping out Dr. Matthews was that he could get Matt to do favors like this operation for Lou Green. Rudy might have tackled the job himself but he was not too familiar with joint surgery, and preferred to take no chances.

They had had Lou at the hospital for a week, now, but his blood count was still low, he was generally in lousy shape, scared, and tortured by the excruciating pain of the slightest movement in his swollen joints; he couldn't afford to keep the bed in the hospital any longer, so they might as well tackle the job.

Even Aline thought it was a simple arthritis, though as a matter of fact the poor kid was suffering from a neglected g.c. infection. Got himself a dose from some prostitute and ashamed to take his fears to a doctor.

Rudy had a couple of calls to make first: a girl that worked trimming hats, couldn't even ask her for anything, those milliners were out on strike. And there was Sam Eisen's father, down with stomach ulcers. It was a wonder Jews didn't get them a hundred percent, with their sour tomato diets. It was a bad case—neglected. An operation might have been avoided if Eisen had had decent medical care, but now it looked inevitable. The man was cadaverous-looking, hollow-eyed, a wonder he had escaped t.b.

Four other stops; at one of them he accepted two dollars. Another would pay, some time.

It wasn't the money. Going around to these old patients of Meyerson, around Sixteenth Street and in the poor Jewish section on the Northwest Side, a man got so tired of seeing slow neglect, and waste of life. Hernias that would have been simple, safe repairs in their early stages, neglected until they were fifty percent fatalities. Rotting tumors . . .

Well, a doctor saw only the worst side of life.

He stopped at Mercy Hospital. The instruments of the great Dr. John B. Murphy had been willed to the hospital; a few of the city's surgeons were permitted the use of them. Knowing how Matt loved to handle the Murphy tools, Rudy borrowed the bone-chisels in his name. They were a set of beauties, especially tempered silvery steel.

Lou's blood count was still none too favorable. "All set?" he inquired, looking gamely at Rudy.

"Sure, this is nothing." Rudy gave him a sedative, and went to scrub up. Dr. Matthews had just arrived and was changing to his whites. He was boiling with anger about the case of Dr. Niles being expelled from the medical society, and could talk about nothing else.

A lot of the town's philanthropists like Marshall Field the umptieth and Harold McCormick had got behind an organization known as the Social Health Institute, which treated venereal diseases. It was not a charity, but a pay clinic where decent treatment could be had at little cost. You saw the ads in men's washrooms—a beautiful bride and groom pictured under the caption, *Don't Spoil Her Life*, etc. Rudy had always figured it was a good thing, took care of a lot of venereal cases that would otherwise be neglected. Why, if Lou Green had gone to the place when he first got his dose, he wouldn't be on a cart now, headed for the operating room. The Social Health Institute also ran full-page scare-ads in the daily papers.

Now, Dr. Arthur Niles, Chicago's leading gynecologist, had allowed his name to be used, as among the sponsors, in those ads. Promptly, the Chicago Society of Physicians and Surgeons had him up for advertising, and expelled him for breach of ethics! Automatically, he was expelled from the Society of American Physicians and Surgeons, too.

"There isn't a more ethical man in the profession!" Dr. Matthews raged. "It's just a cheap idiotic trick by some of those damn Madison Street syph doctors who are afraid the Social Health will take away their business! To keep them in, and throw out a man like Niles!" He went on raging about the stupid reactionary gang in control of that medical society, about how they impeded every step in the advance of medicine; he was still growling when they got into the operating room.

The tanks of ethylene were ready. "Going to use that Chicago gas?" Rudy jibed, thinking to calm Matt a little by starting the usual kidding.

"Not unless you've got some of that hot air from Northwestern," Dr. Matthews responded.

"Saline or glucose, doctor?" Rudy asked.

"Either one."

Rudy found Lou's vein, and inserted the tube, letting the saline solution dribble slowly into his blood.

Dr. Matthews made the opening incision.

Lou's tissues were flabby, pale, fatty, weak stuff. To Rudy, the internes seemed slow with the retractors. One of them, a long-necked fellow, was surely a bad interne. It seemed to Rudy that they didn't come any more like they had been in his bunch, alert, ambitious, never enough of work.

Matt worked with his usual beautiful, cool precision. He had a Murphy chisel in his hand, and with three sharp strokes cut away the overgrowth of bone that clogged the joint. A nurse took the whitish, spongy sliver. Matt worked the joint. It was still a bit stiff.

"Want to finish?" he offered Rudy the chisel. Rudy couldn't help feeling an electric thrill when he clasped the John B. Murphy instrument.

"Well let's see some of that fancy Northwestern technique," Matt kidded.

Rudy nicked out the last bit of sick bone.

This moment felt good. The ritual of antisepsis working so perfectly, gloves and sterile towels and clamps and tweezer-grasped gut. Like kosher and unkosher, Rudy always thought. Like a taboo game played when you were a kid: hopping on the sidewalk squares, first one touches a line is out.

The internes began to sew up, taking stitches far from the edge of the cut, as the weak tissues, like decaying cloth, might not hold the seam.

Rudy stood watching Lou. He remembered how tough his own unmarried years had been, remembered nights when cold water, when walking around the room, hadn't helped.

Why, he had known Lou since he was a kid; they had been members of the same club, he was his doctor now, he knew all about the guy, and what was there to know? An empty life, like grayish mucky water—nothing there. Used to hang around with Lou Margolis—the two Lous. But this one didn't have the stuff. Did everybody have to be a genius, a superman, couldn't you just be an ordinary guy like Lou Green and get along?

He pitied Lou, saw him unable to satisfy such a simple need as love, picking up some two-dollar punk on Clark Street, then hiding, nursing his clap. . . .

So they had expelled Dr. Niles.

"I think we can release the constrictor now," Dr. Matthews said.

The nurse bent and unclasped the band around the thigh, allowing the blood to flow back into the leg. Now was the crucial moment. Had they cut a vein, a nerve?

Rudy touched Lou's exposed toe. It paled, and, barely discernible, darkened as the blood flowed back into the touched spot.

"It's all right," he reported.

Matt stood by him and watched the test repeated.

"Yep," he agreed, with the excitement that came at the successful turn of even the most routine of operations.

Just then the nurse said: "I can't get any pulse."

For an instant Rudy lost his presence of mind. He caught himself as Matt was already ordering: "Set up another jar of saline solution on the other side."

It was just in instants, moments like that, that Rudy doubted if he would ever be really tops. Although he too had had the right impulse: he had noticed even as Matt spoke that the saline had run out. Lou simply needed more liquid.

The anæsthetist's brow was in a deep V. One of the nurses was swiftly replacing the empty jar. Another was setting up the extra jar. But the red-necked interne stood paralyzed, hands hanging.

"Better get that into him," Dr. Matthews ordered. At the same moment the interne's stitches broke, and a jet of blood spurted. "There you are with your Northwestern stitches." Matt coolly tried to kid the internes out of their jitters. "Of course I can't really blame you. These tissues are awfully friable. How is the solution going?"

Rudy, holding the incision together as Matt hastily patched the seam, glanced over and saw the red-necked interne jabbing Lou's arm. He made three attempts, and failed to find the vein. Rudy took the needle, found the vein. The liquid started into the bloodstream.

"Yes," Matt said, relieved.

In a few moments, the anæsthetist raised her head, pleased.

"I thought he would come back," Matt said for the benefit of the internes. "After all, the leg is one-fourth of the body. All that blood rushing down into the leg, when we removed the constrictor."

That was the only reprimand he gave the nurse for removing the constrictor all at once. She should have known enough to let the blood back gradually.

The interne who had blown up was drawing off his gloves. With professional adeptness, he squeezed the air down to flop out the rubber fingers. He left the room, without asking.

Matt fussed around the table, doing a number of things he could have left for the nurses, the technicians. It was that feeling of not wanting to leave a good job, so soon.

He leaned over Lou's face; ethylene wore off quickly, Lou was already coming back.

Matt looked to Rudy. In that look there was the intimacy of what the two of them had done. "Back again," Matt said, with that clipped, sarcastic look that sometimes touched his lips. It was just between them: after all, what was this worth, and why did they do it?

The dogma sprang to Rudy's mind: "There is nothing more valuable than human life."

Why, sure, Lou Green was young, and all life was ahead of him; why, there were wretches that they had pulled through, sclerotic old men who were dying piecemeal, there was John D. Rockefeller clutching to this earth, that was one thing you could never stop to question.

Yes, they had done a swell bit of work there, pulled him back from the brink. But catching Matt's dubious look, Rudy knew he too was thinking: what if they had missed, that moment, what if they had been too slow? And a little treatment a year ago would have spared the whole risk.

The nurse was humming:

"Diamond bracelets Woolworth doesn't sell,
Baby . . ."

Mitch Wilner's report was short, scientifically worded, and completely devoid of any elaborations about his work.

When he had written it out, he had been unable to avoid the feeling of amazement that two years of research should boil down to these few typewritten pages, or, really, to these few tables of figures. But, after all, Einstein's theory had occupied only three pages of print.

Two years? Wasn't it more? Actually, one thing led back into another, till he might go back, step by step, through his research to the first time he had looked through a microscope, in Joe Freedman's basement.

He was wearing his tux, because there was a reception after the meeting.

As he stood up there on the platform, so young, just a kid among all these corpulent and bald and wheezy doctors, it was a thrill to see him. His thick dark mustache bragged of full serious manhood, his forehead had come out strongly molded, as his hairline had slightly receded; he was handsome, standing there.

And as Mitch read his paper before the medical society, Sylvia felt herself brimming over with waves of smiles. This bare report was nothing like the long job he had described to her, and yet all these men must know intuitively every step that Mitch had followed, to bring them these few significant numbers.

She could feel herself inside of Mitch's mind, feel his mind reviewing, as he read, the gradual conception of his idea, going back even to that day when they had played tennis, and he had taken the cellophane from her cigarette package, to use in his dialysis.

"As we compare the two tables . . ." Mitch said, up there on the platform. And Sylvia seemed to be living that night when Mitch had tabulated his results for an entire month, and placed them alongside the results on an identical set of experiments run four months previously, and found that the two sets did not check.

And how, when he was half asleep, the two tables had seemed to be poised over him, and suddenly, idiotically, the whole thing was clear to him. One was through rubber, one was through cellophane.

Regularly, less antitoxin had remained in the samples after the cellophane dialysis.

She could just imagine Mitch sitting up in bed, then turning on his light and putting on his clothes, ready to rush over to the lab, as though with the wild purpose of getting back all the tap water that had run out through the drain in the last six months.

But instead, he had simply turned on the light and gone over the two tables again. There could be no other answer. He could trap the pure antitoxin between cellophane and rubber, as between a larger and a smaller sieve.

Sylvia felt as though she must have been with Mitch on that night of conception, almost as though that must have been their wedding night. And then had come the day when he had noticed a slight fogginess in the dialysis water; and the tense resolution to keep his hands off, to let the process go on another twenty-four hours for surer results; and then the moment when he held a tiny white residue in a test-tube, a patch of unknown powder, that might be the pure antitoxin itself! The results had been meager, but had indicated that his theory was correct.

Then more months of fixing, patching, correcting, trying over, and yes, the substance caught in the water retained the antitoxic factor, but feebly. He tried various other mediums, collodion, sheepskin in place of the rubber, thin cellophane, thick cellophane, two-day dialysis, three-day, four-, five-, six-, ten-day washes. In his most favorable set of runs, he had coaxed a larger proportion of antitoxin out of the serum than the scientists of the Hebrew University had been able to do with their method. And his method had the advantage of simplicity.

True, it was still far from practical. Most of the antitoxin either remained in the serum, or was destroyed. Another year . . .

A murmur went through the hall as Mitch finished. "Beautiful piece of work," she heard a man behind her say, and she wanted to cry out: "He's mine, he's mine."

She felt a hand cover hers, and squeeze. She had completely forgotten Aline and Rudy. Rudy was beaming. Aline was squeezing her hand and looking at her with a real understanding expression. Sylvia experienced a sudden rush of love for Aline; she had always underestimated Aline.

They had got Mitch back, as he finished with the flock of questioners, and, as they were leaving the hall, Rudy was greeted by Dr. Matthews.

"Hello, hello!" He knew Mitch too and, turning to Sylvia, said: "And is this Mrs. Wilner?"

It seemed so natural. Sylvia mentally whispered to Mitch: "Oh let's make it soon, now, soon!"

"Nice report," Dr. Matthews said to Mitch. "Are you going to go on with it?"

"Well, I have hopes of spending next year at Rochester," Mitch smiled.

Then it was coming through! Sylvia knew that Mitch would not have mentioned it unless it was practically certain. Dr. Durand, of Rochester, was doing the same kind of research, and Mitch had applied for a job with him. The pay would even be enough to let them get married. Thirty a week. Once Joe had wondered if they could do it on fifty a week.

Now, with these results, Dr. Durand could scarcely refuse Mitch the appointment.

They had made their way to the coffee shop. "Did you catch Glenn Frank's talk this afternoon?" Dr. Matthews asked, and Sylvia was a little amazed that he could get off the subject of Mitch's research so quickly.

"No," Rudy said. "I was sorry to miss it, did he have anything to say?"

What could Glenn Frank tell them, Sylvia felt Mitch's attitude, he might be a university president but in medicine he was only a layman.

"He had plenty to say," Dr. Matthews laughed. "He started quite a wild argument on the floor. He didn't mention the Niles case but there was no mistaking what he was talking about! According to him, if we don't find some way ourselves of making medicine available to the people, we'll all be working for the government in a couple of years. He believes socialized medicine is inevitable unless we build up things like the Social Health clinic. Instead of being kicked out Dr. Niles ought to be made president of the S.A.P.S. and we might get somewhere!"

"Is that so?" Rudy said. "Say, I'm sorry I missed his talk."

"But under socialized medicine everybody would be reduced to the same level. Like postmen. What would become of research?" Mitch pointed out.

"Those who would be fitted for research, would do research. Which is not always possible nowadays," Dr. Matthews smiled.

"The only way to accomplish anything is to increase the efficiency of medical science," Mitch said. "The trouble is not with the way we administer our knowledge, but that we don't know enough."

"You haven't tried to practice yet, Mitch," Rudy remarked, and Sylvia thought maybe Rudy was a little jealous of Mitch, today.

"Well, but look," Dr. Matthews said. "The city is overpopulated with doctors, most of whom just manage to make a living, and yet there are thousands of people who lack adequate medical attention."

"The doctors and the patients ought to get together," Aline said in her innocent way, and they all laughed.

"Well, I'm afraid Glenn Frank doesn't know much about the problem," Mitch said. "He's got some radical ideas, but he doesn't realize how conservative medical men are."

"That, unfortunately, is where we agree," Dr. Matthews said, and Sylvia thought he was really a charming person. He came of a distinguished family too, university professors, he was a marvelous connection. After they were married and back from Rochester, she would have Rudy and Aline bring him to dinner.

The envelope was from Rochester. Mitch opened it with pounding joy. It would be like his ticket to the hall of the elect.

He had read the few courteous lines and his head was still pounding. People talked of times when you couldn't believe what you saw. It was a fact. You couldn't believe.

He knew the reason. When no real reason was stated in a case of this kind, there was only the truth.

Fellows had warned him, hinted, but he had laughed it off saying that a man's Jewishness might be the deciding factor against him when all else was even. But they never refused a man who was really tops! And Dr. Durand had encouraged him, admitted that he wanted further work done on the problem. That time he had visited Rochester, with Rudy and the fellows, Dr. Durand had practically invited him.

There could be no other reason, and still he couldn't believe it. With the work he had done, the papers he had published . . .

They might be justified in having a quota. He wasn't arguing about that. After all, sometimes it did seem as though the Jews might overrun the profession.

But when a man really had something to contribute! You didn't stop him, just because he was a Jew.

He was numb for days. Too late now to apply anywhere else. He had been so confident. He might as well give up, and start to practice.

When the best men in the profession could be like that, what was the use?

. . . Marry, and have a corner office, and tend Jews with sour-pickle ulcers.

Rose and her younger sister, Mae, went into the hallway to greet the latest arrivals at Mae's trousseau party. It was Sylvia Abramson, and she had brought along Sorka Rosen. (Mort's latest, and I understand it's serious this time!) Rose led them into the bedroom, where they dropped their fur coats and could be heard exclaiming: oh, it's cute, oh, it's darling, oh, it's too cute for words, over Mae's collection of wicked honeymoon lingerie.

"Rose doesn't seem to mind in the least," Thelma remarked.

"Well, she had her chance with Manny," Lil Klein put in, eying Thelma. "I told her someone else would snap him up if she let him go."

Thelma cawed. "Some bargain!" she jested.

"My, you would think this was the old country!" Aline criticized them. "Why be so old-fashioned! What if her kid sister does get married first! Does that make her an old maid? Why, Rose is just a kid!"

"She's twenty-six."

"What is he anyway? In business?" Thelma queried, about Mae's fiancé.

"A C.P.A. They make plenty. He's a graduate of Wisconsin, too."

Rose came in, holding a twin-pointed brassiere. "Look what Syl brought Mae. Isn't it cute?"

"It's positively wicked!" Thelma chirped.

"You have to have them with the new molded gowns," Ev said.

"My, how times change!" Lil said, remembering how she had been forced to flatten her full young breasts in the boyish-form days.

"Why didn't you ask me? I could have got them for you wholesale," Ev remarked to Sylvia.

The chattering heightened, and for a moment it seemed to Rose like the old days when they were girls together, and something bright and warm seemed to flow, when they all got into a room, clacking, dishing. Only now, they were all married, or at least engaged, except herself. They seemed to exude a different effluvium. They were all so safe, so sure of themselves, and at the same time their voices were sharper, occasionally flashing out like claws at each other.

First Aline, and then Celia, had been her chum, and each had promised to reveal to her that intimate secret after marriage, and both, in an unaccountable way, had failed her. She wouldn't even expect anything of her sister.

Why, Ev and Lil had children, and Celia was carrying hers, and Aline would have a child; Rose had even heard it whispered that Lindy's wife was—you know. Everybody was having babies.

And she was just getting to be an old maid schoolteacher. Always the teasing brats at school, or the family at supper, or the new prospect with his slicked hair, and herself putting on the glad girlish face and parroting: Oh, I'd love to, I'd love to! for any date.

They were gabbing about the opening of the new opera. "All society will be there," Lil said. "Rose, are you going?"

"Why, I don't know yet," Rose said. "I haven't decided." The eternal stall of a girl who hasn't been asked, but still has hopes.

"Of course Mort has to go," Sylvia said. "You know he's become a regular first-nighter. But I don't think Mitch can afford the tickets."

"It's simply terrible. Ten dollars a seat."

"Well, it's for charity."

"You going with your folks, Cele?"

"I'm not sure. We were asked to join the Deutsches' party," Celia said, dropping the swanky name casually.

"I heard that the acoustics in the new auditorium are terrible," Thelma Kassell authoritatively remarked.

It had been like that ever since the first night he had laid her in Sam's office. Nothing got a rise out of her. Here he was blowing fifty bucks to a scalper for tickets to the big opening of the opera, and she would probably take it like tickets for a movie.

He wasn't kicking about the dough, as right now he was cashing in. Some of the boys were running a cigar store racket and needed legal advice to the tune of a century a week, and Sol Meisel's troubles in the cleaning business were a little legal gold mine, and the drive on crime was a gift of the gods, as all he had to do was drop in on Jake's coffee shop, see who was missing, prepare a habeas, pull the boys out of jail, and collect. He had plenty of places to spend the money, as he was sending his youngest brother through medical school, and setting a brother-in-law up in the gents' furnishing business, and the old lady needed operations all the time, and the old man was out of a job again.

But the way Gwenda acted he might as well have stuck her in a two-buck flop as in the Northmoor Arms; and she got no more kick out of eating at the Blackstone than at Thompson's.

Sometimes when he walked into that swell room at the Northmoor, the same hotel where Bugs Hogan kept his fireless cooker, Runt figured out the cost: a hundred and twenty a month was thirty bucks a week just for rent, and if he had her twice a week that was fifteen bucks a shot and, hell, for fifteen bucks he could get a lay that would be something, instead of this limp hunk of white meat, with her enigmatic Garbo silence. Even Garbo was talking now.

But every once in a while she would reward him with a dim, remote smile; ha! a sign of life! and he would throw out forty bucks more for lingerie.

He couldn't figure her at all. Two years now. She never mentioned her folks; and if he asked, all he got was a pained: "Please, I would rather not discuss it."

He couldn't tell whether she went for him at all, or not. Like when Shorty the vaudeville actor had tipped him off how to add an inch to his height by wearing military heels; Gwenda had picked up the shoes and run her finger around the heels, looking at him with that wan Garbo smile. He had felt smaller than ever, but she had trailed over and run her hand through his hair, and when he kissed her he had felt something like a flutter in her mouth, as though the muscles around her mouth were dead from lack of use—like the muscles in people's ears—and she was trying to make them come back, and kiss.

"Get yourself some new glad rags, baby, this is going to be some party!" he said, exhibiting the ducats to the opera opening, and slipped her a hundred-dollar check.

And when she stepped out in her new dress, he had to hand it to himself for picking a classy number. She looked like she had been poured into that piece of black satin, the gown flowed down her lean mare's thighs to actually make a froth at her feet, the silver slippers peeking out, like little white stones on a midnight beach. When she walked, her slim legs were suggestively clear against the dress, and he thought: the heck with short skirts.

Women were the nuts, the way they knew how to show you everything even when seeming to hide it all.

As she sat down and crossed her legs, he noticed the low heels on her formal slippers. She caught his look.

"Thank the Lord dresses are long again," she said. "Now I can wear low heels and they don't show. I hate to walk on stilts."

Dave Plotkin's sweet mama would knock their eyes out tonight!

Runt was feeling so swell, wearing his coat with the big fur collar, his woman wearing her golden mink. The icy night was like a black marble wall enclosing the city; automobile lights mirrored on the marble street; and street lamps spaced away like a chain of giant pearls. He gave a panhandler four bits.

The low sweet call of cab whistles sounded from neighboring hotels, and to these was added the Northmoor doorman's whistle, for Dave Plotkin and his dame. There was a quick crunch of tire chains, and the shining yellow door was held open. Forgotten, the cabby days! He could ride in Yellow or Checker, what the hell!

Runt was feeling swell as the cab churned over the Michigan bridge— go easy here, the rubber paving blocks are skiddy—and swell because he knew his city, knew the very pavement on the bridge—feeling so swell he said stop here awhile, because he just wanted to look, and admire the bulwarks of the Loop.

"Gee, it certainly looks great!" He opened the door, and took a drink of the icy air, and the sight of the buildings was cold and deep in him, like the bracing air, and there was an exhilaration, a pride sweeping through him like the great sweeping arc of the Lindbergh beacon on the sky.

They were parked at the turn of the river. Across, the wide wings of the Merchandise Mart were rising, the building spreading so wide that you didn't realize it was skyscraper high, the biggest building in the world! And around the bend were the two great towers over the river, the Opera and the News, facing each other; and back eastward were the fine new buildings on the Drive, Builders' Building, and prick-pointed Mather Tower, and the London Guarantee, and Three-Thirty-Three, and inside the Loop, a whole forest of towers, the Methodist spire, and the Morrison, and think of the five-crowned Pure Oil Building, the Carbon and Carbide, the new Jewelers' Building—oh, Chicago!

"Jeez, some town!" Runt said.

And the Sun Goes Down

There was a daylight blaze under the spur of the El on Market Street; white fingers of movie lights traveled caressingly over the facade of the huge new Opera Building. Beyond, the light faded away into a bluish haze that engulfed the crummy waterfront warehouses, ancient, decaying dumps.

Crowds, bleak-faced in the cold night, stomping against the chill that penetrated the soles of their shoes, pressed from all sides toward the wooden ramp fronting the new building. Hooves resounded on the wood, as mounted police held clear the entrance. The limousines made a smooth throbbing sound over the ramp.

Newsreel cameras were mounted over the sidewalk.

"So maybe he lost ten or twenty millions, what's it to him?" Lou was remarking with clever nonchalance, as he stepped from the car into the blaze of movie lights. He put up his hand to balance his new silk topper.

"Just like a Hollywood opening," Celia said, surveying the banks of staring faces.

Rose stepped onto the pavement, still giddy with the last-minute reprieve that had brought her a fill-in date for Celia's guest, trying not to worry about her unimpressive formal in all this rush of splendor, still undecided whether to be natural, or to try to put on a sweetness act for Mac Hirschberger, whom she would probably never see again anyway, so why not be natural?

Celia and Mrs. Moscowitz looked as swell as any society dames, standing regal in their knee-length ermine wraps, under which projected the glittering filmy net of their new gowns, and the spike-like gleam of their heels, so high they were practically stilts. Twenty dollars a pair, Rose knew.

The newsreel cameras, fooled for a moment, ground Rube Moscowitz's party.

They certainly looked classy, the six of them, strolling into the blazing white foyer, past the blink and wink of newspaper flashlights, entering Samuel Insull's new opera house.

"He didn't lose so much," Rube Moscowitz said authoritatively. "His stocks are nearly back to where they were before the slide. Say, he could put up three more operas like this and never notice it."

"Well, this is your chance to sell out," Lou suggested.

Rube chortled. "I'm rid of half of it already," he said. "I'm sinking my dough in real estate."

"Look, mother," Celia whispered. They turned and stared at a party getting out of a long black limousine. The newspaper photographers were around them like a swarm of insane monkeys, and the newsreel trucks attacked, their cameras following every turn of the group.

"I bet it's Mrs. Rockefeller McCormick," Celia murmured.

"She doesn't look crazy enough to be a McCormick to me," Rose remarked, feeling her liveliness returning.

Her partner gave her an appreciative glance.

"Remember that one that married the old Swiss riding master?" Celia said. "What ever became of her? . . . And Harold McCormick with his monkey glands!"

Gosh, it seemed long ago!

"Well, I guess they can afford to be crazy," Mrs. Moscowitz remarked, backing away as the ritzy party came toward them.

Celia put her hand to her diamond necklace. For an instant, she had felt dowdy.

". . . In the gorgeous lobby is a scene of splendor surpassing the glory of the court of King Louis the Fourteenth," gasped the radio voice. "And now, the scions of one of Chicago's wealthiest and most exclusive families . . ."

"Your ex is getting so busy he can't even take care of his practice," Mr. Klein remarked, coming into the frontroom. "Joe Goldman went up to give him a case, but Sam was in court trying to get off a couple of radicals. So Goldman took his business someplace else."

"I don't know what's the matter with that fellow!" Lil said, exasperated. "He doesn't get anything for defending those damn fools!"

"I think he will lose the Atlas Coal Company too," Mr. Klein mentioned.

"Well, *I* certainly didn't lose anything. Anyway, I'm not interested. I'm not interested! I'm listening to the radio, father!" she snapped.

"What's the matter with your friend, Harry Perlin?"

"Nothing, he's a dope. That's all."

"I see another stockbroker shot himself. He was living in the Del Roi Hotel." He offered her the paper. "Despondent on account of his ill health," Mr. Klein quoted wryly.

"Father, please let me listen!" Lil cried, striking away the newspaper.

". . . is wearing a gorgeous creation direct from Paris, and her famous three hundred thousand dollar diamonds . . ."

"I thought they weren't going to have any boxes," Rose said.

"Oh, they had to put them in, the last minute," Mac Hirschberger informed her. "See, they had a lot of private stalls built back there under the balcony, but the society folks said nix, nobody could see them in those stalls. So Sammy had to yank out ten rows of seats and rebuild the entire main floor, with the boxes in the middle, where they can be seen."

Like a jewel-crusted belt across the middle of the auditorium, the row of boxes stretched, studded with the tiara'd heads of society dames.

"Wait for me inside. Back in a minute." Mort dropped Sorka with Mitch and Sylvia, and drove off to park the car. He found a spot in an alley. A youngish figure in a thin, torn overcoat approached.

"Watch your car, mister?"

"Naw," he said. It made him sore, to have these self-appointed car watchers try to shake him down, in every alley, and under Wacker Drive.

The fellow was shivering, he noticed as he walked away. Well, he'd give him something if he was still there when he came for the car.

In the two blocks to the theater, Mort was approached three times. " 'Nya spare a dime, mister?" He gave the second one a dime, but felt annoyed at the third.

"Wow, it's cold!" he said, rushing into the lobby, where he met the others. "My ears are frozen."

"The J.S.S.B. is simply swamped with people begging for coal," Sylvia remarked.

"Look. Over there. That's Irene Castle McLaughlin," Sorka whispered.

As they paraded down the aisle Celia remembered how, long ago, she had been simply overwhelmed by the grandeur of the opening of the Chicago Theater. How young and green she had been!

It was as she had thought: everybody who was anybody wore tails. She exchanged a triumphant glance with Lou, and looked daggers at her father, who had insisted that a tux was good enough. She maneuvered to get him into a seat quickly. Once seated, she turned for a long, slow survey of the glittering audience. She spotted the Deutsches talking to some of the Rosenwalds. She caught and returned several greeting smiles—the lips pulled wide and pressed into a grimace, the head nodding slightly.

"For cry sake!" Lou said. "Look who's here!" and chuckled.

Celia followed his glance. Several rows back, she caught a glimpse of the clamp-jawed, scraped-looking face of Runt Plotkin! She glazed her eyes and turned as he nearly caught her gaze.

"Can you beat it!" she said. "Of all the crust!"

"Friends of mine," Runt said. "That's Lou Margolis. I went to law school with him, and that's his father-in-law with him, the big heavy guy, that's Rube Moscowitz, he's a big-shot politician. He and Insull are like this!" Runt showed two fingers. "Want to meet them?"

"All right," she said, in her low disinterested voice.

He squirmed in his seat. "Jeez, some show, hey, babe? Lots of judges here. There's Judge Noonan. Hey. I bet the Genna boys would have liked this, they were nuts about opera!"

Suddenly, a rush of murmurs swept the vast auditorium, then there was a hushed gasp.

Proud, with his patrician white mustache, and a kingly mild smile on his pinkish face, Samuel Insull appeared in a center box. He was surrounded by potentates in full dress, and women who had that finely groomed society look of having been made to appear much handsomer than they are.

"There he is. Shall we say hello to him now?" Mrs. Moscowitz fluttered.

"No, not now. In the intermission." Rube was visibly confused.

The auditorium darkened. There was some opera singing. And when the lights went on between the acts, they had the same feeling as when the curtain goes up for a show.

Who had come late, in the ritziest boxes?

"Oh, I know who it is. I saw her picture in the rotogravure," Celia said, watching a young woman who sat beautifully erect, in the third box.

"Millicent Stone," Rose reported. "She was supposed to marry some society guy but they called the wedding off all of a sudden."

"Why?"

"Three guesses."

"They've been calling off an awful lot of society weddings in the last few months," Celia observed.

"Beaver!" Lou claimed, spotting J. Hamilton Lewis.

They joined the glittering parade into the lobby.

Rube, Lou, and Mac went for the men's room.

Rube recognized a couple of the county commissioners.

"Looks like they're holding a meeting here," Lou cracked.

"Yah. Probably trying to figure out where to get the next payroll," Rube laughed.

"I see where they're trying to put across a twenty percent pay cut," Lou said. "But where will they get the other eighty?"

"Why don't they take a bucket out in the lobby and collect a few diamonds. That would keep them going for quite a while," Mac Hirschberger cracked.

"Hi, Rube," one of the commissioners said.

"Hi there, you old Turk!"

There was a lot of backslapping.

"What I mean is, Pat Hurley is absolutely right!" a pot-bellied commissioner was holding forth. "The country is just as rich as it was before the crash. That stands to reason, don't it?"

The lobby was as crowded as State and Madison on a Saturday noon. From all sides came the popping of flashlights. Frenzied little women with pads of notepaper dashed to the sides of the photographed ones, asked a few respectful questions, and departed.

"Aren't those your friends?" Gwenda said, as they passed in crosscurrent with the Moscowitzes.

"Oh, sure," Runt said. Suddenly he felt hesitant about introducing her. But what the hell!

"Hello, Lou, hello, Celia," he said. "Wantcha to meet a friend of mine . . ."

The crowd held them prisoned for a moment, facing each other.

Lou dropped a cold nod, and turned away.

Runt went furiously red in the face. He looked at Gwenda. She was blowing out smoke, indolently.

At last the crowd pulled the two groups apart.

"Do you think we ought to go over now?" Celia said.

"Maybe we ought not to bother him," Mrs. Moscowitz wondered, nervously. "He's got so many people."

"I dunno," Rube said. "He sent me the tickets."

"Well, I think he might notice if we didn't even say hello. After all, he came to my wedding," Celia observed.

Just as they were starting toward the Insull box, the lights dimmed.

They acted easier toward each other.

In the swirling mob pushing out of the theater, under the jagged crying of taxi whistles, of horns, the Abramson party ran full tilt into the Moscowitz party.

And after the chirps, squeaks, and cries of greeting, the comments of gorgeous, wonderful, why it just looks like everybody was here tonight, it was decided that, since it would be ages before they could get their cars, they might as well walk over to the Bismarck and all have coffee together.

Rube and Mrs. Moscowitz took a cab; Celia saw that there was little chance of hitching on to the Deutsches' party, and so, why not, all the young folks went walking swiftly together, up Madison Street.

If You Had Bad Luck in the Market, Try
Good Luck (Oleomargarine) at Home!

"And did you see Mrs. Potter Palmer?" Celia was saying, and Sorka was saying: "But the most gorgeous thing was that fishnet gown that Adrienne Franks was wearing," and Mort had just stopped, annoyed, yet digging into his pocket for change, and Lou Margolis was insisting: "They ought to keep these guys off the streets," and Rose was walking close to Mac Hirschberger and her light, pretty laugh was sounding when with one accord, as though they felt an impulse rushing in the cold air against their cheeks, the girls, then the men, looked upward. Rose shrieked, and huddled against her escort. Sylvia stopped in her tracks, pulling Mitch to a stop.

After the shriek, there was a queer instant of silence, of actual waiting. The whole street, frozen in the clarity of the cold night, seemed to be waiting. Street cars, automobiles, people walking, all, to the mind remembered, were clenched in an instant immobility.

Some saw the body plunging bulletlike toward the pavement. Others felt, rather than saw, and experienced the scene as a whole: the spattered body on the pavement. Right at my feet! right at my feet! each mind insisted.

They had all shrunk together, huddled into a group.

A man had jumped from a twenty-third-story hotel window.

BOOK FOUR

Each in His Place

HOME, HOME

THEY took a slow boat home.

On the boat, Alvin was sour all the time. If he let himself be dragged along to play shuffleboard, all his shots were short. Or suddenly he would make a vicious push, smacking the disk to the end of the deck, and throw down his stick.

He rarely talked. What was worth talking about? Eunice was greatly excited about Ernest Hemingway's *Farewell to Arms*.

"Crap!" he said.

"But how can you say that, you haven't read the book!"

"Crap!"

Eunice discussed him with Joe. "He seems to have lost all interest in life. I don't think it's just because we're going home. He started to be this way months ago. He even lost interest in food," Eunice explained. "You know how Al used to make such a fuss about restaurants in Paris. But lately he'd even eat at a Duval."

Joe laughed. "Maybe he's decided to change his act," he said. "You know Alvin. He has to be different every year."

They exchanged a glance of worried understanding.

Being on a boat, so small, out where all around is ocean, Alvin thought constantly of himself, so small, in relation to the universe. He thought over his whole life and saw that he had done nothing. He had never finished anything he had started. And now? What was there for him, back in Chicago? If the factory was going bust, as the old man wrote, then he certainly wouldn't have a chance to revive that modernistic line.

And what friends would he have in Chicago? Those old kids from the bunch? Stock's stodgy symphony every Saturday night? Bury himself in Chicago. Like those guys that let themselves be buried alive in a coffin. People paid a dime to peep at them.

Limp in a deck chair, eyes half shut, Alvin wished never to think or feel any more, but only wash along like the sea.

Joe flopped into the next chair.

Alvin squirmed. Joe's vitality irked him; the swell bronze of him, just from Palestine. Sure, gape at him, Eunice, take it in. Let him show you how he's bronze all over, his ass too, all in that beautiful golden shade, you bitch, ask him, he'll show you!

"Play some deck tennis?" Joe suggested. "Eunice is coming up."

Alvin grunted negatively.

They lay for a while, silent.

"What the hell do you want to go back to Chicago for?" Alvin snapped. "There's nothing for you there." And added maliciously: "She's getting married."

"Well, all I want is to pick up some dough and maybe go back to Palestine," said Joe.

"You know there's a depression," Alvin remarked. "There was a stock-market crash."

"Oh, well."

"What the hell do you want to go back and live in Palestine for?" Alvin persisted querulously. "Do they have to cut your balls off before you have sense enough to keep out? Not that I'd mind. . . . Why don't you go to Russia?"

"Why don't you?" Joe responded.

Alvin shot him a hot, nervous look. "Aw, shut up."

Eunice came along the deck. She wore a tan pullover; her wrists protruded delicate and white. Joe joined her at the rail, leaning, staring at the leaden ocean.

"He must be a hell of a guy to live with," Joe said.

"Uh-huh."

She had always been the *shikseh* Alvin had married, to be looked at only with speculation: how long would it last? But now, talking, she was just a girl tired of uncertainty, a young woman confessing she wanted to settle down, and have kids.

"Well, why don't you?" Joe said. "It might be good for him too."

"He says it's a hell of a cruel thing to bring children into the world."

They shared a grin at the typicality of Alvin's remark.

"Anyway, you don't have to worry about keeping him. He needs you more than you need him."

"Think so?" She touched his hand gratefully, on the rail. "There are times when I know he wishes I were someone else. When your friend Sylvia was in Paris I thought he must have been in love with her once, because he was so mean to her."

"Oh, all of us were," Joe said. "I guess there's a girl like that in every crowd, the one that seems the purest and the sweetest, you know the kind of girl adolescents idealize."

An ideal must remain unattainable. Like Palestine, a love-ideal to the Jews, a mere cohabiting wife to the Arabs, who possessed her.

"It was pretty serious with you, wasn't it?" Eunice pursued, quietly.

"I had it worse than the others," Joe admitted. "But it would never have worked out. Well, she's marrying now."

"I think she's a very sweet girl, and very good-looking," Eunice said. Then she squeezed his hand. "You're a swell guy, Joe."

Yes, any woman would pay tribute to a man who was faithful to love, to ideals. Momentarily, Joe wondered whether all his love had not been a play for this kind of pity and sympathy. And maybe now that he was going back to America, he would start a new, more realistic life.

It was around midnight, and drizzling. The decklights made grayish halos of rain in the pitch-darkness. Cold wet blew against the face. Alvin insisted on taking a final turn.

"Don't you want your slicker?" Eunice asked.

"No," he snapped.

It was odd for him to disregard his clothes.

Joe was half asleep when he heard the tapping.

"Who is it?"

"It's Eunice, Joe."

Hearing a woman's voice, his cabin-mate awoke and gave Joe a look between leering and annoyance.

"I'm worried about Al," Eunice said.

"What time is it?" he asked.

"It's after two. I went up on deck but couldn't find him."

Joe pulled on his pants and a coat, and slipped into the passage. Neither voiced the suspicion, the fear.

The deck was all black, and the mist blown against their faces seemed unreal, unseen. Eunice clutched Joe's hand.

"Did you look on that little afterdeck? You know he sometimes climbs up there," Joe said.

"No. I couldn't see the ladder."

Joe lit a match; the pitiful flame seemed large in that darkness, against their fear.

"Wait here."

Joe immediately made out Alvin's figure. He was sitting precariously on the rail, facing the sea.

Eunice had climbed up the steps; she gasped.

Alvin turned his head. "What the hell do you want?" he growled.

They could think of no joke that would disguise their search. They heard his savage, hurt cry: "Can't you leave me alone!" the cry of a man who is utterly sick of being alone in himself.

Double Wedding

Sylvia sat combing her hair. "Oh, it's so ratty, there's just nothing to do with it at this stage," she sighed. She tried a coil.

Mort stood in the doorway smilingly watching her.

"You're my everything, everything I love . . ."

The honeydrip radio voice pervaded the house, like the scent of a cheap perfume.

"Is that Rudy Vallée?" she asked.

"Thrilled?" Mort said.

Even the voice of the crooner was included in the spreading, generous love of the world that she felt.

"Everything I care for . . ."

"One thing about those low-on-the-neck hats," Sylvia said; "they cover this mess on the back of your neck. And all the girls are letting their hair grow."

"That's right," Mort speculated. "They ought to be good for another season."

Her brother advanced to her dressing table. He took his hand out of his pocket. It held a ring-box.

"Oh, Mort!" she cried, reaching.

His teeth shone, his very mustache glittered.

Sylvia daintily held up the white-gold circlet, whose narrowness emphasized the bold grandeur of the perfect diamond. "She'll love it!" she said, at the same moment laughing at her own inability to suppress a touch of envy because the diamond was three times as large as the one Mitch had been able to afford. And oddly there drifted through her mind the thought that Joe had never given her a ring, and the memory of that time she had given Joe her mother's ring.

"Yep," Mort said. "I decided to make an honest woman out of Sorka." He slid down beside her. "How about making it a double wedding?"

It would be quiet and dignified. Nothing like the public brawls that the Moscowitzes and the Goldbergs had given.

On the morning of the wedding day, Mort came into Sylvia's room grinning. "Want to see something funny?" He held out a small framed picture. It was Peter Arno's cartoon, showing a hot mama poking her bed-fellow, over the caption: "Wake up, you mutt! We're getting married today!"

"Isn't it a scream?" Mort said. "Sorka sent it."

One thing, Mort and Sorka were well matched.

There was a dinner for the three families, in a private salon of the Palmer House.

"Better drink plenty of wine!" Mort said, slapping Mitch on the back. "It helps."

"Baloney, that's just a superstition," Mitch responded. Sylvia was glad to see how he was taking all the kidding like a sport.

"Yah?" Mort laughed. "This is a case of science contradicted by experience!"

Sorka laughed merrily.

Sylvia and Mitch were going to Europe. Mitch had at last consented to accept several months in Vienna for their honeymoon as a wedding present, and once there, Sylvia knew he would forget his bitter disappointment about Rochester. Mort and Sorka were going to Bermuda. But the couples were spending this night in the hotel.

"Better be good, Mitch!" Mort said with double meaning as they parted in the hallway.

Once in their room, Sorka unrolled the marriage certificate. "My! it looks like a diploma!" she jested.

"Behold! the rewards of virtue!" Mort merrily responded. Whoever wanted a bashful, trembling virgin for a bride! "Say, maybe we ought to go in there and give them some instructions!"

"Oh, yeah? What did Mitch go to medical school for?"

Mort stood in the bathroom doorway, watching her undress.

"You know what they really ought to do at weddings is run off one of those movies that show how it's done."

"All right, mister, beat it and let the blushing bride prepare for bed."

"Don't forget that passionate perfume," he said. He stepped out of the bathroom, and began to hum "Body and Soul."

From the bathroom, she joined:

"You know I'm yours for just the taking . . ."

Sorka walked to the window, and looked out on State Street.

"I'm supposed to stand pensively at the window, aren't I?" she said, turning her head to him. Laughing appreciatively, Mort joined her, slipping his arms under her wicked black negligee.

The rooftops were rectangles of snow. Their eyes turned to the white blaze, *CHICAGO*, on the theater sign, and they could read GARBO TALKS.

They kissed.

Playfully, Sorka drew out the rope-tie of Mort's dressing-gown. He grabbed for it, and they had a tug of war.

With the last pull, she capsized, face-down on the bed. "You win!" she gasped, letting go.

"Now I'm going to beat you!" he laughed.

Suddenly they were staring at each other with complete knowingness. His blood pounded. His arm was raised. Mort slid down on the bed beside his wife and both were engulfed in an overwhelming embrace, a happiness in having found something new and complete in each other on their wedding night after all, a confessional of all the potentialities within the human spirit, toward lust, and toward beauty; now they were wedded in knowing each other utterly; each would really know, would take part in anything the other might ever do.

"You're my everything,
Everything I love . . ."

Syl's mind kept singing, while the two of them couldn't stop looking into each other's faces, with flowing, happy self-consciousness.

Only, in spite of the perfection of this pinnacle, the true savoring of the occasion seemed to escape them. It was like staring into the sun, you couldn't see.

"Happy?" Mitch said.

"Oh, yes!"

Each feeling the other's glowing wish for the partner's happiness, deferring each small move, to know the other's wishes, wishing to do as the other wished.

You're my everything . . .

She had saved herself all these years, twenty-six, they had narrowed down to the fine point of this moment, and from here would spread outward again. Truly she had never felt like this with Joe, never wanted this love with Joe. Now it was perfect, two virgins, together. It was beautiful and holy. All the city was covered with snow.

She wanted to be overcome, like a girl of seventeen, all love.

Yet thoughts that she wanted to ban persisted.

They couldn't afford to have a child, yet. Ev Goldberg had twins, Aline was having a baby, and Celia, and even Thelma was due, but she would still have to wait, and wait till Mitch was settled in his work. What were the best years for childbearing? Before thirty. Before thirty, she must have a perfect child, intelligent and beautiful.

"Darling! darling!" she said, pressing him with her hands; suddenly feeling the surge of ecstasy. Oh, why had they had to wait so long, their best years! Now they must make it up to each other in the complete recklessness of their passion. And she was unable to keep herself from murmuring: "Darling, be careful."

The Year They All Had Babies

Lou and his partner Nathan Schaeffer had been on their own for a year, Lou taking along Rube's business and Schaeffer being the son of a judge. They were doing fine, handling the affairs of some of the best families in Chicago. Lou was dashing around full of energy all the time, though he sometimes got a little irritable at night, and he was always taking aspirins.

The best way to get what he wanted was through kidding people, making them laugh, he found, and sometimes he lay awake half the night figuring out just how to get a certain contact, and how to meet that person informally, where he could kid him into the deal. As his lying awake kept Celia awake, they started to use separate bedrooms.

They went out practically every night; Lou was popular everywhere. Occasionally Celia imagined she heard a side remark, oh, she's the daughter of that West Side politician, but really in a tone of appreciation of the way she and Lou had come ahead. Lou was the life of every affair at the club, he was usually master of ceremonies, imitating Harry Richman, and there was always a request for his imitation of Harpo Marx imitating Gandhi "making salt while the sun shines."

In court, too, he knew that a joke at the right time is worth tons of argument. Once he was defending the popular young widow Mrs. Lerner against a group of her husband's relatives who were contesting his will, and it happened that Einstein was visiting Chicago at the time. "This is all a matter of relativity," Lou remarked in court, and the judge laughed so much he didn't listen to the other side and practically handed the case to Lou.

For a week you couldn't go to a bridge party at the Chicago Beach Hotel without hearing someone remark: "It's all a matter of relativity."

Celia was in Charlevoix most of that summer; Lou came down on weekends. When she began to feel dangerously attracted to the bronzed, sailboating Clark Gables, she decided she had better play safe and have a kid. Infants were a nuisance with their howling, and they cramped your style. Still, with a nursemaid it wouldn't be so bad.

They had come from playing a foursome with Archie Stern, a fine contact. Celia was taking a shower; she always got sweaty in the sun.

"Babe, we could have a kid this year," she plopped.

"Huh?" Through the open door she could see Lou pulling on his bathing suit, his skin baby pink outside the suitlines. He was going to peel.

Lou Margolis didn't know whether to act sarcastic or sympathetic throughout his wife's pregnancy. After all, the Indian squaws used to drop them on the road. Celia was large and healthy, she scarcely showed. And when it got big, Lou made a few cracks about watermelons, and let it go at that. She was going to Dr. DeLone, the best man in town. Lou got a lot of laughs, kidding about prunes for dessert.

Once Rube blustered into the office and bellowed: "How's she doing, can you feel it move yet?"

That embarrassed Lou; Rube was a boor.

And on the night when, silently, she took his hand and laid it over her belly, and he felt or imagined he felt a kind of fluid thrusting, Lou was awed, and a bit of ashamed of himself. "Another Benny Friedman, huh, kicking already," he cracked lamely.

He knew it was traditional for the father to walk around sleepless in the hospital corridor, suffering more than the mother during the delivery, and he was a little ashamed because he wasn't worried at all. Lou was doing a crossword puzzle when the Moscowitzes arrived. He was trying to think of a five-letter word for a flower that grows in the desert. And all the while he really felt loving and husbandly toward Celia. He simply knew that she could be trusted to do her part and deliver on the dotted line.

It was a boy, weighing eight pounds, beating the Lindbergh baby by half a pound.

Lou passed out perfectos at the Club. Judge Morgenstern, the aloof, actually came over and patted Lou on the back. "Now that's what I like to see, you young fellows settling down to the really important matters of life, and producing a few smart Jewish lawyers for the coming generation!" he said.

Lou felt that again he and Celia had done the right thing at the right time. Everybody was feeling serious about life these days, and they had shown that the younger generation were not just play-kids.

There was a silly old Jewish superstition that prohibited naming a child for someone who was still alive. But Rube gave the hint that he wouldn't mind, and as they were completely emancipated, they named the kid Reuben.

The old grandfather, Avrum, swore that was bad luck, and vowed he would stay away from the *briss*, but the joke was on him as the circumcision had already been performed at the hospital.

Thelma was scared stiff. She felt obliged to have Rudy Stone, and though she declared she had absolute confidence in him, still you had to admit he was young. Secretly, she paid twenty dollars for a visit to Dr. DeLone, who told her just what Rudy had told her.

She believed in prenatal influence and, as she wanted her daughter to be an opera singer, she spent all of her time listening to the orthophonic, and even in the last stages of pregnancy went downtown to hear Marion Talley though otherwise she was ashamed to be seen on the streets. She absolutely forbade "robot music." When a radio in the building was turned on, she shut all the windows tight and stuffed her ears.

She had a tough delivery. Thirty-six hours of agony. Manny was like a maniac howling for Rudy to do something, but Rudy insisted on waiting. After the five-pound girl was born, Manny calmed down and practically worshiped Rudy for saving his wife and child. "An inexperienced man would have gone in and probably killed the baby, but Rudy handled it perfectly!" he would declare, launching into a long detailed account of the birth.

All he could think about was some clever way of announcing the addition to the family. It had to be cleverer than Lou Margolis's announcement, which consisted of a legal description beginning: "Know all by these presents . . ." and ending with a rigmarole about "the said parents, being parties of the first part," etc. Sealed by a notary public. It certainly was clever.

Manny thought of announcing their child in the guise of a new car: Just received, latest 1930 model self-starter, twelve-cylinder lung-power, beautiful red finish Kassell Combination. . . . But he had got one like that from an automobile salesman.

In the middle of the night, he had the inspiration. Two days later, everyone in the bunch received an envelope from the *NEWS-FLASH* Clipping Agency. It contained a newspaper clipping from the Chicago *Tribune*, dated June 1, 1949. It was headlined:

YOUNGEST OPERA STAR ELOPES
WITH LINDY JR.

And the story ran:

> "The world was agog today over the romantic elopement of Chicago's sensational young diva, Cynthia Kassell, with the brilliant young son of the Lone Eagle, Charles Augustus Lindbergh, Jr. . . . Miss Kassell was born July 21, 1930, the daughter of Thelma and Emanuel Kassell, D.D.S. . . ."

Everybody admitted that was cute.

Aline had a girl, too. She didn't mind being pregnant; it was a nice lazy job; she slopped around the house in her old dresses, their tightness accentuating her condition.

She liked the idea of kids tumbling around the house, and decided she would have three: one for each of them and one extra. Being an active member of Hadassah, she decided she really wanted her children to be brought up Jewish. She named her daughter Naomi after her maternal grandmother.

That summer Estelle got caught. She never knew how it happened. At the time she was private secretary to Albert Venuti, an importer, and it was the first time she had had anything to do with an employer. He was a youngish Italian, with a fine home in Oak Park, a wife and kids. She was actually doing a good job as a secretary and getting only thirty a week. So why—well, there wasn't anyone better around, and she didn't like to be alone.

He was terrified at the news, and acted badly—hinted how did he know it was his doing. Oh, it was all ugly. By the time he made arrangements for her to get it fixed up she was half-minded to light out and have the kid, somewhere. Aline had a kid, and Celia, and all those girls. . . . They were settled, had homes, kids. She barely prevented herself from calling up Sol Meisel.

Venuti said the job cost him a hundred and fifty. It was done in an office on Crawford Avenue by a young blond fellow, who tried to make her, leering all the time.

There wasn't even a place for her to rest. Estelle took a cab to her room and was utterly alone all evening. That rat might at least have called.

And of course she lost her job.

But the Mort Abramsons took the prize. They must have gone right to
work on their wedding night because the delivery was prompt. A ten-pound
boy!

"It takes a man, every time!" Mort crowed.

They named him Raoul, for Israel.

It was wonderful, the feeling that pervaded the bunch. Now they were
all together again, drawn together in the feeling that they were the
generation that counted, young mothers and fathers; the life-insurance ads
were for them, the full-page ads in the *Ladies' Home Journal* showing
happy young mothers and fathers and their kids in the family car were for
them; now they could understand so many things that had seemed
meaningless before, oh, like the *Daily News* page headed Good Foods,
Fine Clothes, Things for the Home, and Your Children; now they saw that
the whole world was really laid out for them, the soup makers and the car
makers were trying to win their approval; they were the young business and
professional men, manufacturers, doctors, lawyers, the best people, the
people who carried on the traditions of the world. They were drawn
together, comparing baby formulas, and How many diapers do you use? I
can't get along with less than three dozen!

They were together again now, and they knew that they had come
through as the real people of the world. Some had gone off and were lost;
Estelle, Alvin Fox; as kids they had foolishly envied those who were rushing
off into the real life outside, to New York, to Europe; but now they knew
they alone had been the wise and the good ones. What did those others
have? Nothing.

All Alone and Feeling Blue

Chicago had never seemed so barren to Joe. But he hung around;
maybe he would pick up a few commissions to do for the Fair.

The near North Side crowd was entirely changed: Indiana was living in
Mexico, and the present crop of bohemians seemed undeveloped, sappy.
Even the Dill Pickle Club was closed. What he wanted was just to sit in
someone's house and gab.

The affair with Eunice was running down. Sometimes he wished it
hadn't begun; instead, he would have been able to hang around their house,
be friendly with Alvin.

He tried to keep from hanging around the Arts Club; it was such a
meager little exhibit he had there.

A couple of evenings he took out Myra Roth, even thought of making a
play for her. It was Myra who had fixed up the Arts Club exhibit; you had
to have pull to get in anywhere. "Let me do things for you, Joe," she
pleaded. She was a swell kid, but neurotic as hell, and that crazy Paris night

was between them. Sometimes Joe even thought of trying to marry her: wasn't that what artists were supposed to do, to solve their difficulties?

So there was the exhibit, and the tea that he managed to grin through. The room swarmed with smart-smelling women, lots of the South Side Jewish crowd, full of expert jabber about Archipenko and Brancusi and Epstein. He knew this was his chance to get in with the crowd, maybe get a few orders for portraits, but they gave him the fidgets, and when they bored at him with "Aren't you a Chicago boy?" he couldn't help feeling Myra must have built him up as a poor West Side lad who had conquered his ghetto background, emerged into the classless realm of art. . . .

Myra had insisted on buying a little Palestinian marble of a dancing *chalutz*, and Aline said she might get the Hadassah to buy one of his Palestinian pieces, for a raffle. No other sales.

Many of the fellows he had known at Illinois were now architects, and though he had to say over his name a few times before they remembered, still, a Guggenheimer was somebody, and entitled to a lunch.

While waiting in the Tavern Club, Joe studied the view. It was a view of all Chicago, but without the detachment of an airplane panorama. From here, he was like a man standing at the head of a stairway, looking over a gathering of people, before going down among them. How flatly level were the roofs! They spread out in a vast semicircle, all clearly and minutely etched, flat rectangles, pierced by an occasional church spire, or by little groups of smokestacks. Chicago! He would never get over Chicago! Seeing it this way, Joe still felt the itch in his hands, to go down there, to make things, to do.

"Well, old Order-of-the-Day! How are you!" He turned to greet Blondy Walsh. "Waiting long?"

"Just got here. I was taking in the view."

"Absolutely marvelous from here. I never get tired of it!" Walsh exclaimed. "Say, I've never forgotten that incident. Order-of-the-Day! Only, you shouldn't have apologized to those damned brass monkeys. What'd you want to crayfish for!"

Joe was startled that an experience he had practically forgotten should remain with this fellow as the one thing identifying him.

"Gosh, this city is developing," Joe said. They stood and gazed over the vast spread of Chicago, westward and northward, and right below, at the tremendous skyscrapers on both sides of the river that girt the Loop. "It hits you between the eyes when you come back," Joe said. "You know I've been away a couple of years. Had a Guggenheim."

"That so! You lucky hound!"

At lunch, Joe didn't know how to get to his objective.

"I notice they're finally rebuilding the Fine Arts in Jackson Park," he remarked.

"Julius Rosenwald is turning it into an industrial museum," Walsh said. "Exhibits of machinery."

"Oh," Joe said. "Well, why not? Signs of the times! What's doing around town?" he finally blurted, feeling he was rushing the topic.

"Nothing much. Things are pretty dead."

"Yah. What is this depression I hear about?"

"That's just it. A depression. A low place."

"Well, there are a lot of new buildings."

"It's all over now," Blondy quoted. "Why, you could go roller skating on almost any floor in the Opera Building. And you know what they say about the Stevens—three thousand empty beds. Count 'em!"

"Well, the Fair will give you fellows plenty to do."

Blondy Walsh shrugged. "Oh, they'll probably go through with it, though on a tenth of the scale they expected."

Joe took a gulp. "Any sculpture?"

Walsh shrugged. He wouldn't advise Joe to count on anything. Certain fellows had the inside track. But if he wanted an introduction . . .

That was how it went on. A fellow spent all his time finding somebody who knew somebody who knew somebody. They took a fellow to lunch at the Tavern Club or at the Cliff Dwellers, and from the skyscraper top looked glassily out over the city and said how dull things were, how there was nothing doing. But anyway a returned Guggenheimer was entitled to a lunch. Though as they signed the five-dollar check, you worried whether they could eat the rest of the week.

With an almost pathetic eagerness, Walsh asked: "Say, did you meet Le Corbusier while you were over there? I'd give my eyeteeth to work with that guy!"

So it was Le Corbusier now. Joe remembered how Blondy had idolized Frank Lloyd Wright, how they had sat up nights, arguing about Wright's antipathy to skyscrapers.

"I saw some Le Corbusier. I think it's a little barren," Joe said. "He could use more sculpture."

Walsh chortled. "There isn't really much place for sculpture nowadays."

"I know," Joe said. "The buildings are too big and the apartments are too little."

"That's a fact," Blondy said. "There isn't much place for sculpture."

The manager of the modernistic little cinema, the Playhouse, was running a series of exhibits of work by Chicago artists, in the silver-leaf lobby of the theater.

Joe consented to exhibit. As it happened, a small aluminum casting of a dancing girl was stolen from the show. The manager disclaimed responsibility. He had been doing Joe a favor, letting him display his work.

Joe was furious. Against the bland shrug of the manager he saw himself, helpless, a peanut artist, whose work could be kicked around.

The family was assembled at Aline's when Joe mentioned the theft.

"Well, anyway, someone likes my stuff," he said ruefully.

The family exploded. Never before had they shown such interest in his work!

"Sue him!" Aline shrieked. "He can't get away with a thing like that!" Where, in the old days, she had always seemed uncertain of herself, she now seemed almost condescending in her advice to her impractical brother.

This was in the time of her pregnancy, and Joe was annoyed because his sister made no efforts to groom herself. Her skin, never especially good, was oily and blotchy now; she used no makeup but a misplaced blob of lipstick. Her housedress was actually fastened with a safety pin, where her girth had expanded. If her slip showed, what the heck, Rudy wasn't going to divorce her because of that.

"You know who can take care of it for you? Lou Margolis!" she announced. "I bet he takes it on a contingency, too. Sue them for a big high price, and with the publicity I bet you sell some stuff, too."

"It's not the loss so much," Joe said, speaking to Rudy, "but the manager ought to be made to realize that he is responsible."

"How do you know that the manager didn't swipe it himself and sell it?" Aline went on. "Anyway, I bet Lou and Celia could do a lot for you. You ought to cultivate them. She's in Hadassah and plays bridge with all those South Side sassiety women. And you know Lou is a whole cheese at the Temple. I went to hear Rabbi Wise speak there, and who should be sitting up on the platform but Lou Margolis! He introduced the speaker. He was very clever, too. What was it he said, honey? Oh, yah. The rabbi is the wise man here, so I'll let him do the talking. Wasn't that clever? Get it? Rabbi Wise."

Celia was an organizer in Hadassah's big fifty-dollar-a-plate lunch, Aline pointed out.

"Fifty dollars for a lunch," said Mr. Freedman wryly. "What are they going to serve?"

"I'll take hamburger," Rudy said.

"Joe, you ought to appreciate the Hadassah; why, they run all those hospitals in Palestine," Aline pursued. "Last year there were over six hundred women at the lunch, but this year they want a thousand, even in spite of the depression. Only the leaders of Chicago Jewry are there, and you know it makes a good impression when they see you can afford to give fifty dollars for a lunch. It pays to advertise."

"Is Mrs. Abramson buying a lunch?" Mrs. Freedman asked. "She is getting so stylish."

"Sure, she was at the lunch last year."

"Well, she can afford it. By everyone else is a depression, but their hat factory is making more money all the time."

Joe drank coffee.

"Is Sylvia still in Vienna?" Mrs. Freedman said. "What will he do when he comes back, be a specialist?"

"I think the boys ought to open an office together," Aline popped out. "A real up-to-date spiffy office in a new building . . ."

Would she never stop talking about Mitch and Sylvia?

"Yeah," Rudy said. "On what?"

Later, Joe's mother got him aside. Honestly, maybe he needed a little money? Don't be ashamed, Joe, say honestly. No, no, no, he insisted, he was doing okay. Because if he needed it, she had a little. Thank God, she had saved from the house money all these years, otherwise how would Aline ever have fixed such a big flat?

"You think everything is easy for them? It's not so easy! He has an office with that old *kaker* Dr. Meyerson on Roosevelt Road, and what does he have? Only the cheapest trade, the poorest class of people. I help them a little. Rudy don't know, and your pa don't know, but in the first years, they have to have a maid, and a doctor has to have—well, you know, he's a doctor." She blinked. "So if you need, I have," she smiled. "No, honest, tell me Joe, how much have you got?"

"I've got a couple of hundred dollars," he said. "Don't worry, if I need money I'll ask for it." He passed it off, laughing, but she still looked worried.

The First Hundred Years Are the Hardest

The whole family was waiting at the station, and practically pulled Syl and Mitch off the train. "My, you are handsomer, you have made him fatter, Sylvia." Mrs. Abramson admired her son-in-law.

"Look at me! Don't I get any attention! I've gained six pounds!" Sylvia laughed, and Mrs. Abramson gave her a quick searching look, to see if something might be on the way, as the other couple had already done the trick!

They crowded through the station. Mort stopped at a bright shining Studebaker coupé that stood in front of their Lincoln. He pulled out a bunch of keys.

"Here you are, doctor," he beamed, handing them to Mitch.

For a moment the homecoming couple were mystified. "It's yours, take it away!" Mort repeated.

Syl was the first to utter thanks. "Oh. That's wonderful! Just what Mitch will need, too. Oh—" Tears were in her eyes. To be among people again, people who thought of you, predicted your needs, the blessed family. She kissed them, each one, with a great hug.

"Say," Mitch mumbled. "Say. Well, thanks." He seemed to be uncertain whom to thank, and made it Mr. Abramson.

"Well, get in, try it out, can you drive?" Mr. Abramson said brusquely.

On Madison and Central, in the heart of the neighborhood to which all the better Jewish families were moving, was a store and office building going practically for the mortgages because the speculator had been caught short in the depression. Mr. Freedman bought the building.

And naturally there was a swell set of doctors' offices which the boys could have practically rent-free.

The way Aline saw it, Rudy would be doing Mitch a favor to take him in, but anything to get Rudy away from that old fool Meyerson with his cranky charity patients calling you up at all hours of the night for nothing.

So Rudy went over to see the swell Zeiss Mitch had brought back from Europe.

"It's a beaut, all right." Rudy bent over the double eye-piece.

"That calibration is marvelous. I can't get along without it now," Mitch said. "With a machine like this you can do lens work eight hours straight without getting tired."

"This must have set you back at least a thousand berries."

"It was Syl's folks' wedding present," Mitch admitted. "They figured I could save a lot by picking it up while we were over there."

"Gosh, what lenses!" Rudy finally straightened up. "Well?" he said.

"Well?" Mitch said. The men smiled at each other. "Well, how is the doctor business?"

"There's plenty of business," Rudy said. "But try and collect."

"Well, I might as well pitch in right away."

"The first hundred years are the hardest. . . . Mitch, what do you want to go into practice for? You ought to stay in research, Mitch, a fellow like you."

"Sure," said Mitch bitterly. "I went down to see Nyquist this morning. They've got practically everybody in the lab working on my serum problem."

"No!"

"Yup. It seems it doesn't belong to me at all. It belongs to the Gorham Company. I can't even work on my own discovery! I wanted to work it out on typhus and pneumonia and the rest, besides tetanus. But they're beating me to it."

Rudy nodded sympathetically. The breaks.

"I imagine Gorham'd put you on their staff if you wanted it," he suggested.

"Why should they hire me when they can get the work done on four-hundred-dollar fellowships at the U?" Mitch snapped. "There are plenty of other suckers like I was. Boy, that's sure some racket!"

"Isn't there anything you can do about it?"

Mitch shrugged. "Those big corporations have everything sewn up. I don't care how much Gorham makes on the process if at least they let me work it out! Anyway, it's time I got down to making a living."

"Yah," Rudy said. "That's where we all end up."

The Abramson family insisted on buying an eight-hundred-dollar fluoroscope because there is nothing so impressive as a fluoroscope in a doctor's office. And the Freedmans presented the two young doctors with a new set of office furniture.

Now the Abramson relatives began to get sick. An aunt developed stabs in the side, and the grandmother was nearing death and needed attention for constipation one week and for diarrhea the next; a young cousin was obliging enough to break a leg. But these events were spread over months; Mitch set up a little lab in the office and had plenty of time, too much time, for research.

Don't Forget the Inspiration

Three doors along the corridor were marked, *Margolis and Schaeffer, entrance 912.* Joe was awed.

As he sat waiting, a fellow emerged from an inner room and took his place at a desk near the window. He seemed familiar. Large, fattish, with a sloppy stretch of shirt between vest and pants. Then Joe recognized Big Ears Lou Green. How could anyone have changed so much in these few years! Were they all really so grown, so youthless?

"Lou," Joe called.

Lou Green fell all over him with greetings, back pattings, well, say, well, say, I hear you been all over the world. Then came the usual gap of silence.

"This your office too?" Joe asked, remembering Lou Green had been one of the law crowd.

"Well, yes," Lou said. "I'm working with Lou Margolis."

"Still the two Lous, eh," Joe said inanely.

"You bet."

"Well, we'll have to get together some time," Joe said.

"Oh, sure. Well, how yuh making out?"

"Okay, okay."

"Still making those—those dolls you used to make? I heard that was a pretty good business."

Joe laughed. "Oh, no. I dropped that long ago. I've been doing sculpture."

"Oh," Lou said. "Is there—uh, how is that business?"

"Not so bad," Joe said. "I'm getting along." He realized Lou had caught on that he was not a big shot. At the same time, he was thinking of

Lou as a failure too, guessing that Lou was only something small in this office.

"Mr. Margolis will see you now, Mr. Freedman," the girl sang out.

"Well, happy landings," Lou Green said, awkwardly, as Joe went into the private office. It was a spacious room with two windows facing La Salle Street.

Lou Margolis strode toward Joe with a hawklike smile and an offered cigar. It took only a minute to dispose of old times, with a feeble crack about the Big Ten. Getting down to business, Lou wanted to know how much that stolen statuette was worth.

"It actually cost me only fifty bucks. But the mold is in Paris and so a duplicate might cost more."

"How do you know they kept the mold?" Lou twirked up a corner of his mouth. His attitude was casual, as though he were playing with this small case just out of friendship. "Would five hundred dollars be a fair estimate," Lou said, "if the mold was destroyed?"

"Oh, five hundred isn't too much for a piece like that. I got five hundred bucks for a little radiator cap I did for Viking cars once."

"That's fine," Lou said. "That establishes your price."

As they shook hands, Joe felt he had to turn the meeting away from this trivial business. "How's Celia?" he said.

"Oh, fine. Fine."

"I hear you have an infant."

"Yep! How's your sister? How's Rudy Stone doing?" he asked, with a knowing air.

"Fine," Joe said. "He's doing all right." Just then he remembered he hadn't talked about the fee with Lou. But of course it would be all right.

"Glad to take care of your little affair," Lou said professionally, as Joe left.

It happened that Sam Eisen went often to the Playhouse to see Russian films, and was acquainted with Mr. Nussbaum, the manager. It's a small world, he thought, when he got the sculpture case.

"Why, hello, Joe, how goes it?" Sam said genially, as they met in the courtroom.

"Well, this is a funny way to meet again," Joe said, as they shook hands.

"Looks like a class reunion," Lou Green remarked, and hawed.

"Hiyah, Sam. How goes it?" Lou Margolis greeted him with professional solicitude. "Keeping you busy?"

"Pretty busy," Sam replied. "Say, I just got a nice little reversal on Judge Horowitz. The appellate court bawled him out for his hostile attitude."

"You're certainly getting popular with Horowitz. What was it, another Bolshevik case?"

Sam laughed. It had been the case of the striker beaten up in front of the Abramson factory.

"What do you get out of that stuff?" Lou Margolis asked, patronizingly, glassily, and added: "Well, I'm going to take some dough away from you today."

"I wouldn't be too sure about that," Sam kidded back, slipping into the courtroom manner.

The trial was going along in a very dull way; it was only when Sam began to question him that Joe felt something was happening. He caught on at once to the thought-out line of Sam's attack. Even at the risk of antagonizing the judge, of losing the case, he was sticking to a line of logic that seemed to reach beyond the courtroom. It was as though he were more interested in his idea than in winning this case for his client.

"Mr. Freedman, how much time does it take to make a little statue of this sort?" Sam asked.

"Why, that all depends."

"Well, just give us an idea. One day, a week, how long?"

Joe said: "I never thought of it that way."

"Suppose you think of it now."

Lou Margolis objected to this line of questioning. "This doesn't take into account the matter of inspiration!" he declared.

"We'll come to the inspiration later," Sam said ironically.

The judge leaned toward Joe, smiling with the indulgent respect that laymen show toward artists. "Yes, we mustn't forget about the inspiration," he said with a fat chuckle.

"Well, let us say in hours," Sam questioned. "How many hours of actual labor would there be on the statue in question?"

"Maybe twenty, thirty hours for a figure that size. It might take more time if I happened to get stuck."

"I don't suppose a sculptor works an eight-hour day?"

The court snickered.

"It depends on what else I'm doing," Joe answered.

There was another snicker-laugh. Joe began to feel resentful.

"And I suppose it depends on whether you feel like working?"

"Well, sure."

"Would that cover the question of inspiration? If you feel like working?" Sam asked.

Lou objected.

"Sustained," the judge said, frowning at Sam.

"Then, say, a week would be a liberal estimate for the entire job?"

"For the actual work, yes, but it might be a long time before I got the idea, or another idea."

"Well, how many ideas, of this size, on the average, would you have in a month, Mr. Freedman?"

"I object to this whole line of questioning," Lou Margolis snapped. "It's irrelevant, incompetent, and inconsequential. What does the attorney know about how an artist works?"

"That's just what I'm trying to find out," Sam cut in. "We are trying to determine the value of the object in the only way there is."

"Why, according to that, a painting by Leonardo da Vinci would be evaluated by the square foot, like a job of house painting!" Lou cried.

"Why not?" Sam said.

The court gasped, then laughed at Sam.

"Your honor," Sam argued. "I am prepared to prove that artists like Leonardo da Vinci and Michelangelo actually worked on a time and material basis. Why, Raphael contracted to paint a chapel in the Vatican by the square foot."

"Na, na, objection sustained, this won't get us anywhere," Judge Noonan yawned. He picked up a photograph of the missing statuette, studying it with the careful expression of someone trying not to show a wrong reaction about art. Joe thought he was probably wondering about the model.

"Let's see about the other expenses," Sam went on. "Studio rent, a model—"

"Of course. A model," the judge permitted himself, slyly.

Lou Green horse-laughed.

"Counting time, materials, and overhead, you could knock out a figure like this for about fifty dollars, couldn't you?"

Lou Margolis laughed derisively, and said: "Object."

In his mind, Joe was adding up the thing the way Sam had suggested. But he said: "A sculptor figures his work according to what he can get for it."

"Well, nowadays a sculptor can hardly get anything for his work, isn't that true?" Sam twinkled.

Then the fat, loose-bellied art critic of the *Journal* wobbled up to the stand, as an expert witness for Joe.

"Do you evaluate a work of art in terms of dollars, or of æsthetics?" Sam questioned.

"Æsthetics is my business," the critic admitted.

"Does the æsthetic value always correspond to the dollars and cents value?"

"Not always," the critic said, and raised his brow toward Joe.

Sure, it was all true, but Joe found himself getting sore at Sam. What did all this have to do with a simple case of the exhibitor's responsibility for what he had borrowed? It was Sam's stubbornness that got under your skin.

The way he insisted on sticking to his own line of logic even if the world he was living in was different.

"Your honor," Sam wound up, "there is only one standard of value for any product, and that is the cost of material and labor. If you build a house, that's how you figure the thing, and if you make a pair of shoes, that's how you figure the price, and if you make a statue, it's the same thing. In antique art, there is a rarity value involved, but even Leonardo da Vinci never got the price his pictures bring today. When he was alive and working, he was paid according to the time and materials his work consumed, and we're asking Mr. Freedman to set a fair value on his time."

The judge listened with the indulgent air of one who gives even the wrong side a hearing. As soon as Sam was through, he said: "Find judgment five hundred dollars plaintiff."

"That certainly was a screwy argument Sam put up," Lou Green was saying. "A dollar an hour! What does he think a famous artist is, a bricklayer!"

"Well, he was up a tree," Lou Margolis commented shrewdly. "What he should have done was denied responsibility. There is plenty of precedent proving a borrower is not responsible for what happens to the object he borrows. He could have had an open-and-shut case." His whole face shifted like a wink.

"That so?" Joe said.

"Sure!" Second-the-Motion asserted. "You have to know the law!"

It occurred to Joe, Sam must have known that much law, and passed up that line of argument, on principle.

"How soon do you think I can get the dough?" Joe asked. With the five hundred bucks, he could set up a studio in New York.

"That's something else again," Lou Margolis said. "Nussbaum is about ready to close that place anyway. He don't get any business there with those highbrow foreign pictures. It won't be so easy to collect." They were on the street.

"Let me know how much I owe you," he said to Lou.

"Oh," Lou said patronizingly. "I'll just make it a third!"

Seeing Sam Eisen go into a B/G Coffee Shop, Joe followed and slid onto the next stool.

Somehow fellows like Sam put you on the defensive. Joe found himself wanting in some way to apologize for his connection with Lou Margolis.

"That was quite a theory you had about the value of art," Joe said. He bit into a triple-decker toasted sandwich.

"What's wrong with it? Is there any other way of measuring value?" Sam challenged.

"Oh, it's undoubtedly right, in the long run," Joe admitted, to prove he too had thought about those fundamental things. "The trouble is, even if those things are right, you can't go by them."

"Listen, if someone guaranteed you a fair living wage, and your materials, for the rest of your life, and let you go ahead with your work, would you be satisfied?"

"Lead me to it!" Joe laughed, but nevertheless a vision of a house, and a studio-barn, and a dog passed through his mind.

They crunched toast.

Joe was remembering how Sam had always seemed an intelligent fellow, deeper than the others. For instance, that time he had busted out of the Big Ten, telling them all what fools they were. And down at Urbana, when he had revolted against compulsory military training.

Sam was wondering, was there something to Joe Freedman after all? That time at Urbana, Joe had got into a scrap with the military too, only hadn't Joe finally crawled back?

"The trouble is," Joe added, "that meanwhile we've got to live in the world as it is."

Sam shrugged. He had been through that attitude, too. No one could help you; you had to go through it yourself. He could only watch sympathetically while Joe took the rest of the bumps. He had a hunch Joe would come through all right. Sam smiled, and to Joe the smile appeared enigmatic.

That Old Pal of Mine

"Shut the door, will you!" Lou Green snapped as the old lady padded out of the bedroom.

"But, Louie, why shouldn't it be open so I can hear if you should call me?" his mother pleaded.

"You'll hear me! Oh, shut the door, can't you!"

She softly closed the door.

At least one thing, since he was sick the old lady had come out of her crazy blues. Taking care of him gave her an interest in life.

Lou turned his face toward the closed door. He would hear if anyone came toward the room; he would have time to stop. If he did it at all. He oughtn't to do it so much.

Now he began to struggle with himself, resisting himself, though he knew from the beginning he would yield. For a moment he kept his hands above the quilt. He told himself he had to break the habit. This habit was really what weakened him, kept him from getting well now. He would take his mind off it, he would read.

On the bedside table were *All Quiet on the Western Front*, *Thirteen Women* by Tiffany Thayer, and *The Good Companions*.

Lou tried to read *The Good Companions*, but after a few pages he found himself picturing the scene in *All Quiet on the Western Front* where the soldiers in a hospital turn their backs while the wife of one of them crawls in bed with her husband.

Bet plenty of them turned around and watched.

Lou imagined himself to be that soldier, and the wife was Celia Margolis.

The book fell away, but was near enough to grab and pretend reading.

He would stop before anything happened. Wonder if Rudy Stone could tell. Well, Rudy wasn't coming until tomorrow.

Now it was no longer Celia but Lil Klein with the soldier; now he was Sammy Eisen to whom Lil had been married; why did they get divorced? Bet Sammy couldn't satisfy her. Here's the boy that could have done it, Lil.

Now it was one of Joe Freedman's models, that naked one in the photograph of the statue.

He forced himself to think of other things. If Schaeffer's kid brother was taken on as a clerk in the office, where would he be? Surely he could depend on Lou Margolis to keep him on the job. Suddenly he felt panicky. They really didn't need him in the office. Even the girls knew. Celia knew it too. Celia was against him. Way back when they were all working in the Preiss office with Celia at the switchboard he had known what she was after, crossing her big legs and letting the meat above the garters show, he would have played her himself if she wasn't so fat, and now he'd be where Lou was. She wasn't really so fat, she looked pretty good, even after having a kid; a fellow got older and his ideas about women changed, and he knew those skinny girls flat as a board weren't the ones could give you a good time, it was girls with something to grab hold of, like Celia. . . .

That case in Judge Vories's court of the father that did it to his twelve-year-old daughter and the mother knew they were doing it; *Mother India*, that's where they did it, in India to all the little girls; stop; think of something else; but what can a fellow do, since having that dose he was even scared of going to professionals; jerk a pickup in a back seat; oh, Celia, Aline Freedman, Lil Klein, Chickie in the *Evening American* story when he was a kid, Rita Silver at the office, Mata Hari; that hot actress Jeanne Eagels in *Rain*; that society dame and he was the guide; oh, to be a riding master; Tillie the Toiler, Lillums, and that chorus girl that wanted eight million dollars and a wedding ring for it, that new movie queen with the bubs, and downtown the show he and Lou had seen together, that actress they arrested for it in New York, her high round mushmelons and the soft side-slavering mouth, the mouth, the mouth, and no not Sylvia Abramson or Rose Heller, nothing with girls like them, but bet they could put on a hot party when they got started, and not the girl on the ground floor she was a nice girl, real love with her, Phyllis, Phyllis. From a kid that was what ruined him, made him flunk the bar, made him miss out on everything, oh, what was a fellow supposed to do, oh, get a wife, yah, on twenty-five a week, get a girl, better even go to the whores, two bucks twice a week four bucks yah and get another dose, cost you two hundred smackers, oh, kids all did it, fellows all did it and it never hurt them; but not till this old, twenty-eight, oh— The door opening!

"Sure I know how you feel, I had an old pal hung around my neck for ten years," Curly Gorman commiserated with Lou Margolis. "Every time he lost a job, there he was sitting in my office."

"Howja get rid of him?"

Gorman giggled, the wheezy giggle of a fleshy man. "Listen, Lou, you can't get rid of a *nebich* like that." He winked as he used the Yiddish word. "He finally kicked off, or I'd be supporting him yet. It's worse than a poor relative."

"Well, I'll send him around to your place when he gets out of bed," Lou said. "Anything you can give him is fine."

"You better slip a rabbi a fin to pray he never gets out of bed!" Gorman jested. Funny, gentiles couldn't get it out of their head that if a fellow was a Jew, he went to rabbis. Gorman added: "I can give him one, two bucks a call. I got a lot of processes now, but I don't know how long this run is gonna last."

"Say, two bucks a call, and he can add the dollar ten, he'll be doing fine," Lou said. The dollar ten was the witness's expense-money for getting to court, which the process server usually pocketed. "Say, he'll be making more money than I am!" Lou kidded.

At the beginning, the office girl had called up every day in the name of Lou Margolis to ask how he was getting along. The last couple of days, probably Lou told her to, but that bitch forgot on purpose. Now, hearing the phone ring, Lou Green tried not to get excited.

"Thanks, thanks, he is better, he is doing fine," he heard his mother blurt. "Tell me, why don't you come out and see him, he is such a friend of yours, he is always talking about you—"

"No, no! Shut up!" the invalid growled. But too late. She marched into the bedroom looking as if she had found a million bucks. "He is coming out to see you today," she said.

"For cry sake what did you have to do that for!"

"What's the matter, why shouldn't he come to see you? He is your friend."

"Oh, what is there to see!"

She caught his disgusted look around the place, taking in Estelle's old vanity table, the raggy slip-covered chair, the crummy carpet. She went and got a fancy runner for the dresser.

"What do you care?" she said. "He knows you."

But Lou was thinking of the swell apartment the Margolises had in the Southmoor Hotel, where all those doggy Roths and Strauses lived.

477

Lou came in briskly. "How's the boy?"

The old lady stood there beaming, showing her gold teeth. "And how is your wife? You got a baby already?" Christ, next she would ask them how often they did it. Finally she announced: "Well, I will leave you alone, boys," and went out.

"Well, how the hell are you, Lou?"

"Oh, I'm okay, I could get up now only Rudy Stone says a couple more days in bed to make it safe. He says the flu is liable to come back on you."

"Say, you missed a good one!" Lou Margolis said, and told the joke about the big Negro woman that came before Judge Lyle charged with bigamy. "Nawsah, yo' honuh," Lou mimicked, "Ah's legally mayyed to the both of them!"

"That's a hot one!" the invalid said. And repeated a story of Rudy Stone's about a hick girl that came to the doc's office and she was about four months gone, see. . .

They both laughed. It was like old times. Lou Margolis told a couple more about jigs, and then he asked Lou the riddle about the Arab that told his two sons to race their horses to Mecca, and the one getting there last would get all his money. What were the two words a wise man whispered, which made them ride fast instead of slow?

Lou Green was stumped. He lay staring at the ceiling, thinking, and feeling lazy and good, and that Lou was a pal.

"I give up," he finally said.

"The words were, 'Change horses.' "

"Say, that's a wow. I'll have to remember that!"

There seemed to be nothing more to talk about. "Say, didja notice Red Grange lost all his money in the crash?" Lou Green observed.

"Yah? Well so did Eddie Cantor."

They were big shots, and now they were no better off than he. And he remembered reading in the paper that the team of Gallagher and Shean had split up; they were broke, too. How he and the Sharpshooter used to put that act over with the old bunch!

"How's things at the office?" he asked.

"Oh, pretty tough without you around. But we're managing. Yep, we're pulling through," Lou Margolis kidded.

"Did you get a judgment in the Owens case?"

"Five grand. But the sonofabitch will appeal. Say, you know Schaeffer's kid brother is in the office now."

"Yah?"

"While you're away," Lou Margolis said, helplessly.

Lou Green tried not to show anything. Naturally, Lou Margolis couldn't prevent his partner from taking in his kid brother as clerk.

"Say, Curly Gorman was asking about you the other day. He's got a lot of tough summonses. You could make fifty, sixty a week on them, easy. I figured you could do it on the side." .

Lou brightened. "I'm going to take the bar again as soon as I get out of here. I got a hunch I'll make it this time."

"Sure, why you know more law than half the heels that are practicing," Lou Margolis declared.

After his pal had gone, Lou Green lay back looking at the cracked yellow-painted ceiling. Nobody made fifty bucks a week serving processes.

He just felt sick, sick again, and dopily wished that he would keep on being sick for a long time, for months. When the old lady came in with the soup, he barked at her.

And then, he began to feel sore at the Sharpshooter. He remembered ways he had helped Lou, worked for him for practically nothing when they were first starting the office, plenty of times giving his wages to pay the rent, bluffed for him, shined up to bailiffs, swiped records a couple of times. Why, Lou was stingy, always used to let him get on the car first and pay their fares, when they were coming home from law school together. It was just laying that big bitch Celia that had done the trick for Lou Margolis. And again, Second-the-Motion began to imagine himself showing her what a real man was like.

"I bet you don't get a cent out of them," Aline predicted, pinning her dressing gown together with a five-and-ten brooch. A button had come off, and she hadn't bothered to replace it. "I understand Estelle has left home again. I wonder who's her new one. You'd think she'd at least get wise to herself and cash in, while she's at it."

"Weeelll," Rudy hemmed, checking his vest pocket for the thermometer. He waggled his fingers at the baby. The baby waggled back, and gurgled.

Something was bothering Aline. She remembered. "What did Dr. Matthews want last night, honey?"

"Oh, he's got an idea about getting together a group of doctors. I don't think anything will come of it."

"What for?" Aline was suspicious.

"Well, his idea is to get a bunch of doctors practicing together, downtown, and have a sort of central, efficient medical service. It could be cheap, too. But I don't think he'll ever get the men to go into it."

Aline studied him a moment. "It sounds fishy to me," she said.

"Well, it wouldn't be a bad idea if it could be worked," Rudy said. "The patients would get a hell of a lot more attention, each one from specialists, and cheaper, too. And we would make out better."

"You mean you would bring in your patients and the other fellows would take them away from you."

"No, no, we would get an entirely new class of patients."

Aline blew spilled talc off the dresser top. "Where are you going to get patients from?"

"As an organization, we might even advertise."

She believed in letting Rudy handle his own affairs, but after all, he had a wife and kid. "Wouldn't you get kicked out of the S.A.P.S. like Dr. Niles with that Social Health Institute? Maybe you better not get mixed up in anything, dear. What's the matter with Dr. Matthews, isn't he making enough with his thousand-dollar operations? Honest, that man!"

"This is a new idea, that's all. You know Matt is always interested in a new idea. Anyway, nothing will come of it, so don't get worried," Rudy said. "He just got a bunch of us together, for general discussion."

"But I don't understand him. He makes plenty as it is."

"There wouldn't be any money in it for him. You know how he is. He's a kind of idealist."

She asked: "Who was there?"

"Well, Dr. Rubin, and Mike Swaboda, mostly fellows from my class."

"Was anybody for it?"

"Well, nothing definite and nothing practical anyway," he reassured her. "It was just a discussion. Some of the fellows are having it pretty tough and would try anything. You know Mike is down there on Twenty-Second and Paulina, he said it was a case of giving up his office or his home so he's sleeping in the office. He was kidding about it, but believe me . . ."

"Well, why doesn't he try to practice where people have some money!" Aline criticized. "He ought to have known he'd never make a living off these Polacks. You'll be in the same boat if you hang around with Meyerson long enough." Though he had the new office, Rudy still insisted on giving part of his time to Roosevelt Road.

Rudy waggled his fingers again. The baby waggled back with both hands, lost balance, and keeled over on its side. There was the instant when she was undecided whether to laugh or howl.

"Boom!" Aline hastily chirped to the baby. "Snookums faw down and go boom!"

Its features relaxed.

Rudy clucked contentedly, and started out.

He couldn't understand why Lou Green hadn't shown a better pickup from the flu. "You might as well take it easy a couple more days," Rudy said, screwing together the thermometer case. He smiled down at Lou's pulpy face, noting the yellowish flesh, the insucked lips. He glanced into Lou's eyes. Foggy.

Lou turned his head away, with a sort of ashamed blink.

In that moment, Rudy got the idea that maybe Lou was abusing himself. That might show in his general lassitude, the nervous abrupt movements of his hands. Hardly clinical symptoms, yet they gave Rudy an impression of hidden unhealthiness.

"You ought to get more exercise when you're up again," he ventured.

"I guess I must of been generally run down, worse than I thought," Lou apologized. "I ain't had any real exercise since I used to play handball at the Y with Lou Margolis, before he got hitched."

"It might not be a bad idea to join again," Rudy said. And, in a brotherly tone: "A fellow ought to lead a normal life, Lou; why don't you look around and marry some nice girl? It would be a good thing for you."

"Is that a prescription, doc?" Lou said with wan comedy.

"Well, I won't say it is, but the natural thing is the best," Rudy said, trying not to go too far in his hint.

For a moment Rudy thought of consulting with the mother about her son's habits. But what was the use? Fellows like Lou Green didn't have a chance. They were just dopes. Ever since they were kids, Rudy had known him, a nice good-natured guy, but nothing to take hold of, no ambition.

Well. He made out a prescription for triple bromide, to be taken every few hours. That would quiet the patient, maybe check his habits.

"It's nothing. Just a sedative," he insisted to the worried mother. "He's all right, he can get up Saturday."

She produced two dollar bills. "It's all we got now, doctor, we can pay you more afters."

"That's all right, any time you have it," Rudy said, reassuringly.

He felt embarrassed, saddened by the woman's pathetically worshipful gaze.

Pay-Off

Instead of cooling off, the crime drive was getting hotter every day. They even pulled in a few big shots. Bottles Capone was pulled in a couple of times for packing a rod, and Bugs Hogan once, and nobody was safe. The State's Attorney said: "I've kept my promise, now it's up to the judges."

The new South State Street court was a big show every day. Every time a celebrated hoodlum was hauled into court, the flashlights popped in the corridors, and there were pictures of a lawyer, grinning, arm in arm with someone with a hat in front of his face.

All the big-shot criminal lawyers were busy in the South State Street courts; O'Brien and Ben Short and even Scott Stewart came laughing and joking into the elevators, to take care of little vag charges, or 4210, disorderly, or carrying a concealed weapon.

It was some joke, because the boys had to be let out as fast as they were pulled in; you can't search a man without a warrant, so how could the cops find concealed weapons on them?

All the same, a few small-time mobsters had to take the rap, and everybody was laying low. In fact a general exodus had begun, the small-timers were beating it out of town.

Runt Plotkin was right there on the sixth floor with a silk handkerchief in his breast pocket, and a new, unlit corona between his teeth, and the bottom button of his vest unbuttoned, and he strolled the corridors, waiting for his cases to be called. It was pie.

Lou Green came around and admitted he was no longer with Margolis.

"Aw, we had an argument. I ain't gonna take nothing from him!" Lou said. "He thinks he knows it all!"

Maybe Lou Margolis couldn't afford an assistant, but Dave Plotkin was no piker! So Runt gave Lou a job. He needed a man to be on the spot all the time, watch the wagon come in, and get tips from cops and guards as to who was arrested, then Runt could spring them with a habeas, and get their business. As the boys were lamming it out of town, competition was getting tough; every criminal lawyer in town had a man on the spot and an inside wire.

The judge who was hearing most of those cases right then was Leaky Donohue, the old law-school instructor. And after he had let Bottles Capone go once, and Bugs Hogan out once, the heat was on him for fair.

"We are betrayed!" the State's Attorney boomed in the papers.

"We are helpless!" the police force howled.

"We bring them in and the judge lets them out!"

And Donohue was on the spot. The big-shot attorneys came in smooth and smiling. You can't frisk a citizen without a warrant. So he had to say: "Dismissed."

The hoodlums put their hats in front of their faces, and shoved their way through the crowded corridors.

And by the time Runt Plotkin got up before Judge Donohue with his string of third-rate mobsters, old Leaky was fit for an asylum. The newspapers were riding him, the S.A. was riding him, the police were making nasty cracks, and he was the goat.

Runt was defending Loud-Mouth Louie Schechter, a taxi driver who occasionally rolled a drunken patron.

And so it was, when Ben Short had puffily departed, and Scott Stewart had practically flicked his cigarette in the judge's face, that Loud-Mouth stood before the bench.

Runt stepped up and nonchalantly made the usual motion to dismiss.

Donohue stood up and glared. "What do you mean, dismiss? He's a known criminal. He has a record. Where's the arresting officer?"

A cop pushed forward and began to make his bored spiel.

"You can't hold this man, your honor," Runt interposed. "It's against the constitution."

Leaky Donohue leaned way over. "It's you and your kind, the vermin of the legal profession, that are responsible for this situation!" he screamed. Pointing dramatically at Runt, he went on: "There is the criminal! What can we do? We are helpless as long as this condition is tolerated! We have the police! We have the courts! But it's these cheap criminal lawyers that prevent us from cleaning up crime in Chicago."

Runt listened, growing red but grinning superciliously all the while. Some grandstand play! That *dreck* Donohue was the one to holler! Why, he had taught most of the lawyers their tricks!

"You can't hold this man, judge," he repeated coolly. "He was arrested without a warrant."

"I'm going to hold you for contempt of court! Every one of you cheap shysters ought to be put in jail!" the judge cried, as a couple of newspapermen drifted back into the courtroom.

"You can't do that!" Runt shouted.

"I can't, huh!" Leaky reared up, his eyes snapping with glee at having found this way of taking the heat off himself. "All right, Plotkin! I'm going to make an example of you! You fellows are the ones who are really responsible for the criminal situation in this city! The police can bring the men in, but as long as you vermin are here to get them out, the police and the courts are helpless. You fellows all ought to be behind the bars!" he roared.

"You can't do this to me! I have my rights! I'll take it up with the Bar Association," Runt sputtered.

"Two hundred dollars for contempt!" Donohue snapped venomously, banging his gavel. "Lock him up, Mr. Bailiff!"

"You can't do this to me! You can't do this to me!" Runt cried, lurching around and shaking his fist at the judge. "I'll get you for this!"

"Five hundred," Leaky said.

Runt was conscious of the stupid, surprised look on the face of his client, and of the awake, shocked air in the entire courtroom. "Get Lou Green," he shouted to Loud-Mouth. "He'll take care of it."

There was some vag in the cell but Runt wouldn't even talk to him. He walked back and forth, fuming. Why should he be the goat? The judge was in a spot, sure. He couldn't pick on any of the big-shot attorneys, so Plotkin had to be the goat! That sonofabitch Donohue still had it in for him from the time he refused to contribute to his petty rackets in the law school, that bastard, flunking everybody so he could make two bucks a head extra when they took the exam over. So now Leaky was out to get him! He'd show him! Why the publicity on this case would make him a big-time lawyer, the guy that talked right back to the judges! He would haul Leaky up before the Bar Association for this!

It was two hours before Lou Green came around with the dough. He had borrowed it from Arthur Tracey, a big-shot gang lawyer. That was the stuff!

Runt walked out, swaggering. In the corridor, a couple of reporters and photographers shoved up to him. "The judge was just making a grandstand play," Runt said, holding the cigar out of his mouth as a photographer pushed a Graflex up to his face. "Judge Donohue hasn't got the guts to touch any of the real big-time racketeers. He knows he has fallen down on the job, so he is trying to blame it on the legal profession. Why, this boy I was defending is just a hard-working taxi driver pulled in so the cops could show an arrest. The whole crime drive is the bunk. It's a merry-go-round."

The evening papers were hot with the big campaign against criminal lawyers. Judge Donohue called upon the Bar Association to root them out. Leading citizens, politicians, business men were quoted vituperating the "lowest scum of the legal profession." Leaky Donohue was in for a column, raving about the "Plotkin type of shyster, graduated from some diploma mill."

That was swell, Runt figured. Now he was right up in the headlines, the cases would roll into the office. But the rush of cases failed to materialize. "They're scared of coming to you," Lou Green reported. "They say you got in bad with the judge."

Runt wasn't worrying. Red Tracey and Maxie Novak and some of the big guys who had never so much as talked to him before met him in the corridor, slapped him on the back, and said: "That's telling them, Plotsy." What the hell did he want with those fifty-buck cases anyway? Big stuff would come to him now.

They were at the Chicago, and it was the scene where Little Cæsar stands on a chair, preening, while the tailor hustles around his legs, fixing the natty cut of the pants. He's about my build, Runt was thinking, forgetting it was an actor, Edward G. Robinson in the part, but comparing himself with the gang chief. A short fellow, a runt, but with a pair of football shoulders.

"Y' know, I could go for him," Gwenda murmured into his ear. When they were seated, with her long legs slid forward, you couldn't tell she was much taller. And she added: "Y' know, Dave, he's about the same build as you."

She was acting good tonight; Runt wondered what would be the payoff, she must have some fancy idea back in her dumb dome.

"All right, you mugs, get going!" the little commander barked at his mob. And though the scene was nothing like what Runt had ever witnessed, in his contacts with racketeers and criminals, he believed the movie, believed this was the real inside big-time stuff, the contacts he had never made.

Napoleon was a little guy too.

And though you knew that Little Cæsar would die soon, nailed against a wall by a spread of machine-gun bullets, or tossed, an indistinguishable black bundle, from a speeding black car, it didn't matter: what was death anyway, what difference how it came or how soon in this tough and scraggy town, so long as you made something out of life while it lasted? Sure, Runt thought, what the hell is there for me to live for? To be dangled and clawed by this dumb bitch for the sake of a lay once a week, to argue my guts out before some cheap lousy judge for a measly fifty bucks—yah, try and collect even that—to keep some lug out of the can? The trouble is, I am too easy, too good to people, I let everybody step on me, God damn, the way to blast through life is behind a cannon.

Everybody hanging onto him, bloodsuckers draining him dry, sending a kid brother through medical school, setting a *shlemiel* brother-in-law up in a cigar store and having to pay for his smokes when he could get them free from the old man, paying the rent at home, fifty bucks for the privilege of sleeping on a lousy daybed, everybody sucking him dry, just because his name was in the papers he was supposed to be rolling in dough, laying out thirty-five a week for that fathead Lou Green, and nothing coming in, he was too easy, from now on he was going to get tough.

The sirening cars. The tearing swerve around corners. Now Little Cæsar would get his. The tattle of guns.

Gwenda clawed his arm, and buried her face in his neck. She couldn't watch death.

On the screen the figure slumped, and Runt felt almost as though welcome bullets were tearing his flesh, finishing him in a grand burst of raging blood.

"Is it over?" she whispered into his neck.

"Yah, yah, it's all over."

She lifted her head.

"Oh, I don't feel like going home yet, I feel like doing something," Gwenda miawled.

Sure. Get him so worn out he wouldn't enjoy it when they finally got there.

"Honest, you make me feel like an old married woman, go to a movie and home to bed," she complained.

"Well, nuts, what is there to do?"

"How about the Chez? I feel like dancing."

Sure, push her around the floor, looking like a midget. And drop twenty bucks when collections were tough. "Aw, not tonight, baby," he pleaded, not wanting to get her sore, or she wouldn't come across.

"All right, honey," she suddenly conceded.

Too easy. She must be after something.

She stepped around in her scanties while she boredly fixed him a gin drink. He didn't like to see her this way, being sloppy, leaving her dress in a puddle where she stepped out of it. And it looked indecent to him.

"Gee, baby, I'm sick of this town," Gwenda said. "Aren't you going to take a vacation or anything?"

"Well, I can't get away right now, I'm working on a big deal, but if it goes through we can—"

"Yah, I heard that one before. Listen, I wanna get out and see the world."

So that was what she was after. But he was flat. And, damn it, he would stick here and scrap it out!

Runt picked up the newspaper. "Well I see Post and Gatty made it, whyncha pick one of them for a boy friend, if you wanna see the world, around the world in eight days," he jested.

"Maybe I will. Listen, baby, let's go on one of those cocktail cruises to Bermuda, huh?"

"Sure, I'll go. Who's gonna pay the bills?"

"I can get someone to pay my bills for me any time."

"Oh, yeah?"

"If you think I'm gonna waste my life sitting around this dump listening to your troubles—"

"That's right. Like I always said. Just a tramp. Anybody that pays for it can have it."

"Listen, baby, I'll go out with whoever I please. . . ."

Damn bitch, she knew he hated to be called baby.

He gulped, and slammed down the empty glass. "Say, listen, Cinderella, you're not putting anything over on me. I know who you're stepping with. I know it every time. I got ways of finding out all I wanna know."

She displayed her mysterious Garbo smile. "Oh, yeah?"

"Yeah. Every time you try and two-time me."

"Dave, I've been square with you, that's one thing, and you know it."

He sneered, like Little Cæsar. "Next time you want to split your crotch on a bicycle, you better do it in private."

She sighed, exasperated, disgusted. "Why, Speedy is a friend of yours, isn't he? So I went out with him a couple of times."

"You don't have to tell me, I know all about it!" he glittered ominously.

"So you know!" she cried.

She was getting even with him all right, since that first time he laid her on the floor of Sam Eisen's office, she had been getting even ever since. Three years! And what had he got out of it! "Aw, let's can it," Runt capitulated. "Honest, kid, you know things ain't so good for me right now, all the boys are laying low. Why, Swanson even got Al scared, but just as soon as this blows over—"

"Yah. You and Al are like this!" She held up two joined fingers.

"Well, I got some information, understand. In a couple of months it'll all be over and—"

"All right! So you've got nothing to do for a couple of months. So let's get out of here and have some fun."

"Well, I've got to make some collections."

"And I have to stick around here and fry while you make your cheesy collections? I'm going to Bermuda."

"I'm in a little tight spot, see, and you've got to stick by me."

"What I do it for I don't know. Three years I've wasted." She sat at her vanity and picked at her fingernails.

She was yielding. After all she wasn't a bad sport. And suddenly feeling tired, and wanting friendship too, and what the hell, three years, that was longer than lots of people stayed married, Runt had an idea.

"Listen, kid, what's the good of scrapping around like this?" He offered peace. "Christ, we got along for three years, we might even get hitched, some time. . . ."

She stared at him. "What the hell would I want to marry you for? What a laugh!"

Runt thought she was kidding. "Say, why not?" he said, suddenly seeing his situation clearly. "It's just the same as if we're married anyway. I ain't playing around with anyone else. . . . And what the hell, we could live"— cheaper, he was going to say, but halted as he saw her doubling into laughter, wave after wave of laughter.

"Well, what's so funny . . .?"

"Why, you—" she sputtered, trying to force a few words between her laughing spasms, "you little Jew runt—"

He jumped up. But as he did so, she arose, too, the better to get out her laughter. The insult of her height over him completed his fury. He wanted, blindly, to cut her down. Runt grabbed, but she fended her reedy forearms up in front of her face; he grabbed her wrists, pulled her arms down, and with the same motion forced her down sidewise onto the bed. Then he put both her wrists together, locked in his one fist; her hands had oddly the gesture of praying. With his free hand he deliberately slapped her face, twice. The hard sounds rose over the dithering of the radio:

"How much do I love you, I'll tell you no lie—

How deep is the ocean, how high is the sky . . .?"

She squirmed desperately; he could see the red marks of his fingers on her wrists. He could murder her, choke her to death with his free hand. The desire glowed like pleasure in his blood. It wasn't only Gwenda. In her throat he could grip the whole lousy world, judges, bailiffs, crooks, he could squelch it under the power of his hand. What was the use of trying to be good to people, violence was all they could understand, murder was all they were worth. Little Cæsar was right!

She looked up at him, gog-eyed; at least death would bring some life, living terror into her damned bored face. Jew runt, huh!

Jew runt. He couldn't control his tears of anger, hurt, confusion. He let go of her, and got out of the place.

The cases didn't come. He showed himself around the courts, stood around in the cigar store, and shot off his mouth, about Baer, sure, a Jewish champion again. "Say, this guy Baer is the first real fighter since Dempsey. Say, he can take Schmeling with one hand, and how that guy will schmell when he gets through with him!" And all the time he figured the boys were wise to his decline. "How's it?" Maxie Novak would salute him in the hallways, "keeping you busy?" and Runt would bomb off as if he had six cases on the calendar: "Sure, sure, all I can handle."

And they were still going to haul him before the grievance committee. Well, let them, he hadn't done a damn thing the big shots weren't doing every day! All it would take was a little drag, and he'd be exonerated. What he needed was a little drag with those stuffed shirts. He thought of Lou Margolis, who was in with the whole tribe, but the hell, he'd be disbarred before he'd kiss-ass to that two-faced mutt.

Hours, he didn't know what to do with himself. No mama now. And he felt kind of funny, showing himself around Jake's place. He felt lonely, no place to go.

Once, Runt saw Sam Eisen coming out of the South State Street court, and walked along with Sam.

"How's it?" he asked. "What are you doing these days?"

"Oh, I get along," Sam replied.

He wondered, could Sam help him? Did Sam have any drag? There were a couple of big-shot lawyers behind those liberal committees Sam was on.

It was late in the afternoon, and loneliness was before him again. Sam had got divorced, too, he remembered; Sam must know how it was, to be like this, the world against you, and without a woman, too.

They turned up to Michigan Avenue.

"I'll tell you, Plotsy," Sam was saying analytically. "You don't even understand what are the forces that are bearing down on you."

"Sure I know," Runt cried with warm agreement. "They have to make a show of cleaning up the criminal law racket so they pick on some little guy like me."

"But what do you think is back of this clean-up campaign?" Sam persisted. "Do you think they have suddenly got religion or something?"

"Aw, it's just a lot of bunk," Runt said. "They have to make a noise."

"Sure, but why? Why are they suddenly worried about crime and criminal lawyers?" Sam asked rhetorically. "For ten years they let the mobsters hog everything and it was kosher. But suddenly they wake up, *vei is mir*, there's a Bugs Hogan in Chicago, there's a Spike O'Donnell, and a Capone, there are lawyers that aid and abet these birds! Why all the commotion? What's all the shooting for?" Sam confronted Runt. "There are over eight million people out of work in this country, Plotsy, and there's a lot of trouble going on, and this winter it's going to be even worse." They had crossed over to Grant Park, walking past the statue of a general on a horse. As always, bums were drowsing on the little mound beneath the statue. Runt remembered when he had been a kid and had come downtown, he had never seen a hill in his life, and had thought, gee, so that's what a hill is like.

"There has to be a noise made about something," Sam was saying, "to keep the mind of the public off the real troubles. So they are cleaning up crime, and criminal lawyers, and you have to get it in the neck."

"Not me!" Runt declared. "I'm not going to take the rap!" . . . Sam was getting to be like all the Bolsheviks; if you cut your little finger peeling an apple, it was the fault of the capitalist system. They blamed everything on the depression.

Walking there along the grass, Runt had an impression he had always longed for the peace and cleanliness of the country, for real mountains. "That's what I'd like to do, just roam around the country," he said. "Maybe after this little trouble is over, I'll go out someplace and commune with nature."

There was a new statue of Abraham Lincoln, a seated figure. They were certainly improving Grant Park.

"Why don't you get wise to yourself?" Sam suddenly demanded. "Go to the big shots in your line. Tracey and those guys. They'll help you, out of self-preservation. Because if things get worse, they're the next victims. You have to understand the forces behind these things, Plotsy."

Runt felt his strength returning. He could already see himself backed up by all the great criminal lawyers, even Darrow, what was Darrow but a criminal lawyer! And he could see himself, small, solid, a Napoleon, getting up before the committee and making a ringing plea for the honor of the criminal branch of the profession. Why, Abraham Lincoln was a criminal lawyer!

"Criminal law, and equity, it's all the same thing as far as I am concerned," Sam was saying. "Our kind of law has nothing to do with justice. It deals only with property." They stood for a while looking at the swell stretch of shops and hotels, the Athletic Club Building, and Orchestra Hall, across Michigan Avenue. "Take Loud-Mouth for an illustration," Sam went on. "He was trying to take away another man's property at the point of a gun. It's all a question of possession, of property. Your practice, or mine, or Lou Margolis's, or anybody's—it's all the same thing. In court, they try to take it away from each other with legal papers. Civil suits, criminal, probate, it's all the same thing. Possession isn't nine-tenths of the law, it's ten. There's no question of justice involved. For instance, this morning I was in Russo's court on divorce. But the busted marriage was nothing. It's who is going to keep the furniture that we argue about; property, possession, that's all there can be in this kind of life. It's in damage suits, and replevins, bankruptcies, everything—one way of stealing is as criminal as another." They strode toward the lake. "Abolish private property, and what use is there for lawyers? None. We're the biggest parasite class, next to the capitalists, that exists."

They walked along, gloomily. Some swell yachts were moored in the basin.

"Well, I notice you're not turning away any customers yourself, Sam," Runt tried to kid him.

But Sam took it seriously. "Naturally, I have to live. My only excuse to my conscience is that I am using my legal training to help out, wherever I can."

"You mean all this defending that you do is straight, Sam, you don't get anything for all that stuff? Why you must spend all your time on that stuff. Don't you even get expenses?" Runt said admiringly.

"Well, naturally we get expenses," Sam said.

"Hah!" Runt raised a brow.

"If you mean court costs and stenographers and that stuff. If the committee has a little money they cover it, and if we have, we cover it."

"Well, I dunno," Runt said sympathetically. He took out a cigar and bit off the end. "I tell you, Sam, when I get time I want to read up on that stuff. You know I was always interested in justice for the underdog, Sam, that's why I got into this lousy criminal law."

"Sure, I know, Plotsy. And if you remember, I started that way myself, remember those old days when I used to go over and act as free defender in the South Clark Street court? Only I saw pretty soon that criminal law is a blind alley."

"Yah, look what it got me into." He felt warm toward Sam; they were old, true friends who had been through life and taken the bumps. As he saw it now, Sam was the only one of the old bunch who had really come through solid. He wondered about Sam and his divorce, and wished he knew how to talk about women, maybe bring up the subject of Gwenda.

"You've got the right idea, Sam. I give you credit. That's all we are is a lot of parasites."

They were walking along the outer drive, heads bare in the breeze; a limousine was crawling along the road about five miles an hour.

"Well, they certainly fixed it up swell along here," Runt said. "That's something. And they're going to have a swell spot for the World's Fair, too."

"Yah, it's something," Sam smiled dryly. "Half a million dollars a mile."

Runt noticed the limousine had turned and was coming back toward them. They watched, idly. Sunken in the back of the car was a great hulk of a man, worn as an empty sack; his loose cheeks hung, colorless, dead flesh. His eyes, though open, were unseeing. Even the slow drive of the car seemed a strain on him.

It was Big Bill Thompson.

And the sight of Big Bill, used up, defeated, affected them both. Look at the titan now. The *Tribune* had won that taxpayer's suit against him and got a judgment for millions. Big Bill was still supposed to be in office but since the reform crowd had got in all around him he paid no attention to his duties. Ettelson was acting mayor[1]. There had been strange rumors about Big Bill. He was sick. He was in a sanatorium. "I heard he was going nuts," Runt said.

Riding five miles an hour, up and down that precious outer drive he had built—Big Bill the Builder.

The whole world of Chicago, of America, suddenly appeared to Runt as sick and done for. Yah, the Little Cæsar crap. The Abe Lincoln bunk over there.

"That's all we are," he repeated. "A lot of parasites."

Sam was smiling.

---

[1] Chicago Corporation Counsel Samuel Ettelson was named Acting Mayor in late July of 1929, while Mayor Thompson recuperated from ill health.

CHICAGO, THE BEAUTIFUL

THE first couple of years Lou watched Rube dodge the income tax he was still kind of scared of Rube and didn't dare make any suggestions. But this year Lou was worried, and mentioned that it might be better for Rube to transfer the money into certain channels that were tax-free, instead of just failing to report his income.

"Aw, why crap around?" Rube said. "I lost enough on the stock market so I shouldn't have to pay any income tax. Who's going to poke into my business anyway?"

Besides, how was he supposed to report these extra items of income? It just might be embarrassing to certain people if he listed certain funds.

And nobody else was doing it. Why, compared to the crowd on the Park Board and the Sanitary Board he was a piker. Say, they ran up a cost of eight million bucks building a million-dollar stadium and you didn't see that seven million on anybody's income tax, did you? Why, the Sanitary Board had spent a million bucks a mile building a bridle path along the canal. Boy, that's where the dough was, Rube said, regretfully. In the building, not in the junk business. And you didn't see those boys writing it all down in numbers on an income-tax blank! Why, there would be hell to pay!

There was nothing to worry about. The boys certainly weren't going to blab on each other.

Coming home, Lou's mind was still full of trying to handle that crazy fool. He found Celia in the bedroom, stretched on the chaise, reading another murder story. The baby was on the rug, and, recognizing him, crawled toward him. Lou picked him up; feeling the infant on his hands quieted his nerves a little.

Walking around, he said: "Listen, your old man is going to get into trouble monkeying around with the income tax. Them days are over."

"Whyn't you tell him?" she mumbled, without interrupting her reading.

"You know your father! Nobody can tell him anything!" He pulled Junior's hands out of his hair. "Say, mister, I'm losing it fast enough without your assistance."

Celia finally put aside the book. "How much is he holding out?"

"There's at least forty thousand I know of. Probably more. He's just liable to waltz himself right into Leavenworth."

"Oh, if they catch him they'll just make him pay it, that's all," Celia said reassuringly. "Isn't there something he could do with the money so it wouldn't be taxed?"

"Sure, he could do what Rockefeller and Rosenwald and all the rest of them do, put it in a Foundation, or shift it to a trust fund for his beloved daughter. I told him all that last year."

"Well, I can't do anything about it," Celia said placidly. "Anyway, who would snitch on him? Who knows how much he makes?"

Lou laughed cynically. "There are people that have a pretty fair idea."

"Who, for instance?"

"Pete Grinnell knows how much he collected off the ward."

"Why, Pete and my father have been friends all their lives. He's like one of the family."

"Don't be dumb!" Lou snapped. "He would stick a knife in his back any night, and you can hardly blame him after the way Rube double-crossed him last election. I told him—"

"Yah, yah, you told him." She was sick of listening to that argument. She had heard nothing but that all year, and now the election was over, the argument was still going on. So suppose Pete Grinnell had been an alderman all his life! All the more reason why he should give somebody else a chance. And after all it was a Jewish neighborhood. And like her father said, if he had the choice he would have supported Pete, but that fellow Diskin they had elected to Pete's job had some kind of pull with a lot of big unions.

"Pete won't do anything. He's a gentleman," she repeated.

"There are plenty of other people that know. Rube has been doing a lot of mortgage business with old man Klein on Roosevelt Road, and what about myself? I know how much he makes."

Celia laughed. "Well, if you're all he's got to worry about! We're going over to the Sterns' tonight," she ended.

"Yah? How much do I have to lose tonight?"

"It's a kind of a celebration. Louise Stern is so tickled about Hadassah; you know we took in practically fifty thousand dollars at the lunch, in spite of the depression."

"Say, if those Sterns ever get broke, they can make a good living at bridge. There's something a little too psychic about that psychic bid they've got."

"I think she gives him signals," Celia said. "But what's the diff? It's worth it. . . . Rose and Mac are coming here first."

"Why don't they get hitched and get it over with?"

"Well, maybe his folks don't think Rose is swell enough."

"His folks! Why, the original Hirschberger was a pushcart peddler," Lou sneered.

"What's Mac doing now, anyway?" Celia asked.

"I don't think he's doing so hot. You don't see him around anywhere anymore."

For almost two years, since that night the opera opened, Rose had been going with Mac. She had just been on the borderline when she met him, twenty-six, when a girl begins to get scared, and now that he had used up two more years, well, if anything happened now, she was sunk.

But she never grudged risking these years. He was tall and bony, like a New Englander, and he wore tweedy clothes carelessly; his features were large and sort of American, but there was an ironic Jewish look on his face. Mac knew all kinds of personal anecdotes about famous people, yet without pretending that he was their buddy; he mimicked Rudy Vallée with excruciating quavers, and if anyone mentioned Bobby Jones, the golfer, he knew how much Bobby Jones was getting for his golf articles. Being in the publicity business, he got main-floor tickets to all the shows and fights, and they were always going places and doing things.

She couldn't tell why he was interested in her except right off he had said he liked them tall and willowy. He was swell with her, treating her like a pal, no slobbery necking. He liked to talk and relax with her.

But lately she knew things weren't breaking so swell for Mac. He and two other fellows ran an office; it broke up, and the other fellows stole the customers. "What the hell, let them have them," he bluffed. "Maybe now I'll have sense enough to go into something that has a right to call itself a business."

Publicity was just a racket, he said, a colossal bluff. All you had to do was hire a clipping agency. And when some stuff accidentally got in the papers, you sent the clippings to your client and said: "Look what I did!"

"You know, it's a marvel to me they don't get wise! And the more you soak them the more they think of you!" He told how a department store which could have had a twenty-five dollar a week office girl to do all the publicity it needed had paid a thousand a month for the "service." And it wasn't his relative's store, either; "The Hirschbergers are too wise."

"You know, I go around from day to day thinking at any moment, presto, changeo, the whole game will bust like a balloon. Any minute the big business boys will open their eyes and get wise. Meanwhile, why shouldn't I grab off my share?" Only right now his share seemed to be pretty small.

His dates had always started with dinner. But last week, taking her to see *Grand Hotel*, he had met her at the theater. Almost every morning she awoke feeling worried about him.

Maybe because of seeing what was happening to her father. At the start, he had charged upon the depression, rushing down to his furniture store at eight every morning, coming home late for dinner every night. But now, after a year, he wasn't in such a hurry in the morning. "If this keeps up, I might as well close up the store and retire, I am semi-retired anyway," was his standard, wistful jest. Rose loved the stubborn bit of accent that remained in her father's speech; somehow it was like his short, upright gray hair, stiff as iron filings.

But suppose he did close the business? Suppose he sat around the house, worn out, an old man suddenly. It was a good thing she had kept on teaching. At least she could borrow on her unpaid salary. Maybe they would let her help out at home, but a fellow like Mac would never let her help.

Rose drove to school every morning with three other girls who taught at the Sholto. Ruthie Lipschultz had a junky old Dodge, and they shared expenses.

Mrs. Kirsh, in the back seat, was reading the *Tribune*. "Girls!" she gasped. "They're going to fire all the married schoolteachers!"

Rose was frightened by the look that remained, for an instant, on Mrs. Kirsh's face.

"Can't they realize a married woman needs the money more, she has a husband to support!" Minna Jacobson half kidded. "Why don't they fire the plutocrats like Rose, all she needs her money for is stockings."

"One twelve, Rose, shell out," Ruth Lipschultz demanded. "That's exactly thirty-eight cents apiece." She wrote into her little notebook.

Rose felt guilty pocketing the change from a five.

"It must be awful for a man," Rose said, thinking to comfort Mrs. Kirsh, "having to let his wife support him."

"Oh, God, sometimes I think he isn't even trying to get anything!" Mrs. Kirsh burst out. Then controlling herself: "That's just how crazy it gets you."

"Mygod, where is all the money! The money must be somewhere!" Minna Jacobson cried.

"They can't collect the real estate taxes," Ruthie said matter-of-factly. "That's why the city can't pay us."

At Celia's, Mac burst into the bedroom and woke the baby. He was swell with kids; Rose loved to watch him. He gave a screaming imitation of a woman cooing at a baby, making all the faces.

"Yours is so peppy," Rose cried. "You know Aline's baby is awfully cute, but she can't even stand up yet!"

"They're the same age, aren't they?" Celia remarked proudly.

"How is Rudy doing?" Lou asked.

"Oh, fair. They have a maid."

The Sterns were discussing the thing about Runt Plotkin in the papers.

"If that happens to a Gentile, it's nothing, but when it's a Jew, that means we're all crooks and shysters," Lou fumed.

"Well, aren't we?" Mac cracked.

"You have to admit that Dave Plotkin's background was a handicap," Celia covered the remark, addressing herself to the Sterns.

"You can't blame everything on a man's environment," Lou remarked judiciously. "Another person might come from exactly the same background and amount to something. When you get right down to it, it's a question of character."

"What will they do to him, send him to jail?" Rose asked.

"No, he'll probably just have to pay his fine. But we ought to kick all those racketeering shysters out of the bar!" Dismissing the subject, he remarked to Archie Stern: "Well, I see S.W. paid seventeen million bucks' interest today."

"Yah, they were so surprised to be able to meet the interest, they had to buy a full page ad to brag about it," Mac jested.

"Well, forty years without a single loss to an investor," Lou quoted the Straus slogan.

They all laughed.

"Would you advise me to buy real estate bonds?" Mac kidded the host.

"Well, we're still doing business," Stern parried Mac's remark, dryly. "Say, I heard a good one today," he went on, and told the riddle about the two Arabs racing to Mecca.

Lou Margolis pretended not to have heard it before, and guessed the answer.

There was something too intense about Mac. Rose and he were having a small winning streak and he was pushing it, making side bets on the hands, keeping track of his winnings to the cent. He usually never knew where he stood till a game was over.

"Seriously," Mac kiddingly kept after Stern, "how long can they go on paying interest out of the income from new sales?"

Stern took it as a joke.

"Oh, I heard of the swellest new game," Celia proposed.

"What is it?"

"It's called Murder."

The group had become extremely animated, their eyes were excited, their movements spasmic. "Oh, I just know you've always wanted to murder me," everybody was saying to everybody else, and: "Just wait till those lights are out!" When they were roaming around the apartment, waiting for the murder to happen, Rose got to feeling a real terror, the kind she had felt that morning looking at Mrs. Kirsh's face, the kind that was inside her all the time now: it was real, now, real. This was the way people were.

There was a shriek. Involuntarily, Rose shrieked, too.

On the way home, Rose and Mac stopped downtown; he wanted a drink. All evening she had become more and more certain that he was in trouble. Now, without knowing why, she started to tell him about Mrs. Kirsh. "Half of the girls where I teach are supporting their husbands," Rose said. "It would be awful if they were fired."

They were looking at each other. She knew that what she was trying to say was no use.

"Have they any kids?" Mac asked.

"Yes. One."

Mac's lips tightened.

They drank again, and talked of other things. As they were about to leave, Rose had a sudden impulse, she knew she shouldn't obey it, and yet she was afraid that if she didn't bring the question up this time he might never understand, might leave her because of misunderstanding.

She reached alongside his hand for the check. "Let's make it Dutch from now on," she said. "Please, Mac."

He grinned lopsidedly. "Oh, it's not that bad," he remarked, and took the check.

She knew, instantly, that she had spoiled everything. She would probably never see him again.

The whole world was tightening, closing in, closing, with drawstrings pulling tighter, always a squeeze tighter.

Endurance Record

If he could scramble through summer, and it would not be so hard now that spring was come, Harry Perlin figured on maybe hitching a trailer onto the coupé, and loading up with Close-A-Doors and heading west. Selling a few as he went along, paying his way and maybe even sending a little money home. He'd have a compact little shop fixed up in the trailer, too, and when he sold out all his Close-A-Doors, he'd camp somewhere, and set up his little machine shop under a spreading tree, and using the Chevvy's motor for power, he'd put together some more Close-A-Doors, and keep on rolling. Roaming the country, living in camps, broiling steaks over campfires, just being footloose and free from all care.

Every night, sitting under the stars. It would be a beautiful kind of trip for a long all-summer honeymoon. A kid like Jackie would have the time of his life on a trip like that; having Jackie along would make it perfect.

And for a while, as summer came on, it looked like Harry's dreams might come true.

In April, a snappy fellow named Hubert Dupres came around, sent by Harry's brother. Dupres had been let out of a bond house, and was willing to try selling anything. He proved to be a whizz. Inside of three weeks he had the crew really turning in sales. Naturally Dupres had to get a sales manager's commission, and when this was added to the salesman's commission, there wasn't much left for Harry. Nevertheless, during May he was clearing a hundred dollars a week.

All of his schemes for enlarging were bubbling in his head again. He saw himself building a factory. He snatched moments to work on models for other inventions; for instance, the dashboard emergency brake. Why, way back in college he had had an idea for an automatic furnace-stoker and had let it go, and look, the Iron Fireman had made millions!

Maybe he would be able to take that roaming honeymoon without even trying to sell anything on the road. Just live on the profits of his invention.

And at the end of May, Dupres quit.

"What's the matter, Hugh, haven't I treated you fair and square?" Harry pleaded.

"Oh, sure, oh, sure." Dupres's twirly mustache danced with his smily talk. "You're okay, Perlin, no kicks. Only, you know I was just filling in time. This backdoor stuff is no game for me." As he stood there, vibrating one leg, the crease in his pants rippled distractingly. Harry glanced down at the fellow's suede sport shoes.

"Going back in the bond business?" he asked respectfully, thinking maybe the depression was really over, as Hoover had stated, and stocks must be turning up. Why, only last week S. W. Straus and Company, for whom his brother worked, had put a full-page ad in the paper saying they were sending out seventeen million dollars in interest alone, to their customers.

"Well, I've got a pretty good proposition," Dupres said, with the same smile. He hopped into his car and was off.

During the next week a couple of the best salesmen also quit. When the third fellow left, Harry felt uneasy, but he hated to mention his suspicion. Mack brought it up. "Say, maybe your pal Hubert is trying to pull a fast one?"

Harry was worried enough to ask his brother: "Say, Vic, do you know what your pal Dupres is doing?"

"Who?"

"My sales manager. He quit. The fellow you sent around a couple of months ago."

"Search me. I didn't know that guy, somebody brought him around. He couldn't sell any more bonds. I don't know who could. Why?"

"Nothing."

The next couple of weeks, sales fell off, and it was the same old struggle, working hard and just barely keeping going.

Harry had been sort of shy about seeing Lil too often, as long as he wasn't solidly on his feet. He got terribly excited when she phoned. He rushed right over. She showed him an ad she had clipped out of the *Tribune*. "Look, Harry, isn't this your invention?"

He knew, before he even actually took in the ad. The thing was called Sesame. There was a picture of wide-open garage doors. And an inset picture of a spring lock with extending levers, like his own Close-A-Door. The Sesame sold for five dollars.

His guts quivered. His eyes bored through the illustration, as though they could rip the cover off the device, and examine the interior mechanism.

Who was the Eagle Mfg. Corp.? How could they possibly sell the thing for five dollars?

He had to get a hold of one of those things and tear it open.

"Gee, thanks, thanks for telling me, I didn't see it," he said to Lil; she was sweet, she was on the lookout for him.

"They can't get away with it!" Lil cried indignantly. "You can sue them. And do you know, you can get an injunction right away to keep them from selling any. You've got it patented, haven't you?"

"Oh, sure. That was the first thing I did." All the trouble he had had with that patent rushed in review through his mind, every time Runt had sent papers to Washington they had scared him, referring to some previous patent but always the reference had been to something totally different, and finally the patent had been granted. He could almost feel under his finger-tips the raised letters, Reg. U.S. Pat., as they stood out on each of the castings.

"Who got the patent for you?"

"Dave Plotkin."

"What!" she groaned. "I bet it isn't worth a nickel!"

"He's a lawyer, isn't he?"

"Oh, you," she said disgustedly. "An ordinary lawyer is no good on a patent. You have to have a special patent lawyer. There are a million ways of breaking a patent. Why, he had no right to do that to you. Sam would have sent you to a patent lawyer."

"But I got the patent all right," he insisted.

She ticked her lips, impatiently. "Better let me get a patent lawyer on the job. At least I know something about lawyers."

What hurt most of all was the idea of going out and paying five dollars to those bastards to get a sample of their product. Their office was in the old Monadnock Building; still, they might have plenty of money.

The place was jammed with young fellows, the line overflowed into the hall. They all had that stiff shined-up appearance of fellows applying for a job. They eyed him, estimating him as competition.

"Yes?" the girl said.

Harry had an idea. "Is Mr. Dupres here?" he shot at her.

"Is it in regard to a position on the sales staff?"

So it was Dupres all right!

"No. I want to see him. My name is Perlin."

"I'm sorry, Mr. Dupres hasn't come in yet," she said.

Harry caught sight of a sample Sesame on the desk behind the girl. It was cheap-looking, tin; those puny rods would never hold a door open, they'd bend or snap. For a moment he felt elated, relieved. But what did the customers know? These things were being sold. The whole market would be ruined.

"Was it in regard to taking out an agency?" the girl inquired.

"No. I just want one of these things. I'll buy one," he blundered.

"Well, uh, we don't usually handle retail sales in this office but—maybe I can accommodate you."

Harry waited. He wanted to yell out: Everybody, this is a fake! I've got the genuine article! I invented it! You can't go out and sell this junk!

A boy appeared with the package. Harry handed over five dollars, and rushed out. His car was parked on Plymouth Court. He fished out a screwdriver and pliers, and sat there taking the gadget apart.

What a gyp! Why the spring would hardly close a screen door! The whole thing would fall apart in a week! People would never buy such a piece of crap!

Still, he knew. It would sell. And people would get stung with these lousy Sesames, and be so sore they'd never even look at the genuine article. He knew in his bones that this was the way it would happen.

But he would fight that robber! To his last nickel!

Harry scrambled the lock together, leaving half the bolts unfastened. He started for Runt Plotkin's office but remembered Lil's advice. And all that stuff about Runt in the papers. But if Runt was in trouble, this was the time he needed help, needed people to have faith in him.

Perplexed, Harry drove west, to consult Lil.

She couldn't understand what strange hold Runt Plotkin had on people. First Sam, and now Harry Perlin, always wanting to go out of their way to help out that crook! Maybe it was some kind of fascination, a hypnotism, like Rasputin.

"How can you even think of letting him handle your case?" she screeched at Harry.

"Well, it's just, I don't know who to go to," he said, confused. Lawyers, and courts . . . he saw himself already defeated.

How different he was from Sam, she thought. Harry was almost too easy, giving up before the fight. "I know lots of lawyers. Let's see," she figured. This was a chance to go to someone new, to open the world a crack. Lately, it had seemed to Lil she was living in a closed world, and the world was closing in smaller and smaller, shutting her in this flat with her father and the kid, and movies once a week to the old Central Park Theater, and a date with Harry, and making him think she was busy with all kinds of dates other nights. Did it mean you were getting old, as the world closed in, you didn't meet any new people; or was it just the depression, people hiding off by themselves?

So there was a fellow named Jerry Bass who was supposed to be very brilliant and smart; she had been dying to meet Jerry Bass. Who could tell what might happen? And he was certainly a more successful lawyer than Sam Eisen.

Lil looked awfully sweet, wearing a white linen jacket with puffed sleeves, and a mannish felt hat. They talked very little about the case, but mostly about people they knew, while Harry sat silent. "Oh, what I don't know about law! I bet I could go into practice myself!" Lil rolled on. "You know, my former husband was a lawyer, Sam Eisen. Do you ever see him?"

He took Harry's case, for fifty dollars and a contingency.

And all the way home she was thinking, she wasn't so old, only twenty-six, why shouldn't life open for her? Some people might think that Sam was more attractive than Jerry Bass, Sam was better built but in a way Jerry Bass was handsomer. Wouldn't Sam be peeved if he heard she got married to a successful lawyer, like Jerry Bass, someone who was going up in the world? Wouldn't everybody be surprised!

Harry and his brother had each been giving their mother ten dollars a week, and as she didn't have any rent to pay, this was enough for their housekeeping. The rent from the upstairs flat was supposed to pay the expenses of the building, but it had been reduced three times in the last couple of years, so that now it was only thirty dollars, and redecorating had cost sixty dollars, so there was hardly enough to keep the building running, and the taxes were raised every year.

And on top of the tax bill, Harry was behind two hundred dollars on his note to Mr. Klein.

One day Mr. Klein phoned. "What's the matter, Harry? I haven't seen you lately."

"Well, you know how it is. I'm busy in the shop almost every evening."

"Then business must be good with you, ha ha."

"Oh, it doesn't mean a thing." Harry tried to return the laugh.

"Well, maybe you ought to have a secretary, to keep track of your bills and things," Mr. Klein hinted jovially. "A man sometimes forgets."

"Oh, I'm not forgetting," Harry quavered, wondering if Lil was listening in, sure, she must have typed the letter reminding him his note was overdue.

"Well, Harry, you know if it was myself I wouldn't bother you about this note of yours." Mr. Klein's voice had turned grayish, weary. "But the fact is I took in a silent partner, so you see I got nothing to say about it . . ."

Harry knew whom he meant. Rube Moscowitz.

"Yah, that's all right. I think I can take care of it next week. You see, I just paid a big real estate tax," he bluffed in case Lil was listening.

"Taxes, are you crazy, nobody is paying taxes now!" cried Mr. Klein. "All the real estate owners are fighting the taxes, and he goes ahead and pays it!"

"Well, what else could I do?" Harry faltered.

"What else! Give it to me, I can use the money!" Mr. Klein had recovered his hard jocular tone.

"I'll try and have it next week," Harry repeated.

"If you haven't got it all, bring a payment. Whatever you got," Mr. Klein ended, lightly.

"Uh, give my regards to Lil," Harry said, sure she was listening.

"What's the matter, Harry, aren't your ships floating?" his mother asked, as she served the *kreplach* soup.

He wanted to spill all his troubles to somebody, and yet he felt angry because she had guessed he was worried.

"Nothing, nothing, I'm tired, that's all," he snapped.

When she went back into the kitchen, he said to his brother: "Vic, can you scrape up some dough, it's for the taxes and a note that's behind, I've been carrying everything myself, but now I can't any more—"

"Why come to me about it!" Vic snapped.

Harry reddened. "I thought maybe you could borrow it somewhere at the office."

"The office! Don't make me laugh!"

"But you're getting paid, aren't you?"

"They put me back on commission!" Victor stormed. "I ain't made a dime all summer. What the hell do you think I am!" He jumped up from the table and walked around the room, his eyes blazing as though everything were Harry's fault.

"Ask the old lady," he suddenly suggested. "She's got it socked away someplace."

As though she had been waiting to be summoned, the mother came into the room, then. "Harry, listen, if you need money I have a little money," she said. "If you need money, take from me."

After all he was going to use the money to save the house, which was her house, so after all he was using the money for her. "Well, ma, we need over two hundred dollars," he admitted.

"Son, I have four hundred dollars. I will bring it to you, and when you need it, use it. What do I need it for? My little dance on this earth is nearly done."

"Where have you got the money?" Victor asked. "In the bank?"

"In the Liberty Bank. Tomorrow, I will get it out."

"You shouldn't keep it there anyway," Victor said. "These little banks may go bust any day. Put it in the Postal Savings. Let's see your bankbook."

She didn't show them the bankbook. Perhaps, as Victor suspected, she had more than four hundred. Trust a Jewish mother to have a few *kniplach* tied away, saved out of the house money, in God knows how many years, sometimes a dollar, sometimes a nickel a week.

"I don't know whether to pay the taxes or the note," Harry said.

"Don't be a dope. Everybody is holding out on taxes. Why, the Field estate hasn't paid a nickel on millions' worth of property," Vic said. "And I don't see any sense in paying that note either, throwing good money after bad. They'll get the house, anyway, on that dumb mortgage you took out."

"I don't know," Harry said. There was only eight hundred dollars more to pay off. Why let the building go for eight hundred dollars? And besides, by the next quarter, business might pick up.

He had the money for her father, Lil knew, because otherwise Harry wouldn't ask her to go out with him; poor fellow, he was so sensitive. And afterward her father came out of his office wearing that expression of momentary respite, like a patient in a dentist chair between drillings.

It was still light when they were driving out to the airfield to watch the endurance flyers break the world's record. They had taken Jackie along, and it felt nice to be with a man, like a little family. Jackie was so excited about the flyers, squirming his head through the car window, that she was sure he would break his neck.

Lil was still puzzled where Harry had got the money, for she sensed that his business hadn't brought in that much profit.

"How's business these days?" she ventured.

"Oh, not so good," he said. Why didn't he ever bluff, like a smart business man? "Those guys got all my best salesmen, with their five-dollar lock."

"Well, listen, Harry," she sympathized, "I hope you didn't strain yourself to make that payment to my father. You know he would have waited."

"Oh, that's all right. It was my brother's money," he answered, blushing.

"Listen, why don't you make yours cheaper, and sell it for five dollars, and compete with them?" she suggested, with animation.

"No, I'd have to put out as junky a thing as theirs," Harry said.

"I hear they're not doing so good," Lil said. "Jerry Bass told me, he has been asking around about them. I told you he was a smart lawyer."

"Oh, when did you see him?" Harry bit.

"Oh, I've been seeing him."

He drove silently. And Lil thought, it was no use, she just couldn't live the rest of her life with a man who gave up so easily, he would never amount to anything, she was certain.

"He says that's a terribly dumb patent Runt Plotkin got for you. He says they might claim a different principle of construction."

"I don't see how they can!" Harry exclaimed. "The only thing different they have is the lock, and it's one that I wouldn't use because it's too cheesy."

"Isn't it wonderful out?" Lil said, breathing so her bosom rose sharp against her summer print silk. "Gee, even when you only get a little bit out of the city, the sky is all different."

Harry too drew a deep breath. He thought he caught the scent of her, floating soft, like the dusk. And her hair, sweetly aired. Such little moments of her renewed his hope.

"Hey! I see it! I see it!" Jackie yelled, nearly falling out of the car, pointing upward.

Harry pulled to the side of the road, and stopped. The kid jumped out, and the two of them watched from the seat.

"It's like a bee, going around around, listen to it," Lil said.

Harry looked at his wrist-watch. "In another half-hour, they'll break the record."

"Seven-fifty-three!" Jackie informed them. "Bang!"

"I heard one of them has a terrible toothache," Lil commented. "Can you imagine! I'd have come down long ago."

"Gee, he's low," Harry said.

The kid danced on the road. "He's coming down! He's coming down!" the kid yelled. "Ma, I'm gonna be an aviator!"

"You can almost see the name on it!" Harry declared. And though the lettering was only a blur, he quoted, *City of Chicago.*"

"*City of Chicago!*" Lil repeated. In spite of being wise, and knowing it was only a publicity stunt, it made her feel something. Imagine, hour after hour, and in the night-time too, all night long, and day after day, droning around up there, circling and circling the city, to bring the world's record to the city of Chicago.

"They're coming down!" Jackie cried, alarmed.

"Oh, no, they won't, not till they break the record." Harry looked at his watch again.

The plane swooped dangerously low, and their hearts swooped, but at the last moment, teasingly, the plane rose, and dipped, and rose again, and drove upward.

Now it was out of sight.

Harry was explaining in detail, to Jackie, how a second plane went up with gas, and how the gas was transferred to the endurance plane, in mid-air. Harry got along with the kid. Better than Sam. How could a father be so unnatural, never even coming out to visit his son?

"Aw, I bet they come down and sleep in the middle of the night when nobody is watching!" Jackie said brightly.

504

Lil leaned forward and turned on the radio that Harry had installed in his car. The nut. Still, it was convenient.

"When it's ten o'clock we climb the stair,
  We never knock 'cause nobody is there—
  Just me and my shadow, all alone and feeling blue."

"Look, the refueling plane is taking off!" Harry said.

Cars had parked all along the road, and there was a special parking space on the aviation field, jammed with cars.

They had their eyes on Harry's wrist-watch. As the moment came when the record was smashed, an immense shout went up from the field; they could hear it a mile away. And all the cars began to honk, and Jackie honked and honked the horn of Harry's car.

In that noise, darting up from all around, happy as a New Year's celebration, Harry felt himself reviving, his ambition returning, he too would win out, and records were still to be broken.

"I'll bet they go on all night," he said. "They'll put up a real record."

"Well, don't forget we can't stay all night," Lil said.

Jackie had run off again, straining after the riding lights of the plane, starlike in the growing dark. Harry suddenly felt boldened, full, sure of life. And with an awkward rush, he pulled Lil to him. "When we're married we can," he blurted.

She went stiff under his arm. All her prospects balanced before her, and in that instant she was sure she would risk this safe, small future, for what she really wanted. "I wasn't aware we were going to be married," she said, and watched him wither.

Oh, she knew already that there was no chance with Jerry Bass, he was engaged, but there must be others, others. She could imagine Ev Goldberg and all the kids in the bunch saying: "Oh, Lil? She finally got married again, to Harry Perlin. Oh, they get along, but you know, he'll never amount to much." And Sam would hear about it, and shrug.

Harry had withdrawn his arm.

Driving back, they heard the rising and falling drone of the circling record-breakers overhead, and they occasionally glimpsed the red and green lights, like smooth-sailing stars against the furnace-reddened haze of the South Chicago sky.

What little work there was to do, Harry could have done himself, but he left it for Mack, to keep Mack occupied, while he sat fretting in the cubbyhole office. To kill time, Harry read the newspapers through and through, even reading the financial pages, looking up General Electric stock, on which his brother had lost so much money; it was 57 now. Once it had been over 300!

There were always charts on the financial pages. And they always showed a toboggan line, but with a tiny up-pointed hook at the bottom.

If he could only hang on for another few months, until the lawsuit was settled, he might even collect thousands of dollars in damages. Then he would call up Lil again. . . .

When the mail came in every morning, Mack would have some excuse for hanging around the office, till he saw if any checks came in. He was worried about being paid.

Then one day Harry had to say it. "Listen, Mack, you know how things are. Maybe you better look around for something else. The while, we can sort of divvy up whatever comes in."

"Oh, sure," Mack said. "Oh, sure."

Then he could only pay Mack half salaries, then only a few bucks whenever he had it. Every time Mack stepped out, Harry figured at last he would find something, but no such luck.

A grocer in the block had a truck that needed overhauling, and Harry asked for the job. He picked up other odd jobs of car and radio repairing, and kept going.

In the evening, he didn't want to face anybody, so he hung around the shop. He renewed his activity as an amateur radio operator, becoming an active HAM again. Sitting at his key, with the old earphones clamped around his head, Harry lost his loneliness; and sitting awake long hours, he wore himself out, and broke down sexual desires.

He checked off all the far corners of the world which he had contacted: a tiny village that he could hardly find on the map of Australia, and Irkutsk, Siberia, towns in Alaska and Brazil; he checked off all the well-known HAM stations in the U.S.A. Every time he caught a new signal, he lived the beginner's excitement all over again, of wondering where it was from, and who was on the other end. It was like those old days when he had had his set in the Big Ten basement, and gone over there so often, why, he used to be stuck on Aline Freedman then, ha ha, and she was married and had a kid.

Once Harry picked up a QSL and started talking and after a while the sender said: "Can you dance, oh, how I would like to go dancing," and Harry flashed: "RUAYL?" and the Young Lady's answer came back: "Yes, IMAYL," and then they kidded back and forth, about how tall and what color eyes, and he ended up by asking for her photograph.

And he actually got a snapshot of a nice-looking girl from Lititz, Pennsylvania, signed TNX for QSL. Her name was Aileen Quigley—a *shikseh*, so it probably would never develop into anything serious.

On winter nights Harry figured that in spring he could sell the Chevvy for around two hundred; it was in perfect condition. Then he would buy a junky car for about fifty bucks, fix it up, and build him a trailer, and he'd roam the country, carefree, calling on all the HAM operators he knew over the air, maybe even the girl in Pennsylvania. . . .

At home, one morning Vic pulled all his shirts out of the drawer, throwing them on the floor one after another. "What's the idea, ma!" he shouted. "Did you change laundries? I can't wear a collar like this!"

The collars all looked floppy, inexpertly pressed.

Then Harry realized his mother was ironing their shirts herself.

"You shouldn't do it, ma," he remonstrated.

"Well, I was trying to save a little on the laundry bill," she admitted. "Shirts is twelve cents, and for the two of you—"

"What's the matter, aren't we giving you enough for the house?" Harry asked.

Then, as his mother evaded his eyes, Harry guessed that his brother hadn't been paying his share of the house money, maybe for a long while.

"What can he do? He isn't working," the mother said. "Harry, he has to ask me even for carfare. And you know how independent he is. It hurts him."

There were times when Harry wished for a long illness for himself. Maybe nothing fatal, not t.b. or anything painful, but a long slow illness, a long long time in bed, resting, and letting someone else worry.

Golden Anniversary

The testimonial dinner tendered to Samuel Insull on the fiftieth, the golden, anniversary of his entry into the business of electric light and power was surely the greatest and most munificent banquet in the history of the world.

In a bygone age, all the world's potentates gathered in the feasting tent of Alexander the Great and ate flesh and drank wine in his honor. To the courts of King Solomon, in his glory, came sultans and desert chieftains; in gaudy striped robes, in jeweled turbans, they sat cross-legged in his halls, and feasted. But this motley crowd in fantastic yellows and purples was merely picturesque as the marketplace; true dignity lives in formal black and white.

The nobles who flourished their lacy wrists at the lavish courts of the Louis, the Cossack hetmans whose boots stamped through the murky halls of the mad Peters, and the armored knights who toasted good King Arthur were few in number, and small in their allegiance, compared to the seven hundred tycoons who gathered at the golden anniversary of Samuel Insull, in Chicago.

The banquet was held in the great hall of the Palmer House. Hadassah might brag of seating one thousand people to luncheon, fifty dollars for each plate. But as far as numbers go, you can see five thousand people fed in the breadline any day. And as for the fifty dollars, what did they get for it but a piece of whitefish[1]? And when you figure the total cost of this jubilee

---

[1] The first edition of this book served "a couple of lamb chops"; later editions

dinner, the cost of bringing each guest on Pullmans and by airways from all ends of the United States and Canada, when you figure the value of their time, days coming here, and days going home, just for the purpose of being present at the dinner, it comes to much more than fifty dollars a plate.

Who shall total the numbers of capons and pigeons slain, the army of cooks and waiters, or the pounds of salt alone, contained in seven hundred individual shakers? That is the work of publicity men; give a part-time job to some snappy young Mac Hirschberger, and he'll total the gargantuan preparations.

But consider the guests, the seven hundred! Streaming into Chicago, the hub, the radial center, out of which flow the lines of light and power, the cables of control, Chicago, the vertex of the Insull empire! Each guest is a potentate, come to pledge himself at the golden anniversary of the emperor! Each, in his own right, a corporation director.

Chairmen of boards, and chairmen of consolidated boards, presidents of corporations, and vice-presidents who in the corporate universe are more powerful than presidents! Men of girth, substantial and solid, with broad gleaming curves of shirtfront and solitary diamond studs. No drunken orgy, no saturnalia in the guise of a business convention. For this is a sober banquet, of honor and of awe for the emperor. They, the satraps, and he, the sultan.

Just look at some of those names! Rube Moscowitz scarcely has the right to be listed among them, for he is no director of an Insull corporation, but it is a symbol of the democracy of the empire that he, on the personal memory of the kindly, golden-yeared titan, is invited to the dinner.

Here are the heads of Ottawa Power and Light, of Eastern Consolidated Electric, of Illinois Utilities, of the People's Light and Power of Indiana, here is Maine Electricity, and Wisconsin Power, and Michigan Light, waterfalls and rivers are owned over these signatures, they press the buttons over platoons of dynamos, and at their will the vital juice would vanish from untold miles of wire, the lights in that great chandelier would die, the city would be dark, the El and street cars would stand paralyzed, the interurban trains would stand paralyzed, and in forty states of the United States, and in the provinces of Canada, homes and factories would darken, and machines would stop.

Coming slightly early, Mr. and Mrs. Reuben Moscowitz could walk the length of that banqueting hall, taking in the glories, for this was something to describe to their children, and this was something that Celia Moscowitz would describe to their children's children, and it might be related down through the ages: the glorious golden anniversary dinner of the head of the empire of light and power.

Mr. and Mrs. Reuben Moscowitz were one couple among the swarm of satraps that shuffled around that vast banqueting hall, admiring the order of

changed this to "a piece of whitefish."

the tables. For upon each table was a cut-out map of a state, and wherever there was an Insull light and power plant, an electric light burned in the map, and wherever there was an Insull trolley line, a miniature, lighted car traveled back and forth on a track!

"There ain't a thing wrong with Insull properties!" Rube Moscowitz declared to his wife, refuting the hints and whispers of his lawyer son-in-law, Lou Margolis, for lawyers are notoriously suspicious. "While everything else has been crashing, smashing, and the stock market went all to hell, look at Insull, look at Consolidated Gas today, it's still above two hundred. While everybody else is going to smash, he's buying up, he's buying cheap. And when this is over he'll own practically all the power in the United States!"

A Texan satrap, round-faced and round-bellied, had heard the words of Rube Moscowitz, and spoke: "Why, this is the one thing people got to have. Power. Why, I never saw it this way till I see it here! Here we've got the rivers, the waterworks, the natural resources of this country! You can't go beyond that, no, sir! Once you have the natural resources sewn up, you're set!"

"If you've got any loose change you better put it right into Insull securities," Rube Moscowitz advised. "The old boy is smart! Know what he's been doing, this depression? He lets a lot of rumors get started, you know, whispering around against him, he has it started himself! Then his stocks go down and he buys them back himself for fifty cents on the dollar! He's going to control the whole works himself! Insull is like Henry Ford! He'll tell those Wall Street bankers to go climb a tree when they try to get control of his companies!"

The men agreed. A whole group of them agreed, for there was now a cluster around Mr. and Mrs. Moscowitz, as it was whispered that the big Jewish fellow was a Chicago man, a close confidant of the boss in his political activities; and she was a queen, there were so few women in the hall, most of the satraps having come a long way across country, without their women. The brightness and tulle-soft presence of a woman, a queen!

"They're all set to dig the subway in Chicago, here," Rube informed them. "That's the next big job for Chicago. Took a long time to get around to it but the plans are all set now and everything is okay. The old man got what he wanted, too; when that subway is finished he's going to be running every scrap of transportation in Chicago."

"Great thing for business!" was the opinion.

"Dig Chicago out of the depression!" Rube Moscowitz repeated the universal slogan.

And now, a universal murmur of expectancy spread through the hall.

There was a pulling of chairs, a taking of places.

"I'm going to squeeze some of my money out of that gypper, Klein," Rube confided to his wife as they went to their seats at the long white table below the platformed speaker's table. "I'm afraid of those mortgages of his.

Too much Jewish monkey business. I'm going to put my dough back where it's safe. When you got the waterfalls and the natural resources backing you up, you can't go wrong, depression or no depression."

They sat.

Now a hush fell upon the assembly. All eyes were directed to the center of the raised table, where two chairs remained vacant. Right in front of them burned a plain electric light.

"Ain't that appropriate?" Rube's neighbor whispered solemnly. "The old man started with Edison, you know. That's where he got his start, with Thomas Edison!"

And now, a murmur rippled over the hush from end to end of the hall, and there was the accompanying tinkle of glassware being set down carefully so as to make no sound.

Arm in arm with his wife, the old man entered. His infant-soft skin glowed effulgent as an electric light; the fine white hairs of his patrician mustache gleamed silkenly, and they could see the flat cool flakes of his cerulean blue eyes.

The couple came to their places at the table.

With common accord, all the assembled banqueters, the seven hundred, arose to their feet in tribute.

The baby-smooth skin of the old man glowed even brighter. His lips parted in a smile of satisfaction, of acceptance.

"One thing you have to say about the old man," Rube whispered, awed. "He's got class."

"Confidence," quoted one of those cynical newspapermen at the press table, "is restored."

Rube was so excited he reached for the pickle dish.

"Rube!" his wife cautioned, stopping his hand. "Your ulcers."

Marshall Joffre died.
Thomas A. Edison died.
Julius Rosenwald died.

Them Days Is Gone Forever

In the Knickerbocker Hotel on the Gold Coast there was a meeting of nearly a hundred men. They were nervous and circled in little groups. There were rumors that Al himself would appear to put his proposition before them. Sol could imagine him at this moment, emerging from his armored fort, that hotel on Twenty-Third and Michigan, stepping into his bullet-proof car, and guarded by two other cars, shooting through the traffic.

"Na, he is a nice fellow, nothing like you think," Korshak reassured everybody.

Dr. Hart, whom they had all made czar of their industry, looked worried.

Cut prices, he said, that's the only way to bring back business.

Capone said raise prices. Sew everything up tight, and the public will have to come across.

A buck? Make it two bucks a suit. Why be pikers?

The proposition was to give Capone full charge of the industry.

They now paid two percent of their gross to the Association. Make it five percent and he would take care of everything.

"There won't be any trouble," he guaranteed. "Everybody will charge the same price."

"Look at my business!" Korshak was his advertisement. "Since I have Al for a partner, I got no trouble."

But everybody felt scared. The big independent Korshak had finally come into the Association, sure, but now he wanted to run the whole industry.

And two bucks a suit—them days were gone forever. People would begin parcel-posting their work out of town again.

Sol listened here, listened there.

"We'll let him state his proposition, we'll listen to him," old man Weiner said. "That's business, we'll listen to anybody."

"Once he gets in, we'll never get him out," Sam Kantrowitz feared.

"Al is on the run, that's why he's trying to muscle in on us!"

"You can't bottle up a whole industry!" that Dr. Hart was explaining. "You can't just name a price, any price, two dollars, five dollars a suit, that has nothing to do with the cost of the job."

"Why not!" Wolper maintained. "If everybody sticks to the same price, and who is going to break the price, with Al in charge?"

"You just can't do it!" that Dr. Hart said, almost crying. "You can't separate the price from the cost." A reasonable profit, he kept yelling, and Sol figured that was okay, a reasonable profit. The whole trouble with the industry was that everybody got away from the natural price level, the doc kept yelling. And you can't fight nature. If you bottle up the price in Chicago, they'll begin parcel-posting the jobs out of town, there is always somebody somewhere that will lower the prices, and the goods is like a river, it flows to its natural level.

Sol's head was whirling, with trying to keep up with the doc, and with the excitement of waiting for Al to show up, in person.

His coming was like nothing Sol had figured. A couple of guys shoved through the room, and there he was on the platform. The guys around him looked like anybody else, plain guys in business suits.

Al himself didn't make any speeches. He sat with his hands on his knees, creasing up his face in a smile, like he wanted to make a good impression. He certainly was a heavyweight.

He sat there while one of the big shots made a speech, giving his proposition. The room was getting hot, as though everybody was breathing double-fast. "Can't we get a fan going here, can't we get a fan going here?" a guy next to Sol bothered, and before Sol knew it he was running around trying to get a janitor or somebody to start a couple of fans that were mounted over the doors, and he forgot to watch Al.

He couldn't get the fans started, and anyway the talking was over, now it was up to them for a vote. Capone and his guys went into a side room with Korshak and Wolper; the big man was wiping his face all the time. Suddenly Sol got the idea Capone wasn't so much. You could hear gurgly laughter from him in the other room; but Sol got the idea here he was asking them for something and they could say no.

The vote was practically unanimous for turning him down.

Them days is gone forever.

ALL GOOD MEN

RUDY was tired of doing nothing, so he walked into Mitch Wilner's office. Even Mitch had got beyond the stage of trying to keep himself busy during office hours. He was just sitting there, studying the lights in the movie sign, across the street.

He started when the door opened, and reached for a book; but, seeing Rudy, dropped the pretense.

"Say, doc," Rudy began. He hesitated to suggest anything to Mitch. Yet he hated to see a man like Mitch wasting himself, sitting around. "I've got a proposition."

"Anything for cash," Mitch jested wanly. "Abortions and mayhem included."

"It isn't that bad," Rudy said. "I was talking with Matthews—"

"Uh huh." Mitch seemed a little guarded. Maybe he knew what was coming.

"You know, it's quite awhile now he's been monkeying with an idea. The main part of it is, how to be a doctor and still make a living," Rudy said.

"What is he, a magician?"

"No, listen. He has an idea about establishing a downtown clinic . . ." Rudy saw Mitch freezing up as he spoke. Doggedly, he went on explaining Matthews's plan for a downtown pay clinic. The doctors would get salaries, and the patients would have the advantage of being treated by specialists at low cost.

"Are you going to go into this, Rudy?" Mitch asked, apprehensively.

"I'm not sure. It looks like a good idea to me. Lord knows, somebody has to do something pretty soon, about pulling this profession out of the hole."

"I wouldn't advise you to go into it," Mitch said, straightening. "I think it would be fatal to you."

Rudy raised his brows.

"You might just as well be a clerk in a department store," Mitch said. "Where's the future in it? It's even worse than some of these cockeyed schemes for socialized medicine. You'd be working your head off on an eight-hour day trying to take care of more patients per hour like a guy on the Ford production line."

"I'd rather be working hard than be sitting around," Rudy said. "For one thing, you forget everything you ever learned, sitting around. And a steady salary looks pretty good to me."

"Sure. Go work for a boss, like a chain-store dentist! Why, it would be the worst cheapening the profession ever got. The S.A.P.S. would never stand for it, they'd kick you out in a minute!"

These arguments were already familiar to Rudy, as naturally they occurred to every doctor right off. And he knew the answers. There wouldn't be any boss, the doctors would run the place themselves, and would keep up a high professional standard.

"I haven't signed up myself, Mitch, and I never may. But it doesn't hurt to go to a few meetings. I'd like you to come along once, Mitch, just to sort of look over the fellows and advise me on the thing. In a thing like this a fellow can't always trust himself."

"I'll tell you right now," Mitch said. "Steer clear of it." He gazed at the movie sign. Norma Shearer in *Strangers May Kiss*. "Everybody has it tough the first couple of years. I'm going to stick it out!"

Rudy couldn't help saying: "I've been at this a couple of years more than you, Mitch, and I know this isn't just a sample of the tough first years that everybody has, because I was doing better than this two years ago. There's something rotten in Denmark, and it's up to us to figure a way out."

"You'll figure your way out of the medical profession," Mitch said. "Do you want to be classed with a lot of quacks?"

At nine-thirty, when he closed the office, Rudy drove down to Roosevelt Road. The windows of Meyerson's office were dark.

The orange-red scrawl of Walgreen's neon sign pulsated feverishly, drawing the eye from the pallid white lights of other stores. Palmolive soap was piled in the window, as the cut-rate item of the week. Walgreen's was selling ten-cent bars two for eleven.

Catty-corner, was Mrs. Kagen's sign, *Cut Rate Drugs*, with dead bulbs like flyspots on the letters. Maybe a couple of those new neon signs in her window would pep up trade, Rudy reflected. Have to keep up with the times.

Anyway this was a dead corner now. Even the radical soapbox orators had been chased away, lately.

Old Doc Meyerson was there all right, dutifully puffing on one of the ten-cent stogies he constantly consumed, to give Mrs. Kagen a little trade. Though he knew that smoking didn't help his wearying heart.

"Hello, doctor, how's your lungs and liver?" Rudy recited his old formula.

"Hi, doc," old Meyerson greeted him. "Get lonesome in your spiffy new office?"

"Good evening, Mrs. Kagen," Rudy shouted. Turned away, she had not noticed his entrance. The old lady was getting pretty deaf.

"Hello, Rudy!" She beamed. "How is your wife, doctor?" Rudy was always touched by the pride in her voice when she called him doctor, just like his own mother.

He reported that Aline was coming along fine.

"The second one!" she clucked, eying him limpidly, philosophically. "They are all having babies, all those children that used to live around here."

"Yah. Nobody learned them better," Dr. Meyerson grunted. "Maybe it's my fault!"

"Go on!"

"Well, Rudy, how's business? Maybe my friend Moscowitz has come to you with his ulcers?" It was a sour joke with Meyerson, that Rube was taking his ulcers around to every specialist in the city. "For twenty years I was good enough for him and his ulcers. But if he has to eat up all the sour tomatoes that Kantor has left over, the Mayo brothers won't help him either!" If there was one thing the old doc knew about, it was stomach ulcers, the Jewish delight. And as for the Moscowitz family, who had been his chief paying patients, he knew every crease in their bellies.

"Here, Rudy, drink something." The old lady came from behind the soda fountain with a chocolate soda.

"Say! What's the idea! I can wait on myself if I want something!" he accepted it, noticing her hand was unsteady now. "Thanks, Mrs. Kagen." Their eyes met for a moment, and all the actual questions they wanted to ask each other were there.

She shrugged her shoulders, and arranged her little old-fashioned shawl.

Meyerson resumed a discussion that had evidently been going on when Rudy entered. "Why not go to Klein and explain it to him just the way it stands with you?" the old doctor advised Mrs. Kagen. "Maybe he'll take whatever you can give him, until summer. And then you'll have the soda fountain trade."

She looked at Rudy as though to say: well, from you I have nothing to hide. "I talked to Mr. Klein already," she said. "He is willing to let me off twenty-five dollars, now, and I should renew the lease for that price, a hundred and twenty-five." Her mild, tired eyes appealed to the two men.

Rudy knew she could never make it any more.

"A hundred and a quarter?" Meyerson bellowed. "What is he, meshuga? Who will pay him that kind of rent nowadays? Roosevelt Road isn't State Street!"

It was funny about an old storekeeper like Mrs. Kagen; though you saw things getting worse and worse, closing tighter, you always figured that an old storekeeper can keep going.

"What can he help himself?" Mrs. Kagen spoke of the landlord. "Klein is in the soup too, rents are down, and he has nothing from his properties. His girl is divorced, and is living home with him."

"Well, what's the use of shlepping along another month and another month? Sell the store right away, go live with your girl, play with your grandchildren, and take it easy in your old age," Dr. Meyerson advised.

"Sell it?" she snorted. "Who will buy a drug store across from a Walgreen's? And I should be a burden on their hands!"

A kid came in, wearing a frightened look that Rudy identified from his drug clerk days. It meant credit. The kid had a prescription. He looked shyly at Dr. Meyerson, muttered: "Hullo, doctor."

"Hello. How is your sister?"

"She's the same," he piped.

"Is this one of yours?" Mrs. Kagen asked, taking the prescription.

The kid went to the far end of the corner, ashamed, to do his bargaining. Mrs. Kagen called: "Harry!" and a skinny-necked fellow in a white coat emerged from behind the prescription partition; he was blinking, and Rudy was certain that he had his *Path* spread open back there. One thing about working for Mrs. Kagen, a fellow got plenty of time to study.

"How goes it?" Rudy greeted him.

"Okay." And Rudy saw himself plugging away, only a few years ago. What was it all for? To have to allow your wife to accept presents from her folks in order to run the house? To have to accept a practically rent-free office in your father-in-law's building? He had done twice as well managing a pharmacy.

"Say, doc." He broached the subject of the clinic to Meyerson, explaining Dr. Matthews's plan.

Dr. Meyerson listened, the white ash of his cigar dribbling onto his lapels.

"Well, what are you asking me?" He wiggled his ferocious brows at Rudy, as of old. And it seemed to Rudy that he had made a fool of himself in even suggesting such a radical idea to an old-timer. If Mitch couldn't see the idea, the old doc would certainly think it was nuts.

"What do you think the attitude of the profession will be?" Rudy asked.

"The profession?" Dr. Meyerson spat. "Ask me better, what will be the attitude of a stableful of jackasses! If anybody that smells a little strange comes near them, they kick him in the belly, even if he is bringing them a pail of oats."

"Oh. So you don't think . . .?"

"Rudy, what is the difference what an old stinker like me thinks? It's a good thing I am old, and I can still stumble around and finish up what I have to do, and if the world wants to commit suicide, let it go ahead! I don't have to worry any more. But if I was starting out in your time, and if there was a new idea, I would listen to it." He ruminated. "Dr. Matthews is a good man."

"That's it!" Rudy said. "That's why I have confidence! After all, it's only a question of the kind of fellows we get into the thing!"

Dr. Meyerson stared at him, and snorted in a way that reminded Rudy of an old actor that used to be in the movies. What was his name? Theodore Roberts.

The kid trotted out with his medicine, and Mrs. Kagen came back to them. "He had only thirty cents. What do you have to prescribe codeine for!" she chided Meyerson. "Always the most expensive drugs!"

"Why don't you try a special every week, Mrs. Kagen?" Rudy suggested. "You've got a lot of old stock, put it on sale and get rid of it. Walgreen is selling Palmolive for six cents this week."

She shook her head, wonderingly. "They have to lose on that soap. For six cents, they have to lose."

"Sure," Rudy said. "But it brings people into the store, and you know how they can make it up on other stuff."

She said wearily: "Ach, Walgreen's. First when they opened there I tried to fight them, but what use is it?"

"How is your grandson? When does he graduate from school?" Dr. Meyerson changed the subject.

She smiled, reviving. "This year. This June. He is the smartest boy in his class! He is going to be a doctor!"

Just to keep Rudy from joining anything impulsively, Mitch came along to a meeting of the group of doctors, at the Morrison. About twenty men were already present when Mitch and Rudy entered. They recognized many of their schoolmates.

"Hi, Rudy!"

"Hi, Mitch! How's the old boy!" Was there a touch of astonishment in their voices, at seeing Mitch Wilner, top man of his class, come along? "Say, how did you ever come out on that protein-free serum?" Dr. Swaboda inquired, still with his old-mannish trick of peering through his foggy unwiped glasses.

That touched a sore spot. Mitch told bitterly how he had been squeezed out of his own research. "The worst of it is they're not even using the stuff!" he complained, remembering disconnectedly that time in class when Nyquist told how he had unwittingly held back the use of insulin a dozen years. But at least Mike Swaboda had recalled his discovery.

Curly Seabury slapped him on the back. "Hullo, Mitch, you old wench-grabber, what are you doing here!"

A vague uneasiness, perhaps guilt, was apparent in the kidding surprise with which those who had come greeted each other.

"I'm checking up for the S.A.P.S.," Mitch kidded. He looked over the men. Weintraub, an old classmate, was here. And Larry Gans, that dope who had nearly killed the dog, the time Nyquist demonstrated insulin. If that was the kind of guy they were getting . . .!

Finally Dr. Matthews hustled in. With him was a hyperthyroid individual who looked like a big-shot executive. There was a stir as most of them recognized Dr. Gordon Orr, who had made quite a name for himself in the Chicago health department. Since the last election, Dr. Orr was out of office.

"Orr hasn't practiced for twenty years, if he ever did practice," Mitch commented, to Rudy. "What do you want him for?"

Disregarding the rostrum, Dr. Matthews sat amongst the other doctors, so that they became an informal circle. Then he explained the idea of the meeting, simply and quickly: "I don't have to tell you fellows how things are. There are too many patients without doctors and too many doctors without patients. Our idea is not socialized medicine, but the one thing that may save us from socialized medicine, if it comes to that. What we want to do is apply modern, mass-production methods, if you please, to our cranky old craft."

He explained the central office, the salary system. "I don't think there's a doctor in the world who wouldn't rather take care of twenty patients a day for twenty dollars, than four patients a day for the same money. Anyway that's my feeling. My practice is where I learn, where I keep alive. . . . In a thing like this, nobody has to accept work outside of his field, for fear of losing a patient. Every patient will get the right kind of care, every man can practice his own specialty and still make a good living. And we can keep the costs low." He glowed with the beautiful simplicity of the plan.

"Every doctor in town would be gunning for us," Swaboda said.

There was a murmur of agreement; he had spoken the objection in every mind.

"Now, wait. We're not going to take the bread out of anybody's mouth. You fellows know whom we would be taking care of. Walking patients. People who are neglecting themselves because they don't want to go to free clinics and who won't call you till they're sick in bed. I think we'd get business that isn't going to anybody, in the present setup."

"After all," pointed out Dr. Kahan, "this is only a small step further than most of us have gone already. We all share offices with somebody or other, we all have a scale of fees." There was a laugh. "Well, a sliding scale," he amended. "So why shouldn't we share offices with a bigger group, and use a business system?"

It was then that smiling Curly Seabury, who had his father's practice to inherit anyway, and seemed to have come to these meetings out of a sympathetic curiosity, arose and said: "It's all well and fine to talk of mass production." He used the term with the accent of amused open-mindedness with which so many people whose own lives were above the current economic turmoil were beginning to use the catch phrases of economics. "Mass production means lots of customers. Now, if the doctors can't get enough paying patients in their own neighborhood, where they are known, how do you figure to bring the same doctors downtown where nobody knows them, and have them reach five times as many patients?"

"How? We'll let them know!" Dr. Orr banged out. He arose, as if recognizing that the moment had come for him to take charge of things. His nervous little body sparked confidence. He was like a super sales manager. There was a freshening and tensing of the atmosphere.

"Let them know? You mean—uh—through the usual channels?" Swaboda piped.

"I mean through the channels that every other business uses," Orr stated flatly. "I mean advertise!"

For an instant nothing was heard but the squeaking of chair-legs on the floor, as the men settled back, shifted, getting into position for the real battle of the evening, squinting to see how this one or that one had taken the idea.

Swaboda was the first to leap up. Shaking his head, like a shocked female, he pawed for his hat and coat. Rudy intercepted him. The damn fool! What did he have to lose, with his one-dollar Polack trade, and sleeping in his office?

"I still have some professional ethics!" Swaboda fumed, twisting his head up on his stringy neck. "I'm no goddam barber's chair dentist, or a goiter-pill quack!"

"Sure, I know, Mike," Rudy soothed him. "But maybe something can be worked out. Why not wait and hear the rest?"

"I've heard enough!" Swaboda growled, hesitating.

While he talked to Swaboda, the thought flashed through Rudy's mind, like a sign passed on a rushing train, that here he was working for the idea as though he had already definitely signed up.

The meeting had broken into half a dozen little groups, each of which heaved with quarrelsome discussion.

In one corner, Dr. Willie Horgan cried that he wasn't afraid of the S.A.P.S. but he was against advertising purely and simply because it was a waste of money, didn't do a damn bit of good.

In another corner, Dr. Weintraub insisted: Wasn't the Mayo clinic in Rochester the same kind of thing they wanted to build? And hadn't the Mayos advertised all over the country, for years!

Curly Seabury, still with the smiling attitude of a friendly visiting critic, was telling Dr. Matthews: "You know you can't get away with advertising. It's one of the fundamental traditions of the profession. . . ."

"The hell with the fundamental traditions!" Matthews cried, standing up and trying to get the attention of the meeting again. "Once it was a fundamental tradition to ride around in a horse and buggy! Anyway, fellows, we're not talking about personal advertising but about institutional advertising. The Social Health Institute right here in town has been advertising for years—"

"Yah, and what about Arthur Niles!" Swaboda squawked. "He was kicked out of the S.A.P.S. for only sponsoring the Social Health."

"It didn't hurt him any, did it?" Kahan snapped. "If that Gold Coast crowd want to be jackasses, okay by me!"

"Well, if you want this to be another g.u.[1] clinic!" Dr. Ryce sneered.

"Nothing of the sort! nothing of the sort!" Orr jumped in. "The Social Health is established and doing a swell job in its field. Now we are going after a bigger idea . . ."

"Anyway, we can't go by the experiences of the Social Health Institute," Dr. Ryce insisted. A person with a venereal disease was not an individual problem but a community problem, he pointed out. Therefore the medical profession and society in general welcomed every effort to control venereal disease. But general disease was related to individuals, not to society. . . .

"That's precisely the question. Why doesn't the health of each individual affect all of society?" Matthews glowed with an impatient idealism.

At this moment Dr. Orr slapped his palm twice against the table-top, and brought the meeting to order.

"Fellows, we're never going to get anywhere with these debates on ideals and ethics. I take it for granted we wouldn't be here if we didn't all have something of the idealist in our make-up. But we've got some practical matters to take up here. Now the question of advertising came up. Well, we're going to have to advertise, in one way or another, and you might as well make up your mind to it that we're going to have to battle the S.A.P.S. anyway, so if you want to keep out of the fight—okay. Nobody has signed anything. If your attitude on the question of advertising lets you out, you're free to leave, and no hard feelings." He didn't wait for anybody to leave, but plunged ahead. "On the practical side, we have to figure out, how are we going to get this thing started? How is it going to operate? How much are we going to make?"

There was a stir of interest. "Now some of us don't have to go into this. Some of us are making a living." He got a laugh. "But even those of us who have a practice can never be free from worrying how long we're going to keep it, so why not have a system that gives us some security? I maintain the healthiest attitude to take is that we're in this to make medicine pay."

A couple of the men left. The rest seemed to be warming again into a homogeneous circle. Swaboda, still in his hat and coat, guardedly kept Mitch between himself and Rudy.

Orr had definite plans. First, the whole apparatus had to be adjusted to produce a certain minimum salary for the staff.

"I've put it at fifty dollars a week, minimum, at the start," Dr. Orr stated. "This entire scheme is not worth while if we can't make at least that much. As we get going, of course we can raise it to seventy-five and I think a hundred would be about right."

Again, the chairs scraped. There were quips all around the room as they compared this prospect to what they were earning.

"Is that fifty a week, every week?"

---

[1] "g.u." = "genitourinary".

And no expenses! Rents, gasoline, even such minor nuisances as gowns, applicators, linens, would be taken care of outside the salary.

Rudy figured he was averaging thirty-five, forty a week, but he must be doing better than most of the boys.

"Suppose each doctor puts in, say, six hours a day," Orr had it figured out. An average treatment took fifteen, twenty minutes—ample time for most things. No hurrying, no rushing. That meant a doctor could easily handle twenty a day; at a dollar a visit, the doctor would be bringing in at least twenty dollars a day!

The actual figures, showing them how easily the money could accumulate, stimulated a quicker, warmer discussion.

"Why, we could have plenty of lab assistants and give everybody blood and urine tests; we could give them lots more than we can on our own," Dr. Swaboda suddenly defended the plan.

"What about hospitalization?"

Dr. Orr had looked into that, too. His plan was that they hook up with some small hospital, which would take care of all their patients at low rates. "We could probably give a complete maternity service, with hospitalization, for about fifty dollars," he said.

"How?" Swaboda asked, startled.

"Mass production!" Dr. Ryce laughed. "Mussolini would go for that!"

One after the other, the men were throwing in suggestions, reminders, and with each comment, it seemed to strike them as a group that here was a new advantage to the idea: they could have an X-ray lab right in the plant, and give the stuff to the patients at practically cost price; their patients wouldn't have to stint on electrocardiograms, basals; they could have technicians around to do all the routine work. . . .

And as they thought of these things, and added each detail to the plans, the thing began to look so good, not only for the doctors, but so good in itself, so useful, that a kind of happiness was felt in the group. They were exciting each other more and more, Rudy thought, feeling within himself that strange keen pleasure that was so rare, an exquisite brotherly feeling, knowing these were all good men, that they really wanted to do their work well, that they were keen to have all the equipment, everything right, to do the best kind of work, that they would get their highest pleasure out of running an A No. 1 clinic, and really taking fine care of a lot of patients, at using all their ability in work. Talking, throwing in ideas like the others, Rudy was beautifully warmed, as a man can be so few times in his life, by the belief, the certainty, that people were good, that if they were only given the means to identify their own with the cause of humanity, they would always choose to do that which was for the general happiness of the human race.

Objections were flung up, too. Some of the men screamed at the idea of including a dental clinic, others argued hotly that dentistry was really a part of medicine; gradually the affirmative was winning, the criticism came more in the nature of shaping the plan, than of opposition.

Dr. Orr outlined the scheme of operation: "Now, what do we need to get started? I figure, about fifty thousand dollars. We want to start this thing right. . . ."

He himself was ready to raise half of the initial capital. He expected they would be able to raise the rest. They would form a corporation, which would own the equipment, lease offices, etc. . . . Then the staff of doctors would form another company, which would operate the clinic.

He certainly had thought of everything.

All they had to do was jump off!

Before they left, Dr. Matthews had a word, on the side, with Rudy. "I think we're really going to get going this time. Looks like it, huh?" He was eager, excited, yet trying to keep a scientific calm, and for the first time Rudy felt they were talking on exactly the same plane, on a basis of equality, as partners. Certainly Matt was not the sort of person ever to high-hat anyone, but Rudy's feeling of awe toward him, and maybe a sort of respect for Matthews's *goyishness* and American forefathers, had persisted until now.

"What about your friend?" Matthews asked. "We need a good allergist!"

Oddly, the idea of Mitch Wilner joining this kind of enterprise seemed completely wrong.

Rudy said: "I could speak to him, but I don't think he's exactly our type of man, for this."

He and Matthews exchanged understanding smiles.

"What do you want to get mixed up with Orr for?" Mitch said, as they were on the way home. "That guy is just a politician."

Actually, Rudy was figuring whether he could raise five hundred dollars, to put into the venture. "He's okay," he defended Orr. "We need a man like him to get this thing going. You saw the way he had it all worked out. Why, Matthews has been talking about it for a year, but it takes a man with a business mind, an administrator, to put the thing into motion."

"And guys like Gans!" Mitch sneered.

"Who said he was in?" Rudy was impatient. "Somebody brought him along to the meeting, that's all!"

Mitch looked hopelessly at Rudy, giving him up as a lost cause. "It's all right to be idealistic," he said, "but you're risking your whole career."

Rudy was driving; he kept his eyes straight ahead. "Well, Mitch, as I see it, somebody has to take the first step, and if it's up to us, it's up to us."

"I wouldn't do a thing like that," Mitch said. "You can't tell what may happen. A couple of big shots like Orr may get control of the outfit and then where will you be? And even if it goes over, it means burying yourself.

So you'll make fifty bucks a week, so what? I wouldn't do it for a hundred a week."

"I know. It's not the kind of thing for a fellow like you," Rudy said. "Honest, Mitch, I wouldn't recommend a fellow like you going into this."

Why not? why not? he was thinking. What was so different about Mitch? Weren't they practicing in the same office? Oddly, his mind shot back to a moment ten, eleven years ago, when they had just been starting university. Mitch had come around to the drug store to consult with Rudy about schools. He remembered, how even Rush had seemed inadequate for Mitch. Everything had to be the best, for Mitch; and he had Sylvia too. But he worked hard, he deserved all he got.

"No, it wouldn't be the kind of thing for you," he repeated, and wondered what future he was expecting for Mitch Wilner.

"Look what you're risking," Mitch persisted. "At least you're making a living now, and if this thing fails and the S.A.P.S. has thrown you out in the meantime, where will you be?"

"I can keep my own practice and take care of it on the side, at the start," Rudy said. Here he was doubling up on jobs again, as usual. "And what can the S.A.P.S. do to me?" He had a green light, but he slowed down anyway at intersections. "And with top-notch men like Matthews coming into this, what can they kick about? As I see it, this kind of group practice is the coming thing."

"Well, maybe, for the run of practitioners," Mitch said, with unconscious disdain. And Rudy realized that their relationship had changed, too. Rationalize as he might, he now felt inferior to Mitch.

And why? Because he subordinated science to being human, to making a decent living, to curing people's sickness, however little?

Wasn't it something to be alive to human needs, to be daring enough to force these rotten times to yield a decent living, to find new ways to adapt their profession to circumstance? If a man like Matthews could devote himself to this end of medicine, wasn't it the most important aspect of medicine today?

In the mornings, Alvin allowed himself a kind of melancholy pleasure. During the entire run along the outer drive, from Fifty-First to the turn by the new Field Museum, his mind played at random upon the subject of himself. Driving required just enough attention to occupy the superficial brain, and left the mind to make random tracks, like the abstract scribbling his hand made while he listened on a telephone.

The tiny Austin, symbolic of his view of himself as small, small potatoes, was carried along in the forty-mile-an-hour traffic; four abreast, the cars hummed down the speedway, and so even was the traffic that it seemed they were carried on a moving street. There was something fantastic and laughable in the float of automobiles, each bearing a man or two toward the Loop. Alvin decided it was because there were no houses, no people, along this drive; removed from the city, it was in itself an abstract presentation of the idea: the machine age. Men carried in cars four abreast, to the maw of the city.

There was a turn, just beyond Fiftieth Street, where the Loop sprang into view, a cluster of skyscrapers rearing up from the lake, like the famed view of the skyscrapers on lower Manhattan. Every morning, as the car made the turn and the range of buildings stood in view, it was as though the contact between himself and reality was renewed. It made him feel that there was beauty that men made in spite of themselves, in their haphazard blundering and groping, and that even his own confused and disordered life might, if he could ever obtain the proper perspective, stand up as a designed and integrated range of towers.

The pleasure of the view was sweet and private. Days the buildings glittered blindingly, days he could count every southern window in the Loop, days the towers faded away in mist, and one strange time, when a pall of I.C. smoke cut off the lower part of the view, Alvin saw the nest of pinnacles and spires airily afloat upon a cumulus cloud.

It was a daily renewal of himself, and a view he would not confide to anyone. He knew Eunice would have loved it, loved to share it with him, yet he jealously kept it from her. Once or twice he thought: Joe Freedman would appreciate this.

Passing the grounds where the World's Fair was to be, he noticed that some progress had been made upon the steel framework of a few buildings. Maybe they would get going on the Fair after all, in spite of the depression, though there was only about a year left to prepare, and the ground looked desolate, like a job given up for hopeless.

If everything was going to be modernistic, there was a good chance they would use modern furniture, and maybe he could get rid of some of those chromium-pipe chairs that the old man had stored in the warehouse. It would be a vindication, to sell them after all; he had just been five years ahead of his time.

Here was the business invading his mind again; just a business man. He fixed his mind on world trends, a trick he had been cultivating lately to get outside of his self. . . . What if there was a war with Japan? Would it be the final world conflict? It might break at any moment, with the disorder at Shanghai. If it happened, would he be brave enough to go and join the Russians?

Then who would run the factory? Oh, it was an ironic turn that had revealed him, the eccentric, the arty wastrel, as the responsible, reliable, conservative member of the family, the good son upon whom all now depended, while that steady old business man, his father, was acting like a lunatic.

Sometimes Alvin thought his father had secretly gone across the line to actual madness, knew himself to be insane, but still managed to present the exterior of a normal, depression-worried manufacturer.

For the Old Fox had lost his sense of values. One day he would rush out and buy the latest automatic self-feeding and self-operating lathe, in a crazy effort to save on labor cost, although there was nothing for the lathe to feed itself upon; then he would prowl around the factory, shutting off wasted lights. Wherever he went, he left a swath of darkness behind him; the hallways were dark; every few minutes the Old Fox would go into the men's room and snap off the light. "He's probably dying to do it in the ladies' room, only he hasn't got quite that crazy yet," Alvin jested.

They were actually sending a warship to Shanghai. This wasn't the old Hearst war scare. But would the U.S. and England actually help Russia fight Japan? . . . This was a sort of game that you played; when your own life was dead, you lived vicariously in the world's life, in its conflicts. Your own life wasn't worth resisting. You didn't even try to break away from your wife any more; the preliminaries with a new woman, any woman, weren't worth the effort. You admitted there were certain fulfillments you would never have. You realized you were one of those damned Jews with a creative urge toward life, and no specific talent, so the best thing was to lie low, submerge, live at a small level, so your urge would not be excited. Be a good boy, run the factory. And watch the world.

The Old Fox's memory was going, too. It had always been his pride that he was a walking filing system. He was a census bureau of the folding chair population of the United States. If questioned, he could remember the size of any order he had received in the last twenty years, and sometimes even the date of shipment. It had been his game to call out these figures, and then have Mrs. Gessler, his office girl, go to the files and check them. But now he had lapses when he couldn't remember what he had done ten minutes ago.

The most touching thing was that, at times, he realized his weakness. When costs were to be computed, he would come into Alvin's little office, and stand beside his desk, his hands full of catalogues and price lists. "My head is full of worries, I cannot concentrate, here, Alvin, do me a favor." Or when the rare buyer came to the factory, even though it was someone he had dealt with for years, the Old Fox would lead him to Alvin and, dropping his arm on his son's shoulder, would say: "You see, it's fine to have a son in the business. Me, maybe, you can chew down, you old *ganef*, but my son is of the new-style business men, no rebates!" He would chuckle, his healthy underchins wobbling a little, and yet to Alvin there was something of terror in this relinquishment, for his father was not old. His eyes would be opaque, you couldn't see into them.

A business that has been running for twenty years doesn't stop all at once; a few orders, even a few payments, still leaked in. But no new hotels, no new restaurants, no new funeral parlors were opening, nobody wanted chairs. Everybody said no.

Sometimes it occurred to Alvin on these morning rides that the trouble with the world was that it had become negative by habit. Men had forgotten how to say yes. Hour after hour, day after day, over the phone, and through letters, business men went through their formula of queries, and ended saying no. He was doing the same thing. If the phone rang, he had a no on his tongue. If a salesman entered, his no was ready. Suppose, suddenly, by decree, everybody took to saying yes. Suppose the world turned affirmative! The skyscrapers, the railroad tracks and trains, the huge electric signs that men had created, all shouted yes to man's powers, and yet here he was discouraged, hopeless, negative, a no-sayer.

Overnight, if people began to say yes, factories would go into production, each would create a demand for the goods of the other, men would be hired, things would be bought. . . .

I'll be making speeches at the Rotary Club next, Alvin checked himself. They'll call me America's Yes Man!

Once there had been over a hundred men working at the factory, but now there were less than fifty, and among them Alvin had to stagger days and half days, to spread out employment. And in spite of the large sign, No Help Wanted, that he had hung on the factory entrance, people trickled in asking for jobs, and everyone they dealt with in business, and fellows he hadn't heard from in years, but had known in college, called up to find out whether he might need a stenographer, a salesman, a night watchman, a truck driver, called up for themselves, for friends, sent friends with letters. And you could tell everybody expected no for an answer, but the ritual had to be performed: hello, glad to see you, sorry, no.

Meanwhile, the relatives had to be supported: the old man's brothers, who had so long been used to their stipend from their rich brother who owned a factory, and certain other onhangers, here an aunt, there a cousin, who had attached themselves to the ship. The old man had wanted Alvin to draw sixty a week. "Take, take, while there's anything left, we might as well live, you earn it, it's only fair," but Alvin experienced a sense of guilt at taking more than the barest minimum. Every time he had to let another of the Czech carpenters go, Alvin felt as though he himself were taking that man's bread. He knew it was absurd, and yet he saw himself guiltily as one who didn't produce, as a paper-juggler, a member of the ruling class that had stupidly brought the world to this state of hunger.

He was drawing a nominal thirty-five a week, although he knew that even in these times they couldn't get someone to do his job for less than fifty.

This is the humility, the self-abasement I got from that shot of mysticism, of Christianity, in Paris, he analyzed himself. To eat simply, to live frugally, to be blameless, had become a fetish with him, as though he were expiating the sins of mankind.

Jesus Christ complex, he knew.

But in this last year he was doing a lot of serious, heavy reading, living to himself, assuring himself he needed nobody, few friends, only books and a few fine Bach records.

He was reading the *Decline of the West* and Karl Marx and Gestalt psychology. It was all very tedious stuff. But it was authority.

And as he sped over the ramp, and took Roosevelt Road across the wasteland of tracks and the river, through the district of warehouses and shanties, to the factory, his mind would turn to business again. It seemed to Alvin that, false modesty aside, he could admit his mind was far superior to that of most business men; they were cunning, shrewd, and they knew their fields, but they lacked imagination. Surely he could think of something, ferret out some channels of business unfound by others, and sneak his little factory out of the general bog.

In the factory, he liked the smell of sawdust in his nostrils, the acrid odor of the paintroom, the rhythm of wooden and metal noises. The depression, he liked to think, has brought the intellectual into contact with reality. The running of the world had been left to business men and politicians, while the keen minds went into universities, sciences, arts. Economists had worked in the abstract. But the depression had given tremendous publicity to the mechanics of the world, and forced the intellectuals into a field where they could be of use.

One idea Alvin had was to follow the real estate news of leases on stores and offices; and on a few of these leads, lately, he had been able to sell some of the modernistic stuff that was in the warehouse. The sale of those pieces, even if the sum was insignificant, was always a personal victory. When he read of two floors leased to the Medical Alliance, he had a hunch, and instead of sending the salesman, went to see them himself.

The modern note was what they wanted, Dr. Orr agreed, and ordered chairs for their reception room and waiting rooms.

Alvin came down personally to see the pieces installed, and ran into Rudy Stone.

They greeted each other, well, well, well, while Alvin wondered at the prosaic-minded fellow he had known joining an experiment of this kind. Maybe he had underestimated Rudy, and the ordinary guys in that old crowd. They were still the foundation of society, out of them still came adaptability.

Aline had come down to inspect the spiffy modern furniture, and now she descended upon Alvin. "Well, if it isn't the Duke! Where have you been keeping yourself all these years! You're a swell one!" She wore one of the latest cockleshell hats, ridiculous over her large, fleshening face.

"Honey, I hope you made him give a special price," she half kidded. "Of course I think the modernistic is the only thing for an office, but I don't think it's appropriate for the home!"

She made Alvin promise to bring out Eunice: "You're still married to that—to the same one, aren't you?" She cocked her eye at him.

"Oh, yes, strange as it may seem," Alvin said.

"Oh, I didn't mean—" She was really embarrassed. "Any children?"

"Nope," said Alvin. "None that I know of."

"What's the matter, doesn't your wife want any?" Aline asked. Then she saw she had put her foot in it. "Well, you must come over some time. Why not be friendly?"

Aline liked to have people around, to be friendly, and now her girl chum Rose was her big problem. She had tried every man in her own set, and where to snare and snag new men was a question. But Aline would never give up, until Rose, like the rest of the girls, was married.

And on this occasion, because the man was a little—you know—Aline was wondering whether just to have the man and Rose come over, or to have them meet in a group of people.

"What do you think, Rudy?" she worried.

Even while sitting in the beauty shop with a pot over her head, Rose heard nothing but talk about the kidnaping; one woman had a child that age, and some had heard the kidnaped child was deformed, and hinted that the father himself had made away with it, and the beauty operator told a tale of a jilted old flame of Lindy's, now getting her revenge. . . .

The horror accumulated in Rose. She thought of all her girl friends who had babies about that age; Aline, and Celia Moscowitz, and Ora Abramson—as Sorka now called herself. She thought of how, in her youth, Lindy had been her hero. And it was just this horrible thing that completed the cumulative rottenness of the world.

The depression, and her father reducing his store to half-size, and seeing kids come hungry to school, and now even the teachers' fund for lunches was gone, and being unpaid for so long, everything together made her feel like she was going to have a nervous breakdown. How could one hope for anything in such a rotten world? How could she go on hoping for romance and happiness? Fat chance that this man would be different from any of the others.

"Listen, dearie, you ought to have your hair molded. It's the latest thing, very artistic," the operator said, and because a girl couldn't afford to pass up even the smallest chance, Rose consented. As the woman began long preparations with steam and towels around her head, Rose tried to figure up how many hundreds, thousands of dollars had gone into dates like this, with her sitting in beauty shops, and fellows buying tickets and getting suits pressed and paying checks in cabarets, ten years of dates, always the same pretending, and always nothing in the end.

When her younger sister had married she should have known she was an old maid. Why didn't she give up, and take it easy?

Rose got off the bus a block too soon, and walked the rest of the way, to bring the blood up to her cheeks. As she came into the hallway, she peeked into the living room. Evidently the prospect hadn't yet arrived. Rudy was sitting there in serious conversation with a pudgy, gray-headed man.

Aline swept Rose toward the bedroom, taking her coat.

"Kid! Your hair looks marvelous! Well, how do you like him?"

Rose stared at Aline, bewildered. Then she knew. That old man talking to Rudy.

"Rose! He's a big-shot gland specialist and even in these times his income last year was over ten thousand . . . Oh, he isn't as old as he looks!" Aline chirped, herding Rose into the hallway. "He's so kind-hearted, and, kid, I know he's dying to get married, he loves children . . ."

They entered the living room. The visitor arose. Of course he was short, too.

Rose managed to put on a smile.

"Dr. Hyman, I want you to meet a friend of ours . . ."

"Please to meet you." He spoke with a trace of Yiddish accent, like her father.

She excused herself, and went to the bathroom, and cried.

But when Aline found her, she had recovered her poise, her famous humor.

"Kid, it's no use," Rose said, controlled, cheerful. "I might as well buy a dog."

Aline stared at her. Sometimes she didn't quite get Rose's remarks, but anyway she was glad she had had it on a Sunday so more people would be there.

She was going to be just natural with Alvin and his wife. For in spite of all his big ambitions, and living in Paris, and his gentile wife, how had he ended up? Helping out in his father's factory, like Mort Abramson or anyone else. At that, Mort was probably a lot more successful.

Naomi was at the window. "Baby, baby," she announced, and Aline saw Mort and Ora parading up the sidewalk with their carriage.

"Isn't she smart!" Aline demanded. "Naomi recognized them!"

Alvin drove up just then, and as she saw him crawl out of that ridiculous little car, Aline remembered that long ago he had gone with Ora. And instantly she speculated whether something, you know, interesting might not happen through their meeting again.

Alvin's wife was dressed in a blue ensemble, really very tasty except her hat was out of style.

Meeting this way on the street, there were gay greetings, attention being centered on the sumptuous baby carriage.

It was glossy black, with an adjustable hood that had windows and blinds. It had rubber tires almost as thick as on a car, and wonderful springs, and four-wheel brakes, and compartments for didies, and the kid's initials emblazoned on its side in a coat of arms!

"Free wheeling! Floating power!" Mort kiddingly extolled the virtues of the carriage. "Wanta trade for that perambulator you got there?" he offered, laughing at Alvin's Austin.

"Hello, Alvin, don't you recognize your old friends?" a cool voice said. Sylvia was bending over the carriage, pulling Ora's baby out of the swathings of silk and woolly woolly blankets, and as she straightened, he anticipated that she might look like a young mother, but she was still a girl, virginal, handling someone else's baby.

"Where's your husband?" Aline demanded of Sylvia.

"Oh, my husband," Sylvia lightly disparaged. "I hardly ever see him."

"Don't tell me he's got a call."

"No such luck. He's gone over to the office to do some lab work."

"Isn't the whole week enough for him?" Aline scolded. "You haven't got him trained right."

"Oh, he works so hard!" Sylvia said a little desperately. "Monday night it's the medical society, and Tuesday it's the Society of Allergists, and every other night he keeps office hours. . . ."

"What does it get him?" Mort declared flatly.

"Well, it's his work, and I won't interfere," Sylvia insisted. And added: "He's coming over later."

"What you need is some lessons in how to keep hubby at home," Ora insinuated, eying Eunice all the while.

They had changed so little. Mort still had an unlined, youthful face, though the eyes seemed to be a little deeper, giving the nose more prominence, and on the whole making him look more distinctly Jewish. Ora was noticeably thicker in the waist, more *zaftig* than ever, but you would hardly have expected she had had a child.

But why shouldn't the young mothers of this generation keep their figures? Ora always contended. Look how many movie stars had had children, and people didn't even know that they were mothers! Why, even Marlene Dietrich had a kid.

Only women of the ignorant foreign classes let themselves go once they got married, they had too many kids. Women who insisted on having the best care hardly even showed they were mothers, except for the natural maturity of their shapes, which was supposed to make women more attractive, anyway.

They started talking about the Lindbergh kidnaping[2].

---

[2] The 20-month-old son of Charles Lindbergh was abducted from the family home in New Jersey on March 1, 1932, and a ransom note was found. The search for the child and his kidnaper was an ongoing major news story as events unfolded.

"No one can really understand how horrible it is, except a mother!" Ora exclaimed theatrically, to Eunice, yet including the company. "My boy is about the same age, and believe me, my heart is still frozen with fear!"

"I haven't let my kids out of my sight since it happened," Aline affirmed. "I remember when Lindy landed in Paris. Gosh, what excitement! You remember, Celia Moscowitz and Lou Margolis were married at the Drake practically that same night and everybody was there! Well, it just goes to show what you get for being famous."

"And I understand she is in such a delicate condition," Ora said, "according to Walter Winchell."

"You know what those Hitlerites are saying in Germany about the kidnaping?" Mort offered. "They say some Jew stole the baby, for a ritual murder. Because it came so close to Passover."

"What those idiots won't invent!" Sylvia said.

"Oh, what's the diff? Nobody believes such things nowadays," yawned Aline.

Dr. Hyman shook his head. "It is fantastic, what people will believe. If Hitler should ever come into power, God help the German Jews."

"He won't come into power," Mort stated flatly. "He missed his best chance in their last election. That was his high point. From now on his movement is on the wane."

"I don't know," Alvin said. "What other alternative is there in Germany?"

"Oh, it's just a lot of bunk. They'd never do anything," Aline remarked, contentedly.

"If a Jew is caught with a German girl, those Nazis beat him up," Mort said.

They all smiled at Eunice to assure her they had completely forgotten she was a gentile.

"I heard that Al Capone was behind the Lindbergh kidnaping." Rose relieved the strain. "I heard he promised to return the child if they drop the charges against him."

"Fantastic! Fantastic!" Dr. Hyman said.

"Oh, they blame everything on Al Capone!" Sylvia agreed.

"That's not so crazy," Mort pointed out. "Capone is in a spot. They've really got him this time, with that income tax charge. You can't monkey with the federal government. He's just desperate enough to pull something like that."

"They'll never keep him in jail," Aline said. "He has too much pull."

"No, times have changed," Mort declared. "Capone is through and he knows it."

Alvin was remembering—when was it, seven, eight years ago?—that the bunch of them had lain around Clarendon Beach, discussing the Leopold Loeb case. And just as that case had perfectly fitted its time, so the

Lindbergh case appeared to him as the final gesture of that cruel jungle era of America, when every man snatched what he could, a railroad, a bank, or a child to hold for ransom. And that it had happened to Lindbergh, the enchanted Boy Scout of the epoch, was one of those beautiful symbolisms that cannot be invented except by reality.

"I think the baby is dead, murdered," Alvin declared. There was a shudder. "The kidnaper just wanted to take revenge on the world."

"How about some bridge?" Aline suggested. "We can have two tables."

There was a great shuffling around. Chairs had to be brought from the dining room.

"I saw the swellest bridge outfits at Field's," Ora reported, eying Aline's banged old folding table. "Chairs and table to match, in red leather, with chromium edges!"

"Aren't you putting out any bridge sets? That's what you ought to do, clean up on the bridge craze," Mort advised Alvin. "Get the Culbertsons to endorse them. Fox chairs for foxy bridge!"

"Yah, we could have an endurance tournament," Alvin attempted to kid the idea, resenting its coming from Mort, knowing that he really ought to go after the bridge craze business.

The cards were made in Japan, and Dr. Hyman started talking of the militaristic Japanese.

"A war might not be such a bad thing," Mort said. "It would end the depression, anyway."

"How can you talk like that?" Sylvia cried.

"Well, I mean between Russia and Japan, or England and Japan, or anybody."

"We would have to get into it," Alvin said.

"Not me, I got a kid," Mort said.

"Daddy, what are you going to do in the next war?" Ora paraphrased, brightly, giving Alvin the eye.

"Listen, the depression can't be so bad," Aline said. "Why, if there are so many people out of jobs, is it so hard to get a maid?"

"That's right!" Ora concurred. "I had two maids quit last month, and I'm not hard to please. You can't help thinking they just don't want to work."

"I'm paying four dollars, with room and board," Aline said. "Believe me, you'd think some people would be glad to work just for room and board, in these times. Still I can't get anybody."

"Is that all maids get?" Eunice inquired.

The girls stared at her, realizing she had no maid.

"The last maid we had, Mort sent me from the shop," Ora said. "She was only making eight dollars a week there, so it was really a worthwhile change for her."

"Eight dollars?" Sylvia said, surprised. She had thought the girls made at least ten, twelve dollars.

"We had to give them a ten percent cut," said Mort. "Everybody else did."

"Well, at least you pay them," Rose put in. "We got two cuts, one ten percent, and one fifteen, and we don't even get paid."

"They paid the police though, your father got some money, didn't he?" Mort asked Ora.

"Well, they'd better pay the police!" Alvin said ominously.

Just then a baby was heard, crying. "That's Jo-Jo," Aline said. "Let him yell himself out, and he'll stop."

All pretended not to be disturbed. Mort fan-shuffled the cards, with the expertness of a poker player who, when wangled into bridge, has only the card shuffling as an opportunity for the display of his skill.

Sylvia was dummy. She got up.

"Don't you dare go in there!" Aline admonished. "You'll ruin all my training!"

Between hands, Aline went to fix some refreshments. Stopping in the bedroom to look at the baby, she found Sylvia there. They were drawn together, feeling tender toward each other, as though they understood and agreed now on the similar purpose of their lives.

"Listen, kid, Mitch was talking to me about Rudy's clinic," Sylvia confided. "Mitch says that at all the hospitals they're against it, they're going to refuse patients from any of those doctors."

Aline refused to worry. "Well, I know," she said, "but Rudy is so crazy about Dr. Matthews he'll do anything he says. And it got started fine, you know it looks like it's going over."

"Mitch says they're even kidding him, about having an office together with Rudy."

Aline gave her a quick, measuring glance.

"I just told you so you'll know what's going on," Sylvia said simply. "Of course Mitch will stick by Rudy."

"Well, I'll tell you," Aline said loyally. "I was against it a little at first but I believe in letting Rudy make his own decisions. And as long as he keeps his own practice on the side, we're safe."

The babies looked so sweet, all in a row asleep. Naomi opened her eyes and reached in a warm darling way for her mother.

"Gee, I envy you," Sylvia said. "If anybody kidnaps her, you'll know it's me!"

"Well, what are you waiting for?" Aline hinted.

"Oh, we can't yet. He's so independent. He wants to wait until he's sure he's making enough." She lifted the child, loving to feel the limp weight of the drowsy body against her shoulders.

"Alvin has changed," Sylvia said. "Don't you think?"

"Oh he's still such a show-off," Aline said. "I wonder how they get along together? I heard they were separated when they were in Paris, and she was living with another fellow."

"I never thought they'd last this long," said Sylvia. "Alvin is so erratic. I guess he probably realized he needs her."

"She's all right, for a *shikseh*, though a little snobbish," Aline said.

Rudy and Dr. Hyman had got off into a medical discussion, and Alvin found himself with Mort.

"Well, how's business?" Mort asked intimately, as if now for a while they could get down to the real facts of life, man to man.

"Pretty lousy," Alvin said.

"Say, you could do a lot of business at the Fair, with that modernistic line of yours," Mort advised.

Alvin warmed. "You know, I introduced that modern stuff five years ago, but it's just beginning to take."

"That Fair is going to bring a lot of business to Chicago, it's going to be the turning point in the depression," Mort stated. "It'll put a lot of men to work," he added, showing that deep down he really worried about all the suffering people.

"I wanted to put out a modern line especially for the Fair; but I can't get my father to see it," Alvin said.

Mort smoked. "That's the way it is, when you go into your father's business, everybody thinks you have a snap, but it's only something else to contend with."

And suddenly Alvin felt caught; Mort had drawn him in. To Mort, to the rest of them, this was his final place in the scheme of things: a fellow that had been taken into his father's business, because he'd never have amounted to anything on his own. All his cleverness, all his originality, was nothing beside the main point. Though he might have radical opinions, talk was harmless. See, they would have him in their homes, be friends, for by the conditions of his life he was one of them, and when it came to action he would have to do as they did.

And the bewildering thing was that Mort didn't see himself as defeated though he considered Alvin defeated. Life was perfectly okay with Mort.

Rose said she had learned a new game at some friends of Celia's: Murder.

"Oh, good!" Ora cried gayly, winking to Alvin. "I want to kill my husband!"

As they left, Mort said to Alvin: "Why don't you trade in that cheese-box? I trade my Chevvy in every year, it works out cheaper that way when you figure depreciation. And you always have a new car."

There was one apple seller who wrote signs on his boxes. Sometimes he even wrote poems, printing out the words in colored chalk. Once he put up his prices like a stock market report:

APPLES   High—5¢   Low—5¢   Closing—5¢

Another time he printed:

Roses are red
Violets are blue
I am broke
And how are you?

Lou Margolis made it a point to patronize this apple seller, stopping for an apple every day as he went into the building.

"It just goes to show," Lou said to Celia, "if a fellow has initiative, he stands out. Even that guy that sells apples. I bet he sells twice as many as the other fellows, just by using a little initiative and making those signs. You watch, before he's through he'll have a whole string of apple stands," he predicted.

Assuming the air of a well-fixed fellow, Lou Green started a conversation.

"How ya makin' out?"

"Not so good, not so good today. Getting too warm, people figure they don't have to help you out. Gets warmer, I'm gonna push off."

"How much you make on a box?"

"Figuring carfare and everything, about a buck twenty-five."

"Sell a box today?"

"Na. 'Sa racket," he complained. "They had a lot of apples to get rid of. They didn't give 'em to us, did they? Made us stand around all winter, freeze our balls, to push off their goddam apples."

"Yah," Lou said, and walked off. Anyway there was no percentage in selling apples.

It was crazy of him to think of such a thing. Even these fellows were hitting the road.

If he had some money, now spring was coming, he could start a miniature golf links. You could rent a lot for a few dollars a month.

Nah.

He meandered into the city hall, stood around the corridor, maybe he would see somebody he knew.

He figured whether he should stall around until his girl got through working. She was the switchboard girl in a big office in the London Guarantee Building. Then if he rode home on the El with her, he'd have to pay her fare. A quarter was all he had.

So he stood around remembering how nice it had been when he was convalescing from the flu, and Phyllis didn't have a job then, she lived downstairs and used to come up and sit by his bed and monkey around hours at a time. That was when he fell in love; she was so sweet even though she was dumb and believed he was a practicing lawyer.

If he met her tonight she'd want to see Greta Garbo in *As You Desire Me*; she had already hinted several times, so he had better steer clear.

After a while he went through a cigar store into a bookie's joint where he once in a while bet a buck; he stood there sharing the warm excitement.

Since Lou's recovery, the old sullen hatred had come back into the house. Old man Green was getting more and more irregular with house money; some weeks it was only five dollars. Mrs. Green took whatever he left, silently, and somehow provided food for the week. But on the week when he left nothing at all, there was an explosion in the Green household. The mother waited until Friday, when Estelle still dragged herself home for dinner.

"We got nothing," she said.

"What's the matter now?" Estelle inquired.

"What do you expect me to make, food out of my fingers? Now he doesn't bring anything home any more."

Lou and Estelle looked at their father. They realized he looked different: tired, meek, and his face was yellowish.

"What do you think I'm doing, taking vacations in Florida!" he defended himself to his children. "Times are tough. If I clear ten dollars a week it's a big week! I been to a doctor. I can't stand on my feet all day. I got neuralgia."

"Well, pa, ma can't run the house on nothing," Estelle mediated.

"I'm doing all I can! A man slaves all his life, he expects some help in his old age! You're working, you could come home and live, and help keep up the house," he complained.

"Why me! Why me all the time!" Estelle cried. Suddenly she turned on Lou. "Look at him! Sits around! I never saw such a useless idiot! He's the son in the family, but I should come home again and slave to support him! Mama's boy! Why don't you get some gumption! He has a girl friend, so if she wants him to take her to the movies she has to pay for the tickets. I know, she told me! Mygod, what a man!"

Lou rushed out of the room.

It was terrible, how they hated each other, there was nothing in the house but hatred, and yet there they were stuck together, a family.

He didn't even have the nerve to shove off empty; he told the old lady he had to have some money, don't ask me why; I've got to have it, I tell you. She gave him that hopeless look, as though she blamed her own fate to obey more than she blamed his asking, and shuffled to her bedroom. He heard a dresser drawer squeaking, and finally she returned with a knotted handkerchief, at which her fingers worked. *"Na"* she said. The bills were tightly wadded. A ten, a five, and three ones.

"Thanks, ma. I have to have it. I can't tell you, but it'll be all right."

She gave him that same hopeless look.

He had an old knapsack that he had used years ago on a camping trip with Lou Margolis and some of the boys. He put some shirts inside it. He figured he'd better not hitchhike as his knee was sort of bum; that operation hadn't quite fixed it, so he'd better ride the rods.

The train swung, the boxcars hanging onto each other as in a desperate game of snap-the-whip; Lou felt his shoulders bruised from the sides of the reefer. His hands were gritty, he was thirsty and throbbing with nausea. Every few minutes he put his fingers under his belt where he had sewn the money. He almost wanted it to be gone. What would he do when he was dead-broke and on his own? Might as well find out sooner as later.

"Hey, Chicago, got a smoke?"

He tried to make his voice strong. "Naw. I gave you my last."

They might be toughs, though you heard that the fellows on the road now were just ordinary guys out of luck, even college boys, and you heard lots of girls were in the boxcars and could be had, sometimes the fellows ganged up on them. Sometimes they were nice girls, too, just out of luck, and maybe he would meet such a one, a girl like Phyllis, that he would rescue from the gang, and have for himself.

"Where to, Chicago?"

"I'm hitting for the coast," he said. "Gonna get on a boat."

"Yah? You a sailor?"

"No."

"What's your racket?"

"I used to be a lawyer."

There was a laugh, raucous, yet tinged with respect.

Eighteen dollars. If he spent only fifty cents a day, he ought to get on a boat before it was gone. And passing through Hollywood, who could tell, maybe something would happen.

A form lurched toward him, his blanket was grabbed off.

"Hey! Gimme that back!"

"Possession is nine-tenths of the law, ain't it!" The tough howled at his own joke, and shuffled to the other end of the car with Lou's blanket.

The night winds went through Lou's clothes.

And finally, in San Francisco, he dragged along the waterfront, not knowing how to ask for what he wanted. In a coffee shop a guy told him: "You can't get no ship without papers, but if you wanna try, go up to the hall," and gave him an address.

A card game was going on; groups of men stood around; nobody paid any attention to him. Lou saw a wicket like a pay window. "Is this where I ask about getting on a ship?" he piped.

A fellow with a dead cigar in his mouth came leisurely around the partition, looked him over, and said wearily: "What you done till now?"

"I worked in a law office."

The fellow shrugged. "Well, you ain't a kid. Lots of kids come around here looking for the romance of the sea. I could take your ten bucks, fella, but it's a year before you get a ship, if ever."

"Well, I—"

"Nah. Figure you went to sea and came back, and start off from there," the union man said, and walked away.

Lou passed his days wandering around the city in a sort of delirium; he hadn't gotten over the two weeks on the road, the long stretches without food or water, the nights with his knees up against his chin, trying to keep warm, to sleep. His bones still felt all brittle and out of joint. His knee bothered him from so much walking. He developed a stiff-legged limp. He hung around the city hall because seeing the same kind of people, lawyers and runners and politicians with sidewise mouths, made him feel almost like he was back in Chicago. Vague lopsided plans clouded through his mind; he would practice law here, no one would ever bother to check up on him, he'd become a big shot in San Francisco and send checks home to the family.

One day he got a terrible yen for a Jewish corned beef sandwich on Jewish rye. He roamed the town, found a real Jewish delicatessen, and broke all his rules, spending forty cents, buying a quarter of a pound of corned beef, a rye bread, and a sour tomato, and gorging.

He had three bucks left, so he decided to try sleeping out. It got cold here at night, with a chill creeping fog that penetrated the bones. Around 2 a.m. he drifted into a restaurant and had coffee and sat around for an hour, and drifted out again, and limped around the streets for a long time, and sat against a doorjamb in an alleyway, and woke up and drifted around again, drifted down to the shore, and sat huddled against a wall while the pukey dawn came.

Lou went a day without food before he could panhandle.

Finally he shuffled alongside a man and murmured: "Say, mister, spare a dime?" And glubbed the word: "Coffee."

The man didn't break his stride, was gone. But at least he knew he could ask. When someone gave him a nickel, Lou wanted to explain all about himself, that he was a lawyer, not an ordinary tramp, but the fellow didn't wait to listen.

When Lou saw a policeman, he hustled away.

There was a wide sign, *Jesus Saves*, across the front of the mission, and just inside the door a little man with an oleomargarine smile held out his hand, saying: "Welcome, brother."

Lou wondered if going inside meant he was being converted. Maybe he should tell the guy he was Jewish.

As he seated himself on a backless bench, Lou, out of habit, twitched up his trouser-legs, which still showed faint creases.

Partly Lou felt as though he were just a curiosity seeker on South State Street. The preacher talked, and then at one point the bums all prodded each other, and began to hum and mumble:

> ". . . marching as to war . . .
> . . . Jeeeesus
> marching on before . . .
>
> . . . peeeple
> join our happy throng . . ."

And finally each got a bowl of soup and a hunk of bread.

"The Lord is your refuge. It is never too late to return to the Lord," the preacher said seriously, giving Lou a slip of paper with a number. A guy with the reddish scrubbed look that bums get when they stay clean led Lou to the army cot.

Afterwards Lou couldn't understand why he had lived through all those nights out in the open, only to get the pains during his first night on a bed. He awoke in pain in the middle of that night; it was like a sword being stuck through his chest, and then being slowly pulled back through the flesh, and out, and in again.

And with the torture of pain was a feverish terror, because he had no idea what time it was, whether near the beginning or end of night. He heard acutely, and it seemed to him that the noises in the room were like the groans of death. One man snored with protracted, catchy gasps, growing louder and louder until they broke, and Lou shuddered, waiting each time for the break, as for the peak of the stabbing pain in his own body.

Half rising, Lou swung his legs over the side of the cot, to run, flee— but the pain came again, and he fell back on the cot, squirming in agony.

At last the pains diminished, as though the sword had made its grooves; Lou lay inert. He noticed now that a light was burning in the doorway, and he saw the deep cleft faces of the sleepers. Their flesh fallen loose in their helpless, deathly sleep, their complete hopelessness exposed, they looked like cadavers on dissecting tables.

He had to call to himself: "Be a man! A man!" to keep himself from screaming.

Oh, he was sick, and alone, and away from home.

Then what if he died like this?

Oh, if he could live, he would be a different man, not a shitheel tagging after Lou Margolis; he would be some use in the world, have Phyllis be his wife, if he lived through this night he would pass the bar, conquer the depression, make a living for himself and his wife, raise kids. It would all be good.

A bell clanged, men crawled around pulling on clothes. He knew he was too sick to get up.

The mission man came through the room, with the same pressed smile like a mistake on his face. Lou felt his eyes closing.

From then on it was a whirl of thermometers, and people talking over him, and answering with name and address, and finally he was in a dump that smelled like County Hospital; it was pleurisy, from sleeping out, from his flu; the pains got worse; and he was being wheeled, he saw the ceiling moving over him, a yellow ceiling, then a dirty green ceiling along a corridor, then a white ceiling. "Breathe deep!" He breathed, each breath a rattle of knives in his chest. But he breathed wishing it would be all over, he had nothing to lose. And neither did the world.

"He's a good boy," he heard a nurse say.

A nurse was there. "Be careful, don't move around. There's a drain in your side."

A couple of days later they tilted him up, and he began to follow the talk in the ward. After a while a letter came with a money order for seventy-five dollars, to get him home. He could see the old lady digging out her last *knippel* from its hiding place.

He felt lighter altogether, relieved of the burden of himself. From now on he had a good excuse.

As Good As Gold

All their fathers had their money in real estate, and as real estate crashed, they scuttled for cover.

Mr. Freedman lost the fine new building of offices and stores, on Madison Street, in which his son-in-law Rudy Stone still had an office with Mitch Wilner. He had put twenty thousand dollars into the purchase, above sixty-five thousand in mortgages. The building went into receivership.

He had an apartment building, in which the family lived, which he had heavily mortgaged in order to buy the Madison Street office building, so now he lost the apartment building too.

He owned first mortgage gold bonds on a large apartment hotel, but when he tried to cash these, they proved worthless; the hotel was going into receivership.

"I don't understand!" Aline exclaimed. "When he owns a building he loses it to the mortgagors, and when he owns a mortgage he loses that too.

So who is getting everything? Where did all the money go? I thought gold bonds were supposed to be as good as gold."

Mort Abramson attempted the explanation. "The values have changed," he said.

"Huh?"

"They thought it was worth eighty-five thousand, but it's worth only about half that amount."

"Isn't it the same building?" Aline said naïvely.

"The rents are down," Mort said. "He was getting two hundred for the corner store and now he only gets a hundred and a quarter."

Sylvia put in: "But isn't a building valued according to how much it costs to put up? Plus the cost of the lot?"

Mort said: "If the rents bring in a profit on a hundred thousand, it's worth a hundred thousand. If they only pay interest on fifty thousand, it's worth fifty thousand."

"So if the rents go down, the value goes down," Sylvia concluded, like a schoolgirl.

Then they puzzled, what is a property *really* worth?

"There isn't any real value," Sylvia decided. "It's all imaginary. Is that why the crash came, Mort, because one month everybody accepted one set of values, and then they all decided maybe they were wrong?"

"Something like that," Mort said. "Now is a good time to buy real estate."

"It's too deep for me." Aline gave up. "All I know is my father lost all his money, it's lucky he still has his lousy business."

The Abramsons did not lose so much, because all their money was in their business; the only real estate they owned was small residential property.

But Rose Heller's father lost the building in which he had his furniture store, and it was rumored that they might actually have to live on Rose's earnings.

And the biggest losers were Moscowitz and Klein.

Mr. Klein was like a man whose house is caving in, and who pulls a pillar out of one side and tries to prop up the other side, then pulls both pillars away from there, trying to prop up the middle.

The building on Roosevelt Road, in which he lived, was going. The store for which Mrs. Kagen had once paid a hundred and fifty had been vacant for six months after she had moved out, and was now rented for seventy dollars to a chain grocery. He had a large bank mortgage on this property.

His North Side flats, where Lil and Sam once had lived, were bonded. He owned a row of two-story houses near Columbus Park, people had bought them on payments and now could not meet their payments.

His loan and mortgage business was on the rocks. The personal loans were practically a dead loss. There was a line of stores on Sheridan Road, on which he held a ten-thousand-dollar second mortgage, and the only way he could save it was to take over the first mortgage and the stores entirely.

So he spent his days juggling, and his nights juggling, figuring if he had better let the apartment house go, and try to hang onto the stores, or, God, what should he do? He borrowed on his life insurance, sold his dead wife's jewelry, but no use.

"I should have known," he kept saying, recalling that time he got caught in the crash of the Florida real estate boom. "This time I should have known when to get out. I could have cleaned up and got out."

And all the time, Moscowitz was on his neck.

For at the same time that real estate was collapsing, Insull stocks were collapsing. And Rube Moscowitz, wanting to save the stocks he had on margin, kept calling Klein, demanding money from that quarter of a million he had invested as Klein's silent partner.

What could he do? Klein cried: "Lil, don't answer."

He rushed out of the office, spent whole days running from one bank to another, from one tenant to another. "Give me ten dollars, five dollars, I'll take anything on account!"

He was out of luck.

From the whole mess of properties, loans, bonds, only one thing crazily remained. It was a cold-water flat building on Thirteenth Street, the one in the slums, where Sam Eisen had hated to collect rent. Once in some juggling of his assets he had put it in Lil's name, for convenience. And when he asked her now to sign it over to him, she said: "No."

Lil saw the way things were going. He would only lose this too. Why throw good money after bad?

Then one day Rube Moscowitz came in looking for her father. Moscowitz was like a mad bull.

"I don't care where he is! Get him! Get him! Don't sit there!" he roared, and she pretended to make telephone calls.

Finally he began to call her father names. A crook. A swindler, a louse, a two-bit Hebe, a double-crossing Shylock, he would have her father put in jail. "I got the goods on him! You tell him I got the goods on him! There's a law in this state! I can have him put in the penitentiary for usury! He knows where I am! You tell him I want to see him damn quick!"

He stormed out.

Lil sat, trembling. She wanted to call Sam. Oh, why wasn't Sam here, now they were in this mess?

At last her father returned. He looked thinner than ever, in his flat double-breasted suit. "Pa, you better see Moscowitz right away, he was here and—" Her lips trembled, she couldn't finish.

Mr. Klein came over and stroked his daughter's hair.

"One thing, I can show where everything went. Everything is on the level," he said, going.

Lil sat on pins and needles. She was afraid something would happen. Murder, suicide.

But sooner than she had expected, her father was back, with Rube Moscowitz himself. She saw her father pulling out documents, proving where the money was invested. Finally they called Lou Margolis.

Lou arrived very much at ease and cheerful. He said: "Hello, Lil! How are you!" as though they had last seen each other yesterday. She noticed his hair was combed across bald temples. The men came out into the larger office and she heard everything.

Lou said it wasn't especially her father's fault, real estate was collapsing everywhere.

"The best thing you can do," he finally advised, "is throw these buildings into receivership, and try and get yourself appointed receiver."

She had always known Lou was brilliant, and would have the right idea.

He explained that where they held first mortgages it would be a cinch to get receiverships and even on some of the second it might be managed. "We can take these cases to Judge Schaeffer. He's hearing a lot of receivership suits."

Judge Schaeffer! His partner's father.

So after all things weren't so bad. They would get something out of the wreck. Was she relieved!

Although it would take time. It would take months before money started coming in and things were pieced together again, and in the meantime her father had lost a fortune. She figured he had lost about a quarter of a million dollars of his own.

"It was spread out too thin," he said.

The kid knew what was going on. It made her laugh and cry the time they were starting to his regular Saturday afternoon movie, and he said: "Ma, we don't have to go."

"Why, Jackie, don't you want to go?"

"Oh, I can get along without it, if it costs too much."

She said: "He's so wise for his age. He understands so much."

They were living on the scraps of rent that Mr. Klein still managed to collect. Lil saw that her father was a little too old to start over, from the beginning. So she had her eyes open for something.

Lou Margolis had formed a company called the Aetna Receivers, which was Rube Moscowitz and her father, though Lou was the one that knew all about it as it was complicated legal work. He got those Sheridan Road stores into receivership, too.

In that building was Madam Marie's Dress Shoppe, and Madam Marie had not paid rent for several months. So Lil had an inspiration.

Madam Marie was evicted, but all of the fixtures in the place were attached, to apply to the rent. It was a most elegant shoppe, done in modern style with a silver-leaf interior and indirect lighting, and personal fitting rooms furnished like boudoirs. It made the Evelyn Shoppes look like Maxwell Street.

The Edgewater was only a block away. Lil decided she would specialize in elegant and daring things, lovely underthings and luxurious house pajamas, in a very expensive line, because people with money were the only ones that could afford to buy things and they bought only expensive things.

She needed some starting capital, so she went down to look over her apartment house on Thirteenth Street. Some of the families owed several months' rent.

The building was a wreck. The mailboxes were ripped out of the walls, and the hallway was so filthy she knew she would smell when she came out of the place. The lath showed where plaster had been kicked from the walls. It was so dark she nearly broke her ankle.

She knocked on a door, and an old woman appeared. When Lil identified herself, she had to listen to an endless tirade about leaky faucets and she had to look at the clogged toilet and finally the old woman told her she had been living there for twenty years but now if niggers were allowed in the block she would move. Nevertheless, Lil collected thirty dollars from the old lady. Her flat was clean, and smelled of home-baked bread and somehow made Lil remember her childhood and her mother, and living in a stove-heated flat like this.

In one back flat there was hardly a stick of furniture, actually they used packing boxes for chairs! And three flats of the twelve were vacant.

But Lil had collected seventy-five dollars, and promises of more. She dug up the janitor, an Italian who lived in the basement. In his kitchen was a double bed, and also a folding bed.

"Lady, how I'm gonna rent these here empty flats?" he demanded. "You got niggers, two houses in the block already got niggers. The white people don't move around here no more."

"Rent the empty flats to niggers then," she said.

"Me? Oh, no. Oh, no. I don't carry no garbage for no dirty niggers!" He drew himself up, dignified.

So she got rid of him, and let a Negro janitor have the basement apartment. And then one of the upstairs flats was rented to a Negro who paid twenty dollars, instead of fifteen. He had a steady job running an elevator in an apartment hotel, he had two kids, and those Negroes dressed better and kept the house cleaner than most of the whites in the building, she declared.

Once the Negro moved in, the whites stopped paying rent.

"Of all the nerve!" Lil cried. "Let them move out!" She would fill the house with Negroes and get twice as much out of it.

But it seemed that the whites could bear living with Negroes, as long as they had no rent to pay.

The worst ones were the Vespuccis, the Italian family that used boxes for furniture. They had even torn down a couple of closet doors, and burned the wood for heat! The man was a plasterer out of work, the woman did a little scrubbing but was sick most of the time. There were a couple of tough kids, about fourteen. They were getting food from the relief. And by now they owed Lil four months' rent.

"Please, don't put me to the added expense of throwing you out, do me a favor, move! I'll even pay for the express wagon!" she begged.

As if they had anything to put on an express wagon but the old iron stove. And where would they move?

So there was nothing to do but pay fifteen dollars for an eviction order, and hope the other tenants would take the hint.

Meanwhile Lil had bought some lovely things for the shoppe, and discovered where she could get beautiful hand-knitted dresses made to order for practically nothing, and she had changed the name to simply *Lillian's*. She got a mailing list of everyone living in the Edgewater Beach.

It was a thrill, sitting all one evening at her own desk in the shoppe that was ready to open, with big boy Jackie sitting opposite her, and the mailing list between them, and a great stack of the expensive linen-paper envelopes, like the kind used for the spiffiest formal wedding announcements. She hadn't even had such expensive envelopes for her own wedding.

She inspected Jackie's carefully rounded Palmer script, as he addressed envelopes. "Oh, Jackie! That's beautiful! Tell me when you're tired, darling."

Maybe Sam Eisen couldn't make a success as a lawyer, and Harry Perlin was a flop as a business man, and her own father had failed, but she would show the world!

Pie in the Sky

Sam's office-mates had gone, and he was sitting alone reading *Tobacco Road* when Ella Bodansky arrived. She slumped into the nearest chair, and edged off her slippers. Heaving a loud sigh of relief, she wiggled her toes.

"They've increased our case loads," she mentioned. "Orphan Annie gave me six new ones today. Looks like winter is coming."

Sam shut the book.

"Those damn fools!" she flared. "If we refused to carry any more cases, they'd have to put on more workers. But we've got a lot of nitwits that think they're in a mission or something. Sushul workers," she mimicked. "Hurry up, Sam, I'm starved."

"Well, put your shoes on."

"Where we gonna eat?"

"How about Childs'?"

She made a face. "There's something too damn virginal about Childs'. Let's go to Deutsch's."

In the elevator she regaled him with a story about one of her clients. "Sam, you'll die. You know that family I've been telling you about—we call the old lady Minnie the Moocher? Vespucci, their name is. She's got a couple of boys—and are they a riot! You don't have to tell them anything! They tore down the doors for firewood! So she's been getting eviction notices, and they're actually going to put her out on the street this time. So she keeps screaming: why don't the relief pay her rent? 'Go out and make a fuss, make them take care of you,' I told her. They can't get a cheaper place than the one she's in, they might as well keep her there."

"Where is it?"

"It's an old dump on Thirteenth Street, it's been filling up with Negroes lately. So she's getting chauvinistic and insists on being moved."

"Thirteenth?" Sam said with a premonition. "How far up have the Negroes come?"

"Oh, it's near Wood Street."

"I bet I know the building. A yellow brick, on the north side of the street?"

"Yah. But how—?"

"Nothing. I used to collect rent for a real estate agent around there," Sam said. Such coincidences were meaningless, except to show a fellow how slow his growth had been.

"So you know what Minnie the Moocher does? She hauls something out of her buzzoom, and the look on her face, I thought it might be some of the Lindbergh ransom money, but when she got it unfolded it was a leaflet for a demonstration."

Sam chuckled. "Yah?"

"Al Howard has been organizing the Unemployed Council around there. . . . So Minnie confides in me, real secret-like"—Ella stage-whispered—" 'My kid, he bring this home, lady. Is these them Bolsheviks?' "

They laughed together.

"So she was afraid if she got caught at a demonstration she would be taken off relief. I pumped her up a little," Ella confessed. Then remembering a detail, she laughed. "Oh, and, Sam, they had the entire streetcleaning department around the station today. If there is a stick or a pebble left in the whole neighborhood it would take a detective to find it! I never saw that street so clean!"

"Is that a fact?" Sam grinned, but with a touch of melancholy. "Looks like they're preparing a reception."

"Yah. I guess the I.L.D. better scare up some bail money," she said wryly.

"You better tell Minnie the Moocher to bring her own bricks," Sam kidded.

It was a day in the middle of October, and Harry Perlin took a walk. It was a random walk, and yet a number of unadmitted reasons made him go the way he went.

He was thinking: should he sell the car; and it was natural to walk, thinking this out. As if the car were already gone.

What use would it be to sell the old bus, the house was being foreclosed anyway, and a hundred bucks would make no difference.

He walked through Douglas Park, and on down toward the lower West Side, just to see what the old neighborhood was like. Some of those old buildings weren't half bad, even though stove-heated. He could probably get a flat for fifteen, twenty dollars. Good enough for him and the old lady, now that Vic was married to a meal ticket and off their shoulders.

And he was thinking: maybe, instead of moving, they should break up the household altogether, his mother could go and stay with his married sister, and he could put a cot in the shop.

She still had a little pair of diamond earrings that she could sell to pay a little for her keep, and he would pay a little for her, too.

For himself, he could manage to get through the winter. He could build some auto radios and sell them. Maybe it would even grow to a business. Everybody said business would pick up after the election.

And in the spring he could pick up a jallopy, fix it up, and shove off, roaming the country all summer, as he had always wanted to do.

Thirteenth Street didn't look so bad. Though he had heard coons were filtering in.

Harry was going along, thinking over his troubles, when he saw a bunch of cops standing in front of a building. There was a relief station sign on the building. Harry stared at the sign with a funny feeling of covered-up fear.

He could see two cops in the upstairs windows of the building, and even while he watched, another detail of cops sauntered around the corner, with the lazy bored air of cops.

Did they always have police at the relief station, or was something happening? He noticed a few people dribbling around a vacant lot, casting wary glances at the cops, scattering but hanging around.

Harry approached a cop and asked: "What's going on?"

The policeman gave him a funny look, and shrugged. Feeling uncomfortable, Harry moved along.

On the corner, he asked a young fellow in a sweater: "What's up?"

"They're having some kind of demonstration."

"Oh," Harry said. A handbill lay on the sidewalk; standing over it he read:

DEMAND
ADEQUATE RELIEF
STOP ALL EVICTIONS
JOIN THE UNEMPLOYED COUNCIL . . .

So Harry figured he would stick around and see what one of these demonstrations looked like.

There still seemed to be more cops around than anything else. But a few people were collected at the vacant lot, across the street from the relief station. A short, hollow-cheeked fellow without a hat was talking. There used to be more people than that around the soapbox orators on Roosevelt Road.

Harry drifted along, but couldn't quite leave.

An old Dodge was parked around the corner. A fellow and a couple of girls sat inside watching the scene. They looked Jewish, so Harry stood near them.

"Has anybody started to talk yet?" one of the girls asked him. She was wearing a raccoon coat.

"No," Harry said.

"I never saw so many cops," the other girl laughed. "Rusty must be sitting in his office with a machine gun guarding the door."

"Yah, and I bet Orphan Annie has barricaded herself in the ladies' room!" the girl in the raccoon coat joked.

Harry gathered they were social workers.

"What can Rusty do?" the fellow at the wheel said boredly. "He can only hand out what he gets."

"Don't you worry. If he squawks downtown, they'll do something about it. How are they going to know, unless somebody squawks? Remember when they tried that ten percent relief cut? I told all my clients to go out and yell their heads off."

"I wouldn't brag about it, Bodansky," the fellow said. "Somebody is liable to hear you broadcasting."

"Nuts."

"Say, wait a minute, isn't that Captain Wiley?" The girl in the raccoon coat leaned out, squinting. She wore glasses, but Harry thought she had a very sweet face.

"Yah, that looks like him."

A police captain was crossing the street toward the gathering demonstrators.

"I believe he's actually going to talk to them."

"Go on, drive over, Louie, let's see what's going on."

"Uh-uh. This is close enough. Lousy as it is, I value my job."

The girl with glasses smiled at Harry. "See what he says," she suggested.

Harry ambled over. Everything seemed strangely easy, and even dull. The hollow-cheeked leader had come forward to meet the officer.

"Go on, get your meeting started and get it over with, I'm not going to hang around here all day," the captain said with what seemed like good humor. "Get on your soapbox."

"We want to see the district—" the leader began.

"Yah, yah, I know all about it. . . . Hey!" the captain called across the street. "Bring the comrade a chair, here, he ain't even brought along his soapbox!"

There was a blurt of laughter along the street. Encouraged, the people shuffled into the vacant lot—women in mangy sweaters, men in coats different from pants, lots of neighborhood kids, some of them on their home-made scooters, a few Negro women and here and there a more neatly dressed person, just curious.

A cop came out of the relief building carrying a wooden folding chair; he placed it in the middle of the vacant lot.

"How's that?" the captain said with mock solicitude.

"Thanks," the leader replied.

"All right. We'll give you twenty minutes. Then scatter." The captain went back to the station. He watched, from the stairs.

The cops were certainly being decent, Harry thought. The people had crowded around the speaker, who stood on the folding chair, yelling the usual stuff. "Comrades, a lot of you here are living on food cards, faced with eviction. We want a committee to go in there and demand . . ."

Harry was just going back to the girls in the car when he noticed some of the cops crossing to listen to the orator.

Then more cops crossed, and fringed the crowd.

Puzzled, and uneasy, Harry stood frozen to the sidewalk.

A cop yelled at the speaker: "Hey! Come down offa there!"

Harry turned to walk away. He was no part of this. He walked square into a cop.

"Where you going, comrade?" the young cop asked with heavy sarcasm.

Before Harry could answer he was shoved; stumbling backward, he lost his balance and sprawled on the pavement, his mouth still open to explain himself.

And before he could get up, he heard feet; the rest of the cops were running at the crowd; Harry scuttled aside on all fours. A heavy shoe scraped his ankle.

Now Harry managed to get to his feet. The whole scene had changed. Cops were already dragging people off the lot; almost on top of him, a huge fat woman in a dirty dark red sweater buttoned awry was squirming in the grip of a cop who held her two arms from behind. She was squalling in Italian. In the same flash, and while he was thinking: why, the cops told them to go ahead, and then jumped them! Harry saw a man wrench a cop's stick from him and swing it wildly. He caught snatches of yells, grunting, and a kid's scream; but the general impression was of a scuttling, scared silence.

Harry realized he was in the midst of a riot, the kind of thing that was in the papers about radicals, reds, only these were just people from around the block, and why had it turned into a riot?

Someone running hurtled against him, whirling him around. He saw a few figures escaping into passageways. He saw two cops chasing a Negro, catching him, distinctly heard the clop of stick on skull as the Negro went down. That was within ten feet of the Dodge, which was just moving away.

Harry started to run, to catch the car, to go with them. His sleeve tore half off his coat as he was jerked back. A cop on each side of him, he was rustled across the street. A final push landed him into a small group of people already rounded up. He felt himself all over everybody's feet.

"I—I—excuse me—" he blurted, automatically.

Then he saw that they were being guarded by cops with drawn guns.

This was the first moment when a furious emotion of complete outrage flooded Harry. Nobody had to guard him with guns! At the same time he bitterly realized it was useless to try to explain anything.

Across the street, a free-for-all had developed. He saw a woman momentarily detached from the crowd fling something in the face of a cop coming toward her. The cop bent double with his arm covering his eyes.

A knowing, suppressed chortle went through the arrested group. "Pepper."

Now the fight was in clumps, like football pile-ons. As they disentangled, some broken-looking human would be dragged up and half kicked, half carried across the street.

Suddenly a wild, gloating yell arose. And Harry saw that one of those pulled out of a pile was in uniform. His coat in shreds, blood dripping from a claw-nailed tear in his cheek.

"It's the captain!" the word went around with exultation, and fear.

"Hope they tore his eyes out!" someone muttered.

"Yah? We'll get it if he's hurt!"

A paddy wagon had appeared; it must have been waiting. As Harry was booted up the step, he received a fist-clout on the side of his head.

"You don't have to hit people!" he found himself screaming, as he tumbled into the wagon. Queerly, he immediately felt a sense of protection, being safe inside the wagon with all the others.

They were still arguing about how the police themselves gave the guy the chair and told him to talk!

—The bastards! the double-crossing bastards!

Just then, a semiconscious figure was hurled like a sack into the wagon. It was the speaker. They made room for him, pulled him onto the seat. He was bleeding from a matted bruise on the side of his head. As the patrol pulled away, Harry's last glimpse was of a terrified kid hanging onto an arrested mother.

The crowded truck lurched, the prisoners swayed in a solid mass. Everybody was sizing up everybody else.

—Hey, my eye look bad?

—Hey, you're bleeding from your mouth.

—Where they taking us?

—Fillmore, I guess.

A woman said: "Listen, everybody. In case you don't know what to do. All you have to tell them is a name. You don't even have to give your right name. In case you got a job or anything, you can give a fake name."

There was a nervous laugh all around. —Got a job!

She was around thirty, very ordinary-looking but with a nice face. She seemed sort of optimistic, as though so far everything was going along as she had expected. Harry wondered whether she was a communist organizer, doing this every day.

The fat Italian woman suddenly opened an old handbag she carried, held it low over the floor, and shook out the contents.

"That's right. Get rid of that pepper." Murmurs and chuckles went through the wagon. A few people pulled leaflets from their pockets and tore them to bits.

This was the real thing now, Harry felt; revolutionists destroying the evidence. He began to search his pockets, thinking to destroy everything that identified him. But he was just an honest law-abiding citizen who had been taking a walk on the street, and he wasn't going to hide like a criminal.

"Listen, if anybody gets out, call up the I.L.D." The leader gave them a phone number. "Just say what station we're at. They'll know what to do."

By now, the vestige of shame at being in a paddy wagon was entirely gone; many were even joking a little about this, their first trip.

The patrol stopped. A half-bald fellow, nearest the door, peered through the glass and said: "O-o. We got a reception committee."

Then the rest of the prisoners saw about a dozen cops laughingly forming two lines on the stairs of the station.

"Got any Hebes there, Mac?"

"Sure, Hebes and shines!"

"How can you tell them apart?"

"Come on, comrade, come on, don't be bashful!"

The bald-headed fellow clung to the wagon, but a cop gave him a shove that sent him stumbling into the gantlet. They heard his first animal bellow as he was lost to sight under the jumble of knees and boots. A stick thudded.

A little girl, arrested with her mother, suddenly began to scream: "Ma! Ma! Ma!" exactly like a sheep about to be slaughtered.

One after another they were pulled from the wagon and shoved through the merry line of clouting and kicking cops. Harry saw the figures emerge stumbling through the doorway into the police station. In the first rush of terror he hadn't realized they were beating the women same as the men.

"Come on! Come on!" Even until this instant he had believed this wouldn't happen to him.

He felt himself whirled, pushed, and, ducking and hiding his eyes, he rushed through the gantlet; one kick landed square on his rump, a knee cracked into his crotch, and as he reached the door Harry felt a stick tear at his ear, bounce off his shoulder. The pain in the shoulder began a moment afterward, and increased, and increased.

One at a time they were pushed into a smaller room, where the arrest slips were being made out. The guy at the desk looked fairly decent to Harry.

"Your name?"

He had been trying to think of a fake name, but said: "Harry Perlin."

"What's that, another sheeny?" cracked a smart-lipped dick. "Harry Perlinsky, huh."

"Well, Perlin, where do you live?"

He gave his address.

"Way up near Crawford, huh? So what were you doing down around Wood Street?" the dick at the desk asked mildly.

Just then Harry felt a hand in his pocket. He stood, biting his lip, while the detective fished out the contents of all his pockets. They examined his address book.

"Any hot Jewish mamas in there?" the comical one inquired.

They threw all his stuff on the desk, like junk.

They seemed to forget him while greeting the nice woman who had been in the wagon. Molly Bernstein was her name.

"Well, well, look who's here! We got some of your nigger pals on the men's side, Molly, would you like to be transferred for the night?"

"Are you going to book me or not?" she asked coldly.

"Sure, glad to oblige. Forty-two ten and illegal assembly," the cop named the charges. "Say, Molly, who is this Perlinsky, a new comrade?"

She shrugged.

Harry was wondering whether he should try to get in touch with Mort Abramson, whose father-in-law was Sergeant Rosen. That would show these bastards he had pull. But in a way he was ashamed to have it known that this had happened to him.

The woman was led away.

"So you were just out for a walk, eh?" The seated one turned to Harry. "Where do you work?"

"I work for myself."

"Well, what were you doing in that neighborhood?"

"I thought maybe I would look for an apartment around there."

They laughed at his excuse.

"But I didn't do anything! I didn't even know there was a demonstration there. First thing I knew I was hit on the head and thrown into the wagon," Harry cried.

"You live near Crawford and you were way down on Wood Street and didn't know a thing about it," the fellow said sweetly.

"Go on, smart guy!" The tough one booted him toward the cells.

Harry looked frantically back toward the kindlier cop. But he was laughing.

The row of iron cages looked odd because they had roofs under the ceiling. With a bunch of other men, he was herded past several empty cells, then shoved, about ten into a two-man cell. Harry noted the lidless toilet sitting in a puddle of urine-water.

"Is Mike Burns here? Put him on the bench. Come on, lie down, feller." They stretched out the hollow-cheeked speaker. Blood had dried under his nostrils.

"Get some water."

A couple of fellows yelled: "Hey! Water! There's a sick man here!"

"Aw, piss on him," the cop said, walking away.

Harry edged over to the back of the cell. Fellows were talking.

"This is nothing; ever been in Bridewell?"

"Was you in the old section?"

"Yah. South cell block."

"Brother, you know it!" a black fellow commented, holding his nose.

The second wagonload had arrived. The fat turnkey appeared herding another group toward their cell.

"You can't put any more in here!"

"We can't breathe now!"

As the shouting and cursing doubled, the rest were taken to a further cell.

Again the yell began: "Water! There's a man sick! He's passed out! Goddam it, we asked for water!"

"Water! Water!" the men began to shout in unison. "Water!" Their fists pounded on the iron partitions of the cells. From other cells, voices joined.

Harry found himself yelling hoarsely, furiously, with the others; damn it, they had to give people water!

"Aw, pipe down." The guard appeared, carrying a pail half full of water.

An intimate sense of victory, however small, spread through the group.

Mike Burns was asking the newcomers: "Anybody see Al Howard? Was he in your wagon?"

A dumb guy kept asking, from one to the other: "What'd they pinch me for? Huh?"

Then, from somewhere in the line of cells, they heard a whistled tune. It sounded familiar, but Harry couldn't place it.

"That must be Al!" Mike Burns said, relieved.

The tune was picked up on all sides, soon the whole jail seemed to be swinging in whistled rhythm.

"What's the name of that song?" Harry asked a curly-headed fellow, who looked okay.

"That? That's the 'International'."

"Oh." Harry felt a guilty ignorance.

They must be whistling as a signal to each other that they were there.

"Get hurt much?" the fellow asked.

"Na. I got one bounce on the shoulder, must be black and blue," Harry said; in the excitement, he had forgotten the pain, but now it cut into him.

"They get tough every time they catch the whites in a Negro district," the fellow said. "They picked us up at a Scottsboro demonstration a couple of weeks ago, it was on the South Side and, boy, that's where the cops can give it to you." He laughed. "They came in the cell and made all us white fellows kiss the Negroes."

Harry squirmed. And at the same time he was wondering: what was the Scottsboro case?

He first realized that there were several Negroes in the cell. Since he was a kid he had a notion that if you got close to them, they stank.

A paunchy Italian pressed against Harry. "Say," he whispered. "What we in here for? I was a-coming home, that's all."

"There was a riot and they picked up everybody on the street," Harry said.

The Italian said: "This is a free country. I can walk on the street!"

"Well, these are bad times and they have to be careful," Harry defended the police. "Still, treatment like this would make somebody turn into a communist, instead of keeping him from it."

"They got to have a Mussolini here, they don't have no monkey business," the Italian said.

"Once the election is over things will be quieter and business will pick up," Harry said. "An election year is always bad for business."

"Who you voting for? Roosevelt?"

"I think so," Harry said. "He's a good man. Though you can't blame Hoover for everything. He was just unlucky to be in there at the wrong time."

"Roosevelt is gonna bring back the wine," the Italian said. "That's gonna give everybody work."

The curly-headed fellow laughed.

"Sure! You got to have thousands people raise the grapes, make the wine, make the beer. . . . And storekeepers! That's enough jobs for everybody!"

"What do you think?" Harry asked the curly-headed fellow, though he supposed the guy was a communist.

The fellow shrugged. "What's the difference who gets in, the same people own the country."

"Well, no," Harry maintained. "I think Roosevelt is going to do something. I think he has the right idea. The forgotten man," he ended, lamely.

—How long they gonna keep us here?

—They didn't book us yet.

—Whadaya mean? They can't hold you without booking you!

—You're here, aintcha?

—Sonofabitch!

From the other side of the building, where the women were penned, singing was heard:

"Work and pray,
Live on hay . . ."

—Those girls got a lot of pep.

—Molly Bernstein is in there with them.

The whole jail was picking up the song. The voices all taken together were strangely light-hearted, and strong.

"You'll get pie in the sky
When you die—
It's a lie!"

A shrill yell rose:

"We want Captain Wiley,
We want Captain Wiley,
With a rope around his neck!"

The men laughed, and responded with the same cheer for Mayor Cermak[3].

The cheering went on, from side to side, till they had honored relief officials and politicians and the red squad and the racket squad and Morgan and Rockefeller and McCormick. Pretty soon they were tired of thinking up new ones, and the women changed to a chant:

"Black and white,

---

[3] Anton Cermak was Mayor of Chicago from 1931 until his assassination in 1933 (he was shot on February 15 and died on March 6).

Unite and fight!
Black and white,
Unite and fight!"

They chanted with rising swinging voices while the jailers yelled: "Shut up, you goddamn bitches."

"You got to hand it to the girls, they certainly know how to keep up their spirits," Harry said to the curly-headed fellow.

In the wagon again, going to the central detective bureau, friends who had been in different cells met, a wife found her husband. "Did they hurt you?" "Are you all right?" And lots of them greeted a smiling Negro, Al Howard, who told them he had been picked up as he got off a street car.

Al Howard sort of took charge of the group. He spoke with a Harvard accent. "Now, when they question you in the bureau, they will taunt you and insult you, but you must be careful not to lose your temper, as that is just what they want. Sometimes it helps you if you maintain a sarcastic attitude and even answer them with contempt." There was laughter. "Of course they will ask if you are a member of the Communist Party." Al Howard looked over the group in the wagon. "There are no party members here, are there?" he said slyly, and the laughter rose.

Harry wondered if there were, and how many?

"Have they got a right to fingerprint us?" one fellow asked.

"They have no right to do so unless you have been convicted of a criminal offense, but the fact is that they will fingerprint us unless they are too lazy, as there are quite a few of us today."

"I'll sue them for false arrest!" one man declared. The more experienced smiled at him tolerantly.

"Hey. Will they beat us up?"

"They may beat you," Al Howard said calmly. "I understand that a few of the police were injured today, and it is probable that their colleagues don't feel very friendly towards us." His voice dropped to an extremely impersonal tone. "Sometimes they resort to torture."

Harry started. Torture? What did the Negro mean? Cigarettes burned against the soles of your feet, like gangsters did? No, cops weren't supposed to do anything that left marks. The rubber hose? Something about Al Howard's voice made him sure the fellow spoke from experience.

"Another thing they may do," Al Howard said, "is subject you to the show-up. Remember that the most important thing is to distinguish yourself at once from the other prisoners, who are usually thieves and criminals of that type. You must make it plain that you are a political prisoner."

Several were confused. He explained: "The danger to us is that sometimes an excited or hysterical person may think he recognizes you as the thug who held him up in a dark alley. If anyone even says you are of the same build as his attacker, the police have an excuse to try to sweat a

556

confession out of you, or to charge you with the crime. And then is when they may resort to torture."

"Uh-huh. The third degree."

"Therefore," Al Howard pointed out, "as soon as I step onto the platform, I make it a point to say: 'I am a communist, and was arrested at a demonstration.' But I am already a known communist. Naturally those of you who are not communist needn't say so. You can say you were arrested at a demonstration in front of a relief station."

They all began rehearsing what they would say.

Harry could already feel himself under those glaring white lights. He would hold up his head and tell them a thing or two! He was no criminal!

As they arrived behind the station, the curly-headed fellow remarked: "I helped put up this building."

"Huh?" Harry asked surprised.

"I'm a structural steel worker. I worked on this job, let's see, it was in twenty-seven, I think."

They were taken up a freight elevator into a large vacant room. A dick entered and called off a couple of names—a man and wife.

"Logan your alderman?" he asked.

"Oh! He got our call!"

"Go on, beat it," he said.

They strayed out, glancing back at the others kind of apologetically.

Again, Harry was led into an office. The same detectives were present, plus a lot of others. He'd already heard they were calling in every squad leader to identify the rioters. Sergeant Rosen of the racket squad was there, as he was supposed to be an expert on the West Side. He was a chunky man with black eyebrows, and he talked to Harry in a fatherly way. "Now you look to be a nice decent fella. Whataya wanna go around with those radicals for? You know an officer was hurt today?"

"I'm sorry," Harry said. So this was Mort's father-in-law.

There was an obscene laugh from the smart cop. "He's sorry he didn't kill him."

The tough detective suddenly shoved a length of pipe in front of Harry's face. "What did you carry this for?"

"Why—I—I never saw that—"

"I suppose you didn't sock anybody with it either?" The detective swung the pipe, as if to sock Harry.

Harry looked appealingly to Rosen.

"You could kill a man with this! Feel it!" Harry felt it crack against his elbow. His crazy-bone pained maddeningly.

"Nah, nah," Sergeant Rosen mildly reproved the cop.

The wild pain made tears spring out of his eyes. Angered because he couldn't help crying before these men, frantic with the drilling pain, and all the while conscious of the torn sleeve that made him look like some cheap radical, Harry let loose a hysterical, half-screaming, half-sniffling speech. "What right have you to hit me! You haven't even any right to arrest me! I was just walking along the street! I'm a respectable citizen! This is a free country but you cops act like a bunch of—of—"

"Cossacks, hah?" the smart dick offered, with Jewish intonation.

"You think you can get away with this stuff! Why don't you tell those men of yours to have some respect for people's rights! I saw them beat up women and children—"

"Outside, outside." One of the dicks was shoving him, while the fatherly Sergeant Rosen looked at him sadly.

They waited, in a bull-pen behind the fingerprint room. A sour-faced racketeer was pacing, cursing. His lawyer was late.

"What's all this?" he demanded of the jailer.

"Bunch of reds."

The racketeer gave them a contemptuous look, shrugged, and paced the other end of the pen.

A cop grabbed Harry's wrists, seized his fingers one at a time, pressed them down on the inkpad, pressed them onto the paper.

Of the whole day, this was the most outraged moment. Harry felt his very toes contracted in fury.

The cop flung his hand loose. Harry stood, trying to keep his inky fingers away from his clothes.

"Over there," one of the fellows indicated a bucket on the floor. It contained mechanic's soap. For a moment, the familiar grit on his palms eased him.

The phone rang while Sam was in the bathroom. It was his habit to relax and read the evening paper slowly, even to the dull paragraphs under the picture of virtuous-looking girls, captioned: "Plan Sorority Dance." The paper was full of piteous tales about what Hitler was doing to the Jews, but not a word about the thousands of communists being hounded and tortured to death. Naturally, they simply didn't exist as objects of pity for the capitalist press. Well, sometimes it was funny. Here was Samuel Insull dancing all over Europe, with the U.S. agents begging him to stand still and be extradited. The old man must be having the laugh of his life. What a swindle!

Sam had already read the half-column of drivel about "police battling red rioters" in front of a relief station. So he expected that Ella would be phoning.

"Listen, dear, they've got the Fillmore Street station full, and I'm going over to Ruth's to see if we can fix up some food for them. So I won't be home for supper. Do you know where we can get some cash for bail?"

Ella got excited like a neophyte each time. With so many arrested, it was futile to attempt to raise cash bail. One night in jail never killed anybody. Anyway the bonds would be doubled tomorrow, when they asked for a jury trial, so the best tactic was to round up real estate bonds, instead of wasting time collecting a few dollars.

"A couple of cops got hurt and the squad was simply murderous. We saw it. We've got to get Mike out at least."

"Well, I only have three bucks," Sam said.

"It's all right, I'll get some. And Al wants to know if you can come down in the morning for the hearing."

"All right," Sam said. "How many have they got?"

"They're still holding about twenty-five. There's some meat loaf in the oven and why don't you open a can of corn?" she ended.

Sam wandered to the icebox. He didn't like eating alone. But at least he was eating, while in Germany . . .

In spite of the biting smell of the jail disinfectant, which seemed to increase with the night, in spite of the crawly damp air, a human warmth pervaded the jail. There was still a little singing, but of all kinds of songs, Girl Scout songs and "Lydia Pinkham."

"Say," Harry asked Curly, "what's the difference between communism and socialism?"

Curly smiled resignedly, and began.

All the while someone was singing:

"Minnie had a heart as big as a whale . . ."

It was after eight o'clock when the two girls appeared carrying a basket loaded with food and milk bottles. "Hi, Ella!" Al Howard greeted her. "Don't tell me the I.L.D. is functioning!"

"On about one cylinder."

"Boys, we eat!"

"Oh, hello," the girls said. Harry recognized them. "We tried to wait for you this morning, but—"

"That's all right. I know how it is."

Roast beef and corned beef sandwiches, paper cups, went through the bars. "We got enough bail for three, and we may be able to scare up enough for one or two more, before midnight."

"You better take Mike out right away. He's hurt bad."

They offered to take Harry out, as it was his first time, but he said to use the money for one of the women. "If you will call up my sister, I think she is getting the money. I already tried to get one message to her."

Around eleven o'clock, his sister came rushing in, guided by that girl Ruth Lipschultz. "Well, of all things, well, of all things!"

"I got fifteen from a neighbor, and we had some money we took in in the store today. Listen, Harry, you didn't really have anything to do with all those radicals, did you?"

"Even if I did!" he cried.

"You know where to come for the hearing in the morning," Ruth Lipschultz reminded him. "Our lawyer will be there, so don't worry."

"Maybe we better get our own lawyer," Eda said suspiciously.

"Don't worry," Ruth pacified his sister. "Tomorrow is only the preliminary hearing. And our best lawyer, Mr. Eisen, is coming down."

"Eisen?" Harry repeated. "Is that Sam Eisen?"

"You know him?"

"Sure. Why, I used to hang around in the same bunch with him. Well, that certainly is a coincidence!"

The courtroom was so jammed that getting through the door was like wriggling into a street car during rush hour. As usual, the judge was late.

"Hello, mister!" Harry turned his head. He was right in front of Ruth Lipschultz. "We certainly packed the courtroom, didn't we!" she said proudly. "And on such short notice, too."

Harry didn't quite understand what she meant, but the courtroom was undoubtedly packed.

"With Judge Horowitz you can't take any chances. He's a louse of the first water," she commented.

There was a fellow in a light brown suit, with muddy spots all over the lapels. That was yesterday's blood, Harry realized.

"I'm supposed to be sick this morning," Ruth confided. There was something so nice and simple about the remarks she dropped. As though they knew each other pretty well.

Then Harry saw Sam Eisen wedging through the door. He felt a rush of pride for Sam, the way all these people were depending on him.

"Hiyah, Sam!" Harry said.

"Hello. Hello, Harry!"

"Well, looks like I'm one of your cases!" Harry blushed.

"Yes, my wife was telling me she met you, last night."

So Sam was married again? To that other girl, who had brought the sandwiches? For an instant, Harry had thought of Lil, and whether they could be jealous over her.

"Oh, say, Sam, it's a coincidence—I was going to get in touch with you anyway about our house. We had a mortgage . . ." He explained the situation.

"There's not much you can do. I can put in an answer for you and get a couple of delays—five or six months, maybe. Then maybe we can arrange to have you live in the house on a low rental, as caretaker." Then he answered someone else: "I think he'll dismiss about half of them, the ones that haven't been in before. But you can't tell. He may get snotty and hold everybody, just to tie up the bail money."

The door to the judge's chambers opened, and Harry recognized the man who came out. It was the smart-aleck dick from the squad.

"Aha!" Ruth said. "Beal."

"He does that every time," Sam declared.

Ruth explained to Harry: "The interested parties are not supposed to talk to the judge before a case."

"Oh. I heard Horowitz wasn't so bad, Sam," Harry mentioned. "Isn't he from the West Side?"

"That lousy cheap ward politician!" Sam cried. "Why he was nearly thrown into jail a couple of years ago when he was mixed up in that election scandal, remember when a Negro was killed? Now he's a patriot all of a sudden, a defender of Americanism!"

Harry was worried. "Will he be tough?"

"He can't do anything to you because we're going to demand a jury trial and that takes it over to the criminal court, outside of his jurisdiction. But he's sore as hell at me because I got him censured by the appellate judges two years ago when I was trying Beal and Maserow for beating up a striker."

A gavel rapped. The court clerk, a guy in a greenish suit, with a poolroom face, mumbled the hearye's and banged the gavel again, and those who had seats plopped down. The rest of the crowd pressed forward like water in a tilted bottle.

Now Harry saw Judge Horowitz. A little Yid with narrow eyes and a wide nasty mouth, making popping, sucking noises.

"Clear the aisles, I'm going to arrest everybody that don't get out of the aisles," he sang, with Maxwell Street intonation. There was a slight compression of the crowd backward.

Some cops led in the prisoners who had spent the night in jail. The men looked bedraggled and unshaven, as though they had been in for a week.

A newspaper photographer was standing behind the judge, screwing a flashlight bulb into a holder. Those bulbs were certainly an improvement on the dangerous old-style flashlight powder, Harry reflected.

The clerk began to call names. "Mary Agnostino. Come on up here when your name is called!" he bawled angrily. He got to Mike Burns.

"He's in the hospital," Sam stated, handing up a slip of paper. "He had two ribs broken by the police."

Judge Horowitz snatched the paper. "That's enough! How do you know who broke his ribs!"

". . . Harry Perlin."

Prepared though he was, the sound of his own name, in court, brought a feeling of shock and fright, and in spite of what he had seen of the judge, a momentary emotion of respect.

About a dozen defendants were now squeezed before the bench. The judge leaned forward. "Any communists here?"

There was a snicker from the courtroom, widening into a general laugh.

The smart-aleck dick whispered to the judge, nodding at a few of the defendants. The judge blinked, understandingly. Then he singled out the fellow with the bespattered lapels. "You don't look like a red," Judge Horowitz declared. "You look like a decent American. What were you doing around there? Are you on relief?"

The fellow was about to answer.

"We're not trying the case, your honor," Sam interposed. "These defendants ask—"

Judge Horowitz nearly leaped across the bench. "Whose courtroom is this, yours or mine?"

Sam repeated firmly: "We are not trying this case. We ask—"

"Oh, we're not, eh? Listen here, Eisen, I've had enough of you. One more word out of you and I'll hold you in contempt."

"I'm representing these people."

"You're representing nobody as far as this court is concerned, understand? I'm not listening to you! I don't even hear what you say!" the judge yelled, rearing in his seat, and glaring through Sam as though he didn't exist.

There was a gasp throughout the courtroom.

Judge Horowitz settled back, wriggled his neck, and made an audible remark about I.L.D. shysters. Then he orated: "I know all about it! You poor people are letting yourself be a tool in the hands of a lot of red agitators that are trying to take advantage of the depression to make trouble! . . ."

The flashlight went off, catching Judge Horowitz patriotically haranguing the red rioters. He held his pose, blinked, and went on with his speech.

"Your honor, this is not a trial!" Sam interposed.

Horowitz paused, mouth open. The blood of rage could actually be seen rising through his face. "Eisen! I don't hear you! In my court, you can talk your head off and I don't hear you!"

"I'm asking for a jury trial for my clients."

"You can talk your head off! I don't hear you!" The judge put his hands to his ears.

A wave of laughter rolled over the courtroom. The gavel rapped.

"Bailiff! Take him into custody! I'm holding you for contempt, Eisen! Take him out! Lock him up! Go on!"

". . . my constitutional rights!" Sam shouted.

"You ain't got no rights! Reds and radicals got no rights!" Judge Horowitz informed him.

"Insist on a jury trial!" Sam called to his clients. "Get Al Littinger. He's down in Haley's court!"

"You can't beat up police officers and then come in here and expect to run the court!" Judge Horowitz bawled. "Nobody can scare me! I am running this court, and not no communist shysters! Now, you people, I know all about you! I know which ones are the trouble-makers. You don't need those red lawyers to come here and get you into trouble. I'm going to show you what I'll do for you. I'm going to leave go the first offenders because you don't even understand what those agitators are doing to you. But let this be a lesson to you! If you ever get mixed up with these reds again, remember, we are wise to you! Call the next bunch!"

Harry hardly understood that he was free. Was this the way courts were run?

The clerk was calling out other names. Harry found himself beside Ruth again.

"Oh, good, they got Al Littinger," she murmured, as a fellow with a briefcase popped his way through the crowd.

Of the twenty-five who had been booked, eleven were held for jury trial. Their bail was raised to one hundred dollars. Among them were Al Howard, Curly, and the woman, Molly Bernstein. Harry figured that he could let them use the fifty dollars there had been on him; he had to sell his car anyway and would pay his sister back out of that.

He found himself in a jammed elevator, with Ruth.

"What will they do to Sam Eisen?" he said.

"I don't know. Listen, let's make some phone calls. I'll call the Civil Liberties, this is something they ought to come in on. And listen, we're going to call the judge. First I'll call, then you call."

She called, insisting it was some personal message, and actually got the judge on the wire. "Judge Horowitz?" she said sweetly, and made a triumphant face to Harry. "I am calling on behalf of several thousand members of the I.L.D. to protest against the arrest of our lawyer, Sam Eisen—"

Evidently the judge had exploded. She made a laughing face, and hung up.

"Now wait a few minutes and you try."

The judge didn't come this time, but Harry talked to the clerk.

They kept on calling, practicing accents. On the seventh call, the clerk answered with a string of oaths that practically burned up the wires.

Harry was laughing now so he could hardly speak into the phone. Presently they began to get busy signals. "I guess we're not the only ones," he said.

She was driving west, so he rode along. Her old Dodge stuttered.

"Your carburetor and timing need adjusting," Harry said. "I could fix it for you some time."

"Will you? That's swell."

He felt nervy, and alive again.

> Dancing in the dark till the tune ends,
> Dancing in the dark and it soon ends
> . . . We're dancing in the dark . . .

Lil's new friend was named Irwin Reese. He was a jobber in lingerie and while everybody was going broke he had made a fortune in hostess pajamas. They had become acquainted when he gave her a line of credit practically on sight because, he said: "I always go by intuition."

Irwin had a long spoonlike face. Lil thought a blond mustache, like his, always gave a man a refined air. He drove a Cadillac which he had bought for a song on a repossess.

Of him, Lil declared: "He may not be a lawyer or a doctor but, believe me, a smart business man is more important than any of those things. Look what happened to all those lawyers and doctors during the depression! But while everybody was going down, Irwin went up. You have to admit it takes a genius to go up in times like these."

And she had taken a new lease on life. She felt like a wise, worldly heroine in a book by Ursula Parrott. She used dresses and lingerie out of her stock, and when she put on the dog with Irwin, going to the Edgewater or the Del Roi, she was right there with the best of them.

"He de do, do hi de hee!" Cab Calloway shrieked, and from the floor Lil joined the chorus:

> "Minnie had a heart as big as a whale!"

He was a swell dancer, light as a girl; Sam had never taken her dancing.

Oh, all of a sudden everybody was cheerful. Maybe it was because the election was over, and, honest, it looked like Roosevelt was going to do something. It looked like winter was over, here comes the spring.

> "Happy days are here again,
> The skies above are clear again . . ."

And Irwin cleverly chimed in:

> "The world is drinking beer again!"

She laughed a high free laugh at his wit.

She loved to have men say nice things to her, especially in a sophisticated way, as when he glanced frankly downward at her breasts, the full inner curves of which were displayed *à la* Jean Harlow, and said: "If you don't mind my saying so, from a purely æsthetic point of view, the breastworks are very beautiful."

That thrilled her. Sam had used to be crazy about them.

> "Just a low down hoochie coocher . . ."

Lil smiled happily to Irwin and said: "Do you know how I feel tonight? Remember when it was fashionable to be flat as a board, and we used to have to wear those tight bandeaux, well, I feel like, all of a sudden after all these years of repression, I can open up and what a relief!"

She heaved a deep breath, swelling her breast. They both laughed.

"And the boys all used to mooch her . . ."

As they sat down, Irwin looked at her dreamily, and said: "You know, I've just had an inspiration."

"Tell me."

He leaned forward. "The bust is coming back," he said. "Women want to be women again. Now you, my beautiful, you're an exception, you're perfectly formed and don't need anything. But what they want now is a brassiere that builds it up, that shows it off, now that women realize a man wants a girl that's got something to show, huh?"

"Uh-huh," she said, considering seriously. "You know, Irwin, that's a wonderful idea. It's a fact most girls ruined their busts with those tight bandeaux and now they need something for the new styles."

"We'll uplift the nation," he said wittily, and made a note. He certainly never let anything slip past him.

Then he looked up with an apologetic smile and said: "That's all the business for today, Mrs. Eisen."

Inexplicably she had felt her dark mood returning, and just as he called her by her married name, she became sad.

He caught her mood—he was so sensitive to moods—and, reaching for her hand, said: "Lillian, sometimes I think you are really not the gay little woman that you seem, but that you are putting up a brave front, covering a wound. I don't want to intrude in your personal affairs, but you know I am your friend."

She was so touched, she wanted to cry, and did sob, a tiny bit. "Oh, Irwin," she said, "it's just that he's made such a mess of things, for me! I should think he'd have at least some consideration for his child, oh, when I think of Jackie having to face those kids in school . . . But he's so heartless! It's unnatural! He never even comes to see his son!"

"You're speaking of your former husband?" Irwin said soothingly. "Of the incident in the paper?"

She turned her face away, and uttered a little chain of sobs. "Why does he do such things! When we were together he never thought of such things! Radicalism!"

"Lillian," he said. "I'm going to speak to you severely. You must put him out of your life and out of your mind, completely. Why, you're young, just a girl, all life is ahead of you! You know, a woman of your nature shouldn't be alone. You've starved yourself for love, Lillian. Tell me, frankly, we're not children—don't you sometimes feel the need of a man?"

So he too had figured out she was a swell setup, a young divorcee in need of a man. But maybe it wasn't just a line with him, he looked so sincere.

He lifted his drink. "Now I'm the doctor. From now on, nothing but gayety and happiness! Lillian, do you know my motto? To hell with the rest of the world, we have no one to live for but ourselves!"

They clinked glasses.

"You're just an old smoothie," she sang meaningly, "and I'm an old softie . . ."

He suggested that they leave. "I have no etchings but I really have a wonderful collection of symphony records."

In her deepest tones, she said: "Irwin, I hope we mean more to each other than just that?"

He responded nobly: "Darling," and squeezed her hand.

She felt sure she could handle him, because he would always have to make the noble gesture, for himself.

Talk about Friends

Scrap iron was so low it wasn't worth the space it took up in the yards. And Rube Moscowitz didn't want to hear about it. Another subject he didn't want to hear about was Samuel Insull. Or real estate. Nobody ever knew what was safe to mention in his presence.

Occasionally he let up the gates by referring to Insull himself. He never spoke the name, but called him the Sonofabitch. He'd say: "Well, I see his son took a satchelful of kale over to the Sonofabitch in Paris." Or: "That Sonofabitch has bribed the whole government of Greece, they'll never get him out of there." When it was rumored that Sir Basil Zaharoff, the mystery man of Europe, was helping Insull with funds, Rube said: "Sure, the Loyal Brotherhood of Sonsabitches."

Lou Margolis heard that Pete Grinnell was dropping remarks about "getting even with a certain double-crossing kike politician." The only chance of Pete's making trouble was if he got the Republicans to investigate Rube before they went out of office.

"The dumb ox, I told him to pay his income tax!" Lou insisted.

"But what will they do to him?" Celia saw her father in the penitentiary next to Al Capone.

"They'd probably make a deal with him," Lou said. "He'd have to pay up though."

"Lou. You better tell him. At least if he knows, maybe he can—"

"What?"

"Well, he could get out of the country."

"Yah. Maybe Sammy Insull will give him a berth on that boat," Lou said. Then laughed, at the clever idea. He would have to spring it to the crowd, some time. The Insull Line, Limited, sailing from noplace to nowhere, guaranteed never to touch port. Make your reservations early.

Rube came barging into the office. "Say," he demanded, "who is this Sam Eisen?"

"Sam? Oh he's just a kid used to hang around Roosevelt Road."

"Yah. What is he, a Bolshevik?"

"Naw," Lou yawned. "He's just got some liberal ideas, likes to fool around and get his name in the paper."

"Then what the hell did Horowitz want to throw him in the can for?"

"He must of got fresh, Sam is a good jury lawyer, but he don't know how to handle a judge." He didn't have all day to discuss Sam Eisen.

"Well, listen, tell Horowitz to lay off that kid," Rube said mysteriously.

"Since when are you protecting Sam Eisen?" Lou laughed.

"Aw, listen, I been getting a lot of calls. The alderman put the heat on, too. He thinks Horowitz listens to me. Can't those Bar Association bums tell Horowitz to behave himself like a judge for a change?"

"What does the alderman care about Sam Eisen?"

"Well, the unions have got after him. Those cloaks and suit makers are all a bunch of Bolsheviks anyway. Looks like your pal has got a lot of friends."

And while Rube was talking about friends, Lou thought he might as well tip him off about Grinnell.

Rube jumped up and strode around the office laughing. "That's a hot one! Holy *shlimazel*, that takes the cake! So they want an income tax! I lose my shirt, and they're going to get me for my income tax! What is this, a gag! Say, I'm no racketeer!" He stopped in his tracks, and stared at the wall with the precise expression of a bull staring at a red rag.

"Oh, there's nothing to it," Lou said. "Still maybe it would be safer if you made a deal. Cermak could fix it up in Washington for you."

"I don't need anybody to go to Washington!" Rube boasted. "I can go to them myself. But what the —— kind of a deal am I gonna make? I ain't got a cent! Where am I going to get them fifty thousand bucks back income tax!"

Lou himself was surprised at the amount.

Rube stared at him angrily, then began ranting. "Swell friends a man got! I spend my life working for that Sonofabitch, I do all his dirty work, if it wasn't for me how many times would he have been stuck for a franchise to run his lousy El, and what do I get for it? When I need him, he runs out on me! Sneaking out of the back door of that hotel in Greece dressed in skirts!" Rube laughed hysterically, as if it were exactly at that moment in his comic opera flight that the financier had deserted him. "Tips he gives me! I'm on his private list for his stocks! On his sucker list, the Sonofabitch! Why didn't he tell me he was bust? He knew goddam well he was bust when he threw that million-dollar dinner in the Palmer House! Stuffed squab! Everything is fine and dandy! The emperor of the United States and Canada, with seven hundred ambassadors, the Sonofabitch! He owns the rivers! He owns lakes! What'd he have to bluff *me* for? Strangers, all right, what the hell, anybody that plays the market deserves what they get! But I wasn't playing the market! I was investing in a friend! The Sonofabitch! The double-crossing Sonofabitch!"

"Well, listen, Rube," Lou tried to pacify him, "they'll get him. Don't worry. They'll catch up with him."

"Lemme get my hands on him. I'd just like to pull out those goddam white whiskers of his! And another pal! Grinnell! My *goyishe* friend! That cheap ward-heeler, I kept him up there for twenty years! Could I help it if the people got sick of his graft? Did I put up another candidate? So he's going to get me! I'll show him! I've got friends in the administration . . ."

But he stopped, as though struck by the word friends.

Because of his year of big worries, Runt Plotkin was prematurely graying around the temples. Seeing him thus, Sam Eisen couldn't suppress an inward smile, for the graying temples created precisely the impression of scholarly refinement for which Runt had always seemed to long.

Hearing of Sam's arrest, Runt Plotkin had been the first to phone and offer assistance. Hadn't he too been thrown in the can by a crazy judge? He came around to compare details. For himself, things were turning out okay. He had taken Sam's advice and gone to the top-notch criminal lawyers. He had lost his practice, being under a shadow for months while he was battling Judge Donohue's trumped-up charges, but now he had been exonerated, he could start all over.

"You know what I'm gonna do? I'm going to haul Donohue before the committee! You ought to complain on Horowitz too! They got too much power! Imagine, guys like that can throw you in the can, any time they feel like!"

"They only took me down to the bailiff's office and I sat there for a couple of hours," Sam belittled his incarceration.

"Yeah?" Runt's cigar wiggled. "They threw me in a cell, the sonsabitches!" Yet he seemed a bit proud of this further persecution. "What happened to your case anyway?"

"Horowitz finally dismissed it," Sam laughed. "He got so many kicks, he had to back out some way. I was surprised myself, at the amount of response we got. His bailiff told Al Littinger that Horowitz never got so much mail in his life. They got protests from way up in Seattle, even; at the start there they were getting about fifty letters a day!"

"You don't say so! You fellows have certainly got an organization!" Runt marveled.

"I don't even know myself where they all came from. The *Daily Worker* just had a squib about the case, urging readers to send in letters of protest to the judge."

"I guess those communists are pretty well organized all over the country?" Runt hinted.

"Some of it came from unions. My father is secretary of his local, he's a buttonhole maker, and he got them to squawk. You know the storekeepers and small manufacturers all moved out of the West Side and now it's full of operators and pressers. So they finally got in their own alderman for the ward. And Rube Moscowitz has to listen to him."

"Yah," Runt said, "when a thing like this happens you find out who are your friends. You fellows have got the right idea. Organization." He puffed, and smiled at Sam. "Say," he said confidentially, "I hear Roosevelt is gonna come out with a five-year plan, like Russia."

Sam Eisen was discussing Runt Plotkin with some of the I.L.D. lawyers. "No," Sam insisted. "A man like that can have a lot of good stuff. He's all right, he's beginning to see things. We ought not to be scornful of his type."

They looked at Sam as though he were soft.

Teachers on Parade

Everybody in Greeley High thought Ben Meisel was nothing but a selfish fat slob, and he knew it. He could see it in their faces when they looked right past him in the corridors; he could hear it in the silences that fell when he approached.

Sure, they were sore because he had saved his money and didn't need to pledge his unpaid salary for sixty percent cash. They were sore because he knew enough to keep his in the Postal Savings. That time when he was a kid and the Sixteenth Street Bank had failed had been enough for him. They were sore because he had no family to support. Well, who told them all to get married and have kids!

Ben passed the open door of Mr. Beaseley's room. Several of the younger men teachers were unwrapping sandwiches, opening milk bottles. But they didn't come there just to eat lunch. He knew they were fixing up some kind of scheme. A gym teacher at Edison High had started an action committee, and now they were trying to start them in all the schools.

As if the teachers didn't have enough organizations already. The Federation was supposed to be pulling wires to get their pay, and the union waited for the Federation to do something, and the Men Teachers couldn't do anything unless the others would co-operate. It was all a laugh. He wouldn't even waste a dollar on dues. When the school board had the money it would pay; until then, twenty unions wouldn't help.

He was sick of everybody in the lunchroom counting every mouthful he ate. The hell with them! He loaded soup on his tray and pointed to the pork chops. The boy put on one.

"Two," Ben said, conscious of Mr. Doonis behind him, watching.

The hell with them. Eating was the only fun he got out of life. The rest of them had things like families, loves, ambitions, and eating was just a stop for gas, to them. But he didn't have anything else and he was entitled to his one pleasure. The best moment was when he secretly opened the top button of his pants.

Ben took two helpings of gingerbread, sliding them onto a single plate.

"Fifty-five!" the cashier sang out, which was about as high as a check could be in that place.

And "Fourteen!" for Mr. Doonis, who had an egg sandwich and a glass of milk.

Ben steered toward an unoccupied end of the teachers' table. But Mr. Doonis kept near him. "I see Miss Crowley isn't with us again today," Mr. Doonis remarked, as he waited for Ben to unload.

Miss Crowley was the old maid French teacher, for years the self-appointed hostess of the luncheon table.

Among the teachers, there had been those like Miss Crowley who hugged their private misery throughout the crisis, shut-mouthed, seeming to grow tighter, bleaker, every day. And there were those who shouted their downward progress to each other: "Well! I sold the old bus today, got sixty-five from a dealer!" or: "Well, I borrowed the last nickel on my insurance!"

And yet, in some mysterious way, all knew what happened to the silent ones, too; the stages of their despair were whispered about with a kind of sympathy, and yet a kind of triumph. Until the final stage when there was a sudden shedding of pride, a joining of the crowd, a breakdown recital of the whole fierce struggle, revealing details that the crowd, who thought they knew all, had until then not known.

Ben ate steadily, his eyes on his plate. Sbarboro, a printing teacher, noisily slapped his tray down next to Ben. "Well, you going to march in the parade, Speedy?" Sbarboro kidded him with his brother's nickname.

There was a stir of interest along the table. "What parade?"

Sbarboro usually lunched with the Beaseley crowd in 311. All he had on his tray was a cup of coffee. He hauled a sandwich out of a pocket.

"Oh, we're having a parade," he said lightly, his eyes sweeping the table. "Soon as it dries up a little, so we don't all catch pneumonia through the holes in our shoes."

Miss Leiter, the assistant principal, came along with her tray.

Sbarboro aimed the next remark at her. "I'm gonna get the boys in the band to come out. We're going to parade right down to the city hall, and ask for our pay."

"I never heard of such a thing!" Miss Leiter cried. "Haven't you men any dignity left?"

"It's all that fellow Davis at Edison. He must be a communist!" Mrs. Flanagan declared.

"Oh, no, he's a Methodist," Sbarboro informed her. "His father is a minister in Evanston!"

"We all want our pay," Miss Leiter declared. "But everybody knows the city treasury is empty. What good is it going to do to make a disgrace of yourselves?"

"They could raise ten million dollars to build a Coney Island out on the lakefront; they can raise a few million for our back pay," Sbarboro said.

"What has the Fair got to do with our pay? That money was privately subscribed!"

"We don't give a damn where the money comes from," Sbarboro declared. "If we yell loud enough, they'll find a way to pay us!"

"That's the attitude of a barbarian," Miss Leiter said.

"We'll walk out and shut up the schools," Sbarboro snapped. "We should have done it long ago."

"Mr. Sbarboro! We're not common laborers, I hope. We don't go out on strike!" Mrs. Flanagan's eyes were popping.

"Please!" Miss Leiter hissed. "The pupils!"

A hush had fallen all over the lunchroom. The kids were listening.

"Will you have some of this rice pudding? It's good," Miss Leiter said elaborately to Mrs. Flanagan.

"No, thank you," Mrs. Flanagan said. "Really I don't care for any."

Everyone seemed unable to keep his eyes off the dish of rice pudding.

"Say, you certainly must have something on the kid that dishes out the gingerbread," Sbarboro observed loudly as Ben started on his double portion. Now all the eyes swung to Ben's plate.

Damn them! It was his money.

Sbarboro jogged his elbow. "No kidding. Wanta come in on that parade?"

"No," Ben said.

"Do you good. Work off some of that fat!" Sbarboro jabbed his paunch.

As Ben passed room 311, Miss Graham, standing in the doorway, called him: "Oh, Mr. Meisel, would you like a piece of home-made cake?"

"I . . . No, thanks, I . . ." he blundered.

"Come on! I made it myself!" Her voice was so pure, too; like a singing brook, he thought. She put her hand on his sleeve and he was in the room. A bunch of teachers were around the table hastily signing their names on one of those eternal pay petitions.

Her voice was so silvery. "Would you like to sign?"

After this crisis was over the board would check up on those names and kick out those who had signed. Anyway, if their threat did any good, he'd get paid too, without having signed.

The second bell rang. He rushed out.

He went out of his way to pass Miss Crowley's room. She was just coming in from the street. Her umbrella was wet.

"Been for a walk!" she announced, belligerently. "Helps digestion." Standing stiff as a bone, in her gray Civil-Warish dress, she stared through him, daring contradiction.

His hand was on the piece of cake in his pocket. He didn't know how to offer it to the old lady. Aw, the hell, she must have had some lunch in her room. Ben stepped into the men's room and crammed the whole chunk into his mouth.

They were all at a Jewish charities benefit night of *The Good Earth*. Mrs. Moscowitz was enjoying Nazimova very much. "Look how Chinese she looks, and you know she is Jewish."

"What do you mean, she is Jewish!"

"Of course," Rube asserted. "All the big American actors are Jewish. Maurice Schwartz, and Paul Muni, and Charlie Chaplin, and Douglas Fairbanks—"

"I heard he and Mary Pickford are getting a divorce," Celia mentioned.

"No!" There was an awed gasp all around them.

This was like the end, the very end of everything. Mary and Doug busting up!

Lou leafed the program, and noticed the Camel ad. "It's fun to be fooled," it said, showing the trick of cutting a woman in two.

Rube caught his arm. "Listen, Horner is here tonight, maybe I ought to try to talk to him?"

"Don't worry," Lou said. Everybody was staring at the new Jewish governor. "We'll stall it till Roosevelt takes office, then we'll make a deal."

"What's the use of making a deal, I haven't got any dough to pay them," Rube whined.

"Keep your shirt on. I think I got an idea. . . . How much did you clear on those receiverships so far?"

"What's the good of the receiverships? I can't cash in on them," Rube complained. "So I'll milk a few thousand out of the properties. That don't help me."

"Maybe you could cash in on them," Lou said quietly, as the curtain went up.

"Huh?" Rube barked.

During the entire act, Rube Moscowitz writhed as in torture. The instant the applause started, while the curtain was descending, he whirled on Lou. "What do you mean, cash in? I can't sell those receiverships, can I?"

"I wouldn't know anything about it," Lou said suggestively.

"Aw, who would buy them? Anyway, I'd have to give half to that louse Klein."

"Why would you?" Lou suggested again.

The Aetna Corporation, salvaged out of the wreck of Klein's mortgage business, had gradually come into control of receiverships on a few million dollars' worth of property. If Rube Moscowitz could influence a judge to transfer those receiverships to another party, wouldn't the deal be worth something to that party? Say, about a hundred grand?

"I know just the customer! Jaffe. His bank is going bust anyway. He might as well do me a favor before it crashes," Rube said. "And those receiverships are good as gold. Lou, that's a wonderful idea. Boy, will it burn up that bastard Klein! All I got to tell him is the judge transferred the receiverships away from us! Huh?"

"I don't know anything about it," Lou reiterated, glancing down at the Camel ad. The girl was twisted in such a way that the sword never touched her.

"She's all right," Celia was saying patronizingly of Nazimova. "But she's getting old. Did you see those wrinkles around her eyes, even through the makeup? That's why I like close seats, you can see everything."

Ruthie drove the car behind the school, and carefully locked all the doors and windows; even her old junkpile wasn't safe from stripping. The kids in the neighborhood were getting wilder all the time; just savages, she and Rose agreed.

The building was one of those put up during Big Bill the Builder's boom. Recently, the collapse of a wall in a South Side school had led to an investigation. Four new buildings had been condemned. Samples of cement had crumbled in the engineer's fingers. Some of the old hen teachers were so frightened that they went around on tiptoe for fear of falling through the floors. Elephantine Mrs. Leland had been shifted from her upstairs room to the first floor—as a safety measure, Rose Heller claimed.

Now that the children were onto the fact that many of their teachers were stone-broke, a queer vengeful glee pervaded the school. At last their teachers were no better than themselves. Rose got the feeling of humanity being really like a pack of animals, fighting, snatching food from each other's mouths.

She was struggling with the windowpole when Rocco, her monitor, came in. Now she was a teacher, and had a teacher's pet.

"Don't you want to help me, Rocco?" Rose asked.

He unenthusiastically took the pole from her, inserted the tip, and pulled. The window jammed.

"You aren't very strong today," Rose said.

"Nome," he murmured. His face was white.

"What's the matter, Rocco?"

"Nothin'." He gave an angry tug to the pole. The window creaked downward a few inches, and stuck again.

"Thank you, that'll do," Rose said.

He replaced the pole.

The class was cranky, unresponsive. She sent some kids to the board to do problems.

A girl with patched stockings came in with a note from Miss Mac, calling a meeting at noon. As Rose initialed it, she looked up, hearing a howl from Mildred Pinto, who had returned to her seat.

"Teacher! Somebody stole my lunch!" Before Rose could get down the aisle the girl had whirled on Rocco, whose desk was opposite hers, shrieking: "He did it! He did it! You dirty sonofagun! Thief! Thief! Thief!"

"Quiet!" Rose screamed. This was the limit. The limit.

"It was right here in my desk," Mildred wailed. "She saw him! Josie, you saw him! Rocco did it!"

"Teacher, I saw him. He grabbed it. I saw him! Rocco is a robber! Rocco is a robber!" Josie chanted. The class took up the song. "Rocco is a robber! Rocco is a robber!"

Rose pressed her palms to her ears. "Children! Please! Quiet!" she begged, on the verge of hysteria. "Rocco, did you take anything from Mildred's desk?"

Her favorite budged his lips: "Nome."

Rose looked into his desk. It was empty.

"He's sitting on it!" Josie shrieked.

Rose looked at Rocco. He had gone white. "Stand up," she commanded.

He didn't move.

"Rocco, you've always been such a good boy. Stand up."

"Teacher's pet! Yah, yah! Rocco is a robber!" they were singing.

"Look me in the eyes. Rocco! Are you sitting on her lunch?"

A cruel laugh, child-cruel, spread through the room.

Rose seized Rocco's chin, turning up his face. His eyes were swimming in tears.

"Answer me, Rocco, or do you want to go to the principal's office?" she ended in a high, blurred sob. Gripping his shoulders, she tried to pull him off the seat. He fought, clinging with both hands to the edges of his desk. She wrenched one of his hands free. He collapsed on the floor, bawling convulsively.

A newspaper-wrapped sandwich toppled off the edge of the seat.

"There, I told you!" Mildred cried, grabbing the packet.

"Rocco! Stand up like a man!" Rose repeated, but her voice was hardly a whisper. She stooped, trying to lift him. The room had quieted; all were attentive to Rocco's convulsive cracked sobs, the racked sound of a boy trying in spite of every other shame to be manly and keep himself from crying. Crackling across this was the sound of the newspaper as Mildred unwrapped her lunch to make sure it had not been harmed.

"Rocco, tell me why you did it and I won't send you downstairs," Rose implored, crouching near the huddled, convulsive figure. Maybe she was an old maid imagining each kid to be her own. But what if she had married and her child came to this hunger? The wall between her and this was so perilously thin! A sick feeling passed through her breast, just as though a child had mouthed it there, and found it empty.

Rocco had managed to control his sobbing by now. Huddled into a ball, he clung to the iron leg of the schooldesk.

Suddenly Rose doubled down on the floor and, putting her arms around him, whispered: "Tell me what's the trouble, Rocco, I won't punish you. Are you hungry? Are you really that hungry? Did you have any breakfast?"

He tried to wrench away, compressing himself into an even smaller entity.

"Teacher, I know!" Frances Del Angelo cried, standing erect as if to recite. "I live in their building, teacher, they ain't got nothing to eat. His father got no work, and his mother was working scrubbing but now she ain't got no work. I know. That's all he had to eat was the school lunch and now we don't get no more school lunch."

Rose got to her feet. She went to her desk, took out her purse. She took a quarter, but put it back and found a half-dollar. Oh, what was the use, how long would it last!

She knelt by the boy again. "Here, Rocco. Why didn't you tell me you were hungry?" His damp fist closed around the half-dollar. He still didn't dare look into her face, but slunk out of the room, stupefied and ashamed. At the far end, a hand caught out for him. "Rocco, how much she give you?" But he tore away.

Rose walked back to her desk and rapped for attention. She saw her purse lying in the open drawer and, as she sat down, she closed the drawer and, with a despairing feeling, turned the key in the lock.

Miss Mac was so distracted she didn't even notice that Ruth Lipschultz was smoking. "Of course the Board of Education is not really responsible," she reminded the teachers. "They are under no obligation to feed the children."

"Well, neither are we, but we fed them," Bessie Stewart said.

"What I want to know is why aren't these children fed at home? Those families are supposed to be getting relief," Miss Greenberg said.

"Yah, and we're supposed to be getting paid," Ruth sneered.

"We ought to march those hungry kids right down to the city fathers and dump them in their laps," Miss Greenberg declared.

"That's not such a bad idea!" Ruth snapped.

"Don't be absurd! What are we, Bolsheviks, starting hunger marches?"

"The kids are hungry, aren't they?"

"Girls! I don't approve of this!" Miss Mac snapped.

"If we had our pay, we could at least keep up the free lunch," Jean Huboda said.

"I heard that the high school teachers are going to parade downtown to demand their pay," Ruth said. "I think we ought to take the children right along, and show the world!"

Most of the women looked scared.

"There'll be no parading from this school," Miss Mac said firmly. "Girls, it's equally difficult for all of us, but we must have patience a while longer. Miss Haley is doing everything she can—"

"Miss Haley!" Ruth sneered. "We ought to march right down to the mayor's office!"

"Yah?" Bessie said, wearily, shoving a newspaper toward them. "The mayor is in Florida, vacationing."

Late in the afternoon Rose felt herself getting sick, out of sheer nervous exhaustion, though it was a week early. Her pains were always terrible, knocking her out for two or three days. By the time the final bell rang she just wanted to crawl in bed and die. The muscular burst of the released children breaking out of the room was the last blow.

Coming into the house, she sensed something was wrong. Her mother, always bustling, was so subdued.

"Rose, didn't you see in the paper, the Jaffe Bank closed today," she said, awed and bitter. "When pa comes home, don't let him talk about it, try to cheer him up."

And now it seemed as though the ordered world were coming to an end. It was as though skyscrapers were toppling, first the Board of Trade Building, then the Morrison, the Pure Oil, then in a giant crash the London Guarantee, the Wrigley, the Opera Building, everything crashing and smashing, in an open-armed rush toward extinction.

A whole chain of neighborhood banks closed. Then a downtown bank closed.

The nation held its breath, hoping. Just hang on a few days more, till the inauguration. Overnight, the magic of a smile, and all will be well again. You have to collect the cards, sweep the table bare, before shuffling out the new deal.

Mort Abramson, poker shark, had one pet remark: "But the chips stay where they were."

So everybody was waiting and it was zero hour. Among others down there was Mayor Cermak of Chicago. He was right close to the new President. And who could tell but probably one of the little matters he might mention would be about a Chicago politician, Reuben Moscowitz, a good fellow who had been a little careless about his income tax but who was willing to make a deal now and pay up. And that little matter would be fixed without the waste of public investigation. Say, fifty thousand in Liberty Bonds that Rube had fortunately drawn out of the Jaffe Bank, a few days before it closed. And the new deal would begin. People would breathe again, freely.

Then as the President's party appeared at one of the pre-inauguration ceremonies, a crazy man stood up on a bench and fired point-blank at the new President[4]. The shot hit Mayor Cermak of Chicago, and his dying words were published all over the land.

"I am glad it was me and not him."

In Chicago, Runt Plotkin got the lowdown on the mayor's words. Take it from him: "They got me!" was what Chicago's mayor said.

Sure, it was the destiny of Chicago to save the nation. It was not Philadelphia or Pittsburgh, but Chicago blood that saved America.

But suppose the mayor had not had an opportunity to mention, before he died, that a good fellow and loyal party man in Chicago was ready to fix up his income tax? Who would now front for Rube Moscowitz?

Lou Margolis quoted Shakespeare: "Beware the ides of March."

Then all the banks were closed. The President was saved, and before he began to pitch his inning he called time out, closing all the banks. "Count your chips, boys," he said.

Everybody was cheerful. So damn cheerful. For this was the way of the American people, pack them in on a rush-hour street car, jam elbows in backs, kick knees in nuts, and it's comical—hail, hail, the gang's all here! Go to war laughing!

And the good old American principle of all men are equal was re-established. All a man owned was the cash in his pocket. The richest were the poorest, for everybody knows that millionaires carry scarcely any cash about them, signing checks wherever they go. It was said that Edsel Ford had to borrow half a buck from the black boy that shined his shoes, to pay a taxi driver.

Everybody was friendly. Everybody was solicitous. Aline called up Sylvia and said: "Have you got any money? I was lucky I had just cashed a check for twenty dollars, I can let you have five."

[4] On February 15, 1933, Giuseppe Zangara attempted to shoot president-elect Roosevelt as he made a speech in Miami. A shot hit Chicago Mayor Cermak, who died 19 days later. Zangara was executed on March 20.

Sol Meisel distributed all the cash in the place among his employees, keeping no more for himself than for each worker.

"I had to borrow sixty cents from my stenographer or I wouldn't have had any lunch," Lou Margolis laughingly reported to Celia. "Lucky I've got an I.C. ticket!"

"I hope things keep on this way," Mitch Wilner told Sylvia. "Nobody even asks for money. I had the garage fill up the car with gas and oil."

Oh, it was democracy. All the cash anybody needed was street car fare. And if the banks never opened, the street cars would have to carry passengers free.

Why should any banks reopen? Harry Perlin said to Ruth: "The whole trouble with the world is money. What do we need money for? We're getting along without it!"

The *Tribune* issued scrip to all its employees.

USE YOUR CHARGE ACCOUNTS, the department stores thundered in full-page ads.

Ha ha. That's good! Our charge accounts!

We'll Take Checks! the theaters advertised.

Ha ha! That's good! Checks.

You had to have cash to go to the movies.

Alvin Fox saw his father standing by the window, hour after hour, looking vacantly upon the street. They had been hopeful of some orders from the Fair that was so near opening. But now, "Who is buying anything? Nobody."

A man couldn't be judged by his actions these days, everybody was acting nutty. Yet a queer avoidance was felt all through the factory. Scarcely anyone went into the old man's office.

Alvin was going to suggest to the old man that he take a vacation, stay home for a few days. He entered his father's office and saw the Old Fox at his desk. He was busily tearing sheets of paper into strips, against a ruler. Alvin stood frozen, listening to the ripping sounds.

The old man looked up. His expression was cheerful, beaming.

And Alvin knew that his father had gone over the edge, at last.

"Do you want some money?" the old man said, waving the bits of blank paper. "I am making money. Here, Alvin, pay the payroll, pay everybody. Thousand-dollar bills!"

> Dancing in the dark till the tune ends,
> Dancing in the dark and it soon ends . . .

Restlessness pervaded the school, like on the days before summer vacation. The corridors were astir with kids running messages between teachers. A girl from Ruth's class brought a note to Rose. "Don't sign anything," it read. Rose was mystified. The room was a hive of whispers. She couldn't think.

A moment later a monitor brought a note around from the principal's office. "It has come to my attention that certain agitators have asked teachers to leave their classes today. Needless to say I expect all teachers to hold classes and keep order as usual. Our plight is no excuse for a relaxation of loyalty."

Rose saw only three sets of initials on the note. She handed it back without signing it. "All right, girlie," she said.

The girl suppressed a giggle, made a knowing face, and bounded out of the room. The kids jumped in their seats.

"Order, order!" Rose rapped her ruler on her desk.

Rocco had his hand up.

"Teacher, kin we strike too? Kin we go in the parade?"

Tears welled to her eyes.

"Yah, yah!" they all yelled. "Teacher! Leave us go in the parade!"

The fire bell sounded. Whooping, the kids burst out of the room. The corridors were full of kids howling and singing: "We strike! We strike! Yay! Yay! Yay!" and making obscene noises with their lips.

Several teachers ran along the corridors trying to quiet the children while others stood in their doorways laughing dizzily. It was rumored that Ruth Lipschultz had rung the gong.

Bessie Stewart seized Rose's elbow. "Half the schools are out! Come on, let's go!"

In the excitement, more joined, even lame old Mrs. Carey was swept into their group.

They piled into Ruth's car till they hung out the doors.

"Us too! Us too!" Kids swarmed around the car, ran after it for blocks.

As they neared the Loop, they could already feel the pulse of a crowd converging. On some of the streets they saw marching platoons of teachers. Hastily lettered placards rode over their heads.

FREE EDUCATION. THAT'S US!

PAY THE TEACHERS!

WHO GOT OUR MONEY?

A whole group, swinging up Jackson, wore armbands reading *Unpaid Teacher*. They were from Edison High. Ruthie piloted the car through Jackson to Grant Park and swept up behind the pair of monuments of Indians on horseback. "Liberty Square!" the plaza had suddenly been christened. It was swarming with teachers. A pupil with his hands full of the armbands, probably printed in a school printshop, ran up to them.

"Me! Me!" Rose reached and got one. A choking, sweet emotion of friendliness flooded her.

They seemed different from teachers. Their faces were awake. The men had color on their lips again. A group sang:

"Hallelujah, give us a handout . . ."

They were suddenly in line, parading down Michigan. There was even a band—and another band—slamming out the music of "Marching through Georgia." Three high school bands! Rose could have hugged every one of those kids!

In the line, marching, Rose caught sight of a group of teachers from Ogden High, her own high school teachers, and only for an instant did it make her feel old and destined to teach school eternally, like them. Her high spirits carried her beyond that thought. She wanted to make herself known to them, to show them how she was one with them now!

An awful lot of policemen had appeared on the sidewalks.

"Pay the police!" a bunch of teachers sang out, and the whole column took up the chant: "Pay the teachers! Pay the police!"

The cops laughed, and were with them. Michigan Avenue traffic was halted for them. State Street was cleared for them!

The sidewalks were lining thicker with people, and remarks were heard, cheering them on: "Go to it, girls!"

The big sooty pillars of the city hall came into sight.

Ella rushed into Sam's office charged with excitement. "Isn't it wonderful!" She pulled him to the window. They could see the parade coming up Washington Street.

Sam always had an instant emotional response to scenes of unison, newsreels of crowds always electrified him, but he knew he was a sucker for such things, now, and while the sight of the parading teachers raised his pulse, he tried to calm Ella, saying: "Wait! Wait! The revolution isn't here yet!"

"But look at them! Schoolteachers! And they're absolutely militant!"

"Yah," Sam said. "But once they get their pay, you'll see they'll sit right back and be the most reactionary group in the city."

"Oh, Sam, don't be such a pessimist! At least they're using mass action!"

He shrugged, and indicated the newspaper on his desk. "They just convicted the Scottsboro boys again," he said. But she refused to be downhearted.

"They'll never hang!" she cried, and pulled him out of the office.

"They won't even get into the city hall," Sam said.

"Well, that'll teach them something, too."

Ben Meisel wasn't going to march in their fool parade, but he might as well go downtown and watch. Probably half of them would get arrested, and thrown out of their jobs.

He was in a kosher-style restaurant on Wells Street, eating a salami omelet, when he heard shouting on the street. The waiter went to the door. A customer left his food and went to the door.

"It's the teachers," the counterman said. "I don't blame them. It's a shame."

Ben kept himself from eating faster. But when he was finished, they were still marching. A group from his own school passed, actually holding aloft a banner marked Greeley High. Sbarboro was holding one end of the banner. Miss Graham saw him, and waved for him to come along. She shouted something, but an El passed overhead and drowned her voice.

Ben drew back on the sidewalk. He walked in the direction they were going.

A lot of cops were around the city hall entrance, but made no effort to stop them. The teachers swept into the corridors.

—We want the mayor!

—He'll see us all right, all right!

Rose, hanging onto Ruth Lipschultz, found herself pulled along on the very heels of the leaders of the parade. They crowded the wide yellowish corridors, jammed into the elevators.

Nobody seemed to be sure who was mayor, since Cermak's assassination.

"Last week it was Corr[5]. This week it's Kelly[6]. They're just passing the buck. What's the difference who it is! We want our dough!"

"They've got seventeen million dollars in a reserve fund; they can use it to pay us!"

They were at the door to the mayor's offices. A plump Irishman said: "He's talking to the governor right now! He's trying to get the dough for you!" At last he gave up, and admitted a committee to the mayor.

The hundred in the hallway settled back, waited. The women sang:

> "Who's afraid of the big bad wolf,
> Big bad wolf . . ."

and the men responded:

> "*Who's* afraid . . .?"

The group came out of the mayor's office. Davis, the leader, stood on something, sending his voice down the hall.

"They're trying to raise the money. They're going to issue tax warrants—"

"We heard that one before!"

They had practically captured the city hall, yet what could they do with it?

---

[5] Frank Corr was acting Mayor of Chicago following the assassination of Mayor Cermak, and held the post from March 15, 1933 to April 8, 1933.
[6] Edward Kelly was Mayor of Chicago from 1933 to 1947.

Down the hallway, down the elevators, out to the crowd that still loitered on the street the story was relayed: tax anticipation warrants. Seventy cents on the dollar.

Now the cops began to ease them out of the city hall. They wandered down through the building, in dissatisfied groups. On Randolph Street they were collecting again. Feeling that they weren't through, that something had to be done.

—Tax warrants . . .

—We're the suckers!

—Why don't they pay their taxes!

As if by instinct, they were surging down the block toward the Chicago Title and Trust Company. The teachers flowed onto the sidewalk. There it was—a building—a front of large brown stones.

"They're holding back millions in taxes," a speaker cried; he was standing on a *Help Keep the City Clean* box. "All those estates—the McCormick estates, the Field estates—they're holding back millions in taxes. . . ."

Through the main floor windows, rows and rows of desks could be seen, and a cashier's cage.

Ben Meisel had walked along this far, satisfied in himself that the parade was a fiasco, glad he hadn't joined.

Someone was making a speech, yelling about real estate barons.

A brick crashed through the plate-glass window.

A mounted cop rode onto the sidewalk. The horse's hoof grazed Ben's toes. He howled higher than all the screaming.

The shattering glass released the last barrier of timidity in the teachers. And yet there seemed nothing to attack, no point at which they could seize, take what was coming to them.

—The banks! Let's talk to the bankers!

—Charley Dawes!

—Melvin Traylor!

Rose found herself with Ruthie again. A teacher with gray bobbed hair was explaining harshly: "Sure I was right in the mayor's office. He calls up the banker. Mel, he says, it's Mel and Ed with them, that's who's running this town, Mel, Ed . . ."

"To the board!"

They were moving. Some were falling away, going off by twos and fours, but Rose was happy, she didn't want this to stop, they must storm on and on, and achieve!

They invaded the LaSalle-Wacker Building. The Board of Education office seemed deserted.

"They're here all right."

Up among the leaders she heard: "They've got to be here. Waterman is on the carpet today. He told me."

Waterman, an assistant principal, had talked over WCFL and made it strong.

"They're here all right—they've got him in there somewhere!"

Rose, excited and disheveled, was in the thick of the band that rushed the board rooms. Somebody put his fist through the glass panel and opened the door from the inside.

They swarmed into the room. It was empty. The men teachers were furious now. One of them picked up a typewriter and banged it to the floor. They rushed through the board rooms, and flung open a last door. They saw several men, in arrested motion, as if they had been running to jump out the windows. Waterman gawked, like one rescued from the gallows.

Awkwardly, a sense of order, of dignity, was restored. Mr. Davis and his committee extricated themselves from the crowd. One of them had his tie jerked around his neck, and was embarrassedly straightening it.

"What do you want us to do? Do you want us to close the schools?" the president of the board cried, defensively belligerent.

"Yes!" a chorus roared. They were standing on chairs, on desks.

"We're holding a meeting right now, if you'll allow us to—"

"Pay or strike!" a man teacher shouted.

The shout was taken up, resounding through the halls.

Davis jumped on a chair and reported to the teachers: "He says they're trying to arrange a loan. They want a few days' time."

"Vote strike if they don't come across," someone shouted from the crowd.

The actual motion was scarcely heard, in the shouts of strike.

A few days later the teachers got paid for two months of the previous year. The pay was in tax warrants which the banks guaranteed at par.

A CENTURY OF PROGRESS[1]

Ruth LIPSCHULTZ gave Harry the tip about the job at the Fair. "Can you get down there?" He searched his pockets. One dime. "I can get down but I'll have to walk back," he laughed.

"Listen, I just cashed a tax warrant. . . ." She crushed a dollar into his palm. Even in this emergency he felt funny about taking money from a girl.

Trucks were slamming between buildings in all stages of construction. It was like the old days, hearing the banging stutter of rivet hammers.

To see a bunch of dago carpenters sitting on a pile of lumber eating their chunky sandwiches; to see a man go up to another guy in overalls who had both hands working, and good-naturedly rifle him for a fag, gosh, it felt good again.

Summer, winter, spring, baby!

Harry threaded his way among stacks of sheetrock, over ankle-snaring cables; he dodged handtrucks and wheelbarrows and asked a dozen guys for Mr. Nagle.

They were building the Fair now, everything the last minute! Let the banks shut, let all the paper bunk about credit and gold values go to hell, Roosevelt was going to make things hum, everybody was starting with him from scratch again. Go, Chicago! with ye olde I Will spirit! Chicago would show them how it was done!

The building was filled with the beautiful cacophony of buzz saws, hammers near and distant, the hiss and spark of welders.

A fellow in a vest studded with colored drawing pencils, lugging a roll of blueprints, yelled: "Sure, I'm Nagle. Whatyawant?"

Every two words, somebody would interrupt Nagle, asking for instructions.

"Tell you what I need. Got six exhibits building and expect two more in this week, Johnson toothpaste and the Lever silk mills. I need an all-around man to sort of keep things humming."

He began explaining the fur exhibit to Harry, carving counters, showcases, movie screens out of the air. Harry made a suggestion: "Wouldn't more people see the movie screen from two lanes instead of one, if it was faced the other way?"

"By golly!" Nagle spread blueprints on the floor. Could be done, it could be done. . . .

---

[1] "A Century of Progress" was the name of the World's Fair held in Chicago from 1933 to 1934.

A harassed messenger rushed up to Nagle, summoning him to another job. "Well, listen, what's your name, Perlin? Harry—well, listen, Harry, if anyone wants me I'm in the canning exhibit. And say, if they deliver some reflectors, sign for them, will you? Fine!"

Harry took off his coat. He was working!

It turned out to be only twenty-five a week, but a fellow hardly even thought of money, it was the feeling of his brains being oiled and used again, of wheels beginning to turn.

"Honest, I think Roosevelt is going to make a difference!" he said to Ruth. He felt so good he could dance. Even the schoolteachers were getting their back pay, everything was working out fine. "I think maybe things will be all right now."

She smiled, knowingly.

Bull Market in Bulls

In New York, a fellow always has three or four deals coming to a head, converging toward one decisive day that'll make or break him; and how can he work today when any moment Keller of Paramount may call saying the job is okay, five hundred a week for supervising sculptural ornament on sets, and it's practically a sure thing because Keller is an old Paris friend of Myra Roth, maybe she slept with him; and in a couple of years you could retire with Hollywood dough and have a studio-barn and a dog and really do sculpture.

And the Whitney Museum ought to answer today, they're buying younger Americans, they've already bought a Moore and a Ben-Shmuel so they ought to buy; and that Radio City contract still might come through, and ask Solomon Weiss for that contact on *Vanity Fair*, they might bite on the new idea of using sculptured caricatures of Hitler, Jimmy Durante, Roosevelt.

Have to take the penguin ashtray model up to Solomon Weiss anyway, at least that's good for twenty-five bucks. Down to the last buck again.

In New York nobody is in their office before eleven, so you waste the morning. All out of ideas for those lousy ashtrays. The one of a monkey with a curly tail to hook around chair-arms was a natural, and this penguin ought to go since Rockwell Kent brought on the penguin craze from wherever it is that he goes to lay the Eskimo gals, penguin earrings, and penguin ice-cream molds for bridge parties.

"I hope you will not sell me anything today," Solomon Weiss puffs out each word like a careful smoke ring; the fat bastard is a good contact because he might always get back his swanky art gallery. On his desk is a cute tin and wire ashtray of a charging bull, which Joe recognizes as the work of a nance that has been selling Weiss lately. Weiss examines the penguin unhappily. "My dear fellow, why penguins, even the dime stores are full of penguins, I am wondering even if it will be worth the expense of casting?" Make bulls, he says, everybody is reading Mr. Hemingway's book, and he permits himself a pun: "There is a bull market in bulls."

All right the next one is a bull but how about twenty-five bucks for the penguin? Then Weiss begins to cry on your shoulder: if business keeps on like this, he will be peddling from door to door with a basket. And he offers fifteen bucks. "I have now many clever artists who will supply me at this price."

That damn little fairy with his cut-out tin! The little turds! They always have some rich sucker supporting them, but they have to nance around and ruin the market, sell for any price just so they can wave a check and be real professional artists selling their work! A year ago Weiss paid fifty bucks for a model.

Can't haggle when you're broke.

The Paramount guy has suddenly been called to Hollywood, and *Vanity Fair* suggests *The New Yorker*, and Radio City after six phone calls says call in the afternoon.

Joe walked around Radio City, goddam the bastards, it was impressive. God, yes, it was great. He walked around the long blocks, studying the sculptural ornament. Maybe he was jealous, but all of this stuff seemed dead. All so smooth, so clever, fitting too well as mere decoration of these buildings. All so goddam modern. Joe thought of how when cathedrals were built, a great sculpture had resulted. Who would ever cross oceans to look at these carved lintels of flying gods with zigzag beards? Cleverness, cleverness, skill, but nowhere the feeling of beauty carefully uncovered.

Yes, here they had restored a little function to the artist in America. But what did it amount to? Work for maybe a dozen artists, chiseled down on their prices with talk about the publicity value. And the fat mural contracts had gone to foreigners.

Joe crossed Sixth Avenue. Directly opposite this hundred-million-dollar monument to modernism was the street of nickel hamburger joints, crowded with jobhunters, hanging around dishwasher employment agencies. Standing eating a Nedick hot dog, he was figuring what was the use of kidding himself. The Paramount thing would be no and the Radio City thing would be no and he'd be lucky to get a job as a window dresser. There was a lousy bus agency sign, *Chicago, $12.00.*

That was the day Mort Abramson phoned. Maybe Mort was calling for Sylvia, maybe she was separated from Mitch, maybe Mitch had died.

Maybe the call, the link with her, meant the Radio City thing would come through. Like that time, in a crisis, meeting her uncle on the Safed road.

Mort was coming around for dinner. Joe couldn't work. He went into Stewart's, got coffee. It was rumored Stewart's was going to require a minimum check of fifteen cents, to get rid of the villagers. He glanced around. Same freaks, fairies and lesbians, phah! Christ, others must see him as one of these, a hanger-on at Stewart's.

Suppose he went back to Chicago? On fifteen bucks? Joe came home broke, they would tell Sylvia. "My bank failed," he could say.

From a rear table, Ted Baron, a John Reeder, slid over. Now Ted would stare at him with that sad accusatory eye: why didn't he create proletarian art? He could just see himself turning out stumpy square-headed proletarians; why the hell did their figures always have to be lumpy and scowling? There were plenty of workers in New York too, millions of scrawny-necked clerks and Joan-Crawford-mouthy department store girls but who ever saw one that looked like a figure out of a John Reed exhibition?

Where was the meaning of it? Where the beauty? Where did it relate to America? Hell, from his very first figure he had worked for an attachment to life, to reality, trying to do that flophouse bum. (Too bad Mr. Freedman didn't have a branch flophouse in New York, his son might need it soon.) And what about that heroic figure of a pioneer that he had left in Palestine? But no, they had to teach him about proletarian art.

They were organizing a show, Ted Baron said. At the New School. What the hell was the use of exhibiting? Where was the sculpture going? Into what public parks? Into whose garden? Where, in the modern cubbyhole apartments?

And, sure, Ted had come into the place without a nickel and was just sitting there until someone would take his check and bail him out. Joe was burned up. Why did they all look to him. Joe Freedman always got along, everybody figured. Teaching in the Y.M.H.A., or making ashtrays. A Guggenheimer. They couldn't forget it. Four years gone and they acted as though he was still living on the dough.

Ted offered to show him his new figure: "This is a big baby, five feet."

Damn them, while he ran his ass off with ashtrays and window-trimming jobs, they sat on their cans and worked. At mealtimes someone always came along with a sandwich. At least they were doing sculpture.

Gradually a fellow gave up his dream of a big skylight studio high enough for twelve-foot monuments, with a balcony bedroom. But if at least you had your own bath, you had an apartment; you could ask girls up. This place would impress Mort. The building even boasted a canopy. It had been remodeled during the boom, cut up into tiny one-room studios, each with a closet turned into a bathroom. The rent was only twenty-five bucks, as the building was now in receivership. And who would ever tell Mort he was two months behind?

Mort entered, instantly appraising the room. He had not grown fat, Joe noticed. One thing the modern spirit had accomplished. And the diet ads. The slightest sign of fat was kidded off a person.

They shook hands. Joe saw the heavy gold band on Mort's marriage finger. He would do that.

"How goes it?" Mort said.

"Okay."

"Doing any sculpture?" Mort walked around the room.

"There isn't any room in this dump for a big figure. I've been doing mostly commercial stuff anyway. I do my own stuff in summer."

Mort stopped before the head of Ann, the one thing Joe had kept out of storage.

"Looks cute. Who is she?" He glanced suggestively at Joe.

"A girl I knew," Joe said coolly.

Mort stood in the center of the room. Probably figuring the rent of the place.

"I hear you're a pappy," Joe said.

"Yep. Two, now!"

The question Joe burned to ask seemed so palpable to him that it must weight the air. But surely if she had a child, he would have heard.

Mort didn't know whether he ought to talk about Sylvia. The place wasn't much but these village dumps were supposed to rent high. That studio bed looked like it was put to good use.

"Can I take a leak?" he asked.

There was a bathroom. Tiny, but white-tiled. On the back of the door was a douche-bag. Aha. Trust Joe. Maybe Joe would fix up a party. Might as well get a change of diet while in New York. Joe must have a bookful of numbers. Artists got them easy.

Emerging, he said: "Let's eat."

It was just then, on Mort's profile, that Joe noticed change: a fullness of the jowls, meaty, well fed, and juicy health around the mouth: meat eating.

He wasn't going to put on a show for Mort. He took him to a German bakery-restaurant.

"Beef stew and noodles," Joe ordered from the forty-cent supper. The waitress wiped soup spillings off the table. Mort ordered a T-bone steak, rare.

"How's business?" Joe asked, with sarcastic inflection.

"We're doing pretty good," Mort admitted. "I have to make a couple of trips to New York every season to keep up with the styles."

"To swipe them, you mean."

"Sure. It's done in the best houses."

"Well, for cry sake, put an end to this Empress Eugénie stuff," Joe pleaded. "I feel lopsided from watching cows balancing chips on their heads."

"It won't last much longer," was Mort's opinion. "That girl in the Camel ad, wearing a man's felt, started a new craze. What's a good show in town? I saw *Another Language* last night. It's got a sculptor in it. Made me think of you. Did you see it?"

"That goo!" Joe groaned.

"My wife is interested in the theater, you know," Mort said.

The waitress brought their orders. The steak wasn't rare enough. Mort complained.

"This isn't the Red Star Inn," Joe commented. "You takes what you gets and you likes it."

Mort felt Joe's antagonism. He didn't know why Joe resented him anyway. He had always felt friendly toward the fellow. It couldn't be that childhood romance with Sylvia, why, men their age knew that the whole thing about love was—well, after being married a few years you saw it differently.

He tried to loosen things with a Mae West joke, the one about her declining to address the Minute Men, with the remark: "I like a man who takes his time."

Joe smiled wanly.

Mort talked about the old gang. Alvin's old man was in an asylum. Went nuts in the bank holiday, started passing out million-dollar checks.

"Heard about your friend Sam?" he tried. "He got thrown in the can for defending some communists. Didn't he try a case you were interested in, once?"

"Yah," Joe said. "He wanted to determine the value of art according to a wage scale. He wasn't so crazy either."

Mort felt even more uneasy. He guessed they just weren't the same kind of people any more. Too bad. They might have had a party. "Coming to the Fair?" he asked, to break the damn silence.

"I thought I might go to Chicago for a while," Joe remarked. "There ought to be a lot of sculpture to do around the Fair."

"Sure. Say, I could give you some ins." Mort felt they were getting together again. "Why don't you fly back with me?"

"Well . . ."

Mort took a box out of his pocket and swallowed some bicarb, explaining he had to take it at every meal, for his nervous stomach. "I always go by air now; it hardly costs more than the Century, and when you figure the time it saves you, it's cheaper. It's the only way to travel."

"Yah." Joe eyed him queerly. "I'll bet."

Joe said he had a class and they parted. Mort was relieved. The guy gave him a pain. People like Joe just didn't know how to enjoy life.

Mort hailed a cab. He could ask the driver if he knew a good place in Harlem. But naw, a married man couldn't take chances. There was a radio going in the cab; some husky-voiced mama was singing "The Best Things in Life Are Free."

Rolling off the bus, Joe scarcely knew whether it was night or day. His throat and belly and nostrils were permeated with the taste, feel, smell of exhaust. Grasping his one suitcase, he staggered for some coffee. Thirty hours! The grime was in his hair. He drank the coffee scalding, but couldn't cut the bus taste off his tongue.

Washing and slicking a little in the bus station lavatory, Joe Freedman walked to the El. Chicago again.

This time Blondy Walsh didn't ask him to lunches. "Hello, Joe, you're just the guy I want. I need some twelve-inch manikins . . ." Walsh had scaled down his skyscraper architecture to the size of advertising displays, for the Fair. A radio exhibit was to show a native in a jungle beating a signal drum, and Eddie Cantor broadcasting to the modern family.

"Want to work by the piece or by the hour?" Joe was asked.

Skyride

Lou Green was thinking maybe a job as one of these rickshaw boys would be good, keep him working out in the open, build up his physique again. Even though he'd have to wear those crazy red pants. And who could tell—a millionaire's daughter might get into his rickshaw and . . .

There was a line all the way outside the building. The employment manager gave him the X-ray eye.

"I'll tell you," he said, "we have so many applicants, we're taking college boys only."

A neon tube is a burning gaseous vacancy, Alvin thought. That's me.

The neon lights streaked the young night like vivid scars. Orange, yellow, red, their pulsations were like the electric nervous beat within himself. There was a fire close-circuited within him, consuming nothing, yet pulsing ceaselessly in confinement, an angry, unknowable electricity, racing in circles, no place to escape, no destination.

He waited near the entrance to the Chinese pagoda. Because she had not wanted him to call for her at the Stadium where she was rehearsing, Alvin scented that Ora would affect a married woman's air of intrigue. Why monkey with her? He knew that this kind of thing was no longer what he wanted.

"... to the faraway Boss in the sky
Where the strays are branded and counted . . ."

Science and invention! he might point out ironically. And here was the Buddhist temple, a vaunted triumph because it had been built in the ancient way—without the use of a single nail!

"... there go I
A-headin' for the last roundup ..."

The song howled from the chain of loudspeaker posts. Progress! In the old days you could walk away from the bandstand, but now the posts carried the blare wherever you hid.

He caught sight of Ora leaving two girls, just letting them glimpse her meeting a man.

"Those girls are so dumb, it's a pain!" Ora cried. "I don't know why I bother with the whole thing except they're so hopelessly in need of people with even a little stage experience, and after all it's for a noble cause."

Hilariously, she described the clumsiness of the girls in the Miriam's Dance chorus. "Actually they don't know their right foot from their left!"

"Git along, little dogie, git along, git along ..."

A dogie is not a little dog but an orphaned calf, Alvin remembered.

"But you can't help being thrilled!" Ora continued. "When so many people are working together, there's something about it—are you bored, Alvin?" She warmed along his side. "I never know what you're thinking."

"I gave up thinking long ago," he replied in the required manner. He could make her watch his every remark, for a sign of his father's insanity.

In the Italian restaurant they sat by a window over the lagoon, so they could see the fireworks. Ora removed her white jacket and settled back, giving him a provocative glance. Her bare arms looked squashy near the shoulders, the "soft well-rounded arms" of the young matron. His glance traveled to the Chinese red of her fingernails, splayed on the table.

"Aren't they barbarian?" She tensed the claws. "They make me feel so savage, so female!"

She attacked her spaghetti. "One thing Mae West did for her sex," she said. "Figures are coming back. I can eat again! Those Palestinian dances are certainly strenuous—and I'll have to be in the modern numbers too, they're so short on leaders."

Why must he try to make her? Why was it taken for granted that chasing another woman was a thing in itself worth while, especially if she were a married woman?

With surprise, Alvin watched his own reactions. Here was a pretty woman offering herself for the game and he just wasn't interested.

"I could kill Mort," she said. "He knows I'm just dying to see some decent theater again, there has hardly been a show in town all winter, Chicago has just become the sticks, but he'll never take me to New York with him. I bet he has a wench there. After all Mort is just a business man."

"So am I," Alvin reminded her.

"Let's break loose, Alvin," she suggested. "I feel like doing something wild."

The stream of people in search of pleasure conveyed only an impression of anxiety to him, they seemed so afraid of missing something, of not getting everything their half buck entitled them to; even the crowd in the Streets of Paris depressed him: the lumpish dull faces of three girls in houri pants doing a routine tease while a barker yapped—there was the whole of life. Lose yourself in humanity.

In the Rat Cellar, supposed to be like a Paris dive, a pair did the usual Apache dance, and a girl in a Mae West costume sang:

> "Eadie was a lady,
> Though her past was shady,
> Eadie had class with a capital K . . ."

"You were in Paris for quite a while, weren't you?" Ora kept on. "Did you ever see Gertrude Stein? Is there really such a person as Alice B. Toklas?"

"Eadie did things in a ladylike way . . ."

He remembered a Paris dive he had wandered into once, that first night with Joe Freedman in Paris—they had certainly done all the dumb standard things, to Europe in a cattleboat —and wandering into the Noctambules to lose his cherry to some five-franc whore. A wonder he hadn't caught the clap.

Ora was telling a Mae West joke. About how she went to a house-party in England and spent all her time sliding down barristers. Only, he remembered having heard the same joke about Dorothy Parker, a few years ago.

He drove Ora home. As she leaned against him in the car, there were still the dim flushes of desire, and, poor kid, she was only lonesome too.

"Want to come in for a drink?" He went in.

"Just a moment till I fulfill my matronly duty," and she stepped into a bedroom and saw that her sleeping babies were okay. The apartment seemed hushed. Ora came out humming, with the radio:

> "Little man, you're crying,
> I know why you're blue,
> Someone took your kiddy car away . . ."

He squeezed her hand and said good-by.

She struck a final pose in the doorway, hand on sidethrust hip, the red nails gleaming. "Come up and see me some time," she quoted, with the Mae West lip twitch.

Alvin felt the sickness of the entire world within himself.

Rudy emerged from his office. As he crossed the waiting room, he stopped a few times to greet patients. "How are you today, Mrs. Kelleher, are you getting that dental work done? Good. I thought that was at the bottom of your trouble." And: "How do you like Dr. Swaboda, Mrs. Patlak? Fine!"

The large waiting room was almost filled, and there was a stir of steady activity. The waits were not long. It tickled him to feel the satisfaction, the approval, in the mood of the patients. Their attitude was so completely different from the hopeless hopefulness of those who waited on the benches of free hospital clinics.

It was a good feeling to be busy all day, to be exercising the best of his skill. And there was no chance for the suspicious antagonism that could develop between doctor and patient when the doctor was worrying about bill beaters, and the patient was wondering if he would be overcharged, and if the doc really could take care of his case or was just stringing him along for the fee, instead of sending him to someone else.

It was good to sense the rapidly growing confidence of the patients, in spite of the ceaseless slander of the Alliance by the rest of the medical profession. Sometimes there was even a laugh, as today when a hefty housewife burst out frankly, after his examination: "Doctor, I'll be honest with you, I didn't know whether to have confidence or not, when I came in here, but I thought, I'll take a chance. I been to enough doctors in my life so I can tell when a man knows his business. And I figured if I don't like it I don't have to let them do anything to me. Eh?"

"Sure thing," he said.

"Well, I'm satisfied. I was suspicious, but now I see this is on the up and up."

He could have hugged that dame.

And it was good to feel that they had done right in taking a chance on their convictions; they had hit it right, and the clinic was going over. They had been through their horrors. From the moment the doors were opened, the campaign of vilification by Dr. Feldner and his clique had begun. At first it was funny, then it was unbelievable, then it was utterly frightening to the men that the self-appointed guardians of the profession should expend so much energy in opposing this innocent little institution. Within a week Alliance men saw how really drastic their move had been: they had cut themselves off from their profession, and if this venture failed, they were out in the cold. One by one, they had to drop their hospital staff connections, their teaching positions; they were even hesitant to show themselves at clinical demonstrations. Swaboda bitterly jested about getting a false beard and sneaking in to watch Dr. Feldner do a tubal pregnancy.

And they knew it would take only one medical mischance to wreck them. There was the scare a month after the clinic opened, when a fever rash broke out among the new-born babies at the little hospital to which they sent all their patients since that clique of medical bigwigs had succeeded in getting every large hospital in the city to close its doors to them. It was not a bad little hospital, in fact it was as high in standard as most fancily endowed institutions, but they had all been used to working in the big-name places. Perusi practically lived in that infant ward. Once, coming down in the middle of the night, Rudy had found Swaboda there too, hunched over a crib while Perusi slept in raucous exhaustion on a table. Any other hospital might lose a few babies, but if they had even the shadow of an epidemic, they were done for.

Finally it was Weintraub who had had the bright and simple idea of transferring the infants from the first to the top floor, where fewer nurses would pass through the room, and in the quieter and better-isolated ward the kids had all recovered.

It was maddening that the fate of their enterprise, more, of their entire idea, should hang on some idiotic little thing like that. But they had pulled through that crisis, and the crisis of fear that had attacked the men when they were actually expelled from their medical societies.

Matt had pulled them out of that one. Instead of letting himself be automatically dropped, he had demanded trial. Then Swaboda, Rudy, and Perusi had challenged their cases, and all four had come up before the regional council of the S.A.P.S.

There was only one formal charge against them: advertising.

The trial took place in that same assembly room where Mitch had delivered his report. There sat the full council of the Chicago district, ten rows of them: a sanhedrin.

Rudy had been afraid he would be unable to look the men in the face. But, instead, it was easy. They were the older men, some had been his teachers, he had worked with others in the clinics; Dr. Feldner, blow-faced and swollen with indignation, glared at him and Matthews. Then, just as he heard his name called, he caught sight of old Doc Meyerson. Meyerson wiggled his spiny brows, and grinned to him. Rudy had to turn his head to keep his eyes from filming over.

The charges had scarcely been read before Swaboda was on his feet, tearing the roof off the place. "You're not trying us!" he cried. "We're trying you! Every patient lying in County for lack of adequate preventive care is trying the S.A.P.S.! Every tubercular, every paretic, is trying your so-called medical organization for consistently opposing every advance in the medical profession. Go all the way back in history! Organized medicine fought Lister, it fought Pasteur—" Rudy had never known this was in Swaboda. That Polack was aflame with eloquence. "Every doctor's wife who has to make over her last year's hat, and serve hash five times a week so he can pay rent on his office, is trying you. Four months ago I slept in my office to save room rent. Now I'm making a living, and doing some good to the community. What's wrong with that? We're trying every doctor here who has to use guesswork when he wants an electrocardiogram because he hasn't got the apparatus and his patient can't afford to pay high technicians' fees. We're trying every internalist who handles a surgeon's knife because he needs the fee for the operation, and just hopes nothing will go wrong. We're trying every bunk-artist consultant—"

594

There was a smothered gasp, for sitting up there was none other than Dr. Veirtel, a notorious fee-splitting consultant who had nothing but a solemn face to contribute to any diagnosis.

Swaboda finally ran out of fury. Like most amateur orators, he swept along on his passion until he came to a point where he had nothing more to say, and ended lamely in mid-sentence.

There was one more defense. Matthews spoke with a cold, idealistic venom. He had prepared himself, and he told them a few facts.

"We are charged with breach of ethics by advertising," he answered them directly to the point. "Gentlemen, you don't need us to show you anything about advertising." He pulled a copy of a local medical society magazine out of his pocket, and slapped it open at an ad. " 'Twin-Spring Waters Cure Diabetes!' " he read. An uneasy laugh arose. Then he showed them, in their own state and regional medical magazines, ads for extracts that cured high blood pressure, for pills that restored lost manhood, and where more dignified products appeared. What of that stamp of approval which was given to national brands of drugs, canned goods, and synthetic foods? No charge at all, he reminded them, except a five-hundred-dollar fee for editorial supervision on each full-page ad.

"Is it advertising, gentlemen, when men who do not and have never practiced medicine, men who make no claims to attainments in research, can go out and collect thousand-dollar checks for lecture appearances, in the name of organized medicine? Or is it advertising when the director of one of the largest hospitals in Chicago pays a publicity man a retainer of one hundred and fifty dollars a month? Perhaps to keep his name out of the papers?" They knew whom he meant all right. And there were plenty more sitting right there whose names might have been called on that same score, except that they were paying less to their publicity agents. "Is it advertising when the Rochester clinic donates a twenty-five-thousand-dollar transparent man to the World's Fair, on condition that the name of the donor be mentioned at every demonstration?" Was it advertising when a former national president of a medical organization appeared on the back page of a popular magazine, the proud endorser of a five-cent soap?

Why all this crusade, why all this furious battle against a few dozen men whose sole crime was to publish a list of their services and fees?

Only one force was behind this persecution. "We don't blame this body individually. Gentlemen, we are sorry for you. We've been in this organization and we know who runs it. We know its uses. In the vulgar world, they have a word for a man who gets hold of an organization and manipulates it for his own profit. They call him a racketeer. You, and we, are being victimized by men who are advertising themselves by means of the Society of American Physicians and Surgeons to the point where their income from lectures and writings in some cases sounds like a movie star's income! Gentlemen, you are allowing yourselves to be led around by the nose by men some of whom have never practiced medicine. They determine your policies and interpret ethics for you. A medical body should be concerned with the practice of medicine; we think we are contributing something to that practice and would welcome an investigation. But if the only thing this medical society thinks about is the advertising business, we are well out of it."

The four culprits had to leave the room while the vote was taken. Swaboda didn't want to wait, but Matthews insisted. When they were readmitted, the hall seethed with guilt and suppression. Veirtel read the verdict. Expulsion, fifty-one to twenty-three.

Matthews couldn't resist his parting shot. "Gentlemen, as we leave the S.A.P.S. we are at last confirmed in our suspicion about the name. You read it the way it's spelled."

After that, the rest of the members of the Alliance received their expulsions with pride.

Already, they knew they were being sympathetically watched by some of the saner members of the profession. Many were beginning to send their patients down for X-rays and other technical work, which the clinic did at a third the customary rates. There were even inquiries from groups of doctors in other cities, who were projecting similar ventures.

Naturally, the S.A.P.S. filed suit to enjoin them, as a corporation, from the practice of medicine. But by now lawsuits, slander, snubs, were standard; the men paid little attention, unless there was a new humorous angle. Only, fundamentally, Rudy still could not understand why anyone should want to stop a thing that was doing good, a thing that the people wanted. It didn't scare him so much now; rather, it was a puzzle to him, in human behavior.

And as things were going better for himself, with a decent regular salary in addition to some outside practice in the evenings, he wanted to see his friend Mitch Wilner better fixed, and he was constantly trying to shove patients over to Mitch.

It happened that Rudy heard of an opportunity for Mitch.

"There's an opening on the staff at Israel, Rudy," Dr. Matthews announced, with a sarcastic smile, one morning.

Rudy guessed that Matthews had finally been dropped, after refusing many hints that he resign.

"What did they do?" Rudy asked. But already it had occurred to him that here was an opportunity for Mitch Wilner.

"A former patient of mine went to see Dr. Feldner yesterday," Dr. Matthews said, "and Feldner refused to treat him, because he had been a patient of the clinic."

Rudy whistled. And such were the ethical men, who were kicking the Alliance members out of their societies!

596

"So I finally resigned," Matthews said. "They've got a meeting this week and I was going to make them kick me off the staff, but I thought in this instance it was stronger to resign."

"Going to take any action against Feldner?"

Matthews smiled bitterly. "The only action I'd like to take would change the shape of his pig's snout."

Matthews's place would probably be filled from the associate staff, leaving a vacancy there, and why shouldn't Mitch get that? To be on Israel's staff of fancy Jewish physicians was just what Mitch should aim for. This would be the first step.

He could phone Mitch. But Mitch would only make out an application, and sit waiting. Rudy doffed his lab coat, and rushed right over to the Field Annex Building. Mitch was sitting there reading *The Coming Struggle for Power*. "Mygod, I thought it was a patient! What's up?"

Rudy explained.

"Gee, that's swell of you to come over and tip me off," Mitch said. "I'll put in an application. But you know it's sure to go to one of their favorite sons, in that dump."

"Now, Mitch, listen to your old uncle Rudy. With your swell research record and the work you did in Vienna you've got a good chance. It's still recent enough to count. But it won't count if you sit on your can and wait for them to come to you. For once you've got to push yourself. You've got to go and call on Feldner and Berliner and every member of the staff. You've got to tell them you want that appointment."

Mitch looked pained. "I can't do that, Rudy. I can't go around blowing my own horn; and you know their reaction to self-advertising."

Both suddenly realized the implication that might be put upon Mitch's remark. That was the ugliness of the crazy code of "professional ethics" that had been drilled into them like some medieval dueling code. Rudy passed over it. He hitched his chair up to Mitch. "Listen, you lunkhead. This is your chance. If you don't do it, by God, I'll make Sylvia go around and interview those guys for you. . . ."

Mitch shuddered even though it was a joke.

"After all, Mitch, we owe it to the profession to get a good man in there!" Rudy kidded, and then, deeply serious: "Just take my advice on this one thing."

Looking somewhat frightened, Mitch said: "Okay. I don't think it'll do any good, but just to show you what a dope you are, I'll go through with it."

"Shake. Now, you're gonna call up Frankau and make an appointment, right now while I'm here, so you don't back out on me." Rudy handed him the phone.

Mort drove into the parking space behind the Pasteur monument. "Half a buck for parking," he beefed. "And on public property. Some pal of Kelly's is making a fortune out of this concession."

And, indeed, southward was a black sea of automobiles. As the bunch emerged from the car, Sylvia paused to look at the statue: a classic-robed female, reaching a leaf of laurel up to the bust of Pasteur. Joe was back in Chicago; he might even be here at the Fair for Jewish Day.

Joe might be a maker of monuments, but her Mitch would be like Pasteur, one to whom monuments were made.

Aline touched her elbow. "Look, there's Dr. Feldner."

The portly surgeon of the Israel Hospital staff was coming toward them, accompanied by his family. "Say hello to him," Aline prompted Rudy. Dr. Feldner would surely recognize his former interne.

Dr. Feldner paused and greeted Mitch.

"You remember Dr. Stone," Mitch said. There was an awful silence. Why, Rudy had put in eight hours a week on free clinics there, and seen Dr. Feldner daily.

Dr. Feldner stared at Rudy, finally nodded icily in an obvious concession to the presence of the women.

Sylvia couldn't help wishing they hadn't been with Rudy. Dr. Feldner might somehow connect Mitch with the idea of the clinic. And right now, when that staff position was being decided.

When the Jews start out to do something, they certainly put it over! The attendance record of the Fair had been smashed, the entire Jewish population of the city seemed to have turned out, and special trains had brought Jews from all over America, to see the great Jewish pageant, to show Hitler, to answer Hitler! Harry Perlin, on the job in Johnson's toothpaste booth, had twice run out of the souvenir photos of Toothsome Tillie. The whole crew was wilted, sweating.

Aline sank onto the stone seat with a great sigh of relief. "I could even sit down on a board full of nails, like that Hindu in the Believe It or Not place. I never walked so much in my life."

"There must be a hundred thousand people here," Mort estimated. "They ought to clear as much as fifty grand."

"Say, I sold ten tickets myself, and believe me it was some job," Aline bragged. "Everybody I tried to sell them to had some for sale themselves."

"Well, everybody is here; why don't they start?" Mr. Abramson complained.

"It starts half-past eight Jewish time," Mort jested.

"Wait! It isn't even dark yet."

They could see a few pale stars in the sky over the lake; and in the bluish dusk the classic pillars of the Stadium were beautiful. Sylvia and Mitch touched hands, remembering Greece on their honeymoon. And on their right rose the modernistic towers of the skyride, outlined in neon lights. They could read the names on the cars shuttling calmly between the towers: Kingfish, Amos, Andy.

Looking around the whole stadium, all filled with Jews, it was inspiring. They were a nation, too!

Just then a droning like coming thunder was heard; and the flight of Italian planes appeared low in the sky. In a giant arrowhead formation, all twenty-five planes that had crossed the ocean, led by General Balbo.

"Oh, the sky is dark with them!" cried old Mrs. Perlin, utterly amazed. Standing with her future daughter-in-law, high in the dollar-and-a-half tiers, she looked sweet and tiny, like a picture-book version of the old-country mother. Her face quivered between delight and fear. "They are coming so close!"

Harry Perlin, just off duty, was running up the Stadium ramps when he heard the coming planes; as he panted into the open, the concerted roar of the squadron was so great he could feel the beat of the noise on his face. It was great, great, a salute to the Jewish Day.

"They come all the way from Italy, ma!" he cried.

Naïve wonder spread on her face. "From Italia? So many! I never saw before, only in the movies."

The flight of planes roaring, the charge of all their splendidly functioning motors pulsing in his blood! The fullness and triumph of the modern world of machines! And Ruth and his mother together. And just the fact of all these people here, all these Jews, raised a gladness in him.

Now, in a thing like this where all the Jews, old greenhorns and young college atheists, got together, there was no longer a shame of the parents. Even his mother's religious *shaitel* seemed right to him. Ruth had said she was sweet.

He would never be as whole again as he was today. It was now or never, if they were going to get married, because now he had a job, and why wait till bad times came back?

"Imagine, all of them came over the ocean without a single accident!" Ruth said.

"Sure! They could send over a thousand!" Harry declared proudly, as if this were his own accomplishment.

The planes circled, and swept off, to their landing field.

"Imagine!" Celia remarked. "I'll bet there'll be regular airlines to Europe soon."

"Sure, that's what the Lindberghs are supposed to be flying around the world for."

"Didn't she just have another baby?" Mrs. Moscowitz exclaimed.

"Think what those planes could do to this crowd if they were all loaded with gas," Lou suggested.

"A squad like that could wipe out Chicago," Rube Moscowitz said.

"Oh, why bring that up!" Celia responded. "I think it was very nice of Mussolini to send them. It's a gesture of friendship."

"There's the whole Moscowitz tribe," Mort observed, "right below us in those ten-dollar box seats. I guess Rube is trying to get rid of his money before he has to turn it over to the government."

"What do you mean?" asked Sylvia.

"Rube Moscowitz is getting into some trouble about his income tax. He forgot to mention a few hundred-thousand-dollar items."

"Say! That's a serious thing!"

"Well, who would give him away? He's so popular, he hasn't any enemies," Aline pointed out.

"Yah? What about that Irish alderman he double-crossed? And old man Klein is burned up because of a dirty trick Rube pulled on him; they were partners in some receiverships and Rube sold them to Jaffe's bank, leaving Klein out cold. Rube got about a quarter of a million dollars out of the deal, just before the bank closed."

"That fox!" Mrs. Abramson said admiringly. "Some trick!"

"You mean Lil Klein's father?" Aline asked.

"Kid, whatever became of her?" Sylvia inquired.

"Kid, I heard she's getting married again but I don't know to who!"

"But you don't mean to say that Rube Moscowitz may actually go to jail?" Sylvia asked Mort.

"Oh, he has too much political pull!" Aline interposed.

"I'm not so sure about that. When Cermak got bumped off, the Irish got back into control. They're sick of having the Jews and the Polacks and the dagos running politics, the Cermaks and Zintacks and Moscowitzes, so now that the Irish are in control again, Rube can't expect any favors. He's no good to them anyway since Insull is *kaput*."

"Oh, Lou Margolis will probably find some technicality for Rube to wiggle out of his case." Sylvia was confident.

"It's after nine o'clock," Mr. Abramson complained.

Just then the *shofar* blew.

The quavering and uncertain sound spread thinly over the field, and then like a Jew encouraged by tolerance, it stiffened, and rose between a wail and a brag. Carried strongly now, the full-blown call of the ram's horn grew through a hundred amplifiers, and filled the Stadium and rolled over the entire World's Fair.

This was the one truly Jewish sound in the world; no other people owned, no other people fitted, the cry of the ram's horn.

Lil Eisen was with her new friend, Irwin, watching the folk dances in the quaint old Belgian village, and she heard the ram's horn's wailing, broadcast over the loudspeaker system, and she laughed.

"Hurray for the Fourth of July!"

And her friend squeezed her hand because she was so cute and clever, and what a smart little business woman!

She made a resolve that she would find a good modern Hebrew Sunday school, for Jackie; later in life, if he wished, he could forget all about Jewishness, but after all maybe there was something to it.

"Why so pensive?" Irwin said.

Alvin and Eunice heard the *shofar's* call; they were walking along the top wall of the Stadium, for Alvin had had to buy a couple of tickets for the firm. The sound spiraled around them, and Alvin realized that in all her years of being married to a Jew, Eunice had not until now heard the *shofar* sound.

"That's the ram's horn, isn't it?" she asked with the intelligent curiosity of a good-willed stranger.

"Yes, I haven't heard it for years. They blow it on holidays."

"Oh, on Yom Kippur?" she essayed.

"No, on Rosh Hashanah—New Year's. To blow in the new year."

"It's exciting," she said.

Let her have the kid this time; a little half-Jew who would be free of racial sentiment. That was the best thing after all.

The whitish outlines of the pillars were still visible against the vapory, warm night air. Shrouded figures could be discerned crossing the field, taking their places on the stages.

Then was felt the eager, twittering Jewishness of the crowd, all assembled with their dollars that would take German Jewish refugees to Palestine; in the anticipatory pause there was felt the all-inclusiveness of these months of communal preparations, the hundreds of daughters in all the Junior Hadassah clubs and in all the temple dramatic clubs who had rushed to rehearsals, the swarm of separate little hopes of meeting new boy friends and new girl friends in this activity, the swarm of little plots and cabals, the little loves and necking parties and even marriages that had grown out of this activity; the ticket selling; the innumerable phone calls that had been made, each with its conditions of social politics, shaming people into more expensive tickets, the whispers and campaigns and comparison, oh, for such a wonderful cause. . . . And now, the whole Jewish community of Chicago collected in this darkness, waiting, while southward, over the World's Fair lagoon, Fourth of July firecrackers streaked in parabolas.

Below the stands, it had been a terrific day of last-minute troubles. A truck, arriving with the huge image of Moloch constructed by Joe Freedman, crashed right through the pavement of the eight-million-dollar stadium. It turned out that the concrete floor was only half as thick as specified. But meanwhile Joe labored among the cheesecloth Miriams and bearded patriarchs, patching up his Moloch. At last, resting, he looked up into the great circle of filled seats, and remembered the amphitheater in Mount Scopus, filled with Jews from Jerusalem, and it was the same crowd. Why, in Chicago there were about as many Jews as in all of Palestine.

A mellifluous voice intoned: "And it was said: *Vayheey ohr*—and there was light . . ."

Gradually, a dawn of light came up, revealing a swaying gray mass creeping, unfolding like primeval waves. This was the birth of humanity, of themselves, a Jewish humanity, way back there in the deserts of Chaldea somewhere.

"There are over three hundred people on that stage," Mort said. "Every ten is in the charge of a leader. Ora is in charge of a group, there."

And suddenly his mind went to the shop. "You know who I think is the trouble-maker?" he whispered to his mother. "I think Pauline Stopa is organizing the girls. She's the only one they'd listen to."

"It's not Pauline. I talked to her yesterday," Mrs. Abramson said.

In his mind, Mort listed over the other workers in the shop.

A chorus sang.

"That's real ancient Hebrew music," Celia mentioned. "It was dug up in Palestine."

"Yah?" Lou cracked. "How was it buried? On phonograph records?"

Now came a procession of long-braided virgins dragging the colossal idol, Moloch.

"Ora's leading one of those crews of virgins," Mort informed them. "I guess she's been fooling me all these years," he cracked.

There was a girl for you! Tosses off a couple of kids, and her figure snaps back tight and lithe as a girl's, full of pep and dance.

"The trouble is that dope we got down there in Washington," Mrs. Abramson mused. "What is he doing for the Association? Whatever Roosevelt tells him, he says fine. A yes man we don't need to send to Washington."

"They've got a union all set," Mort revealed. "They're just waiting for those codes to come out. They'll strike the same day."

"A President we needed, to give them excuses to strike," Mrs. Abramson complained.

"Ah, it's the same as four years ago, they won't get to first base," Mort said.

A theatrical fire hissed in the huge maw of the Moloch, and the Virgin was sacrificed.

"Give me the old days!" Mort smacked his lips.

It was the scene of the Spanish expulsion of the Jews.

"Look at Spain now," Lou Margolis said. "They never amounted to anything since they expelled the Jews. The same thing will happen to Germany."

"How do I know they're even trying?" Rube complained nervously. "Those Irishmen have got it in for us. They claim they talked to Washington but how do I know they ain't giving me the run-around? Anyway, what can they do? They barely got their own income taxes fixed up. If it wasn't for the cardinal and those Catholic votes they'd be out of luck. Y' think they can ask the cardinal to put it in for a Hebe?"

On the stage, a little Jew smothered under a bearskin was prancing, while Cossacks snapped long whips about his legs.

"You think this is exaggerated?" said Mr. Abramson. "I have seen this myself, in my young days in Russia."

"And right today!" Rudy put in. "I saw a picture of a poor old German Jew harnessed to a garbage wagon, dragging it through the street."

"Thank God, my kids will never know of such things," Aline said. "In America such things don't happen."

"Yah! What about the Ku-Klux Klan?" Sylvia reminded her. "And when a doctor can't get into Rochester just because he's a Jew?"

"Well, I don't see many gentiles on the Israel staff," Aline countered.

"Those *Daitche Yehudim*," sneered Mrs. Abramson. "I am not saying Hitler is right, but if it had to happen to Jews someplace, then they are the ones that deserve it most. So high class! A Russian Jew, to them, was to spit on."

"Don't worry," Sylvia said. "Now they remember they are Jews like anybody else."

"They're even taking Russian Jews into the Prima Club," Mort revealed. "They had such a big mortgage on their new downtown building. I understand Lou Margolis is a member."

"When this is over, let's all go to the Streets of Paris," Aline suggested. "I want to see that fan dancer they arrested last week. What's her name? Sally Rand. Do you think she really comes out naked?"

"It's just a publicity stunt," Sylvia said.

"Ora knows all about it. She was there," Aline insinuated, glancing at Mort.

"Maybe it would pay us to send our own man to Washington to see what they are putting in those codes," Mrs. Abramson worried. "Better to spend a little money now than to spend a fortune fighting it afterwards."

"A real *Chassidishe nigun!*" Mr. Abramson repeated, humming with the singer a wordless melody that he remembered from his Talmud days.

"Dai, dai,
Da da dee dee dee. . . ."

People, people! It was the thickness of them, the swarming fullness of this vast Stadium, stirring one to a strange sweet kind of racial love. They were stamping through the Palestinian settler's *hora* now, the field was a sworl of circles. Emotion rose out of the Stadium, rolled over the field like an intoxicating vapor, drugging all.

The whole pageant was rushing through Joe's blood, all his life, and the life of the race that made him. He recalled his own journey, seeking and seeking, going backward on the trail that the Jews had traveled, to Poland, to Bialystok, and then he had had to go again, to Palestine. Now, here, it added up.

Jews, shopkeepers and buttonhole makers, and their educated American children; there seemed a goodness in people when they came together in celebration of themselves. Perhaps they were mistakenly united in this common tradition of their past, in wandering, suffering, learning; perhaps it was from this feeling of cultural equality that the poor buttonhole makers got the delusion of living in a world of human equality. But granting error, and pathos, and clumsiness, and cheating sentimentality, and stampeding emotion, this was beauty too. And at a moment like this, a man didn't want to let go of the world. However silly and involved and stupid human motives might become, there was a life-lust that rolled all into one.

A hand pulled him into the whirl. Joe sang out a Palestinian cry, and danced like a real *chalutz*. The faces all around him, all, all were beautiful.

The crowd tore around Alvin. Some were surging downward, to join the dancers on the field. Others were driving, twisting toward exits. He drew back with Eunice, to a place high on the ledge of the Stadium.

Jews, always afire, damn Jewish Fourth of July.

Moments, there, he had been touched. But what did it all prove? Look at them, with their sweat-beaded faces, their belching corned beef breaths, fat, fat, an ugly people. Clutching pop bottles. What did it all prove, except that the Jews had always been a race of intruders? Even that first time in Palestine, they had been the invaders, taking the land away from the Canaanites, the Philistines, the native tribes. And now again, they would take it away from the Arabs.

What would happen when the swarm of German Jews landed in Palestine?

"You'll see," he predicted to Eunice. "They'll send thousands of German Jews over there, and it'll be worse than in 1929. The Arabs will have an excuse."

"But where else can they go?" Eunice said.

Where? They could disappear. As he saw it now, disappearance was the eventual answer. Eventually, why not now, ha ha. Sure, the Soviets might toy with a Jewish colony in Siberia, but in a few generations that too would be Russianized.

"Oh, it's exciting," Eunice said, looking down onto the self-intoxicated crowd.

"Let's get the hell out of here," he said. In the crowd-stream, paunches pressed against him, he could hardly keep from striking out, tearing a space for himself, so he could be free, alone.

For Them, the Lights Turn Green

Even at State and Wacker, a block below the millinery district, the sidewalks were thick with strikers.

Mort headed into a parking station. "You know it actually pays them to tear down these old buildings and use the lots for parking stations," he said, keeping cool.

As they emerged into Wabash Avenue, his mother took his arm. The street was crammed. In the summer heat, the coatless men, the flocks of girls in cotton dresses, made a holiday mood. At Wacker and Wabash, there was a crowd of workers around a speaker. But some also loitered along the parapet, staring down at the river, laughing at the Negroes jigging on the quay to advertise fifty-cent speedboat excursions. A group of girl pickets were walking, arms locked around each other, singing:

"Who's afraid of the big bad wolf,
The big bad wolf, big bad wolf,
WHO'S afraid—"

"Some strike!" Mort said. "They think it's a picnic."

"In the beginning, they always think it's a picnic. Wait, wait, these dumb *shiksehs* never were on a strike before," Mrs. Abramson said. "Why do they leave them block the streets?"

Several mounted police skirted the crowd, and a squad car nosed along Wacker Drive.

The workers seemed cheerful and absolutely confident of an easy victory. Why, the head of the employers' association, Scherer, had already started to negotiate, recognizing the union! Wasn't the NRA[2] with them? Wasn't the President with them?

"And I voted for the sonofagun!" Mort growled.

He slid through the crowd, his mother following in the path he made. They had almost reached the Milliners' Building when someone who had worked in their shop recognized them.

---

[2] The National Recovery Administration was a controversial agency established by Roosevelt in 1933 to fix the economy by eliminating "cut-throat competition." It was ruled unconstitutional by the Supreme Court in 1935.

"A boss! A boss!"

For an instant Mort felt utter fright. They'd be torn limb from limb. He scuttled desperately toward the guarded building. But instead, a path opened as though no one wanted to be contaminated by their touch.

"Who's afraid of the big bad wolf,

Big bad wolf . . .?"

The song was flung, laughing, howling, after the Abramsons, who hurried, stony-faced, into the building. The lobby was painfully quiet, like on a Sunday. No crowd shaking dice around the cigar stand.

But in the offices of the Vogel Millinery, a tumultuous meeting was in progress. Here were the insurgent employers, disgusted with the conciliatory tactics of Scherer. Why, his Western Association wasn't even going to put up a fight! Scherer was ready to sign anything, just because the walkout was in the busy season. The room throbbed with August heat and boiling tempers. Mort pitched into the discussion. "What do we need the Western for! To lay down on us?"

"Sure, Abramson, you can talk!" snapped Vogel, flailing his arms, showing wide stains in his armpits. "Out there on the West Side, a couple of pickets around the shop is nothing; and anyway you got a father-in-law on the police force to give you protection. But here they got us by the nuts. Excuse me, Mrs. Abramson. They got the whole millinery industry in these two-three blocks, and with that mob out there, right in the Loop too, we got a swell chance to bring in new operators. All we did was lock ourselves in jail for them!"

"Who told you all to locate in one building?" Mort said, triumphantly, feeling the tables turned from four years ago, when his isolation had been an advantage to the strikers. "There's plenty of room to spread out over the city, but you had to put your shops in a bottle for them!"

"All right, all right, you were wise, you knew exactly that it was going to be a strike this year!" Willis Cohen snapped. "But we ain't here to talk about that. Are you settling with them, or not?"

"Why should we settle?" Mrs. Abramson cried. "They ain't got twenty girls out of three hundred in our shop."

"Don't give us any bunk. I know you ain't got ten regular girls on your machines," Vogel cried.

"Aph!" Mort said. "They aren't striking. They're afraid of trouble, so they stay home. The big majority of our hands will come back on the same wage, with an open shop, as soon as it is quiet."

"Yah, but you know what will happen when Scherer settles with the union?" old Baruch Neiman taunted him. "The union will be strong and they will send all their forces out to the West Side, and then you will be in the soup."

"We're not worried," Mort parried. "Chicago isn't the only place where you can run a factory."

What? Hah? There was a swarm of curiosity. He let it be understood that they had another plant all set, in a near-by small town like, say, Aurora, where farm girls would work for practically nothing, and the union would have some job getting to them. Sure, all the bosses had considered this strategy, but it took the Abramsons to lead the way.

Vogel was pounding the table. "We have to decide on some action. If the Western settles the strike, are we sticking with them or not?"

"This strike is not the only question!" Mort declared. "We've got to have a fighter, not a yes man! We have to fight the whole principle of the NRA! The whole thing is unconstitutional. We have to have an organization that will go down to Washington and fight for us! What is Scherer? A messenger that brings us codes from the government, telling us how to run our business!"

"Those bestids sold us out to the New York crowd. The New Yorkers made the millinery code, they made everything for themselves," yelled Simonovitch, a little Maxwell Street Yid whose hideaway sweatshop, once a joke, had quadrupled production during the strike.

"They are giving us a differential on wages," Willis Cohen pointed out.

"A couple of cents a hour!" Simonovitch hooted. "If we got to pay a wage scale, the whole Tchicago business is *kaput*."

"Listen, we all know this by now!" Mort shouted. "The main thing is to figure out a program."

"The hell with the Western! We make our own association!" Simonovitch cried.

"The hell with the blue eagle[3] too. A *shvantz*[4] they ought to have for an insignia, not a blue eagle!"

"Sixty cents an hour for those girls, the union is crazy. What are they going to do with the money!"

"Buy hats!" There was a sickly laugh.

"I am offering my girls forty cents," Mrs. Abramson said. "That is plenty. If they want to come back, all right, if not, there are thousands of Polacks."

"Wait! Order! Let's do this with a system. If we got to have a new organization, we got to have a chairman!"

Mort emerged as one of the ruling committee of three; he knew he could swing old Baruch Neiman, and Vogel would have to come along his way. Why, he would be the key man in the whole industry, west of New York! He was a general now. He was fighting for the freedom of the business man. What use were the codes but to protect the weak, to flatten out competition, to reward incompetence? Nobody was going to tell him how to run his business!

---

[3] The blue eagle was symbol of NRA compliance, posted everywhere.
[4] "Shvantz" = "Phallus."

A swarm of manufacturers buzzed after him into the hallway, each trying to tweak him aside, to beg a secret favor, since the Abramson shop was running full blast: fill a little order for me, my best customers, I don't want to lose them; look, Mort, you can swipe all my new off-the-face models, only fill this order for me!

Once Syl drove along to the factory. The usual greeting awaited the car:

"Yay! The boss!"

"Hey, Abramson! you stink!"

"Mort, I'm sick of it!" Sylvia said, seeing the injunction on the door as if it were a sign of plague. "Can't you put an end to it! The other shops settled with them, and they're getting along."

"Say, are you crazy too?" He slammed the car door.

A trouble-maker he had fired the day before walked alongside them, sticking up his palms, Yid fashion. "Vot do you vant from me, go vay, boyis!" he mimed.

"Hey, Abramson, why don't you come down alone once!"

"He even sleeps with his mother, for protection!"

There was a universal Bronx cheer.

Mort rushed into the factory, and phoned a strikebreaking agency on West Madison. The lousy Antisemites. Now they would get it.

All through the meal they carefully avoided talking about what was in the paper. They were elaborately polite, like strangers to each other. Ora had invited them over in honor of Mitch's appointment to Israel. The conversation staggered. Had they seen the new rage, Katharine Hepburn? And the Piccoli marionettes, they were cute. In the parlor Sylvia picked up Ora's copy of *Anthony Adverse.*

"Finished yet?"

"Say, give me time. I'm young yet!" Ora joked.

"Don't forget I'm next on it," Sylvia said. "I don't understand why anybody wants to write such a long book."

"So you'll have to buy it instead of getting it out of the rental library," Mort said. It was almost the first time he had spoken, that evening. His voice was high-pitched. He took the book from Sylvia. "Here's the good part. Did you see this, doctor?" He found the passage giving a full description of sexual intercourse, in terms of a flower opening.

Sylvia looked away, with a brief, aloof smile.

"Have you read *Little Man, What Now?*" Mitch interposed.

"I'm sick of these depression novels," Mort said, explosively. So what? So it was in the papers. BATTLE STRIKERS! Nobody had been killed, had they? There were strikes all over the country, thanks to the NRA. He was no exception. Look at the trouble in the Kohler plumbing fixture plant, and that guy was known all over the world for the idealistic way he treated his employees, building a model village for them.

"The trouble is it doesn't give any solution," Ora complained.

"Well, is there any solution, in our present system?" Mitch said.

That made Mort boil. He knew what was coming. They were all going to parade their idealism before him, their socialism, their communism, their technocracy, sure, everybody was an unselfish angel, as long as Mort supplied the money. Mitch was going to be a big-shot doctor now, a member of the Israel staff, a lofty humanity saver; and he was just a measly business man.

"I'm as idealistic as the next guy!" Mort burst out. "But I'm sick and tired of all this crap about systems. We've got a system. The only trouble is nobody will let it alone. If you have one system you've got to stay within the rules of that system. You can't play poker by the rules of bridge."

"Maybe that's what's wrong with your bridge game, dear," Sylvia joshed Mitch, trying to ease the situation.

Mort continued: "If the capitalist system is based on class warfare, then that's the way the balance is maintained. Let the classes scrap it out, it doesn't hurt. The government has no right to step in and help either side. It has to be a neutral referee. Otherwise it upsets the whole system, and the result is the kind of mess we're getting into now. I'm not arguing about communism or socialism or any damn thing. If the people wanted communism it would be here."

Mitch hooted.

"But as long as the capitalist system is maintained, it has to be allowed to work naturally. When the government steps in and jacks up wages artificially, it gums up the works."

"You mean you don't believe in capitalism, but as long as we have it you want it to be capitalistic?" Mitch suggested.

Sylvia and Ora laughed appreciatively. Mort's hand trembled with anger, as he lit a cigarette.

"I saw an article in *The Nation*," Ora said, "claiming the NRA is a frameup by the big producers, to put the little fellows out of business. It doesn't even help labor. In most trades the NRA scale is lower than what they were getting already!"

"Yah? That's what you know about it!" Mort exclaimed. "They tried to organize a millinery union here a couple of years ago and got the pants beat off them. They went out on strike the day the NRA went in effect, and they got doubled wages. If we have to keep on paying the scale, then the whole Chicago millinery industry will be squeezed out by New York because cheaper labor was all we had on them."

"I thought only the sweatshops would be squeezed out," Mitch said.

Mort glared at him. "Our girls were making twelve, fifteen, eighteen dollars a week," he informed Mitch coldly, not bothering to mention the eight-dollar checks. "The work is light. Practically anybody can learn in a couple of days. Now, if they were satisfied to work for that money, and they didn't need any more money, why make trouble? These girls aren't supporting families. They don't even have to support themselves. They live with their families. You can talk a lot of baloney about a living wage but the fact is these *shiksehs* work for spending money, that's all, they spend it on clothes and junk. They don't need their jobs so much. Look at the big turnover we have. If they needed their jobs they would keep them. The girls just work a couple of years till they get a chance to marry."

"That's right," Ora conceded. "The government is just pampering them. Why, our maid quit last week—why should she work, she said, when she can get more money on relief?"

"That isn't the argument." Mitch quietly disregarded her. "Whether they need the money or not is no excuse for underpaying them."

"Who said we're underpaying them!" Mort shrieked.

Instead of coming over on his side, Sylvia inquired coolly: "But Mort, if the other shops can pay the union wages, why can't we?"

Mort thought he would choke them. Choke them all. They, the defenders of the poor! Ora, with her fancy dancing lessons and her nursemaid, and Mitch, the fancy doctor who couldn't pay his bills! While he, the one that earned the money for them all, was the capitalistic ogre!

"Nobody can pay those wages!" he shouted. "But we're the only ones with the guts to fight it! They're all losing money. Their expenses are doubled, and yet they can't raise their prices."

"Why not?" Mitch said. "The idea is that if higher wages are paid people will have more money to buy things."

Sylvia saw Mort's apoplectic expression. "I guess we just don't understand economics," she said, hoping to end the discussion. She picked up a piece of a jigsaw puzzle and tried to fit it into the half-finished pattern.

"You ought to read Veblen's *Theory of the Leisure Class*," Ora remarked innocently. "He had it all figured out. There has to be a class of girls working for twelve dollars a week in order that there may be a class of people sending their children to the university."

So now they were all going to parade their education on him, Mitch and Sylvia with their Phi Beta Kappa keys, and Ora with her graduate studies! "Sure, and who supports the universities? The business man!" Mort snapped. "Maybe it would all be perfect under communism but the system we live under, it happens to be the business man that bears the brunt of the trouble and worry, who has to keep the whole works going. Where would the arts be, and the sciences? Who paid the bills for all those guys that laid around Paris making art and literature, yah, and it takes a doctor ten years to go through school and then he has to be supported five years before he makes a living—if ever!"

Mitch had turned dead-white. But Mort continued, madly: "Sure, it's a swell ride! Everything is taken care of! The lights turn green for you as you go along! You end up as a high-class specialist in a fancy hospital. You don't soil your hands with money! That makes you superior to the guy that runs a sweatshop to support you—"

Mitch jumped up.

"Mort, what's got into you!" Sylvia cried. "I think you ought to apologize."

"Like hell I will! For once I'll talk! I'm the dirty dog, the lousy boss, the strikebreaker! I haven't even got a college degree! I'm not making any great discoveries to save the world from flea bites! You can all be idealists, sure, be radicals even, go on, read the *New Masses*, as long as the factory pays for the subscription. I'm sick of the whole damn business!" His voice broke and trailed off, his anger piping into self-pity. "You think everything is my fault! You think I want to hire thugs to beat people up! Why don't you understand the things in your own life . . .?"

"He's overworked. He's nervous with that crazy strike." Sylvia was assuring Ora.

"You know he doesn't mean it," Ora was assuring Mitch.

"We were going anyway," Mitch said, controlled. "I've got to get to sleep early. I'm at the dispensary tomorrow morning." He raised his voice slightly, talking at Mort: "Girls that get twelve dollars a week can't afford to pay doctor bills. They have to come to a free dispensary."

The two couples separated.

As they came to their car, Mitch stopped. Sylvia understood. He was thinking: "Mort paid for the car."

"Let me drive?" she offered.

What could they say to each other? Now they had finally parted from Mort, too. An unutterable grief filled her. Not only because of what had just happened, but all of life seemed to be that way, lately; you began with something, and lost, and lost; little by little, this sense of love and home and friendship was pieced away, like a whole sheet of paper torn, and the pieces torn, and their pieces torn, and torn.

When she had her child, they would just live alone, the three of them, close, close to themselves.

There was no place on the Fair ground for employees to eat except the fancy-priced restaurants where a meal was at least seventy-five cents.

So for lunch Harry would just grab a hamburger and eat it walking, using his half-hour to see the Fair. He was nuts about the Dymaxion car, declaring he always had contended the motor belonged in the rear, and he spent several lunch hours watching the demonstration of the automatic telephone switchboard. But on this day he meandered into a great hall filled with agricultural machinery. There was a historical series, from the first McCormick reaper with its wooden parts to a huge modern combine that did the work of fifty men, cutting, binding, thrashing, sacking, all in one machine. There was the latest agricultural invention, a cotton-picking machine, the product of years of experiment.

Harry became excited. He had never realized that farming could be entirely mechanical. He began to dream again, seeing himself and Ruth out of the harsh city, established in a modernistic glass house, raising kids in the sunlight. And he would have a great barn full of machinery, he would ride out over his fields doing everything by the latest methods, he would have a shop of his own where he would tinker and repair; evenings and Sundays he would build himself a streamlined Dymaxion car. What was the use of slaving, wasting your life in the city! Remember that exhibit in the Hall of Science, showing lungs from a city man, soot black, beside the clean gray-pink lungs of a man who had lived in the country all his life!

That would be the perfect way to live, combining machinery and nature. . . . He had to rush back to his job of handing out Toothsome Tillie souvenirs to the visitors in Johnson's Brite-White Toothpaste exhibit.

The Very Guts Corrupted

Dr. Feldner's speech was the most open and vicious attack yet made upon the clinic. When the men came down that morning, it seemed that even the stenographers and the elevator boys were whispering about the news reports of the speech. And in spite of sympathy, little wells of silence fell about those who had been named by name.

Addressing a medical convention, Dr. Feldner had commented upon an ad offering a "free dental X-ray" with every five-dollar examination by the Medical Alliance.

"Bargain counter medicine dispensed by misfits and incompetents" . . . "frauds, quacks, and charlatans" they were called. Dr. Orr, "politician and promoter," was lambasted for an entire paragraph. Dr. Matthews was called a pseudo-idealist with the type of irresponsible originality dangerous to anyone under his knife. Drs. Stone and Swaboda were cited, and the rest of the doctors grouped as a "lot of half-baked graduates from second-class schools." All of them were put in the same class as chain-store dentists, Crazy Crystal mineral waters, spiritualist healers, and peddlers of Indian medicines.

The accusation struck home. For several months Rudy had been dissatisfied with the clinic's advertising, written by an "expert" whom Dr. Orr had hired for six thousand a year. It was, in fact, bargain counter advertising.

The epithets were libelous and could be proven so. Why, every man in the place came from a first-class medical school and most of them had interned in top hospitals. The fellows were burned up. Mike Swaboda rushed into Rudy's office, ready to collect a gang, go down to the convention, and challenge the entire Feldner crowd. Matthews was attempting to sneer off the whole thing with cool intellectual superiority. "Why pay attention to those smart-aleck has-beens?" he said. "They passed out with the Mencken age. All those buffoons ever knew how to do was to attract attention to themselves by insulting people. Feldner has a Gold Coast practice, and likes to get his name in the papers. It's only to be expected that when we tackle the real problems, those smart-aleck advanced thinkers of the Mencken era turn out to be the most reactionary rats in the country. Let him rave. We just have to do our work, and when the profession catches up with us, as it will have to, they'll all be out on their fat cans."

But Rudy insisted: "The fact is that our advertising *is* lousy and that gives him an opportunity to attack us. We've kicked about those ads ourselves. Have we got anything to say about how this place is run, or what?"

The whole matter would surely be the big topic of discussion at lunch. Maybe they could finally have it out about Orr's advertising policy, as well as a few other funny things about Orr's management.

Manny Kassell, the dentist, got into the elevator as Rudy and a bunch of the doctors were going down to eat. As they were on different floors, there was only casual working contact between the doctors and dentists. Too, the doctors seemed to have preserved their professional scorn for the tooth-choppers, mere mechanics. Just as the office girls went off in one little group, and the lab girls in another, so the doctors and dentists kept their separate social groups at lunchtime and after work. But now it occurred to Rudy that the dentists ought to be in on this. He knew Manny Kassell from years ago, Manny had always been sort of one of the bunch, and had come into the clinic largely on Rudy's say-so.

"Eating? Come with us," Rudy suggested.

As they got to Grayson's restaurant on Wabash, Manny hesitated.

"Come on, we always eat here," Rudy said. He saw Manny looking at the window price-list. The place served a good lunch, the cheapest sixty cents.

Manny went in with them. He had changed a lot since the old days when he was such a grand kidder. Well, they had had a lot of worries with a sickly baby.

As Manny sat next to him, Rudy noticed him worrying over the menu, and suddenly understood that he must be looking for something cheaper than the sixty-cent lunch.

The dentists were getting only thirty a week. Why, the dental department was bringing in a large profit! Imagine, the man couldn't even afford a decent lunch. And now Rudy noticed that Manny was no longer the flashy dresser either, but looked drab, worn.

Almost immediately the fellows were lighting into Dr. Orr. Sure, the Feldner crowd were a bunch of lice, "but why should we expose ourselves, why give them anything to work on? Those ads are atrocious."

"Who is that advertising punk he put on for six thousand a year? I could write better ads myself!" Swaboda asserted.

"Yes, but you aren't Dr. Orr's city hall buddy."

"Oho," the murmur went around.

"And a couple of ohos."

And why should Orr be getting more money than the rest of them?

"After all, he's built up the clinic—"

"*He's* built it up!" When they had sweated blood, risked their careers, their savings, the safety of their families!

"And another thing." Rudy spoke. "There's a condition been going on that I am personally ashamed of! We've got trained men working in the place for thirty dollars a week! When we started, some of us took pretty low salaries too, for a while. But it was understood as soon as we got going everybody would get a respectable wage. The dentists are still working for thirty a week, and Orr has refused to raise them."

The fellows glanced at Manny, and bit into their veal cutlets.

"We'll have to look into that," Matthews said coolly. "But we must realize the clinic is not yet safe. We've got to have a fighting reserve for one thing—"

"I notice there's no reserve when it comes to Dr. Orr's salary," Weintraub remarked.

"He's building a reserve there, too. A thousand smackers a month," Swaboda snapped.

The kicks became general. Why should Orr hand himself five times as much as they were making? Sure he handled the business end, and probably got himself plenty of rake-off on the purchases too.

"Why, it's a crime! We've got dental men working at less than truck drivers' wages, while that guy gets away with graft," Swaboda insisted.

"Just a minute, fellows," Matthews said. "Remember this, Dr. Orr is working as an executive, and twelve thousand a year is not such a hell of a big salary for an executive. And, besides, he's entitled to something for organizing and getting the finances for the clinic."

"Executive? You mean executioner! We've kicked a thousand times about those bargain counter ads! Free dental X-rays! You can't blame Feldner! If that's the only way to develop the place, we'd rather quit!" Perusi yelled. "Haven't we got anything to say about the way the place is run? I thought it was supposed to be operated on a group plan. What does he think he is, our boss!"

"It is a group. But we can't jump on our director like this," Dr. Matthews defended Orr. Their judgment was hasty, he insisted. Orr was basically honest and certainly essential to the organization. True, he had his faults. But most of the men were not in a position to realize all Orr was doing. He, Matthews, had worked along with Orr from the very start, and they'd have to take his word for it—Orr was not trying to boss the clinic.

All these complaints could be taken up at a staff meeting. "I'll agree to this," Matthews said. "There certainly should be a closer supervision of advertising; undoubtedly Kerrigan, being a layman, doesn't understand our point of view."

The staff meeting of the Medical Alliance was confused, tumultuous, and painful. Matthews pleaded with them not to relinquish the ideal which had brought them together, in a series of squabbles about personalities. Orr presided, listening with a tolerant smirk to the charges against his administration. Showing them that he was a man who could take criticism in a big way, he admitted that the advertising had been at fault. "Kerrigan is a swell ad writer, a twenty-thousand-a-year man, and we're lucky to have him," he stated. "And he has been writing copy that sells the clinic. We can't blame him for being an ad writer instead of a doctor. He'll write any kind of ads we tell him to."

Dr. Orr consented to a committee of three to consult on, and okay all advertisements before they were released for publication. Having made that concession, he surveyed the men, laughing easily, as though to show them what fools they had been to make all this fuss. Why let Feldner get their goat? They had known what to expect and would just have to stick together and take it.

It was then that Rudy arose with a motion that the dentists receive salaries comparable to those of the doctors.

Orr was startled. "We can't consider that at a general meeting," he announced. He would think the thing over. But he couldn't hold out much hope, as the organization was just about paying its way now, and any raises would have to come out of their own pockets.

"You're getting a thousand a month!" Swaboda challenged.

Orr glared. "I'm not discussing my salary!"

"Well, we are."

Perusi jumped up. "We're all doing the same amount of work here! Why should one man get five times as much as another!"

The meeting was blown wide open. Why, some of those punks hadn't made twenty dollars a week and were getting sixty now, what were they kicking about, Orr pointedly flung at Swaboda. He, Orr, had done all this for them! He, Orr, had developed the clinic and as long as he, Orr, was director . . .

"All right," Swaboda said. "We'll change that, too. Everybody has a vote in this thing."

Matthews was painedly trying to quiet them. To squabble about money! To wreck their whole organization on a salary fight!

Weintraub pulled Rudy aside. "We can't put him out," he explained. "He owns half the stock."

Rudy was puzzled. "We each have an equal vote," he repeated.

"Yah, that's in the operating company but the owning company is different."

Rudy wasn't so sure. Why, the one thing they had insisted on was that everybody have a voice in the policies. The two of them got into a confused discussion.

Orr was still standing up there, banging the gavel. "I've fought and I've slaved for this idea," the director orated. "You fellows know that the clinic is a big thing with me, maybe the biggest thing in my life. I'm in the front, taking the fire, and that's okay, I'll stay out in front. I know you men have made sacrifices to be with me, and, why, we've only begun to fight. Let's not break up on petty details. . . ." He welcomed a committee to discuss the question of salaries. The meeting broke up with the feeling that everything had changed; the glow was gone. They had thought they were doing something together, and here they had a boss. Did he own the place?

They didn't know just where they stood. Then they were shown.

A kid named Willie Statler had a four-dollar-a-week room in Mr. Freedman's Star Hotel; he was a busboy at the Del Roi, and used to come back to his room every afternoon to rest between shifts. He was a friendly kid. He always brought along some fruit swiped from the iceroom.

"Well, how's business?" Mr. Freedman asked.

"They're full up over there. The hotel is full of hicks. This Fair sure did something for the Chicago hotels. I heard it pulled them all out of the red," said Willie Statler, giving Mr. Freedman some grapes as big as plums.

"Well, what are you kicking about, you got a job too, didn't you?" Mr. Freedman pointed out.

"Some job!" Statler grunted. "That basement kitchen is flooded from a busted sewer. Phew!" He touched his nose.

Suddenly he put his hand to his belly and ran for the can. A couple of old bums sitting in the lobby laughed.

When Statler emerged, looking white as a sidewalk, Freedman asked: "Say, are you sick? What's the matter with you?"

"It must be something I et. Working in that garbage, it's no wonder. Boy, if those people in the fancy restaurants could see where that crap they eat comes out of!"

"It wasn't something you drank, huh?"

"Na, I ain't had a drink in a week."

"I got a son-in-law is a doctor." Mr. Freedman gave him the card.

An hour later Nigger John came down the stairs and reported. "Say, boss, that kid is sure sick. *Oy gevalt!* I dunno what he got left to push out! He's been in that can six times in the last half-hour!" and he laughed. "He's layin' on the bed now sick as a dog. He wants a doctor, boss."

"I'll call my son-in-law," Mr. Freedman said.

On his way home from the clinic, Rudy stopped into the flophouse.

Willie Statler was up, and determined to go back to work though still woozy. He admitted he had been sick and getting sicker during the last few days, with increasing spells of diarrhea.

It looked like some simple digestive disorder; maybe the kid had been drinking the green rotgut that was being pushed out with the end of Prohibition. Rudy prescribed a soft diet, and asked the kid to come into the clinic the next day, for routine tests.

"He's a good kid," Mr. Freedman said. "He makes sixteen dollars a week there, and sends some of the money home. He's from Omaha."

But by the next day Willie Statler was worse. He couldn't come to the clinic. Rudy found him in bed, his complexion greenish, his lips dry. "Doc, I ain't got any insides left. Honest to Christ, I feel like I crapped out all my guts. I can't take it."

It was one of those times when a doctor feels maybe he ought to know, but he doesn't know what's wrong. Could it be ulcers? Maybe even appendicitis, though that wasn't indicated. Rudy took blood and urine samples, and told the kid to stay in bed. A South State Street dump was a hell of a place for a sick man, but he didn't quite feel justified in hospitalizing the case. The next day there was no improvement. At lunch, in connection with some joke about diarrhea, Rudy mentioned the case.

"Say, did you get a sample of the feces?" Dr. Swaboda piped. Swaboda would be sure to pop out with some rare oriental disease. But just for the hell of it, Rudy got a smear for Swaboda.

Pridefully excited, Swaby dragged Rudy to a microscope. "What do you call that?"

Rudy looked. It was something he should know.

"Looks like amoeba," he said, puzzled.

"Right on the head. You probably never saw this before, except in pictures. That's the first case I've seen in six years. But it takes a County man, Rudy, it takes a County man. We had a case of amoebic dysentery in 1927. Only one I ever saw."

Like perhaps three-fourths of the doctors in Chicago, Rudy had never run into this tropical disease. He remembered it now, in the books.

Swaboda was so excited by the rare find that he made Rudy take him over to the flophouse. The first question Swaby popped at the boy was: "Ever been a sailor?"

The sick kid looked puzzled. "Me? No. I come from Omaha."

Then where the devil could he have picked up a tropical disease? Swaboda studied the case record. "Work at the Del Roi Hotel, huh?"

"I'm a busboy."

Swaboda snapped his fingers. "Rudy, I'm a sonofagun if that case we had at County didn't work at the Del Roi or one of those downtown hotels. I remember it distinctly. I think he was a cook."

"What was his name?"

"How should I know? . . . Say, your pal Mitch Wilner might remember something about it."

They phoned Mitch. He did remember the case of amœbic dysentery, because it had been so rare. "It responds pretty well if you get it early enough," he said. "Though it can be fatal. That guy got over it." That was all he recalled.

"Gosh, I'd like to get ahold of that case record," Rudy said.

"Yah. It might be handy." They returned to the patient. Swaboda said: "Say, Willie, anybody else sick up there where you work?"

"Yah. There was another guy was sick, but he quit. I don't know what happened to him. Hey, is this serious, doc?"

"No. You'll be okay in a week or so. That's all, just one more guy?"

"Well, I ain't been there very long. It's a wonder everybody don't get sick in that dump. The plumbing is so lousy, there's garbage all over the floor. You can stick a fork right through those lousy old pipes. They got the holes plugged up with rags or anything. The Department of Health ought to make them fix that old plumbing," Willie complained, but added knowingly: "I suppose they smeared the inspector."

"Why, Christ, that disease may have been nesting in the Del Roi basement the last ten years," Swaboda said.

They called attention to the case, in the routine report to the Board of Health.

The kid was coming along all right, and they might have let the thing go, when old man Freedman came down with dysentery.

He had seen the kid getting well, and therefore began with a scorn of the disease. "It goes through you and that's all," he insisted. Even though he had a doctor for a son-in-law, Mr. Freedman was one of those people who feel they can't really be sick unless they admit it by going to a physician. He had never missed a day at the hotel, the last twenty years, and why get himself laid up—the disease would pass of itself.

It was Nigger John who phoned Rudy; the old man had fainted on the toilet.

Rudy found him laid out on one of his nicked enameled cots.

Over a week, Freedman's case failed to respond. Rudy tried emetine, every known agent. He looked up the disease in tropical literature. No use. Freedman's intestines were in awful shape anyhow; how he had appeared in fair health all these years was a mystery. The combination of heavy Jewish cooking at home with South State Street slime at lunch would have corroded a cast-iron stomach. On top of everything, he was, like so many

Jews, a magnesia drinker, and had been drinking the stuff like pop. Now nothing would work on him. The amœbas seemed to be multiplying, infecting the intestinal walls.

There was no one who could give advice. If there was something to go by, even the record of that case at County!

It was practically insane to expect to find a County Hospital case record, but on a wild chance Rudy went down with Swaboda. Part of the records for that year were bundled away in stacks in the basement, others were "filed" in a switchboard room. The walls were lined with ancient, broken drawers, cram-full. No index. They opened the cases at random, pulled out yellowing, dusty sheets. The closest they came was finding a box of records for that same year, containing mostly fracture cases.

"What a system!" Swaboda growled. "Maybe somebody here remembers something. Let's see if any of the old nurses are around."

They ran into a supervisor who remembered Swaby. She was a heavy-ankled old warhorse, with a megaphone voice. She didn't remember the case. "Doc, you should be here now. Some fun. All we got is pellagra. I got three wards full of them and there's more coming in every day. I never saw anything like it. They're all plain starved, that's all. If it keeps up I don't know where I'll put them."

An inflated interne gave them a rigmarole about the fancy injections that County was developing, for the treatment of diet insufficiency. "Did you see Dr. Hendricks' article in the *Courier*?" he said. "He's getting a big reputation in this field. Of course he has a great opportunity here. Plenty of material to work with."

They walked through the ward of starved and emaciated, whites on one side, Negroes on the other. A radio was on.

"Who's afraid of the big bad wolf,
    Big bad wolf—"

"Listen," said single-minded Swaboda, "you heard of any cases of amœbic dysentery around here?"

"Yep!" the interne glowed. "We've got one! A pip!"

"Where did he work?"

Since Rudy began dragging Manny Kassell out to the house on mysterious conspiratorial meetings that had something to do with the clinic, Aline had been seeing more of Thelma. Their little girls were the same age and just in that angelic period when they were so cute and a pure joy.

What if Thelma was only the wife of a dentist! If the boys could practice together, why, their wives could go out together.

They were showing their kiddies the transparent man, in the Hall of Science. An automatic voice came out of the man, explaining his digestive process, while lights went on inside him. There were only two dolls like this in the world; they cost thousands of dollars.

They saw Sylvia studying the medical exhibits, and had a picnic watching her as she carefully read all that long scientific junk on the cards under each exhibit. She was fairly far gone, but not really big yet.

"I guess she's trying to make sure he'll be another medical genius," said Aline.

Sylvia moved on to a display of photographs of the great men of medicine.

"They used to come over all the time, but I never see them any more," Aline said. "I suppose she is afraid Mitch will be kicked out of Israel if he even breathes the same air as a doctor from the Alliance."

Sylvia almost bumped into them. "Well, have you picked out a place for Mitch, there?" Aline kidded, while they fell all over each other with greetings. "Where have you been keeping yourself?"

"Honest, Aline, Mitch has been so busy since he got on the Israel staff. They call him night and day. . . . How's your father?"

"Not so hot," Aline admitted. "Rudy says they may have to operate."

Sylvia was sympathetic.

"Well, I'm glad to hear Mitch is so busy," Aline remarked. And added with her awful frankness—you could never be sure whether it was dumbness or being mean—"I thought maybe you were avoiding us because Mitch was afraid of fraternizing with his former office-mate. I know how careful doctors have to be about who they are seen with."

Sylvia flushed. "Oh, Aline, you know Mitch is all for Rudy! Even if he might think Rudy made a mistake in joining the clinic. Honest, you know I don't like to go out by myself, and Mitch is never free." She couldn't help adding with a thrust of pride: "He's teaching at Rush now, too."

The kid was tugging at Aline; she felt cross; her sleeves were tight and hot. "Maybe Rudy is making a mistake," she said tartly, "but at least he and the boys are making a living. You don't have to bunk me, Sylvia! Rudy was on the staff too and they hauled him out four nights a week, for nothing; I never saw such a crazy profession! They put you on their staff and you have the privilege of putting in sixteen more hours a week and burning up gas rushing back and forth to the hospital, and if you want an even greater honor you can go and teach at a medical school free of charge! Do you think he ever got any patients out of it? No! For my part, Mitch can have all the professional honors! I am proud of my husband for having some gumption!"

Sylvia was flabbergasted. "But, Aline, I have nothing against the boys downtown. I wish them the best of luck!"

"I know, I know, Sylvia," Aline said. "You and Mitch were always superior to everybody else, so we poor simple folks will just have to find friends in our own class."

Thelma, dreadfully upset by the whole situation, for which she felt sort of responsible, as the wife of a dentist championed by doctors, blurted that she had to take Cynthia because Cynthia had to go.

Aline gathered up Naomi, and they marched off.

Sylvia leaned against the wall. There was no place to sit down. The whole world was misunderstanding her and Mitch, lately. The minute you began to go up, angry arms from all around tugged and dragged at you, to keep you amongst mediocrity.

She tried to fix her attention upon a display showing how a single rat off a ship could spread typhus all over Chicago if not for the marvelous methods of the public health sanitation.

The executive committee met in Dr. Matthews's office.

"The kid went back and talked to the men around the kitchen," Rudy reported. "It seems the health department finally got wise. All the men had examinations. A bunch of them got laid off."

"That means they're carriers," Matthews said. He was even more excited than Swaboda about the epidemic. It was his idealistic nature. "But aren't they doing anything else about it?"

"They're painting the basement kitchens now," Rudy said wryly.

"That hotel ought to be closed!" Matthews cried, his nose twitching angrily. "Why, every resident of the hotel may be infected! And what about the thousands of people who've stayed there during the Fair—they've probably spread the disease all over the country! And anybody that happens to eat at the Del Roi is exposed to it! Why, I've eaten there myself, many times!"

"And the worst of it is," said Rudy, still under the chill realization that, but for an accident, he might not have diagnosed the disease, "hardly anybody practicing in this country would be likely to recognize it if they saw it. There may be deaths already, attributed to other causes."

"I don't understand this! There ought to be a public warning! What's the health department waiting for?" Matthews snapped.

"The end of the Fair," Swaboda said, simply.

Matthews threw down his pencil. Of course. If any public announcement was made, panic fear would sweep the country. The Fair would be deserted. Millions of dollars would be lost to Chicago business men.

"And don't forget, they may want to have a Fair next year too," Swaboda added.

"The Dawes family hasn't quite recouped its stock market losses," Weintraub mentioned. "Another year would just about do the trick for them, with their fat concessions."

"Does the S.A.P.S.—?" Matthews began. But obviously they must know.

"Well, we've done our part," Rudy said. "We've notified the authorities and it's up to them to warn the public."

"But they can't just let these people walk around . . ." Matthews worried.

"Why couldn't we make a public statement?" Swaboda suggested.

The idea soaked in for a moment.

"It would certainly put the clinic on the map," Weintraub said, gleaming.

"That's not the point," Matthews snapped.

Dr. Orr had been unusually silent. Now he cried: "Right! We don't want to make any announcements. It's none of our business."

"I didn't say that," Matthews contradicted him. "I said if we made the announcement, it would not be for the publicity value to ourselves. This is a public matter. They may be able to shut up everybody else but nobody is going to shut us up."

"Wait a minute! We're not making any statements about any epidemics!" Orr jumped up, as if to guard the door. "I've already talked to the health department," he informed them, while glaring at Rudy. "They called up about these cases you fellows reported. In the first place, I don't find those cases listed as patients. Am I supposed to know what's going on here or . . .?"

"I treated them," Rudy gulped, and the others started to talk at the same time, trying to explain how the thing had come up, and that one of the patients was Rudy's own father-in-law. But their heated talk only heightened the confusion, even making it seem as though Rudy were taking patients away from the clinic.

"Nobody has any right to make any statements in the name of this institution!" Orr insisted. "We haven't made any investigation. We have no authority to say that—"

"But we did, we went down there in the basement!" Swaboda yelled.

"And anyway the health department is on the job," Orr out-yelled them. "There's no sense in alarming the public. The department has got a list of everybody that stayed at the Del Roi. They're going to get in touch with every single one of them and tell them if they feel sick to have their doctor communicate with the Chicago health department. Then those doctors will be told to look for dysentery."

Matthews's eyes seemed to burst out of their sockets. "What about the carriers?" he demanded. "By this time they may have passed it on to thousands who were never near the Fair. What about the people who just ate at the Del Roi without being registered there? Why, they can't reach half the people that were exposed! The only way to do it is by a public announcement."

"The health department has known about this for weeks! They're hushing it up!" Rudy charged, appalled.

"Listen, calm down, Rudy," Orr advised. "You're looking at this from a personal standpoint. The fact is the health department has everything under control at the Del Roi. They're notifying public health officials all over the country to be on the lookout for amœbic dysentery, and that's enough. A public announcement would just scare the population. It would do more harm than good."

"It's not going to scare any amœbas into them," Matthews said. "All it would harm is the Fair. There's only a few more weeks to the Fair and they can afford a loss to prevent a national epidemic."

"The health department is in charge of this situation and we have no right to interfere," Orr insisted, and they had to admit that was reasonable. "We can't go off half-cocked. A couple of you went over there and took a look. But the health department has made a thorough investigation, and that's that. Listen, you men know I have no reason to cover them up." True. After all that crowd were his political enemies. They had ousted him. "But I've been a public health man myself and I know that there are certain things that have to be taken into consideration that ordinarily a doc doesn't come into contact with. It's a different kind of problem and you can't handle it like you would an individual case. So I say the health department is entitled to handle it their own way."

Swaboda seemed to be convinced. Even Rudy couldn't help feeling that Orr was sincere, and in a way, correct.

"Besides, fellows," Orr concluded, "we've got to play ball once in a while. We've got to take the hotels into account. We've got plenty of fight on our hands right now. Why, if we buck the health department they can put us out of business. We can't bust out with a scare about an epidemic just because there were one or two cases."

Matthews leaped up. "Play ball! I'm not playing ball with people's lives! So we have to malpractice in order to stay in good with the city hall! Not me! I don't give a damn about the Chicago real estate situation or the Chicago hotels either!"

"The trouble with you is you're too idealistic," Orr said lightly.

"All right! I'm idealistic!" Matthews flared. "I'm idealistic enough to prevent other people from getting into the state that Rudy Stone's father-in-law is in this minute. That man may die! We're making an announcement, and right now!" Matthews reached for the phone. Orr grabbed it.

"The hell we are! This organization has made no investigation of those cases—"

"I've seen those cases and that's enough for me!" Matthews pulled at the telephone.

"You're not the Medical Alliance—" Orr shouted.

"We saw them too," Swaboda cut in.

Rudy tried to speak calmly. "Dr. Orr, I think the majority is in favor."

"Don't give me any of that stuff! I'm boss here and I—"

"Boss!" the men echoed.

Matthews stood frozen, his mouth open.

"Boss, huh?" Swaboda repeated. "A thousand a month."

"I see," Matthews said, painedly. "The boys tried to tell me a few things before, but I couldn't believe them. So you're the boss, Dr. Orr? So you're running the place?"

"Well, someone has to run it," Orr maintained truculently.

"I see," Matthews repeated. "And I suppose that's why we have to advertise eyeglass frames instead of our optical services. Well, Dr. Orr, I never intended to compete with the Jiffy eyeglass stores. I'm not going to have my friends greet me on the street as Dr. Jiffy. . . ."

"That last ad was okayed by your committee!" Orr bellowed, evidently glad to get off the subject of the epidemic.

"It was not!" the men shouted in unison.

"Are you calling me a liar?" Orr challenged.

"Yes! And plenty else!" Matthews answered. "Are you being cut in, for your efforts on behalf of the hotels?"

Orr charged at him, flailing wildly. Rudy jumped up, catching at Orr's arm, and was swung against a desk. The men leaped on Dr. Orr, as Dr. Matthews struck, hitting him in the eye.

A wild grunting curse burst from the director. With tiger strength, he pulled the whole lot of them along the floor as he strained at Matthews. There was a quaking, hot-breathing moment as the men realized, and stood by what they had done. Orr's muscles relaxed. They let go of him, and he walked out.

The doctors began to speak in hard, over-calm voices. Somehow they felt a little ashamed. You couldn't say Orr had been altogether wrong in his attitude on the epidemic. Maybe a more formal investigation would have been in order. But it was the way he had acted, trying to boss them. Everything had come to a head—all the other grievances. It was too late to go back on themselves now. Maybe Matt shouldn't have hit him.

Matthews, Swaboda, and Rudy sat down to prepare a statement to the press.

They called an immediate emergency meeting of the staff. Dr. Orr was ousted from the position of director. A trembling triumph pervaded the clinic; whispers, and little laughs about Orr's black eye. So they had a boss, huh!

And yet there was no feeling of safety. A man like that, a big shot, a high-pressure man, would find a way to strike back.

Aw, what could he do! They had the votes.

Rudy, Mike Swaboda, Perusi, stayed downtown, talking endlessly. They got the early morning papers, tore through them. The statement about amœbic dysentery had not been used. They had an uneasy feeling that Orr had understood the situation better than themselves. Well, maybe the papers would print it after they had had a chance to check up on it. They bought edition after edition. Nothing on the epidemic.

But there, in a tone of contained glee, was a cute story about a rift in the "cafeteria medicine" clinic. There were little paragraphs about the black eyes that appeared "when doctors disagree."

Feldner was blabbing all over town about quacks scrapping amongst themselves. Dr. Orr's black eye had become a black eye for the clinic. The whispering affected the patients. Business fell off. Puzzled glances, whispers, giggles filled the place.

They heard nothing from Orr. Rudy began to get worried. Their failure to get news of the epidemic published had somehow invested the whole affair with failure.

Dr. Orr struck. He called a meeting of stockholders.

Only then, the fellows learned what they had let themselves in for. He really was the boss. Together, they had sunk over thirty thousand dollars into common stock, while he had bought ten thousand dollars' worth of preferred, giving him a fifty-one percent control over the company that owned the lease and the equipment. Dr. Orr voted himself back into the directorship. He returned to the office, where he held long, mysterious conferences with strangers.

Even Rudy's calm self-control was cracked. He had started the men on this revolt; what good had it done! Orr would probably fire them one by one. They had let go of their private practices.

Mr. Freedman was in the hospital. The only thing to do seemed to be to shut off a part of his intestines, giving them a functional rest and a chance to combat the amœba. But he was in no shape for an operation. He had little resistance; it seemed that his business losses during the last few years had sapped him.

Rudy felt that Mrs. Freedman distrusted his care of her husband, yet was afraid to insult her son-in-law by calling another doctor. She was suspicious of their hospital; why couldn't her husband be taken to Israel? And though she would have paid five hundred dollars to have Matthews operate at Israel, she was even suspicious of Matthews, as a clinic man.

It was this that was most galling of all. The unrelenting unfair campaign of slander had finally infected the public with distrust of the Medical Alliance. "Cheap medicine"—"advertisers"—"quacks"—and the recent publicity had given Feldner his final bombshell: scrapping amongst themselves! God, people were stupid! There was a woman, Matthews's patient, whose X-ray clearly showed gallstones. But she wouldn't believe a clinic doctor—she took herself to a heart specialist who assured her that she had no gallstones but only a nervous condition of the heart. She came back to spit the story at Matthews. "My doctor says he don't care what your X-ray shows, I ain't got gallstones! You people just want to get my money!"

"What's the use!" Matthews said bitterly. "Who are we doing all this for?"

Rudy, too, had plenty of experiences of that rotting doubt. His own mother-in-law—when he and Matt were breaking themselves to pieces, trying, doing everything they could for Mr. Freedman. He scarcely slept, those weeks. Aline would try to calm him, stroking his back slowly, but it was no use. Everything had gone wrong at the same time. And what tortured him most was that nothing was being done about the epidemic.

"You did all you could, dear," Aline kept telling him, and, yes, checking the problem from every direction, he had done all he could. But he hadn't won out.

He had one more idea. For days he debated with himself, prevented himself from drawing Mitch into the tangle. But finally he had to do it.

"Mitch, I'm going to ask you to do something tough."

Rudy outlined the situation on amœbic dysentery. "It's got me nuts. Old man Freedman may not pull through. It's on my mind all the time. I'll tell you what I want you to do, Mitch. I don't know whether the S.A.P.S. is officially aware of the business or not, but if the whole question was thrown up at a meeting they would have to take action. I'd do it myself if I was still in the organization. As it is, I want you to do it."

Mitch asked for time to think it over.

The greatest art exhibition of all time, a seventy-five-million-dollar collection of old and modern masters had been assembled at the Chicago Art Institute as part of the Fair. Never before had a mere art exhibition in America drawn such droves. It was the hit of the Fair. Just proved that art went right to the hearts of the big public.

Joe and Alvin wandered through the halls. One masterpiece after another. In sculpture, Michelangelo, Rodin—breathtaking. And yet all it did to Joe was screw up his anger. Hundreds of thousands, millions, for these dead, while he frittered away his time making ten-dollar figurines.

"Sonofabitch! It makes me sick! Let's get out of here!" he growled.

Mitch and Sylvia lay in bed. "You mustn't!" she insisted. "Mitch, you've had enough bad breaks. Years you wasted on that serum, and what did you get out of it? Now, just when you've got a start, you can't risk it by getting in bad. We deserve a little peace, Mitch."

"It isn't that," he worried. "If I thought it was the right thing, I'd do it. But nothing can be accomplished that way. You can't make people do things by antagonizing them. Rudy and his bunch are going off half-cocked. This thing has to be investigated in the regular way. We've got committees for such things. I can't just jump up on the floor and yell."

"Of course. It would just get you in bad. I can't understand Rudy. He's gone bugs on this subject." She snapped out the light.

"And after all, maybe the health department's method is okay," Mitch said. "We aren't in the Middle Ages, when epidemics were uncontrollable. The whole science of public health is outside of our field. We can't interfere with their methods. After all, if this thing could become an epidemic, it should have shown up more in the last couple of years. According to Swaboda, that case we had in County was from the same source. If it doesn't spread any faster than that, there's no sense in alarming the whole country over a few isolated cases. The health department may be right. And you can't really say they're suppressing it when they've informed health officers all over the country. I understand they already have the thing under control. Deaths are falling off."

"How many have there been?" she asked.

"Nobody knows exactly. I think about twenty cases were reported, over the country."

"The S.A.P.S. must know what's going on. If they don't want to do anything about it, your protest won't make them."

Still his mind seemed uneasy. "I'll write a letter to the society, asking if the matter has been investigated," Mitch concluded. "That's the proper procedure."

She wondered whether Joe's father was going to die. Then she curled against Mitch. "It's such a crazy world," she said. "We have to be careful, darling. Don't let's leave it wreck us."

Revolt of Doctors

As Rudy came to work he saw Dr. Matthews standing in the lobby, away from the elevator bank, grinning.

"Coming up?" Rudy asked.

"I can't. I'm fired," Matthews announced. "And there is a large gentleman at the door, to see that I don't molest the peace of the clinic."

"I'll quit too," Rudy said. A wife and two kids and a third coming, and start to hunt for practice. Discredited by the S.A.P.S. He couldn't ask Mitch to turn back the practice he had given him. He couldn't ask anything of Mitch any more. It had been within Mitch Wilner's right to refuse that crazy request, at that, he had done something, and of course they were all still friendly but . . .

"Maybe you won't have to quit," Matthews hinted.

"Huh? . . . Oh."

Matthews rode up with him and watched him get his notice. Four or five other doctors, arriving for work, were in the elevator. The men rode down with the two fired leaders.

An impromptu meeting was held in the lobby. As the other staff members arrived, they joined. Rudy and Matthews were commissioned to look for a large set of offices.

The revolt of the doctors took place on Saturday night. Every man in the staff, with the exception of two known stoolpigeons to the boss, had secretly joined the new organization.

The office girls had got wind of the affair and sent Miss Squires and Mrs. Ritter as a delegation, asking that the girls be taken along. Even the handyman was with them!

Rudy was one of the group selected to swipe the records. They arrived at the old building separately. The night doorman might have been a little puzzled by the fact that each of the doctors brought along a suitcase. But it was none of his business.

Swaboda and Matthews were already upstairs when Rudy stepped off the elevator. They were merrily stuffing their bags with case records.

"Take the current patients first," Matthews instructed, and Rudy took from M to R.

> "We're gonna shuffle off
> To Buffalo—"

Swaby chanted. He slammed his suitcase shut. It took some effort to lock the bulging lid.

> "I'll go home and get my panties,
> You go home and get your scanties,
> And away we'll go—
> MMM-mmm."

He staggered with the suitcase.

Manny Kassell arrived, carrying his suitcase with an air of guilt. Miss Squires was with him.

"Don't forget those envelopes!" She darted at a pile of boxes near the addressograph machine. "They're all addressed." She squealed with laughter. "The girls nearly died. Addressing them on his time!" The envelopes were to bear letters to all the patients, informing them that their doctors had moved, and to report to the new address for further treatments.

> "And the train goes slow—
> Oooo-ooo."

The whole bunch of them picked up the chorus:

> "To Niagara in a sleeper,
> There's no honeymoon that's cheaper . . ."

"You fellows look like you're going on a trip," the nightman said as they signed out.

"Yep. A little hunting trip, we're all going together," Matthews said, convulsing Swaboda.

The new offices, a block up Wabash, were in happy pandemonium. In one corner, at a table improvised over trestles, sat a crew of office girls inserting names on the mimeographed letters that were to go out that night. Shirtsleeved doctors and dentists were stumbling all over the place pushing around insane assortments of medical and dental equipment. On top of all worked an overtime crew of painters. The amateur furniture movers were continually stumbling over tarpaulins, ropes, ladder-legs. Two dentists and the pharmacist were sweating behind a complicated dental chair which had somehow got stuck under a painter's scaffold. Finally Hank, the handyman, solved the situation by putting the chair into reclining position, and riding it under. What a genius! Every few minutes, calls for help came from the elevator, as men arrived with examining tables, instrument stands, therapeutic lamps rescued from their home basement or borrowed from friends' offices. Dr. Harrows, the Roentgenologist, commandeered a crew to go and get an X-ray machine. "It's sort of antiquated but it'll be all right till we can get a new one delivered. There's not much my box can't do anyway." Rudy joined the crew. They nearly tore apart the walls of Harrows's old office, pulling out the wiring and the rheostats, and when it came to loading the machine onto Harrows's Buick, there was a problem! Most of the pieces were finally squeezed into the back, with a violent disregard for the upholstery. The last minute, Harrows threw away all restraint and donated a fancy all-positions examining table which weighed a ton and had more levers than a human had bones. This was fantastically loaded onto the roof of the car. Rudy rode on the running board, hopefully clutching a leg of the table, to keep it from sliding off the roof. "Buick ought to get this for an ad!" he cried. On top of everything, Weintraub had the crazy idea of stopping for a sterilizing cabinet which he had left with a friend.

Matthews contributed a fluoroscope; Mitch, hearing what was going on, insisted that Rudy take a metabolimeter they had owned in common. By midnight, the new set of offices was a warehouse of sterilizing cabinets, scales, and trick physical therapy units; enamelware kicked underfoot, extension cords lay in snares. Doctors were helping the girls fold letters and lick envelopes. Several wives bustled around measuring windows for curtains. Matthews sat happily on the floor enameling the blistered legs of an instrument table. He was humming: "Who's Afraid of the Big Bad Wolf?"

A messenger boy came, delivering some stationery. "Who's the boss here?" he asked. "There ain't no boss!" a half-dozen men gleefully chorused at the bewildered kid. "Whatchagot?"

Rudy caught a look at himself in the mirror. He brushed his cowlick up from his forehead. He was smudged, stained, and smeared. His back ached from pushing furniture. There were blisters on his hands.

Matthews leaped up, having completed his job. His eye roved over the establishment. One way or another, the stuff had fallen into place. The offices looked equipped.

"Pretty good, huh?" he grinned. "How about some coffee?"

"Yeah, verily!" Swaboda exclaimed.

"Hey! Who's gonna mail these letters! They have to go out tonight!" Tillie Squires insisted.

They grabbed armfuls of letters.

The gang was still singing that nutty song as they invaded Thompson's:

> "And away we'll go—
> Mmmm-mmm . . .
> Off to Buffalo—
> Ooo-ooo!"

Aline took charge of everything. The funeral was to be by Elfman, who, though still located on crummy old Roosevelt Road, handled all the best Jewish funerals. And though naturally she was feeling terrible, she wasn't going to let him take advantage of their sorrow; everybody knew you had to watch Elfman or he would sting you. So she took him aside into the bedroom and had a little subdued argument with him.

"Of course we want everything nice," she informed him, "but," smiling wanly, "you know we're not millionaires. And he didn't leave much—not that it matters—but all he left was his insurance and he borrowed on that. So you understand, Mr. Elfman . . .?"

"Oh, I understand, I understand, I knew your father for twenty years. I went to the same *shul* with him. Trust me, everything will be satisfactory." He trotted toward the parlor; but she stopped him and got an exact price. From four hundred dollars, she got him down to three hundred for the same casket and service.

"I see you are your father's daughter," he complimented Aline.

Aline was proud of her mother, too. Mrs. Freedman was not carrying on, screaming and tearing her hair as was expected of the foreign-born. She sat quite dignified, her hands in her lap, a large, still figure. In fact, she looked like those pictures of Gertrude Stein.

Many old friends and neighbors came and went, and over and over the tale was repeated: "Those murderers from the Fair. They killed him. They had to have a Fair. So they couldn't tell the public it was an epidemic. He caught it from the boy that was working in the Del Roi Hotel. How many died all over the country, who knows? Maybe hundreds."

"Oh, they tried to save him. Two operations. But what could they do? He got complications, he caught pneumonia. . . . He was always working. Whoever knew him even to take off a whole Sunday?"

And now Aline and Joe could realize how little they had ever seen of their father, how little even their mother had seen of him. Now in the end, everybody conceded—a good man. A daughter married to a doctor. A son an artist.

When the men from the hotel called up and asked if they could come out, Aline was momentarily stumped. How would it look—to have those

South State Street bums standing around? All her friends were here too. Nevertheless she decided to be broad-minded. She said yes.

Rudy remained in the background. Now that it was all over there was no longer any suggestion of distrust in Mrs. Freedman. "You did all you could; it was God's will." Yet he was a doctor who had lost a patient.

He stood on the back porch. Naomi somehow sensed the gravity of the day. Baby Jonathan rolled about her, cublike, but she refused to wrestle with him.

Rudy looked through a newspaper. "No more cases of amœbic dysentery," a health official was quoted. And a column of praise for the day and night activity by which the health department had checked the disease. Yes, this the papers would publish. No more cases! Why, Mitch had told him yesterday of several out at Billings, among them the famous professor, Robert Morss Lovett[5].

Yes, they had painted that lousy kitchen and shifted the twenty-six infected food handlers to other jobs and called the epidemic over. Only, the disease had continued to appear in the hotel. Why, it was carried in the very ice-water that the bell boys rushed up to the hot rooms, those sweltering August and September days. Willie Statler could have told them, from the first. The lousy, corroded sewer pipes ran right over the ice-water tank, dripping amœba-infested slime, and the lid of the tank was not watertight! Call for ice-water, pure, clean!

Joe killed time in a movie. Lately he had been going to movies a lot. He hardly bothered to notice the names of the pictures; all movies were essentially the same anyway, and he relaxed in a kind of movie torpor, letting time flow.

And now his father was dead. Joe could make no meaning out of death. He had seen too little of his father. Joe couldn't go home and face all the sorrowing Jews, so he delayed, taking in a movie. This was a movie called *Freaks*, a weird horror enacted by limbless creatures, midgets, pinheads whose idiot faces seemed just wiped of drool. The story was of how a normal, beautiful girl, an equestrienne in the circus, married a midget, planning to get his savings for her lover. Then the freaks, instinctively bound together, took it upon themselves to protect the honor of the midget. Gradually their circle closed upon the normal girl and her normal lover. Horribly, helplessly, she was being drawn in among the freaks until she too would be one of their kind. And on a night of utter terror, the mute, the limbless, the idiot pinheaded, the half-animal, sprang upon the

---

[5] Robert Morss Lovett was a professor at the University of Chicago when Meyer Levin was a student there. He lived until 1956; perhaps he contracted dysentery and recovered? The description of the appearance of dysentery at the Century of Progresss exhibition, the news of which was largely suppressed until the season closed, is historically accurate.

healthy lovers; the man was cut to pieces, buried in slime and mud. The unfaithful woman was captured, and upon her the freaks worked their final, ghastly revenge. From that night forward she too was one of them: there, in a fenced pit, she cackled and flapped—a creature with the face of a woman, the body of a hen.

And this gruesome parable had not been made as art, but as a sideshow novelty, a shocker to catch dollars.

She was beautiful, and she became a creature with the face of a woman, and the body of a hen.

At his father's funeral. She would surely be there. Now he would gaze down into the pit, and see her with her hen's body, and be freed of his long sickness of love.

In front of the house, Joe met Nigger John.

"Hello, Mr. Freedman," the Negro said. He wore a hesitant look.

"Were you upstairs?" Joe asked.

"I didn't know if it was all right."

"Come on," Joe said.

On the stairs, John said, hesitantly: "Say, maybe I ain't ought to ask this from you folks, say, you know he used to like to hear me when I sing '*Eli, Eli*'. You know how your old man give me the name, the Shvartzer Yid." His voice trailed off, appealing.

"You want to sing, huh?" Joe said.

"I don't know if you folks would think that was all right, for me to do."

The flat was crowded; nobody seemed to notice the entrance of the Negro. Aline jumped at Joe. "Where have you been! Oh! We were worried!"

"Well, I'm here!" he said.

His mother arose and embraced him, straining tightly, and weeping a little. Joe noticed the pictures turned to the wall, the mirror covered with a sheet. Now his mother would go and live with Aline, spend her time taking care of Aline's kids.

So he was practically through with the family.

That little, taciturn man, scarcely ever at home, had in his obscure way been the last binding thread. In a pinch, a fellow could go home, the old man still made a living.

It had been as simple as that.

And now maybe for the first time he felt full dependence upon himself, manhood at thirty.

The men from the hotel stood in a compact group, against a far wall. Joe recognized them by sight: Azelli, an eccentric who saved newspapers and was the Star's only "steady boarder"; and drunken Mike, whom the old man had had to kick out so many times, and whose eyes were whisky-glazed now; and the Irishman, an onhanger of mysterious connections, probably a pimp. They were gotten up to look respectable, and yet an air of wildness and of furtive uncertainty hung about them. Perhaps they owned the old man more clearly than all his family and clan; by far the greater part of his time had been spent among them, and surely they knew things about him that none of the family knew.

The Negro had drawn toward them for shelter.

Joe approached them.

"He was the best guy on the street," the Irishman said.

"Your father was the best friend I ever had, boy," Mike declared.

"He never gave anybody no trouble," the Irishman said.

It became clear to Joe, how his father had been; in the dregs of South State Street, among tubercular whores, pimps, beggars, bums, Old Man Freedman had remained simply a good Jew.

Joe stopped his sister, and said: "He wants to sing '*Eli, Eli.*' The Shvartzer Yid."

"What?" She was horrified. "Oh, no. I'm broad-minded, but that wouldn't be appropriate. We can't let him do it here."

Mrs. Freedman heard them arguing. "Let him, let him," she declared. "He was a good friend of pa's. So long, he worked for him."

Aline made an announcement. "Please, everybody. We are going to listen to John, he worked for my father for many years and he wants to sing '*Eli, Eli,*' for him."

John stepped to the casket and began the heart-throbbing Yiddish song. His voice was full of sorrow. Sniffles were heard throughout the room.

Joe looked out the window, at the U-shaped red brick apartment building across the street. The song, with its quavering sentimentality, its wailing forsaken note, seemed to him not only a requiem for his father, but for the whole time when Jews were like this.

And across the notes of "*Eli, Eli,*" came a wild Tarzan yell from the street, where Aline's Naomi was playing with some kids.

Joe turned and, looking through into the next room, saw that Sylvia had entered during the singing.

It was just as always, just as though the years between had never been; a wave, a force, seemed to sweep through him, momentarily dizzying his mind, first like sheer fright, then it was as though the sustained, paining charge continued in his heart.

He was sure now that this love was a thing outside of his self, beyond any control, and therefore it was no longer important. It was just a reflex action. The idea of love alone was doing this to him. He didn't know Sylvia any more, perhaps had never known what she was like.

She had seen him; so he went into the other room to greet her.

"How have you been, Joe?" she asked.

"All right." With her movement, as she turned toward Joe, he caught the scent of her, cool, and sharp as ever. Could it be, that no other . . .?

"I was going to ask you to come and see us," she said.

Aline was listening, watching, and his mother too. He was sure he was showing no reaction. He was afraid to look directly, fully at Sylvia but just once he glanced quickly up and down, seeing all of her. Her complexion seemed different, perhaps it had lost its eggshell smoothness, and become warmer, more like flesh. And her figure seemed bunchier. It should have been plain to him at the instant; but it was only when she had gone aside, talking with Aline, that Joe realized her condition.

"So I just eat a light supper," Sylvia was saying. "That seems to help."

"Well, I had it easy with my first one but I had awful vomiting spells before Jo-Jo . . ."

"Maybe it's a sign it's a boy," said Sylvia.

Why didn't he feel that horror, the hen in the pit? Why didn't it sweep over him, and cure him with the wild shock? Why hadn't he noticed at once how she waddled, large-bellied, how her skin was coarse, blotched; now it was as though he were watching her carnally with Mitch.

And standing there with Aline, jabbering clinically of nausea, of the color and tenderness of breasts, of what clothes to wear, of drinking hot water, of wine and stool. And coming here to a funeral, wives, wives in their old banal attitudes, carrying the race, always bringing life for death, bringing births to funerals like stale playwrights. . . . Just another female, with a fetus there, glands, and guts, and pumping blood.

The old man's will had been written before the depression. The mother cried, hearing him bequeath the apartment house where they had lived, and which he had lost to the mortgage holder; and the swell store and office building on Madison, now in receivership, threatened with a deficiency attachment. It was as though the old man were alive, listening stony-faced to his will, all that property he had slowly accumulated blown away, a life of struggle blown away, yes, he might just as well have taken it easy.

Joe could walk along South State Street now, and the army recruiting station was in its place, and the hollow-cheeked gals from the ten-cent burlesques, stepping across the street without stockings, and in all their hideous stage paint, didn't bother him, nor the bleary dusty windows of the flophouses. Joe had it figured out now. Two things that had been worked into him since infancy were wrong. The idea of romantic love, from the first fairy-tales to the latest Janet Gaynor movie, told and told as true, was wrong. And the idea of money security, from the first penny bank, was wrong. Now he could walk down this street without that haunting fear of some day becoming like the derelicts who slept in his old man's hotel.

Both those ideas, primary concepts of this civilization, would of course remain in the world. But now they could ride him no more.

He didn't have to use all his force in fighting them any more. Maybe he'd do some sculpture, now.

"Well, he made the front page," Lou Margolis greeted his wife, throwing the *News* toward the couch. She had already seen the paper.

QUIZ MOSCOWITZ ON INCOME TAX

If they didn't go to the Sterns' bridge party tonight it would be the beginning of not going anywhere. Maybe Lou could face it out like a joke. She could hear him, in advance: "Well, my father-in-law has put in a reservation for the cell between Al Capone and Sam Insull."

The maid passed through the room; Celia was certain the girl gave them a funny look.

"What can he do?" Celia said.

Lou shrugged. "There's only one chance, down in Washington. It may be too late now, I told him to clear it up last year, as soon as Roosevelt took office. Once it's in the paper they're on the spot."

"Why didn't he fix it before!" she cried.

"Your old man is such an ox! Just because there's a Jewish governor he thinks nobody can touch him."

"But why all of a sudden? What happened? I don't understand!" she persisted.

"What happened is that, when Cermak kicked off, Kelly and Nash got control of the machine. It's the Irish, that's all." There was always a tussle for control of the state; between the governor of Illinois and the mayor of Chicago; Rube Moscowitz had stuck with the Jewish governor against the new Irish mayor, and as the mayor's gang grew in power, Rube was on the spot. Pete Grinnell was a big shot in the new city hall machine and was crying for revenge. While Rube had been dickering to be allowed to pay back taxes quietly, claiming it was all an oversight, and hadn't Kelly been allowed to correct an income tax error, someone had given the story to the papers. If there was a trial, all the dirt would come up, the tributes from gambling houses in the neighborhood, the rake-offs on contracts, the graft from storekeepers, everything.

The kid, Reuben, pawed over the paper, spelling out the headline. "Moscowitz. Hey, ma! That's my grandaddy! Look, pop! Bigger than Dillinger!"

Celia choked down her involuntary laugh. "He takes after his father," she remarked. "Everything is a joke to him."

A question lay between them; each knew the other couldn't sleep.

If Lou was connected with the case people would sniff: "Huh, Margolis was in on it from the first, helping his father-in-law dodge the income tax, only he didn't do such a good job of it."

But if Lou didn't go, they would say he deserted his father-in-law in his hour of need.

Finally Celia spoke: "I don't know if you ought to go to Washington with him."

"There are a lot of guys that could do him more good," Lou said. "An Irishman, like Jerry McNamara. He could get straight to Farley."

"If he took some other lawyer—and you just went along as a—" friend? relative? adviser?

"Yah, I could go as his valet," Lou cracked.

Rube wouldn't budge out of the compartment. The man acted half insane. Lou wanted to ask him: "What are you trying to do, find out how it feels to be locked in a cell already?"

And he didn't want to be left alone. When Lou got up with the idea of looking over the train, Rube demanded: "Where you going?"

"Take a leak," Lou said.

"You can take one in here," Rube pointed out.

"I'll be right back," Lou said. When he returned he found Rube pacing the compartment. Lou tried to ease him off. "Say, I heard a good one about Mae West in there," he began, and told the story of Mae West and the bull in the pasture. Rube didn't show any sign of hearing the story but at least he sat down. Lou continued, telling about Mae West in an endurance contest, about Mae West and the six acrobats. He added one he had made up himself, about Mae West's telling a bill collector: "Come up and sue me some time!"

All at once Rube Moscowitz began to talk to his son-in-law. "You're a good kid, you're a smart kid," he said. "But lemme tell you something. Never trust anybody. You see what it gets you. I was an easy guy. Rube Moscowitz, everybody said, sure, he'd give you the shirt off his back. And look what it gets you. A knife in the back.

"Pete Grinnell. We treated him like one of the family. He used to eat with us all the time. But when the time comes that he can get something by sticking a knife in your back, he'll do it. Just like look what Hitler is doing to the Jews. They went to war for Germany and they got killed in the war for Germany, but that don't make any difference, all they get is a knife in the back. And a Jew will do it to you too. Look at that bastard Klein. He swindled me out of a fortune with his second mortgages and now if I try to save a little from the wreck, he sues me for what I saved out of the receiverships. It was my money that was lost, wasn't it? I had a right to get back what I could!

"If I had all the money I gave away in my life I would be a rich man, depression or no depression. But does anybody come out to help me? No, they all want to see me in jail. That's what kind of an animal a man is, he ain't worth living. Look what man has done with the world. It's got everything on it. Plenty for everybody to live a healthy life and eat and drink all they want. So all we got is hunger and starvation and wars. You think I don't feel it? I feel it. Right in my neighborhood they come begging to me

636

for relief and I can't even get them enough relief. Even to get bread and beans they have to have a riot in front of the relief station. Roosevelt came in and he was going to fix everything but what have we got? Strikes all over the country. The farmers are spilling the milk on the roads; they got machine guns in every factory. Roosevelt is a good-hearted guy but he is just another politician. They'll knife him in the back the same as they did to me. You want to know what's the trouble? The trouble is with human nature. Man is just a louse and he always will be a louse. They say they got a different system in Russia and everybody thinks about everybody else but I don't believe it. You can't cure the troubles of the world with a new system because man is a traitor, everyone will betray his brother, and that's why things are this way.

"I lived my life, I worked hard, I was on the go all the time, trying to build something big. And what have I got out of life? Friends? I've helped people out of jams that you don't even know about. But is there anyone to go down to Washington with me now? Insull was a bigger man than me, and when the time came they were after him with a knife and he ran to the last corners of the world but they betrayed him even in Turkey. Do you think I sympathize with him? No. He double-crossed me, he sold me stocks when he knew they were going bust, he imposed on me because I was a friend. In this world, there ain't no such thing as a friend."

The train rode on through the bleak bare fields; they saw stray clumps of sagging unpainted farmhouses, and flashes of signboards.

Anyway, Lou thought, it was good Rube had got that speech out of his system. Maybe after eating he would feel better and talk plans. All Rube's philosophy he had figured out before he was in long pants. God, some of that older generation were sentimental saps!

Rube's ulcers were bad. The foods he delighted in, meats he could sink his teeth into, spicy and peppery, accompanied by sour pickles and sour tomatoes, horse radish and mustard, were denied him.

He set down the milk, contemptuously. "Why do they pick on me?" he demanded. "Say, there ain't a guy in office in Chicago that didn't do a little income-tax juggling. Did they go to jail? They fixed it up for everybody; only when I come along, they get tough. I can name you guys that owe millions. But they have to pick on me!"

"I got an idea," Lou suggested. His idea was that Rube should claim he had failed to include certain money in his tax report because the money had been spent in political gifts that had to be kept off the record.

"Sure!" Rube cried. "I must have handed out a hundred grand in the 1930 election. There was a dozen aldermen I had to hold in line for the Sonofabitch, to pass that damn subway deal he wanted."

"You got any evidence?"

"Naw. I got some of it down in that little red book."

"That's all we need!" Lou snapped. "We'll hand them a story about the little red book. They'll be scared to call for it on account of the scandal it would bring onto the party."

Rube gazed through the window. "They won't swallow that crap," he finally said, back to hopelessness. "The first thing they'd do, they'd ask the Sonofabitch if it was straight, and he'd never back me up on it. Just my luck they have to catch him now."

"Maybe he will back you up," Lou said.

"Naw. He's got all he can do to save his own skin; you think he's going to front for me? . . . Anyway, there wasn't that much."

"Well, we can try it. It's our only chance. And especially when we hand them a check along with the story."

"Shit!" Rube suddenly cried, enraged. "Why should I protect anybody! I'll spill the whole tubful of crap! I may go down, but I'll pull some of Kelly's pals down with me!"

This was the thing then that the papers got hold of. How Rube Moscowitz, the junk dealer, had gone down to Washington trying to get out of his income tax case, how he had claimed that Insull paid him to act as his political agent, not with cash, but by giving him immense loads of scrap iron at ridiculously low prices. And the hundreds of thousands of dollars in profits from million-dollar deals in junk couldn't be charged to Rube's income as most of it had to be spent on furthering Insull's political interests.

And the papers had a string of names given by Rube Moscowitz; of Alderman Manciewitz, whose son he had sent through college with Insull money; of Alderman Posner, who had received ten thousand dollars for his election campaign; of Alderman Monahan, who had received five thousand in one election, fifteen thousand in another; and down the list, until practically half of the city council was included.

What howling and laughter and vituperation now arose! Blanket denials, sarcastic comments about the junkman trying to save his skin, trying to get revenge on his political opponents. And the El and street car companies issued statements to prove that he had never bought scrap iron from them below the market price.

So Rube Moscowitz's confession in Washington brought no pardon. He would have to stand trial.

Home, Rube refused to talk to anybody. With morose obstinacy, he came to the table on Friday night and gorged himself with sour tomatoes.

A Party of Lawyers

Even Sam was surprised at the turnout. The long room was crowded. At least three hundred must be present. And all stiff-necked, solemn with the "dignity of the profession." Seeing a few of the white-haired old-timers, Sam knew what a terrific restraint had been overcome, before they allowed themselves to answer the call. Plenty greeted each other with over-loud jests. Notices in the Bar Association, in the city hall, had brought these hundreds, by their presence admittedly desperate.

It didn't take long to break through the crust of pretense and get down to action. They wanted some form of economic help. Let the government make projects for lawyers, too! Committees were appointed to draw up projects. It was a swell, successful meeting; the left-wing crowd remained in control, but they had drawn the real rank and file into their committees.

There, in the doorway, Sam saw Lou Plotkin, a brother of Runt.

"Well, how's Dave doing these days?"

"Not so hot." The kid was frank. "He gets an accident case once in a while. We got another brother interning in a hospital, he tips us off—"

"Why didn't Dave come around?"

"Aw, you know—he's got pride," the kid laughed. "He sent me to represent the family."

"Well, bring him around."

The projects had been drawn up, and the city hall's okay was needed before the federal government could be expected to assign funds. The corporation counsel was stalling. Finally a general delegation took the appeal to his office. Fifty, sixty men went along, and several women lawyers were in the crowd.

Runt Plotkin and his brother were there with Sam. "I know a guy in Gessner's office." Runt promised pull.

Talk was nervous and high-pitched. Archibald Summers, an ancient fixture around the courts, noted for his flowery oratory, was there, and Grace Szieman, an official in the Women's Bar Association—the whole group was far more "respectable" than Sam had dreamed. They filed into the outer chamber and asked to see Gessner.

He was "out." He was "busy." He couldn't see them. They waited. Surprise, outrage grew in that room. Why, they were lawyers, like Gessner himself! Members of the profession!

The clerk, hot, embarrassed, again phoned into the private office. "He says to leave your resolutions, he'll give them every consideration."

Summers arose, formidable in his three-inch starched collar. He began an oration: "I have been a member of this profession—"

Runt cried: "He can't give us the run-around!"

The lawyers pressed toward the desk.

Then the red squad arrived. The dicks began on the lawyers who had remained in the corridor. "What's going on here! Outside! Clear the halls!"

They stomped into the waiting room and began herding the lawyers toward the door. "Outside! You can't mob this office! Outside!"

Maserow, transferred from Rosen's squad, recognized Sam. "Come on, you Bolsheviks! Beat it!"

The lawyers were so ashamed for their city, so utterly, helplessly astonished, that they moved as though guilty at the order of the squad.

Chased out by cops! Not even allowed to present their petition!

"Go on before we run you all in—"

"But these are lawyers, members of the bar, here to—" Grace Szieman began.

"Yah? We don't care who you are! You can't come in here like a mob—"

They let themselves be chased into the elevators. Only when they were on the street did they seem to recover consciousness.

Sam had remained, in spite of the bulldozing of the squad.

"All right, let them have a committee," the clerk said, when only a half-dozen lawyers were left. Runt was there, too, Grace, and Summers, whose collar dripped sweat.

The dicks stayed in the room, keeping an eye on them.

Runt looked toward the elevators. "Well, anyway, now they know what's what," he said to Sam. "Now we know where we stand."

Things for the Home

Aline would have had the party at her house, only, it being but a few months since the death of her father, there might be some criticism. And having the Hadassah benefit party at Thelma's house would be a good opportunity to bring her back into the fold.

"Only we're not Juniors any more, we're in the regular Hadassah," Aline pointed out. Not like those society girls who kept on being members of the Junior League even after they were married and had kids.

Thelma and Manny had practically come to life all over again when the boys formed their own clinic. Now, they could afford to get a girl to stay with the kid, and so they could emerge into the world again, go to shows and affairs with the rest of the bunch. "You know, a little more money makes all the difference."

Another thing, Thelma had just fixed over her house and was aching to show it off. She had got a complete job of redecoration from her landlord, and in modern style, you know, painting the woodwork white, and using wallpaper with a cubistic design. She had bought a set of neo-classic furniture; the chairs had thick white fringe, and were in the Grecian fluted pillar motif, combining the classic with the modernistic. And a single-tone tan rug, which she kept covered with newspapers on ordinary days, as it spotted easily.

Aline had gone with Thelma on all the shopping expeditions. It was Aline who had discovered the interior decorator. His name was Lucius Von Dahl and his interior decorating services were free if you bought the furniture through him. Of course Rose Heller might be offended, but her father's store was just a tiny dump now, full of old-fashioned junk.

Mr. Von Dahl came and spent an entire day arranging the furniture and the lamps and the modernistic pictures. Thelma marked all the placements of furniture so that on cleaning days she could replace them exactly right, for the ensemble.

When they were planning the party to raise money to send young German Jews to Palestine, Aline had an inspiration: "Kid, let's make it a Hard Times party."

That appealed to Thelma, as she liked to be original. "Instead of bothering serving refreshments," Aline elaborated, "we could have a breadline. Wouldn't that be cute!"

Aline had another inspiration. Thelma wouldn't have to get any extra dishes. "We can just serve them on paper plates, and in coffee mugs—you know, like at Thompson's."

So Thelma and Aline hopped into the car and priced mugs at Wiebolt's and then Goldblatt's, and even on Maxwell Street, where they saved thirty cents on the deal. They also bought a booby-prize, the cutest ashtray, in the form of a dog whose hind leg you raised to make him peepee and douse your cigarette.

"It's kind of risqué," Aline worried for a moment, "but our bunch is very broad-minded."

She was so elated with her trophies that she drove right through the Loop making left turns and disregarding the angry whistling of the cops. This was going to be a real cute party.

> He floats through the air with the greatest of ease,
>
> The daring young man on the flying trapeze—

The first sight that greeted the arrivals was a huddled figure in a coat with turned-up collar, seated on the stairs of the two-story red brick building. He had a crate of apples beside him.

"Happo! Best happle! Five cents, one nickel, help the starving Armenians, I mean Hamericans, please buy a happle, mister!" he chanted, as a gang unloaded from a Buick.

"It's Manny!"

"Isn't he a card!"

"Isn't that a cute idea for a Hard Times party? Puts you right in the spirit of the thing," Mrs. Weintraub commented.

"How much are they?" Rudy asked.

"Five cents apiece four for a quarter!" Manny replied glibly.

"Hey, wadya mean four for a quarter!"

"Hokay, tree for a quarter," he conceded, slaying them.

"Peel me a grape!" Mrs. Weintraub cried.

Several bought; the apples had cost Manny four cents apiece but he turned the whole nickel over to Hadassah. So Hadassah made a dollar thirty on apples alone.

Little Joe Springer had appointed himself doorman. "Annie doesn't live here anymore!" he greeted all arrivals. The flat was soon crowded.

The women complimented Thelma on the gorgeous modernistic furnishings. Ora Abramson asked where she had bought the swell reproduction of Bakst.

"I really don't know," Thelma said, "my interior decorator got it for me."

Sol Meisel, of all people, had come tagging along with the Abramsons. Ora said he hung around their house all the time, coming and sitting like a lump. All he talked about was business. They were having some trial downtown, trying to clean up the cleaning racket, and it was dragging along for months. Sol was always coming over to ask Mort's advice. Just give him a half a chance and he would go into that long story about the time a gang tried to hold up one of his trucks on Crawford Avenue, and he fought them bare-handed against their machine guns.

Ora was practically naked, wearing the grass skirt and bandeau which she had got on their honeymoon in Cuba. Mort came in a tux, joking that times were so hard this was the only suit he had left. Most of the men were in overalls that looked very new, though Aline had cut the bottoms of Rudy's overalls into fringes, so they would look ragged. Many of the girls also wore overalls, and Helen Springer looked especially cute because of the very snug fit around her hips. All the men took advantage, patting her rump as they passed.

Aline had come as Mae West, and was dismayed when Bertha Weintraub appeared as Mae West, and with a gorgeous wig à la Belle of the Nineties.

Bertha was in a flirtatious mood, hip-rolling up to the husbands of all the other doctors' wives, lifting her eyebrows and murmuring: "You must come up and see muh some time." Finally she tried it on Mort, who responded with "How about right now!" and dragged her into the bedroom.

"The party's getting hot!" Aline remarked, flushed with pride, as there was nothing like a little necking by oddly assorted husbands and wives to liven up a party, especially when you knew it would lead to nothing serious.

Manny had come in from his apple-selling job, and was ensconced behind the punch bowl. Mort and Bertha had not yet emerged, so Aline drew Manny aside and hinted: "Give Mort something to do." Manny was right up to the situation. Presently Mort appeared, blindfolded, carrying a tin cup. He wore a scrawled sign: "I am blind." He held a clothes line, which was tied to Manny Kassell, on all fours, impersonating the blind man's dog. Manny was a scream, running and nipping at the ankles of the girls. The act was very successful; in the tin cup, Mort collected over a dollar, and several buttons, for the benefit of German Jews going to Palestine.

> Oh, you nasty man,
> Taking your love on the easy plan . . .

Thelma kept worrying if it was time to start refreshments. She had taken a marvelous salad recipe from the page headed "Good Food, Fine Clothes, Things for the Home, and Your Children." That was her favorite page. It also contained society news. This salad had been served at a Junior League bridge, and she had slaved for two days preparing the concoction, which consisted of lettuce cups, with tomato aspic, Norwegian sardines, mixed with chopped nuts, pickles, and pineapple, and topped with whipped cream. She also had corned beef sandwiches.

"Wait, wait," Aline counseled, holding her back. "After the entertainment."

Then who should arrive but Evelyn and Phil Ware. Poor Evelyn had had a cyst and three operations since having those twins, and she was hardly out of the hospital for a month at a time. Her complexion was sallow, her eyes had lost their snap. She was trying to fix things with makeup, and her face was caked and plastered. She had false eyebrows and pasted-on eyelashes. Aline said to Rose Heller: "See, she's wearing one of those fur-lined brassieres, that's what you ought to get, it gives you more bust. It's the thing nowadays."

"You know they had to close up a lot of their shops," Thelma said. "Now all they sell is six-dollar dresses."

> I'll be glad when you're dead, you rascal, you,
> When you're dead in your grave, no more women will you crave,
> I'll be glad when you're dead, you rascal, you!

Phil Ware was the center of a group discussing the Moscowitz case. He still had his Harvard accent. Well, when it came to understanding the fundamental philosophy of law, Phil said, naturally Margolis was handicapped by his lack of education. But when it came to clever technicalities! Why, take the case of that real estate broker, Klein, who had sued Moscowitz for selling a lot of receiverships which they were supposed to have held in common. "Do you know what Lou Margolis did? In order to sue in equity a man must come into court, as we say, with clean hands. Lou Margolis looked up some old property of Klein's and discovered it was three years in arrears in taxes. So as Klein couldn't come into court with clean hands, Lou had his suit against Moscowitz thrown out!"

There was a chuckling appreciation of this clever dodge.

"Do you think Rube Moscowitz will have to go to jail?" Thelma asked.

"Oh, they'll drag the case along in the courts for years," Aline said.

"You know where they got Al Capone working in the jail? In the cleaning plant! That's one business he knows! Haw haw!" Sol offered.

"I bet Insull never goes to jail though," Mort said.

"It's going to be mighty tough to prove anything on Insull," Phil said. "Everything he did was legal."

"I heard that he lost all his own money too. You can't blame him for the crash," Aline commiserated.

"Oh, yah, he's just a poor sweet old man!" Rose scoffed. "It's a wonder how people swallow all that bunk."

"Well, I heard he even had to have his son pay his hotel bills," Aline insisted. "And he takes the bus down to court."

> . . . for the best things in life
> Are free!

"Attention! attention!" Manny had donned a green eyeshade and was now running the Wheel of Chance. Tickets, five cents.

Mort and Phil Ware discussed the NRA. "It can't last," Mort said. "Ford certainly told them where to get off, and what did they do to him? Nothing!"

"I notice you had some labor trouble at your place," Phil Ware commented.

Mort darkened, but shrugged. "I had three hundred new girls broken in inside of a month. I still got a lot of the old ones coming back begging for their jobs."

"Well, you had to raise their wages some, didn't you?"

Mort conceded: "We raised them a little. But those guys with shops downtown still got the union around their necks. Now they're trying to sick section 7A on me, but before they can do anything the whole NRA will bust up. It's ridiculous. You can't control business like that."

"The dress industry is the same way!" Phil Ware said; he was now taking more of an interest in his father-in-law's business. They had quite a heart-to-heart shop talk. Sol Meisel hung on, listening.

"I notice our friends the Wilners didn't come," Aline remarked pointedly to Ora.

"By the way, what's your brother doing?" Ora asked.

"Joe? He's on one of those government projects, doing sculpture."

"You mean, a relief project?" Ora insinuated.

"Oh, no!" Aline flushed; she could have killed Ora, and Joe too. "Only the best artists can get on this project, it's a real honor."

"Number forty-two! The winnuh! Come up and claim your grand prize! A beautiful addition to any household—a useful and ornamental object!" Manny sang out. Amidst much acclaim Phil Ware received the little dog ashtray. There were guffaws as he demonstrated the action of the hind leg. But then, alas, he turned the tray over, and discovered a mark, "Made in Germany."

"Well, well, what's this?" he joked.

Thelma went red. Aline snatched the tray. "The idea! I'll take it back the first thing in the morning, and give them a piece of my mind!"

Ora said Macy's in New York had had so many things returned that they now bought from Czechoslovakia instead of Germany.

"Oh, they feel it, they feel it," was the general opinion, as though they could almost see Hitler writhing under the boycott.

Manny saved the situation again by calling: "Breadline forms to the right!"

Ora caught Mort eating a corned beef sandwich. "Your ulcers," she warned.

"The hell with them! They're my ulcers, not yours!" The meat was thick in the sandwich, as good as the kind you used to get at Kantor's in the old days!

Aline started coaxing Thelma to play something, something classical, and Thelma yielded, though explaining that she hadn't touched the piano for weeks. She played Beethoven's *Moonlight Sonata*, and they all balanced their coffee mugs and tried not to make crunching noises as they surreptitiously took bites of their corned beef sandwiches.

Dr. Weintraub and Joe Springer emerged from the kitchen twanging a whiskbroom, banging a dustpan, imitating cowboys singing:

"Oh, I'm heading for the last roundup
To the faraway Boss in the sky—"

Bertha Weintraub, alias Mae West, joined them, lisping, making wicked eyes. Then she sang:

"I'm gonna kill you just for fun,
The bugs can have you when I'm done,
I'll be glad when you're dead, you rascal, you."

Pennies were pitched, and there were calls of "Come up and see me some time!"

Dr. Weintraub convulsed them, reciting: "Four Prominent Bastards Are We." The party got gay. Rose broke loose and did her imitation fan dance, using a feather duster for a fan. The way she imitated the Sally Rand poses, the way she put her hand to her face in consternation when she dropped her feather duster, it was a scream! She was better than Fanny Brice!

"All the same, it was Sally Rand that put over the Fair," Mort commented, suppressing a belch.

It was a very successful party. Manny counted forty-three dollars and fifteen cents' profit on the gambling, omitting the fifteen dollars' expenses, which he contributed. When people started to go home, Thelma noticed a horrible stain: somebody had spilled coffee on her beautiful new rug, and her heart was broken.

But it was such a fine crowd, young couples, the best people in the world. It was worth it.

The Best Things in Life Are Free

> Work and pray,
> Live on hay—

The party at Al Littinger's house was to raise funds for the appeal of the six who had been convicted in the Thirteenth Street case. They had been held that time Harry Perlin got free.

A scrawled sign in the dining room said: *Gin, tea, milk, whisky, pop, all drinks ten cents.* There were bologna and cheese sandwiches for a dime.

The crowd was cheering on a prize contest, around a vase that stood on the floor. The one that pitched the most nickels into the vase would get a copy of Strachey's *Coming Struggle for Power.*

Ella Bodansky was down on her knees. This was her last nickel. She made elaborate preparations for her final pitch.

"You might as well save that nickel, I was the champion mib shooter on the J.P.I.," Al Littinger kidded.

Ella got a giggling fit. Her nickel hit the vase and rolled off. She wept in mock despair. Al prepared to pitch, singing: "I'm Popeye the Sailorman! I eats my spinach, and with my strong right arm, I pitches my nickels right into the can!" Ella kicked his elbow. "Foul!" he yelled, as the nickel chinked into the vase.

"Sam, Sammy, got any nickels?" Ella begged. "I'll beat those bums yet!"

"Nope, you're a bad risk," Sam refused.

Harry fingered the few coins in his pocket. Ruth had slipped him an extra dollar as they left the house, figuring that was the least they could spend at the party. He couldn't stand it much longer, living off her. She tried to make it easy for him, sometimes putting money in his pocket, or leaving it about in the most unobtrusive way. He had stood it all winter but if he didn't get anything with the Fair reopening he would just go away, disappear or something. The Fair reopening next month was his only hope.

"Well, Harry, what have you been doing all these years?" Rose Heller asked. She had come up with a schoolteacher friend of Ruth's.

"Oh, I had a business of my own for several years. But the depression got me," he said, wondering why he couldn't forget about being a business man, why couldn't he simply tell her the last job he had was counting visitors to a Fair exhibit? Did she know, through her friend, that his wife was supporting him? "I have another invention that I'm working on, a new kind of emergency brake for automobiles, but this time I'm going to try to sell it to a big company, they get everything anyway. Well, and what have you been doing with yourself?"

"Oh, I'm just an old maid schoolteacher," she said gayly.

"I wouldn't say that!"

"Are you a member of the I.L.D.?" Rose asked.

"Well, no . . . I was in this case, though," he added with a feeling of pride.

She hadn't known, and he told her all about the riot. "The cops just jumped them! It was the rawest thing! I never thought about such things until this happened to me. Why, on the South Side in an eviction riot the cops shot three people, in cold blood."

"You don't have to tell me!" Rose said. "We practically had to tear down the Board of Education to get our pay, and we still haven't got it all!"

"I was a witness in the trial," Harry said. "The judge was absolutely unfair."

Sam had joined them, and was explaining about the case to Rose. "It's one of the worst cases we had, because a captain was hurt, and the police are out to get revenge. But they smeared it on too thick this time. They just about handed us a case that any appellate court will have to reverse."

"Do you see any of the old bunch?" Harry asked Rose.

She still saw quite a lot of Aline, Rose admitted. "Oh, they're just comfortable bourgeois. They have three kids now, you know."

"My mother was up to that clinic Rudy is connected with," Harry said. "She had some throat trouble, and they cured it."

"Say, I understand they had some trouble about that clinic?" Sam asked Rose.

Rose explained about the fight with Dr. Orr. Sam got quite excited. It was a perfect Marxian case, he said. "This guy Orr controlled the plant and the machinery, so he tried to exploit the doctors." Only, in this case, the workers were able to go off and set up their own plant. A perfect example! "Maybe now those doctors understand a thing or two!"

"Well, the net result is that it didn't do either of them too much good," Rose pointed out. "All that publicity gave the whole idea of the clinics a black eye and people are leery about going to them."

"Why don't they try to interest labor groups?" Sam wondered.

"That's just what Rudy was talking about," Rose said. "He wants to get contacts with unions. Why don't you get in touch with him?"

Shirley Littinger put on a phonograph record of "Four Prominent Bastards Are We," by Ogden Nash, and was it a hit!

Sam was auctioneer and began by auctioning off the Ogden Nash record. ". . . this private edition of a great American classic," he sang out, "sung by those famous revolutionary artists, Rudy Vallée, Bing Crosby, Eddie Cantor, and Libby Holman!"

Rose bid. A redheaded fellow bid against her.

"Don't go home without the four bastards!" Sam admonished. Rose won the record for a dollar and a half. In great style, Sam auctioned off a "pair of shoelaces worn by Tom Mooney," "seven links from a chain-gang chain," which turned out to be a Woolworth bracelet, a cake baked by Shirley, and a cop's night-stick, said to be a trophy of the Thirteenth Street riot.

Before Rose knew it, Ella had equipped her with a feather duster and a whiskbroom, and she was doing her celebrated imitation of Sally Rand. The redheaded fellow added to the act by jumping on a chair and peering down, in comic efforts to see behind the fans. Rose was giddy and laughing, dancing up to fellows and chucking them under the chin with the feather duster. Everybody was in stitches. She never remembered seeing Sammy Eisen laugh so merrily, he was always such a serious kid. His wife looked like a nice kid too. Pennies were falling all around. Finally she dropped the feather duster and the redheaded fellow gravely offered her a single artificial flower in its place. She struck a September Morn pose with the flower and the whiskbroom and everybody screamed.

They were a swell bunch of kids.

And on the last day of the Fair, they wheeled Rube Moscowitz out of the operating room, his wide-staved chest heaving like the hulk of a foundered, capsized freighter. He was a mound, a hill of rotten guts. His great arms still looked powerful to crush, and full of the juice of life; the heavy flesh of his cheeks hung down around his jowls, leaving clear the bludgeon outline of his skull.

His head was turned, looking out the window of that room high in the tower of the elegant Israel Hospital. Wife, daughter, and son-in-law followed his glance.

Over the acres of I.C. tracks, there was a wonderful view of the Fair. The entire shore and island was a fantastic illumination; threads of neon zigzagging through the phosphorous haze that illuminated the skywall of the night, pierced by shafts and towers, by the great white Havoline thermometer, so tall you could read the temperature a mile away, by arching searchlights. The noises of the Fair reached the hospital like brooming waves.

Rube Moscowitz had no call to die! He could live, all right, or he could turn himself off as those lights were snapped out, die in a last burst of fireworks, with his big politician's hearty laugh blowing over Chicago: sue me now! Ho, ho, Uncle Sam! So you'll stand me in court, a cheat, a grafter, a liar, a tax-dodger! A cell in Alcatraz! Thanks, you can have it! I got a mausoleum in the finest, most exclusive Jewish cemetery in Chicago, I'm all set in Rosevale Rest, I got my lot in a deal years ago, it don't even cost me a cent!

Let them wait with their trial! He had the final ace!

Of thee I sing, baby,
Summer, autumn, winter, spring, baby!—

Harry couldn't resist wiping the broad hood of the gunmetal airflow De Soto, running a cloth over the gentle swell of the fenders. "That's a car!" That was what he would have been like, as an automobile manufacturer! Daring! The first to come out with something new! The public always found out what was good! He would do even more! Like that experimental model in the Ford exhibit. He would place the motor in the rear, that's where the motor belonged. Millions of cars were being made, year after year, made the wrong way, even while engineers knew the right away, just because no one had the nerve to take the daring step.

Boy, to own one of these! To lift the hood and pry into that motor.

He'd get a car again. Some kind of a car. Things wouldn't be so bad from now on.

Curly, the gas attendant, came over. "Well, whatcha doing after tonight, Perlin?"

"I've got a job promised in a South Side garage, there's a fellow thinking of quitting," Harry said. "I've been subbing for him on his night off, it was the same as my night off here."

"Well, that's something, anyway," Curly said.

"Jesus, howdja like to own one of these?" Harry couldn't tear himself away from that De Soto.

"Got anything on for tonight?" Everybody was suddenly friendly, loath to part on the last day of the job.

"Yah, I'm meeting the wife over on the grounds as soon as I'm through."

"She got a friend? I got a bottle," Curly offered, cocking his brow, whistling.

Oh, he floats through the air—

Picking up the *Trib* on the car seat Sam glimpsed the headline, MOSCOWITZ ILL, UNDERGOES OPERATION. He skipped the story, hunting for news of the Spanish revolt. Nothing but yards of crap about Hauptmann and the Lindy ransom money. How could you expect the *Trib* to give the public any real news? Bored, he skimmed the comic strips. Orphan Annie's uncle Warbucks was battling "labor agitators," pictured as thugs who were trying to ruin the factory where that great new invention, a cheap building material that would end the depression, was being produced. Even the comic strips! All the pukey Ella Cinders and Apple Marys and Tailspin Tommies that had invaded the papers, with their war machines, kidnapings, brutalities. What chance did a kid have nowadays?

But there was still Skeezix. Why, he was big, and the baby, Corky, was big—Skeezix was teaching Corky how to read! And Mrs. Walt was fat.

. . . A complete other world he had left behind him. Some time he might go out and see the kid, it would be safe now. But what for? He'd be a stranger.

Well, such individual tragedies were the waste of humanity's slow education.

The kid had looked something like him.

The car had filled, jammed. He got up and gave his seat to an old woman. Hanging onto a strap, lurching, Sam noticed a photo in the paper. Moscow subway opens. He got a kick out of that. He'd have to tell Ella.

The wheels ran a song in his head:

"Git along, little dogie, git along, git along—"

Aline emerged from the grocery, with Naomi and Jo-Jo tagging after her. The air was nippy. "Button your coat, Naomi," she ordered. Then what did Cuteness do? She turned first and gravely buttoned up her little brother's coat! It was a scream! She was so bossy! yet so motherly!

"Ma, did you get my weetsies?" she demanded. She was saving the covers, for a prize doll of Popeye the Sailorman.

"And when she orders me to buy Wheatsies, I have to buy Wheatsies, there's no but about it!" Aline loved to tell her chums.

Oh, now was the most enjoyable age of children. At this age they were cherubs! It was worth all the smelly diapers and getting up to feed them every two hours, they were so delicious and so cute, now.

She bought a fat Saturday paper; there would be a whole page of Apple Mary to read to Naomi, and bundling them into the car she snapped on the radio.

"I saw stars,
I heard the birdies sing,
Tweet-tweet—"

"They want me to stick around tonight," Mitch phoned. "The whole staff is dancing around Rube Moscowitz and they're short of men."

"Of course, if you have to, dear," Sylvia said. "How is Rube, anyway?"

"He's acting funny," Mitch said. "The operation was a success and he ought to pick up, but he just doesn't want to, I guess. They've given him two transfusions."

"Well, I don't blame him. It would be the best thing for him if he kicked off. I bet he's got plenty of insurance, too."

Putting down the French phone slowly, Sylvia felt loneliness settling upon her. She could stand it on other nights but on Saturday nights there was still a kind of habitual stirring in the blood, to do something, go somewhere.

She closed the book she had been reading, *Three Cities*, about a Jew in the Russian revolution. Because she knew she would have to read the time away, the idea of reading nauseated her.

> "When a lovely
> Flame dies,
> Smoke gets in your eyes."

She shut off the radio. Then Sylvia lifted up her baby, and rested her lips against the fuzzy sweet head. She walked around, with her lips against the sweetness.

Time would close in on her, years would close in on her, but she would be safe. No matter what happened in the world, revolutions or no revolutions, they would be safe. In any state of society, men like Mitch would be needed, would be the really good men.

Indiana and Joe were helping each other load their sculpture onto a handtruck. Most of the fellows were taking their stuff off the grounds as nothing would be safe the last night. Indiana had a comical story about Sally Rand, the new art patron. "On the level! Sally is going in for Art in a big way." There was an academic wop whose classical allegorical figures were the joke of the exposition. But Sally had become convinced he was a neglected Michelangelo and was shipping a carload of his stuff to her ranch in California. Indiana was convulsed at the picture of those tombstone Apollos strewn around a fan dancer's ranch. "You better go after her, Joe," he advised. "There's a patron for you!"

Joe was straining a gut lifting his *Flying Tackle* onto the truck. Maybe because he was so tired, the story didn't seem funny. The fan dancer was just the last figure in the idiotic gallery of hoped-for patrons with which an artist deluded himself. From the first day in the Midway studio, grimacing smiles and being nice to visitors because any one of them might turn out to be a patron in search of a worthy subject for largesse. Be nice to the rabbi, Joe, he has a fund for encouragement of Jewish arts; Joe, I'm having you meet Mrs. Schmaltz, if she takes the notion she can really *make* you; Mr. Gloober, Joe, of course he's just a Babbitt, but he has a big shoe factory and I think he's reached the stage where he wants to patronize the arts . . .

"What's so funny about Sally Rand!" Joe snapped, bitterly. "If you ask me, we're the suckers."

Before they knew it they were in a long argument about patrons. "All right, how else are we going to get along?" Indiana challenged.

"Am I supposed to have all the answers? All I know is, I'm on the project."

"Yah, and what are you going to make on the project, drinking fountains for schoolkids, with mickeymouses?"

Joe wasn't prepared to answer. But he had an idea it could be different. What the hell, if the government once and for all admitted that sculpture was a part of the whole scheme, that it had a place in the American layout, and that the mechanics was so arranged now that art must either become a part of the life of the nation, or nothing at all, why, then the government would have to admit there was only one body of people competent to say what art was worth creating. And that body was the artists themselves. No more patrons, no more dealers, no more screwy commercial hookups. The artists would have to find some way of forming their body, some way of working together, taking themselves seriously as a unit. Maybe the Roosevelt boys figured they were only handing out a little relief when they thought up the art projects, but Joe had a hunch that they were more than ready for the artists to make them work out this problem on a permanent and creative basis.

"That's a pretty good little animal," Indiana grudgingly praised his *Flying Tackle*, as if he had never seen it before. "Where did you get the idea?"

Sam was supposed to meet the others in front of the Time-Fortune Building, and then all would go somewhere for dinner, maybe take in the Shakespeare players. During the entire two years, he hadn't been to the Fair, so he'd better take it all in tonight before it was history. The crowd poured along the main drag in ceaseless proliferation; a military band brayed "Tipperary" through the radio posts; he was shoved, jostled, shoved, jostled; already he was shivery with the taut elated nervousness he got in crowds; already he sensed a special impatience, a peevishness, in this pour and pour of people. The crowd was outwardly good-natured, boisterous, on the last leg of a two-year jag, sending off the Fair that saved Chicago, pulled all the hotels out of the red, ended the depression, and yet the crowd was surly, angry. Sam imagined a vengeful note in the jeering comebacks the crowd flung at the barkers, in the cries of fellows after broads; he felt something ominous in the moving, drifting, ceaseless moving of the crowd-stream, people dumbly in search, in need of something they knew they weren't going to find here.

He was standing watching the shifting of enlarged news-photographs on the *March of Time* screen. There was a photograph of rioting in Spain, then the startling actual photograph of King Alexander of Yugoslavia as he fell back, in his car, assassinated. A female voice behind Sam remarked: "Mygod, I'd hate to live in a country where they have things like that, rioting and murders all the time."

"Me too," Estelle placidly agreed with her girl friend. "Oh, kid, wait, I want to see the picture of the Lindy kidnaper. Honest, electrocution is too good for him."

"You know where let's make the fellows take us tonight? The Black Forest. I want to see the ice skating."

"Kid! We better get a move on!" Estelle looked at her watch. "I go on in three minutes."

"I'm gonna kill you just for fun,
The bugs can have you when I'm done—"

". . . but you should have heard her! The utter dumbness of it! Some gum-chewing stenographer probably, but how can people be so blind!" Sam cried, exasperated.

How could anybody shut out the thunder! The whole country was alive, awake, whistling with violence, the Frisco general strike, the textile riots, the farm mortgage revolt, the Minneapolis truck strike, the brewing auto strike, the munitions investigation revealing how banks had made the last war, and were making a war again!

". . . wagon wheels, wagon wheels—"

"As far as the mob is concerned, all that happened last year was the birth of the Dionne quintuplets," Joe Freedman remarked. "A human being has proven herself equal to a she-dog." Sam failed to laugh. Cynicism seemed so fruitless, a lost attitude.

"You can't expect the mass of people to realize what's going on," Joe said. "Think over all the people you know. What are they interested in?" His own mind ranged, not over the people he knew immediately, but of the old bunch he had known, grown up with. "Bridge, and Burns and Allen."

"I know, I know," Sam said, "yet a fellow can't help feeling the least people can do is realize what's going on, and think of themselves in relation to that—to that process."

They were on the balcony of the electrical building, and could look across the decorative lagoon with its rainbow fountains, across to the main drag of the Fair, and beyond that, glimpse the drab background of Chicago.

Joe was justifying himself now, assuring himself that he had always instinctively understood that process, the long historical process Trotsky raved about in his autobiography, that he had always instinctively allied himself to the truth. For instance, way back at Illinois there had been that incident when he had bucked the military training. Sam had done the same thing. Thinking back, now, it seemed he and Sam should have been more strongly allied, then, but perhaps they hadn't understood the full import of what they were doing. Now, on all the country's campuses kids were making a fuss, taking peace vows. Joe felt himself a forerunner.

You couldn't expect everyone to drop everything and work for a Utopia. In any revolution, the vast bulk of the populace, it seemed to Joe, sat behind shuttered windows waiting for the scrap to be over. The best you could expect would be for those who sat behind the windows to be sympathetic, even ready to take a pot shot at the existing order, to welcome a society that would divide things more equally.

It seemed to him that, broadly, humanity could be divided into two types: the unworthy and the worthy. The unworthy were the mere lumps of selfish human flesh. The worthy were those who were at least aware of the streams of human life. And he felt that he, himself, was one of those who knew, and was ready. Every man didn't have to agitate, to be with the revolution. In every act of life, there were two ways of going, and if a man consistently, in his own life, in those decisions which confronted him, acted in harmony with the long historical wave toward revolution, why, he could claim integrity in his life. It seemed to Joe that Roosevelt was such a man and that, quietly, the American revolution was going forward.

In the end, Joe remains middle-class, Sam was thinking. He can see and sometimes understand what is going on, but even way back in school in that military training business Joe confused the issue, there was some crap about what kind of theme he could write, instead of a straight question of whether or not we should be forced to drill. He crawled back then, when the dean worked on him. Whimsically, Sam remembered the dean's trick way of telling a fellow he was no gentleman—that invitation to dinner offer, if you were the kind of a boy that behaved. He was almost on the point of asking Joe whether he had ever taken the dean up on that dinner. But he forbore. After all, Joe wasn't a bad guy, he was more sensitive than most of that gang. "Think of the people you know," and you found yourself thinking not of the people you knew today but of the people you grew up with. Because you really knew their class background, Sam decided. Or was it because they were the people you really lived with all your life? Whether near or away from them, you measured yourself by their standards, for those were the ideas you had grown into, when you first became aware of the social world. They were the unchangeable flesh of your mind. And fellows like Joe could be useful; they were the artists; they should reveal. Both men looked up simultaneously. From where they stood, the buildings on the other side were like a single, flung-out construction, splash-colored.

"It's like a bright scarf," Joe remarked, appreciatively.

"Yah. Around the neck of a consumptive," Sam added.

There below stretched the rotting lungs and the rotten guts of Chicago. Close against the bludgeon stone-head, the Loop, lay the decay of the body. North, south, and west, spread the semicircular band of slums: frame houses, deserted blocks, buildings stripped of doors, of windows, of plumbing. It was as though the city were continually working away from the inner corruption of itself, people moving away further north, south, west, leaving a growing, festering wasteland between the new districts and the Loop.

Their parents had moved from Halsted Street to Paulina, to Kedzie, to Crawford, and they had moved from Douglas and Garfield Parks to Columbus Park, and next they would go out to the suburbs; and the Irish had moved southward, leaving their old hovels to the Negroes, and the Germans were scattering northward, and the middle of Chicago decayed. Who ever went through those streets, Wentworth Avenue, Thirteenth Street, Wells Street, following them south, west, north, where buildings leaned and sagged, front steps torn away, tin nailed over holes? And people lived, there were still people to live in all these! Here were still swarms, still coming swarms for Chicago.

"That will all be changed," Joe said. "Did you see those slum rehabilitation plans? I think Roosevelt is really sincere. Why, it's a tremendous job, they've got whole square miles to be torn down and rebuilt, with modern, cheap housing. I know a couple of architects already working on the project."

Sam smiled patiently. "Do you think the real estate men will ever let them do it?" And he could see Lil, holding out for top prices on that old slum property on Thirteenth Street, where he had once had to be the rent-collector.

> "She certainly can
> Can-can—"

Alvin couldn't get away from the old man's patiently humble face. His nerves were raw, unpeeled. Eunice's transparent efforts to calm him, distract his attention, made him scream: "What am I, a baby? You don't have to drag me into their lousy Hall of Science. I haven't seen it and I don't want to see it!" But he dragged along rather than face the effort of thinking of something else to do. They were seeing movies of microscopic water organisms, and against the mechanical voice of the lecturer he heard his father's lucid, serious tones. "Sometimes, like today, I am all right, Alvin. You can see it, don't you? You know what I can even do? I can remember the whole price-list on the merchandise! Ask me, you'll see." And his pleading look. Walking his son as far as the heavy inner door, the one that was locked. "Good-by, Alvin," then turning back, like a host who has seen his guest to the door.

"You can never know! You can never be sure again. Every word he says will seem cuckoo," Alvin muttered.

"Oh, I think he is much better. Obviously better," Eunice said calmly.

In his mind, Alvin was applying the same test to the sane world. If you once suspected it of insanity, everything that was said and done . . . He laughed mirthlessly. Eunice called his attention to a model of the solar system; the planets were corks stuck on the end of wires, and all were dizzily spinning and circling on their various axes in their various orbits and the whole damn spheroid containing all the suns moons earths planets racing in their intersecting paths was turning on itself going somewhere too.

> "There go I,
> Heading for the last roundup,
> Git along, little dogie . . ."

The advertising guy and his wife were swell people. Sophisticated, and nothing got past them. Mort leaned over and with his hand on the guy's wife's knee, said: "Lemme tell you the latest Roosevelt story. I just heard this in Washington. There was a couple had a baby—no, just one baby, they have them one at a time in Washington," he smirked, about papa Dionne.

"So they went to have this baby christened. They argued all night and finally they decided to name him William. They got to the church and the father was holding the kid and the kid was smiling and everything looked like it was going swell. 'What name?' the priest asks, and the father takes a last look at the kid and says: 'Franklin Delano.' When they got out of the place, the mother jumps on him. 'After we decided on William, what's the idea of naming our baby after the President?' 'Well, I'll tell you,' he says, 'I had the name William right on my tongue, but when the time came to speak, I looked down on that kid and he had that big gooey smile on his face and all the time he was peeing all over me.'" Mort stopped, pointedly. The advertising guy guffawed. His cute wife gazed at Mort as though he were revealing new qualities.

The advertising guy agreed the old blue eagle was practically picked clean. Ford had shown Roosevelt where to get off at. And once Roosevelt learned to let business alone, a big revival was coming. A real boom. "We feel it already. Advertising is picking up," he revealed. "Not piker stuff. Big programs."

Mort squeezed the fellow's wife's knee and leaned breathily over the table. "Whadya think of this for a slogan for women's hats?" Mort asked. And sprang it: "The Crowning Glory."

"Swell!" the fellow cried. "That's a knockout! That's as good as Sherwin's Paint—Covers the World. They figure that slogan is worth a million dollars to them!"

"I heard he didn't even need the operation," Harry Perlin declared. "What I think is, he's just committing suicide."

The orchestra leader stepped to the microphone and crooned:

> "I could write a sonnet
> About your Easter bonnet—"

The girls were ordering carefully so their dinners wouldn't come to more than seventy-five cents apiece though about all you could get for that price was a sandwich.

"I haven't got anything against Rube Moscowitz," said Sam Eisen. "As far as I'm concerned he was even a good-hearted guy." Think of that titanic energy, that big-chested laugh, that easy giving, as long as he had enough stowed away in his own pockets, think of the organizing power of a Rube Moscowitz, holding the entire West Side in his palm for twenty years, holding the barbers, the poolroom boys, the grocers, the widows who ran flats, the landlords, everybody together, delivering his ward Democratic even when the whole town went Republican, why, there was a powerful man! In a decent form of society, what tremendous good, what usefulness could be gained from a man with so much energy!

"Walking in the Easter parade!"

"He's involved in some sort of scandal, isn't he?" Dr. Feldner inquired casually, as they met in the hallway.

"Yes. I guess he figures there isn't much left to live for," Mitch said.

"We might as well order up an oxygen tent."

> "The moon is low—
> Stars up above . . .
> . . . love . . ."

The solid crowd moved as though on an automatic conveyor, a mass of gog-eyed stupid faces trying to swallow everything in the last minute.

". . . the paste that gives your teeth a treat," chanted the talking automaton of the Tooth Paste Man, across the aisle, and the loudspeaker from Meyer Levin's[6] marionette show squawk-lisped: "I caught Twillinger the bank robber because I can run faster with Buster Brown shoes. Ask mother to buy you Buster Brown—"

In the next section, Estelle was modeling furs. She and Peggy alternated on a turntable which carried them around in front of the public, and then behind a screen.

Estelle was tight. She hadn't had more than a couple of swigs but there was something in the air tonight, a last-night craziness that got you drunk. As she stroked the sumptuous silver fox with a movement that was supposed to make them take their eyes off her fanny and concentrate on the furs, she staggered. A guffaw and a cheer went up.

She had gone around three times now, and each time she was carried backstage there was Peggy, still lying in a clinch with the boy friend.

Hatch, the manager of the display, had completely let his hair down. Every time the turntable brought her back, he shoved a bottle at her. This time she took a long gulp; she barely had time to toss him the bottle and turn her face to the public.

Whistles and "Hey, share it, baby!" greeted her. Someone threw a rubber onto the stage. In back, Hatch was singing:

> "East Side, West Side,
> All around the town—"

Peggy and her boy friend were still lying there pasted together.

"Hey!" Estelle jumped down and kicked them. "Come up for air! I need some help!"

"Help! Help! Fire!" Hatch grabbed Estelle's fur and draped it around his own neck, striking a Mae West pose as the stage went around with him.

From then on it was a riot. Even the Negro porter went nuts, putting on a fur and doing a tap dance. A pie-eyed college boy jumped onto the stage from in front, and tried to get fresh.

> "You, you, you, you—
> Oooo! You nasty man!"

---

[6] Note the author's historical reference to his presence at the Fair.

It was nearly closing time, so Hatch pressed a button and stopped the turntable.

Peggy and her boy friend, they said they were engaged, rolled under the platform.

"Yeah, boy, go to it!" Hatch encouraged.

"What's the matter with yourself?" the fellow ribbed Hatch.

Estelle was in the tiny dressing room pulling off the ritzy gown in which she modeled.

"Say, I've been trying to make this redhead all summer and a lot of good I did myself," Hatch affirmed.

"Well, tonight's your last chance!" Estelle called. "You better not waste it! I like 'em tall, dark, and handsome!" She was in her two-way stretch and studied herself critically: was she getting middle-aged spread?

"Here I come!" Hatch pulled aside the curtain and grabbed her as though he meant business.

It was a crazy night and the last night and what the hell do you live for anyway! She didn't care if they rolled on the floor with the other couple, she didn't care if the nigger watched them go to it, she was all set and who would ever know!

"Taking your love on the easy plan—"

The next-door radio was going and as it was still really early, she couldn't ask them to shut it off. Though she might as well go to bed; nothing to do.

Next year maybe they could move out to Oak Park. Mitch was gradually centralizing all his practice downtown, and would be able to give up the West Side office. You could rent a whole house in the suburbs as cheaply as a flat in town. And with a child, you really needed a house. It would be their home.

> . . . Anything but love, baby,
> That's the only thing I've plenty of, baby—

Runt paid Lou Green's way in. "If I can find my sister I can collect a few bucks," Lou mumbled.

"Oh, that's okay, I'm flush," Runt declared. The pin-game business looked like a million. They couldn't get you on gambling either because he was prepared to prove in court it was a game of skill.

Lou had never yet seen Sally Rand. "Hey, can you see her hair down there?" he asked again.

"Aw, she ain't much," Runt said authoritatively. "She got fat legs. They got her in a blue light so you don't hardly see anything."

"I bet she shaves it off," Lou suggested.

"I want to see those Shakespeare players again before they close up," Runt said. "That's one thing you can't beat, the old Bard of Avon. Packs 'em in every time! 'To be, or not to be—' "

"Save that for the court," Lou flattered.

> Scheme a while,
> Dream a while—

"It's a natural!" Pisano insisted. "Look, Solly, this kid can ride. I wouldn't team you with a coaster. And he's got a Hebe schnozzle you can see from the bleachers. Those Germans took firsts in every race last year, and with you and Morey riding to beat the Nazis, will we pack them in! Remember how the Baer-Schmeling fight packed them in!"

"Say, Maxie Baer can take on any two heavies you can name and punch them out of the ring!" Sol asserted.

"Sure! You got a Jewish champ. Now you can go in and take the riding championship too. I tell you one thing, Solly, this Nazi business makes your people come out and root for their boys!"

"Yah, but I can't afford to ride with no punk," Sol insisted. "And not for that money."

"Listen." Pisano bit his cigar. "Maybe he's doing you a favor. You ain't been on a track for three years, and this kid is right in the pink. How do I know he won't have to carry you?" He added, concerned: "How's the old pump these days? Okay?"

Sol howled. "I can get on a bike today and ride circles around any man you got. There never was a thing wrong with my heart! Listen, Wop, I'm through with the lousy cleaning business. They cleaned me out. Carl Stockholm can have it. Jeez, I don't know how he does it. He got the whole contract for the Fair. Did you see the plant he's got on the grounds? High-class stuff!"

"Sure, Carl is a swell guy and a good business man. But you were never a business man, Solly. I don't know where they got the idea a Hebe has to be a good business man. I could take you any day! Remember the time you offered me fifty-fifty!"

They laughed. "Well, I'm going back on the track," Sol said. "That's where I belong! Christ, they're starting a price war again and I give up. Those guys are cleaning suits three for a buck! and we used to get a dollar seventy-five a suit!"

"What'd I tell yuh? I told yuh what happened to Mike Daly when he tried to run a chicken farm, I told you all the boys, sooner or later, they find it out—if there's one thing you can do, stick to it. Listen, Solly, you paid a lot for your experience but now you're a wiser man. Ride a couple of races on this contract and by the time the Garden race comes around you'll be back with the top boys, five hundred a day."

"Four months that trial took!" Sol ruefully remembered. "It was the longest trial they ever had in Chicago. It cost a hundred grand. And did they get anything on those racketeers? No!"

"Sure, forget it, forget it. Solly, we always wanted to have a Hebe team, and now we're set!"

Sol was beginning to feel free again. He could hear the whir of wheels behind him, the shrieking of girls' voices. "Boy! I ain't had a good piece of tail since my last ride," he said.

". . . Bringing you the tunes of yesteryear!" the announcer spoke.
     ". . . He beats me too, what can I do,
     He's my man . . ."
"Turn it softer, please, Rose," her father said, so she turned the radio down. Gee, those tunes made her feel old.

There was a model of an atom. Stemming out on wires from the dense nucleus were little corks representing electrons. And in life, all were in motion. Exactly like the planets in the solar systems, Alvin reflected; the electrons moved in their excited orbits, turned and whirled on themselves. There was only one simple pattern, repeated in various dimensions, in various thematic treatments, in the shapes and movements of life. And if the electrons in a body-atom moved on the same general scheme as planets in a sky-system, why couldn't you say that the human being, on his social plane, moved in the same kind of pattern? Why couldn't you view society as a physical pattern, and people as these excited electrons, circling around their nuclei? And each bunch of electrons, forming a social atom, joined in motion with similar atoms, forming a class of society; and the classes of society, whirled into a planetary unit, were humanity, and where was humanity going?

He was pleased with the conceit.

Couldn't you say, then, that all human society, taken as a whole, was turning, toward somewhere? Like the infinite electron jittering in its path, within an earth that was spinning and circling in a system that was as a whole spinning and circling within another infinite system.

Or take the men in the factory, each an electron excited by wages, and they communicated their excitation to a broader structure, a union, that carried them into its orbit that was carried again turning and circling as part of a whole economic globe, and that too was turning in some vast and ponderous movement that man could measure only by inches, along the ages.—A century of progress. But movement, direction was there.

"Feeling better?" Eunice asked. "I thought you'd calm down after you got some food inside you."

     I remember every little thing you used to do,
     Every road I walk along I've walked along with you—

And something large. A large figure, a colossus, but this time he would make it really big in conception, feeling! In Palestine he had made something that meant something to the country, to the people, to himself, and now he was ready for America. None of your squeezed, flattened men wrapped around cogwheels. And none of your bunchy-muscled proletarians swinging the pickax. Then, smoothly riding through space in the skyride

660

car, over the lake of color, the red and yellow lightnings, the field of white, the firework parabolas. Joe got an idea. A kind of Paul Bunyan. A body electric. A colossus not only of the backwoods but out of Whitman, too, and out of electricity and Boulder Dam, a striding man of power. Done in large masses, carved with an honest, native simplicity. They could have their Mestrovic Indians—he would yet leave a monument in Chicago!

On the U.S. art project. Maybe he could rent a little house, near enough to the city. A house and a barn, for himself the year around. Working in the barn. And maybe in summer he'd plant a little garden. And there'd be a woman in the house.

> I played the market down the street,
> That's a game I couldn't beat,
> I bought Amalgamated Heat—
>   I faw down and go boom!

The toy worked on a spring. It was a model of a naked plump lady, squatting on her hams. A key wound it up. And then a little rod sticking up her crotch stirred the hips of the soft rubber statuette round and round while the body rose and fell suggestively and even the breasts seemed to wobble. If you put your hand on the rubber, it was warm and soft, it was flesh.

On the base was printed, "Souvenir of a Century of Progress."

Ben Meisel released the spring and let the little lady wriggle her sitting buttocks against his palm.

> Git along, little dogie, git along, git along,
> Git along, little dogie, git along,
> Git along, little dogie . . .

"The party's getting rough!" Lou Green yowled, dodging a Streets of Paris sign that tumbled down on top of two guys yanking at it with their canes. Then, catching the idea, he leaped for a lamp post, climbed up, gave a Tarzan yell, and sent the modernistic glass fixture hurtling to the ground, what a smash!

He slid down. Runt, Estelle, and her gang were gone. The hell with them! A crowd-swirl sucked him along; a drunken bunch of guys was storming the Streets of Paris. Zowie, through a plate-glass window! He tumbled through with the mob. "Where are those girls!"

> Ah, sweet mystery of life . . .

"I always did have a yen for you," Runt confessed, bumping his body into Estelle as they danced, and cupping his hand under her breast.

He didn't have to think he could make her just because he helped out that lousy brother of hers! She yanked herself away, and with a silly titter, stumbled across the floor into the arms of a total stranger. The man dragged her to a table bedecked with a sign: LADIES' ROOM, torn off a wall somewhere.

You are an aaaaangellll . . .

Everybody was in the streets of the Fair. And the angry river was in flood. Bulbs, windows, smashed. Every toilet sign had been yanked from the walls and lanes. Now a fever of destruction was loose that was no playful hunt for souvenirs. Kiosks were kicked apart, overturned along the ways. Fellows piled up onto each other's backs, smashing whatever could be reached.

Grotesquely, as from a row of battered teeth, two letters remained over the door to the Hall of Science: . . I E . . .

Now holes began to appear in walls. Pieces of lighting fixtures, exhibit stands littered the grass. Nothing that could be smashed by humans, aided by planks, canes, crowbars, remained intact. The sullen anger that Sam had felt in the crowd earlier in the day was loose now, flowing unchecked, high on hysterical laughter.

. . . the night was made for love . . .

It was time for the midnight splurge of fireworks that was officially to end the Fair. Sam, Alvin, and Joe managed to get up on the skyride observation tower. Below them, the crowd-streams radiated star-fashion along the paths; the movement of people was like pulsations along charged cables.

They were discussing Roosevelt. "But you have to admit he is liberal-minded. He is doing things in a modern way. He's at least making an attempt to cope with the situation," Joe said.

"He's putting on a good show," Alvin remarked.

"That's just it!" Sam cried, shivering with the crowd's angry fever, feeling able to clarify worlds. "They had the Fair for a year and then there was nothing to do, so they had the Fair for another year. But you can't make a show of things forever. Roosevelt may even be elected to another term. But in the end people get the idea. Look at that crowd. They get the idea now. The Fair is over and what's on the other side? Not a damn thing. It was all artificial, a lot of bunk, and now they're still out in the cold. They thought they were in another world, halls of science, fountains, houses of tomorrow, but they know where they are now. There's something in that crowd—"

Across the lagoon, a rocket zoomed, bursting into a shower of yellow, blue, green, red fire flashes that rained beautifully against the night.

An aaahhh hushed the crowd.

Volleys of rockets filled the sky.

. . . the best things in life
Are free . . .

The couples got switched, and separated, and miraculously bumped into each other, swirled against each other in the crowd-stream. There wasn't much territory Mort had not explored on the ad fellow's wife, and he knew when her husband went out of town. As the foursome bumped together, Mort gazed with half-drunken keenness into Ora's face, and he thought he saw the cat-cream look there, oh, the same look he had planted on the face of the other guy's wife. The rage was just mounting in his head, when Ora distracted them crying: "Oh, look, I never saw this place before!" It was a log cabin, with a sign saying this was a reproduction of the cabin of Chicago's first citizen, Jean Baptiste Point de Saible.

"Isn't it cute?" Ora said, and gave the ad man a look, oh, to lay in a place like this away from all the world.

"I understand de Saible was a Negro," the ad man remarked, with the super-gravity of the slightly stewed.

"Naw!" Mort cried.

"Absolutely. He was a fur trader, and the first white man to inhabit Chicago!"

Mort guffawed. "The first white man! he was a nigger and the first white man . . ." The women tittered. The ad man got the joke and he too began to laugh. The four of them united, hugging each other and laughing till they forgot what they were laughing at.

> The call of the West . . .
> Our lips close pressed . . .

"Whadaya wanna go here for? It's just a dump." Estelle stumbled hanging onto her unknown pal as he yanked her toward the log palisades. They had made the rounds of the villages, one after another, Italian village, Irish village, Streets of Paris, Bowery, and here they were at Old Fort Dearborn!

"Shhh! We're the Indians!" They Indian-stalked around the wall and they crept under a locked turnstile. The place was deserted. They scuttled across the parade grounds and sneaked into a log building. They climbed up some stairs to a watch tower and there the fellow lit a match, and there was an army cot. Estelle sank upon it dizzily, and giddily her mind was singing, a crowd outside was cayoodling:

> ". . . the world's all right
> 'Cause I'm in love!"

. . . with anybody, everybody. . . . Just for tonight! Ishkabibble!

Getting into the car, Lou Margolis looked toward the Fair grounds and reflected it was too bad, Rube could have made a good hunk of money out of the scrap iron of the Fair.

"I don't care what anybody says," Celia burst out. "He was a good man. The life he had to lead, there were lots of things he had to do to play the game, but in the main he was good to everybody, he helped the poor, my father was generous, he was a good man."

Summer, autumn, winter, spring, baby!

There were wild, night-torn hours. The huge mob that had jammed the streets of the Fair slowly contracted, congealed, until only the night-hunters, the bloody-eyed, remained. In the Black Forest, incendiary flames arose. In the Streets of Paris there was a free-for-all; tables were smashed on backs and heads, a grabbing hand ripped Estelle's gown, and the cold air met her breasts; a mob got hold of a fire hose and doused a squad of cops; the free-for-all was carried from the Streets of Paris to the Bowery; Runt pushed through crowds, grabbed girls, got socked; he was out for a hunk, he was out for a new piece of tail; Mitch Wilner got home late and found milk and a sandwich waiting for him, and even though he undressed noiselessly in the dark, his wife stirred and said: "Darling" when he got into bed; Mort and his crowd whizzed down Sheridan Road at sixty-five in the new airflow De Soto, the hell with the stoplights, the auto-radio was on and they all sang with the radio:

". . . the faraway Boss . . ."

Lou Green was yanked awake by a cop, and found that he had passed out against the imitation log palisades of Old Fort Dearborn, somewhere a loudspeaker was hoarsely braying a twanging cowboy song:

". . . where the strays are branded and counted . . ."

Harry Perlin couldn't sleep; worrying about tomorrow, he lay awake listening acutely: a car was parked on the street for a while, it had a radio going, people had laughed at him when he started to make car-radios; if he had only had the capital, he'd have shown them, and he listened to the cowboy twang:

"Git along, little dogie, git along, git along,
Git along, little dogie, git along,
Git along, little dogie, git along, git along—"